THE YEAR'S BEST DARK FANTASY & HORROR

2015 Edition

THE YEAR'S BEST DARK FANTASY & HORROR

2015 Edition

EDITED BY PAULA GURAN

PRIME BOOKS

THE YEAR'S BEST DARK FANTASY AND HORROR: 2015

Prime Books
Germantown, MD, USA
www.prime-books.com

For more information, contact Prime Books:
prime@prime-books.com

Print ISBN: 978-1-60701-431-7
Ebook ISBN: 978-1-60701-463-8

In memory of
my cousin Kay,
who introduced me
to science fiction and fantasy
as well as a
great deal more.

Contents

INTRODUCTION

Paula Guran

"I believe in the redeeming power of stories, I believe that stories are incredibly important, possibly in ways we don't understand, in allowing us to make sense of our lives, in allowing us to escape our lives, in giving us empathy and in creating the world that we live in."—Neil Gaiman

It's hard to believe, but we've arrived at the *sixth* volume in this series. It truly does seem like it began much more recently. I have to count the books on my shelves to reassure me of the reality. I hope the continuing success of the series means I am doing *something* right, and that I did it again this time around.

The sheer range of what can be termed dark fantasy or horror is vast. It gives me a great deal of room to fulfill the unique intent of *The Year's Best Dark Fantasy and Horror.* This year, with fiction published in 2014 from a variety of venues, we run the gamut from quiet chills to deeper terror, literary explorations to new-fashioned heroic fantasy, playful subversion to soul-rending scrutiny, historical horror to dark futuristic scenarios, the surreal to the weird west, the demonic to mad science . . . and a great deal more.

Some stories are quickly understood or offer the reader an immediate impact. Others are subtle and some more complicated. A few may require a bit of contemplation to fully appreciate.

The authors include bestsellers, the critically acclaimed, award winners, notable new talent, and a few authors at the start of their careers.

I wish I had the time and space to explain why I selected each and every one of the twenty-six stories and two novellas contained herein—especially if I consider some reviews I've glanced at over the years. My choices may be eclectic—in fact, they are purposefully so because my taste and critical acumen *are* broad ranging—but they are never random. It's difficult to please even one person completely when you are choosing from such diversity. Perhaps that's why I always like to remind folks that the very terms *dark fantasy* and *horror* are highly debatable and constantly changing. There's no single definition of either and your opinion of both depends on your very personal responses and emotions.

And, let's face it: what you learn and feel and think—not only about dark literature, but more profound subjects—change you over the years. What you find to be "the best" in any field is probably not exactly what it once was or will eventually be. Experience alters you, life provides new resonances. Growth is not linear; I feel that, if you are lucky, you grow in many directions like the branches and roots of a tree.

On the other hand, that theory may be completely off base: maybe straight and narrow produces refined taste.

Whatever the case may be, I do agree with the quote from Neil Gaiman that begins this—"stories are incredibly important, possibly in ways we don't understand"—and that this is particularly true when it comes to dark fiction.

If you are new to my ideas about dark fantasy and horror, or if you've been with us for a while but would like a refresher, by the time this tome comes out you can check paulaguran.com/features for several of my (often repetitious) introductions to these annual volumes.

And, as always, I'm also looking for more material to consider, so check that URL for submission guidelines as well.

Paula Guran
11 April 2014

The dead have no choice but to listen . . .

THE QUIET ROOM

V. H. Leslie

"Turn the music down," Terry said, standing on the threshold of his daughter's room. Some unspoken rule forbade him from going in, especially without permission. It was different for mums, he imagined; no part of the house was off limits to them, they could tidy and snoop in equal measure, unchallenged. But for dads, a teenage daughter's room was a minefield, a frightening place that only served as a reminder of how distant the days of childhood were. In truth, he preferred to stay outside.

His daughter, Ava, unaware of his presence, danced uninhibited to the music. The gap in the door allowed him to see more of her body than he would have liked, a body that had somehow grown overnight to replace the goofy child with pigtails and grazed knees. The clothes she wore seemed to belong to that younger Ava as well; too small and too tight, riding up to expose the body that had outgrown them, though Terry knew she'd bought them like that on purpose. Wearing as little as possible was the fashion these days and she was a dedicated follower, like all her friends. He should talk to her about that, about following the herd. But for now he just needed her to stop the music.

Terry rapped the door again. "Ava."

She was deaf to everything but the synthesized wail reverberating from her speakers. Terry raised his voice. "Ava, I won't say it again . . . "

"Dad!" Ava replied. Her voice was louder than Terry's, amplified by embarrassment. "What are you doing up here?"

Terry was always amazed at how easily she could turn things around. Now he was in trouble for trespassing on her space. "Your music—"

"What?" Ava placed a hand behind her ear.

"It's too loud. Just turn it down."

She huffed as she walked to her stereo and turned it off.

"Happy now?" Her question was absurdly loud without the music to compete with.

"Yes," Terry said quietly. A poster of a very young looking man, tanned and shirtless, gazed back from above his daughter's bed. Terry pointed at it. "He'll catch a cold," he said, realizing as soon as he did how old he sounded.

Ava just raised her eyebrows, something she'd perfected to make Terry feel both chastised and insignificant. He wondered if she'd learnt it from Prue.

"You don't think maybe you have too many posters up?" Terry asked.

"It's *my* room, Dad."

It was *his* house, he wanted to say, therefore it was *his* room. But there was no sense in being pedantic. It was important for Ava to feel that she had a place. He supposed it was a good thing Ava had become so territorial about her attic bedroom. The house had so many other good-sized bedrooms on the second floor, but she seemed to intent on having the smallest room, furthest from the nucleus of the house.

"It makes the room look a little crowded is all," he offered. He avoided what he really wanted to say, that he didn't like those half-naked men gazing down at his daughter. But there was no point rehashing an earlier argument; they'd already disagreed about poster-to-wall ratio and Terry had conceded. He couldn't start telling her what to do now.

Ava shrugged in a way that said she didn't care about his opinion. And why should she? He hadn't exerted any kind of influence on her life so far. Why should she listen to him now? Terry realized he was hovering. "Dinner won't be long."

"Okay."

Terry looked around Ava's room one more time, trying not to be disappointed at how much it conformed to a typical adolescent space. As well as the posters of manufactured pop groups on the walls, piles of clothes and shoes crowded the floor. They'd only moved in a few weeks ago and already the room had the worn look of a teenage den. It wasn't just the room but Ava's choice of music he found so annoying. He worried about her taste. Those formative years when he'd been out of her life were responsible for shaping her in all kinds of ways. He couldn't expect to change her overnight. But he wished she would listen to something else.

He made his way back down the stairs, conscious of the volume creeping higher again. It was clear now why she'd been so keen to claim the attic bedroom; it was so she could make as much noise as she wanted.

• • •

Terry walked through the old house, waiting for the pizza delivery boy to arrive with their usual order. It was a big house, bigger than it needed to be for just the two of them.

There had been few properties on the market so close to Ava's school and of those it was the most affordable, though bigger and more expensive than he would have liked. Terry still wasn't accustomed to so much superfluous space. He walked through the house now, opening doors to rooms he wasn't sure how to use, how to fill, moving around the empty spaces before closing the doors once more. It was becoming a habit, a nightly tour. He tried not to think of it as some kind of vigil.

Though the house was old, the rooms lacked period features or individual characteristics. They were uniform, bare, gazing back at him with vacant expressions. All except the music room. He hesitated on the threshold for a moment, drawn by what was on top of the piano. It was the first thing Ava had unpacked, the first thing she'd found a home for but Terry still wasn't used to seeing it. He just hadn't expected to bring Prue with them. The urn was much more plain than he would have expected for Prue. He would have imagined something more showy, more extravagant. But though simple in design, it still made him uneasy. He knew it was only ash and dust but it felt like he was facing an old adversary every time he saw it.

The sooner Ava decided where to scatter her mother's ashes the better. He'd tried to persuade Ava not to put it off, that doing it quickly would help her move on, but really it was because he hated Prue being in their home. The last time they had been under the same roof was thirteen years ago and, with the exception of Ava, he had no happy memories of that time.

Ava couldn't conceive of keeping the urn anywhere else. Prue liked the piano apparently and was especially keen on Liszt. The Prue Terry remembered didn't know the first thing about music, classical or otherwise. Prue's sister was the musical one.

Without looking at the urn, he walked towards the piano and pressed his finger to one of the shiny clean keys, cold beneath his touch. It let out a puff of dust. Terry pressed it again and imagined the effort inside as the mechanics attempted to conjure sound. A second silent exhalation was all he got.

Terry didn't know a thing about pianos but knew this one was busted. He would have thrown it out but for the fact the house was left so vacant, almost unusually so, that its presence seemed all the more engineered. It was almost a relief to find something from its past, even if it was broken. It was odd for a house of this age not to have more relics, Terry thought; old fireplaces, cornicing, fretwork banisters, any would have been typical of this period. The previous owners must have stripped it back to the bare essentials, purging it of its past with copious tins of magnolia. A blank slate.

Terry had moved a lot over the years and most of the homes he'd lived in had retained a few objects from the previous owners; mildewed white goods that were an inconvenience to take, unfashionable light fittings, the odd piece of furniture. And then there were the marks people didn't realize they left behind. Children's measurements on a doorframe, old photographs at the back of a drawer, a dent in the plasterboard from children play fighting too enthusiastically, or from grown-ups fighting for real. Terry liked to trace the narrative of the houses he lived in. The walls whispered their story through such scars.

But this house was silent.

Just like the piano. Terry pressed the key again, half expecting a clear shrill note to contradict him. But he only heard the click of the key as it moved and a whisper of air.

Terry sat on the stool. He wouldn't get rid of it. The piano was the only link to the building's past, a gift from the house. He spread his fingers over the keys, imagining himself a great pianist about to begin a concerto. He lifted his hands above the keyboard ready to bring them down in unison and glanced up at Prue's urn. A shrill electric note echoed through the room.

Terry leapt back from the piano, stumbling over the fallen stool. He hadn't touched the keys and yet a sound filled the house, becoming a tune he began to comprehend—"The Ride of the Valkyries," played on distant tinny notes. The new doorbell Ava had persuaded him to buy. Farcical, like the inside of a musical greeting card.

Terry rose quickly, closing the lid of the piano and hurrying to the front door.

Terry placed the pizzas and the dips on the table. He heard Ava bound down the stairs, surprised that she could hear the jingle of the doorbell over her music at the top of the house. She had a way of sensing food.

Ava piled her plate high, whereas Terry only took one slice at a time.

"You know we're going to have to eat real dinners sometime," Ava said with her mouthful.

"Why?"

"Because they're healthy. You're supposed to make sure I eat right."

"It feels right to me."

"Not for your cholesterol."

Terry, glancing at Ava's plate, thought it a little hypocritical. "Well, what should I cook?"

"Pasta or fish. Vegetables and stuff."

Terry nodded, suitably admonished. He was reminded of one of the last conversations he'd had with Prue, her concern that he spoilt Ava too much.

"What do you normally eat?" she said between noisy mouthfuls. "You know, when you were on your own?"

Terry was quite content with sardines on toast, or pub grub from the local. But he always ordered a takeaway when he had Ava. He saw her so sporadically, sometimes only every couple of weeks that it always felt like a victory. Prue had not made it easy, so he equated seeing his daughter with a kind of celebration. It still felt like that, even though he was well aware they were engaged in a complex renegotiation of their roles. He wasn't used to being a full time father yet. For him, seeing his daughter everyday had not lost its novelty. Though clearly pizza had.

She was still waiting for an answer.

"Oh, this and that," he said.

"Well, why don't we go shopping tomorrow? Get some healthy food in?" Terry smiled; when Ava wasn't being moody or answering back she was actually a pretty nice kid.

"I'd like that."

"I can make my chili surprise."

"What's the surprise?"

"You'll see." Ava smiled. "It was Mum's favorite."

Terry swallowed hard on Ava's use of the past tense but washed it down with his beer. He wouldn't have imagined Prue liking chili, too much spice for her bland palate. He was beginning to realize how little he knew about his ex-wife. They'd been little more than strangers at the end.

Terry smiled, taking the good mood to try to connect with Ava. "So how are you finding it? The house I mean?"

"It's okay. I like my room. But it's not very homey."

"No?"

"It feels empty. Even with all our stuff."

Terry thought about the piano room, the only room that felt occupied.

"Who lived here before?" Ava asked.

"No one, apparently. Not for the last twenty years at least. Just been sitting empty."

"About time we came along then." Ava smiled, helping herself to another slice.

Terry smiled too. When she wasn't in that room of hers he felt like she was actually listening to him. He wondered whether it was time to deliver some fatherly advice, to address the way she dressed, to talk about her tidying her room a little more frequently.

Upstairs, Ava's music blared suddenly. Terry couldn't make out the words but the tune was melancholic, lovesick. Not the kind of music he would have expected.

"Sorry Dad," Ava said, getting up from the table and heading toward the stairs, "I must have forgotten to turn it off."

Terry listened to her footsteps as she ran up the stairs and the music stopped as suddenly as it had started.

Terry decided it was time to unpack the boxes. He'd been so focused on making a home for Ava that he'd literally left his work wrapped up, concealed beneath bubble wrap. Ava was keen for them to fill the house, to get as close to normality as possible. Besides, she would soon be up for school and he couldn't spend another day roaming around the old house, waiting for her to come home.

He took the blade of a pair of scissors to the first taped box, opening it to a host of chinaware. The tiny porcelain cups rattled as he delved inside. He worked in antiques—at least that was what his shop's frontage had said, but it was really bric-a-brac. "Antiques" sounded better; it implied that the object in question was in some way important. Customers wanted to know when items were made, who owned them, and they attributed worth generally to how well those questions were answered. Terry had learnt very early on that you could sell anything if you gave it a story. And what people sought most were unique stories. What Terry tried to do was to offer the mundane, the forgotten, the overlooked a good narrative. He'd largely succeeded. He'd made some exceptional profits on some lesser-known treasures, partly because of his expertise in restoration but mostly due to the caliber of his stories. Making something out of nothing was his trade.

Terry had decided to make this room, one of the many indistinguishable reception rooms, his workshop. He doubted that it had ever been used for that purpose before. The house felt grand, and though it didn't provide many clues, he imagined it had been designed with only luxury in mind. The reception rooms would have been filled with occasional furniture, countless armchairs to nestle into, little mahogany writing desks for penning love letters or replying to dinner invitations. As he unwrapped dainty teacups and their saucers, vases and ornaments, he thought that it was very likely that once the house would have been filled with such knickknacks. Except that now, as he arranged them carefully on the table, they looked out of place. Absence and neglect had filled the house so entirely that everything else seemed like an affront.

"Dad?"

It shocked him into nearly dropping the teacup in his hand. He placed it down carefully. "Ava, you made me jump."

"Sorry. What are you doing?" Framed by the doorway, dressed in her school uniform but still rubbing the sleep from her eyes, she looked more like a child than ever.

"I thought I'd start work today. Come in, come in. Take a look around." He used his best shop voice.

Ava entered the room, picking up bits and pieces that took her fancy. She seemed to like the things that opened and closed, playing with the hinges or the catches, mostly timepieces or ornate pillboxes. She was opening the front of a carriage clock when something in one of the cardboard boxes caught her eye. "What's that?"

Terry pulled it out and dusted it down. It was a black box, decorated with brightly colored images of birds in flight. "It's a music box," he said. "Look . . ." and as he opened it, it began a to play the notes of a lullaby.

"It's beautiful." Ava reached for it. She ran her fingers over the surface.

"It's black lacquer," Terry said, competing with the mechanical tune, "undoubtedly nineteenth century, though the origin is harder to pinpoint. I'd say European, though it looks Japanese. There was a lot of mock oriental stuff then."

"It's beautiful," Ava repeated, holding it in the light. "Look, there's a girl here," she said, delighted at her discovery, "and another this side but with wings." She turned the box around. "Is she an angel?"

Terry put on his glasses and examined it more closely. "I'd forgotten about this piece. No, she's no angel, I think it's Philomela. You see the bird this side?" He pointed. "The girl *is* the bird. She's transforming into it."

"Why?"

Terry shuffled in his chair. "Well, Philomela was very beautiful and her brother in-law wanted her very much. He engineered it so that she was alone in a cabin in the woods where he, er . . . " Terry searched for a euphemism. "Where he had his way with her. Then he cut out her tongue so she could never tell anyone what he'd done."

"Gruesome."

"Yes. But Philomela had a plan. She wove the story of his actions into a tapestry and sent it to her sister, who helped her escape. When the brother-in-law pursued them, the gods took pity on them, transforming them into birds. Philomela was transformed into the nightingale, the bird with the sweetest voice. I suppose to compensate for a life of silence."

Ava smiled. Terry smiled too; he'd omitted the bit about Philomela's sister's revenge on her husband, how she had murdered their son and fed him to his unknowing father.

Somehow infanticide seemed to tarnish the whole story.

Ava picked up the box. "Can I have it?"

Terry shrugged. "Well, I'd say it would fetch at least £200."

"Really?"

"Shall we say . . . a clean bedroom and a hug?"

Ava pretended to think about it. "How about two hugs and I'll wash up instead?"

Terry was so impressed with her bartering skills that he was more than happy to forfeit the clean bedroom. "Deal."

They shook on it.

Ava turned before she got to the door. "One thing I don't get, why a tapestry? It seems like a lot of effort. Why not just write a letter?"

"A letter would have been expected. Only something more subtle would get past the guards. Sometimes we don't see the messages that are right in front of us."

Ava seemed satisfied with that answer and left Terry among his relics.

Terry spent the rest of the day in a frenzy of activity. He'd unpacked most of the boxes and sanded a few smaller pieces of furniture. The room smelt of varnish and woodworm treatment. Ava would be home from school soon and he was looking forward to showing her the progress he'd made. He was repairing a Georgian chest when he first heard the tapping sound. He strained his ears, listening. A dull repetitive tap. Terry walked about the room, checking the various timepieces that were scattered about. It wasn't a ticking. It was hardly noticeable but it was there, a quiet but indisputable *tap, tap, tap.*

He walked out into the hallway. The tapping louder now that he'd left the noise of his workshop behind. It was a noise that would drive him mad if he didn't discover the source.

The doorbell broke him from his reverie and for once he was glad to hear it. Any sound was better than that incessant tapping. He jogged to the door, imagining he had wings like the Valkyries, excited to see Ava after a long day. Except it wasn't Ava. Terry froze. For a moment he thought Prue had come back. That she'd somehow wangled her way back into the world of the living to take Ava from him. Then the woman removed her sunglasses and he could see a younger face, kinder eyes.

Philippa.

"Some Gothic mansion you got here," Prue's sister said, looking the place up and down. "I hope you've had a priest round to bless it."

Terry stood speechless. The resemblance had always been uncanny, though they were not twins. It was as if Prue was resurrected before him, but a younger version, closer to the woman he had married. He'd seen Philippa at the funeral of course, shocked then at how strong the resemblance had become over the years. They kept their distance. They always had.

"Come in," Terry said recovering. They leaned in for an awkward kiss. "If you *dare* . . . " he added in an attempt to relieve the tension.

Philippa raised her eyebrows but followed him inside.

"It's big."

"More rooms than I know what to do with. We have a music room, don't you know."

"A haunted library as well, I suppose, and a madwoman in the attic."

"We definitely have one of those," Terry said, relieved to see Ava coming up the path.

"Aunty Philippa!" Ava ran the rest of the distance.

"Mad as a hatter," Philippa agreed as Ava bounded into her.

"Why don't you give Aunty Philippa the grand tour?" Terry said once the hugging was done.

"Sure," Ava said, straightening her uniform. "If you care to follow me."

Terry and Philippa exchanged glances and fell in step behind her.

"Nice piano," Philippa said, stopping at the music room.

"It was here when we arrived," Terry explained. "The only thing the previous tenants left. But it's broken."

"May I?" Philippa asked, walking to it before Terry could object. She sat and pressed at the keys. Terry was reminded of the tapping noise he'd heard earlier, realizing that it had stopped in the interim.

"Silenced," Philippa said.

"Pardon?"

"I think it's been silenced. It's not broken. It's so people can practice without causing a racket. It can be reversed, I know a guy who could fix it."

"Really?" Ava exclaimed.

"I can teach you, if you like? I used to play." Philipa demonstrated with a silent flourish. "I'm a bit rusty but I'd be willing to share what I know. First things first," she said glancing at the urn, "let's get this piano to make some noise."

Terry found he could tolerate the quiet of the house in the daytime if it meant music in the evenings. Sitting in his workshop he listened to the snatches of melodies next door as Ava took her piano lesson. He could differentiate between them, Philippa's fluid cadenzas and Ava's hesitant and static playing. But Ava was improving. When Philippa left, Ava practiced on her own and he could make out the beginnings of tunes, the foundations of compositions he partially recognized.

It wasn't just the music that he looked forward to but the laughter. The house seemed alive with female voices. Sitting in his workshop he listened to his daughter's voice, laughing over the sound of the piano, and thought it was the most beautiful sound he had ever heard.

"Aunty Philippa said I need to practice more," Ava said at dinner.

"You play every day as it is," Terry replied, though he didn't mind Philippa's sudden involvement. In fact, he was surprised how naturally she slipped into their lives. It was important for Ava to have some familiarity, he reasoned. He helped himself to more of Ava's signature dish, the surprise being copious amounts of jalapeños. His mouth made an O shape as he tried to breathe through the heat.

"But I want to get really good," Ava insisted. "I need to work on my tempo apparently and not rush the rests."

" 'Rests?' "

"The silent bits in between the playing. Aunty Philippa says silence is as important as the sound the notes make. She told me about this composer who wrote a composition of four minutes and thirty-three seconds of silence."

"I bet the audience wanted their money back."

"It was revolutionary."

"You can't compose silence," Terry said, pouring himself a glass of water. "It just exists. He didn't create anything that wasn't already there."

"But it wasn't there. Not until the composer closed the lid of the piano to mark the beginning of the movement. People listened more patiently than they would anywhere else because they were in a concert hall. Can you imagine how long four minutes of silence must have felt when you expected music?"

Terry thought of how quiet the house was in the daytime when he was alone in his workshop. But even then there were the sounds of sanding wood, the ticking of clocks.

"Except it wasn't silence," Ava continued. "People shifted in their seats, coughed. Some even walked out. That was the music he wanted the audience to listen to."

"Sounds a little lazy if you ask me," said Terry. "He wasn't the author of those sounds, he didn't plan that the man in the back row would cough, or that the lady at the front would tut."

"But he created the opportunity for those sounds, they never would have existed if he hadn't made the silence."

Terry looked at his daughter. He hadn't expected to have such a thought provoking conversation over dinner. Though still in her school uniform, she suddenly looked like a young woman and unmistakably like her mother.

That night Terry dreamt of the music room. It was full of people, dressed in black, sitting around the piano as if for a recital. Terry walked among them, noticing how still they all sat, their heads cast down. He saw instruments in their laps or at their feet. He tripped over a cello, the strings catching on his trousers, but it didn't make a sound. Nor did the cellist stoop to pick up the instrument. It was so quiet that even the sound of his footsteps seemed to have been silenced somehow. Terry stamped his foot, trying to make as much noise as he could, and when that failed he knocked over a set of cymbals, expecting the vibrations to shatter the silence. But nothing dented the stillness of the room. He tried to address the gathering but his voice faltered, the people didn't even look at him. Terry grabbed the nearest man by his lapels and shook him roughly, but the man merely stared back vacantly. Terry tried to scream into the man's face, pouring all his confusion and rage into one almighty cry, but no sound came and his throat became hoarse with the effort.

In the background he heard the piano.

Dissonant notes at first, but gradually they merged to form the beginnings of a melody. He avoided looking at what was on top of the piano but glanced across at the keyboard. The lid was down. To signify the beginning of the movement, he remembered. But how could that be? The melody began to gain speed, the volume creeping higher and higher, the playing becoming more crazed, more erratic, building toward an inevitable and deafening crescendo—

Terry sat bolt upright in bed.

He breathed deeply, trying to steady himself, fancying he could hear the sound of his racing heartbeat. As it slowed he was conscious of another sound. He strained his ears and thought he heard the same dissonant notes from his dream.

It was the piano.

It echoed through the corridors of the old house, drifting up the stairs, filling the rooms and recesses with its melancholic air. Ava. Terry pulled aside the covers and began down the stairs.

He pushed his dream to the back of his mind as he followed the melody to the music room, opening the door with a thud.

The music stopped.

"Ava?"

Ava sat at the piano in her nightclothes. Her fingers were stretched out on the polished veneer of the piano lid. Had she closed it suddenly when he entered the room?

Terry walked towards her in the silence. She opened her eyes slowly as if waking up. She looked around dazedly at her surroundings.

"It's okay," Terry soothed, placing his arm around her, gently bringing her to her feet. "You've had a bad dream. Let's get you back to bed."

As he closed the door, he looked one last time at the piano but saw only the urn.

Ava was quieter than normal the next day. She looked tired, as if she hadn't slept at all. There was no laughter during the piano lesson that evening either. Listening in his workshop, Terry could only hear Philippa's voice giving instructions between the playing. At the end of the lesson Terry walked Philippa to the door.

"Is everything okay with Ava?" she asked before she left. "She seemed a little subdued."

Terry shrugged. He wasn't ready to verbalize his concerns. "Teenagers," he offered.

Philippa looked at Terry for longer than was necessary before saying her goodbyes.

Walking back inside, Terry couldn't quiet his qualms. Ava had hardly uttered a word to him all day. Even at dinnertime, when she was usually so chatty. And she'd hardly touched her food. If something was on her mind he wanted her to be able to talk to him about it. He wondered if she could. She'd always had Prue befo . . .

Shhhhh!

He stopped in his tracks.

He was outside the music room. For a moment he thought he must have been speaking aloud, that Ava overhearing must have shushed him. But listening now, all he could hear was Ava's playing. He edged closer to the door. For a moment he was sure he heard two voices instead of one. Whispers, muffled by the sound of the piano. And in the background, a soft syllable. *Shhh. Shhh. Shhhhhhh!*

Terry opened the door.

Ava sat at the piano. The lid was closed.

"Who were you talking to, Ava?"

Ava looked at her father bemused.

"Ava?"

Ava shook her head and made her way up the stairs to her bedroom.

The silent treatment continued for the rest of the week. Terry was reminded of Prue's sullen moods when they'd been together. She could go weeks without speaking to him if she wanted to. It was the worst kind of punishment. Terry hadn't expected Ava to inherit her mother's morose temperament; she'd always seemed so much more like him. Terry would have preferred Ava to shout at him, or skulk up to her bedroom and play her abysmal music as loud as her speakers would allow. But the house was as silent as his daughter.

The only exception was her piano lessons, when for a brief hour the house was filled with gentle refrains and familiar melodies. When Philippa left, Ava practiced on her own, always the same song; the one he'd heard her play when sleepwalking. A sad, slow air that gradually built, stopping frustratingly short, just before the final crescendo.

Terry wished she would play something else but she was as deaf to that request as she was to his pleas to open up.

The only time Ava said anything now, apart from the monosyllabic replies to his questions, was when she was alone at the piano. Listening at the door, Terry was sure he could hear whispers, hushed beneath the dark melody that had come to haunt him.

He resolved to speak to Philippa about it. Maybe she'd noticed something strange during their piano lessons.

Seizing the next available opportunity, he took Philippa into his workroom and closed the door.

"Well, she follows instructions," Philippa assured him, "but she doesn't say any more than is absolutely necessary. Her playing though . . . "

"Yes, she's very good," Terry conceded. "Except that when she practices, she only plays the same tune over and over. It's driving me mad."

Philippa asked him if he could identify it. He hummed it instead, feeling a little self-conscious.

Philippa looked away. She shrugged after a few moments. "Sorry, I don't recognize it. Listen, I'm sure whatever this is will blow over. Ava is adjusting." She placed her hand on his arm. "She's been through an awful lot."

Terry leaned in closer, "That's not all. When you're gone I hear her talking in the piano room. Talking to . . . "

Philippa nodded. "I don't think you need to worry about that. She's obviously not ready to let go of Prue just yet. At least she's talking."

"I suppose." But Terry couldn't see past how morbid it was.

"Besides, why do you think people visit gravestones?" Philippa continued. "They offload. The dead have no choice but to listen."

When Ava went to school that day Terry went straight to the piano room. He needed to address the strange influence the urn was having on his daughter. Despite what Philippa said, there was something unnatural about the communication in the piano room.

He didn't give much credence to the supernatural, but he knew how stubborn Prue had been in life, and if anyone would flout the laws of death it would be her. He'd thought about replacing Prue's ashes with soil or something, wondering if getting rid of them would somehow restore normality. But it all seemed so underhand. He wanted to resolve this civilly, parent to parent. He'd practiced the words in his workroom but now, in the presence of Prue's urn, he was at a loss. He stared at the floor.

They'd managed to avoid each other pretty well over the years. When he picked up Ava he usually stayed in the car and honked the horn. But with death, a strange desire to see his ex-wife had overwhelmed him. He wanted to see what she'd become, to look down on the woman who had caused him so much misery. He remembered the last time he'd seen her in the Chapel of Rest; standing over her, he'd felt a strange sense of victory, one which hadn't involved the courts or social services. He'd won the right to his daughter just by waiting it out.

Prue had looked different, slightly bloated. He wasn't sure whether she'd put weight on over the years or if it was the effect of death. He'd read somewhere that a corpse had many of its fluids removed, to stop the natural bloating that sets in with rigor mortis and the body was pumped full of embalming fluid. He knew the dead were dressed up like this for the viewing public, a strange kind of charade; an attempt to stop the clock, to avoid the inevitable putrescence. Her face had been painted an unnatural shade, her skin alive with an artificial glow. He'd wanted to touch her cheek to see if it felt the same but he knew it would be cold and he didn't want to ruin the illusion.

He thought about how her body would have been doused in disinfectant and germicidal solutions. The body he had lain with, made love to in the back of his first car. The embalmer massaging the legs and arms the way he had once caressed them. The eyes posed shut with an eye cap. Worst of all was the mouth. The mouth he'd kissed. The mouth that whispered *I love you, I'm having a baby,* the mouth that had screamed at him a hundred times, or closed tightly in disappointment or anger when they'd exhausted words. All the things it had left unsaid, sown shut with ligature and a needle or stuck together with adhesive. He had known then, without any doubt, that Prue was gone. That the body before him was only an echo of her, the undertaker's artifice. In death the real face crumbles, the mouth rolls open, gawping in a way that Prue herself would have described as uncouth, expelling the soul with its final breath.

Back in his workroom, Terry finally began to relax. He wasn't sure if it was because he was surrounded by the tools of his trade, the reassuring ticking of the carriage clocks, or the silent narratives of the objects he'd resurrected, whatever it was, he felt consoled. He rummaged through his toolbox, forgetting what he was looking for but enjoying the sound of metal rattling. He wanted to make some noise. He felt like celebrating. He'd finally given Prue a piece of his mind after all these years.

He'd felt ridiculous at first, of course, speaking to the urn, saying the words aloud in the quiet room. It was absurd. But it was better than staying silent on the subject. It became easier when he imagined Prue in the Chapel of Rest. Then the words had poured out of him. They gushed uncensored from his lips, thirteen years' worth of latent discontent suddenly given voice. He'd shouted and sworn, threatened to scatter her ashes to the corners of the earth unless she left their daughter alone. The dead have no choice but to listen and he left the room feeling as if he'd finally vanquished his demons. That by speaking his mind he'd performed some kind of exorcism, that the house would finally be free of its strange deathly silence. The sudden blare of music startled him.

Terry put his hands to his ears, shocked at how loud it was. It thundered down from the attic, louder than anything he had heard before. It made his heart race, filling him with an urgency to make it stop.

He raced up the stairs, towards its source. It was too loud for any melody, for words. It was an alarm, a war cry, an enormous echoing din.

Bursting into Ava's room Terry made straight for the stereo and turned it off. He sat panting on her bed, listening to his relaxing heartbeat, savoring the new silence.

When he finally looked up, he received his second shock of the morning: Ava's bedroom was completely transformed. Her clothes were neatly folded, the debris that had previously crowded the carpet put away. Her desk was clear of makeup and CDs, and in their stead were a pile of schoolbooks and a neatly arranged pad of A4 paper. Terry stood and turned. The room was immaculate, spotless. Apart from the work on her desk, there was nothing else in the room. Even her picture frames had been removed, the walls bare.

For a moment Terry wondered what Ava's room had been like when she lived with Prue. He'd never asked her. He imagined that Prue would've run a pretty tight ship. He doubted she'd be allowed posters on the walls, to leave clothes on the floor. Maybe these months living with him had been a rebellion against her mother. And if so, why had she reverted back?

Terry shook his head, bemused. He should've been glad that the images of bronzed hunks had been removed from his daughter's room, but it was all so sudden. And where had all of it gone?

Terry crouched, pulling aside the duvet to peer under Ava's bed, wondering if Prue had also snooped through their daughter's things. The space under the bed was pretty much empty as well, containing only the discarded rolled up posters and the music box.

Terry retrieved it and brushed it down, the black lacquer gleaming underneath the dust. He thought for a moment that maybe he shouldn't open it, that maybe it would contain something private, a diary or a keepsake. Maybe something that would explain her strange behavior, he thought, justifying his desire to unclasp it.

Empty.

He waited for the mechanical notes to begin playing. He wound the spring and opened the box again, expecting the action to spur the steel mechanism inside. But no sound came. Terry opened and closed it a few more times, each time anticipating the tinny mechanical melody. But it was silent. He'd take it to his workshop and see if he could fix it, wondering all while why Ava hadn't told him it was broken.

Terry ordered pizza that night on purpose, hoping that it would incite Ava to criticize him about his cholesterol again. But she ate her slice in silence, cutting it into small neat pieces instead of picking it up with her hands like she used to. He wasn't sure whether to come clean about going into her room—she'd always been pretty protective about her private space—but she'd soon discover her music box gone and besides, any reaction was better than none. "I went into your room today," Terry said, breaking the silence. "You left your music on."

Ava continued eating.

"Your room looks pretty tidy. I'm glad you took my advice." But he wasn't glad at all. He preferred it when it was a tip, when she played her music really loud and ate her food with noisy mouthfuls.

Ava glared at him but still she didn't say anything.

"Anyway, I've taken the music box." Terry knew she'd know now that he'd been snooping under her bed, but he didn't care. "You should have told me it was broken. I'll try and get it fixed, if that's what you want?"

Ava put her cutlery down and looked at him again. Her eyes were softer this time, almost imploring. It frustrated him more than her anger.

"Ava, for goodness' sake, what's wrong?" he said. He heard his words reverberating in his head. He waited a few moments for her to reply and when she didn't, he stood. "Talk to me!" he yelled, knocking his plate off the table in his rage. It fell to the floor, shattering into pieces.

Ava raised her hands to her ears, closing her eyes.

"Ava, I didn't mean to scare you."

But she was up from the table in a flash, running up the stairs to the attic.

Terry watched her go, then he stooped to pick up the shards of crockery. He wondered at Ava's reaction to the noise. For though his rage had been voluble, and he watched the plate shatter, he couldn't remember it making a sound.

Terry gradually became accustomed to the silence. He went about his day as if his world had been muted. As if a strange cloud had descended over them, cushioning the usual sounds a household made. Ava withdrew into the silence, into the attic, only appearing for her piano lesson or for meals. He spent so little time with his daughter it was almost as if Prue had never died.

Terry sat in his workroom, listening, waiting for Ava's piano lesson to begin. Nothing happened for a while and then he heard Philippa's raised voice and footsteps on the stairs, heading to the attic. He headed to the music room, finding Philippa sat alone on the piano stool.

"What happened?"

"It's broken, I don't know how." She lifted the lid and pressed a key to demonstrate. "It's impossible, unless someone came in here and silenced it."

Terry sat down beside her, thinking about how his attempts to fix the music box had also failed.

"So Ava's still not talking," Philippa observed, "what's her problem anyway?"

Terry shrugged. He spread his fingers over the keys, pretending to be able to play. Without any sound it was easier to imagine the melody in his head, the melody Ava usually practiced. The imagined music distracted him from the alarm that was building up inside. Where was the sound going? Why did the house seem to prefer the quiet?

Philippa placed her hand on Terry's. He stopped moving his fingers in imaginary playing. He let it rest there under hers.

"You know," Philippa whispered, "before she took a vow of silence, Ava told me about why she wanted the attic room. She said that you hear things better at the top, that the acoustics are better the higher you are." She spoke the next words slowly. "The best seats in the house are in the gods." Terry winced. They were Prue's words. Repeated often in mock enthusiasm when they couldn't afford the better seats, lower down. She believed them in the end, doggedly buying the seats the farthest from the stage.

"I lied the other day," Philippa said withdrawing her hand, "about the piece Ava plays all the time. I do recognize it. You do too. How could you have forgotten?"

Terry stared at the piano keys, hearing only silence. And then he was sitting in the theatre, one sister on either side. He watched the orchestra pile in to murmurs from the auditorium. They were dressed in black formal wear, placing their instruments at their feet, or holding them in their laps. The conductor arrived and it became suddenly silent, the musicians and audience hushed. And then the tapping as the conductor counted them in.

They were in the gods of course. It had taken Prue ages to waddle up the stairs. But she couldn't be persuaded otherwise. Besides, they had no money then. She'd placed his hand against her stomach and he felt the baby inside swimming around to the music. At the interval, Philippa volunteered to help him get the ice cream. Prue was relieved to stay where she was.

They'd gone down together.

The theatre had a concave of private boxes. Relics from a time before, closed now for renovation. He was helping to restore them; it was how they'd known about the production in the first place. He was proud of his work. Prue never seemed to want to listen but Philippa was so engrossed holding the pile of ice cream tubs. It would only take him a moment to show her the balustraded parapet, the gilded plasterwork.

He closed the door. The wallpaper was decorated with nightingales.

They just made it back in time for the second half. The ice cream was soft. Prue never said a word.

That night Terry dreamt of the quiet room. He was expecting it, almost hoping for it. He felt as if he were on the wave of Ava's melody, rising and falling, building up to a final, inevitable climax. He didn't want to fight against it any longer. He felt himself carried along by it, up the stairs to his daughter's room, sweeping him across the threshold into the cold, quiet space. The posters were back on the walls. They looked even more obscene than before. He didn't want to see their oiled male torsos, their wanton expressions leering down at his daughter. He ripped one off of the wall, standing back in surprise at what was exposed behind.

A huge gaping hole. An enormous black pit, audibly sucking the air out of the room. He pulled down another and saw a similar void. He tried to peer into the darkness but couldn't see anything, couldn't concentrate on anything but the noise. He removed the other posters, revealing similar vacuums, the sound deafening in the quiet room. Terry felt himself being dragged toward them, pulled toward the unknown.

Beyond the room, beyond the din, he could hear Ava's faint playing, the familiar melody barely a whisper. He latched onto its harmony and filled his mind with it, following its thread. He grabbed hold of the bedstead, then the desk, moving slowly through the room to the hallway, finally shutting the door behind him.

Silence.

He made his way down the stairs to the music room, this time prepared for the congregation inside. They were dressed in black as before, with their heads bent low as if in mourning. Terry didn't waste time trying to talk to them. He walked past them looking for the source of the silence. Ava was at the keyboard, her hands on the lid, her fingers dancing along the surface, playing her silent music. But this time Terry confronted what was on top. He could face Prue now that she was dead.

What he saw made him stagger. If he hadn't been condemned to silence, he would have screamed.

Lying on top of the piano was Prue's corpse. She looked almost as she did in the Chapel of Rest. Her eyes shut, her hands arranged demurely, but her legs wide open, revealing cheap stockings and a glimpse of her underwear. She looked like some slutty nightclub singer. Terry walked around the piano, an absurd bier, staring at the woman he had once loved.

He felt compelled to touch her cold skin, prepared to shatter the illusion. But just as he reached for her, she turned her head towards him and it wasn't Prue's face but Philippa's staring back, opening her lifeless eyes. And as he recoiled from her she opened her mouth, ripping the embalmer's stitches from her lips and letting out the ear-piercing scream he couldn't make.

• • •

Terry woke with the scream in his mind. It was morning and glancing at his alarm clock he realized he had overslept. He wondered why Ava hadn't woken him, remembering then that Ava hadn't said a word to him for over a week. She had probably already left for school with nothing but the silence of the morning for company.

Terry put on his dressing gown and went up to her bedroom. He rapped a few times on the door and opened it, her absence confirming that she had already left. It was still a tidy, blank, shell, an empty cocoon that had facilitated her startling change. Terry wanted to take a sledgehammer to it, to break the unnatural silence with the sound of wood splintering, of plaster falling. He recalled shredding the posters in his dream, the delight it had given him ripping them from the wall, and he remembered the actual posters rolled up under Ava's bed.

He fell to his knees, thrusting his arm into the darkness to retrieve them. He sat on Ava's bed and unrolled the first of them, revealing the image of a bronzed torso, progressing to well-defined shoulders, then a muscular neck with a prominent Adam's apple. He stopped at the head, realizing, as he saw the model's mouth that he was reaching the end of the movement, that everything was beginning to make sense.

The pinup's mouth was scribbled out with black marker pen, the messy scrawl forming a blackened hole. Could Ava have taken the posters down to give him a message, hoping their absence would tell him something, then scribbling on them in case he still didn't see. Sometimes we don't see the messages that are right in front of us, Terry thought, remembering the day he gave Ava the music box. Remembering the story he'd told her about Philomela. How do you ask for help when you are bound to silence? Why not write a message? Too obvious, he remembered telling her, it wouldn't get past the guards.

Terry shook his head. He could talk but he hadn't listened. Not really.

He got to his feet, straining his ears, listening now to the house below. You can hear everything better from the gods.

He heard a sound from the music room. He listened hard, but the silence itself seemed to be getting louder, sonorous, obscuring everything else. It was there underneath, barely a whisper.

Shhhhhh.

Terry raced down the stairs as he had in his dream, conscious that his footsteps on the floorboards emitted no sound. He pushed the door open as soundlessly and saw his daughter sitting at the piano. Her hands were on the piano lid, engaged in silent practice.

Terry hurried to her side, turning her by the shoulders to face him. But her head flopped listlessly. Her eyes observed him vacantly.

"Ava? We have to leave. It's this house."

The silence buzzed around him like an angry swarm.

Shh. Shh. Shh. Shh. Shhhhhhh.

Terry stood, tried to pull her from the piano, but she was a dead weight.

"Ava, come on, we have to go!" He knew he was speaking, he could hear his voice in his head, but the sound he made was swallowed up, absorbed by the quiet of the room.

The silence was enveloping everything, feeding on the sounds they made, stealing them, leaving nothing behind in its wake. A blank slate. Terry tried again to wrench Ava from the piano, from this parasitic house, but silence closed in around them. His mind emptied, blackness swirled instead, accompanied by the sound of air being sucked away. *Shh. Shh. Shh. Shh.*

Terry put his hands to his ears, trying to stop the pain in his head. He reeled against it, falling into the piano, knocking the urn from its perch.

It all happened so slowly in the quiet room that it had the same blurred quality as his dreams. The urn rolled to its side, silently tumbling toward the ground, knocking against the piano lid on its way down and releasing an enormous cloud of ash.

The particles swirled into the air, caught in a whirlwind, and for a brief moment Prue stood before them. She looked at Terry and opened her mouth into an exaggerated smile.

The house, he realized, created the silence for other sounds. Sounds suppressed or obscured, dormant or tacit. Sounds long dead, buried deep in the heart, called back again to speak out, amplified by the vacuous silence of the room.

Ava had tried to warn him, though she'd been bound to silence in her role as dutiful daughter. She'd always been caught between two parents and Terry felt a sudden overwhelming sense of sadness for his daughter.

Prue stopped smiling. Her mouth opened wider and wider, her face collapsing into a yawning, swirling hole. Terry stared into the hollow and saw only the darkness at the heart. A low rumbling like distant thunder emerged from the pit of it, then a cacophonous melancholy strung out into the room. He'd been the author of those sounds he'd realized, of her anguish and grief. But it wasn't too late—

"Prue," he tried to say, but the words couldn't compete with the piercing discord. He placed his hands to his ears. The notes became louder and louder, starting to come together, flowing into the familiar melody. Climbing higher and higher, as if to the gods. The crescendo surged into the room from her mouth, spiraling around as if in flight. The music broke against him like a wave, and in awe he opened his mouth dumbfounded and swallowed it all down.

The dead have no choice but to listen, but Prue always answered back. He should have known she'd want to have the last word.

The sound of the urn shattering broke Ava from her trance. She glanced at the shattered remains on the floor then looked toward her father.

"Dad? Dad?"

Terry could feel the ash in his throat, silted around his larynx. A cloud of ash and dust rested in his gullet. He reached for his voice but felt only his absence. Yet in his mind all he could hear was music.

V. H. Leslie's stories have appeared in *Black Static, Interzone, Weird Fiction Review, Strange Tales IV, Best British Horror,* and *Best British Fantasy.* She has also had fiction and non-fiction published in *Shadows and Tall Trees* and is a columnist for *This is Horror.* She was recently awarded a Hawthornden Fellowship and the Lightship First Chapter Prize; 2015 will see the release of her novella "Bodies of Water" as part of the Remains series from Salt Publishing and her debut short story collection, *Skein and Bone,* from Undertow Books. More information on the author can be found at vhleslie.wordpress.com.

Girder's art challenges people because he fills it
with his turmoil in order to exorcise himself . . .

EMOTIONAL DUES

═══◆═══

Simon Strantzas

Girder looked for somewhere to park. His rusted Chevy felt out of place on the tree-lined Bridle Path, its rust-orange holes like neon lights announcing his presence. He felt the neighbors' eyes spying on him—it was clear to every one of them that the scrawny man in the faded denim jacket and stained pants didn't belong. He wondered if they would feel the same about his paintings. Someday, he mused, they might crawl over one another to have one on their fancy wall. At least, he hoped. Girder took in the Rasp Estate, sitting a few hundred feet away, through his scarred windshield. The red-brick house sprawled, looming above bright emerald grass, its sharp roof knifing into the cerulean sky. He hoped coming had not been a mistake, because it felt like a colossal one.

Girder got out of the car into absolute quiet, his movement causing ripples in the chilled air. Brown and orange leaves were underfoot and everything smelled of sweet decay. The rain from the night before left enough damp that leaves clung to Girder's old shoes as he limped to the passenger side of his car. He shivered his thin jacket closer to squeeze more heat from the worn denim, and then folded down the torn vinyl seat to retrieve the wrapped painting he'd brought. He thought of Raymond, sitting in the back room of the Overground, sipping orange tea while Girder was out in the cold betraying him, and reminded himself he was doing the right thing.

The walk to Rasp's door was a long one, hampered not only by a crooked leg but by the weight of the painting in Girder's weak arms. He had to traverse the distance slowly, his jaw hanging loose as he panted, breath sour and full of worry. Girder wished he could have contacted Mr. Rasp before arriving unannounced at his gate, but there was no listing in the telephone directory, and Girder knew no one who might help. He had no contacts in the community, no one but Mr.

Raymond, who insisted on brokering all deals for Girder's work, and Raymond would not be so quick to be cut out of the equation. Merely asking for Rasp's name had caused the man's drill-hole eyes to blink repeatedly, like an alligator preparing to snap. "It's a habit I'm loath to get into. Everyone is a friend when the gallery's walls are full, but when that work starts to sell, artists quickly forget what it is I do for my commission." Girder had to lie and promise he would not circumvent Raymond before the gallery owner would reveal Rasp's name, an action that later filled him with regret.

Raymond claimed to have met Rasp only once; long enough to show him Girder's work. "How did he know about it?" Girder asked when Raymond, breathlessly, told him the news.

"Do you remember that tall dark man lingering at the show? He works for Rasp. A scout or buyer or some such. I definitely know him from somewhere." Rasp had arrived at the Overground's closing hour, heralded by his assistant. "The fellow made sure no one else was in the gallery before bringing Rasp in. I was quite furious until I realized who he was." Rasp had grimaced at the work on the wall, Raymond said, scowling when he found Girder's abstractions. Then Raymond claimed Rasp's eyes widened as he stared deep into the swirls of paint and immediately insisted he own the series. When Girder arrived at the gallery the next day, Raymond handed him a check. Finally, there were digits enough to reflect what he deserved. For the first time since his father's passing, Girder wished the bastard were still alive. Just so he might finally rub his nose in it.

It was a relief to put the wrapped painting down in front of Rasp's large red door. Needles pricked the length of Girder's knotted arms, and his curved left hip throbbed. He pressed the doorbell, heard a soft chime thud somewhere in the depths of Rasp's estate, and rubbed his hands together for warmth. He rang the bell again and waited. There was no movement. Peering through the circular inset window, he saw nothing but darkness. Perhaps Rasp was not interested in seeing any more of Girder's work. Perhaps there was something to his father's drunken laughter. Perhaps—

The creak of metal hinges, dreadfully cautious of what was to come. A tall thin Asian man appeared, his flesh the sallow tan of someone sheltered from the sun all his life. He wore a pinstriped suit, its sleeves too long, and did not utter a word. Instead, he scoured Girder inscrutably. Girder swallowed, his nerve abandoning him as he stared at those empty eyes.

"Um . . . I'm here to see Mr. Rasp."

It sounded like a question.

The suited man did not react, did not take his eyes from Girder's. He spoke with a hollow voice and an accent Girder couldn't place.

"He does not take visitors."

"But I—I have a painting here I thought he might want to buy."

"Why would he want to do that?"

"Why?" Girder stammered. "Because I'm Girder Schill."

Dark eyes slipped behind narrowed eyelids. Girder shuffled, paper-wrapped parcel at his feet.

"Should I know who that is?"

Girder frowned. His voice betrayed his irritation.

"Mr. Rasp bought some of my paintings from the Overground. I think he might be interested in seeing more."

A noise between a sniffle and a snort. A raised knotted hand.

"Wait here."

The man vanished behind the closed red door. Girder's anger welled; red patterns mixed and swirled with other colors as they crept over his eyes, abstract shapes betraying some secret. Girder willed himself to calm down. He had no conduit for the vision at hand. He could not allow himself an episode without documentation. No puzzles without all the pieces. Girder looked down at where his narrow hands must have been and willed them to appear through the haze. He visualized each digit, forced the vision back to the edges of his sight until it passed. His mouth tasted like a battery. His heart beat wildly. Every muscle in his body tensed and ached. It took ten cold minutes for the door to open and a pale tan hand to beckon, fluttering urgently like a wounded bird.

Through some strange refraction of light, the foyer appeared too large, too long. The ceiling was at least twenty feet from the ground, trimmed with ornate cornicing, and the walls were dark with paint or shadow, lined into nothingness with rows of artwork. A table lamp illuminated the foyer just barely, chasing the darkness to the corners to bide its time. The thin man materialized from the dark like a strange specter.

"Mr. Rasp will be right with you."

Girder's nerves jittered. Rasp could be his salvation. If so, betraying Raymond would be worthwhile, even if the gallerist had been the only one brave enough to show Girder's work. He called it "a violent cacophony of nightmares." For Girder, they were catharsis, rage, and inadequacy painted on canvas; a conduit for his hallucinations, something he barely understood. "It's automatic painting, dear," Raymond said. "All the best do it. It's a money-maker."

Yet that money never came.

"No one likes looking at them, dear," Raymond said, tipsy on champagne as the show closed, his tiny eyes glazed bubbles. "It unnerves them."

And continued to unnerve them over the following days. At least until Rasp arrived.

An unusual odor wafted into the foyer. Damp, meaty, stale; so subtle it might have always been there. A pale shape floated through shadows some distance away, hovering a few feet from the ground like a humming wasp's nest. When further veils pulled back, Girder saw ill-defined features coalesce. From nothing formed what could only be the wrinkled face of the elusive Mr. Rasp.

He was rotund. Confined to a wheelchair pushed by the tall assistant, and cocooned in a heavy indigo robe, Rasp's pale bulbous head was perched on the folds around a bruised throat. No other flesh was exposed. His gloved hands were attached to withered lifeless arms that rested at his side. The wheelchair stopped a few feet from Girder, and the artist had to stifle his reaction. Rasp's flesh was nearly translucent, filled with dark spider-web veins, and his red mouth was an open wound, revealing too many tiny discolored teeth.

"You are Girder Schill?"

The wound spoke with incredulity, the voice harsh, consonants accentuated yet wet. Doubt momentarily infected Girder. He favored his good leg.

"Yes, I am." He belonged there; he repeated it to himself. "I'm sorry for showing up without warning you first."

"Never mind. Never mind." Rasp's head rolled, threatening to fall off his rigid body. "You aren't as I expected you. One builds an image in one's thoughts."

Girder knew that all too well.

"I don't want to take up too much of your time, Mr. Rasp. I have a painting here and I—"

"Nonsense. You aren't taking any of my time at all. Come, you could no doubt use something to drink. You look positively drained."

"Well, I—" Girder started, but Rasp was gone before he could finish. The sound of rubber wheels echoed, voices fading. Only the rows of paintings remained.

Girder carried his package and found Rasp in the sitting room, his tall assistant by his side. The room was bigger than Girder's entire apartment. Yet, in there, Rasp's presence swallowed the space.

"Sit. Nadir will bring something to drink. Do you have anything in particular you'd like?"

"I'll—I mean, I'll have whatever you're having."

"Oh, I won't be drinking with you. Despite how I look I'm on a very strict diet." Yellow smile, dark gums revealed. Still, Girder tried to laugh, though he was certain it sounded forced.

"Just a beer, I guess. If it isn't any trouble."

"None at all. Nadir?" The thin man nodded, almost bowed, then slipped through the doorway. "Now, while we wait, let's take a look at this painting. I'm rather excited, as you can imagine."

Girder stood. Everything rested on how Rasp reacted to the work. Without his patronage, Girder's future was dire. His leg wobbled long enough to catch Rasp's eye. He put it out of his mind and focused on the string tied around the painting's frame, and how it had become knotted. He worked the knot with the tips of his nails, knowing they were far too short, but also that he had no other way of opening the package. The panic was sour in his throat.

"I'd help you but—" Rasp looked down at his own thin withered arms. Girder nodded, then struck upon an idea. Keys from his pocket found the twine, and there followed the sound of a bowstring being plucked. Girder carefully removed the flat brown butcher's paper. Rasp stared hungrily. Girder's stomach growled.

"This one is called 'The Empty House.' It's oil on canvas."

Girder held the painting at arm's length. Rasp's voice wheezed, "Higher, please." Girder lifted until his face was covered. "Nice, nice," Rasp said, then a wet sound like lips being licked. Girder lowered the painting. Rasp looked beatific.

"It's a wonderful piece. Wonderful. Just as I expected. The color, the emotional fury; it's like a late-period Gotlib, or even a Munch—if Munch were any good. Compared to you, though, the two were finger-painting. I can see the emotion here, so much it hurts. Tell me, does it have a story?"

Girder's father's fists. Insults, jeers. A beating that irreparably loosened something in Girder's brain. A cultured veil of fury; abstractions hinting at unfulfilled secrets. Vision that had to be fixed in place with paint to be understood, to be made real. It was his father's dying gift.

"No, there's no story. It's just a painting."

The fat man's laugh sounded like wet choking. Tiny brown teeth bared, a dozen pale lumps struggling for escape against indigo folds. Girder became worried, but as Nadir returned, beer on a small platter, that mirth ebbed.

"It's not customary for me to take visitors here, Mr. Schill, which is why I can't offer you anything more exotic to drink. In truth, Mr. Raymond should not have provided you with any information about me. It causes too many ethical conflicts."

Girder nodded but said nothing. He did not want to accidentally dissuade Mr. Rasp from the purchase. Instead, he slowly sipped at the beer he had been given and tried to keep his sensation of biliousness at bay.

"Normally, I'd have you sent back to Mr. Raymond to arrange the transaction, but your work is something to behold—so emotional!—that I'm willing to cut out the middle man, as it were, so I might get new works more expediently. I assume the rate I paid at the Overground would suffice here? Good! Nadir, take this piece and bring me a check for the normal amount. It seems Mr. Schill and I have come to an agreement." Another smile full of ugly brown teeth. Girder questioned whether what he felt was happiness, especially when he held the check in shaking hands. It was more than Mr. Raymond had ever given him.

"You look pleased, Mr. Schill."

"Oh, I am. Yes. This will help me out a lot."

"Good. I trust then there will be more pieces coming?"

Girder had no doubt.

Girder returned home, energized. Why had he needed the gallery when the direct approach was so lucrative? Rasp would be his salvation, not smug, thieving Mr. Raymond. Girder's work was finally being recognized for its worth; neither Raymond nor his dead idiot of a father could tell him otherwise.

The money paid Girder's outstanding bills, and what remained paid for supplies. Canvases were stretched, paints were mixed; Girder's specters hovered close, revealing themselves only when finally he held his brush. An opaque veil dropped, his eyes clouded. A landscape of colors clashing, a Rorschach of emotion. He worked hard to commit the essence to reality. Weeks passed, but the anger did not. The colors didn't run, didn't move. Instead, they leapt from the brush. Never had the euphoria been so cathartic. Never had the muse guided his arm so exactly. From him pains and sorrows flowed onto canvas. At the end of the fourth week, he awoke on the floor, paint outlining him, muscles aching. The work was done, though he couldn't remember when. Exhausted, he staggered to bed, slept more than a day. His dreams were monochrome.

"Frankly, Mr. Schill, I feared you wouldn't return."

Girder's face could not contain his smile.

"Of course I was going to. I painted this for you."

"Oh, I should hope not. I hope you painted it for yourself. That's where the choicest pieces originate." And Rasp laughed, though it was strange and stuttered. His perched head rolled. Girder averted his eyes, but it was too late. He'd already seen it.

"Nadir, if you'll do the honors."

The tall assistant nodded, then reached to peel the butcher paper from the canvas. As he did so, his sleeve pulled too far back and a flash of skin stained different colors caught Girder's eye. Just as quickly it was gone, replaced with the sight of Rasp expectantly dampening his lips with a sliver of desiccated tongue.

"Well, stand back, man," he urged, and his assistant withdrew a few steps. Rasp looked at the canvas, then at Girder. The look on his face was inscrutable. Girder's mouth was drier than it ever had been.

"Mr. Schill," Rasp began slowly. "What appealed to me most about the pieces of yours I purchased from your friend, Mr. Raymond, was the *emotion* expressed in that work. It was as though your feelings had free rein. Love, hate, anger, jealousy, betrayal—it was all on display in brutally honest detail." Rasp's pale eyes were glassy, a thread of spittle crept from the corner of his bloodless lips. Then his eyes cleared, and he looked hungrily at Girder. "That is the kind of work I'm looking for from you, Mr. Schill, and I have little use for anything else."

"I don't understand." Girder's voice quavered. His father's voice echoed from the caverns of the past. "Is there something wrong?"

"Wrong? Indeed, not. This is perfect."

Perfect. Not a word he'd heard before. The sound of it was strange and joyously unnatural. His father would never have used such a term. He might instead have laughed if he'd heard it uttered, especially in reference to Girder. "You?" he'd say amid drunken punches. "You're joking!" Even in the haze of morning, when the fumes of his father's drinking lingered like an uninvited guest, he might croak, "Sorry, Girder. Nobody's perfect." Years later, Mr. Raymond, who ostensibly worked to promote Girder's art, would echo the sentiment. "Nothing is perfect, love. Your work challenges people because you *bleed* on the canvas; you fill it with your turmoil to exorcise yourself. But that's why no one is buying your paintings. It's because sometimes something nakedly displaying another man's soul is unsettling at best. And at worst, repulsive." But Mr. Rasp had since arrived and offered salvation. A corpulent angel with a lolling head, laughingly making easy what had always been difficult. All Girder deserved was finally handed to him without question. For a moment he almost believed that everything might one day be . . . no, he would not say the word.

"Perfect," Rasp repeated on seeing the unwrapped canvas. "It's absolutely perfect." Girder exhaled and hunger returned to his limbs. *Not long now,* he told them, but they shook in doubt. The painting was a culmination, and those emotions painted an intricate landscape that even he could scarcely believe had been reproduced by his brush. Yet there it was. No doubt the painting looked better than he did: as the paints were mixing in his mind and subsequently drying on the canvas, he did not see a single mirror. Had he, the haggard man staring would have likely been unrecognizable. It came at a great cost to him. Wasn't it reasonable to pass those costs on?

"I'm happy you like the piece, Mr. Rasp, don't get me wrong, but the price on the work in the past—What I mean is, I feel *this* particular piece is bit beyond those in quality, and should maybe command something higher?" Girder's voice wavered and body shook. The speech hadn't been practiced enough, and it was too late to snatch the words back. The white of Rasp's eyes narrowed, his small puckered tongue ran slowly over his lower lip. Nadir remained motionless, but Girder suspected he was affecting a lack of interest. Finally, Rasp bellowed, body rippling with laughter.

"Of course, Mr. Schill. Of course. I wouldn't dream of cheating you on this most exquisite piece. *This* is true genius. Nadir, wouldn't you agree?"

The assistant's eyes barely grazed the painting; instead, they were focused on its nervous painter. Nadir again wore that inscrutable look upon his face. Was it pity? Jealousy? Whatever it might have been, it caused him to utter a few forced words under his breath before he snatched the canvas from Girder.

Relieved as he was of both burdens—that of the painting and of the request for more money—Girder's heart finally slowed enough for his blood to cool. It was only then he wondered if he had been terrified into blindness, for he realized the walls in the sitting room around him were empty of everything but hooks.

"What's happened to the paintings?"

Rasp's gash opened, but instead of words it emitted a violent cough. Nadir appeared instantly, brandishing a handkerchief he had produced from some hidden pocket, and covered Rasp's mouth. Rasp's head and throat heaved, body motionless, and filled the handkerchief with heavy sputum. Girder averted his eyes, but not before he noticed something red seep through, and in his shock mistakenly thought he saw other colors, too. Nadir made the mess vanish into his pocket. Rasp's head hung low when he was done, panting and wheezing. Girder shifted back to his good leg. His bad ached.

"Are you okay?"

"Don't—you needn't worry about me. I'm fine." Rasp's speech was broken, the pale flesh around his mouth wet. "But this brings to mind something I thought I might propose. I wasn't sure I would until I saw this latest work of yours . . . and saw the sorry state of its creator. You look barely able to walk." Girder winced. "For a short time, I think it might be best if you stayed here on the estate to work."

The surprise was not Girder's alone. Nadir's entire reaction crossed his face in an instant. He reacted sharply.

"No."

For whom was the word meant? Girder or Rasp? The painter's crooked leg throbbed. Rasp did not look pleased.

"Ignore him, Mr. Schill. This is an arrangement that can only work to our mutual benefit. You will be freed from the burdens that distract you from your work, and I will be able to watch and help guide you. Of course, you would get a stipend for this, regardless of the amount or quality of work produced."

"I don't know. I'm not sure I feel comfortable—"

"Nonsense. I am not trying to *buy* you." The laugh was unnatural, the sound only an approximation. "Think of it as an artistic retreat. Spend a few weeks here and see what you produce without other worldly concerns. In truth, I'm not certain I can wait another month for a new piece of work, regardless of how much I enjoy this one."

"But a month . . . most of my work takes longer."

"I have plenty of artwork here, enough to sate me if necessary, but nothing so pure as yours, I fear. No, you'll have to concentrate on the job at hand, and the only way to do it is to strip you of your earthly concerns. See what you can accomplish for me."

Nadir glared. Those eyes barraged Girder, searing into him. That alone was reason to decline. But Girder thought of the cold winter knocking, one foot already through his apartment door. He thought of the empty shelves, and his throbbing leg. Still unconvinced, he thought of his father's jeers.

"I suppose a few weeks couldn't hurt."

"Splendid," Rasp said. Nadir's stare made it obvious winter had already arrived.

Nadir's demeanor was unchanged the next day. He helped Girder bring his bags and supplies into the house, but did not speak. Instead, Rasp did the speaking from his chair parked in the doorway, out of the sun.

"Whatever you need, Mr. Schill, to make your stay pleasant, please let Nadir know."

Girder's room was large and faced south to maximize working daylight. A king-size bed, a small chaise longue, a fireplace. The large window overlooked the winter garden; the deep greens vibrant, orange flowers like starbursts. Girder couldn't imagine a better-suited workplace. As promised, there were no distractions in the room; no telephone or radio. The walls were as bare as the sitting room's. Which Girder found odd, considering.

Rasp visited only once. Nadir wheeled him in as Girder was finishing the setup of his workspace.

"Should you feel hungry later, the kitchen is to your left at the end of the hall. It's open to you at any time."

"What time should I be down for dinner?"

Rasp's dark lips curled, quivered. "Not today, I'm afraid. I've made other arrangements. Besides, watching me eat is not something most people would relish. Wouldn't you agree, Nadir?" The tall assistant's face twitched.

"Maybe next time?"

Girder was ashamed of the desperate tone to his voice. Rasp's strange breathing sounded like a giggle.

"Perhaps."

Amply supplied with paint, Girder faced the empty stare of the blank canvas. He sighed. The first brush stroke was the hardest. He did not plot nor plan. Instead, he dredged—pain and frustration . . . He moved his mind into his rotted leg, visualized the nerve endings sparking in the darkness, waited for it all to coalesce. He almost touched the brush to the canvas, but knew the simplest stroke locked out an infinite number of others. He preferred the vast nothingness where it was safe, warm. Protective. A single mark could not be undone. Potential hemorrhaged. He willed the images to come from beneath and feed him. He closed his eyes and waited. Waited. They would come. They always came. He simply had to have faith.

A deep familiar voice echoed in the hall outside the room, and Girder's blood chilled. It couldn't be. Not him. Every inch of skin constricted, trying to shrink Girder from existence. How had he been discovered? All the resolve Girder had built up wavered.

When the inevitable knock arrived, Girder's hesitated. He did not want to face what was beyond. The knock returned, insistent, and he realized there was no escape. Never from him. Girder opened the door and found the two men he least wanted to see: the tall hawkish Nadir, triumphant, a stack of paintings under his thin arm; and the viper-faced Mr. Raymond, whose eyes were spitting above his plaster smile.

"Hello, Girder." The voice tight, his anger barely suppressed. Or was it pleading? Mocking? Was there some plan Raymond had colluded with Nadir to implement? Girder was tired, unable to think straight. Perhaps he was wrong about everything. And yet there Mr. Raymond was, weeks after Girder had last been to the Overground. A haunting of his past betrayal made flesh. One of his many hauntings.

Nadir looked derisive. "I can see you two have a lot to discuss. Thank you for the delivery, Mr. Raymond. Mr. Schill, if you could show him out when you're done?"

Nadir stepped back, absorbed into shadows. Girder fumbled for words as Raymond stared.

"Um . . . I suppose you're wondering . . . "

Raymond's hand struck out and snatched Girder's wrist before he could escape. The gallerist squeezed tight and spoke, his voice a seething whisper.

"I don't know what you're thinking, but you'd better get out of here."

"I'm just doing—"

"I don't care what Rasp has you doing. I don't normally care to be involved in this sort of thing at all—life's too short to mourn a loss—but this isn't right. Selling to him is one thing, but this . . . this place *smells* like a nest of something, though I can't say what. You should leave."

Girder wrested his arm free.

"I *have* to stay," he said, rubbing his wrist. "But it's not for long. All I'm doing is painting a few pieces and then I'm going home. I'll probably have more for you to hang at the Overground in a month or two."

"You know that . . . person? That Nadir fellow? He doesn't look at all familiar to you, does he? No, he probably wouldn't. But I know him well, even if he doesn't remember me. I tried to help him too once. Now look at him."

"What are you—"

"Look at him, Girder. He's used up. A junkie. You'll be too. If you're lucky."

"I appreciate the concern, Mr. Raymond, but—but I think I can decide on my own what's best for me. You—you aren't my . . . "

Girder trailed off. Raymond's eyes had fallen back into half-slits, as though he had crawled back into shed skin. His old carefree face then returned, like a well-worn accessory.

"Sure. That's fine. If you manage to paint something else, dear, be sure to look me up. It was a pleasure working with you." He extended his hand and they shook, then Mr. Raymond wrapped his scarf around his long throat.

"Don't worry. I can show myself out."

"I'll let you know as soon as I have something," Girder said as Mr. Raymond walked down the hall, but the gallerist only offered back a cursory wave, not bothering to turn.

Nadir appeared a moment later, stepping into Girder's room without invitation. Frowning dark cuffs creeping away from his wringing hands.

"Why didn't you leave with him?"

"I know you don't want me here, but I need the money Mr. Rasp is offering." Nadir's expression was full of disgust. He shook his head.

"Everybody always needs something." Nadir casually looked over at Girder's easel and the blank canvas that sat on it, and his face changed.

"What is it?" Girder asked, but Nadir wouldn't stay. He simply looked wide-eyed at Girder, then left, fleeing out the room on spindle legs. Girder closed the door behind him, then to be safe he double-checked the locks.

He could not return to work. His leg throbbed incessantly. Everything was in tatters. But why? For money? Was nearly starving a good enough excuse? He hobbled to the window and peered down at the winter garden. Night had steadily crept in, turning small bushes into shadows, the trees into silhouettes with lifeless branches bent downward in defeat. Girder sighed, finally turned away and saw the blank canvas in the dim room. He had nothing with which to fill it. He had come to the estate hoping his problems would vanish; instead, the isolation amplified them.

It was just after midnight when Girder managed to put brush to canvas. He slipped into an autonomous state, the brush becoming a conduit for his catharsis. He dug deep into the places he'd been twisted by what had been done to him, by what he in turn had done to others. Colors swirled in a tempest of pain behind his eyes. He simply tapped and bled them onto canvas. Each painting was in the end the same: a formless portrait of his father. Girder pressed until exhaustion crept into his senses. It was only then he lay, aching, on the bed. Eyes strained, dry, and swollen, he closed his lids and saw those swirling colors start to fade. But the sound did not. The quiet sound of something wet being dragged.

It was louder in the hallway. Echoes bounced around corridors barely lit by the rising sun. At the other end of the hall was a shut door, and as the bare-footed Girder approached it the noise intensified. He noticed the air was tinged with a sour metallic odor, and he stared at the door to reassure himself it wasn't vibrating. As he reached out to touch it, the sound, all sound, sputtered then stopped. And the world inverted. There was a quiet noise, then the squeak of rubber. Girder saw the beam of light at his feet broken by shadow, and when he looked up Nadir had emerged from the room and stood before him. Sound rushed back with a gasp.

"What are you doing here?"

"I'm sorry, I just . . . " Girder glanced around the shoulder of the tall man and saw Rasp's back as he sat in his chair, a dark wide canvas of indigo. Paintings surrounding him, paintings piled on the floor and against the wall. He appeared to be sweating, his pale skin greasy and rippling like gelatin in disturbance. Nadir's dark shadow obscured the sight.

"Get out of here," the assistant warned. Large hands pounded Girder's chest like two hammers. Girder's mind grappled with what it saw, but it was only after the door had closed that the sight fully developed. Nadir's hands were slick and stained like a bruise, purplish-yellow and red. Girder wondered what had they done.

Mid-afternoon appeared before Rasp did. Girder had hidden all morning— his confusion adding streaks through the colors swirling in his mind's eye— but eventually gnawing hunger overtook him, and he turned to the stocked kitchen. He made a turkey and Swiss sandwich as quickly as he could, anxious to return to his hiding. But the warning squeal of rubber came too late. He looked over his shoulder to see the overweight sweating Rasp and the hovering Nadir in the doorway, both watching him intently. The eyes of the latter narrowed. Rasp's voice was unusually clear.

"I apologize for Nadir's behavior this morning. It was . . . *harsh.*"

"It was my fault. I shouldn't have intruded like that."

"No harm done," Rasp dismissed, and shook his head. Did his pale skin vibrate too long? "How is the work coming? I trust everything is to your satisfaction?"

"Yes, of course. I mean, the work is going well. I think."

"Good, good. I can't wait to see what you have for me." Rasp flashed his blackened gums. Girder shifted uneasily on his weak leg. He rubbed the damaged muscles, the dull sensation giving him comfort.

"I think you'll be pleased when it's done."

"I'm sure I will be. I'm a man of tremendous appetites, as you can tell, and there's little I love more than a fine piece of art. Wouldn't you say so, Nadir?"

Nadir ignored the question.

"Did you know we had a visit yesterday from Mr. Raymond, the dealer from the Overground? Girder and he had a good talk."

"Oh, did they? What did Mr. Raymond have to say to you, my boy? Did he try and steal your talent back from me?"

Discomfited, Girder stumbled.

"No, not really. He seemed fine."

"You can never tell with a *snake* like that one," Rasp chortled, round head bobbing into folds of deep indigo. "He's always trying to slide in where he isn't wanted, isn't he, Nadir?"

Rasp's smile did not make it to the eyes. He wore a pair of gloves that obscured stained flesh.

Rasp continued. "Ah, well. It looks as though we're disturbing you. I merely wanted to let you know that as I feel a smidgen under the weather I may not be able to visit you as often as I'd wished to track your progress. Rest assured, though, Nadir will be here to help you with whatever you may require. I expect only the best from you, Mr. Schill. You are certainly capable of it." He swallowed, small lumps travelling down his throat like swallowed eggs. "Nadir, please take me away so our guest might continue working."

Rasp was wheeled into the dark, the remaining funk that surrounded him dissipating slowly. Girder took the sandwich he'd been making and threw it away. He was no longer hungry.

Time passed. Girder spent the time sequestered, leaving the room rarely. He lived inside a world of color, dreaming it, breathing it, at times unsure what was real. The only interruption was Nadir's begrudging apologies for Rasp. "He doesn't feel well." And, "It's a side-effect of his incapacitation." It didn't concern Girder. Little of the material world did. As long as supplies were by his door each morning, his fever dream would not subside. Should strange wet noises have persisted beyond his door, he was too busy or too tired to notice.

Never had he worked so quickly, with so much complexity. If Rasp wanted emotion, he would get it. Every sting felt, every hurt suffered, raw materials as essential as paint. Girder's father's laugh, the pain from his ruined leg, the glare of Nadir, the doubt of Raymond, all formed a cultured mosaic he alone could see. His scoured soul, his scars mapped in brushstrokes. Cramped fingers became his ultimate medium—the pain bringing tears to his color-blinded eyes.

And two weeks later and twenty pounds lighter, in a spent daze he took in the finished work and smiled.

The smile remained as he sat in the kitchen. Coffee brewed inside while outside the snowstorm did the same. A reticent howl echoed through the estate. Girder felt serene yet looked worse—thickly bearded, eyes bloodshot and dark—but the smile was genuine. For the first in some time, he was at peace. His happiness was the only reason that explained Nadir's noiseless appearance in the kitchen's doorway.

"The painting is done?"

Girder beamed. Nodded.

"Then Mr. Rasp will be pleased."

But once Nadir slipped away to tell Rasp, the realization finally penetrated the fog of denial. Rasp wanted it all, wanted every ounce of Girder, and the artist had been more than willing to dredge it up. But now that the time had come to hand it over—to hand *everything* over . . .

In truth, Girder was spent; there was not another opus in him. He had been burned clean of anger and resentment, welling colors drained from his soul. All of it, all his father's monstrosity, was contained within the painting, all the suffering trapped in the strokes of the brush. The painting hummed with power, and Girder did not want to relinquish it. Not to anyone, even Rasp. Yet that was who had housed him, who had fed him . . . He owed Rasp a great deal, but the price was too high.

An hour later, Nadir delivered Rasp to Girder's room. The porcine man had changed somehow. Both smaller and larger at once. Girder's yellow face alone was gaunt, though it lit when in the presence of the painting. "Absolutely marvelous," Rasp said.

"Nadir told me you were done, but I couldn't have expected this." Lips twitched, dark tongue passed over them nervously. "This is absolutely a masterpiece, Mr. Schill. A venerable masterpiece."

Even Nadir seemed impressed; upon seeing it his face registered genuine, if fleeting, emotion. Perhaps awe? The reaction was both reassuring and disappointing.

"I don't think I could have done it without your hospitality Mr. Rasp. You're generosity may have literally saved me."

"Think nothing of it. Seeing the results just proves I made the right decision." A glance at Nadir; the servant's eyes were elsewhere. "You've outdone yourself, Mr. Schill. I consider this whole endeavor money well spent."

Girder silently cursed. Rasp clearly wanted the painting. Which meant Girder had to gather some nerve.

"Um . . . about that, Mr. Rasp—"

Rasp's head ceased bobbing.

"Now, now. We had a deal, did we not?"

"It's just that—"

"Did I not keep up my end of the bargain, Mr. Girder? I've provided for you all that you've asked, but I didn't do so for your charity."

"Perhaps I could paint you another one? Perhaps something else?"

"No, Mr. Schill. I think the time for that has passed. I must insist. I couldn't possibly let this specific painting escape me."

Girder stammered. Rasp's words cut him short.

"Nadir, come." Rasp whispered into his servant's ear. The tall man smirked, nodded, then left the room. Rasp resumed speaking, albeit in a quieter voice.

"Mr. Schill. I don't appreciate the situation you've placed me in, but I am a fair and reasonable man. I will give you double your normal rate—the rate which Mr. Raymond would charge me—for this painting. I do so, you understand, under duress, and only because I simply cannot wait to see if what you produce next is suitable. I suspect this painting will satiate me for some time—it's so rich, so deep with power. But I think this may be the last time you and I can do business this way. I recommend that after we are done here you make arrangements to return immediately to your home."

Nadir reappeared before Girder could find words to reply. He showed Rasp a checkbook but did not take his eyes from Girder.

"I want you to give him double, Nadir. Plus the stipend I promised. Then I want you to help him load his belongings into his car. He won't be staying with us any longer."

"But Mr. Rasp . . . " Girder couldn't believe the sound of his own warbling voice—everything was falling to pieces. "The snowstorm . . . it's not safe."

Mr. Rasp considered this for a cold moment.

"Very well, Mr. Schill. You may stay an extra night. But tomorrow you must go. And, in the future, you ought to allow Mr. Raymond alone to handle your sales to any prospective buyers."

Girder sat devastated on the bed of his borrowed room. Outside the window was the furious chaos of snow, and despite the fireplace's radiating heat he remained both cold and empty. How had things devolved so quickly? His father's voice echoed, reminding him that he destroyed everything good. Girder didn't have to believe it to know it was true.

He washed face in the small en suite sink, then stared in the mirror at his sagging reflection. Girder was a fool. He had risked everything on a fantasy and a dream, neither of which had come true. There was so much road left ahead, and what did he do? He drove into the desert.

Without Mr. Rasp's aid, what would become of Girder? Would he fade to nothing? Upset, the artist's fingers twitched, craving the security of the brush, the expression of its bristles. But behind closed eyelids nothing waited. No points, no pricks, no colors shifting, swirling, dancing. Even clenched fists rubbing orbital bone made no difference. The visions did not return. He opened his eyes, watched the periphery of his vision crackle with energy as his sight settled. His father's greatest scar had finally faded, and Girder knelt down on his working knee, terrified of what that might mean.

Consumed by listless melancholy, Girder did not immediately notice that the pungent, meaty odor had returned. He opened the door and took a step into the hallway, then stopped. There was nothing but darkness down the empty corridor.

No, not just darkness. The sound of something in the darkness. Something being dragged ever closer.

Girder's vision grew hazy, and he shook his head before retreating. Then he pressed his full weight against his door to fortify the barrier. With his ear to the wood, he once again heard wet sounds and recalled the trail of fluid streaked across the hall. What it suggested was not something he was willing to think about, willing to face. The storm rattled windows and doors, but it was the walls that sounded as though they were being ripped apart.

He opened the door no more than a crack large enough to peer through, but all he saw was a thin slice of shadow. His breathing was turbulent, lungs aching, yet he was too panicked to do anything but stare into the dark. Everything beyond a few feet was lost in a thick unfocused fog. He had to concentrate to see through it, and when the murk parted he saw the dark shadow racing along the hall toward him. Girder withdrew from the door, terrified, almost falling over his crippled leg, and as he did so the wet noises of the house were transformed into those of Nadir's bare footsteps.

Rasp's servant held a large, familiar-looking canvas against his body, shielding it from Girder's view. He rushed down the hall, oblivious to spying, toward Rasp's door at the other end. Nadir struggled with the size of the painting, the encumbrance magnified by the presence of his ill-fitting pinstriped suit. The cuffs rode high as Nadir fussed to maintain his grip, and Girder saw that those dark blotches on Nadir's wrists extended further along his arms. When he reached the end of the hall, Nadir lowered the painting and put his key in the door. Light spilled into the hallway, and Nadir picked up the painting, then disappeared into the room. The low humming buzz returned, lasting for almost two hours, while unsteady light slipped from the crack beneath Rasp's door.

An idea occurred to Girder, one that didn't fill him with pride for considering, but he knew he had been left with few options. When without warning the buzz abruptly ceased, Girder stood and slipped into his shoes. He peered once again through the crack in his door and saw Nadir emerge from the darkened room, sleeves rolled to his elbows. In his hands was the same large canvas he had carried earlier, and he lugged it back down the hallway, only now in a state of either thorough exhaustion or inebriation. He slowed only briefly as he neared Girder's door and scowled in its direction, then continued without losing a step. Girder watched him round the corner at the end of the hall, vanishing into shadows filled with the storm's white noise.

He had to discover where his paintings were being kept. Part of him tried to justify his quest with the knowledge that he would never be in the presence of the pieces again, so he deserved to see them one last time. But even as he crept behind Nadir he knew it was untrue. Girder could never abandon something that was so much a part of him. He might just as well be leaving behind his soul. Based merely on Rasp's reaction earlier, there was no way the fat man would part with the painting now that he had it, so Girder would simply be forced to take it and hope for the best. The biggest difficulty would be getting it to the car in the storm, but he would find a way. He had to.

It did not take long for Girder to discover the hiding place. He had barely rounded the corner of the hallway when Nadir stepped empty-handed from a shadowed nook. There was no time to pivot on his crippled leg before Girder was seen, so he immediately did his best to affect an expression of confusion and exhaustion. It seemed to make Nadir more suspicious. The assistant rolled down his sleeves as he spoke.

"What are you doing up?"

"I couldn't sleep, so I thought I'd spend one last night looking around. I'm going to miss being here."

Nadir narrowed his eyes.

"It's probably better you go."

"Better for whom?"

Girder tried not to blink, but he was outclassed by Nadir. It was like staring into the uncaring face of a reptile.

"Are you packed?" Nadir asked, finally breaking the quiet.

"Yes. Everything but my easel and artwork."

"Go to your room now and get some sleep. Be ready to leave at nine," he said, and waited until Girder left first. He followed Girder the entire way, waiting until he was back behind the closed bedroom door. Girder heard breathing outside the door for half an hour, waiting for Girder to fall asleep. Despite his best efforts, Girder almost did, which left him disoriented when awakened by the quiet sounds of Nadir abandoning his post and giving Girder the freedom to explore.

The long hallway was worse when empty, and Girder's slow walk only increased his terror of being discovered. He stayed in the shadows as much as possible and kept his ears attuned to any noises that might betray he was being watched. When he finally turned the corner he stopped and checked back where he'd come from to ensure no one was there. He heard a faint knocking sound, as though the storm were intensifying. Then he turned back to the shadowed nook and the nearly invisible door hidden within.

It was made to be unnoticeable; its color, and the shadows, perpetually shielding it from ignorant eyes. The structure itself was incongruous, as though an afterthought. Perhaps it was an illusion of the slanted ceiling, but the hidden door's corners appeared flush, and its knob sunk deep in the dark. Girder's hand faltered. Behind him the knocking had faded, leaving only the static of the storming snow in the distance. He pulled the door carefully, but at first it didn't move, as though being held shut from the inside. Then the resistance gave, and it swung open so suddenly Girder nearly fell.

In the dark he saw a stack of wood-framed canvases leaned against the wall, but it wasn't until he discovered a small light switch that he realized how many were truly there. Numerous piles of canvases, a hundred or more, covered almost every inch of the room. Some were in piles on the floor; others were stacked against the wall a dozen deep. All were face down, as though to protect them. Girder had never been in the presence of so many paintings at once outside a museum, and after the shock dissipated, he wondered how many of them were his.

In the far corner, he spied a facedown painting whose shape struck him oddly familiar. Hadn't he stretched a canvas like that in the past? He stepped forward and flipped the piece over, only to find himself puzzled. It couldn't be right. He flipped over the painting's neighbor, turning the canvas face up, and then flipped over the one beside that. He flipped all the paintings around him, but the result was the same: they were blank. All of them. Not painted over, but never having been painted on to begin with, as if they were all that remained of former paintings that no longer existed. They were empty; only a foul-smelling tallow remained, covering the canvases, sticking to his hands.

Girder paced inside his room, mourned over what he'd seen; so many paintings destroyed—and who knew how many of his own. If there was any consolation it was that he could not find anything shaped like his last painting, his masterpiece, among them. It had been spared, but he didn't know for how long. He had to rescue it. There was no money in the world that meant more to him than that artwork. The painting held so much of him; its absence left him hollow. It needed to be retrieved.

Out the window drifts of snow accumulated in the storm. The world conspired to trap him while his soul screamed for flight. He could not leave without the painting. It was clear his survival depended upon it.

Girder stepped into the hall, put his bag down quietly. He had packed everything he could carry, left behind what he could not. The house was quieter than he had ever known it; the air's stillness lent a foreboding atmosphere that his intentions further cultured. He crept down the hall toward the Rasp's room, the source of that dreadful buzzing. At the door he listened for eternity, waiting for an indication he'd been caught, but nothing came. He tried the knob, eyes narrow in the hope that the door was not locked.

The knob turned and a bolt slid back with a faint click.

Girder opened the door only enough to slip inside. The veils were drawn, blocking all but the thinnest sliver of light. Navigating the dark was difficult, so he clung close to the wall, moved around the room toward where he remembered the stack of paintings were. He almost stumbled over something lumpy lying across the floor but managed to right himself in time. He waited, but heard no sign that he'd been discovered. He was completely alone.

Girder moved with one arm stretched outward, feeling his way. The painting could be anywhere, and though he knew it was intact, it was also vulnerable. He felt it calling like a piece of him that had been lost or gone missing. Girder concentrated on the sensation in the blind dark and reached out a final time, groping desperately in the void. He was thus amazed when his fingers grazed rough canvas, ever so slightly, and he knew instinctively he had found what he had sought for so long.

Nothing else moved in the dark. He picked up the canvas and experienced the immediate connection with something long lost. The painting for which Rasp had paid could not be sold. Girder would sooner have sold his soul. Both he and it had to leave the house immediately.

Touching the wall, inching forward to where the door should be waiting, he found nothing. The wall seemed to stretch forever, without end. And yet he couldn't even see the sliver of light from the hallway beneath the edge of the door. The only illumination in the room was from the reflection of the snowstorm, though Girder was not sure how it could be slipping in: there were no windows in the room.

Girder forced himself to remain calm and focus simply on finding the light switch. A brief flick would be long enough to get his bearings in the empty room. He put the painting down, ran his hands along the smooth walls, and limped onward. Was it indeed the room he'd been in earlier? It had to be. There was only one hallway between his room and Rasp's, and it wasn't possible to become lost so easily. And yet, nothing seemed familiar. Not the room's size nor shape nor layout. Nothing but Girder's mounting panic. He desperately wanted to escape the confines of the dark, his unintentional prison, and watched for the tinniest fragment of light.

There was no time in the dark. Minutes were days, and as the static of snow reached new heights outside, Girder's fingers skittered over the walls, looking for the hidden switch. They found it quite by surprise, having almost given up the search, and Girder huddled close to it for fear he might become lost once more. A quick burst, he promised himself. A single quick burst of light to fix his environment, eliminate its oneiricism. Long enough to gauge his location, but not long enough to arouse suspicion. One burst would tell him everything. He counted down in his head, opened his eyes wide to take in as much information as possible, then flicked the lights on and off so rapidly he didn't initially see anything at all. But his eyes were like instant photographs, and in the darkness a horrifying negative developed.

The room had shrunk, folding in on itself. Far smaller than he recalled, far smaller than could have been possible to navigate. Paintings were stacked everywhere, and as the image in his mind's eye formed it was clear his painting, his masterpiece, was among them. But what horrified him was not the clutter or the impossible size of his surroundings; it was what stood at the room's center—a large shadow around which Girder had circled while looking for the exit. It resolved slower than the rest of the items around it, yet Girder concentrated on that particular shadow the hardest, transfixed by his sense of dread. The thing was large, and at first indescribable. Only as features solidified from out of the darkness did Girder realize that what he stared at was Rasp, slumped in his wheelchair. Or at least what was left of Rasp.

The corpulent body sat motionless, dressed in the same encompassing purple robes, his lifeless arms on the wheelchairs handles, his feet on the tiny steps. Everything was as it should have been. Except his head. His head was gone, and only a hole remained.

The air was sucked from Girder's lungs; replaced with ice. He closed his eyes, but in the darkness it did not matter, the image remained burned on his retina, developing further instead of fading. Girder could see things he had not initially: the tiny undone clasps that ran up the front of Rasp's robes; the cauterized hole of a neck, red and puckered. Without Rasp's head, bobbing as he spoke, his body appeared artificial, a mere costume. But if that were the case, what did it disguise? And, more frighteningly, what had happened to whatever wore it?

Girder heard that wet sound again, like something dragged across the floor, so near it would be upon him at any moment. He reached down to retrieve the painting at his feet and prayed he could escape without turning on the light. He couldn't bear to see Rasp's body again. But without that second look, relying only on his quickly fading memories, he misjudged his dash and grazed something that could only have been the headless body. There was no sound from the heavy mass beyond a heavy sigh, but something fell behind Girder, hitting the floor with a sound like hollow wood, and Girder knew there was no time left for him.

He groped for his final painting, finding it where he imagined the doorknob to be. The wet sound recurred louder and faster, and he scrambled out and into the dark hallway.

He ran blindly, unsure of where he was going. The hallway looked different in the night—corners where there shouldn't have been, solid walls that ought to have been doors. And with each crooked step rattling in his head, with each breath wheezing in his ears, he heard the wet sound, rasping as if it too were breathless.

The painting under his arm made flight difficult, but it did not occur to Girder to drop it, to throw it aside. Everything he was, everything he had become since suffering under his father's fists was in it, and he would let no one steal it from him. He held the canvas tight, pushed it against the air that tried to knock it loose, to slow him down. Even when that scrambling wetness was overhead, echoing in his ears from above, he couldn't think of releasing the painting. From somewhere there was a hiss through ravaged flesh, a final rally before the deadliest blow, and Girder's bent leg finally faltered—a part of his soul already surrendering to his end.

But the hands that thrust out for him, dragged him into the light, were not from beyond. They were long-fingered and multicolored, and attached to narrow arms of similar complexion. Girder saw little else as he was flung sideways, the canvas slipping from his numb fingers as he tumbled over tangled limbs and onto the hard floor. The air filled with screeching, desperation denied, and Girder's tearing eyes stung from exertion. He could not comprehend what was happening, his head swimming, delirious from impossibilities. All connection to reality slipped away, and it was only the solid smack of a flat hand against his face that focused him. But when the truth solidified, he felt no better off.

Nadir stumbled from the door, his eyes red and rheumy, his thick black hair twisted. He had stripped down to his undershirt, and for the first time Girder saw the intricate tattoos that stretched all the way from wrists to shoulders, interrupted only by the length of plastic tubing tied around one arm.

"You're safe here, for now," Nadir slurred, then picked up his glass of liquor from a table covered with needles and spoons and slumped into his only chair. Above his head and on every wall painted artwork hovered like unfamiliar cherubs.

"What's happening?" was all Girder's terror would allow him to say.

"What's happening?" Nadir mocked. "What do you think is happening? Rasp wants what's his. That's all he ever wants."

"I don't understand. What is he?"

Nadir staggered, tried to refill his tumbler from the dark glass bottle of bourbon on his table, but most of it merely spilled past. Nadir was oblivious to his failure.

"You ruined everything. You had no right. No right." He coughed violently, then took another gulp of his drink before pointing at the paintings above. "You should never have come here. I should have stopped you, I should have made you leave, or killed you when you didn't. I should have reached my fingers around your throat and squeezed!" Nadir's eyes bulged as he said it, his fist clenched so tight it paled, and Girder scrambled to his knees. The storm on Nadir's face passed instantly, and he slid down into his chair. "Everything is ruined. Everything. I remember what it was like, I remember the joy and freedom, before I gave myself over. I believed it all because I was nearly as blind as you. It cost me everything. So long now I'd forgotten. Then you come in here—" Nadir's eyes flared again, the bleariness replaced by something worse as they focused on Girder—"you come here and knocked on the door and demanded it all for yourself. You walk by my work, even here, in my own private inch of this circus, and you ignore it, laugh at it, diminish it, and think you're something more than you are. You're so desperate for it that the trap isn't even baited before you walk into it. You come and chaos comes with you."

Nadir stood and downed the rest of his bourbon. He looked at Girder, but it was clear he didn't see him. Those bloodshot watering eyes looked right through to someplace cold and dark. He sniffled, and Girder pawed for his painting and dragged it closer. A ripple appeared on Nadir's face, beginning around the edges of his swollen eyes and moving outward. Skin and meat and teeth trembled, a swell of emotion that was focused on the fallen Girder. The artist's fear returned, pulling the cloak of colors over his eyes, and before he went blind he scrambled to his feet, painting hugged close. Even behind that returning veil, Nadir's shaking fury made him appear twelve feet tall.

"Why didn't you leave when you had the chance? Why didn't you save yourself as I couldn't? Why did you have to upset and awaken it?"

"What is it?" Girder pleaded. "What is it?"

But Nadir did not answer. Instead, he threw his empty tumbler at the floor and lunged at Girder, long fingers like painted claws, eyes rolled up in glassy hate. Girder stepped back and instinctively reacted, swinging the painting in his hands as hard as he could. Canvas split and frame cracked. All Girder had was destroyed in an uncontrolled instant, and Nadir fell to the ground, wailing, cursing. Then a wave of convulsions took hold, and while his neck muscles spasmed, he spewed foul liquid over the floor, wave after wave, but did not take his hate-filled eyes from Girder. Instead, he crawled forward, reaching for the terrified artist. Girder could not think, only react. He stepped back, still brandishing a piece of shattered wooden frame, and hit the weakened Nadir with it until splinters flew and Nadir's body slumped. Once the convulsions ceased, the veil of colors dropped from Girder's eyes. He let go of the bloody piece of wood, and it splattered on the floor. Girder knew he had to escape, but when he reached the door his slick hands were unable to twist the knob. He was trapped. Then, beneath his touch, the door vibrated; a pounding that echoed the rush of blood in his ears. It was the sound of something trying to get inside the room.

Girder heard the sickly slurp as he backed away, the drooling suck of ravenousness, and the door visibly rattled with each blow.

His head raced with terrified thoughts of all Nadir had warned.

"It's gone!" he pleaded. "It's gone! I don't have it! There's nothing here for you!"

But the pounding did not stop. The wooden doorframe split; the air crackled, full of pungency. Girder rushed around the room, around the incapacitated Nadir, looking for some weapon to protect himself from Rasp or whatever it was that was coming through the door. All he found was a slim dull knife, one he could barely hold in his tired, bloodied hands.

The banging, that ugly noise intensified, interspersed with the door being clawed. Girder noticed the doorframe separate from the wall with each succeeding blow, pulling away and opening the entrance that much further. Girder hunkered behind a fallen piece of furniture and waited, thin dull knife dancing in his trembling hand. Unexpectedly, he imagined his father kneeling in his place.

What came though the torn opening on that final blow was nothing Girder was prepared for. It had the face and head of Elias Rasp, but contorted and stretched, the skin like vellum, the eyes dead and staring wide. But the head was supported by the blackest flesh, wrinkled and covered in a bloody sheen. Its conical body, nearly three foot long, twisted as it reached its tail, an appendage that flicked spasmodically while hundreds of long spindly legs carried the creature scurrying toward Nadir's unmoving body. And the torn and broken remnants of the painting he still wore. A trail of greasiness followed after, but the thing with Rasp's face was not slowed by it. Unencumbered by its previous corpulent body, it moved with precision, black tongue hanging limply from a dislocated jaw. The knife slipped from Girder's hand, his fear too great to control himself.

The thing stopped a few feet short of Nadir's body, its oversized head cocking too far, and rolled its cataracted eye. Girder stared, transfixed, as the thing perched on Nadir's face and spun its head in the other direction, jaw to its back, eyes moving skyward, and from the grey skin on the rear of the presumable skull a thin spongy gland pushed out. It then gathered its legs to itself and hunkered to feed.

But it was not the bloodied Nadir who was the meal; it was what remained of Girder's masterpiece. Colors from the torn canvas bled, then faded from the surface as the sickening mouthparts pulsated over the rough canvas. Ropes of greasy slime slid forth as it moved, removing the hours and days and weeks of Girder's work, and with each pulse the creature seemed to grow fuller. It fed off everything Girder had given, and the sight left the artist cold and emptied. He reached down to retrieve the dull knife, his grip that much more sure.

The Rasp-thing fed, the smell and sound of it overpowering, as Girder crept behind it. Each staggered step reminded him of the games Rasp had played over the intervening weeks, of the disappointment in Mr. Raymond's eyes, of the way his father had—as they all did—of diminishing him, of making him believe he was less than he was. They had all stolen so much from Girder, taken so much *of* him, and given him nothing in return.

Except that was not true.

His father *had* given him two things.

The first, a connection to his emotions so strong that a veil of burning red rage consumed his sight; the second, an understanding of how a person's hands might quickly inflict the maximum amount of damage.

He stepped over Nadir's prone body and into range; Rasp's dull dead eyes rolled and glared. Its jaw quivered, tongue lolled.

It knew.

Girder could no longer hesitate.

The slim dull knife stabbed black flesh repeatedly, throwing indescribable color across the walls. The creature gurgled, squealed, spun in circles as the foul liquid spurted. It darted and Girder leapt back, but with broken body and legs it managed only circles, spraying everything. Girder nearly slid in the mixture of hemolymph, grease, and bile as he struggled, his nerve gone and twisted leg screaming. But the damage to the Rasp-thing was done, and as it slowed its mindless convulsions the vestigial face on its back flickered and twitched with ebbing control. It was only when it had ceased moving beyond an occasional dying tic that Girder was brave enough to crush it beneath the weight of Nadir's empty chair.

Girder stood panting on wobbling legs, taking in what lay before him. Nadir, broken and unbreathing. Rasp, a severed head crushed to a soft lump. Blood and vomit and colors spread across the canvas of floors and walls, and upon them an abstract expressionist composition unlike any other revealed itself. Girder observed the patterns, breaks, details of flecks and spots, and read their meaning. The composition's intent was clear. It spoke directly to him. It spoke of freedom, of release, of a life finally his own. While outside the storm raged fiercely, inside Girder's great tumult was finally at an end.

Simon Strantzas is the author of *Burnt Black Suns* (Hippocampus Press, 2014), *Nightingale Songs* (Dark Regions Press, 2011), *Cold to the Touch* (Tartarus Press, 2009), and *Beneath the Surface* (Humdrumming, 2008), as well as the editor of *Aickman's Heirs* (Undertow Publications, 2015) and *Shadows Edge* (Gray Friar Press, 2013). His writing has been reprinted in *The Mammoth Book of Best New Horror*, *The Best Horror of the Year*, *The Year's Best Weird Fiction*, and *The Year's Best Dark Fantasy & Horror*. It has been translated into other languages; and been nominated for the British Fantasy Award. He lives in Toronto, Canada, with his wife and an unyielding hunger for the flesh of the living.

He had nothing except taunting dreams of castles and meadows and the screams
of dragons, fading so fast he could barely remember the sound at all . . .

THE SCREAMS OF DRAGONS

Kelley Armstrong

"And the second plague that is in thy dominion, behold it is a dragon.
And another dragon of a foreign race is fighting with it, and striving to
overcome it. And therefore does your dragon make a fearful outcry."
—*Cyfranc Lludd a Llefelys*, translated by Lady Charlotte Guest

When he was young, other children talked of their dreams, of candy-floss
mountains and puppies that talked and long-lost relatives bearing new bicycles
and purses filled with crisp dollar bills. He did not have those dreams. His
nights were filled with golden castles and endless meadows and the screams
of dragons.

The castles and the meadows came unbidden, beginning when he was too
young to know what a castle or a meadow was, but in his dreams he'd race
through them, endlessly playing, endlessly laughing. And then he'd wake to
his cold, dark room, stinking of piss and sour milk, and he'd roar with rage
and frustration. Even when he stopped, the cries were replaced by sulking,
aggrieved silence. Never laughter. He only laughed in his dreams. Only played
in his dreams. Only was happy in his dreams.

The dragons came later.

He presumed he'd first heard the story of the dragons in Cainsville. Visits
to family there were the high points of his young life. While Cainsville had no
golden castles or endless meadows, the fields and the forests, the spires and the
gargoyles reminded him of his dreams, and calmed him and made him, if not
happy, at least content.

They treated him differently in Cainsville, too. He was special there. A
pampered little prince, his mother would say, shaking her head. The local
elders paid attention to him, listened to him, sought him out. Better still, they

did not do the same to his sister, Natalie. The Gnat, he called her—constantly buzzing about, useless and pestering. At home, *she* was the pampered one. His parents never seemed to know what to make of him, his discontent and his silences, and so they showered his bouncing, giggling little sister with double the love, double the attention.

In Cainsville the old people told him stories. Of King Arthur's court, they said, but when he looked up their tales later, they were not quite the same. Theirs were stories of knights and magic, but lions too and giants and faeries and, sometimes, dragons. That was why he was certain they'd told him this particular tale, even if he could not remember the exact circumstances. It was about another king, beset by three plagues. One was a race of people who could hear everything he said. The third was disappearing foodstuffs and impending starvation. The second was a terrible scream that turned out to be two dragons, fighting. And that was when he began to dream of the screams of dragons.

He did not actually *hear* the screams. He could not imagine such a thing, because he had no idea what a dragon's scream would sound like. He asked his parents and his grandmother and even his Sunday school teacher, but they didn't seem to understand the question. Even at night, his sleep was often filled with nothing but his small self, racing here and there, searching for the screams of dragons. He would ask and he would ask, but no one could ever tell him.

When he was almost eight, his grandmother noticed his sleepless nights. When she asked what was wrong, he knew better than to talk about the dragons, but he began to think maybe he should tell her of the other dreams, the ones of golden palaces and endless meadows. One night, when his parents were out, he waited until the Gnat fell asleep. Then he padded into the living room, the feet on his sleeper whispering against the floor. His grandmother didn't notice at first—she was too busy watching "The Dick Van Dyke Show." He couldn't understand the fascination with television. The moving pictures were dull gray, the laughter harsh and fake. He supposed they were for those who didn't dream of gold and green, of sunlight and music.

He walked up beside her. He did not sneak or creep, but she was so absorbed in her show that when he appeared at her shoulder, she shrieked and in her face, he saw something he'd never seen before. Fear. It fascinated him, and he stared at it, even as she relaxed and said, "Bobby? You gave me quite a start. What's wrong, dear?"

"I can't sleep," he said. "I have dreams."

"Bad dreams?"

He shook his head. "Good ones."

Her old face creased in a frown. "And they keep you awake?"

"No," he said. "They make me sad."

She clucked and pulled him onto the chair, tucking him in beside her. "Tell Gran all about them."

He did, and as he talked, he saw that look return. The fear. He decided he must be mistaken. He hadn't mentioned the dragons. The rest was wondrous and good. Yet the more he talked, the more frightened she became, until finally she pushed him from the chair and said, "It's time for bed."

"What's wrong?"

She said, "Nothing," but her look said there was something very, very wrong.

For the next few weeks, his grandmother was a hawk, circling him endlessly, occasionally swooping down and snatching him up in her claws. Most times, she avoided him directly, though he'd catch her watching him. Studying him. Scrutinizing him. Once they were alone in the house, she'd swoop. She'd interrogate him about the dreams, unearthing every last detail, even the ones he thought he'd forgotten.

On the nights when his parents were gone, she insisted on drawing his baths, adding in some liquid from a bottle and making the baths so hot they scalded him and when he cried, she seemed satisfied. Satisfied and a little frightened.

The strangest of all came nearly a month after he'd told her of the dreams. She'd made stew for dinner and she served it in eggshells. When she brought them to the table, the Gnat laughed in delight.

"That's funny," she said. "They're so cute, Gran."

His grandmother only nodded absently at the Gnat. Her watery blue eyes were fixed on him.

"What do you think of it, Bobby?" she asked.

"I . . . " He stared at the egg, propped up in a little juice glass, the brown stew steaming inside the shell. "I don't understand. Why is it in an egg?"

"For fun, dummy." His sister shook her head at their grandmother. "Bobby's never fun." She pulled a face at him. "Boring Bobby."

His grandmother shushed her, gaze still on him. "You think it's strange."

"It is," he said.

"Have you ever seen anything like this before?"

"No."

She waited, as if expecting more. Then she prompted, "You would say, then, that you've never, in all your years, seen something like this."

It seemed an odd way to word it, but he nodded.

And with that, finally, she seemed satisfied. She plunked down into her chair, exhaling, before turning to him and saying, "Go to your room. I don't want to see you until morning."

He glanced up, startled. "What did I—?"

"To your room. You aren't one of us. I'll not have you eat with us. Now off with you."

He pushed his chair back and slowly rose to his feet.

The Gnat stuck out her tongue when their grandmother wasn't looking. "Can I have his egg?"

"Of course, dear," Gran said as he shuffled from the kitchen.

The next morning, instead of going to school, his grandmother took him to church. It was not Sunday. It was not even Friday. As soon as he saw the spires of the cathedral, he began to shake. He'd done something wrong, horribly wrong. He'd lain awake half the night trying to figure out what he could have done to deserve bed without dinner, but there was nothing. She'd fed him stew in an eggshell and, while perplexed, he had still been very polite and respectful about it.

The trouble had started with telling her about the dreams, but who could find fault with tales of castles and meadows, music and laughter?

Perhaps she was going senile. It had happened to an old man down the street. They'd found him in their yard, wearing a diaper and asking about his wife, who'd died years ago. If that had happened to his grandmother, Father Joseph would see it.

Certainly, he seemed to, given the expression on Father Joseph's face after Gran talked to him alone in the priest's office. Father Joseph emerged as if in a trance, and Gran had to direct him to the pew where Bobby waited.

"See?" she said, waving her hand at Bobby.

The priest looked straight at him, but seemed lost in his thoughts. "No, I'm afraid I don't, Mrs. Sheehan."

Gran's voice snapped with impatience. "It's obvious he's not ours. Neither his mother nor his father nor any of his grandparents have blond hair. Or dark eyes."

Sweat beaded on the priest's forehead and he tugged his collar. "True, but children do not always resemble their parents, for a variety of reasons, none of them laying any blame at the foot of the child."

"Are you suggesting my daughter-in-law was unfaithful?"

Father Joseph's eyes widened. "No, of course not. But the ways of genetics—like the ways of God—are not always knowable. Your daughter-in-law does have light hair, and I believe she has a brother who is blond. If my recollection of science is correct, dark eyes are the dominant type, and I'm quite certain if you searched the family tree beyond parents and grandparents you would find your answer."

"I have my answer," she said, straightening. "He is a changeling."

Two drops of sweat burst simultaneously and dribbled down the priest's face. "I . . . I do not wish to question your beliefs, Mrs. Sheehan. I know such folk wisdom is common in the . . . more rural regions of your homeland—"

"Because it is wisdom. Forgotten wisdom. I've tested him, Father. I gave him dinner in an eggshell, as I explained."

"Yes, but . . . " The priest snuck a glance around, as if hoping for divine intervention—or a needy parishioner to stumble in, requiring his immediate attention. "I know that is the custom, but I cannot say I rightly understand it."

"What is there to understand?" She put her hands on her narrow hips. "It's a test. I gave him stew in eggshells, and he said he'd never seen anything like it. That's what a changeling will say."

"I beg your pardon, ma'am, but I believe that's what anyone would say, given their meal served in an egg."

She glowered at him. "I put him in a tub with foxglove, too, and he became ill."

"Foxglove?" The priest's eyes rounded again. "Is that not a poison?"

"It is if you're a changeling. I also gave him one of my heart pills, because it's made from digitalis, which is also foxglove. My pill made him sick."

"You gave . . . " For the first time since he'd come in, Father Joseph looked at Bobby, really looked at him. "You gave your grandson your heart medication? That could kill a boy—"

"He isn't a boy. He's one of the Fair Folk." Gran met Bobby's gaze. "An abomination."

Now Father Joseph's face flushed, his eyes snapping. "No, he is a child. You will not speak of him that way, certainly not in front of him. I'm trying to be respectful, Mrs. Sheehan. You are entitled to your superstitions and folksy tales, but not if they involve poisoning an innocent child." He knelt in front of Bobby. "You're going to come into my office now, son, and we'll call your parents. Is your mother at work?"

He nodded.

"Do you know the number?"

He nodded again.

The priest took Bobby's hand and, without another word, led him away as his grandmother watched, her eyes narrowing.

That was the beginning of "the bad time," as his parents called it, whispered words, even years later, their eyes downcast, as if in shame. The situation did not end with that visit to the priest. His grandmother would not drop the accusation. He was a changeling. A faerie child dropped into their care, her real grandson spirited away by the Fair Folk. Finally, his parents broke down and asked the priest to perform some ritual—any ritual—to calm his grandmother's nerves. The priest refused. To do so would be to lend credence to the preposterous accusation and could permanently scar the child's psyche.

The fight continued. He heard his parents talking late at night about the shame, the great shame of it all. They were intelligent, educated people. His father was a scientist, his mother the lead secretary in her firm. They were not ignorant peasants, and it angered them that Father Joseph didn't understand what they were asking—not to "fix" their son but simply to pretend to, for the harmony of the household.

They took their request to a second priest, and somehow—for years afterward, everyone would blame someone else for this—a journalist got hold of the story. It made one of the Chicago newspapers, in an article mocking the family and their "Old World" ways. His family was so humiliated they moved. His grandmother grumbled that his parents made too big a fuss out of the whole thing. It didn't matter. They moved, and they were all forbidden to speak of it again.

That did not mean no one spoke of it. The Gnat did. When she was in a good mood, she'd settle for mocking him, calling him a faerie child, asking him where he kept his wings, pinching his back to see if she could find them. When she was in a rare foul temper, she'd tell him their grandmother was right, he was a monster and didn't belong, that their parents only had one real child. And even if it was all nonsense, as his mother and father claimed, *that* part was true—he no longer felt part of the family. They might not think him a changeling, but they all, in their own ways, blamed him. His parents blamed him for their humiliation. The Gnat blamed him for having to leave her friends and move. And his grandmother blamed him for whatever slight she could pin at his feet, and then she punished him for it.

He came to realize that the punishments were the purpose of the accusations rather than the result. His grandmother wanted an excuse to strap him or send him to bed without dinner. At first, he presumed she was upset because no one believed her story. That did not anger him. Nothing really angered him. Like happiness, the emotion was too intense, too uncomfortable. He looked at his sister, dancing about, chattering and giggling, and he thought her a fool. He looked at his grandmother, raging and snapping against him, and thought her the same. Foolish and weak, easily overcome by emotion.

He did not accept the punishments stoically, though. While he never complained, with each hungry night or sore bottom, something inside him hardened a bit more. He saw his grandmother, fumbling in her frustration, venting it on him, and he did not pity her. He hated her. He hated his parents, too, for pretending not to see the welts or the unfinished dinners. Most of all, he hated the Gnat, because she saw it all and delighted in it. She would watch him beaten to near tears with the strap, and then tell their grandmother that he'd broken her doll the week before, earning him three more lashes.

While there was certainly vindictiveness in the punishments, it seemed his grandmother actually had a greater plan. He realized this when she decided, one Sunday, that the two of them should take a trip to Cainsville. He even got to sit in the front seat of the station wagon, for the first time ever.

"Do you think I've mistreated you lately?" she asked as she drove.

It seemed a question not deserving a reply, so he didn't give one.

"Have you earned those punishments?" she said. "Did you do everything I said you did? That Natalie said you did?"

He sensed a trick, and again he didn't answer. She reached over and pinched his thigh hard enough to bring tears to his eyes.

"I asked you a question, parasite."

He glanced over.

"You know what that means, don't you?" she said. "Parasite?"

"I know many words."

Her lips twisted. "You do. Far more than a child should know. Because you are not a child. You are a parasite, put into our house to eat our food and sleep in our beds."

"There's no such thing as faeries."

She pinched him again, twisting the skin. He only glanced over with a look that had her releasing him fast, hand snapping back onto the steering wheel.

"You're a monster," she said. "Do you know that?"

No, you are, he thought, but he said nothing, staring instead at the passing scenery as they left the city. She drove onto the highway before she spoke again.

"You don't think you deserve to be punished, do you? You think I'm accusing you of things you didn't do, and your little sister is joining in, and your parents are turning a blind eye. Is that what you think?"

He shrugged.

"If it is, then you should tell someone," she said. "Someone who can help you."

He stayed quiet. There was a trick here, a dangerous one, and he might be smart for a little boy, as everyone told him, but he was not smart enough for this. So he kept his mouth shut. She drove a while longer before speaking again.

"You like the folks in Cainsville, don't you? The town elders."

Finally, something he could safely answer. She could find no fault in him liking old people. With relief, he nodded.

"They like you, too. They think you're special." Her hands tightened on the wheel. "I know why, too. I'm not a foolish old woman. I'm just as smart as you, boy. Especially when it comes to puzzles, and I've solved this one. I know where you came from."

He tried not to sigh, as the conversation swung back to dangerous territory. Perhaps he should be frightened, but after months of this, he was only tired.

"Do they ask you about us?" she said. "When they take you off on your special walks? Do they ask after your family?"

He nodded. "They ask if you are all well."

"And how we're treating you?"

He hesitated. It seemed an odd question, and he sensed the snare wire sneaking around his ankle again. After a moment, he shook his head. "They only ask if you're well and how I'm doing. How I like school and that."

"They're being careful," she muttered under her breath. "But they still ask how he is. Checking up on him."

"Gran?"

She tensed as he called her that. She always did these days and it was possible, just possible, that he used it more often because of that.

"You understand what honesty is, don't you, boy?"

He nodded.

"And respect for your elders."

It took him a half-second, but he nodded to this as well.

"Then you know you have to tell the truth when an adult asks you a question. You need to be honest, even if it might get someone in trouble. Always remember that."

While he liked all the elders in Cainsville, Mrs. Yates was his favorite, and he got the feeling he was hers, too. There had been a time when his grandmother had seemed almost jealous of her, when she would huff and sniff and say she thought Mrs. Yates was a very peculiar old woman. His parents had paid little attention—Gran had made it quite clear she thought everyone a little peculiar in Cainsville.

"There are no churches," she'd say. And his mother would sigh and explain—once again—that the town had started off too small for churches and by the time it was large enough, there was no place to put them, the settlement being nestled in the fork of a river, with marshy ground on the only open side. People still went to church. Just somewhere else.

It was his mother whose family was from Cainsville. Gran only accompanied them because she didn't like to be left out of family trips. She didn't like the town and she certainly didn't like Mrs. Yates. But that day, as she went off to visit his great-aunt, Gran sent him off with two dollars and a suggestion that he go see what Mrs. Yates was up to. Just be back by four so they could make it home in time for Sunday dinner.

He went to the new diner first. That's what everyone in Cainsville called it. The "new" diner, though it'd been there as long as he could remember. It still smelled new—the lemon-polished linoleum floors, the shiny red leather booths and even shinier chrome-plated chairs. The elders could often be found there, sipping tea by the windows as they watched the town go by. "Holding court," his grandmother would sniff—watching for mischief and waiting for folks to come by and pay their respects, like they were lords and ladies. He didn't see that at all. To him, they were simply there, in case anyone needed them.

Today, he found Mrs. Yates in her usual place. He thought she'd be surprised to see him, but she only smiled, her old face lighting up as she motioned him over.

"Mr. Shaw said he spotted your car coming into town," she said. "But I scarce dared believe it. Did I hear the rest right, too? Your gran brought you?"

He nodded.

"Does she know you're here?"

"She said I could come talk to you if I wanted."

Then he got his look of surprise, a widening of her blue eyes. "Did she now?"

He nodded again, and he expected her to be pleased, but while her eyes stayed kind, they narrowed too, as she surveyed him.

"Is everything all right, Bobby?"

He nodded without hesitation. Gran thought she was clever in her plan, that he would tattle on her to Mrs. Yates without realizing that's exactly what she wanted. He had no idea what she hoped to gain, but if Gran wanted it, he wasn't doing it.

"Are you sure?" Mrs. Yates said, those bright eyes piercing his. "Nothing is amiss at home?"

He shrugged. "My sister's annoying, but that's old news."

He thought she'd laugh, pat his arm and move on. That's what other grown-ups would do. But Mrs. Yates was not like other grown-ups, which was probably why he liked her so much. She kept studying him until, finally, she squeezed his shoulder and said, "All right, Bobby. If that's what you want. Now, do you have your list of gargoyles?"

He pulled the tattered notebook from his back pocket. He'd been working on it since he was old enough to write. Cainsville had gargoyles. Lots of them. For protection, the old people would say with a wink. Every year, as part of the May Day festival, children could show the elders their lists of all the gargoyles they'd located, and the winner would take a prize. If you found all of them, you'd get an actual gargoyle modeled after you. That hardly ever happened— there were only a few in town. It sounded easy, finding them all, and it should be, except many hid. There were gargoyles you could only see in the day or at night or when the light hit a certain way or, sometimes, just by chance. He'd been compiling his list for almost four years and he only had half of them, but he'd still come in second place last year.

"Let's go gargoyle hunting." Mrs. Yates got to her feet without groaning or pushing herself up, the way Gran and other old people did. She just stood, as easily as he would, and started for the door. "Now remember, I can't point them out to you. That's against the rules." She leaned down and whispered, "But I might give you a hint for one. Just one."

Behind them, the other elders chuckled, and Bobby and Mrs. Yates headed out into town.

He found one more gargoyle to add to his list, and he didn't even need Mrs. Yates's hint, so she promised to keep it for next time. They were going back to the diner and the promise of milkshakes when Mrs. Yates glanced down the walkway leading behind the bank.

"I think I hear the girls," she said. "Why don't you go play with them a while, and then bring them to the diner and we'll all have milkshakes."

He hesitated.

"You like Rose and Hannah, don't you?"

He nodded, and her smile broadened, telling him this was the right answer, so he added, "They're nice," to please her.

"They're very nice," she said. "I like to see you playing with them, Bobby.

It's not easy for some children to find playmates. Some boys and girls are different, and other children don't always like different. You'll appreciate it more someday, when being different helps you stand out. But children don't always want to stand out, do they?"

He shook his head. She understood, as she always did. His parents lied and tried to pretend he wasn't different. She acknowledged it and understood it and made him feel better about it.

"Do you want to go play with the girls?"

He nodded. He *did* like the girls—Hannah, at least. What bothered him was the prospect of sharing Mrs. Yates with them later. But it would make her happy, and he was still her special favorite, so he shouldn't complain.

"Off you go then. Come to the diner later and we'll have those milkshakes."

Mrs. Yates said Hannah and Rose were in the small park behind the bank. They were often there on the swings, and when he rounded the corner, that's where he expected to see them. The swings were empty, though. He looked around the park, bordered by a fence topped with chimera heads. Walkways branched off in every compass direction. He heard Rose's voice, coming from the one leading to Rowan Street.

The girls crouched beside a toppled cardboard box. Hannah was reaching in and talking. He liked Hannah. Everyone liked Hannah. His mother said she reminded her of The Gnat, but she couldn't be more wrong. Yes, Hannah was pretty, with brown curls and dark eyes and freckles across her nose. And, like The Gnat, she was always laughing, always bouncing around, chattering. But with Hannah, it was *real*. The Gnat only acted that way because it tricked people into liking her.

Rose was different. Very different. She was a year younger than Bobby and Hannah, but she acted like a teenager, and she looked at you like she could see right through you and wasn't sure she liked what she saw. She had black straight hair and weirdly cold blue eyes that blasted through him. She wasn't pretty and she never giggled—she rarely even laughed, unless she was with Hannah.

Rose saw him coming first, though it always felt like "saw" wasn't the right word. Rose seemed to sense him coming. She stood and when she fixed those blue eyes on him, he quailed as he always did, falling back a step before reminding himself he had done nothing wrong. Rose only tilted her head, and when she spoke, her rough voice was kind.

"Are you okay, Bobby?"

"Sure."

Her lips pursed, as if calling him a liar, then she waved for him to join them. As he stepped up beside the girls, he was chagrined to realize that as much as he'd grown in the last few months, Rose had grown more. She might be only seven and a girl, but he barely came up to her eyebrows. She moved back to let him stand beside Hannah.

"See what we found?" Hannah said.

It was a cat, with four kittens, all tabbies like the momma, except the smallest, which was ink black.

"Show him what you can do," Rose said.

Hannah glanced up, her forehead creasing with worry.

"Go on," Rose said. "Bobby can keep a secret. Show him."

He looked at Rose, and she nodded, giving him a small smile—a sympathetic smile, as if she knew what he was going through and wanted Hannah to share her secret to make him feel better. He bristled. He didn't want her sympathy. Didn't need it. But he did want the secret, so he let Rose cajole Hannah until she blurted it out.

"I can talk to animals." Hannah paused, face reddening. "No, that doesn't sound right. It's not like Dr. Dolittle. I don't hear them talk. Animals don't talk. But they do . . . " She turned to Rose. "What's the word you used?"

"Communicate."

Hannah nodded. "They communicate. I can understand them, and they can understand me."

He must have seemed skeptical, because her face went the color of apples in autumn.

"See?" she hissed at Rose. "This is why I can't tell anyone. They'll think I'm crazy."

"I don't think you're crazy," he said. "But you're right—you probably shouldn't tell anyone else."

Hannah's gaze dropped, and he felt bad. Like maybe he should tell her about the dreams and how he admitted it to Gran, and what happened next.

Did they know what happened? His grandmother always said Cainsville was a "backwater nowhere" town, where they lived like they weren't sixty miles from one of the biggest cities in America. Gran said they were ignorant, and they liked it that way. They didn't read newspapers, didn't listen to the news or even watch it on television. That wasn't true. He'd once told Mrs. Yates about going to the site of the World Fair, and she'd known all about it. She'd told him stories about the fair, the sights and sounds and even the smells. He'd gotten an A on his paper and his teacher said it was almost like he'd been there. He'd asked Mrs. Yates if *she'd* been there, and she'd laughed and said she wasn't *that* old. No one was. So people in Cainsville weren't ignorant, but he supposed that knowing about the 1893 World Fair wasn't the same as knowing what his teacher called "current events."

"You shouldn't tell everyone," Rose said to Hannah. "Definitely not anyone outside Cainsville. But no one here will think you're crazy." She nudged Hannah with her sneaker. "Tell him about the black kitten."

Hannah took more prodding, but when Bobby expressed an interest, she finally stood and said, "He's sick. Momma Cat is worried he's going to die. He doesn't get enough to eat because he's smaller than the others."

"He's not that much smaller."

"He's different," Rose said. "That's why they won't let him eat very much. I think he's a matagot. That's what we were talking about when you came up."

"A matagot?"

"Magician's cat," Rose said, as matter-of-factly as if she'd said the cat was a Siamese. "It's a spirit that's taken the form of a black cat."

"They say that if you keep one and treat it well, it will reward you with a gold piece every day," Hannah said.

"Gold?" he said.

Something in his tone made Rose tense—or maybe it was the way he looked at the black kitten. Hannah only giggled.

"It's not true, silly," Hannah said. "Magic doesn't work that way. Not real magic."

"What do you know about real magic?"

She shrugged. "Enough. I know it can make gargoyles disappear in daylight and tomato plants grow straight and true. I know it can let some people read omens—like old Mrs. Carew—and some see the future, like Rose's Nana Walsh."

He turned to Rose. "Your grandmother can see the future?"

"Futures," she said. "There's more than one. It's all about choices."

He didn't understand that, but pushed on. "If I asked her to see my futures—"

"You can't," Hannah cut in. "Not unless you can talk to ghosts. I'm not sure anyone can talk to ghosts. If there are ghosts." She turned to Rose, as if she was the older, wiser girl.

"There are," Rose said. "Those with the sight sometimes say they see them. Others can, too. But most times when a person says they're seeing ghosts it's their imagination. Even if you can talk to them I'm not sure why you'd want to."

Hannah nodded, and his gaze shot from one girl to the other, unable to believe they were talking about such things seriously. Kids at school would call them babies for believing in magic. His parents would call it ungodly. His grandmother would probably call them changelings.

"About the cat. The . . . matagot." He stumbled over the foreign word.

"We don't know if it is one," Rose said. "Hannah says his mother thinks he's strange. She still loves him, though."

"As she should," Hannah said. "There's nothing wrong with strange."

Rose nodded. "But we're worried."

"Very worried." Hannah knelt beside the box where the mother cat was licking the black kitten's head. "Momma Cat is even more worried. Aren't you?"

The cat *mrrowed* deep in its throat and looked up at Hannah. Then she nosed the kitten away from her side.

"I think she's going to drive it off," Bobby said. "They do that sometimes. With the weak, the ones that are different."

Hannah shook her head, curls bouncing. "No, she's asking me to take it."

"You should," Rose said. "Your parents would let you."

"I know. I just hate taking a kitten from its mother."

The cat nosed the kitten again and meowed. Hannah nodded, said, "I understand," and very gently lifted the little black ball in both hands. The cat meowed again, but it didn't sound like protest. She gave the black kitten one last look, then shifted, letting its siblings fill the empty space against her belly.

"You'll need to feed it with a dropper," Rose said. "We can get books at the library and talk to the vet when she comes back through town."

Hannah nodded. "I'll take him home first and ask Mom to watch him."

They got to the end of the walkway before they seemed to realize he wasn't following. They turned.

"Do you want to come with us?" Hannah asked.

He did, but he wanted the milkshake with Mrs. Yates too, and if the girls were busy, he'd get the old woman all to himself.

"I told Mrs. Yates I'd meet her at the diner," he said, not mentioning the milkshakes.

Rose nodded. "Then you should do that. We'll see you later."

"Is your family coming for Samhain?" Hannah asked.

"I think we are."

Hannah smiled. "I hope so."

"Make sure you do," Rose said. "It's more fun when you're here."

He couldn't tell if she meant it or was just being nice, but it felt good to hear her say it and even better when Hannah nodded enthusiastically. He said he'd be back for Samhain, and went to find Mrs. Yates.

On the way home, his grandmother asked about his visit with Mrs. Yates. She was trying to get him to admit that he'd tattled on her. Even if he had, he certainly wouldn't admit it. His grandmother might say he was too smart for his age, but sometimes she acted as if he was dumber than The Gnat. Finally, she pulled off the highway, turned in her seat and said, "Did Mrs. Yates ask how things were at home?"

"Yes."

"And what did you tell her?"

"That they were fine."

She put her hand on his shoulder. It was the first time since he'd admitted to the dreams that she'd voluntarily touched him, except to pinch or slap.

"You know it's a sin to lie, Bobby."

"I do."

"Then tell me the truth. Did you say more?"

He hesitated. Nibbled his lip. Then said, "I told her Natalie was being a pest."

Her mouth pressed into a thin line. "That's not what I mean."

"But you asked—"

"Did you say *anything* more?"

"No." He hid his smile. "Not a word."

A month later, as Samhain drew near, he mentioned it over dinner.

"We aren't going," his mother said quietly.

"What?"

"Gran feels Cainsville isn't a good influence on you right now."

He shot a look at his grandmother, who returned a small, smug smile and ate another forkful of peas.

"Remember what happened when you visited last month?" his father said. "You came home and you were quite a little terror."

That was a lie. His grandmother had punished him twice as much after they got back, making up twice as many stories about him misbehaving. He'd thought she was just angry because her plan—whatever it had been—failed.

Gran's smile widened, her false teeth shining as she watched him.

"I don't care," the Gnat said. "I hate Cainsville. It's boring."

His grandmother patted her head. "I agree."

He shot to his feet.

"Bobby . . . " his father said.

"May I be excused?" he asked.

His father sighed. "If you're done."

Bobby walked to his room, trying very hard not to run in and slam the door. Once he got there, he fell facedown on his bed. The door clicked open. His grandmother walked in.

"You're a very stupid little beast," she said. "You should have told the elders. They'd take you back."

He flipped over to look at her.

"If you're being mistreated, they'll take you back," she said. "But you didn't tell them, so now we have to wait for them to come to us. I'll make sure they come to us."

His grandmother soon discovered another flaw in her plan. Two, actually. First, that whoever she thought would "come for him" was not coming, no matter how harsh her punishments. Second, that his parents' blindness had limits.

As the months of abuse had passed, he'd come to accept that his parents weren't really as oblivious as they pretended. Nor were they as enlightened as they thought. Even if they'd never admit it, there seemed to be a part of them that thought his grandmother's wild accusation was true. Or perhaps it was not that they actually believed him a changeling faerie child, but that they thought there was something wrong, terribly wrong, with him. He was different. Odd. Too distant and too cold. His sister hated him. Other children avoided him. Like animals, they sensed something was off and steered clear. Perhaps, then, the beatings would help. Not that they'd ever admit such a thing—heavens no, they were modern parents—but if he didn't complain, then perhaps neither should they.

They did have limits, though. When the sore spots became bruises and then welts, they objected. What would the neighbors think? Or, worse, his teachers, who might call children's services. Hadn't the family been through enough? Gran could punish him if he misbehaved, but she must use a lighter hand.

That did not solve the problem, but it opened a door. A possibility. That door cracked open a little more when his mother received a call at work from one of the elders, who wondered why they hadn't seen the Sheehan family in so long. Was everything all right? His mother said it was, but when she reported the call at home, over dinner, his grandmother fairly gnashed her teeth. His mother noticed and asked what was wrong, and Gran said nothing but still, his mother *had* noticed. He tucked that away and remembered it.

Christmas came, and he waited until he was alone in the house with his mother, and asked if they'd visit family in Cainsville. His mother wavered. And he was ready.

"Your grandmother doesn't think you're ready," she said as they sat in front of the television, wrapping gifts.

"I've been much better," he said.

"I'm not sure that you have."

He stretched tape over a seam. "I don't think I'm as bad as Gran says. I think she's still mad at me because we had to move."

A soft sigh, but his mother said nothing. He finished his package and took another.

"I think she might exaggerate sometimes," he said quietly. "I think Natalie might, too. I sometimes get the feeling they don't like me very much."

Of course his mother had to protest that, but her protests were muted, as if she couldn't work up true conviction.

"If you don't see me misbehaving, maybe I'm not," he said. "I do, sometimes. All kids do. But maybe it's not quite as much as Gran and Natalie say."

He worded it all so carefully. Not blaming anyone. Only giving his opinion, as a child. His mother went silent, wrapping her gift while nibbling her lower lip, the same way he did when he was thinking.

"I have friends in Cainsville," he said. "Little girls who like playing with me. They're very nice girls."

"Hannah and Rose," his mother said. "I like Hannah. Rose is . . . "

"Different," he said. "Like me. But she's not mean and she doesn't misbehave. She hardly ever gets in trouble. Even less than Hannah."

"Rose is a very serious girl," she said. "Like you. I can see why you'd like her."

"I do. I miss them. I promise if we go to Cainsville, I'll be better than ever." He clipped off a piece of ribbon. "And they *are* your family. You want to see them. Gran never liked Cainsville, so she's happy if we don't go."

"That's true," his mother murmured, and with that, he knew he'd won an ally in his fight to return to Cainsville. But as he soon learned, it hardly mattered at all. His mother had a job, just like a man, but she didn't make a lot of money, and his father always joked that it was more a hobby than an occupation, which made his mother angry. That meant, though, that his father was the head of the house. As it should be, Gran would say, and she could, because there was only one person his father always listened to—his own mother, Gran. If Bobby's grandmother said no to Cainsville, then they would not be going to Cainsville and that was that.

Gran said no to Cainsville.

No to Cainsville for the holidays. No to Cainsville for Candlemas. No to Cainsville for May Day.

It was the last that broke him. May Day was his favorite holiday, with the gargoyle hunt contest, which he was almost certain to win this year, according to Mrs. Yates.

He *would* go to Cainsville for May Day. All he had to do was eliminate the obstacle.

Everyone always told him how smart he was. Part of that was his memory. He heard things, and if he thought they might be important, he filed the information away as neatly as his father filed papers in his basement office. A year ago, his grandmother had admitted to feeding him one of her heart medicine pills. Father Joseph had been horrified—digitalis was foxglove, which was poison. Bobby had mentally filed those details and now, when he needed it, he tugged them out and set off for the library, where he read everything he found on the subject. Then he began stealing pills from Gran's bottle, one every third day. After two weeks, he had enough. He ground them up and put them in her dinner. And she died. There were a few steps in between—the heart attack, the ambulance, the hospital bed, his parents and the Gnat sobbing and praying—but in the end, he got what he wanted. Gran died and the obstacle was removed, and with it, he got an unexpected gift, one that made him wish he'd taken this step months ago, because as his grandmother breathed her last and he stood beside her bed, watching, he finally heard the screams of dragons.

It started slow, quiet even. Like a humming deep in his skull. Then it grew and the humming became a strange vibrating cry, somewhere between a roar and a scream. Finally, when it crescendoed, he couldn't even have said what it sounded like. It was all sounds, at once, so loud that he burst out in a sob, hands going to his ears as he doubled over.

His mother caught him and held him and rubbed his back and said it would be okay, it would all be okay, Gran was in a better place now. Yet the dragons kept screaming until he pushed her aside and ran from the hospital room. He ran and he ran until he was out some back door, in a tiny yard. Then he collapsed, hugging his knees as he listened to the dragons.

That's what he did—he listened. He didn't try to block them, to stop them.

This was what he'd dreamed of and now he had it, and it was horrible and terrible and incredible all at once. He hunkered down there, committing them to memory as methodically as he had the dreams of golden palaces and endless meadows. Finally, when they faded, he went back inside, snuffling and gasping for breath, his face streaked with tears. His parents found him like that, grieving they thought, and it was what they wanted to see, proof that he was just a normal little boy, and they were, in their own grief, happy.

He waited until three days after the funeral to broach the subject of Cainsville. He would have liked to have waited longer, but it was already April 27, and he'd given great thought to the exact timing—how late could he wait before it was too late to plan a May Day trip? April 27 seemed right.

After he'd gone to bed, he slipped back out and found his parents in the living room, reading. He stood between them and cleared his throat.

"Yes, Bobby?" his mother said, lowering her book.

"I've been thinking," he said. "Natalie's so upset about Gran. We all are, of course, but Natalie most of all."

His mother sighed. "I know."

"So I was thinking of ways to cheer her up."

As he expected, this was about the best thing he could have said. His mother's eyes lit up and his father lowered his newspaper.

"It's May Day this weekend," Bobby said. "I know Natalie thinks Cainsville is boring, but she always liked May Day."

"That's true." His mother snuck a glance at his father. "Last year, she asked if we were going before Bobby did."

"I thought we might go," he said. "For Natalie."

His father smiled and reached to rumple Bobby's hair. "That's a fine idea, son. I believe we will."

Rose knew what he'd done. He saw it in her eyes as he walked over to her and Hannah, cutting flowers before the May Day festivities began. Rose saw him coming and straightened fast, fixing him with those pale blue eyes. Then she laid her hand on Hannah's shoulder, as if ready to tug her friend away.

Hannah looked up at Rose's touch. She saw him and grinned, a bright sunshine grin, as she rose and brushed off the bare knees under her short, flowered dress. Rose kept hold of her friend's shoulder, though, and squeezed. Hannah hesitated.

He stopped short. Then he glanced to the side, pretending he'd heard someone call his name, an excuse to walk away. He headed toward one of the elders, setting out pies. The pie table was close enough for him to hear the girls.

Rose spoke first. "I had a dream about Bobby," she whispered.

Hannah giggled. "He is kind of cute."

"Not like *that*."

Hannah went serious. "You mean one of *those* dreams?"

"I don't know. There were dragons."

He stiffened and stood there, blueberry pie in hand, straining to listen to the girls behind him.

"Dragons?" Hannah said.

"He was hunting them."

"I bet they were *gargoyles*. He's really good at finding them. He has twice as many as I do, and he doesn't even live here."

"He killed one," Rose said.

"A gargoyle?"

"A dragon. An old one. She was blocking his way, and he fed her foxglove flowers, and she started to scream."

His stomach twisted so suddenly that he doubled over, the elder grabbing his arm to steady him, asking if he was all right, and he said yes, quickly, pushing her off as politely as he could and taking another pie from the box as he struggled to listen.

"That's one freaky dream, Rosie," Hannah was saying.

"I know."

"I think it just means he's going to win the gargoyle contest."

"Probably, but it felt like . . . " Rose drifted off. "No, I'm being stupid."

"You're never stupid. You just think too much sometimes."

Rose chuckled. "My mom says the same thing."

"Because she's smart, like you. Now, let's go ask if Bobby wants to come see Mattie."

The tap-tap of fancy shoes. Then a finger poked his back.

"Bobby?"

He turned to Hannah, smiling at him.

"We're glad you came," she said. "We missed you."

He nodded.

"It's not time for the festival yet. Do you want to come see Mattie?"

"That's what she named the kitten," Rose said, walking up behind her friend. "Short for matagot."

"No, short for Matthew."

Rose rolled her eyes. "Whatever you say."

Hannah pretended to swat her, then put her arm through Bobby's. As she did, Rose tensed and rocked forward, like she wanted to pull Hannah away. She stopped herself, but fixed him with that strange look. Like she knew what he'd done. With that look, he knew Rose had a power, like Hannah. And him? He had nothing except taunting dreams of castles and meadows, and the screams of dragons, fading so fast he could barely remember the sound at all.

"Smile, Bobby," Hannah said, squeezing his arm. "It's May Day, and we're going to have fun." She grinned. "We'll always have fun together."

He won the gargoyle hunt that year. The next year, too. They went to Cainsville for all the festivals and sometimes he and his mother just went to visit. Life was good, and not just because Gran was dead and he'd gotten Cainsville back, but because he'd learned a valuable lesson. He did not have powers. He would likely never have them. But he did have a power inside him—the screams of dragons.

He would admit that when he killed his grandmother, he thought he'd suffer for it. He'd be caught and even if he wasn't, it would be as Father Joseph preached—he would be forever damned in the prison of his own mind, tormented by his sins. Father Joseph had lied. Or, more likely, he simply didn't understand boys like Bobby.

No one ever suspected anything but a natural death, and his life turned for the better after that. He learned how to win his parents' sympathy if not their love. To turn them, just a little, to his side, away from the Gnat. He learned, too, how to deal with her. That took longer and started at school, with other children, the ones who bullied and taunted him.

He decided to show those children why he should not be bullied or taunted. One by one, he showed them. Little things for some, like spoiling a lunch every day. Bigger things for others. With one boy, he loosened the seat on his bike, and he fell and hit his head on the curb and had to go away, people whispering that he'd never be quite right again.

Bobby took his revenge, and then let the boys know it was him, and when they tattled, he cried and pretended he didn't know what was happening, why they were accusing him—they'd always hated him, always mocked and beat him, and the teachers knew that was true, and his tears and his lies were good enough to convince them that he was the victim. Each time he won, he would hear the dragons scream again, and he'd know he'd done well.

Once he'd perfected his game, he played it against the Gnat. For her eighth birthday, their parents gave her a pretty little parakeet that she adored. One day, after she'd called him a monster and scratched him hard enough to draw blood, he warned that she shouldn't let the bird fly about, it might fly right out the door.

"I'm not stupid," she said. "I don't open the doors when she's out." She paused, then scowled at him. "And you'd better not either."

"I wouldn't do that," he said. And the next time she let the bird out, he lured it with treats to his parents room, where the window was open, just enough.

He even helped her search for her bird. Then she discovered the open window.

"You did it!" she shouted.

She rushed at him, fingers like claws, scratching down his arm. He howled. His parents came running. The Gnat pointed at the window.

"Look what he did. He let her out!"

His father cleared his throat. "I'm afraid I left that open, sweetheart."

"You shouldn't have let the bird out of her cage," his mother said, steering The Gnat off with promises of ice cream. "You know we warned you about that."

The Gnat turned to him. He smiled, just for a second, just enough to let her know. Then he joined them in the kitchen where his mother gave him extra ice cream for being so nice and helping his little sister hunt for her bird.

The Gnat wasn't that easily cowed. She only grew craftier. Six months later, their parents bought her another parakeet. She kept it in its cage and warned him that if it escaped, they'd all know who did it. He told her to be nicer to him and that wouldn't be a problem. She laughed. Three months later, she came home from school to find her bird lying on the floor of its cage, dead. His parents called it a natural death. The Gnat knew better, and after that, she stayed as far from him as she could.

While his life outside Cainsville improved, his visits to the town darkened, as if there was a finite amount of good in his life, and to shift more to one place robbed it from the other.

He blamed Rose. After her dream of the dragon, she'd been nicer to him, apparently deciding it had been no more than a dream. Unlike Hannah's power, Rose's came in fits and starts, mingling prophecy and fantasy.

But then, after he did particularly bad things back home—like loosening the bike seat or killing the bird—he'd come to Cainsville and she'd stare at him, as if trying to peer into his soul. After a few times, she seemed to decide that where there were dragons, there was fire, and if she was having these dreams, they meant something. Something bad.

Rose started avoiding him. Worse, she made Hannah do the same. He'd come to town and they'd be off someplace and no one knew where to find them—not until it was nearly time for him to go, and they'd appear, and Rose would say, "Oh, are you leaving? So sorry we missed you."

Soon, it wasn't just Rose looking at him funny. All the elders did. Still, Mrs. Yates stuck by him, meeting him each time he visited, taking him for walks. Only now her questions weren't quite so gentle. *Is everything all right, Bobby? Are you sure? Is there anything you want to tell me? Anything at all?*

It didn't help that he'd begun doing things even he knew were wrong. It wasn't his fault. The dreams of golden castles and endless meadows had begun to fade when he'd turned nine. It did not directly coincide with the first screams of the dragons, but it was close enough that he'd suspected there was a correlation. Even when he stopped tormenting his tormenters, and let the screams of dragons ebb, the dreams of the golden world continued to fade, until he was forced to accept that it was simply the passing of time. As he aged, those childish fancies slid away, and all he had left were the dragons. So he indulged them. Fed them well and learned to delight in their screams as much as he had those pretty dreams.

There were times when he swore he could hear his grandmother's voice in his ear, calling him a nasty boy, a wicked boy. And when he did, he would smile, knowing he was feeding the dragons properly. But they took much feeding, and it wasn't long before no one tormented him and there were no worthy targets for his wickedness. He had to find targets and, increasingly, they were less worthy, until finally, by the time he turned twelve, many were innocent of any crime against him. But the dragons had to be fed.

That summer, his mother took him to Cainsville two days after he'd done something particularly wicked, particularly cruel, and when he arrived at the new diner, the elders were not there. Even Mrs. Yates was gone. He'd walked to her house and then to the schoolyard, where they sometimes sat and watched the children play. He found her there, with the others, as a group of little ones played tag.

When she saw him, she'd risen, walked over and said he should go to the new diner and have a milkshake and she'd meet him there later. She'd even given him three dollars for the treat. But he'd looked at the children, and he'd looked at her, standing between him and the little ones, guarding them against him, and he'd let the three bills fall to the ground and stalked off to talk to Rose.

He found her at her one brother's place. Rose was the youngest. A "whoops" everyone said, and he hadn't known what that meant until he was old enough to understand where babies came from and figured out that she'd been an accident, born when her mother was nearly fifty. This brother was twenty-nine, married, with a little girl of his own. That's where Rose was—babysitting her niece.

Bobby snuck around back and found the little girl playing in a sandbox. She couldn't be more than three, thin with black hair. He watched her and considered all the ways he could repay Rose for her treachery.

"What are you doing here?" a low voice came from behind him. He turned to see Rose, coming out of the house with a sipping cup and a bottle of Coke. Like Mrs. Yates, she moved between him and the child. Then she leaned over and whispered, "Take this and go inside, Seanna. I'll be there in a minute, and we'll read a book together."

She handed the little girl the sipping cup and watched her toddle off. Then she turned to him. "Why are you here, Bobby?"

"I want to know what you told the elders about me."

"About you?" Her face screwed up. "Nothing. Why?"

He stepped toward her. "I know you told them something."

She stood her ground, chin lifting, pale eyes meeting his. "Is there something to tell?"

"No."

"Then you don't have anything to worry about."

She started to turn away. He grabbed her elbow. She threw him off fast, dropping the bottle and not even flinching when it shattered on the paving stones.

"I didn't tell anyone anything," she said. "I don't have anything to tell."

"Bull. I've seen the way you look at me, and now they're doing it, too."

"Maybe because we're all wondering what's wrong. Why you've changed. You used to be a scared little boy, and now you're not, and that would be good, but there's this thing you do, staring at people with this expression in your eyes and . . . " She inhaled. "I didn't tell the elders anything."

"Yes, you did. You had a vision about me. A fake vision. And you told."

"No, I didn't. Now, I can't leave Seanna alone—"

He grabbed her wrist, fingers digging in as he wrenched her back to face him. "Tell me."

She struggled in his grip. "Let me—"

He slapped her, so hard her head whipped around, and when it whipped back, there was a snarl on her lips. She kicked and clawed, and he released her fast, stepping back. She hit him then. Like a boy. Plowed him in the jaw and when he fell, she stood over him and bent down.

"You ever hit me again, Bobby Sheehan, and I'll give you a choice. Either you'll confess it to the elders or I'll thrash you so hard you'll wish you *had* confessed. I didn't tattle on you. Now leave me alone."

"You think you're so special," he called as she climbed the back steps. "You and your second sight."

"Special?" She gave a strange little laugh, and when she turned, she looked ten years older. "No, Bobby Sheehan, I don't think I'm special. Most times, I think I'm cursed. I know you're jealous of us, with our powers, but you wouldn't want them. Not for a second. It changes everything." She glanced down at him, still on the ground. "Be happy with what you have."

He was not happy with what he had. As the year passed, he became even less happy with it, more convinced that Rose and the elders were spying on him from afar. Spying on his thoughts. This was not paranoia. Twice, after he'd done something moderately wicked, his mother got a call at work. Once from Mrs. Yates and once from Rose's mother.

"Just asking how you are," his mother said over dinner after the second call. She slid him a secret smile. "I think Rose might be sweet on you. She seems like a nice girl."

"Her family's not nice," the Gnat said as she took a forkful of meatloaf. "Her one brother's in jail."

His mother looked over sharply. "No, he isn't. He's in the army. Don't spread nasty gossip—"

"It's not gossip. I heard it in town. He's in jail for fraud, and so was Rose's dad, for a while, years ago, and no one thinks there's anything weird about that. I overheard someone say the whole family is into stuff like that. They're con artists. Only the people saying it acted like it was a regular job." She scrunched up her freckled nose. "Isn't that freaky? The whole town is—"

"Enough," his mother said. "I think someone's pulling your leg, young lady. There is nothing wrong with Rose Walsh or her family. They're fine people."

For once, he believed the Gnat. He'd wondered about Rose's brother ever since he took off a few years ago and Rose said he'd joined the army to fight in Vietnam, but he'd been over thirty, awfully old to sign up.

Con artists. That explained a lot. Rose was conning the elders right now, telling them stories about him. Trying to con him, too, into not wanting powers. He did. He wanted them more than anything. And he was going to find a way to get them.

He spent months researching how to steal powers and learned nothing useful. It did not seem as if it could be done, and the more he failed to find an answer, the more the jealousy gnawed at him, and the harder it was to focus on keeping the dragons fed and happy. He had to do worse and worse things, and it made him feel even guiltier about them. Together with the jealousy, it was like his stomach was on fire all the time. He couldn't eat. He started losing weight.

He had to go back to Cainsville. At the very least, the visit would calm the gnawing in his stomach and let him eat. He would talk his mother into a special trip to Cainsville and he would go see Hannah. Not the elders. Not Mrs. Yates. Certainly not Rose. No, he'd visit Hannah. She'd help him set things right.

His plan worked so beautifully that he felt as if the success was a sign. His luck was turning. He asked his mother to go and off they went that Sunday. He arrived to hear that Rose was in the city, and he found Hannah in the playground, tending to an injured baby owl.

"Did a cat get it?" he asked as he walked over.

She'd started at the sound of a voice, and he expected that when she saw it was him, she'd smile. She didn't. She scooped up the owl and stood.

"Bobby," she said. "I didn't know you were coming today."

"Surprise." He grinned, but she didn't grin back. Didn't even fake it. Just watched him as he opened the gate and walked in. "Is the owl all right?"

She hesitated, then shook her head. "Something got him. Maybe a cat. He's dying." Another pause. "That's the worst part. When they're hurt and I can't help."

"You can put it out of its misery."

She almost dropped the fledgling. "What?"

"I can do it. Mercifully. Then you won't need to feel bad because you can't help."

She stared at him like he'd suggested murdering her mother for pocket change. One of the dragons roared, a white-hot burst of flame that blazed through him.

"I'm thinking of you," he said, glowering at her.

"And I'm *not*. That isn't how it works. Rose said you . . . " she trailed off.

"Rose said *what*?" He stepped forward.

Hannah shrank, but only a little, before straightening. "That you don't understand about the powers. You think they're this great gift. There are good parts, sure, but bad, too. Lots of bad. I woke up in the middle of the night last week because a dog had been hit by a car. I ran out of the house and my mom helped me take it to the vet's, but there was nothing we could do. It was horrible. Just horrible. And I felt it—all of it. But the only thing that made that dog feel better was having me there through the whole thing, no matter how hard it was. So I did it. Because that's my responsibility."

Then you're a fool, he thought. *The dog wouldn't have helped you. It would have left you by the road to die.* He didn't say that, because when he looked at her, getting worked up, all he could think was how pretty she'd gotten. Prettier than any girl in his class, and he wanted to reach out and touch her, and when the impulse came, it was like throwing open a locked door. This was how he could steal her power. Touch her, kiss her . . .

He bit his lip and rocked back on his heels. "I'm sorry, Hannah. I wasn't thinking. My dad always said a quick death is better than suffering, and that's what I meant. Help you *and* help the baby owl." He met her gaze. "I'm sorry."

She nodded. "It's all right. I'm just feeling bad about it." She set the fledgling back on the ground.

"I know." He stepped closer. "I wish I could make you feel better."

Another nod, and in a blink, he was there, his arms going around her, his lips to hers. It wasn't the first time he kissed a girl. He'd done more than kiss them, too. Sometimes that was him being wicked, but most times, he didn't need to be—he knew how to say the right things. A little charmer, that's what his mother called him, obviously relieved that her sullen boy had turned out so well.

So he kissed Hannah. It was a good kiss. A sweet and gentle one, for a sweet and gentle girl. But she jerked back and pushed him away hard, as if he'd jumped on her.

"I-I'm sorry, Bobby," she said. "I have a boyfriend."

He was about to say "Who?" when he saw her expression.

Liar.

The dragon whipped its tail inside him, lighting his gut on fire. He forced it to settle. He wouldn't be wicked with Hannah. He just wouldn't. Not unless he had to.

"It's Rose, isn't it?" he said, stepping back, looking down at his sneakers. "She doesn't like me. She has dreams about me—about a dragon. She told me that, but I don't understand what it means."

"She doesn't either. What did she tell you?"

He shrugged and continued the lie. "Something about a dragon. That's all I know."

"It's two dragons. She dreams they're fighting over you and screaming awful screams. Then one wins and it . . . it . . . "

"It what?"

"Devours you," she blurted. "We don't know what it means."

"What do the elders say?"

"Elders?" She frowned at him. "We wouldn't tell the elders. Rose looked it up in books. She has lots of books from her Nana. Some talk about the sight and dreams, but she can't figure this one out."

"So she's never told the elders? About me?"

"Of course not. What's there to tell?"

He bit his lip. "I get the feeling Rose doesn't like me very much anymore." He lifted his gaze to hers. "I get the feeling you don't either."

"I . . . " She swallowed. "I'm fine, Bobby, I just—"

He grabbed her around the waist and kissed her again. This time when she struggled he held on, kept kissing her, and the more she fought, the more certain he was that this was the answer. She had the power. Touch her. Kiss her—

She kneed him between the legs.

He gasped and fell back. "You little—"

"What's happened to you, Bobby?" she said as she scooped up the bird and backed away. "You never used to be like this."

"I just wanted to kiss you. You didn't need to—"

"That wasn't kissing me. That was hurting me. You want to know why I don't like you as much?" She held up the owl. "Because they don't. The animals. You scare them and you scare me."

She cradled the fledgling against her chest and ran off, leaving him there, gasping for breath in the playground.

He started walking, not knowing where he was going, spurred by the fire in his gut, a fire that seeped into his brain, blinding him. When the rage-fog cleared, he found himself on Hannah's street. And there, crossing the road, was what he'd come to find, though he only knew as he saw it.

The black cat. Hannah's matagot kitten. A middle-aged cat now, slinking arrogantly across the street without even bothering to look, as if no car would dare mow it down.

He followed the beast, waiting for it to get to a secluded spot. In Cainsville, though, there weren't any secluded spots. When he'd been young, he'd felt as if he was being merely observed, someone always watching over him, keeping him safe, and he'd loved that. Now it felt as if he was being spied on, judgmental eyes tracking his every move. They weren't, of course. As he moved, he'd sometimes see someone peek out from a house, but they'd only smile and nod. He might be thirteen, but here he was still a child, innocently out playing hide-and-seek or tag with his friends. He could cut through yards and steal behind garages and no one would ever come out to warn him off as they would in the city.

Eventually, the cat stopped prowling, and did so in one of the rare secluded spots around—the yard of an empty house. Cainsville had a few of them, not abandoned but empty. This one was surrounded by a rare solid fence for privacy, and once Bobby was in that yard, he was hidden. That is where the beast stopped to clean itself, proving that whatever airs cats might put on, they were very stupid beasts.

As he crept up behind the cat, his hands flexed at his sides. He had to grab it just right or it would yowl. Pounce and snatch. That was the trick. Scoop it up by the neck, away from scrabbling claws and then squeeze. It was simpler than one might think, particularly when the beast was so preoccupied that it didn't turn even when his foot accidentally scraped a paving stone.

He got as close as he dared. Then he sprang.

The cat whipped around and leaped at him. The shock of seeing that stopped him for a split second, and before he could recover, the cat was on him, scratching and biting, and it was like Rose and Hannah all over again, fighting like wild animals, only this animal had razor claws and fangs, and when he finally threw the beast off, blood dripped from his arms and his face.

He ran at the cat, but it bounded away, leaped onto the fence and turned to hiss at him, almost halfheartedly, as if he wasn't worth the effort. He glowered at the beast then stomped toward the gate. When he swung it open, someone was standing there. Three someones. Mrs. Yates and two of the other elders.

"What have you done, Bobby?" Mrs. Yates said, her voice low.

"Me?" He lifted his blood-streaked hands. "Ask that damned cat. I was trying to rescue it for Hannah."

"No," she said. "That isn't what you were doing at all."

"I don't know what you mean. If Hannah told you—"

"Hannah told us nothing. She doesn't need to. We know."

He looked at her, and then at the other two elders, and he knew, too. Knew the truth he hadn't dared admit. The girls weren't tattling on him. It was the elders, burrowing into his head, reading all his most wicked thoughts, seeing all his most wicked deeds.

He managed to pull himself up straight and say, "You're all crazy." Then he pushed past them and raced back to his mother.

It was the old story. The one where he'd first heard about the screams of dragons. It was coming true. All of it. First the dragons. Then his stomach, twisting and hurting so much these days that he couldn't eat—just like the king couldn't eat because his food went missing. Now the people who could hear everything. The elders and Rose. They knew what he was doing even when he didn't speak a word. He could not escape them, again like the king in the story.

That's why he used to dream of castles. He wasn't a changeling child. He was a king—or he had been—and the old story was replaying itself, consuming him and his life.

After that last trip to Cainsville, the elders were no longer content with the occasional call to check on him. Twice they'd shown up at his house. His *house.* Mrs. Yates had taken him aside and tried to talk to him, prodding him hard now with her questions, telling him she was worried, *so worried.* If only he'd talk to them, they might be able to help.

Liar.

They didn't care about him. They came as a warning. Letting him know they were in his head, watching and judging. Letting him know they were going to win. He was just a little boy. He would be consumed by them—the dragons—as Rose's dreams predicted. It all made sense now, or it did, the more he thought about it, obsessed on it, dreamed of it. It was like a puzzle where the pieces don't seem to fit, but you just had to be smart and twist them around until they did.

He went to the library and dug until he found the story in an old book of legends. He'd vaguely recalled that the king had stopped his enemies—those who could hear everything—by feeding them something. Apparently, he'd fed them food made from very special insects. Bobby read that, and he went home to sleep on it, and when he woke, he knew exactly what he had to do.

It was May Day again. This year, the Gnat had decided not to come. She'd been at a friend's place and called to say she was spending the night and skipping the trip. He'd given the news to his parents when they returned from a bridge party.

The next morning, his mother started fussing, worrying that the Gnat would change her mind as soon as they'd left for Cainsville.

"She'd call before that," his father said. "She's a big girl."

"I can phone and ask if you want," Bobby said.

"Would you? That's sweet." She patted his back as he walked past. "Whose house did you say she was at again?"

He answered from the next room, his reply garbled, but his mother only said, "Oh, that's right. Now, does anyone know where we left the tanning lotion? I want to get started early this year. Wait, I think Natalie had it . . . "

A few minutes later he found her in his sister's room. "She's not there. I remember her saying something about going to the roller rink."

His mother sighed. "I wish she wouldn't. Those places seem so unhealthy for girls, with the lights all off and so many boys . . . "

"I can talk to her about it tomorrow if you're worried."

Another pat as she zoomed past, tanning lotion in hand. "Thank you, dear. You're a good brother, even if she doesn't always appreciate you. Did you pack that pie you made?"

"Pie?" His father appeared in the doorway. "Bobby made pie? Apple, I hope."

"Shepherd's pie," his mother said. "He made it last night while we were out. Didn't you notice the mess when we got home?" She glanced over. "So you *did* find hamburger meat in the freezer."

"One last package, like I said."

"I was so certain we'd run out." She headed for the hall. "All right. Time to go."

The waitresses at the new diner let him warm his casserole in the oven. He was sitting in the back, watching the timer, when the door swung open and Rose burst in, Hannah at her heels.

"That smells good," Hannah said. "Is it true? You made pie?"

"Shepherd's pie. I hope you're not still mad at me. I'm . . . " He lowered his voice as he walked toward her. "Sorry about the last time. That's why I made the pie. For you and Rose. To say I'm sorry. For the elders, too. I don't want anyone to be mad at me." He gazed into her eyes. "I hope you'll have some."

She seemed nervous, but forced a smile. "Sure, Bobby. And I'm sorry, if I overreacted. You scared me and—"

"What have you done?"

It was Rose. She hadn't spoken since she'd entered. He hadn't even glanced her way, seeing only Hannah. Now he looked over to see her standing in front of the oven, staring at it. When she turned to him, her face was even paler than usual, her blue eyes bulging.

"What have you done, Bobby?" she whispered.

"Done? What—"

"I had a dream," she said. "Last night."

"More dragons," he scoffed. "Dreams of me and screaming dragons."

"No." Her horrified gaze never left his. "It wasn't dragons I heard screaming."

"Whatever." He turned away. "You're crazy. Your whole family is crazy."

"Where's your sister, Bobby?"

He shrugged, his back still to Rose. "She stayed home."

"Where is your sister?" she said each word slowly, carefully, and he was about to reply when the door opened again. He turned as Mrs. Yates and two of the elders walked in. They seemed concerned. Only that. Then they stopped, mid-stride. They inhaled, nostrils flaring, and when they turned to him again, horror filled their eyes, the same horror that crackled from Rose's wide-eyed stare.

"Bobby," Mrs. Yates said. "What have you done?"

He wheeled and raced out the back door.

Before he knew it, he found himself back where he'd been the last time, in the backyard of the empty house. He looked around wildly, saw a break in the lattice work under the deck, and crawled through, wood snapping as he pushed his way in, splinters digging in, blood welling up.

When he got inside, he turned around and huddled there, hugging knees that stank of dirt, his arms striped with blood.

Blood.

He remembered the blood.

He shot forward, gagging, stomach clenching, head pounding, the images slamming against his skull. He kept gagging until he threw up. Then he sat there, hugging his legs again as the tears rolled down his face.

Gran was right.

I am a monster.

And I don't even know how it happened.

"Bobby?"

It was Mrs. Yates. He scuttled backward, but she walked straight to the hole and bent to peer in. She smiled, but it was such a terribly sad smile that he wished she'd scowl instead, scowl and rage and call him the monster he was.

"I am so sorry, Bobby," she said. "I don't know . . . " She inhaled. "I won't make excuses. We could tell things weren't . . . We had no idea how bad . . . " Another inhalation, breath whistling. "I'm so, so sorry. I wish I'd known. I wish I could have helped."

He said nothing, just kept clutching his knees.

"I can't stop what's going to happen now, Bobby. I wish I could. I would give anything to fix this. But I can't. I can only make it easier."

He started to shake, holding his legs so tight his arms hurt.

"I read those newspaper articles," she said. "About your grandmother. What she said. Your dreams. We should have talked about that. Perhaps if we'd talked . . . " She shook her head, then peered in at him. "You dreamed of golden castles, didn't you? Castles and meadows and streams."

"And dragons," he whispered.

She went still. Completely, unnaturally still. "Dragons?"

He nodded. "I dream of dragons screaming. And then I wasn't dreaming and they still screamed."

"You should have told—" She cut herself short, chin dipping. "Let's not talk about the dragons. You won't hear them anymore. I promise. But the castles. You liked the castles?"

He nodded.

"Would you like to see them?"

"They're gone. They went away."

She inched a little closer to the gap in the lattice. "I can bring them back. Back as bright as they ever were. Castles and meadows, cool breezes and warm sunshine. Laughter and play, music and dancing. Is that what you remember?"

He nodded.

"Would you like to go there?"

"Yes."

She ducked her head and crawled under with him. In one hand, she held a bottle. She pulled out the stopper and held the bottle out to him. The liquid inside seemed to glow, and when he looked up at her, she seemed to glow, too, the wrinkles on her face smoothing.

"Do you trust me, Bobby?"

He nodded.

"Then drink that. Drink it, and you'll see the castles again. You'll go there, and you won't ever need to come back."

He took the bottle, and he drank it all in one gulp. As soon as he did, the dragons stopped screaming, and he saw Mrs. Yates, glowing, every inch of her glowing, like sunlight trapped under her skin, her eyes filling with it, drawing him in as she reached out to hug him. He fell into her arms, and the glow consumed everything, the world turned to gold, and when he opened his eyes, he was sitting on sun-warmed grass, staring up at a castle, and a girl laughed behind him and said, "Come and play, Bobby." He turned, and she looked like Hannah but not quite, and she smiled at him, the way Hannah used to smile at him. He pushed to his feet and raced after her as she ran off, laughing.

And that was where he stayed, just as Mrs. Yates promised. Endless days in a world of gold and sunshine, days that ran together and had no end. Every now and then he would fall asleep in a lush meadow or in a chamber in the beautiful castle, and when he did, his dreams were terrible nightmares, where he was bound to a hospital bed, screaming about dragons. But the nights never lasted long, and soon he was back in his world of castles and meadows, running, chasing, playing, dancing until he forgot what the screams of dragons sounded like, forgot he'd ever heard them and forgot everything else—his grandmother, his sister, his parents, the girls, Mrs. Yates—all of it gone, wisps of a dream that faded into nothing, leaving him exactly where he'd always wanted to be.

New York Times #1 bestseller **Kelley Armstrong** has been telling stories since before she could write. Her earliest written efforts were disastrous: if asked for a story about girls and dolls, her story would—much to her teachers' dismay— feature undead girls and evil dolls. She grew up and kept writing and now lives in southwest Ontario with a husband and children who do not mind that she continues to spin tales of the supernatural while safely locked away in the basement. Armstrong is best known for her thirteen Otherworld urban fantasy novels (on which the SyFy series *Bitten* was based). The third in her Cainsville series—the world in which this story is set—will be published this year. She has also authored six novels for her Darkest Powers series and the Age of Legends trilogy, both for teens. For younger readers, she coauthored (with Melissa Marrs) the Blackwell Pages trilogy.

Few souls are practiced at fighting off an invasion . . .

DREAMER

Brandon Sanderson

"I've got him!" I yelled into the phone as I scrambled down the street. "Forty-ninth and Broadway!" I shoved my way through an Asian family on the way home from the market. Their bags went flying, oranges spilling onto the street and bouncing in front of honking cabs.

Accented curses chased me as I lowered the phone and sprinted after my prey, a youth in a green sports jacket and cap. A bright yellow glow surrounded him, my indication of his true identity.

I wore the body of a businessman, late thirties, lean and trim. Fortunately for me, this guy hit the gym. I dashed around a corner at speed, my quarry curving and dodging between the theater district's early evening crowds. Buildings towered around us, blazing with the lights of fervent advertising.

Phi glanced over his shoulder at me. I thought I caught a look of surprise on his lean face. He'd know me from my glow, of course—the one visible only to others like us.

I jumped over a metal construction barrier, landing in the street, where I dashed out around the crowds. A chorus of honks and yells accompanied me as I gained, step-by-step, on Phi. It's hard to lose a man in Manhattan. There aren't alleyways to duck into, and the crowds don't help hide us from one another.

Phi ducked right, shoving his way through a glass door and into a diner.

What the hell? I thought, chasing after, throwing my shoulder against the door and pushing into the restaurant. Was he going to try to get out another way? That—

Phi stood just inside, arm leveled toward me, a handgun pointed at my head. I pulled to a stop, gaping for a moment, before he shot me point-blank in the head.

Disorientation.

I thrashed about, losing sense of location, purpose, even *self* as I was ejected from the dying body. For a few primal moments, I couldn't think.

I was a rat in the darkness, desperately seeking light.

Glows all around. The warmth of souls. One rose from the body I'd left, the soul of the man to whom it had really belonged. That was brilliant yellow, and now untouchable. Unsavory, also. I needed *warmth*.

I charged for a body, no purpose behind my choice beyond pure instinct. I latched on, a lion on the gazelle, ripping and battering against the consciousness there, forcing it down. It didn't want to let me in, but I *needed* that warmth.

I won. In this primal state, I usually do. Few souls are practiced at fighting off an invasion. Consciousness returned like water seeping underneath a door. Panic, horror—the lingering emotions of the soul who had held this body before me, like the scent of a woman's perfume after she leaves the room.

As I gained full control, vision returned. I was sitting in one of the diner's seats looking down at the corpse of the body I'd been wearing-the body Phi had killed.

Damn, I thought, chewing the last bite of food the woman had been eating as I asserted control. It left a faint taste of honey and pastry in the mouth. *Phi had a gun.* That meant the body he'd taken had happened to have one. Lucky bastard.

A group of old women in cardigans and headscarves squawked in the seats around me, speaking a language I didn't know. Other people shouted and screamed, backing away from the body. Phi was gone, of course. He'd known the best way to lose me was to kill my body.

Blood seeped out of the corpse and onto the chipped tile floor. Damn.

It had been a good body—I'd gotten lucky with that one. I shook my head, lifting the purse beside me—I assumed it belonged to the woman whose body I'd taken—and began to dig inside. I was an old lady, like the others at the table. I could see that much in the window's reflection.

Come on, I thought, standing up and continuing to search in the purse. *Come on . . . There!* I pulled out a mobile phone.

I was in luck. It was an old flip kind, not a smartphone, which meant it wasn't locked or passcoded. Ignoring the yells of the old lady's dining companions, I walked around the corpse on the floor, stepping out onto the street.

My exit started a flood, like I was the cork popped from shaken champagne. People left the diner in a run, many white-faced, a few clutching children.

I dialed Longshot's number. She was the one Phi was hunting, but she wanted to be useful. We often left one of our number back in a situation like this anyway, using him or her to coordinate. With the rest of us jumping bodies and finding new mobile phones, the best way to stay in touch was to have one person keep a set number and phone, taking calls from the other four and relaying messages.

The phone picked up after one ring.

"It's Dreamer," I said.

"Dreamer?" Longshot wore a body with a smooth, feminine voice.

"You sound like an old lady."

"That's because I am one. Now." My voice bore a faint accent from the soul that had held this body. Things like that stayed. Muscle memory, accents, anything not entirely conscious. Not languages, unfortunately, but some skills. I'd once stayed in the body of a fine pianist for a couple of weeks playing music alone as the ability slowly seeped away from me.

"What happened?" Longshot demanded.

"His body had a gun. He ducked into a restaurant and popped me in the head when I followed. I don't know which way he went after that."

"Damn. Just a sec. I need to warn the others that he's armed."

"This could be a good thing," I said, glancing to the side as a couple of cops pushed through the growing crowd. "The mortal police will be after him now."

"Unless he Bolts from his body."

"He's on his third body already," I said. "He doesn't have many to spare. Besides, Bolting would risk losing the gun. I think he'll stick to the same body. He's brash."

"You sure?"

"I know him better than anyone, Longshot."

"Yeah, okay," she said, but I could hear the implication in her voice.

He knows you too, Dreamer, and he got you. Again.

I lowered the phone as Longshot hung up and began calling the other three. I itched to be off, chasing Phi down again, but I had to be smarter than that. We knew where he was going—his goal would be Longshot, who hid atop a building nearby, unable to move. What we needed to do was make it tough for him to get to her.

Phi wouldn't escape me this time. No more failures. No more excuses.

"Excuse me?" I said, hobbling over to one of the police officers trying to manage the crowd. Damn, but this body was weak. "Officer? I saw the man who did this."

The officer turned toward me. It's still surreal to me how people's responses to me change depending on the body I'm wearing. This man puffed himself up, trying to look as if he was in control. "Ma'am?" he asked.

"I saw him," I repeated. "Short wiry fellow. Tan skin, maybe Indian, with a green jacket and cap. Lean face, high cheekbones, short hair. Perhaps five foot five."

The cop stared at me dumbly for a moment. "Uh, I'd better write this down."

It took a good five minutes for them to get down my description. Five minutes, with Phi running who knows where. Longshot didn't call me, though, so I didn't have anywhere to go. I'd know soon after one of the others spotted him. Two of the others would be out like I was, hunting Phi on the streets. One last man, TheGannon, guarded the approach to Longshot's position.

A team of five to deal with one man, but Phi was slippery. *Damn it.* I couldn't believe he'd gotten the drop on me again.

I was finishing my description of his body for the sixth time when Longshot finally called me. I stepped away from the officers as they got corroborating information from other diner patrons and called in the description. An ambulance had arrived, for all the good it would do.

"Yeah?" I said into the phone.

"Icer decided to get a vantage atop a building on Broadway. She caught sight of our man moving down the street, almost at Forty-seventh. Moving slowly, like he's trying to not draw attention. You were right, he's in the same body as before."

"Awesome," I said.

"Icer is on her way down to hunt him. You're not going to let your past issues with Phi get in the way, are you, Dreamer? Phi—"

"I put the cops on his trail," I said. "I'm Bolting, but I'll keep this phone."

"Dreamer! You'll be on your last body. Don't—"

I closed the phone, turning back to the policemen. I chose a muscular man with dark skin. He wore a white shirt instead of blue, and the others had called him Lieutenant.

"Officer," I said, hobbling up, trying to get his attention without alerting the other police.

"Yes, ma'am," he said distractedly.

I faked a stumble, and he reached down. I grabbed his wrist.

And attacked.

It's harder when you're already in a body. The soul immediately gets attached to the body, and forcing out and into something else can be tough. Besides, when you're out of a body, the primal self takes hold, and it helps you—nearly mindless though you are—*claw* your way through another soul's defenses

Some people say you can control the primal, body-less self. Learn to think while in that mode. I'd never been able to do it. Anyway, I had a body already, and part of my energy had to be dedicated to holding down the soul inside, that of the old lady. At the same time, I had to attack the police officer and force his soul aside.

The man gasped, eyes opening wide. Damn. His soul was tough. I strained, like a man straddling between two distant footholds, and shoved. It was like trying to push down a brick wall.

I will get him, this time! I thought, straining, then finally toppling that wall and slipping into the new body.

The disorientation was over more quickly this time. The officer stumbled as he lost control of his limbs, but I had the body before he dropped. I caught myself on a planter, going down on one knee, but didn't collapse fully.

"Lorenzo?" one of the others called. "You okay?" They'd covered the corpse with a white blanket. It lay just inside the door to the diner.

Fleeing people had tracked blood out in a mess of footprints, but some diner occupants and employees still huddled inside the restaurant, shocked by the horror of the death. I could remember that fear, vaguely, from when I'd been alive. The fear of death, the fear of the unknown.

They had no idea.

I nodded to the other officers, standing back up, and when they weren't looking I slid the phone out of the hand of the old lady. She stood frozen and slack-jawed. Her soul would reassert itself over the next hour or so, but she wouldn't remember anything from our time together.

I pocketed the phone and began to jog away.

"Lieutenant?" one of the officers called.

"I have a lead," I said. "Keep going here."

"But—"

I left them at a run. The police thought the killing to be a gang-related hit, and so far, they hadn't shut down the streets or anything. Maybe they would, but it was better for me if they didn't. That would mean more bodies for my team to use, if they needed to.

The cop's body felt strong and energetic, I was left with the faint impression of a melody the cop had been singing in his head before I stole it. That and . . . a face. Wife? Girlfriend? No, it was gone. A fleeting image lost to the ether.

I jogged around the corner, keeping an eye out for the glow of a body that was possessed. This area was close to Longshot's building. If Phi got to her . . .

She wouldn't have a chance against him. I slowed my pace as I reached the place where Icer had spotted Phi. There was no sign of either one.

I wove through the crowds of lively, chattering people. The cop was tall, giving me a good vantage. It was strange how unaware people were.

Two streets over, people stood in chaos, horror, or disbelief. Here, everyone was laughing and anticipating a night at a show. Street vendors cheerfully took tourist money, and dull-eyed people earning minimum wage handed out pamphlets nobody wanted to read.

Phi would be close. Longshot's building was just down the street, with her atop it. He would case the area, planning how to attack.

I waited, anxious, tense. I waited until the earbud I wore—tapped into the official police channels—spouted a specific phrase. "Marks here. I think I see him. Broadway and Forty-seventh, by the information center."

I started running.

"Don't engage him," the voices crackled on the line. "Wait for backup."

"Lieutenant Lorenzo here," I shouted into the microphone. "Ignore that order, Marks. He's more dangerous than we thought. Take him down, if you can!"

Others on the line started arguing with me, talking about "protocol," but I ignored them. I unholstered this body's gun and checked to make sure it was loaded. *Now we're both armed, Phi,* I thought. I charged around a corner, people flinging themselves out of my way once they saw the uniform and the gun raised beside my head. The shouts that chased me this time were of a different type—less outraged, more shocked.

Gunfire ahead. For a moment, I hoped Marks the cop had done as I told him, but then I saw a glowing yellow figure drop to the ground. It wasn't Phi.

Icer, I thought with annoyance. Indeed, Phi—still wearing the body with the green jacket—scrambled down the street after dropping Icer. I didn't have a very clear shot, but I took it anyway, pulling to a halt, raising the gun, and firing the entire clip.

This body had practiced with a gun. I was far more accurate than I had any right to be, bullets spraying the walls—and, unfortunately, crowd right near Phi. I didn't hit him. I got so close, but I didn't hit.

"Damn it!" I said, charging after him. The crowds nearby were screaming, throwing themselves to the ground or running in stooped postures. Phi was heading straight toward Longshot's building.

Another gunshot popped in the air. I moved to dodge by reflex, but then saw Phi drop in a spray of blood.

What?

A cop stood up from beside a planter, looking white in the face. That would be Marks, the one who had called in the sighting. The cop raised his head in horror, looking around at the mess. People groaning from gunfire gone wild, the dead body Icer had been using, and now the fallen Phi.

The cop walked toward Phi's body.

"No!" I yelled, I scrambled for my microphone, running forward.

"Someone tell Marks to stay back! Marks!"

He stiffened, then dropped. I cursed, trying to reach him, but there were so many people about, huddling, looking for cover, getting in my way. I drew closer, fighting through them, in time to see the body of Marks—a young, redheaded man with a spindly figure stand up again and turn in my direction. Phi was on his fourth body. He lowered Marks's gun toward me.

Not again, you bastard, I thought, throwing myself to the side as four shots fired into the crowd. Only four—the gun had been partially empty.

I came up from my roll, thankful that Lorenzo was so athletic. My body knew what to do better than I did. Phi was already off and barreling toward Longshot. No subterfuge now, no casing the place. He knew that shots fired into a crowd would make this place go dangerous very, very quickly.

I ran after him, yelling into my microphone, "Marks has been working with the target. I repeat, Marks has been working with the target. In pursuit."

Well, that might just sow more chaos. I wasn't certain. I pulled my earbud out as I gave pursuit. The mobile phone from the old lady was ringing. I put it to my head as I ran.

"Icer is down," Longshot said. "It was her third."

Damn. I was out of breath.

"I think he got Rabies too," she told me. "He was only on his second body, but I can't reach him. He must not have a phone yet. It's you, Dreamer."

"TheGannon?"

"Gone," Longshot said softly.

"What the hell do you mean, gone?" I demanded, puffing.

"You don't want to know."

Damn, damn, damn! TheGannon was our door guard. "Phi is still armed," I told Longshot. "If he gets to you, try your best."

"Okay."

I pocketed the phone, holstered my gun, and gave the run everything I had.

The street had gone to chaos quickly. With the wounded lying about, the people dropping papers and possessions as they ran and screamed, the cars stropping and people hiding inside, you'd have thought it was a war zone. I guess it kind of was.

I slid across the hood of a car, keeping pace with Phi—even gaining on him a tad—as he reached the target building. He didn't go inside, however. Instead, he pushed into the building *next* to it, a low office building with reflective glass windows.

He doesn't know that TheGannon is gone, I realized, charging after. *He's trying to keep himself from being pinned.* The office building and the target were similar in height. He could easily jump from one roof to the next.

He still had a lead on me, and it was a good minute or so before I hit the door, shoving my way in. This time I watched for an ambush. I didn't find one; instead, I saw a door on the other side of the entryway swinging shut.

"What's going on here!" a security guard demanded, standing beside his desk near the door.

"Police business," I yelled. "That doorway? It's a stairwell to the roof?"

"Yeah. I gave your buddy the key."

Damn. He could reach the roof, lock me out, and then jump over and take out Longshot. Phi was a clever one, I had to give him that much credit.

I entered the stairwell. I couldn't worry about gunfire. I had to charge up those steps as fast as I could. If he shot me, he shot me. There was a chance that would happen, but if he got to the roof, I lost. And I would not let him get away again!

I heard puffing and footfalls above me as I took the steps. My body was in better shape than his, but I'd been running longer than he had.

Still, talking to the guard must have slowed him down, and I seemed to be gaining on him.

I rounded another corner in the white-painted stairwell, passing graffiti and concrete corners that hadn't seen a mop in ages. I was gaining on him. In fact, when I neared the top floor, I heard rattling as he worked on the door.

No! I forced my way up the last flight of stairs, reaching the top right as Phi pushed it closed on the other side. I slammed into it, exploding out onto the rooftop before Phi could lock it.

He stumbled away, red hair plastered to his head with sweat, shoulders slumping from fatigue. He tried to get out his gun, fiddling with an extra clip, but I tackled him.

"You're mine, this time," I growled, holding him to the rooftop. "No slipping away. Not again."

He spat in my eye.

Admittedly, I wasn't expecting that. I pulled back in revulsion, and he kicked me in the leg, shoving me off and throwing me to the side.

I cursed, wiping my eye, scrambling after him as he ran across the roof. The target building was next door, maybe five feet below this one, no gap between. My body's muscles were straining after that climb. I could still hear shouts from the chaos below, sirens wailing in the distance.

Phi jumped onto the rooftop. I followed. Longshot was there, wearing a young woman's body, backed up against the far corner of the building. Phi ran for her.

I screamed and threw myself forward, plowing into him just before he reached her.

And that tossed both of us off the building.

It was the only thing I could have done. If I'd gone slower, he'd have reached her. At this speed, I couldn't control my momentum. We fell in a heartbeat and crashed to the ground.

Disorientation.

Primal forces, driving me toward heat and warmth.

No. That was my last.

The thought bubbled up from deep within. Some say it's possible to control the primal self, the freed self.

I lashed out this direction, then that, but somehow held control. I could see Phi's spirit moving turgidly toward a body, and I somehow forced myself to follow. Two glowing fields, like translucent mold, seeping along the ground unseen to mortal eyes. Still a chase. A chase I would win.

I reached him just before he got to the warmth, and I latched on. I held tightly, clinging to him, and like an unwieldy weight, stopped him from getting into the body. He battered at me, clawed at me, but I just *held on*. I'd lost knowledge of did what I did, but I held on. For a time, at least. An eternity I could not count.

Finally, he slipped away, as he always does.

I found another warmth, then opened my eyes to a smiling face.

"Longshot?" I said, disoriented. I was lying on the ground in a new body, a construction worker, it appeared. The contest was over; I'd be allowed this body now.

"You did it," she said, glowing. "You held him down long enough for Rabies to get here! Once Phi got control of his last body, Rabies already had it in custody! You won, Dreamer."

"He cheated."

I sat up. Phi sat there in the body of another construction worker; the two men had been taking cover here, it appeared, near the base of the building. I could tell it was him. My brother always has this self-satisfied leer on his face, and I could recognize him in any body.

"What? That's nonsense." The businesswoman would be Icer, from that tone in her voice. She sat on the edge of a planter nearby. "We got you, Phi."

"He shot into the crowd!" Phi said.

"So did you!" I said, climbing to my feet with Longshot's help. After spending so long . . . too long . . . outside a body, the warmth felt good.

It had probably been only a few minutes, but that was an eternity without a body.

"You were playing detective, Dave," Phi said, pointing at me. "I was criminal. I can shoot innocents. You can't."

"By whose rules?" Icer demanded.

"Everyone's rules!" Phi said, throwing up his hands. "You've got five, I'm only one. The criminal has to have a few advantages. That's why I can kill, and you can't."

"It's five on one," I said, "because you bragged you could take us all on your own, Phi."

"You cheated," he said, leaning back. "Flat-out."

"Man," Rabies said, wearing the body of a thick-armed black man. He stood a little off from us, looking at the chaos of Broadway, with police, ambulances. "We kind of caused a mess, didn't we?"

"We need to ban guns," Longshot said.

"You *always* say that," Phi replied.

"Look," Longshot said. We won't be able to use Manhattan for months."

"Eh," Phi said. "I'm doing a race with TheGannon across the country next. What do I care?"

"What happened to TheGannon, anyway?" Icer asked.

Longshot grimaced. "We had an argument. He left."

"He bugged out in the middle of a game?" Icer said. "Damn that kid. We should never have invited him."

"They're coming over here," Rabies said. "To check on the bodies of the two cops. We should split."

"Meet up in Jersey?" Longshot asked.

We all nodded, and the glowing individuals went their separate ways. They'd probably dump these bodies soon, working their way out of the city by hopping from person to person in whatever way suited them.

I ended up going with Phi. Side by side, walking away from the dead cops, hoping nobody would stop us. I was tired, and Bolting to another body didn't sound pleasant.

"I *did* get you," I told him.

"You tried hard, I'll give you that."

"I won, Phi. Can't you just admit that?"

He just grinned. "I'11 tell you what. Footrace to Jersey. No limit on bodies. And just for you, no guns. Loser admits defeat." With that, he took off.

I sighed, shaking my head, watching my older brother go. A footrace? That meant no cars, no subways. We'd have to run the entire way, jumping into new bodies every few minutes as the ones we were using grew exhausted—like a poltergeist version of a relay race.

Phi never knew when to stop. I didn't remember a lot about when we'd been alive, back when our capture the flag games had been limited to controllers and a flatscreen—but I did know he'd been like this then, too.

Well, I could beat him in a footrace. He wasn't nearly as good at those as he was at capture the flag.

I'd win this time, and then he'd see.

Bestselling author **Brandon Sanderson** has published eight solo novels for adults including *Warbreaker, Elantris,* two books of The Stormlight Archive series—*The Way of Kings* and *Words of Radiance*—and the Mistborn books—*The Well of Ascension, The Hero of Ages, The Alloy of Law, and Shadows of Self.* For young adults he has authored *The Rithmatist* and two Reckoners science fiction novels—*Steelheart* and *Firefight*—as well as four books in the middle-grade Alcatraz Smedry series. He was chosen to complete the final three novels of Robert Jordan's The Wheel of Time series. He lives in Utah with his wife and children. Sanderson teaches creative writing at Brigham Young University.

*The cut in my finger doesn't close for weeks. The hole in my soul
remains the equivalent of a sucking chest wound . . .*

(LITTLE MISS) QUEEN OF DARKNESS

LAIRD BARRON

I: Initiation

I write this: *The cops don't know what really happened in Eagle Talon. Lies, all
lies. Ask Jessica, if I ever see her again.* This isn't about Eagle Talon, however. I've
never even been. No sir, Bob, if it's about anything, it's about that debutante
ball Zane throws in his basement at the tail end of high school, 1998. The
unfinished basement with the raw earth and a tunnel that smells of mildew
and dankness. The tunnel is maybe three by three and is actually a cleft in the
rock of the hill upon which this house rests.

I can't forget that hole in the ground. It drills through my mind.

Yeah, Shit Creek describes an imperfect circle right back to the bad old
days. Oh, the party is rad, though: heavy metal, booze, drugs, psychedelic
lights. The kids slam-dancing. Me with my hand on Stu Whitlock's hip the
whole time and nobody the wiser. Then that damned hick brat Dave Teague
racing overhead, naked and covered in blood (so the legend goes), screaming
his head off. Ruins everything . . .

I also write: *People call it this or that, but our club doesn't have a name. It
didn't originate in Alaska. It was around before Alaska. We don't suckle at the
breast of a god, it suckles at ours.* Unfortunately, devoid of context, that stuff
reads like the Unabomber's doodles.

Next, I make a list. Were I to title it, the title would be "People Who
Died," like the song. Such an everyman tune because everybody can relate,
right? The partial list is scribbled in a black moleskin notebook. I've left
bloody fingerprints on the pages. Many of the names are illegible from the
smears, or redaction with a magic marker. Names changed to protect the

guilty. Four remain intact in truth and form. Hell if I know whether that's significant or not.

Zane Tooms & Julie Vellum: They could've been the power couple from the lowest circle of Hell. Alas, Zane already had a loyalist and Julie's not the kind to need any. These are your villains. Nuff said.

Steely J: Just about tall enough to play pro basketball. He's Zane's major domo. The Renfield to Zane's Dracula. Loyal through thick and thin—and I'm not kidding, I literally mean that. We called Zane Fat Boy Tooms until his folks croaked and he started in with the horse de-wormer and got slenderized. Steely J stuck with him down the line. Steely is what you might call inscrutable. Looks nice, dresses nice, and plays nice, if a teensy bit of a cold fish. His features lag behind whatever message his brain is sending. Somebody behind the curtain throws a switch and he smiles. Or, he smiles and picks up a claw hammer and comes for you. The Sandburg poem about fog creeping on little cat feet? That's Steely J. Except six-six with a hammer.

Vadim: My buddy Vadim often brags that he's an expert in Savate. He paid two hundred dollars for a six week course at a strip mall. I let him drag me in once to meet the instructor (mainly I wanted to ogle some studly hotties kicking and stretching, but whatev) and the dude had a bunch of diplomas, certificates, and autographed photos of macho celebrities I didn't care to recognize. The French version of hi-ya for an hour. Bo-oring.

The strip mall closed shop when the economy cratered in '09. Not before Vadim got what he needed, however. He asserts that Savate is the elite of the elite fighting arts, natch. I don't know my foot from my elbow when it comes to violence. I'm a lover, always have been. That's why I keep the numbers of a few bigger, tougher friends in my Rolodex.

Vadim talks lots of shit every time we go clubbing and the fraternity bros start hitting on me, which they totally do. I clutch his sleeve and say, "Whoa, there stud. They're just being friendly. Get mama another margarita, 'kay?" Vadim shoots the bros a venomous parting glare and then toddles off to fetch my drink. His thighs bulge his cargo pants so that he really does toddle. I think of it as having my own Siberian tiger on a leash, except with pouty, pouty lips, and six-pack abs! Nice while it lasted. He's dead too.

End of list.

Go back, not the whole way, not to high school. Three and a half years is far enough. We have gathered, dearly beloved. Gathered to sign on the dotted line and change the course of our stars forever. What a load of crap. *I'm* motivated by fascination, boredom, skepticism. Some of the others are buggy-eyed true believers. Have at it, morons.

The sun is bleeding out all over the Chugach Mountains. An inlet, ice-toothed and serpentine, lies below us somewhere, wrapped by mist that's freezing into black pearl. I'm not captivated by the austere beauty of the far north as seen through frosty picture windows. My feet are cold and I'm bored. I'm an L.A. girl trapped inside an L.A. boy. This arctic weather is for the birds.

Julie Five says to me, "Oh, Ed, quit sulking. You detest it so much, why'd you come? Nut up or shut up." She finishes me off with a sweet as pie smile. I beam one right back. Anybody more than arms-length away might get the impression we're peaches and cream. Big sister, little brother at worst. Then again, it's an intimate gathering of former classmates. Most of the others know how it is with us because it's been this way with us since junior high. Her nickname is JV, but I call her Julie Five. Our mutual acquaintance, the lamentably absent Jessica M, coined that bit of mockery. Sure, we're supposed to pity Julie Five for cowering in a closet while her lover got noisily disemboweled by the Eagle Talon Ripper in the winter of 2012, but her sob story doesn't move me—"victim-of-unspeakable-tragedy" is scraping the bottom of the barrel on a white trash reality show. Her sneaky path to fifteen minutes of fame and she didn't even try to stop the murdering bastard. Oh, dear heavens, no—she left that chore to her archrival, Jessica M, the girl who got the cover of *Black Belt Magazine* and interviews with every cable news show in existence. Good for Jess. Screw Julie Five. She's cowardly, treacherous, and mean. She like totally vacillates between vocal fry and ending every sentence on a rising note. Basically the darkest valley girl in the history of valley girls. I'd feed her a cup of lye if I had some.

Our host, Zane Tooms, stares at the sunset the way a man with an appointment compulsively checks his watch. He's dressed in a white shirt and black pants. No shoes. He never wears shoes at home. His shirt is unbuttoned two notches. A metallic chain gleams from the opening. I've seen the pendant when Zane had his shirt off—a smallish lump of vaguely horrid metal, or bone. Its color shifts, the film of a lizard's eye rolling aside. He folds his napkin, rises from his seat (throne) at the head of the table, and walks further into the decrepit mansion.

The house juts from a knoll with an impressive view of tidal flats and occasionally the water. The knoll was a bear den until hunters exterminated the bears and poured concrete back in when-the-hell-ever. Exactly the kind of place natives would say, "Don't build here! Bad medicine!" White Man doesn't give a shit about any of that and here we are. Even so, the Tooms residence lacks the sinister gravitas of a classic, gothic haunted castle. Made over once too often, the latest reconstructive surgery has rendered it a weird amalgam of art deco and 60s kitsch. His home might have been cozy in its heyday. He let it go to seed after the senior Toomses shuffled into the next life. He travels and can't be bothered with upkeep. I've told him he needs a decorator because the ambiance sucks. Frontier chic it is not. Swear to god he doesn't even live here, it's so borderline derelict. If Zane confessed he only showed up to unlock the joint and turn on the lights half an hour before his guests arrived, I wouldn't be shocked.

The basement is carved into the den itself and mostly unfinished. Lots of exposed beams, pipes, and dirt. I shudder to think. Tunnels bore past the glow of any lamp. Can't say I'm impressed with the remote location or the bear catacombs. Way too rustic for this girl. What does impress me is Zane himself. These days, after slimming his chubby cheeks and beer gut, he's drop dead gorgeous. A walking, talking Ken Doll; brunet model. He oozes primal charisma. Night and day from the acne-riddled, blimpo Zane that we knew and abhorred as kids. I'd kill to learn his secret and that's part of why I RSVP'd yes on the invitation last month; why I ditched everything I had cooking in Cali and came like a dog to her master's whistle.

Steely J gives us a significant nod. We guests push away from half-empty plates and migrate into the parlor, wine coolers and rum and cokes in hand. I loathe the parlor. It's cold and dank, the books are moldy, and the stuffed moose head that presides here has gone blind with rot. The notion of accidently brushing against something icky gives me the shivers.

Zane unlocks a cabinet and sets a jewelry box upon the big circular granite table we're seated around. The table is slightly concave. Several parallel grooves radiate from the edge to a depression in the center. As for the jewelry case, it is an unpleasant box with the lacquer stripped. The wood is scored and blanched by patterns of fungal decay. An eighteenth-century caravel's lost antique dredged from the muck at the bottom of Cook Inlet in 1979, or so my peeps testify. Inside the box, a ring nests in crushed velvet. An indelicate description for those playing at home—its color is similar to a blood clot glistening against tissue paper. He plucks the ring and casually passes it to Morton, just like that. No formalities whatsoever.

"Damn, it's heavy," Morton says. Morton always sounds bemused or surprised.

"Don't drop it," Julie Five says. She's cool and eager. She gave Morton a hummer last August while we were all on a tour bus at Denali State Park. They speak to each other with barely restrained antipathy. "Drop it, and it's ten demerits." Gawd, I hate her smug, bitchy tone. I hate that Morton accepted her blowjob and turned me down flat. Heel.

"By the way, the table isn't granite," Zane says as if he's peeked into my brain. His gaze is cruel. "Another rock entirely. There are chains of sea caves in the Aleutians. This table is carved from the bedrock of those caves. Men died acquiring this on my behalf." He looks at Morton. "Okay, Mort. Time to get bitten." He is indulgent, yet commanding. Two decades in Europe, and farther abroad, will do that to a guy, I suppose. Julie Five says Zane spent months lost in a desert and went barking mad. Eating-his-own-shoelaces fucked in the head. Wouldn't guess it to feast your eyes upon him, or maybe you would. The corners of his eyes twitch if you catch it at the right moment.

Morton makes a show of examining the ring, as if a middle manager role at an office supply store qualifies him to appraise jewelry. He's enjoying the spotlight. "Is this the Ouroboros?"

"Don't be ridiculous." Zane's sneer almost spoils the plastic charm of his perma-smile. I've long assumed his genial urbanity is a façade for darker impulses. Doesn't bother me. Everybody has got another side. It's exciting.

"If there were a *real* Dracula Ring, this would be the one," Julie Five says. "Lugosi's was pretty. Fake. Fake. Fake." She rocks, barely suppressed. Her face is so very animated. I've seen that expression. It's the wide-eyed, lips slightly parted expression women at boxing matches wear. I'm sure the rich hoes in Rome did it the same when they attended the gladiatorial games.

The ring is formed of thick, intertwined strands of corroded iron. There's a jagged gap opposite the shank. Whether from damage or by design, I haven't a clue. The shank is set with the aforementioned gory gemstone that also, if you squint, resembles a death's head in the way a thundercloud might resemble the skull of an angry god. The stone fitfully glints with the light from the table lamp. Almost a twin to the pendant hanging from Zane's neck.

"I thought it'd be a thumb prick." Morton slips the ring onto his finger.

"Ha ha, you said *prick*." I laugh, but not really. No, not really.

"Dude," Vadim says with ample foreboding. "This shit is how you get sepsis or peritonitis or something."

"Quiet, punk, you're next." Julie Five grins at him. I think of a northern pike opening its needle-fanged jaws to slurp down a hook.

Zane raises his eyebrow. "A dribble of claret for the cause seems reasonable. The price for betrayal is a blood eagle. JV's idea. Be warned."

"What's a blood eagle?" I say.

"You don't want one," Vadim says.

Steely J excuses himself. He steps through a panel near a bookcase and that's the last I see of him. I think it's the very last time *anybody* sees him for a few years. Candice, his latest girlfriend remains at the table with an expression of abandonment. She's had too many wine coolers.

Neither Clint nor Leo speak. They're nervous, I can tell. Leo is a bit green around the gills. Real hard cases. Both of them agitated and wheedled to be included, and now their knees are knocking. And why are they spooked? The ceremony is bullshit. High school melodrama. This is supposed to be mock serious, like fucking about with Ouija boards and séances or homoerotic fraternity paddling rituals.

"Seven is a good number," Zane says. He's not counting himself, obviously. He's playing Satan. "Seven were the apprentices in the Devil's Grotto."

"Power number, baby," Julie Five says, Ed McMahon to his Johnny Carson.

We all stare at one another. Similar to gazing into a mirror—after a while, everybody is as plastic as Zane. I poke Morton in the ribs. Somebody has to be the first to leap and he's it. He makes a fist. Blood begins to flow. The blind moose watches as we each take our turn.

God, do You remember my third year in college when I saved that little old lady who fell on the ice in front of a moose that had wandered into town? I threw snowballs and shrieked until it ambled away into the trees. Surely, if You're the real deal You were there. God, please be real. Please help me now. Because I can't see anything. I'm flopped on my belly atop a heap of corpses. That can't be right. The dark is sticky. Warm, inanimate flesh yields beneath me. My pinky slips into someone's dead staring eye. Eyelashes bat against my knuckle.

Zane kisses my cheek. I'd recognize his Rico Suave cologne anywhere, even here. He says, "Welcome and congratulations. You're part of it. You'll always be part of it. I'll see you at the party. Guest of honor, Ed."

The rest of the night is a blank. Or a hole. So, thanks for that, God. If you exist, which I figure you don't. The cut in my finger doesn't close for weeks. The hole in my soul remains the equivalent of a sucking chest wound.

II: Culling

Zane Tooms makes the CNN ticker three and a half years later.

Kind of a funny story. A terrific day until that point. I spend it shopping for vintage LPs at this fat cat record producer's annual garage sale. Vinyl is my true addiction. Stronger and purer than my fondness for baby dykes, or even my love of a self-effacing bear with real taste in the arts. I spend weekends with my boyfriend Tony at his Malibu beach house. This summer my theme resounds courtesy of The Kinks: "Little Miss Queen of Darkness." I don't really identify. Drag isn't my thing and any sadness in my eyes is liable to be incidental tearing from my extra lush lashes. Nope, I love the song because its lyrics are true poetry. Poetry is distinctly lacking in this modern world. Barbarians have sacked the music industry, despoiled Hollywood. Publishing is a joke with celebrity tell-alls and Dan Brown as the punchline.

I'm lamenting these facts while sprawled on the sofa in Tony's giant game room. The news hits as I'm raising a mojito to my lips. Hard to believe my eyes. I didn't believe them either, though, when the accusations of seventy counts of Rohypnol-facilitated rape first came down to the clack of a magistrate's gavel. Apparently that dark side of Zane's was worse than I thought. Theory goes that seventy is a conservative estimate—who knows how many victims he's left scattered across Europe.

Now Zane is dead. The DEA and Mexican police shot him a bajillion times in some fleabag hotel in Mexico City. I don't know how to feel. There's a tiny white scar on the underside of my middle finger. I look at it and wonder if he ever raped *me*. Doubtful. Despite all indications, evidence is he didn't swing for dudes. Like I said, I don't know how to feel.

"Ha! Hell yes! I told you they'd get that rat bastard!" Tony wanders in from the shower and does a sack dance in celebration. He played ball for the Forty-Niners. His gut is enormous. The old me, lily-fresh college grad, would've cared. The worn and worried me is more concerned with Tony's heart. He's a kindly soul, his celebration of Zane's demise notwithstanding. Tony heard the stories and paid for my therapy. He's earned the right to cry, "Ding-dong!" etcetera.

Oops.

The doorbell rings and it's Julie Five on the step. I almost swoon at the shock.

"So, we meet again." She's wearing sunglasses and a white sundress. Her skin is softer and pinker than I recall. Time has rejuvenated her or she's gotten on the E. Bathory program. A midnight-blue Mustang is parked in the drive with the top down. The hood symbol looks more like a particular malformed death's head than any mustang. Three and a half years might as well be three and a half days. She makes a moue of her lips. I don't offer my cheek for the courtesy peck, no way. I'd rather let a tarantula sit on my face.

She crowds me backward. Her shadow crosses mine and my legs go weak and I collapse upon the rug where sunlight pools on nice days. This is California, so yes, the sunlight is doing that right now. She steps over my supine form and I get a peek at her goods, like it or not. Red panties to match her scary-long fingernails. The sun filtering through the fabric of the dress turns everything to crimson. She reaches into a demure handbag and produces the iron ring. Slides it onto the third finger of her left hand. She looms above me, smiling in a way I don't recognize from her repertoire. If evil and cruelty can mature the way wine does, then here you go. This goddamned cask of Amontillado's got cobwebs all over it.

"What's going on?" Tony arrives, half-naked and thundering. He quickly takes in the situation and gets right in her personal space. "Who the hell are you?"

I'm afraid he'll hit her, shatter her smirk with his mallet fist. I'm terrified he won't. Either way, it doesn't matter. I can't move, can't speak. My body is cold from the inside out.

"You're Anthony. Hello." She extends her hand.

He brushes her gesture aside. "And you're Julie. Yeah, I recognize you. Step, lady. You aren't welcome."

"C'mon, stud. Put her there." She smirks mischievously and reaches for him again. The light in the room dims because she's sucking it into her eyes. She snags his hand and clasps it tight with both of hers the way politicians do, the way a black widow fastens to her prey. Squeezes so hard that blood drips from their joined fingers. That's the end. Tony sways in place and she stands on tiptoes to whisper into his ear. It goes on for maybe ten seconds until she releases him and steps back.

"Oh, wow," he says. Tony usually talks loud enough to break your eardrums. This is a mousy little whisper. "I'm sorry. I didn't know." His face changes as he turns away. His skin tightens and his mouth and eyes stretch at the corners, but I only catch a glimpse. He shambles toward the living room, gone forever.

"Not with a bang but a whimper," Julie Five says, quoting the only Eliot she's likely memorized. Julie didn't use her own brain to get through college. She relied upon cunning and nascent savagery. The light in the room drains away and she floats above me, a pale gemstone revolving against the void. She draws the dwindling heat from my bones and into her huge, luminous eyes.

I belatedly notice the feathered dart protruding from my breast. Steely J drifts from the unknowable depths, pistol in hand. He salutes me and drapes his arm around Julie Five's waist.

I am very, very tired.

They wink, synchronized, and I wink out.

• • •

Vadim talks while he carries me in his arms, the Bride of Frankenstein.

"There are these worm things, or leech things, neither, but you get the picture, and they detach or are expelled from a central mass. These worms, or leeches, crawl inside you through whatever opening is available. The urethra and the anus are likely access ways. That's what happened to the dinosaurs. It's one theory. I think it works."

"Put me down, man." My voice is hoarse and my skull aches. My breast muscle hurts too. Whatever Steely J hit me with packs a nasty hangover.

We stand there, wherever there is. An abandoned hotel lobby? Lots of dust, boarded windows, and the light fixtures are fubar. Bright though, because sunlight streams through cracks and crevices. I ask the obvious and he shrugs. He too received a visit from Julie Five and a follow-up dart from Steely J. Like me, he came to in this place.

"Uh-oh."

I follow Vadim's gaze and see a thick man all in black standing on the mezzanine steps. His face is pale and freaky as shit. The flesh is so tight, his eyes stretch to slits, their corners near his temples. A machete dangles from his fist. Blood drips from the blade.

"Tony?" Right size, wrong face, except maybe it was the right face, I'd seen it changing at the casa . . .

"Tony isn't Tony no more. That's Mr. Flat Affect." Vadim grips my arm. "Let's book."

We book. I try the obvious things—exterior door handles are locked and chained from the outside; the windows are barred. I glimpse a dry pool in the courtyard. The yard has gone Planet of the Apes. Grass run riot. The palm trees are dull yellow. Mort is spiked halfway up the bole of the biggest tree. He's covered in dried blood, but I recognize his voice when he calls for help, for god, for death. There are several more people nailed to trees. Harder to identify. I don't want to know.

Before long, I stop to catch my breath.

"This is about the ritual."

"Duh," Vadim says. "The goon is one of Zane's pets, or something like that."

"But why are they after us? We're part of the inner circle, right? Ground floor of the new order and all that jazz?" I hadn't taken it seriously, had only gone along because of the pressure. I hadn't swallowed ZT's apocalypse fantasies. Now, here I am trying to lawyer my way out of getting murdered.

"He lied. We're the blood in the blood pact."

"Pact with whom?"

He gives me a sad look for not paying attention during class.

Another Mr. Flat Affect saunters through a door and confronts us. He too wields a machete. However, he's clad in a white paper suit. The suit is streaked and grimy. It's a bad moment, but Savate! I expect great things from Vadim's size-eleven Doc Martens. Vadim yells, "Oh fuck!" and elaborately gathers himself like he's tossing a kaber and snaps this kind of slow-mo roundhouse kick that misses by a mile. Maybe a mile and a half. He lands on his ass. And it would be hilarious except I'm shitting my capris. Mr. Flat Affect doesn't hurry; I doubt he ever hurries. He raises the machete and splits my best friend's skull. Does him like the islanders do with coconuts, with a lazy overhand chop. *Kerthunk.* The killer pauses to savor the gurgling and spurting.

Doc Martens are peachy. I swear by Nikes. Canary yellow with Velcro, nobody's got time for laces. I put mine to their best use—slapping tile at a high rate.

III: The Bear Catacombs

I run through an archway and am back in Alaska in the Toombs family basement. The bear catacombs. It has to be a nightmare because I instantly recognize the late 90s. Sister, those were bad times for yours truly—nobody told me "it gets better," they told me to sit down and keep my mouth shut.

A party is in progress—music on full blast, lights ablaze, half the kids from our high school graduating class doing the bump and grind. Zane lurks on the fringes, a loud, fat, glittery-eyed kid. His smile is sly. He's exactly as I remember, only more so.

There my high school self is, on the edge, crushed against a skinny senior track star. My hair is dreadful in spiked hair and a lime mesh tank top, and Stu Whitlock flaunts a mullet. Merciful Jesus, I had no idea I had so much to apologize for.

The band grinds to a halt and the lead singer chugs from a bottle of whiskey. My youthful double disappears up the stairs. A few seconds later, the shrieks begin. That would be Dave Teague, naked and insane, busting a move for the front door. I remember the rest with unpleasant clarity—there's a hot blond Ukrainian transfer student lying mangled and murdered in a bed on the top floor. Some lowlife snuffed her and tried for the daily double with Dave. The killer is in fact shambling after Dave into the night. In a few minutes, state troopers scrag the psycho killer on the access road. I also recall that someone mentions the psycho's face is white with greasepaint, or he wears a mask, and shit, it hits me—Mr. Flat Affect has been with us since when.

Mind. Blown.

"La!" Julie Five steps from the crowd. Modern day Julie Five, fully envenomed, egg sac probably full to bursting. She was sort of a cute kid. Not anymore. She grins and tweaks my nose. Her fingers are icy. "You're bleeding, sweetie."

The blood is Vadim's—I've come through so far without a scratch, and that's ironic, because I'd bruise if somebody stuck a pea under my mattress. I'm speechless, unable to twitch, Julie Five seems to have that effect on my nervous system. Behind her, kids begin milling around the exposed section of wall where the pipes and tree roots form a maw. There's some scuffling and I see my erstwhile date Stu Whitlock crawl inside. He's followed by that beefy guy who played linebacker the year we went to state. Then another, and another, wriggling like sperm to fit through the crack in the earth, burrowing their way to god knows where. Doesn't take long for the last pair of legs to disappear into the darkness and it's us chickens left behind in an empty basement.

Mr. Flat Affect emerges from the corner where the coats are piled. Sways in place, devilish gaze locked on me. He's a meat suit and whatever powers him came from the deep earth. I whimper.

"Don't be afraid," Julie Five says. "You made the cut. We wouldn't dream of harming a hair on your frosty little head. You're our final girl. I always hoped you would be." She takes my hand, leads me upstairs, and seats me in the parlor at a plain wooden table. The moon glows hard in the upper corner of a bay window. Its light seems to recede, shrinking to a dot as I watch. She removes a black moleskin notebook from her purse, opens it before me, and clicks the action on a ballpoint pen, places it beside the notebook. "Your memoir. It will be important someday, after everyone has forgotten how all this started. There's a fire safe in the den."

Two more Mr. Flat Affects have noiselessly appeared at her flanks. One in white, the other black. Their expressions are identically monstrous. She links arms with them and they glide into the shadows. "Good luck," she says from somewhere. Her voice echoes as if bouncing around a canyon. "Enjoy yourself."

I do as she says and write down what I know. I stash the notebook in the fire safe. Sun devours moon and the second decade of the twenty-first century absorbs the 1990s. The Tooms mansion decays around me. The table becomes stone and the stuffed moose head wilts unto a living death. I'm once again thirty-something and utterly fabulous despite the bags under my eyes, the tremor in my hand, and the caked-on gore.

Steely J, Julie Five, and Zane Tooms are long gone. The others remain as remains—Vadim, Morton, Candice, Clint, and Leo. Bloated, purple-black, in a pile near the hearth. Candice's shoe has fallen off.

Had the poison been in the ring or the liquor? The ring is how I bet. My crazy-person epistle isn't going to do me any favors in a court of law. Story like mine is a one-way trip to the booby hatch. What will happen to me when the authorities make the scene? That gets an answer when the pair of troopers roll up to investigate after the anonymous call. They are none too reassured by my appearance and wild story. Two seconds after they nearly trip over the pile of corpses, I'm staring down the barrels of automatic pistols.

My finger bleeds from a wound that will never close. I make a fist without a thought as I mumble apologies for being here in this house of horrors, wrong place, wrong time—oh, so most def the wrong time. I needn't bother. The tearing pain in my hand lends an edge to my voice. My breath steams, a dark cone, and both troopers shudder in unison. Their guns clatter on the floor. Color drains from those well-fed faces, skin snaps tight and their eyes, their mouths, shiver and stretch. The transformation requires mere seconds. Their peculiar, *click-clicking* thoughts scritch and buzz inside my own psychic killing jar. They are mine, like it or not.

I *do* like it, though. A bunch.

Mist covers the world below this lonely hilltop. It's bitter cold and I'm barely dressed, yet it doesn't touch me. Nothing can. I am Bela Lugosi's most famous character reborn and reinterpreted. The Tooms estate is my mansion on the moor, my gothic castle. Time has slipped and I wonder if Tony is still out there in Malibu, waiting to meet me and fall in love. Do I care? Must I?

Who originally said some men want to watch the world burn? Whomever, he meant assholes like Zane and Julie. They chose me, corrupted me, and invested in me some profane force. Its trickle charge impresses my brain with visions of debauched revelry, of global massacre, fire, and slavery. Do my minor part to spread mayhem and terror and a few years down the road I can be on the ground floor of a magnificent dystopian clique. I can be a lord of darkness with minions and everything.

What shall I do with such incalculable power?

"Fix me a cosmopolitan," I say to ex-trooper, ex-human, Numero Uno. He does and it's passable.

There are numerous doors inside the Tooms mansion, to say nothing of the crack that splinters through bedrock and who knows where from there. I could wreak havoc in the name of diabolical progress. Or I could flap my arms and fly to Hollywood, whisper in the right ears and watch a sea change transform the industry. Or I could return to my senior year and seize Stu Whitaker by more than the hip, tell Father dearest to get bent with a martini in one hand and a smoldering joint in the other.

Decisions, decisions, you know?

Laird Barron is the author of several books, including *The Croning, Occultation,* and *The Beautiful Thing That Awaits Us All.* His work has also appeared in many magazines and anthologies. An expatriate Alaskan, Barron currently resides in upstate New York.

EDITORIAL NOTE: *Between 1804 and 1856 about nine thousand women were confined in the thirteen penal colonies of New South Wales and Van Diemen's Land in Australia. These facilities were called "factories" because they were places of production. The inmates were assigned jobs ranging from needlework and spinning to rock breaking and "picking" oakum. An estimated twelve to twenty percent of modern-day Australians are descended from these women.*

THE FEMALE FACTORY

Lisa L. Hannett & Angela Slatter

The isolation cell had fallen into disuse since Mrs. Avice Welles, purported widow, had become Matron of the Bridewell Female Factory. It wasn't that her reign was any gentler or kinder at the Van Diemen's Land facility, but she had other methods of reprimand and rehabilitation upon which she preferred to rely. Indeed, some of the inmates, grownup and child alike, had come to think fondly of the old lockup. As with most nostalgia, it conveniently forgot there was nowhere for the breeze to go in the two by three space, that it soon became stuffy, somehow both stifling and cold. In winter, snow and sleet came through the rusted bars like an unwelcome guest, and any rations served to prisoners being punished within were less in both quantity and quality than what was scraped up at Cook's table, and much more liable to contain weevils and maggots.

And it was also conveniently forgotten that the isolation cell was designed as a place of lost hope.

Bridewell grew from the earth like a polyp of stone and mortar. Set at the feet of gently rolling hills, on gold and green land, it was lapped by the waters of Mason Cove. If the inmates should so choose—and be in a position to do so—they could cast their eyes seaward and find the Isle of the Dead, crouching low and dark, clutching its inhabitants firmly in its earthen breast.

Around it, the landscape was quilted with fences, the earth plotted and parceled, presented as gifts to notable sailors. A good mile away was the township, far enough from the incarcerated to feel superior, but close enough to access their labor with speed. Though wood and wire demarcated *ours* from *theirs*, Nature provided no real barriers against attacks by the local Mouheneener tribe—nor against convict escape.

Bridewell's perimeter was made of mottled sandstone, topped with a crust of broken glass. Beside the main gate, shut and barred now for the night, a single torch hung from the stone's sheer face, its tiny fire reflected in the shallows of the empty cove. There were no finger-holds to be found in the walls, no crevices in which to jam the toe of a pointed boot, no ropes long or sturdy enough to surmount those jagged heights. With the men's barracks within spitting distance, it was by necessity, so Superintendent Rook always said, that the ramparts were erected thus, *To protect the women from harassment.*

Inside, the Factory was more yard than structure. The Matron's tiny cottage shared the same wall as a small kitchen block, a washhouse, and a miniscule shed. On the north side, in the furthest crook, a single privy reeked six days out of seven. Downwind from the long-drop, Bridewell's isolation cell stood on its own, weeds making merry around it. Slightly off-center, surrounded by a sea of sand and pea shell gravel, loomed the women's quarters. A broad rectangular building with gabled roofs left, right, and middle, it housed as many souls as Her Majesty saw fit to banish across the seas. Hardened criminals shared the same corridor as the Second class girls, all of whom were separated from the fancy ladies—those in First class, whose chambers were closest to the dining hall, whose doors weren't always locked behind them, who had permission to marry, who didn't work their hands raw picking oakum or breaking rocks, and who got red calico jackets, muslin frills, bonnets (bonnets!) and gingham handkerchiefs to wear to Church on Sunday.

Beyond the workhouse and rooms, tucked close beside the washhouse, a small gate was set in the western wall. Its frame was warped, the wood sun-bleached, the hinges liable to creak if Bert forgot to grease them once a week with the pat of butter he got with his bread. Tonight, the door hadn't complained as it was pushed open after curfew. It swung shut just as quietly behind the children as they snuck out of the compound, creeping past the Surgeon's cottage and barn-turned-workshop, past the stockyard and the Constables' hut, past the gallows and beyond. Down to the shore, to the thin jetty and one of the large dory boats used for trips to the Isle of the Dead.

Ned and Alf were the biggest so they sat on the middle thwart, each plying an oar. Bert, aft, navigated, with Millie beside him. Victoria and Little Sarah huddled fore, the latter sitting in the wheelbarrow they'd brought along. Big Sarah and all five Marys had stayed behind, lucky enough to draw the long straws in the lottery, but unlucky enough to have to wait in the shadows for the others' return. No one fought to go out to the island, even though there were benefits if they did. It was cold, so cold on the water, and the children considered themselves blessed if they avoided catching a chill. Jack and Harry and Abigail had gone that way, not long ago, shivering themselves into the grave.

Once they'd beached on the small shingle, the band trooped up to where freshly dug earth betrayed the resting place of the lately departed Ada Habel. If that didn't make it easy enough to find, the fact they'd visited the plot right next to it last week (one Hippolyte Pollitt) certainly helped—and neither of these women had been buried close to the others. Armed with spades slightly too big for their frames, Bert and Alf faced each other across Miss Habel's grave and began digging. At first it was easy enough work—the criminal had been found only yesterday, suspended between heaven and earth by her garters. But there was so much soil, newly turned though it was, and the body buried so deep. They were sweating hard before long.

"Get lower," Bert grumped at Millie and Victoria, who were crouched by the graveside holding lanterns to help the boys see. The beam could be spotted across the water quite easily if the sentries were sober and paying attention.

The piss-yellow light did nothing to improve Miss Habel's appearance. Frowning, Bert brushed the dirt from her cheeks. Every dead female he saw seemed to look like his departed mother. He knew it was not so, *could not* be so—but in the three years since Mary Ann Ross's death, he'd forgotten her features. They'd drifted away, eroded by time, and other women's faces had left something in their place. The picture in his mind was now a piecemeal thing, a nose from one, eyes from another, cheekbones from yet another still . . . even the mouth, the top lip and lower sourced from different women.

Though her face was gone, Bert remembered every secret she'd told him.

The return journey was no easier or faster, certainly no warmer. By the time they'd heaved Ada Habel and her meager belongings into the barrow, rowed until their arms burned, and, aided by the waiting Marys and Big Sarah, pushed the dug-up to the rear entrance of the doctor's surgery, Little Sarah was shaking so badly her teeth went *rat-a-tat-tat*. Millie and Victoria tried to get some warmth into her, rubbing her limbs though their own hands were icy.

Bert knocked, two soft raps; even at this time of night *he* wouldn't be abed. Almost instantly the portal swung wide and Dr. Nelson Dalkeith stepped forth. Quickly, wordlessly, he ushered them around to the barn, refusing to speak until the door was firmly shut behind them.

The children looked about, as if they'd never seen this room before. But it was the same as it had ever been; only the displays changed, the bodies and their state of dissection. Heads down, they wheeled Ada Habel to the middle table and hefted her onto it with a good deal of thudding and thumping.

"Good show, Albert," Dr. Dalkeith said absentmindedly. No one called Bert that. *Albert*, as inscribed in full in Superintendent Rook's registry, picked at random from a list of other, unwanted monikers. Not inherited, not given with love. Just given. The good doctor's Scottish burr dragged the name out, made it sound even more foreign. The man was tall and strapping—or so Bert had heard the girls say—and he dressed well, though he often smelled of malt and burnt tobacco. His eyes were brown and kind, if unfocused, his hair and beard a red-gold that drew attention. He fished about in his vest pocket and pulled forth five sovereigns. "For Matron Welles. Oh and here's tuppence apiece for your efforts."

"Thank you, sir," said Bert, making the coins disappear with a dexterity that his mother had never had, else she might have kept out of jail.

Dr. Dalkeith's large, red-knuckled hand reached into his trouser pocket and brought forth a battered brown paper packet. One by one he gave each of the children a piece of boiled taffy, a treat for their industrious Burking. Even as he handed out the last bonbon, his fingers twitched, gaze sliding towards the saws and knives, scalpels and clamps on the wheeled bench beside Ada Habel's unlovely head.

"Millie?" whispered Bert, directing her with his eyes to a dismembered corpse waiting to be scooped and barrowed off to an abandoned pile. "Get the arm."

Reliable Millie always did as she was told, no questions asked, especially if it was Bert doing the telling. Without hesitation, she tiptoed to the heap, freed the pale blue limb and held it snug behind her. Bert looked back at Dr. Dalkeith. Past experience told him the direction the man's mind was taking. Past experience told him their mutual mistress would not be pleased to find the corpse chopped up without her say-so. He said, "Shall I tell Matron Welles to come at the usual time?"

"Oh, yes. Please do." The man sounded disappointed, but he was back in the room now, fully, not in the airy place he drifted when engaged in his researches. He herded them out, snuffed the lantern hanging from the eaves, then closed and bolted the door.

There was neither warmth nor light to welcome them home. A single barred window faced the door, the rusted iron rungs relics of earlier days, when these quarters had been used for storage. No glass filled the frame; mosquitoes and flies buzzed in on streaks of silvered blue summer nights, but not in winter. Wielding a twig broom before them, Big Sarah took a few swings in the darkness to make sure the Constables weren't there, crouched in the near-black, poised to scare them. Rats scurried up the small room's clapboard walls and scratched along wooden rafters as the bristles whipped through the air, meeting no resistance.

"It's safe," Sarah said, stepping fully inside to lean the broom against the jamb. Eyes adjusting to the gloom, the children felt the way to their bed, sweeping the dirt floor in great arcs with their toes. There were no separate pallets in here, just a pile of sacking and old cloth in one corner, a combination of fresh and rank straw beneath to give some padding against the hard ground. When all twelve were sitting cross-legged in a circle on their rough mattress, Victoria scraped a pilfered match along the bottom of her shoe. The tiny flame flared like hope; in its glow, Millie handed Bert the arm so he could examine it more closely. Turning it over, once, twice, the boy nodded, pleased, though the hand was crabbed, the fingers clawed—that could be replaced.

None of them asked what he was doing or why he'd wanted such a grisly souvenir. Though not the oldest among them, Bert had proved himself time and again to be their natural leader. Though they burned with curiosity, no one followed him when he snuck back outside, only to reappear a few minutes later, the arm no longer in evidence.

If they had faith in nothing else in their small world, they had faith in Bert.

Dawn had barely broken, but Matron Welles was already dressed and seated at her small desk, making entries in the Superintendent's journal. Absentminded fool that he was, Martin Rook couldn't be relied upon to keep Bridewell's daily records—but Avice was pleased to benefit from his idiocy. After years in his service—rather, *at his side*—Rook trusted her to oversee the schedules and inventories, to keep the women and children in check. Such trust was far more valuable than a larger cottage, she told herself, or even promotion. Within Bridewell's walls, the old duffer's trust gave her unprecedented freedom.

Leaning over the hard-covered black journal, Avice formed each letter carefully. The knowledge of how to write had been hard-won; she took great pride in her copperplate script. She had done well for herself, she had worked so hard; and would do better still.

18 May 1852
Ada Habel (female convict, Third class: prostitution, assault) found dead by Taskmistress Fiona. Suicide by hanging. Buried in unhallowed ground on the insistence of the Reverend Tanner.

Pausing to replenish the inkwell, Avice admired the pot's violet glass and the filigreed silverwork chased up its bulbous belly all the way to the inscribed cap. The initials weren't hers, though they were close enough; the beautiful *A.N.D.* reminded the Matron there was nothing wrong in the slightest with asking for more. From lid to base, it was a perfect heirloom . . . as was the chain of black pearls Avice wore under her collar, the cameo ring on her pinkie finger, the opal-tipped pin in her thick dark bun. The women who'd owned these trinkets before her—*no, not* owned, she corrected, held *maybe*, purloined *most likely*—had had no real right to them in the first place. Once they'd passed through Bridewell's gates, these delinquents became the Governor's burden and property. By extension, they were also the Principal Superintendent's, the Superintendent's, and *hers*.

The same, Matron Welles thought, *applied to said criminals' worldly goods.*

It wasn't theft, she thought, so much as preservation. The lonely dead had no belongings, therefore they could not be stolen from.

Buried in unhallowed ground on the insistence of the Reverend Tanner. Changing her mind, Avice dragged the full stop into a comma and added, *with no more than the sin in her heart and the devil's mark on her neck.* She made a mental note to search the children's mattress, if they failed to produce Miss Habel's grave goods in the morning.

> *Taskwork Reckoning—Labor Effectiveness—Needlework.*
>   *1. Caps Ladies Night; 10 hr days.*
>   *a. 1st Class, Maximum: 6/16*
>   *b. 2nd Class, Medium: 6/16*
>   *c. 3rd Class, Minimum: 4/16*
>   *2. Cases Pillow; 10 hr days.*
>   *a. 1st Class, Maximum: 3*

b. *2nd Class, Medium: 2 4/16*
c. *3rd Class, Minimum: 1 8/16*
3. *Collors Gents; 10 hr days.*
   a. *1st Class, Maximum: 3*
   b. *2nd Class, Medium: 2 4/16*
   c. *3rd Class, Minimum: 1 8/16*

Running down the list—from caps, collors, cuffs, and drawers to flannels and trowsers, shifts, and waistcoats, petticoats to pinbefores, for ladies and gents, children and infants—Avice wondered if it was worth noting the division of labor, one more time, for Martin Rook's sake. If she could simply hand the diaries directly to Principal Superintendent Skaille she needn't bother, but Rook . . . Inevitably, he'd come knocking at her cottage door of an evening, enquiring about the First class output versus the Crime Class. Maintaining the pretense of control.

Maximum, see? she'd tell him again and again, pointing at the journal. *The First class women*—she refused to call them ladies—*spend the full length of their days with soft work. All ten hours. Embroidery and sewing, a little light housekeeping . . .* She'd repress a sigh as Martin began kissing the nape of her neck, and insist he focus when he'd ramble about books going missing from his library and other nonsense. *Miss Fiona doesn't pamper the other lasses so; well before noon, the Third class girls are spinning and reeling and carding wool, churning laundry . . .* Clenching her teeth, she'd try not to flinch as Martin's beard bristled against her cheek. *And they're picking rope and oakum with the orphans . . .*

Aren't they too old to be here still? he'd sometimes say, or, stupidly, *Where are their mothers?*

They're orphans, *sir. And there's no space for them at the Queen's School.*

No room at the inn, eh?

It didn't matter what she said, Avice thought with a heavy heart. Night after night Martin would come to her door, play the buffoon with rough questions and rougher kisses, and wouldn't leave until both were answered.

Candlelight made Avice's pale flesh glow, clean as soap. She admired her small, neat hands with their soft skin, grateful she did not have to work as the low women did, griming their digits black on nasty, tarred ropes. Their fingernails and prints cracking, no matter how much lanolin was massaged into them at day's end, tips rough as saltbush, scratching if they happened to brush loose strands back from the children's faces. Unconsciously, the Matron tucked a few wisps behind her ears. Her fingers were the finest cotton against her temple, and she was glad, so glad, they looked nothing like her mother's.

After dusting the page with pounce to dry the ink, she shook the fine cuttlefish powder from the volume then closed it with a thump. The clock on the narrow mantle told her it was fifteen minutes until half-five; fifteen minutes until muster. The timepiece was pretty, despite the thin crack in its glass; a discarded item once belonging to the Superintendent's dead wife.

Looking over her shoulder at the door, she made sure the key was still turned, then gave her sole window a quick glance—no lurking shadows. Her own journal, navy cover, gilt on the spine, lay in a secret drawer she'd had built in her desk long ago, when Martin was in Hobart for a fortnight and she'd been given sole charge of Bridewell, including its visiting carpenters.

Avice took a deep breath and steadied her hands; they always shook when she made these notations. She regretted, yet again, that she had no measurements for her mother's head, nothing precise, only the memory of a small skull with a slightly conical bent (selfishness, treachery, deceit), a snub nose, heavy brow, and tapering chin (ingratitude, criminal tendencies). She remembered, or was certain she did, how the area at the base of Hattie Welles' ears had been indented—a ridge that clearly indicated she was an unfit mother . . . It all went some way to explaining how the woman wound up at the end of a hangman's noose.

Surely, Avice thought, these traits suggested an excess development of the *Amativeness locus*—entirely fitting, given Hattie's chosen profession.

Avice carefully inscribed the measurements she'd had Dr. Dalkeith take from the Pollitt woman last week, into a neat column that matched so many others in the book. Today there would be more, she thought, nodding with satisfaction. Ada Habel was sure to give up her secrets before the Surgeon had finished with her. Ada Habel. Yes, the jezebel would help Avice towards the understanding she so desperately craved—nay, *needed*. As her hand resumed its shaking, the swaying pen in her grip keeping time with the clock, the Matron knew it was time to stop. Before she was late to muster. Before her imagination got the better of her.

Briskly she noted the number of excursions she'd sent the children on, what they'd retrieved. After blowing on the ink, she slipped the book back into its cache, then stood and smoothed her skirt, making sure her attire was as perfect as it could be. As her last preparation for the day she took a quick glance in the oval of beaten tin that served as a mirror. The flame guttering on the simple dresser cast weird shadows across her face; the features contorted, then blurred, and Avice couldn't be sure if the grimace she saw was hers or that of an awful ghost. Mouth slightly agape, she blinked rapidly and brought the candle closer, then closer still, to chase away the demon of her vision. Heat threatened the carefully laid curls at her temples, but Avice would not move until she was sure, absolutely, that the fit of darkness had passed.

The clock chimed half-five, its music ever off-tune.

A moment, Avice thought, putting the candlestick down on the desk. Pinching color into her cheeks. Pulling the knot of hair loose and tugging a boar-bristle brush through its black waves.

Hattie Welles never had the chance to go gray, and Avice wondered how long it would be before she outdid her mother in this. Unblinking, focused on the blur of her face, she ached to know if they looked alike. The spare minute passed and passed again while Avice inspected her reflection. Again, memory betrayed her.

The brush clattered onto her dresser. The candle flickered. As the clock ticked and ticked, the Matron scraped her hair back severely, held it in place with pins that dug into her scalp.

The female convicts were housed in Bridewell's central building, divided into three dormitories, each one a little plainer than the last. Outside, the Overseer, William Henry waited, reeking of rum. The Matron gave him a curt nod before entering the women's sleeping quarters, as always processing from First through to the Crime class. A pinch-faced Irish girl with far too many freckles greeted Avice respectfully; Maura, the trusty's name might've been, or possibly Aislyn. Not that it mattered. A *refined* criminal like her would soon be sent out as maid or housemistress to the settlement, and would return to Bridewell only when they were through with her, or when she fell pregnant, whichever came first. There were merely two occasions for noting their names officially, Avice knew: right after the wagons wheeled them into the Factory, and right before the Porter ferried their limp bodies over to the Isle of the Dead.

As she passed through the next dormitory, the Second class watchdog and inmates alike observed the Matron's progress with ill-concealed nerves. She nodded with satisfaction to find no stains on either serge petticoats or jackets, that, to a woman, the hair was coiled neatly beneath calico caps. Aprons were clean and pressed, the thin cloth lying flat on the girls' bellies.

Good, she thought, allowing a smile. Yet when she stepped into the Third class block, she grew distinctly displeased. There was no sign of Miss Fiona, and without supervision, the criminal women were not waiting obediently, arranged in stiff rows. Instead, some lounged on cots, some slouched in high-backed chairs, others laughed loudly with no thought for how they were perceived.

Too late, the Taskmistress's stout form stumbled, puffing, into the room.

"Up, up!" she shouted, flustered, at the rabble. "Up and present yourselves, slatterns!"

The women climbed slowly to their feet and drifted into a disorderly parade for Avice's inspection. Fiona tried desperately to catch her breath. "My apologies, Matron, I was delayed by . . . by . . . "

Avice did not chastise, but gave a sidelong look that silenced her. "That will do, Miss Fiona. Send them all to Labor. I will see you shortly.'

In a little shed by the washhouse, Avice found the children still asleep, worn out from their evening's endeavors. Curled like puppies, they cocooned against each other, the biggest on the outside, the littlies in the middle. One of the girls—a Mary? a Sarah?—was shuddering something fierce. Sweat coated her face; her lips were tinged blue. Hearing the rattle of phlegm in her lungs, Avice hoped it wasn't consumption. It had taken years to cultivate this group's obedience, and their silence. She didn't want to have to purge them all now, simply to avoid the spread of disease.

On the floor she spied trails of dried mud and sand, dragged in from last night's trip to the Isle. Avice pursed her lips. Maybe it wouldn't be such a bad thing after all, getting rid of this lot and raising a newer, more conscientious bunch in their stead. The largest clumps of muck led her straight to Bert, his long body small as he could make it, leaving less surface for the cold to find. Matron Welles leaned forward, careful not to let her skirts touch the fetid straw, and slapped the boy's face as hard as she could.

"Up, up!" she hissed, unconsciously echoing Miss Fiona. She gave a kick for good measure, aimed another at Ned, and yet another at Victoria, catching her in the thigh as she tried to rise. Millie was fastest on her feet and scrambled around in the hay, digging desperately until she located a filthy sack.

"Matron Welles! Look, here are her things." The girl held it up and away from herself, as if by doing so she might avoid violence.

Avice snatched the bag, but could tell by the weight that it held little. "Did you take anything? Was there something good in here?"

Millie shook her head, licked her lips. "No, Matron. That was all. I knew you'd be unhappy. But Bert has the coin."

Avice nodded as the dark-haired boy took Dr. Dalkeith's golds and silvers from his trouser pocket. He diligently placed them, one at a time, into her faintly lined palm.

"Five sovereigns for you, Matron, plus all the money he gave each of us."

"Any more? Don't lie to me, for I'll know."

"No, Matron Welles, nothing more. Where would we hide anything from you?" asked Bert, innocently.

With narrowed eyes, she held his gaze until the boy squirmed, then she turned away, surveying the others. The smallest still lay atop the makeshift bed, her narrow chest fluttering up and down.

"Please, Matron . . . " began one of the older girls. Big Sarah, thought Avice. Or possibly a Mary. "Please let her rest, she's ever so sick."

Another curt nod, and the children breathed a sigh of relief. *Make your farewells while you can,* she thought, resisting the urge to say it aloud. The child wouldn't last until dinner, but the others needed to maintain their focus. Lessons would be most interesting today.

The benches were arranged in a horseshoe around a narrow table in the center of Dr. Dalkeith's workshop. Motes of old feed glinted in the pale yellow filtering down from the skylight, stirred by the children's passing as they'd dragged themselves to the seats. Avice stood beside the Surgeon, holding a handkerchief to her nose. The space was large and cold, yet the smell of cattle bubbled up as if heated, even though it had been years since the building had been used as a barn. Avice was grateful for the chill; it helped her to concentrate, to memorize all the measurements, the alignment, and presentation of the deceased's features so she could transcribe them in her journal later. The children were fidgeting, producing noises like mice in the walls, scratchings and scritchings, but the Matron blocked them out, attention pinned to the unfortunate on the table in front of her. Trying to recall what her mother had really looked like, if she and this woman bore any resemblance, any inherent essence of criminality.

Dr. Dalkeith leaned forward, long fingers hovering over his selection of sharp-edged tools. He lit upon a scalpel, but the Liston knife waited patiently for when joints and bones needed to be separated.

"Measurements, Nelson," murmured Avice. The anatomist met her gaze, his own unfocused, elsewhere. A few blinks later he nodded, let the scalpel go and began the task of gauging all the component parts of Ada Habel's skull, speaking so the Matron might mentally record them. When he'd done, at last, he gave her the kind of look a dog gives its owner, seeking permission to feed, to fetch, to *do*. At her brief nod, he grasped the scalpel once again, placed it at the point beneath Ada Habel's sternum, and began to cut.

Skin, flesh, and fat parted, a layer cake of white, red, and yellow. The Matron was enlisted to sponge any seepage while Dr. Dalkeith snipped and sliced and sawed, though what liquids Miss Habel once had inside her were now thickened, sludges in varying shades of expiration. The notes he took in his own scruffy journal, mid-dissection, were of little interest to Avice, but she watched avidly as he created the accompanying sketches. Unless she was mistaken, the good doctor would soon submit another article to *The Lancet*, since the Royal Society in London had, thus far, consistently rejected his treatises on the theory and practice of surgery. But a paper detailing the physiognomy of transported criminals? *That*, surely, would one day see his name printed in the Society's *Philosophical Transactions*.

For nearly two hours, Matron and Surgeon were bent at their labor while the children, having seen this many times before, were bored. Most perched on the edge of the benches, feigning interest as they listened out for the breakfast bell's ringing. Alf bit his fingernails and collected them in a small pile on the seat beside him. Millie, elbows on knees and chin propped on hands, held her eyelids open by the lashes. The Marys took turns picking nits from each other's braids, while Big Sarah looked on, forlorn, her mind in the infirmary where Avice had consigned Little Sarah. When the Matron had her back turned, Victoria slid an arm through Sarah's and gave her a quick peck on the cheek; the older girl smiled, but it just wasn't the same. Only Bert kept his eyes fixed upon the trio on the low platform. He was sizing up the dug-up's hands as Dr. Dal sawed them through at the wrists. They were strong, the palms square, fingers short and broad. Hardy. Workman-like.

Yes, he thought. They would do nicely.

Once the inmates had had their share of bread and gruel, and they'd all heard Reverend Tanner preach the Good Word, William Henry once more rang the bell, sending the women and children off to their next shift. The Porter wheeled trolleys into the mess hall for the Crime class to load up with dirty dishes. As cutlery clattered on Bridewell's sturdy crocks, Avice retreated to her private quarters, step a little unsteady with excitement. Hands clasped in front of stiff skirts, she had to remind herself to not fidget, not fiddle.

She rounded the corner of the cottage just in time to see Miss Fiona by the door, bent over the lock. Startled, the Taskmistress came up like a jack-in-the-box.

"Matron," she near-shrieked, pushing her hands behind her back. "I came . . . as . . . as you requested."

Fiona's misdemeanor this morning had slipped Avice's mind. That act of forgetting annoyed her almost as much as finding the woman blocking her way when all she wanted was to record Ada Habel's details. It was not like her, to let a sin go unpunished, unmemorialized. She knew she would take her irritation out on Fiona twofold; but not now. Not yet. Writing was the most important thing at that moment, transferring the images from her mind onto paper.

Her palm met Fiona's pockmarked skin, once, twice in quick succession. Sharp and stinging, the slaps left afterimages of the Matron's long fingers on the other woman's cheek, splayed like seagull wings. Fiona clutched her face, expression flushed and wild, as if knowing this small reprimand couldn't possibly be her full punishment. Avice didn't disillusion her.

"Go," she said, elbowing past, then poised to slide the key in. "Ensure the laundry is well under way, the irons heated for pressing. Double loads this morning—if the girls complain, whip them before you join them. I want to see your knuckles red and raw when you come to Superintendent Rook's office at noon."

Unconsciously, Miss Fiona worried at her fists before plunging them into her apron pocket. "Noon, Matron? But the midday meal?"

Avice's back stiffened. *This*, she thought. This is how the Third class learns its idleness. Half-turned, she let the silence stretch as Fiona inched backwards.

"Never fear," she said finally, "the children will make short work of your portion."

Full bellies made Millie and the Marys extra-chatty; the winter cold kept them all alert. Sitting crossed-legged in the yard picking oakum, backs pressed against the north wall, the girls whispered endlessly about Little Sarah. How they'd heard her crying, mewling like the kittens Miss Fiona had found under the kitchen-house last summer. How she'd started coughing and couldn't seem to stop. How it had sounded like drowning cats in a barrel.

"She needs proper treatment," said Victoria softly, prissy as her name.

"She needs attention," agreed Big Sarah. "Not to be stuck in a stuffy room until she suffocates."

"She needs someone other than us to care," said Dark Mary.

Down the line, Bert unraveled tarred ropes with his cracked nails, the shredded cordage spooling into a great nest on the gravel. From the speed with which his blistered fingers moved, it was hard to tell how little attention he was paying his work. He'd get through two pounds today, easy, still manage to eavesdrop on the girls, and further his plans. Like his mother, Albert Edward Ross was a listener. He picked up pieces of information and stored them away, regarded them as his very own treasure house, put all those resources to good use. It was three years since Mary Ann had died in childbed, but she'd managed to pass on all her bits and bobs of gleanings—including what she'd excavated beneath the isolation cell.

As the girls described Sarah's condition in more and more gruesome detail, Bert surveyed the yard. Miss Fiona was nowhere to be seen and neither was Matron Welles. William Henry was off supervising the Second class women—which everyone knew meant he was out behind the old barn siphoning booze from Dr. Dal's stores—and the two Constables had been called to the main house to keep watch on a Third classer who'd tried stabbing Cook with a butter knife for skimping on soup. There were women elbow-deep in laundry vats, women beating the Superintendent's wool rugs, women cording wood, women making trips to and from the well—but they were all too busy, too tired, to care what the orphans were doing.

Keeping close to the wall, Bert crept long-ways around to the isolation cell and, as the other kids watched, he loosened the unlocked chain and slipped inside. Within minutes he was back, breathless and covered in dust. In his outstretched hands, he held a hardcover book.

"Where'd you get that?" Alf asked, and though Bert contemplated saying something snarky, he was too excited to make a jibe. He'd been waiting for the right time to tell the others. He knew they were deathly curious about what he'd been doing with the collection he'd accumulated after their trips to the Isle, but no one had broken rank and demanded to know. That made him proud of them, and himself. Patience was another trait he'd inherited from Mary Ann Ross; the ability to pinpoint the best moment for revelations.

"Found it," he said; another lesson had been not to tell *everything*. Inching closer, he lifted a hand, forestalling questions. "Hold your horses; first, look at this." Scrubbing grimy palms on his trousers, he delicately opened the cover. Inside, the frontispiece showed a stark woodcut of a man—something shaped like a man, at any rate—with scars and stitches running all over his uneven body. One by one, the other kids huddled around the slender book and stared at it, some rapt, some frowning in confusion. "Sit," Bert hissed. "At least *fake* that you're still working." Once they'd settled, he flipped from illustration to illustration, recounting the story he'd invented to accompany the images—

the only story that could possibly fit. Matron Welles' education program had not included reading lessons.

"See, this bloke is awful lonely," Bert said, pointing a sticky finger at the black and white picture in his lap. The ink was dark and thick, but the white around it was so bright the kids felt like squinting. Bert frowned as his thumbs left brown smudges on the paper. "He's gone off to the mountain and left all his family behind. And then we don't see them anymore," he flicked ahead, proving to everyone that these "family" pictures stopped after the first couple of chapters, "so I reckon they all must've died."

The kids nodded; it all made perfect sense.

"So the man," Bert continued, taking a closer look at the etching, "well, he's not really a man yet, I reckon, not much older than Alf . . . So this bloke's maybe eighteen—"

"What's his name, then?" Alf snatched the book from Bert, brought the pages right up close to his nose, as if proximity might help him decrypt the letters squiggling underneath the image.

Bert worried at his lips, then shrugged. "What's it matter? He's just some bloke—it's what he does that's important." He waited for Alf to drop his guard, then yanked the volume back. Gently whisking a few flecks of dirt off its cover, he turned the leaves more slowly, looking for a picture he'd studied longer than the rest. The others gradually shuffled around, forming a ragged circle about him, all the better to hear, all the better to see.

Millie shook her head. "Naw, Bert. Give him a name. Can't keep calling him 'man' and 'bloke' all the time. Gets confusing."

"Reckon his mum must've named him something," said Tall Mary.

"Maybe even a nickname?" said Big Sarah.

"I don't know," Bert said, sighing. "Whatever. What do you want to call him?"

"Kinda looks like Doctor Dal," said Ned, leaning over Bert's shoulder. Tilting his head like he'd seen the doctor do when assessing the dug-ups, the state of their decay, their fitness for his purposes. "Gots round specs just like his, and that same real high forehead, too. And his hair's all short and patchy, same-same. Reckon William Henry's took the shears to his scalp the way he does the three-Cs when they've acted up."

They snorted—thought it funny as hell, the way the low-class women carried on when the Overseer brought out his clippers, with the Reverend beside them getting hot and bothered about vanity and sin. The lot of them, watching the blades scissor away tumble after tumble of long shiny locks. *Rather lose their lives than their hair,* Miss Fiona always mumbled then, looking down her pug nose at the screeching ladies, but keeping a good step back from the Overseer's reach nevertheless.

"All right," said Millie, "so the bloke's name is Dal? Dalkeith?"

Bert shook his head. "Naw, we don't want anyone sticky-beaking, overhearing, then telling Matron we're blabbing about—*you know.*"

Red Mary and Spotty Mary looked over their shoulders, as if expecting Mrs. Welles to materialize. They'd all seen the vivid red stripes across Millie's scrawny back, which appeared the first night Matron accused her of talking out of turn, and many a night thereafter for one transgression or another.

"No," he said again, "let's just call him Frank and get on with it."

The other kids smirked or shrugged or gave no reaction; a name's a name, far as they were concerned. What's important was that everyone had one.

"Right," Bert said, getting his thoughts in order. "So Frank, who's now an orphan in the mountains, takes his shovel and goes on the dig."

Fat Mary dropped the rope she was pretending to untangle, her podgy hands mucky with tar. "He went on the dig? But isn't that kids' work?"

"He's not that old, remember," Bert said, animated now that he was getting to the good part. "But, yeah, he goes out on the dig, more than a few times from the looks of it, and comes back to his little room with all these bodies, right?" He turned the book around, pointed out the silhouetted torsos, arms, legs, heads. "Then he takes his sharp knife and cuts the lot of them up."

"Big deal," said Red Mary. "Doctor Dal does that all the time."

"Yeah, but—"

"Less yapping, more picking," came a gruff voice from afar. As one, the children stood up, forming a human curtain around Bert, giving him a chance to stuff the tome under his shirt before William Henry saw it.

The rest of the afternoon was spent tearing tar and gum from old ropes, feeling like the tacky stuff had glued their jaws shut. Bert fidgeted on the hard packed gravel, watching the Overseer nod on the stool he'd set close by. Just when it seemed the man had dozed off, he'd snort or fart himself awake, preventing any hope they had of talking. It wasn't until sunset, after Miss Fiona clanged them all in for the evening meal, that Bert finally got to finish his thought. The children sat at a small table all their own, in a far corner.

"This bloke doesn't just chop the dug-ups apart and have a good squiz at their guts the way Doctor Dal does," he whispered. Crossing his arms and leaning close, he forced them to listen and listen good. More than ever, it was important they *listened.* "Frank figured out how to sew the pieces back together. You get what I'm saying?"

The kids were tired, eager to wolf down their meager rations and fall into a sleep they hoped wouldn't be interrupted for a few hours at least. Millie's nose was sunburnt, and Red Mary's forehead was blistered and peeling. "No . . . What?" someone said, the words drawn out, edged with a fledgling whine.

Bert raised his eyebrows, his voice so low now they could scarcely hear him. "Frank got himself all the right bits, all the parts, and then stitched himself a new Da."

When he told them the rest—about his mum, Mary Ann, how she'd heard tell of the disused cellar, how she'd got herself sent to the bin regular-like so she could *dig*; about the plans he had; about what they could create down there—they barely dared to exhale in case their pent hopes should fly away on the soft wings of their own breath.

With the scalpel poised a few inches above the corpse's sternum, Dr. Dalkeith's fingers shook. Either the sight of a First class cadaver rattled him— even pregnant, this one had been quite pretty, until the ravages of her final labor took their toll on her—or he'd hit the whiskey hard last night. Avice suspected the latter: another rejection from the hated, the beloved, journal in the *India*'s mail bag had arrived late yesterday, and the Surgeon had hidden for hours thereafter. The Matron resolved to have strong words with him once he'd recovered his equilibrium. Confronting him wouldn't be easy, she knew. He was a stubborn man, self-interested; she would need to appeal to his ego, dangle shiny possibilities, and make them seem like probabilities. A larger budget for his laboratory, perhaps. An upgrade in his facilities. At the very least, a new still.

On the opposite side of the operating theatre, the children sat in their ragged rows, eating the crusts of bread she'd not allowed them to take in the dining hall in the interests of starting the day early. Despite their nocturnal excursions they were alert and attentive, their eyes fever-bright as they watched the Surgeon at his work. It was this very absorption that made Avice suspicious. They'd lost interest in what was done here long ago; almost to a child, they'd suffered dissection fatigue from the sheer number they'd witnessed. Only Bert ever consistently paid attention, and she'd put that down to a prurient curiosity—a clear sign the boy was bound to meet a bad end.

Their engrossment was inordinate and it was, quite frankly, making it hard for Avice to be as heedful as necessary. Eyes reduced to slits, she burned the woman's features into her memory. The skull was fascinating. Large and oval, broader at top than bottom by a great disproportion, the angle of the brow very, very slight, almost as straight as a wall. Heart-shaped, the Romantics would no doubt call this one's face. Cherubic.

"Matron?"

She realized Dr. Dalkeith had called several times. His bushy brows were raised and his blade had advanced to the corpse's gently curved widow's peak. *Mother, may I?* She almost laughed, then gave a curt nod. The doctor peeled the hair away from the crown, the knife's edge dividing flesh and bone. When he'd sawed through the skull and removed its neat little cap with the Liston, he smiled.

"The children might find this interesting," he said, and instructed them to focus on the dead woman's right leg. Slowly, he stuck a long, thin, metal probe into the mushy gray of the exposed brain. When two-thirds of its length had disappeared, he took a deep breath and jiggled it a little. Immediately the children recoiled, as though expecting the creature to twitch and flail on the table; but there was no such movement. Watching the Surgeon practically mash the woman's brain, Avice's heart fluttered, but she managed to keep her lips firmly closed.

"The nervous system can be manipulated after death," Dr. Dalkeith explained in a tone pitched to convince—himself or them, though, Avice couldn't quite determine. "Post-mortem corporal motion," he twisted the rod, but the limbs remained idle, "is a reflection of the body's former activities—a hangover from life, if you will. A man inclined to ride velocipedes, for instance, should have incredibly mobile quadriceps and triceps surae for hours—days, even—after his passing. A sheep-shearer should have enough strength remaining in his shoulders and back to roll himself over at least twice before being confined in his shroud. And a criminal . . . " He paused to retrieve two more skewers from the tray, and embedded them beside the first. "A criminal, with her devious mind, her predilection for sneaking and snatching and throttling and scurrying . . . Well, *her* physique should tell the *liveliest* of stories—wouldn't you think?"

The doctor didn't look up; didn't truly expect a reply. His monologue hardly skipped a beat when Bert piped, "Yes, sir. Yes it should . . . " Instead, he merely nodded, and continued to insert spike after spike into the dead woman's brainpan, until her head bristled like an echidna.

"Manual stimulus alone will not suffice," he muttered, addressing, Avice suspected, neither she nor the children but listeners with no time for his life's work, listeners on the far side of the globe. "As you can clearly see—" again he twisted and shunted the needles with no effect, "this one's a dead fish. *But.*" There seemed to be an exclamation point after that word—*But!*—and the Matron imagined the man lifting his finger in a veritable *a-ha!* of discovery before he retreated to the shadowed end of the barn. Unoiled casters squeaked as he maneuvered an ancient wheeled table toward the light. On it sat a device Avice had seen many times, but never in use: a friction machine of some sort, she recalled him saying, with two upright spindles between which a large metal plate turned on a winch. When the doctor set it in motion, glints of sunlight reflected off the round surface as it spun on its side, like a Catherine Wheel. A smaller disc sat off to the right, connected to the larger by a flexible silver cord. Together the plates turned, getting faster and faster, revolving into a blur of energy.

"But with the addition of a rotating doubler—an electroscope," he clarified, "or somesuch producer of electrostatic induction, we will find the difference remarkable."

Positioned, as she was, behind the doctor, Avice could not see what sleight of hand he performed then—how he linked the device to the exhumed body—except for the scorched metal crimps he clamped onto the skewers protruding from the open scalp. There were wires curling outward, and a few switches at the machine's base, one of which Dr. Dalkeith must have flicked. As the double-wheels increased their spinning, an incredible hum filled the air, a crackle that exploded in a sizzle of sparking *pops*—and there! There!

Bolts of blue fire, blue magic.

Liquid sluiced from the body. A stench of singed offal arose, so powerful that Avice was forced to cover her mouth and nose for fear of retching. The skin around its eyes and mouth blackened, the veins in its pallid neck shone ultramarine, its face had somehow grown more horrific than ever, *afraid* even, as the lids fluttered and the irises rolled madly—while its feet, its hands, the entirety of its lower body *convulsed*.

For a few seconds, no more, the woman on Dr. Dalkeith's table had been resurrected. Her spirit and form arisen.

For a few seconds.

Perhaps.

As the smoke issuing from the skull cleared, Avice was no longer sure she'd seen what she'd seen. The body was slack, its wretched stink enough to conjure hallucinations. The face was scorched beyond recognition and the fluids pooling beneath the table were evidence enough that this—*thing*—was as dead as her own mother.

• • •

"You two, tidy this up."

As the doctor turned away and began to rinse his instruments, Matron Welles couldn't miss the look that passed between the boys tying on their aprons.

She narrowed her eyes. "Hurry. Prayer begins in five minutes. God may possess eternal patience, but Reverend Tanner does not. He will expect you, washed and quiet, in four."

"I'll help," volunteered one of the Marys. Or was it the sole Sarah? As Avice had predicted, the little one hadn't survived the night; she would be planted on the Isle at dusk with a few scant words from the parson. Mary, Sarah, Victoria, whoever it was—after a while, they all looked the same—got up, jostled to the end of the pew, and started to make her way to the Surgeon's table.

"Wait for me," said another Mary—yes, this one was definitely a Mary—chasing after her friend.

But the first girl was none too pleased to see her follower. A scuffle ensued as they pushed to be the biggest help, banging into each other as they vied for leadership. One elbowed the other, who in turn snatched the cap from her counterpart's head, yanking hard on her pigtail. Slaps developed into wrestles, which collided with the bench holding Dr. Dalkeith's instruments. Tools—clean and dirty—skittered to the floor, girls tumbling after them. Arms and legs furiously whirling, aprons loose and petticoats grinding into the sawdust, they rolled around—now one on top, now the other—taking out some childish frustration.

"Enough," Avice said, voice sharp as her stern clap. "That is *no* behavior for young ladies! Get up!"

Again, she clapped her hands, startling the scrappers into submission. White-faced, they rose, clutching the folds of their skirts for dear life. On the other side of the table, Bert and Alf jolted, dropping bits of their burden. Between them, the corpse sagged like a half-empty sack of flour; its crown and heels dragged on the ground, arms flung wide. Slurry trickled from incisions, from orifices. As the boys shuffled to regain their grip, the body's left foot twisted and tore off.

"Sorry, Doctor Dal," Alf mumbled, collecting the appendage and jamming it into his apron pocket. Grasping more firmly around the knees, he scuttled quickly backwards, pulling Bert—clinging to the thing's armpits, walking gingerly to avoid the mangled head—toward the wheelbarrow beside the workshop's back door.

"Not to worry," the Surgeon said, insouciant. "Her sufferings are no longer of this world. Death's a better release than she could have hoped for."

For reasons she couldn't quite articulate, Avice found the doctor's nonchalance offensive in the extreme. True, the woman was a criminal, but even so . . . Had someone stood over Hettie's corpse and said such things? Surely, she thought, surely someone had shown some respect, some compassion—

"Don't take her out *now*, you fools," she snapped, looking up in time to catch Bert and Alf dumping the woman's remains unceremoniously. "Everyone will be going to church in a moment; they'll *see* you. Come back at twilight, before Labor's end." She inhaled, gathered her composure. "Or would you prefer they return early tomorrow, Doctor? Before lessons?"

Wiping his hands on a scrap of linen, the Surgeon seemed not to hear her. One by one, he gathered the fallen scalpels, picks, saws, pliers, and prisebars and polished them on the cloth before laying them out neatly on the tray he'd returned to the workbench. Brow furrowed, he crouched and did a second inspection of the floor, before straightening with a hand-drill in his grasp. He made to carry the lot over to the pitcher and basin, then appeared to change his mind when the peal of a bell struck up the call to prayer.

"Doctor?" Avice said.

"They'll keep," Dalkeith said to himself. Then, louder, "Beauty of this business, Mrs. Welles. Everything will keep . . . "

"But the mess," she insisted, Bridewell's doctrines running through her mind, cleanliness first and foremost. "The boys will dispose of it in the morning, before we reconvene."

"Ah. Tomorrow." Dr. Dalkeith removed his spectacles, smeared them with a rag from his pocket, then perched them once more on the bridge of his crooked nose. "Ashes to ashes, Mrs. Welles. We've come full circle; again, my cold rooms are filled with nothing but dust."

"Very well," Avice said stiffly. "I shall schedule an excursion for this evening."

The Surgeon turned away and continued to polish his tools. "Whatever you wish, Matron." Dalkeith picked up a small, trowel-shaped implement. "Just ensure they remember their spades."

Every night for a fortnight, the children were sent out on the dig.

By the second day they were exhausted, eyes red-ringed, complexions drawn despite the sun burning down as they plied oakum between nerveless fingers. William Henry whipped the boys thrice at Labor for nodding off, and yawning instead of praying morning and evening. The girls endured lectures from Miss Fiona who, in a fit of innovation, reintroduced the use of the isolation cell. In that close space, Millie or Victoria or Sarah or a Mary would peel back one corner of the thin wood camouflaging the hole Mary Ann Ross had dug, and drop whatever limb had been souvenired from Dr. Dalkeith's workshop down into the dark of the cellar.

Matron Welles didn't stop this punishment, but would surreptitiously give extra rations after they'd endured the cell. Twice the first week and three times the second, she'd let them all sleep a few minutes extra—and before bed one night, she'd given Victoria a new lightweight shift and allowed Millie to inherit the old one, even though it was torn and grave-stained. The children couldn't explain the Matron's softened attitude—nor in all honestly could Avice—but neither did they question it. They faced William Henry's floggings and Mrs. Welles' gifts with equal trepidation, equal acceptance.

Driven by their secret goal, they endured.

In the wee hours, Tall Mary and Only Sarah strutted around their quarters, proud as ponies who'd chewed through their bits, showing off the blade they'd pilfered from Dr. Dalkeith's stash during their "wrestling match." Even seen through a fog of exhaustion, the shine hadn't worn off their prize; without fail, they took it out of its hiding place before muster. To boast. To reassure themselves it was still there.

The foot Alf had pocketed had been taken by Bert—as had the next one they'd claimed, along with the set of nearly-pink lungs, the shriveled stomach, the mismatched pair of thighs, one kidney, and a bloated slab of a liver. Once they'd nabbed a full torso—ribs and spine and all!—however, Bert had needed to borrow their strength to transport it underground without causing needless damage. At last he'd led them all, in the darkest part of the night, to that secret, better place. The place his mother had found.

He made quick work of tying the rope he'd acquired at Labor to the iron bars of the isolation cell's door. One by one they'd shimmied after him, into the disused cellar below, and waited near the rope's dangling end, blackness pressing in. It was even colder down here than it was above. A strange smell scampered at their nostrils while Bert lit one of the candle stumps he'd been collecting and storing on earthen shelves. Weak light leapt and danced, throwing shadows across the dirt walls, the fine roots scraggling from the uneven ceiling, the caved-in door, and over the lumpen thing that lay on a length of pilfered canvas covering half of the packed-mud floor. Or, rather, the collection of things that lay there.

Now, as Bert placed the torso between two tanned arms and above a badly sewn pelvis, what had once been a jumble of body parts was taking proper shape. There was a person's core—recognizably female—both legs and both arms, the segments of each joined together. The hands—unwittingly donated by Ada Habel—had at last been neatly stitched onto the disparate wrists, though Bert's needlework was nowhere near as fine as the girls'. It would be up to Millie and Victoria and Sarah to put their embroidery skills to practical use when it came time to assemble the daintier details: innards, facial features, hairline, the seam between neck and shoulders. Soaking in buckets, organs awaited transplantation. All they lacked was a right foot. A head. A gap in the chest waited for just the right heart.

Bert, Alf, and Ned grinned. Millie's own smile broadened as she paced the length of the canvas, examining all angles. The Marys pressed fists to their mouths to stifle giggles, while Victoria held her breath, hands raised as in prayer. Sarah alone stood calmly, off to one side, head cocked in contemplation.

"I wish Little Sarah could have seen this," she said. "She needed her more than we do."

"Not more than," Bert said, his voice gentle as an embrace. "We all need her. We all need her terribly."

Yes, yes, we all do, chorused the others, fervently, until Big Sarah smiled.

Slowly, finally, their new mother was coming together.

Heavy rains kept them from the cellar for three agonizing days. The gravel yard flooded; an ankle-high sea of milky yellow water lapped at Bridewell's main hall, drowning the work lots and the flower garden outside Matron Welles' cottage. Tufts of wool and unraveled rope bobbed on the surface; in the Factory's corner, cascades poured into the long-drop until it overflowed. On Martin Rook's orders, women and children alike were kept indoors—to avoid pleurisy as much as cess.

Despite the Superintendent's best intentions, five workers were lost to fever and ague, one to drowning, and another was struck by lightning as she crossed the yard carrying an armful of copper pans to the kitchen. Bert watched her scalded figure dragged inside and felt a pang of loss. She'd had such a friendly smile, that lady, but it was toasted beyond recognition. Ugly and black. Completely unfit for their patchwork mother, who would only ever look on her children with warmth, or glee, or good-humored mischief. Never with burnt misery.

Bert fretted so much about *her*, waiting unfinished underground, that he lost all appetite. Skinny already, he wizened with worry while Ned and Millie fought over his rations. By the time Matron at last summoned them back to the barn for lessons, he was nearly weak enough to need Dr. Dal's strange machine to give him a jolt.

The Surgeon's boots squelched as he walked around the table, his hands leaving damp prints on the burnished wood surface. Swaying, he braced himself against the corpse before making each cut, blinking and blinking as though to clear the storm from his vision. Sweat plinked from the tip of his nose, stinking like old vinegar. Bubbles gurgled from deep in his belly, popping loud out his throat. When the blade slipped from his fingers, Dr. Dal plunged after it, like Millie's mother had, that time, into the factory well.

Waterlogged, Bert reckoned as the doc swam up to his feet. Soaked to the bone from so many drenched days.

On the other side of the table, Matron's mouth was a firm black line. A dark crease developed between her brows, stayed there. Back straight, she stilled in that way Bert and the other kids knew too well; inside she was coiled like a snake, ready to strike. Out of habit a dozen pairs of small shoulders trembled, preparing for a blow.

"Settle down, little ones," she said, the words strained just shy of soothing. "We won't be long. If you're good and quiet, I'll ask Miss Fiona to bring you a ha'penny bag of boiled sweets next time she goes into town."

"Yes, Matron," said one of the girls, pretending she was easily fooled.

They tried not to squirm, to sit tight and so earn a reward that would never appear, but their agitation, followed by their bodies, rose with the Surgeon's tirade.

Dr. Dalkeith had upgraded from scalpel to handsaw, which he flailed as he interrogated invisible men. Ranting about criminal minds—*their sins come from the minds, not the souls*—he lectured in shouted snippets.

"Gentlemen of the Royal Society," he slurred, "I beseech you. Cast your discerning eyes hither. When it comes down to it . . ." He stopped, swallowed hard and tapped a fist against his sternum. "When it comes to unlawful behavior, the body entire is superfluous. Instinct and intelligence—or lack thereof—are the seeds of misdemeanor. The cranium and what lies within it, I am convinced more than ever, are of the utmost interest. The primary seat of miscreant drive is here," he pointed to the corpse's forehead with the tip of his saw, "and the secondary, it might be argued, is here." This time he jabbed the soft place between the woman's ribs, severing a chunk of her breast in the process. "But our focus today is on the former—should *ever* be on the former. Why waste time? Am I not right, Mrs. Welles?"

Jaw set, the Matron clasped her hands firmly and did not reply.

The Surgeon took no notice. Grunting and puffing, wielding the tool double-fisted, he severed the corpse's head in a matter of minutes then held the thing up by the hair. "Take notes, if you please, Avice. A fascinating specimen, wouldn't you agree, Gentlemen?" Twisting the sample this way and that, he looked at the children as though expecting a response, then nodded as though he'd received one. As the doctor highlighted all aberrant features, Bert watched Mrs. Welles; watched her watching, *taking notes* as Dr. Dal had instructed, without ever writing anything down.

"Proof!" The doctor staggered to a tall apothecary cabinet bracketed by floor-to-ceiling shelves to the left of the workshop. He tucked the head under his arm like a football, occasionally stroking its bedraggled blond hair. With some effort, he unlocked the leadlight doors and flung them wide. Stare fixed on the lowest shelf, he extracted a container twice as big as a chamber pot; lidless glass, dusty but clear, tinted pale greenish-blue. "If mere words cannot persuade you, Gentlemen, I shall endeavor to provide physical proof."

In moments, the head was sealed in the jar—Matron Welles had to melt the wax and affix the treated leather lid, for Dr. Dal had some trouble with the matches—and floating in a potent brine that distorted her once-lovely features, making her look almost as ugly as Millie's mother, pulled too late from the well. *Almost*, but not quite.

"If we get her quick," Bert whispered to Alf, barely allowing his lips to move lest Matron Welles catch him, "she'd be a good face to look on. She'd be a good fit."

Gaze locked on the doctor, who had just thrust the full jar at Matron Welles before lurching over to the settee tucked off in a corner, Alf nodded. He raised his hand, hushing Bert's next question, as the Matron collected a wool blanket and draped it over the doctor's prostrate form, without tenderness. When muffled snores emerged from under the cover, Alf whispered, "Faint, Bert," then balled his hand, turned to his right and punched Ned hard in the stomach.

As air—followed by the extra breakfast rations he'd pigged—whooshed from Ned's mouth, Bert let himself go slack. Closing his eyes, he flopped from the pew, falling with a dull *thwap*. He wasn't sure what Alf planned, but if it needed Bert to be out cold, then he'd play the part convincingly.

Cold seeped through his thin clothes as he lay there, trying not to inhale the smell of Ned's puke. Footsteps clomped nearby as the kids ran from Bert to Mrs. Welles and back, while Alf called out, "They got the sickness, Matron! Just like Little Sarah—they got it real bad. Dr. Dal's got to help them; he's got to give them medicine, and make them better. Dr. Dal! Dr. Dal, wake up!"

If Bert didn't know better, he'd think the note of panic in Alf's voice was pretty bloody compelling. The Marys—bunch of whiners at the best of times—picked up the boy's keening, making a din powerful enough to rouse those out on the Isle. Not strong enough to make Dr. Dalkeith stir, it seemed—which, Bert guessed, was the real reason behind Alf's caterwauling. Testing how deep the doc's sleep was.

"Hush! Hush, now. *Hush*. The Surgeon is . . . " Matron Welles looked around as if searching for the right word. " . . . *indisposed*. He has been working overly hard of late, and needs some rest. Hush! Hush. Alfred, Edward, carry Albert over to the infirmary—can you manage that, Edward?"

Scowling at Alf, Ned clutched his stomach and brought up another splatter of soup and half-chewed bread.

"Fine," the Matron sighed. "Join Albert in the sickroom, but mop up that mess first. You," she said, pointing to Big Sarah, "help take the boys to bed. And you," she pointed, plucked at a name, "Mary—accompany the little ones to the dining hall. William Henry will bring the day's Labor inside; we can't have this infection spoiling the lot of you. And Superintendent Rook will not be pleased if you don't make quota this week. The rains have set us far enough behind . . . "

Her instructions quieted as the Matron led the able children outside. When the pattering of their footfalls had dwindled, Bert risked cracking an eyelid. With a sour expression to match his reek, Ned glared at Alf, who rocked on his heels, practically bouncing with pride.

"There's hessian sacks by the barrow," Alf said. He tilted his chin at Sarah. "Bag that head for us. Reckon doc's pissed enough to forget he even jarred it in the first place."

Bert raised a brow, mutely questioning how Alf could possibly know such a thing.

The boy shrugged, unfazed. "When William Henry gets far gone as the doc has, it knocks a good half hour off his memory at least. All manner of things you can get away with when a man's blind as that."

Between the barn and the infirmary was no place for talk. Without knowing if or when Matron Welles would return to check on them, the boys put on a show of illness while Alf and Sarah carried their burdens in silence.

"Lie still," Alf said to Bert, throwing him down on the nearest cot. The blanket was thick, well-made; the pillow was filled with feather, not straw. Bert had half a mind to *will* himself really sick, just so he could rest here a few days, sleeping in his very own bed—but then he thought of the flood, the cellar, the preserved head, and the mess they'd be in if it all wasn't cleaned up quick-smart.

"I'm too scrawny," Bert said, begrudgingly, when Mary slid the jar under the covers beside him, trying to camouflage its presence with artful tucking and fluffing. "You'll have to give it to Ned."

Twisted on his side, Ned hugged the jar. If anyone checked on them—without looking *too* close—it'd seem Ned was cradling his aching guts, trying to hold them in.

"How long d'you reckon Dr. Dal will be out?" Bert asked, drowsiness warring with his eagerness to reach the cellar.

"Long enough," Alf said. "Give it till evening prayer—if you haven't seen him by then, he'll be done till morning."

"All right," Bert said, gauging the time by the length of the shadows creeping in the infirmary door. "Better get going, else Matron will come hunting you. Me and Ned'll keep care of things here." He snuggled into the mattress. "Meet us later. After moondark. Downstairs."

The panes in the bay window were begrimed with rain-spattered dirt. *The irony,* Avice thought, glancing at the decorative ceiling border, exhortations woven in a pattern of blackberries and pansies: Cleanliness—Godliness—Quietness—Regularity—Submission—Industry. Arms crossed, she stood with her back to the Superintendent's desk, awaiting his return. Taking deep, slow breaths, she let the coals of her anger smolder.

How dare he summon *me like a maid, then leave with nothing more than,* "Stay put!"

Pulling her shawl tightly around her shoulders, Avice gazed outside, keeping an eye on the door's reflection. In the yard, half a dozen Third class women trod widdershins, inside the walls. Barefoot and shorn like lambs, bearing thick iron collars, they drifted like ghosts from corner to corner. *Arson is the perfect crime if you wanted to get caught,* Avice had written in the Superintendent's journal before these particular women were punished.

As the procession paused at the western wall, the small wooden door swung smoothly inward. Through the narrow gap, one of the children slipped, hunched nearly double and wrapped in one of the infirmary's new blankets.

"Edward," she muttered, then corrected: "No. *Albert.*"

Within seconds she had composed the entry for Rook's journal; sick or not, the boy would have to be punished—for theft of the blanket, if not for intentionally infecting Bridewell's vulnerable populace. She tallied the pounds of oakum that would have to be deducted from the daily totals, and added two-thirds of Bert's allotted rations back into general stocks for redistribution. It pained her, after all the effort she'd made with the children this fortnight, that this one remained so headstrong . . .

She considered dashing outside to give the boy his comeuppance—Martin would hardly notice her absence—then saw Bert intercepted by a black-clad form. Taller than any man had a right to be, thin as a bird-gutted scarecrow, Reverend Tanner's wide-brimmed hat obscured the top half of his face and, in this weather, would serve better as an umbrella than a sun-screen. He took up more space with fear than his slight figure alone ever could.

The child struggled to keep his blanket wrapped round him as he tried to sidestep the parson, and Avice chuckled. Official punishments could certainly wait, she decided, until after the Reverend had filled the boy's mind with visions of fire and brimstone.

Which left her here to face Martin Rook, whenever he deigned to return.

"Think of the Devil," she murmured as the office door creaked open.

"Have a seat, Avice," the Superintendent said before she could utter another word. A second later, she was at a loss for anything more than a grunt of surprise. Following quick on Martin's heels was Miss Fiona, rosy-cheeked with self-satisfaction.

"I'll stand, thank you," Avice began.

"Sit." Martin snapped his fingers, as though she were a dog, and pointed at a low stool in front of the desk. "Now, woman."

Not Matron, then. Not Avice. *Woman.*

Rigid with fury, she inclined her head ever so slightly, gripped her skirts and smoothed them beneath her as she sat. Her boots crunched noisily on scattered chips of timber as she adjusted her position; the stool's legs had been hastily shortened, sawn off two-thirds of their regular length. Perhaps Martin had done the job himself, right there, in too great a hurry to sweep the sawdust away. As the Superintendent leaned heavily against the imposing desk, Avice was forced to crane her neck to meet his eyes.

For once, Rook's gaze was lucid. His thinning hair was combed slick, shirt ironed, the tie under his waistcoat knotted impeccably and pinned with a burnished gold rod. When he exhaled, it was through trimmed nostrils, not out of a drooping mouth, and as he spoke Avice caught a whiff of fresh mint.

"I am gravely disappointed with your performance, Mrs. Welles," Martin said, emphasizing the *grave*, which elicited a giggle from Miss Fiona. Lifting his trousers by the pleats to minimize creasing—the way Avice had been *trying* to get him to for *years*—Rook crossed his legs at the ankle, leaned back, and winked at the Taskmistress before plucking a leather-bound volume off the felt blotter.

"Fiona," Avice said, half standing as two and two made four. She'd got him dressed for this meeting; no doubt the strumpet had done her fair share of *undressing* him as well. "What on earth—"

Her thoughts evaporated as Martin Rook placed a pudgy palm on the book, looking for all the world as though he were about to swear an oath. Caressing the cover, he waited for Avice to realize that this journal was fashioned not from black hide stained liberally with Tokay, but was clothed in a rich shade of navy, gilt shimmering on the spine and the paper's cut edges. Not *his*, then, but . . .

"Where did you get that?" she whispered. "Have you sunk so low, Martin, that you must steal from trusted friends?"

By the door, Miss Fiona snorted. Her cracked red hands were greasy with rose-scented lanolin; the uniform she wore was crisp white, the weave finer than any Avice owned.

"I see," the Matron said. Martin had had it stolen. And at such a low price. "You've done well for yourself, Taskmistress."

"*Matron*," Fiona corrected, triumph adding a note of glee to the title. "That's Matron to you, Miss Avice."

"I did everything," Avice said, after the buzzing in her ears subsided, the spots in her vision dispersed. "I liaised with Skaille, oversaw these—" she waved her hand in Fiona's direction "—ingrates. Bridewell has flourished under my care. There are fewer deaths, though intake is up. And the children."

"Indeed. The children. It wasn't like you," the Superintendent said, lip curling, "to be so . . . *caring*."

Avice swallowed bile, remembering Rook's wandering hands, his rancid breath by her ear, the rough scrape of his tongue, and the thrust of him inside her. Remembering all the things she'd done, all the things she'd allowed to be done to her.

"How dare you," she spat, but Martin waggled her diary by one gilded corner.

"Dalkeith's flights of fancy I can ignore; he's a man of science, after all. But you . . . Disappearing each morning? Those urchins at your beck and call?

How could I know you'd been seeking pleasure with necrotic tissue? Couldn't you have simply used the good doctor as a means to cure your frigidity? Then at least I might have benefited from your extra-curricular activities—as you did from mine." Rook smiled warmly at Fiona, who blushed like a schoolgirl instead of the forty-something trollop she was. The idea that he thought she'd enjoyed any of what he'd done to her made Avice's head pound. "But it soon became clear the doctor was not of abiding interest to you, so I asked Fi here to call on you, see what was keeping you so preoccupied of late. And if you should happen to be out when she dropped by, well . . . All the better."

"You had no right," Avice said, trembling.

"You always have undermined my authority, Mrs. Welles. For a while—oh, let's be honest, for *years*—I was content to turn a blind eye. Play the fool to your queen, the jester to your highness. Whatever warmed you, warmed me, *darling*. But I cannot ignore this." He cleared his throat and said, more forcefully, "I did not authorize *this*."

He tossed the diary to Fiona, as though he couldn't bear touching the thing a second longer. "We are not in the business of *creating* criminals, but of *rehabilitating* them. At the very least, it is our mandate not to make them worse."

When the children woke, they found it was to a dull gray day. There was no sign of the sun when Bert poked his head outside their little shed; the rain had once more set in overnight, but it was obvious they'd overslept. Their stomachs told them they'd missed breakfast, which in turn told them they'd not been woken. And *that* told them something had happened to Matron Welles.

Victoria was sent into the storm to scout for information while the others huddled within their four walls, listening to the roiling thunder. It wasn't long before the girl was back, muddy and soaked, babbling how she'd overheard William Henry laughing with the Constables about Avice's fall from grace. How Miss Fiona preened and swanned inspecting the women of all classes, wearing a pretty new outfit.

Initially there was a stunned silence, until first one then the other broke into ragged laughter, interspersed with whoops and tears of joy. All of them, except Bert, who tolerated their noise until he couldn't think.

"Shut it!"

"But, Bert, she's gone! She can't lord it over us anymore," said Millie, trying to make him see reason.

After a short pause, he said, "But we need her, don't you see?"

They all shook their heads in a dogged fashion.

He sighed. "If she's gone who's going to be in charge of us? Who's going to take us to Dr. Dal? He won't be wanting to babysit the likes of us. Welles was the only one to organize things for him."

Turning away, Bert pulled the well-worn book out from beneath their bedding and pinned it down with his knees like a map on the floor, pointing at the page he'd selected like a battlefield commander instructing his troops. The image showed Frank lowering a deep black heart into his creature's splayed ribcage. Lines etched around the organ showed it still beat.

"He's right," sighed Victoria, with a growing dread that seemed to transmit itself to the rest of them.

"We need one last thing—one last fecking thing," despaired Ned.

And then Bert smiled. It was a slow smile, a sure smile, a smile to curdle the blood, but his company took only comfort from it. Millie alone remained belligerently pessimistic, lacking faith.

"Where are we gonna get one of those?" she demanded.

Bert's smile grew wider. "I know where we can find one, barely used. Wait until nightfall."

Avice did not hear the knocking at first, so deeply sunk she was in her misery.

The new Matron will attend to Bridewell's daily reckonings . . .

The new Matron will contact the Queen's Orphan School in Hobart about places for our lost sheep . . .

Constables! Escort Mrs. Welles to her quarters and see to it she doesn't leave.

Was Hettie caught so easily, Avice had wondered, as she was led to her— the new Matron's—cottage. Was she as foolish as her mother? Was that her only inheritance?

That stupid old man, she seethed now, and that even stupider harlot . . .

The tap-tap-tapping finally broke her concentration.

In the sliver betwixt door and frame, Millie's pale face appeared.

"How did you get in?" demanded Avice, and the girl grinned.

"Ned and Alf led 'em off, the Constables. Be quick about it, Matron, if you'd like to make good your escape."

Avice Welles did not need to be told twice. She left everything behind, everything but the small purse of sovereigns Miss Fiona had failed to find stuffed into the mattress. She let go all notes, all researches. She would start again, would recall enough to rebuild.

Following Millie, she kept watch on the girl's thin straight back. She thought how her recent kindnesses to the children had paid off in this act of charity.

Outside, it was raining still. She could barely see a foot in front of her, could only just hear when Millie said, "This way, Matron."

Head down, Avice kept pace with the child's quick step. Around her the other children gathered like misty wet ghosts. When she finally looked up, they were at the isolation cell. Millie smiled. Bert was there, too. He offered his hand as if to help her across a threshold.

"A hiding place, Matron. Not for long, but long enough." Nodding, she took his fingers and stepped over—then found herself falling. Falling so far and so fast, the plummet stopped by a breathtaking hit, a great splash of dirty water. Her leg broke beneath her, one ankle too, but she was too shocked to cry out. Through the pain she noticed a rope snaking from above; the children, one by one, slid down it like monkeys, wet, mud-spattered monkeys all coming into the strange dank room lit by candle stumps.

Bert was first. He sloshed across the cellar and took something from against the wall, then stood in front of her, waiting until the others were safely there to witness. Ned and Alf, Millie and Victoria, Only Sarah, Fat Mary, Red Mary, Tall Mary, Dark Mary, Spotty Mary. In the shadows behind them Avice thought she saw another shape, thin and small, translucent and shivering beyond death: Little Sarah. And there, beside her, features so long forgotten, so long diluted by time, but now undoubtedly her: Hettie.

Avice opened her lips, tried to make a sound, tried to plead, but all she managed was a muted *uhhhnuh* before Bert brought the spade down hard on her head.

From the rickety old fences surrounding the graveyard, Bert had acquired a scrunched roll of barbed wire. Well after curfew, Ned had clambered up on the roof of the isolation cell to affix a star picket of iron there to act as a lightning rod. They'd wrapped the sharp wire around the picket and ran it along the wall, into the lockup, then down, down, down into the hole.

In this storm, no one was outside.

Without Avice Welles, no one bothered with them.

In the puddle-filled cellar, the old Matron had breathed her last, prone in shallow mud. After Bert's final blows had stopped, Victoria and the Marys had watched on, fascinated, as the woman's thickened breath bubbled, ribcage expanding and contracting, both ceasing after one last noisy burst of air.

Behind them, the boys were busy wrapping the new mother in rusted barbed wire. They were careful to ensure the spikes grabbed into the patchwork meat without tearing, equally careful to not let it pierce their own hands. Not always successful in this latter task, they spilled their fresh young blood. Filled with the magic of youth and grief and yearning, it stained the dead flesh, entered wounds that gaped but did not weep. Her recently sewn head, neatly attached by Victoria's fair hand, listed to the side; as if she slept, Bert thought. Her hair had been cropped right before her death. A rough job; chunks had been taken out of her scalp, leaving longer tufts unshorn. Those gashes hadn't had time to heal, nor the raw lacerations around her neck—the iron collar's love-bite, William Henry called it—so these marks, too, were repaired with tidy, meandering stitch-trails. Black and blue threads complemented the black and blue welts on her skin, the black and blue hollows in her lean face.

Bert thought she was beautiful, just as she was. All the children thought she was beautiful.

Ever since Dr. Dal had jolted that dug-up, Bert had thought long and hard about it. Relying on instinct more than logic didn't diminish his confidence in his science. He was *positive* this procedure would work. He'd used a drill to make several small holes in the skull and now inserted, with painstaking care, stolen wires before attaching their free ends to the barbed cage trussing her body.

"I dunno, Bert, I don't want no black-souled mother," sniffed Millie, standing beside him, her patched shoes making ripples in the puddle around the body. Bert gave a sigh of exasperation.

"How many times I gotta tell you? Once the lightning hits, that heart of hers will start pumping and brighten right up. The most brilliant blue-white you ever seen. She'll shine like an angel, and she'll be our proper mum. Trust me."

"What about her foot, Bert?" Ned, checking the wire trailing down from the hole above, nodded towards the ankle which ended only in a stump.

"Never mind. We'll make her one, a wooden one, when she's up and about. Only we need this storm to get her going. We can't wait. And it's only a foot; she don't need a foot to love us."

Ned nodded. Bert sat back and surveyed his handiwork. Only one piece left, and they'd be set. The chest cavity was wide open—Victoria stood at the ready with needle and thread—but they'd not yet taken the heart from Matron. Bert had been so anxious to get the lightning rod in place, to get the framework in place, to take advantage of the weather, he hadn't wanted to waste time. It would all happen so quick, he just *knew* it. After seeing the woman lightning-struck in the courtyard, all he could think about was how random the bolts were, how they had to be ready, ready, ready to take their chance.

Let Mrs. Welles keep that heart safe and fresh until the very last minute, he reckoned.

Millie didn't look convinced, but she shut up and followed him to the corner where the Matron lay like one of Cook's butchered sows. Wielding the filched scalpel and a gutting knife Alf had scavenged from the kitchen, Bert slit the woman's chest, then pried apart her ribs to get at the still-warm organ. Neatly detaching the organ from all the bits and bobs that kept it in situ, he handed the meaty muscle to Millie. "Make yourself useful. Take this over to *her.*"

Obediently, she did so. Waiting beside the wire-wrapped figure, her gaze traveled from the wet heart slicking her hands, dribbling down, down into the gaping cavity there, into the darkness that would soon be filled with this squishy red ticker, with thread and blood, with love. Standing in the freezing stormwater, renegade drops dripped from the open floor above, her thin-soled shoes leaking, Millie shivered, feet so cold she barely felt them. Outside there was a sharp *crack* and an ominous tumbling rumble not long after. Blinking up into the rain, Millie counted half a second between the flash of light in the opening overhead and the rattling boom that followed. Close, so close.

On the opposite side of the mother, Bert paced, craning to see the sky through the cell above. It hadn't really occurred to him that the lightning might not play nice, might not be so willing to come when called, that it would obey only its own elemental rules. Somehow he'd imagined a roiling store of the stuff amassing directly over them, ready to be summoned as needed. But these wild, whiplashing bolts? He had no idea how to get them to go where they needed it most.

A flash of blistering white. Wincing, Bert cowered near the wall next to Alf and two of the Marys. If the previous strike had been loud, he reckoned this one was a ripper. All the children gave little screams of panic, except Ned and Millie, who kept screeching long after the others had calmed.

In the spotted darkness after the blast, they both shook and shuddered, buzzed and smoked. Ned's hands seared to the barbed wire he'd been touching; Millie jittered and juddered in the rainwater pooling around the new mother, who jittered and juddered too, but made no sound. The wires, probes, and metal bindings all crackled and glowed. The heart in Millie's spasming grip burned black and crisped faster than thought.

Then it was done.

It was over.

Millie and Ned fell slowly, wisps of steam coming off them, like souls released.

Bert blinked and swallowed, blinked and swallowed again. The children drifted, half-terrified, half-fascinated, to their fallen mates. Kneeling, they examined them, scrunched their noses at the smell of sodden burnt meat, at the power they'd so briefly harnessed at such a cost. The Marys began to cry first—as always—then Sarah, then Victoria, and finally Alf.

But Bert . . . Bert was processing what he'd seen, even as he stared down at Millie and thought how quiet his life would be without her. Yet, even thinking that, his mind was playing catch-up, replaying what he thought he'd seen. If his eyes hadn't deceived him, that mist, that smoke, that fog, that *essence* from his friends' bodies hadn't gone upwards, but *down*. It hadn't dissipated, but been drawn in. Their spirits, if that's what they were, hadn't gone up to Heaven the way Reverend Tanner insisted, but they hadn't gone to Hell neither. No, they'd only gone as far as the level of his feet before they'd been taken into the patchwork mother.

Slowly, he turned his gaze to where the stitched lady lay.

Slowly, the others followed, their losses suddenly forgotten.

Strange science. Dark magic. Yearning and blood, loss and sacrifice.

The body, their own new mother, still cocooned in the wire frame, was moving.

"Alf?" said Bert.

"Yeah?"

"Hand me them wire clippers."

Angela Slatter is the author of the Aurealis Award-winning *The Girl with No Hands and Other Tales*, the World Fantasy Award finalist *Sourdough and Other Stories*, Aurealis finalist *Midnight and Moonshine* (with Lisa L. Hannett), as well as *Black-Winged Angels*, *The Bitterwood Bible and Other Recountings*, and *The Female Factory* (again with Hannett). In 2015 her story *Of Sorrow and Such* will be one of the inaugural Tor.com novella series. Her short stories have appeared in publications such as *Fantasy*, *Nightmare*, *Lightspeed*, *A Book of Horrors*, and Australian, UK and US "best of" anthologies. She is the first Australian to win a British Fantasy Award, holds an MA and a PhD in

Creative Writing, is a graduate of Clarion South and the Tin House Summer Writers Workshop, and was an inaugural Queensland Writers Fellow.

•

Lisa L. Hannett has had over sixty short stories appear in venues including *Clarkesworld, Fantasy, Weird Tales, Apex, The Year's Best Australian Fantasy and Horror* (2010, 2011 & 2012), and *Imaginarium: Best Canadian Speculative Writing* (2012 & 2013). She has won three Aurealis Awards, including Best Collection for her first book, *Bluegrass Symphony,* which was also nominated for a World Fantasy Award. Her first novel, *Lament for the Afterlife,* is being published by CZP in 2015. You can find her online at lisahannett.com and on Twitter @LisaLHannett.

Balls and ovals of ice clung at the perimeter of the eaves, the edges
of the windows as if whispers and open-mouthed cries had crusted over,
hard ice expressions with hollow lament trapped inside . . .

THE STILL, COLD AIR

Steve Rasnic Tem

Russell took possession of his parents' old house on a cold Monday morning. The air was like a slap across his cheeks. The frost coating the bare dirt yard cracked so loudly under his boots he looked around to see if something else had made the sound. Nothing grew here but a few large trees. His parents had left behind an old washer, a scattering of junk-filled cans and buckets, the front grill of an old Chevrolet, and some moldy, unidentifiable bit of taxidermy. A set of rusted bulkhead doors probably led to the basement. He hadn't wanted the property, and his sisters didn't want him to have it.

"You don't deserve their house, you know," Angela had said, before handing him the keys. "You hated them, didn't you? I mean what else could it be the way you treated them? You must have hated them."

And of course he didn't deserve it. He'd been estranged from them his entire adult life, but he didn't have much choice. Winter was here, and he'd been living out of his car the last three months. Did he hate them? He actually had no idea. The bigger question was why they had willed him their house.

The key was giving him trouble—he examined it—worn thin and scratched up, the lock itself fairly chewed up as well. He eased the key in carefully, feeling for a fit, afraid he was going to snap it. Snow hadn't actually started yet, but tiny bits of ice floated in the air, now and then landing with a sting. Not a good night to spend in the car, especially with his own house at hand, however shabby and worn down. He tilted his head back and looked up at the sky—it wasn't just a snow sky, but a sky on the verge of imminent collapse. The roofline drooped directly above him, the eaves tipped back with the corners sagging even lower. From the street the gray roof looked like an old woman's floppy, misshapen hat, with some fat animal hidden inside to make it bulge along one side. He recognized his father's repair system in that—why replace a broken ceiling joist when you could wrap wire around it or nail on extra scraps of wood to strengthen it or tie it to a roof rafter? The result was that runaway warping as the other roof members generated torque around his amateur repairs. It was a wonder the whole thing hadn't already come crashing down, or some passing inspector hadn't stopped in alarm and condemned the place. The front door suddenly gave way and he stumbled inside.

It opened into the living room, which seemed to be not much warmer than the outside. He flipped on the light and looked around for the thermostat. He had no idea how he was going to pay for heat and electricity. But even if the utility company shut off the power it was still better than living out of his car. Maybe his sisters would help out. Unlikely, but possible.

He could see very little bare wall in the living room. Large bookcases with books jammed in vertically, horizontally, and all angles in between took up most of the area. Much of the remaining wall space was hung with large rugs and woven pieces, and battered overstuffed chairs had been pushed against them, with quilts and towels and blankets and even old clothes wadded behind and in every available space between the furniture. He pulled out a heavy chair and removed the miscellaneous cloth shoved behind it. There was a gap of about two inches between the wall and the floor with frigid air—he guessed from the basement—pouring out. He shoved this insulation back into place as quickly as he could and walked around the perimeter of the room, occasionally getting down on his hands and knees to inspect what his parents had done to block the drafts. In spots, wads of cloth had actually been taped or glued. He stood up and looked at the ceiling—the surface was uneven, dipping and rolling as he scanned from one side to the other, and two of the taller bookcases had been jammed into place to support it. He didn't dare move anything for fear the entire jerry-rigged arrangement would collapse on him.

The wind groaned and whistled on the other side of the door, softly whining through unplugged passages. The walls appeared to shake. The cold found his spine, and brushed up his vertebrae, playing with his nerves.

He understood now why his sisters didn't want the house. What he didn't understand was why they'd been so displeased he'd gotten it. He would have thought they'd find it suitable punishment for his sins, but perhaps his parents hadn't told them everything.

"We're not asking for any money, son. Just some physical help so that I can fix a few things. That's all." His father had sounded frail on that first of numerous calls. Russell almost thought the old man was faking it. But that voice, it sounded—what was the word—shredded?

"No time, Dad," he'd said, although most days it was a struggle just coming up with things to do. "Ask the girls. If not them, they have husbands."

There was a long pause at the other end. "They'd worry too much. They live too far away and I know they'd drop everything, disrupt their lives . . . " He stopped awhile, coughed uncontrollably. "It wouldn't be fair. You live less than a hundred miles away." His mother's voice rose in the background, garbled, indistinct. "Wait a minute, okay?" When he came back he said, "We don't have much, but we'd pay you for your time, feed you, whatever you need."

"I'm pretty busy, Dad, like I said. Look, I'll call you back." He'd called back two days later. "Just can't do it, Dad. What was that you used to say? 'You'll have to figure this one out for yourself.' When I was in jail?" Russell couldn't remember which particular jail term it had been, but that advice had been standard issue for the old man. He hung up, but before he did, he couldn't be sure, but he thought the old guy had been crying.

One of the bookcases had a hole punched through the back to access the thermostat mounted on the wall behind it. He finally heard the furnace fan screech on. A tour of the rest of the house required but a few minutes.

One door went to a dull green bedroom large enough for a full bed and dresser. A square panel in the ceiling provided access to the attic. One day he would check to see how bad it was up there. A narrow path around the bedroom wall led to the house's only bathroom, large enough for one person to stand in, use the toilet or bathe. The porcelain displayed a dull patina of rust stain. Another door off the living room took him into a tiny kitchen with a chipped yellow table.

This was what his parents had moved into after all their resources dried up. What happened to most of their belongings? Maybe they'd been stuffed into basement and attic for more homemade insulation.

He walked to the living room window, showering himself with enormous gray clots of dust as he pulled back the curtain. The new snow had filled the grassless yard quickly, catching in the limbs of the skinny bare trees until they overflowed and leaned. It tumbled out of the sky like rapidly disintegrating hospital linen. He hadn't visited his parents in the hospital. Angela said they'd barely made it through the night after the train went through their car. He'd traveled over that crossing less than a block away to reach this shabby cul-de-sac.

The dense white air sparked with random headlight reflections. He pressed one cheek against the biting glass and looked up through the dark in order to see the edge of the elevated highway a few dozen yards distant. A large truck swung top-heavy and sideways perilously close to the edge of the floating ribbon of dirty concrete, wheels thundering beneath the panicked horn. He imagined he could feel the quieting snow attempt to absorb the sound. His cheek began to numb and his face to twitch before he peeled it away from the pane and pulled the curtain snugly over the night.

As Russell turned around a moment's disorientation made him close his eyes. The effect of the frigid window lingered on his cheek. He raised his hand to rub his face and momentarily lost his balance, opening his eyes with a start. The living room seemed smaller than it had before, as if the intense cold had contracted the walls. That must be an effect of the unfamiliarity of the place. But a small place seemed even smaller if you'd lived in it a number of years as his parents had, as he had in his last apartment. He remembered thinking he'd do anything for just a couple of more square feet. Some days his apartment had felt like nothing more than a tight and clunky, smelly suit he'd been forced to wear. It had embarrassed him to live there.

A cold line glided across his wrist and lingered there, as if it were an absent finger seeking contact. He tensed, waiting for something more but it did not come. He held out his arm like a divining rod and walked helplessly in circles, seeking the source of the cold, feeling led and teased.

He hadn't even noticed that the furnace fan had stopped whining after awhile. He walked over by the heat grate low in the wall. Air hot as flame shot out, carrying long spongy strands of dust like snake spirits. He watched entranced as they first hung up on the grate then spun loose and floated around the room. He'd have to change the filter soon.

He didn't completely trust the already-made bed, but he no longer had sheets of his own. In the car he'd slept in layers of underwear, sweaters, bathrobe, and three coats. The sheets and blankets looked clean enough, but they had that old man smell. More cells dying, and the lungs working harder to push in and out the stale air. He supposed one day he would also smell that way.

He considered turning the heat down before bed, switching off the lights. But heat and lights were a luxury he wished to bathe in.

A sheet had been draped over the small bedside table. Removing it he discovered a small thirteen-inch TV; by maneuvering the coat hanger jammed into the broken aerial he acquired a fuzzy picture, but no sound. For a few minutes he watched a rolling image of a weatherman walking around outside against a sky filled with snow and static. Now and then the static would leak out of the sky and fill the entire frame. He assumed the broadcast was local, but on days like this it was easy to imagine the whole world snowing.

He flipped the set off and settled in. The bed was freezing, the bedroom heat vent broken or clogged. The pillow felt hard, cold and greasy against his neck, a refrigerated pig. He didn't care. He closed his eyes, expecting fatigue and body heat to solve all his problems.

From his nights in his car he naturally fell into a kind of half-sleep. He was vaguely cognizant of a glow from the snow filling the world outside, pushing through the curtains, bathing the interior of the undersized house with its blue-white persistence. He needn't go to a window or open a door to see the increasing accumulation; he could feel it coming down, out of the distant dark and through his half-sleep and covering the dirty, disappointing city, filling this cul-de-sac with swollen empty dreams and erasing the grimiest details. He suffered the weight of it; half hoping it would either kill him or put him unconscious, it scarcely mattered which. He heard the creaking overhead and, sleepily aware of the increasing mass on the malformed roof, he found himself smiling. But although the roof groaned and the walls trembled and sighed, the pitiful structure held, at least for now.

For now but wait but wait—the words dropped into his ears and stayed. They did not bring him fully awake but they made him consider. Two voices fighting for dominance, and vaguely familiar.

In the distant other side of sleep he heard wind gusts under the eaves, pushing against brittle siding. The house stirred but he did not. Waited and waited until there was no hope, whispered with bitter control; he considered he might be in a struggle with his shoulders, trying not to hear. He felt a memory of light warming his eyelids, trying to make him raise them, but he would not.

Then thunder in his head as he fought the suspect sheets that once enshrouded the old couple who'd raised him—And You Left Us Here Alone!

Russell tore the bed clothing from his chest and neck, desperate to breathe. He thought he might have called out—at least he was confident he'd heard a voice so like his own on either this side or the other of the heavy curtains. The bedclothes slid away and off the bed like a sudden failure of skin. He was now cold to his bones and scrambled frantically to drape himself again.

Sounds were muted. He felt curled into the center of a cocoon of hush. Outside the wind slipped off the roof and tumbled. He imagined he could hear the sound of noiseless footsteps creating a progression of holes through the snow and halting outside his window, the depressions filling with shadow.

He eased himself across the bed and pulled a bit of curtain off the window.

Nothing peered in but an oval pattern of rime centered on the pane. Through the empty holes for eyes and mouth he could see the wobble of restless foliage. The wind coughed up billows of powdered snow, walked them across the drifted lawn and abandoned them to the ice-laden streets. In distant neighborhoods the yellow lights blinked and smeared.

The phone rang out jangled and upset. Russell hadn't even known there was a phone, hadn't seen it, and certainly hadn't authorized its connection. But it called out from somewhere within the room. He crawled over the cluttered floor, brushing books, papers, clothes or rags away with the gross movement of hands and arms, swinging and batting in an urgency to kill the obnoxious sound. His fingers brushed the receiver and he jerked it up to his ear.

"Yes . . . "he answered, as if about to be ordered to do something he wanted no part of.

"Russell?" He thought it was one of his sisters, but he didn't know which one. "Are they there? If they are you must let them in. Do you appreciate . . . how cold . . . " The connection filled with waves of static which washed through the receiver and across his chilled arm.

"Angela? Beth?" But there was no answer, and he didn't bother calling out his other sisters' names. Who was coming? And in this weather? He dropped the phone.

Something smacked against the window, flat and unpadded. Russell thought of the unlikely possibility of a bare hand, ungloved, unprotected. His sisters were foolish that way. A trip involving at least three of them, come here to complain or intervene (all under the guise of "helping"), had always been a prospect. Maybe there were things of value still hidden in the house, although he couldn't imagine where, and they wanted their portion. It never paid to underestimate people's greed, even family members'.

There was a chuffing sound outside, like someone struggling through the snow. Or it might have been a panting dog in the next room. Interrupted sleep caused a corruption of the senses, so he could trust his own perceptions no more than the good will of others. But there was that chuffing sound again, a mouth seeking oxygen perhaps, but all it got for its efforts was a throat full of cold. He grabbed for the phone again and dragged it to his ear. The line was still open, with a steady train of distant, oft-repeated soft explosions of air, like a life stuttering out of the world. He laid the receiver gently back into the cradle, not wanting to make a sound, not wanting to encourage any sort of response. Someone wept, either outside the house or inside these poor walls, or inside his head. But he couldn't allow them to freeze, at least not here.

Russell climbed to his feet, feeling around on his body, attempting to bring it to life. He'd gone to bed in his clothes; he didn't own pajamas. He was grateful, but after searching the room in the dim light leaking around the edge of curtain he couldn't find his boots, and he was reluctant to turn on the light. The space under the bed was jammed with plastic bags. He put several over each foot, attempted to tie them into place.

The living room smelled of warm furnace dust and air breaking down into something darker and less useful. He opened the front door slowly and, closing his eyes briefly, let the cold air rush him into its embrace. Sighing, he looked around at the drifts, now a foot high and creeping taller against the house. It should stay this way, he thought, the downy white having transformed the grungy yard into a painting. He recognized a hulking phantom of snow and ice as his car. But the automobile seemed strangely past, a useless memory. One large tree appeared to have given up against the weight of snow and now leaned dangerously close. He saw no signs of his sisters, but he could see the holes they'd made in the snow, the wind not quite having erased their footprints. He heard them whispering, or whimpering around the side of the house. It served them right if they'd gotten themselves into trouble, but he couldn't just leave them there.

The plastic bags kept the damp out, but the lack of boots made him unsteady on his feet. He teetered this way and that, rocking his body through the snow, his view skewed by imbalance. The snow smelled of air cleansed of human contact. The roof loomed, parts sagging with incompetent support. He found himself staring at the perimeter of the eaves, the edges of the windows. Balls and ovals of ice clung there, as if whispers and open-mouthed cries had crusted over, hard ice expressions with hollow lament trapped inside.

A sudden gust of wind picked up with rapid feminine tittering, blew it around the house until the voices became a glacial mist. He arrived too late, the only signs were the curved icicles clawing the edges of the metal basement hatch.

The stuck front door panicked him until he slammed it open with a thrust of shoulder and thigh. He staggered in, the moonlight gathering around him to illuminate the impoverished state of the room. His parents had left him everything, and nothing. He forced the door shut, hearing the splintering as the bottom pushed on the threshold covered with intruding snow. He was still able to latch it, but the effort made him weepy.

The phone was ringing in the bedroom. He stumbled in, sat down on the edge of the unsteady bed and picked it up. The line was dead, the receiver icy against his ear as he listened to the cold empty air. "With no signal, nothing comes across," he thought he said aloud.

In the darkened room he felt the bitter air moving around him. The old house leaked, and he should never have accepted it. As he raised his head and stared at nothing, the shadows began to rearrange. All those years he had successfully kept his distance. He felt so frozen, and all he wanted was not to feel at all. The small house sighed, and then it trembled, and now it seemed no larger than the confines of his head.

He should never have gone out. He should never have come here in the first place. If he had more time maybe he could figure things out, even though figuring things out had never been his strong suit. He'd made so many bad mistakes. And now in the still, cold air he realized he'd let them in.

Steve Rasnic Tem is the author of over 350 published short stories and is a past winner of the Bram Stoker, International Horror Guild, British Fantasy, and World Fantasy Awards. His story collections include *City Fishing*, *The Far Side of the Lake*, *In Concert* (with wife Melanie Tem), *Ugly Behavior*, *Celestial Inventories*, *Onion Songs*, *Twember*, and *Here with the Shadows*. An audio collection, *Invisible*, is also available. His novels include *Excavation*, *The Book of Days*, *Daughters*, *The Man in the Ceiling* (with Melanie Tem), *Deadfall Hotel*, and, most recently, *BloodKin*.

"The Elvis Room"—the one room you save back, in case a president or rock star happens to land unannounced at the front desk . . .

THE ELVIS ROOM

⭤

Stephen Graham Jones

Because of an error in measurement, a matter of less than most machines can even calibrate to, my career in experimental psychology hasn't been a career at all, but a series of nine-month contracts punctuated by weekly-rate hotel rooms.

I'm the mad scientist the tabloids say would "weigh the darkness," yes.

For eight days in August of my twenty-seventh year, newly minted and not unphotogenic, I was something of a sensation, both in the paranormal circles and in syndication as a two hundred and fifty word "story of interest." The directors and the writers were thrilling the audience with their horror stories, but I was putting a scale to that horror. I was making it real.

Of course there were the expected comparisons to 1901, when the human soul had been "weighed"—those famous twenty-one grams, irreproducible in dogs—but my conditions were much more controlled, and not nearly so sensationalistic. Whereas that measurement of twenty-one grams had been either hailed as the triumph of religion over science or bemoaned as that which would finally make faith unnecessary (1901 was the height of the Victorian spiritualism movement), my experiment was pure curiosity: it had grown from a case, from a patient. That's vastly different than presupposing an afterlife, then finding a way to prove it.

Yet the public digested the two exactly the same.

I was able to protect "Mary," anyway. Patient 039—a number I just made up, like the name. Better that this experiment's fallout settle on only one of us.

Her problem was monophobia (also known as "autophobia" or "isolophobia") and extreme nyctophobia. The first is the fear of being alone. The second is fear of the dark, a common, widespread problem, and not just limited to children.

After all, human eyes haven't evolved to penetrate the darkness of the savanna night—or the closet, with the light off—and where we can't see, there our imaginations can populate and propagate. The unseen terrorizes specifically by remaining unseen; it's an axiom for a reason.

And "monophobia" is perhaps not the most apt term for her anxiety, but "paranoia" is so reductive; in actuality, her fear of being alone stemmed from her distinct sense that she was never completely alone.

She had been referred to my sleep lab not because my new colleague thought I could cure her, but because he knew I needed raw data on the fear response: galvanic skin response, respiration, blood pressure. Already I had three lifelong night terror sufferers spending their nights with me for a token bit of my grant monies (fast evaporating). Granted, what I was investigating could be considered peripheral to the major lines of inquiry, most of which involved treating the Big Three (schizophrenia, depression, the dementias), but I was ambitious, was trying to find my fulcrum with which to overturn the world.

My study had been born when a certain pamphlet found its way to my inbox: American Indians on campus were calling for a return to "traditional" hair-lengths. It wasn't for anything religious, but because long hair supposedly magnified the natural world, tuning their scalps in to the slightest breath, forty feet away. It was apocryphal, of course, and very much in keeping with pirates wearing hoops through their ear lobes to sharpen their vision. But what if, right?

My grant was partially funded through the Defense Department, yes. Anything to give soldiers more advantage on the battlefield. Or less disadvantage.

In order to properly track the possibility of this, however, I first had to establish a baseline of physiological responses, which would cumulatively and quantitatively map out what people call the hair on the back of their neck "writhing" or "standing up" to alert them that they're being watched.

And being watched is at the bottom of most cases of nyctophobia: you can't see into the darkness, but you can be seen.

As for Mary, she had long, flowing hair, perhaps even "sensitive" hair— what my then-wife would have said was hair from a shampoo commercial. She had been a twin in the womb, but was the only one born. It was a story she dwelt on, and the source of much of her anxiety.

I admitted her to my lab and she signed all the requisite releases, and that first night I watched her, and followed her readings, and my colleague had been right: there was something distinctly haunted to her demeanor, to her bearing, to her postures, once she'd acclimated to the new room, the cameras. It was in the way she would sometimes look behind her, to what my monitor insisted was just another empty corner.

In the womb with twins, one will often eat the other. It's just the natural course of things.

Her parents never should have told her.

Finally she fell asleep, and all her readings leveled out.

We did this four times, and her charts were beautiful, her terror so unadulterated that I could understand her impulse to trust it.

On the fifth—and fateful—night, then, sitting in the lounge with her, I told her that I could prove to her that her fears were baseless. That she had nothing to be afraid of, or to feel guilty for. To reiterate, here, I wasn't supposed to treat her, just document her. This was strictly outside the purview of my study. But you can only watch someone struggle with a stubborn jar for so long before you offer to help. Especially when the contents of that jar can save their life.

"But she won't show up in pictures," she said, anticipating my methods.

"Because she's not real," I told her.

I was too proud of my discipline, yes. My—and all scientists will admit this, at some level—my denomination.

The human mind was a computer bank, to me. I could simply change the punch cards, reprogram a life. Stimulus-response, the world conforms to reason; I was a product of my lengthy education. There were no dark corners, as far as I was concerned. Just shadows we haven't bothered to shine our lights into yet.

I was going to shine my light into Mary's corner.

She would be a footnote when I finally published, a fortuitous benefactor of the early parts of my study. No, of my *rigor*, and my ability to balance experimental psychology with the individuals it's supposed to eventually benefit.

A friend in another department had a lab where he was measuring atmospheric pressures and the smallest fractions of weights, in an attempt not to find dark matter—though if it resolved in his data, he had assured me he wouldn't complain—but to deliver his findings and conclusions to the Department of Weights and Measures. His findings on decay, on specific gravities, on not only how many angels would fit on a pinhead, but their percent of body fat. His world, infinitesimal as it was, was the physical, while mine was the interior, the, according to public opinion, "subjective." But, in my hubris, I could hotwire them.

Two nights later I led Mary into his chamber and left her there, retreated to the booth with my friend.

Once the pressure settled in the chamber and my friend had established her tare-weight so as to rezero his superfine scales, I had him turn the lights off. My hope was to show Mary that her fears were baseless: the chart of her time in the chamber, in the dark, would be level. No spikes to indicate a presence, malevolent or otherwise. This was all assuming that there actually were no such thing as the immaterial. My grounding for that, which she had to agree with, was that "ghosts" or whatever surely at least interacted with light, yes? Even if they never touched the floor or were completely permeable, holograms in a sense, still, our eyes were built to read surfaces light was reflecting off of, right? Meaning that, if these presences Mary insisted upon were actually there and interacting with her, then they had to be interacting with her through the physical world. Otherwise there could be no interaction.

And of course, once the lights went all the way down to black, Mary's sobbing screams filled the booth.

My friend made to release the door—his laser-cut bars of copper and vanadium never screamed for their lives—but I stayed his hand, convinced that two full minutes of zero change on the charts would prove to Mary that her certainties were all in her head, and could thus be talked through and dealt with in a proper, rational setting rather than continually recoiled from, and allowed to dictate her life. I wanted to give her back control, and the freedom that came with it.

Except—that famous measurement.

Not at the height of Mary's panic attack but right after, something in that darkness of the chamber did in fact move, or seem to.

The atmospheric pressure dilated ever so slightly, as if, perhaps, a hummingbird had opened its mouth, emitted a single, invisible breath.

And the weight shifted in tandem with that.

I, of course, told Mary that the variance on the charts was within the baselines, no environment is truly hermetic, but she fell away from me, ran off across campus in her lab-issue nightgown, to finally get picked up in hysterics at a coffee shop.

When she said my name hours later, through a battery of sedatives and well-meant cups of coffee—does nobody check with anybody else?—I was brought in, and when she argued that my tests had proven what she'd already known, had confirmed her worst fears, that her dead sister was stalking her, my friend was compelled to turn those charts in. Nothing less would satisfy her. And I don't blame him, for handing them over, for admitting to everything; he was going to be in enough hot water for having loaned his equipment out to another department, for an unauthorized rogue experiment, one involving human subjects, when he was only cleared to glove up, handle precious metals.

By the time the night's events were whittled down to two lines on a report, they seemed no less than a revolution.

Once the papers got their hooks into it, my experiment was "proof of ghosts." When I'd been trying to establish the opposite of that.

In a matter of months, my funding disappeared, my papers started getting declined for the conferences, and I had to look further and deeper for teaching opportunities I'd formerly kept in my hip pocket as insurance. And all because my friend's equipment had been so impossibly fine: that much-discussed change in atmospheric pressure—I'd never anticipated that her papillae, expanding into 'goose bumps,' could actually be measured. That didn't explain the subtle addition of weight, but my friend reluctantly opined that it had probably been the result of a moving subject on a scale designed for stationary objects. Inertia and momentum; they don't teach that in Intro Psych.

I didn't seek the fame or notoriety out, but it found me all the same.

My wife left shortly after. It was understandable. My reaction to the published results and to my department's disavowal was, like Mary, to rush back, insist upon the validity of the experiment. In the existence of ghosts, yes. In the undeniability of the data. That the data was more valid, even, if there can be a spectrum or a gradient of validity. Like penicillin, like Teflon, this was something we'd stumbled upon, not something we'd set out to prove.

It was a mismeasurement, though. That wasn't even consensus, it was just assumed. No one was trying to replicate our work.

Public opinion had always seemed vapid, until it was levied against me.

The conferences I began to get invited to for a brief time, they also hosted panels on UFOs and Bigfoot. I was being exiled to the fringes, just another "shrieker," as my major professor used to call them: those who are so far from the center that they have to scream and pull their hair to be heard.

Those conferences, however, unlike the ones I'd always known, paid.

A second wife came and went, not willing to commit to my nomadic lifestyle, to what she called my lingering bitterness, and ten years slipped past, and then five more, and then a sixteenth year, and I still hadn't found that fulcrum I knew had to be there to flip the world over onto its back.

At some point in a fall like this, you stab your hand out for a handhold.

Not from reflex, but because you've been dwelling on notions of redemption for years already. On giving the world its comeuppance.

And so was born my second experiment.

Just like the first, it was born of observation, of happenstance: as my life was more and more spent in hotels, I began to take note of my fellow travelers. To study them and their habits, their small compulsions and superstitions that they probably weren't even aware of. And I began to pick up the lore. Not the usual clutch of urban legends, either—disappearing hitchhikers and the like—though of the same family.

And some assembly was required.

The first component wasn't even a folk tale, it was just something I picked up from a hotel manager's daughter. In trying to negotiate a cheaper rate for my monthly stay than for the weekly I was already being charged, I had to work my way up the administrative stream, as it were. And she was the last step before the main office.

It was all pleasant, of course; I've found that abrasiveness doesn't go nearly as far as a display of academic fatigue with the process, with a sense that the two of you at this table are in this together, and it's not about the two of you at all, but this issue. Of rate.

In watching her page through her binder to show me occupancy trends and the like—she'd come prepared to these negotiations—I noticed there was always one vacancy, even when the final report noted how many people had been turned away.

"The Elvis Room," I said, sitting back.

I'd just made the term up, but it was obvious what it meant: the one room you save back, in case a president or rock star happens to land unannounced at the front desk.

The manager's daughter had laughed and turned the page, and we'd continued with our argument, which finally bled into her mother's office, with the result of five dollars off per week.

It was hardly worth it, had been something of a pyrrhic victory if I'm going to be honest, as well as an indicator of the station I'd fallen to, but that night I couldn't stop thinking about the Elvis Room, as I'd coined it.

Over the next few weeks I consulted with scholars from the humanities, who in turn directed me to texts dealing with urban legends and folk beliefs.

As it turned out, the Elvis Room was from the same branch of formative superstition that kept thirteenth floors of hotels from being called that. I'd heard this years ago, but never investigated. A quick walk through the lobbies of downtown confirmed it, though: the rows of buttons available for passengers to push, they were usually arranged so as to obfuscate that missing, surely evil "13."

We're a funny species.

As for the lore surrounding what I was now confidently calling the Elvis Room, it wasn't something I could glean from a bank of buttons, then grin over to myself.

To find out the truth about it, I had to interview fourteen managers and nearly twice as many assistant managers. Just one disgruntled, former manager would have sufficed, but I had no way of finding such a person. So my approach had to be more scattershot and time-consuming. But such is science.

The assistant manager, who finally admitted that standing orders for the industry were to always leave one room empty, was named . . . Roderick, say. As Roderick understood, the reasons for the Elvis Room had nothing directly to do with "ghosts" or "hauntings" or anything so fantastic. It was just numbers. Statistics.

Once records had started to be kept and, a decade or two after that, collated, then compared from city to city, season to season, chain to chain, the bookkeepers began to notice a certain unsettling trend. In guest fatalities.

So long as one room was left unoccupied, then guests by and large woke up, made it to breakfast. Those instances where a boisterous guest—an Elvis or a president, yes, a cattleman or a couple who couldn't be relegated to the manger—insisted upon registering for that last room, though, well. Nearly without fail, a guest would suffer a stroke or a heart attack in the night, or worse, and the rest of the guests would then be not just inconvenienced by emergency personnel, but spooked, perhaps unlikely to stop by this particular hotel again the next time through.

Which is what it all came down to for the hotels: repeat business. It makes sense for them to leave one room empty, if it means a guest will leave under his or her own power, possibly to return. Guests who are carried out feet-first are poor promotion.

"Is there any pattern to the—the victims?" I asked Roderick.

"What do you mean?" he said back.

He had a way of emphasizing just exactly when you had his full attention. He did it by hardly ever looking at you otherwise.

"Like, is it the guest who takes that last room?" I said. "Or is it someone who's there for a second night? Lone occupancies or doubles? Second floor or twelfth?"

"Online bookings or last-minute, too tired to drive to the next town," Roderick went on, completing my list. He shrugged it off, though: "The pattern is that someone dies," he said, as if I were missing the point.

I thanked him—a good data collector knows when the subject is tapped—promised again to guarantee his anonymity, and passed him the meager sum we'd agreed upon.

Next, I had to crunch the numbers myself. Which involved finding those numbers but—the same way looking over a mathematician's shoulder would be less than gripping—allow me to offer those rough counts are available. Moreover, as near as I could tell from organizing them in columns and rows, Roderick's claim held; in cases of guest deaths, hotels are reluctant to share information, as any press in that regard will perforce be bad press.

I could collect this data myself, however.

I had a theoretical model. The next step was to compare it to observation.

Downtown there was one hotel with a famous glass skywalk across to a coliseum where a certain major music act was performing. I'd seen the lines snaking back from ticket booths all week, and the parking garage next to the coliseum already showed evidence of illegal tents. There were columns in the newspaper about college students renting their apartments for the weekend and getting enough to pay the month's rent.

I'd had enough bad luck. Perhaps I was due a touch of providence. Lady Science will eventually smile down at the strictest of her adherents, yes. The most devout.

It took some work on my part too, however.

At what I deemed the busiest period at the registration desk, when the three clerks manning the counter seemed almost to the end of their shift, perhaps making them less conscientious regarding matters of policy—any problems they cause will be problems for the next shift—I ambled up, began making my case. It took theatrics and intimidation and finally the threat of a diabetic coma (I had purchased the requisite bracelet identification at a thrift store) coupled with assurances that I was not a fan of the music act in question, that this wasn't an emergency born of poor planning or fervid fandom.

I got the Elvis Room.

Walking away from the registration desk, I peeled the wrapper off a bar of candy, bit into it for the glucose. It tasted like victory.

And, while Roderick had no data on which guest is selected to die as punishment for letting that last room go, the fact he didn't know meant that it was rarely, if ever, the Elvis Room.

I slept peacefully. The thread count of the sheets had to be in the thousands.

The next morning found me stationed in the lobby, where not one but two bodies were wheeled through. From, judging by the attendant crying friends, two different rooms.

Going by the age of the mourners, I assumed the bagged bodies were in keeping. Which meant an overdose, most likely, except that one of those friends' shirtfront was still bloody. That the friend wasn't in handcuffs suggested that she'd tried to revive or console the dying. And the blood meant violence. Which was a lot less passive an interference or nudge than I'd suspected.

I wanted to ask, to confirm, except I had to allow the possibility that the culprit was not yet apprehended. Meaning my questioning would put me under suspicion, which would stall the experiment. And right when it was producing such fine results.

Risking my current posting with my absences, I became the oldest fan of this music act, and followed them to their next two cities. The time I wasn't able to get the Elvis Room, there were no bodies. The other time I wasn't able to get it, there was a body, but this was due to the scene I'd seen made at the registration desk, which resulted in the Elvis Room being taken by an obviously pregnant party.

It wasn't the kind of proof that would hold up in a professional journal. But it wasn't anecdotal or apocryphal, either.

I was onto something.

The next vital bit of cultural trivia was delivered to me by a junior in college whose shoes didn't quite match. He was leading a ghost tour in a city I'd just had to move to when my previous posting evaporated in the predictable manner; his outfit's pamphlet had been in the shelf under the night clerk's registration desk. I only went at the last minute, when my neighbors on the fifth floor started into the second episode of their police procedural show on television. It wasn't that I minded the noise, just that I'd already heard that episode, from the last neighbors.

That's unfair, though.

The real reason I wandered out into the night was that I was at the bitter end of two weeks of aimless reworking of the parameters of my work. The momentum was gone, the promise of my early findings about the Elvis Room not leading to an obvious next step, as you always hope will happen.

On the stairs down to street level, I passed only a single other walker. I nodded once and stepped aside, as climbing is more difficult than descending.

The other guest passed without looking up, his hand skating a breath over the dull handrail.

It made me remember my age, grasp the handrail myself.

The bus was right on time, as promised in the pamphlet. I was one of four passengers, and, as the bus was open-top, we were all glad to have worn the light jackets that otherwise would have been unnecessary.

Len, my lore-filled junior, managed to fix our attention on his tip jar four separate times during his well-rehearsed opening remarks, and then, thanks to a headset, he continued to narrate as he drove.

The first stop, of course, was the local cemetery, some of the headstones reaching back to the seventeenth century. Whether the stories he relayed had any basis in fact, I have no idea. Perhaps there really is a coven of vampires buried there. Perhaps there is one more grave than there are headstones. Maybe we should never eat fruit of any tree that grows within that low fence. Maybe the fog there is transportive in nature.

Next was an old convent I didn't know existed. Len painted for us the image of missing children and particularly carnivorous nuns. It was all in good fun. The convent had long been condemned, probably now counting as a historical monument it had so many layers of graffiti festooned on its once-imposing walls.

Three of the other passengers clapped when Len's "surprise" sound effect (a woman's scream) burst through the speakers.

Having our backs straightened was what we had paid for, after all.

Sixteen years ago, I would have wanted to track their galvanic skin response, their respiration, the dilation of their pupils.

Another lifetime.

I was after bigger game now.

And Len, unbeknownst to both of us, was my guide.

Before the next stop, though, I should introduce my third wife. She had been the last to board, and was the least prepared, the least invested in the goings-on. Rather, it seemed this long, meandering bus ride was simply an escape for her. A place to sit where life couldn't harry her.

As I would later come to find out, Len didn't make my third wife pay for these rides. They were her dinner break; she waitressed at the restaurant down the block from my hotel, and traded him baskets of rye bread with spun aluminum cups of whipped butter for the ride.

In the updraft from the bus's open top, her long blond hair lifted like tentacles behind her, and I've always maintained a preference for long hair.

So is love born.

I wasn't very invested in the haunted tour myself. At least, not until the old boarding house.

Because we were in a residential area, Len was able to pull over against the curb and step up from the seat, an open book in his hands. His voice took on shades of the pulpit, of the reverential, of the sour.

The book was thin, available after the tour for ten dollars, no tax.

One chapter contained the reproduction of a journal kept by the former operator of the boarding house in question.

I leaned forward, licked my lips as I do in eagerness, an affectation I'd once been known for, in my first post-doc posting. I didn't even realize I was doing it until the breeze chilled the moisture I'd left.

The passages Len read for us, his voice occasionally falling into a serviceable waver, documented this boarding house operator's observations over the course of seventeen years. And the stories her guests would occasionally share with her.

Because she only had the eight rooms to let, and because the house was creaky even in 1922, she always had a thorough count of her boarders, and a running awareness of who was where and when.

Thus it came as a surprise to her when a boarder would ask about a new boarder they'd passed in the hall, or on the stairway.

There were no new boarders.

With regularity, this continued to happen, year after year. There was never anything malevolent or unsettling about the sightings, either. Only in retrospect did they approach anything spooky. And even then, not necessarily spooky for the boarder, who would assume the landlord was wrong about a new boarder, or hiding a new boarder for reasons all her own. Or it could even be someone who had unaccountably walked in the open front door, used the hall as a hall, then exited out the back.

To this proprietress, though, a Shay Matheson, the accumulation of the sightings led her to form a theory of her "immaterial boarders," as she called them (perhaps a play on "borders," yes): they were simply the souls who had passed on, but for one reason or another, had yet to move on. Perhaps that's how the afterlife works, even; while your paperwork's being processed, your soul weighed against a feather, you while away the days in the waiting room, with the living. As a final goodbye, possibly. Or maybe it's that certain souls have to serve penance with us. Or maybe some people just can't let go as fast as the rest, and so doom themselves to walk the old pathways until they remember what they're supposed to be doing. Where they're supposed to be going.

For the purpose of my experiment, Shay Matheson's conjecture concerning the reason for the walkers' presence was of no use.

Her explanation for their passings in the halls, however, it was a revolution in thinking.

Most who opine on the purpose of ghosts ascribe to them motivations in keeping with our all-too-human motivations. Not Shay Matheson. She understood that the dead are a completely different species.

Her suspicion as to their passings in the halls and on the stairs was that, if her boarder saw this "ghost" and took it for real, for alive, then for a few steps, maybe even a minute or two, this "ghost" could also believe it was alive. She proposed an essentially parasitical relationship, one whereby the host, us, doesn't have to lose nutrition or body mass or reproductive capability, but idle attention. Passing glances. Assumptions.

Further, she proposed that, if this were the case, then these lonely dead people would be drawn to places of crowded anonymity. Her boarding house. Train stations.

Hotels.

Sites where we've been socially conditioned not to engage, which would reveal their essential lack; they're dead, they're ghosts. Sites where you don't question the personhood of that other body in the elevator car, but instead just stare straight ahead, pretending you're all alone.

Your efforts to deny that other rider actual presence is the most obvious statement of that presence.

These spectral walkers are drawn to it like a moth to a candle.

Hotels are their churches.

For steps at a time, they're alive again.

There's a reason that other guest pacing you, three steps ahead, is so silent.

It's that, under his hat, he has no eyes.

Though there were brief nuptials to get through two weeks later, and what we called a placeholder honeymoon up in 566 (room service, room service, room service; apparently waitresses have a fetish for it), my mind was churning with possibility.

I wanted to be with Julia, my new wife—of course—but I also wanted to be out in the halls, putting my research through the paces.

Except for the Heisenberg Principle.

The fact I knew about the walkers introduced something to the experiment which would alter the data in ways that could ruin me a second time.

No, this time my proof had to be irrefutable.

Observational, yes, but also second-hand. From reliable sources.

The most reliable I could find on short notice.

Not hotel employees, trained in the fine art of superstition and possibly trying to drum up tourist dollars, and not paid subjects, willing to tell me whatever I wanted to hear, as I was the one dangling the check. And, as I desperately wanted to hear it, my critical faculties would be compromised from the start, such that I would essentially be colluding with my subjects, suborning perjury, as it were.

It was the first spat of our new marriage.

Without telling Julia the parameters, I poked and prodded her with slight variations on a fixed set of questions. Not so she could be my first subject, but so I could hone the questions.

I needed a set that would elicit candor, that would resist fantasy, and that would operate like those coin sorters, where the pennies all fall into one basin, the quarters another, where a dime is never mistaken for a nickel:

1) How many nights per year, approximately, do you stay in a hotel?

2) For business or personal reasons?

3) How many guests do you think you encounter?

4) Do you pre-book?

You start with the slow pitch, yes, such that they can suspect this just another marketing survey. In the case of this experiment, however, I quickly realized that, once the questions graduated to fast-pitch, they were begging the question:

5) Have you, in your travels, encountered any fellow guests who you later found not to be corporeal?

6) Did you nod to them, or wave, or attempt to converse?

7) If you had a pet, how did that pet react?

8) Would you happen to have a timestamp for this encounter, for purposes of pulling security footage?

I sympathized with Julia, for her annoyance. Reluctant to share the experiment, though, I feigned idle curiosity, fed her the smallest portion: the existence of an Elvis Room in every hotel.

She shrugged and looked at me as if wondering just who she'd married, here.

I shrugged back: here I am, deviant curiosities and all.

During her evening shifts, I would sometimes release my night course an hour early and ease from registration desk to registration desk. At first there was no system; I'd just been driving home when I'd suddenly found myself sitting in the ten-minute lane of a second-rate hotel. Now there was a grid. I was working my way across town, like playing checkers.

That was where the system lost any semblance of rigor, however.

To be more accurate, it wasn't the system that was failing. It was me. Those hours of freedom from teaching, in which I could have been productive, I was, simply put, whiling them away in the lobbies of these hotels.

While there, I found it important to leave my tie knotted close to my throat, and to carry my shoulder bag. Otherwise the evening desk clerk would either query me him- or herself, or have security do so.

My loitering would never have been allowed to continue in Las Vegas, of course. There, if you run one table, you can't just change casinos and do it all over again. Their management talks to each other.

Hotel management doesn't need to be quite so vigilant.

When queried, I had been sent by my current school to meet a visitor, was here on school business. I even had a sign of sorts made up: a piece of copy paper and black marker. Not with a guest name the clerk could check, but for self-identification: the school I was currently contracted with, which my identity card supported, when necessary.

All I had to do was prop the sign up on the end table or couch, and I could sit for an hour, for two if I thought Julia would buy that class had gone long.

I was waiting for inspiration to strike, for the apple to fall, for a disinhibiting symbol to synthesize and simultaneously release the next step of my experiment.

All I had thus far was enough, perhaps, to bolster an article on folklore or urban legends.

What I needed was a revolution, a revelation. A new career, a new life. If the world wouldn't accept me now, then I would change the world, make it hinge upon the results of my experiment.

And, though it goes without saying—and this would never be part of my published findings—I did find myself believing. I had stood there in the lobby of that concert hotel, and watched the bloody-sheeted gurney creak past.

Though I told myself that if I hadn't insisted upon the Elvis Room, someone else surely would have . . . still.

My rational mind argued that the science was worth the sacrifice. That this is what a haunting actually is: torturing yourself with a looped event from the past that your mind can find no easy label for. What doesn't fit, it just bounces around in your head; I'm hardly the first to propose such a theory. Only now, I guess, you could say I was living it.

In a way, then, sitting in these hotel lobbies, it could be construed as a sort of apology—me standing close to a fire I had started, as if the heat could burn the sin away.

Unless I was waiting to overhear a belligerent would-be guest demanding the Elvis Room, then quietly rooting for him or her, and camping out by the coffee machine, waiting for the emergency personnel to arrive.

Three weeks into this cycle, this tailspin, a hotel guest sat down beside me, waited for me look up.

"Sorry I'm late," he said, wowing his eyes out for emphasis. "Guess I fell asleep. It's already midnight for me."

I let my eyes move from his face to the sign that had drawn him to me.

"I'm sorry," I said. "Your ride, he's—I'm waiting for someone else. We house all the college's guests here."

"Oh, man. Who?"

My jaw moved around the shape of an imaginary professor's name, but then I noticed the desk clerk was tuned in, here.

"She's from Biology," I said.

"Two of us?" the man said, and though the muscles forcing my face into a polite smile held, I'm pretty sure, I could feel the scaffolding starting to collapse.

"Let me just—" I said, rising to follow my index finger to the guest phone, stationed near enough the side door I could slip out.

I had the phone to my ear when the clerk tapped me on the shoulder.

I swallowed, re-cradled the receiver.

"Perhaps it would be best if I called your guest for you," he said, reaching across for the phone.

"I don't want to wake her," I said back, my hand holding the receiver down.

The clerk chuckled, didn't want a scene.

"Then maybe it would be best if you were to wait outside. Across the street. There's a bar."

I almost had to grin in thanks.

"I could use a drink," I told him.

He smiled, stepped across to hold the door open for me, and said, "It's good you chose this night. Tomorrow, there's a conference on . . . criminal behavior, I think it is."

"A conference?" I asked, just because it was my slot to fill in our little game of charades.

"Police," the clerk hissed, then pulled the door shut.

Standing on the sidewalk, I smiled, my face suddenly warm in spite of the night air.

Of course.

I needed the most reliable set of sources possible for my experiment. The most no-nonsense, the least prone to invention.

The Policeman's Ball it was.

Three weeks later, I rented a room at the hotel designated for next law enforcement officer's meeting I'd been able to find.

I told Julia it was research. Then, after she left for the restaurant, I withdrew her savings, promising myself to pay her back ten-fold, to deliver her into a life she'd never even guessed at.

Provided she didn't check her balance, press charges.

The conference, as it turned out, was surprisingly easy to infiltrate. I'd assumed law enforcement personnel would have better screening in place, but all I had to do, finally, was ask at lost and found for the convention badge I'd lost, then select the male-named one from the two the desk clerk provided.

After that, I simply camped out in my room Friday and Saturday nights. I couldn't risk sitting in on a talk or a panel, and having someone call me by the name on my lanyard.

Sunday morning, however, I emerged. Not crisp and ironed, as if new-minted, but just as rumpled and ready to go home as the rest of the crowd.

Then I simply requisitioned one of the abandoned tables in the exhibit room and put up the least explanatory of handmade signs: SKETCH ARTIST?

On my table, I had a pad of drawing paper with the top few sheets ripped off. To prime the pump, as it were.

Slowly, they trickled in.

This wasn't a sketch artist conference—do those even exist?—but the conference did bill itself as hosting a set of panels especially dealing with facial recognition, so I gambled that departments would have sent whatever sketch artists they had on contract.

I was right.

They weren't exactly lining up to draw for me, but once word got around about my experiment, and that I was paying forty dollars per—well.

Julia would have been proud, to see her money put to such good use.

And then there was the added draw of competition.

My pitch was that, over the course of the weekend, I'd paid a current parolee to skulk around at the edges, never quite making eye contact or engaging in conversation. But there. Probably only once, so think, remember.

Whichever sketch artist rendered him the best, made him or her the most identifiable—there was going to be a "line-up" during closing ceremonies later this afternoon—would win the three-hundred dollar jackpot.

They didn't care whether I was trying to prove their craft or discredit it. They just shrugged, looked up and to the right more times than not, and began to sketch.

By two o'clock, I had sixteen sketches.

At which point I put up my "back in five" sign, collected the sketches, and made my exit.

I'd already checked out that morning, so I could go immediately to my car.

The plan was to get back to my room with Julia, distract her as well as I could from the chance of thinking about her savings account, then spend the night appreciating these last few drops of a secondhand life. Because it was all about to change.

In order to not contaminate the data-collection phase, I'd not yet taken the next step in the research.

As it turned out, though, now I couldn't wait.

That next step, which a lesser scientist would have started with, was to look up as many of the deaths in that hotel as I could, and then search for faces.

I hadn't done this beforehand as I might then become the "whisperer" to the sketch artists, indicating to them with non-verbal cues that, no, his hair wasn't that long, his jaw more square, her eyes more vulnerable.

Just on the chance of my influencing the sketches, I'd not even looked at them yet, but had insisted the artists do their work with the tablet facing away from me, then fold their work before selling it to me.

Outside the public library, I patted the sketches there on my passenger seat but resisted again. Told myself it would be better science to collect all the dead faces I could, instead of the five or ten that I thought matched what I'd already seen.

When you've been strung up and burned in effigy once, your control parameters the next time out—they can get obsessive, yes.

Whatever helps the experiment, though. That always comes first.

The library finally had to chase me out at closing.

Dime by dime, I'd printed face after face. The first few I'd looked at in an idle way, but two dozen in—the hotel had been in operation for sixty-four years—I'd become an automaton, just click/print, click/print.

With my sheaf of corpses, then, I stumbled out to my car, and finally broke down—as I knew I would—and paged through the sketches, sorting them without meaning to.

Three of the artists had drawn the same man I'd seen over the shoulder of countless news anchors: sunglasses, five o'clock shadow, firm mouth, grim eyes. Perhaps this was the same person of interest they drew every time out, their way of gaming the system. Or maybe criminals actually conformed to a certain appearance, unlikely as that seemed. It wasn't my province to say.

I was here for other reasons. Deeper reasons.

Twelve of the remaining thirteen had drawn a balding man with an almost comically wide mouth, his eyes vague and directed elsewhere, as if the artists hadn't quite "made" them, so could only approximate.

I nodded, smiled.

They were trained to pay attention to distinguishing characteristics, which in turn made them sensitive to faces with characteristics that distinguished those faces. Memorable faces.

It didn't token well for people with wide-set eyes or unfortunate scars, but it did suggest that the more successful criminals could just as easily have been good fits for the FBI: vague, easy-to-forget faces. Nobody special, just part of the background.

This balding man, though—had I seen him, had I left my room and encountered him, I would have remembered him as well.

Under the dim glow of a streetlight, then, at ten minutes till eleven on a Sunday night, I made the discovery of my century: this balding man had died there fourteen years ago. In his sleep.

I let my head fall back and I laughed, and then I looked all around, for someone to share this with.

It was just me, though.

I had figured it out. What no one else had. Sure, two generations ago, boarding-house proprietress Shay Matheson had made intimations in this direction, stabs in the dark, as it were. But this was real, this was verifiable. More, it was repeatable.

That's always the final test.

The world was going to have to accept me back, now.

I knew where its dead were.

Walking through the lobby of what I was now calling my temporary home—our temporary home—a Jerry Lee Lewis song was coming from the night clerk's tinny radio. The night clerk was nowhere to be seen.

I stood and listened to it, felt my eyes unfocus, like . . . I don't know. But something. And then I got it: a paper I'd tried to write in graduate school. Not an article, my major professor assured me, but good as exercise, anyway. And to insulate myself, should I have animal testing issues lobbed my way later in my career.

The paper, which I never completed, as the research wasn't worth running down, had to do with finding dogs and cats retired from laboratory testing. Just surgical cases, nothing pharmaceutical. The same way police dogs are farmed out, to while away their final years.

I knew most lab animals were destroyed once they'd served their purpose. But not always.

My idea was to track some of them down, in their dotage. And, if they'd been conditioned on a certain tone of chime, say, to then strike that chime again, and observe the response. The stated concern was muscle memory, more or less. Really, though, I wanted to watch their eyes. Not to see if that chime was conjuring a specific experiment, but to see if they got a wary look, as if the lab were assembling itself around them again.

That was how I felt, standing at the vacant registration desk: like an old dog hearing an old chime—Jerry Lee Lewis. Contemporary of Elvis Presley. The piano player many said should have been Elvis Presley, if not for his much-publicized marriage.

Listening to him, it was just forced déjà vu, then. Like I was standing at the lip of my world, looking over into the next.

I was tired. It had been a full weekend. My body was crashing from all the adrenaline of discovery.

Julia.

I think I actually said her name out loud, and looked up through four ceilings, four floors. Like she could save me from myself, here.

Because I'd stopped taking the stairs since Shay Matheson's journal, I waited for the elevator, stepped in, and, reliable as ever, it carried me up to my hall.

It was empty. Even the two times I looked behind me.

I tried to laugh at myself, about how stupid I was being.

It was guilt, I knew. A responsible researcher, one who's not in a movie, anyway, knows the first thing you do when you verify a hypothesis is to document it, and seal that away somewhere. Nothing official, just enough so that, if you leave your lab or your office, step in front of a bus—or into a plunging elevator—then the research can survive you.

That's what I was feeling: the weight of being the only one, so far, to know.

It made my head light on my shoulders, my steps ponderous, historic.

Perhaps this was what success felt like.

I'd better get used to it, I told myself, and then, rounding the molded-in pillar to 566, I looked down the hall behind me one more time. Just for superstition.

Empty. As I knew it would be.

Some nights, every step is an experiment.

I shook my head, grinned, and went to insert my keycard. Into the already-open door.

It swung back as if from the weight of my unasked questions.

I swallowed loudly, stepped into the doorway. "Julia?" I called, my voice hushed in that token way, as I had to assume she was sleeping. But I also assumed that she would be eager to wake, to see me.

The lights came on when I touched them, proving this wasn't a horror movie.

The room was as it always was: a sitting area, a kitchen on one wall, the bed against the other.

The bed was made but rumpled, as if someone had laid there.

I touched those wrinkles, touched the edge of the sink as well, as if confirming her absence, and then, nodding to myself, I went back to the door, sure I had the wrong number, had gotten off at the wrong floor.

566.

I shook my head no, tried to play back Julia's schedule, just came up with six o'clock again. It was when she got home every Sunday, because she'd lied to the headwaiter that she was religious. The kind of religious that likes brunch tips, though, right? I think he'd said. It was all because of a show she liked.

I breathed in, breathed out.

"You should be here," I told her, and, still shaking my head no, I stepped across, to deposit my files and sketches on the two-person table.

And that was when I saw it.

A carbon of the withdrawal on her savings account. Dated Saturday morning. When the bank was only open for four scant hours, and all the way across town, at that.

But she'd gone there.

And now she wasn't here.

I wanted to laugh, wanted to cry. Timing, that's all it was. Soon I was going to shower her with money, with respect, with fame. She'd been investing in our future, I wanted to tell her. She just hadn't known it. She'd been ensuring the science could continue.

I didn't know what to do.

Wait until her lunch shift tomorrow, sit at one of her tables? Catch her taking break on the haunted bus tour, start all over again?

I opened the window, telling myself it was to study the city, but I'd read enough studies to know it was either a response to this sense of claustrophobia—opening the window would increase the range of my options, or let me feel like that, anyway—or a result of the way my culture had programmed me: the romantic gestures were ingrained. The city festering below me was supposed to be epic, a big machine I could never stop, my problems just the smallest of cogs.

This is what you do at these moments. You gaze into the distance. You feel sorry for yourself.

And finally, you see yourself in the reflection.

Except, this time, I wasn't alone.

On the bed behind me, sitting with her back to me, was—

"Jules!" I said, spinning around, and then I felt behind me for the wall, for the table, for a part of the real world I could hold onto: Julia had blond hair. It wasn't restaurant policy, but it might as well have been.

The woman who had been on my bed, her hair had been spilling down her back like ink in water, like raven feathers, so black it was almost coming back around to blue. And long enough I could have lost my arm in there.

I shook my head *no, no.*

"You're dead," I told her.

I was talking to Mary.

That's her real name, yes.

I hadn't looked her up in all the years since, because I knew it would be litany of institutions, of séances that were supposed to fix her, of more and more desperate attempts to finally, please, be alone. I hadn't looked her up because, in addition to what she'd been burdened with before coming to me, now she was a laughingstock, as well.

I hadn't looked her up, no, but, in looking up the rest of the dead for my research, my search terms had found her all the same, suicided in a motel room half a country away. Tired of running from whatever had been pursuing her.

Personal demons, I would have said, at the beginning of my career.

When I had a career.

I tried to take a step, to get to the hall, but the muscles of my leg were in revolt, it seemed.

"You're dead!" I said again, to no one.

I scooped up my research, held it close, and finally managed, keeping constant contact with the kitchen-counter, to scrape and slide my way to the door.

An instant before I eased the door shut, the light went off.

I ran, clutching my papers.

Crashing down the stairs two and three at a time, I shifted the sketches and files in order to keep contact with the handrail, and I remembered the gentlemen I had met coming down the stairs the night of my haunted bus tour, the night I met Julia. How his hand had just been skating along the rail, but never quite touching it.

Because he couldn't.

Had he placed himself there to witness, though? Had he been a scout of sorts, from the other side, somehow herding me onto that haunted bus? Did they want me to meet Julia?

I fell down the last flight, collected myself, burst out into the lobby, fully expecting it to be standing room only, packed with the dead, there to receive me in their quiet, patient way. To carry me to their god, or feast on what was left of my reason.

The lobby was empty.

I collected myself as best I could, just caught a falling sketch. It was the sixteenth.

I'd initially dismissed it as incomplete, as too vague to be included in the data set.

Now I saw it for what it was: that same balding man, just featureless in a way. No eyes, no mouth.

But an intent, somehow. A grim intent.

I pushed the sketch away, turned to the registration desk.

The clerk, still half-asleep, was studying me. Trying to fit me into his narrative of the night, it seemed.

"My wife," I said to him, piling my papers on the desk, struggling to corral them, keep them from becoming the avalanche they wanted to be.

"Your wife," he said back to me, my prompt to actually complete this question.

"Did she—did she leave a note?" I said, working so hard to control my voice.

"Oh, oh yeah," he said, narrowing his eyes and looking away. A poker player's gaze. A gunfighter's stare.

I reached across, pulled him to me by his shirtfront, so our faces were close enough I could taste the musty sleep on his breath.

"I can tell the manager you were sleeping on the job, you know," I told him, trying my best to hiss it across.

"No rooms to register, man," he said, breaking my hold, adopting a tone for a moment that I associated with music videos, with "gangster." It was his tough persona, that he usually didn't need for work.

This wasn't a usual night, though.

"No rooms?" I said, panic creeping all the way into my voice, now.

"Your wife, man, she—she knew we always held one back somehow. I figured what the hell, right? Andrew Jackson speaks with the weight of history . . . "

"She's in the Elvis Room?"

"Elvis is in the building?" he said, a smile curling up from the right side of his mouth, his eyes mock-darting to the lobby behind me, for Elvis.

"She's in that last room?" I said.

"With explicit instructions—"

"Which one," I said across to him.

When he just gave me that same stare, I slowly, as if showcasing it, pulled out my wallet, and started laying down Julia's money, twenty by twenty. "Jackson by Jackson," to him. It made it worse.

At two hundred and forty, all of it, the clerk shrugged.

"Guess she didn't say anything about not telling you what floor," he said, pulling the bills across, folding them around his thumb like a Vegas dealer. "Try nine, boss man. Nine might just be your lucky number, tonight."

"Odd or even?" I said.

"Your lucky numbers tonight won't be prime . . . " he said in his best fortune-cookie voice, liking this game so much more than I was. I turned, was already running.

Someone was going to die here tonight, I knew. One way or another. Quiet or loud. Because there are rules. The Elvis Room, it was occupied. And Julia was here. And Mary.

I punched the elevator call button continually until the door dinged open, and it was just sliding shut when a hand stabbed in, caught it.

The clerk, I knew, going back on his deal.

Instead, there was the distinctive sound of gurney wheels.

I knew it from the lobby of that concert hotel.

I went to dislodge the fingers but they were already gone. The door swished shut.

I breathed out, was going to have twenty seconds to myself here. Nearly half a minute to collect myself, to prepare. To settle down.

Except I wasn't alone.

In the distorted reflection afforded by the brass frame around the numbered buttons, I could just see an absolutely still shape in the corner behind me, to the right. Small enough to be miles away, yet necessarily within five feet. Which was one single lunge.

And it wasn't looking down like they're supposed to, either. Like anybody in an elevator is supposed to, living or dead. It was watching me. With the hollow cavities that used to hold eyes.

I spider-walked my fingers down the double-row of buttons, afraid of any sudden motions, of any offensive sounds, and when the elevator jerked up in response to my selection, the lights faltered in exactly the way they never had before, in all my time here. Not a bad connection so much as the light not pushing out far enough from the bulb. A dark flash.

I turned around, protecting the back of my neck with my hands for some reason, but when the light came back, I was alone again.

I told myself I had been alone the whole time. That this was all in my head.

My breath hitched once, twice, and I threw up anyway, my vomit splashing the brass handrail. At the end of it my eyes were crying, my hand shaking.

When the elevator car shuddered to a stop I crowded the door to make my escape.

It opened onto the balding man with the wide mouth. Just standing there, his head lowered as is proper for them, as if death is a lower class, not a separate state, but even lowered, I knew the specific planes and contours of that face. I'd seen it on sketch paper over and over, until I'd felt my own mouth spreading into a rictus, in sympathetic response.

Instead of twitching a shoulder or pulling his mouth improbably wider—I would have screamed—he just stood there, the "5" on the wall over his shoulder indicating that I'd hit the wrong number, that I was on my floor, not Julia's. Not her new one.

Once upon a time, I had told Mary that the dead couldn't hurt you. Even if you could see them somehow, still, how could they interact?

She'd wanted so badly to believe me. She'd wanted so badly for science to save her.

Here was the refutation of my claim, though.

What this dead man was telling me was that I could get off here if I wanted. That I could call it a night, if I was ready to retire. If I could be content with letting them proceed with what they had to do.

He was an usher, fully prepared to nod as I passed, keep his face thankfully hidden.

I could sleep this all off.

Except I couldn't. Because of Julia.

This was no longer an experiment. This was my life.

"Wrong floor," I said, giving my voice the smallest amount of air possible, and like I'd started a great clockwork mechanism, the balding man started to raise his face, and I punched the door-close button deep enough to splinter a fingernail.

I scrabbled for nine and hit it again and again, my lips praying for the first time since childhood. It wasn't words from the Bible but a basic diagnostic procedure. Still, it worked: four dings later, the ninth floor hall opened up before me.

It was empty.

Somehow that was worse.

"Two, three, five, seven," I recited to myself, navigating from side to side, figuring out that the evens were all to my left, even if "2" was stubbornly prime.

I ran past the first three doors, not sure how to conjure Julia. I started hammering on them at the fourth, and went down the hall that way, *bang bang bang* then run, do it again.

Until I got to 922.

It was already open.

There was a burgundy apron with white stitching on the part of the floor I could see. It matched the upholstery of the waiting room benches at Julia's restaurant.

I looked behind me, to the people I'd roused. A woman in her milky nightgown, a man in faded boxer shorts, another man in a suit jacket, his tie loosened for Scotch. They were trying to figure me out, and to map the appropriate response.

"Call security," I told them, holding my empty palm up to show them I wasn't the threat here, and then I shook my head *no* and stepped into the room.

Julia was sleeping just under the sheets like she liked, because of a report she'd seen on hotel comforters. The heater was on to compensate. And the lamp was on because she was alone. And the box of tissues was by the lamp, because of me.

I wanted to tell her everything.

But at street level.

I was three steps into the room when the white sheet she was under began to stain red.

I opened my mouth to . . . I don't know.

The door clicked shut behind me, the light flickered again in that new way it had, and in the flash of darkness before it came back, I saw him. The balding man with the wide mouth, the empty eyes.

He was looking right at me, now. Past his lips, in his mouth, it was the same blackness as behind his eyes. As where his eyes had been.

"We didn't—we didn't mean to, to take the last—" I tried.

The lights came back up and he remained, and the rational part of my brain slowed the scene down, made it make sense: if the dead congregated at hotels so as to be mistaken for real people, then—then they would insist on management leaving a room free.

They could all huddle there. Not sleeping, they don't need to sleep, just standing shoulder to shoulder. Probably all the ones who hadn't ventured out, the ones who hadn't been seen. But this was second best; it was something they remembered from being alive: fresh towels, a crisply made bed. The pad of paper waiting under its pen, the pen you always knock under the bed, never reach down for, afraid of what you'll touch.

Here, if it was empty, the dead could be just like the living, for the night. They were staying in a hotel room. And it looked just like they remembered.

If there weren't any rooms, though, then they'd be forced to walk the halls when none of us were.

It would make them feel even more dead. It would remind them that they had no rooms. That they didn't need them.

At which point, they would start sneaking into rooms, bold and angry, desperate for a room to get empty, so they could pretend until morning again. And one of the rooms would end up empty, one way or another.

Shay Matheson would have seen the truth of it.

And I wished I didn't.

"I won't tell anybody," I said to the man, and he angled his head over, so some of his dead blood spilled from the corner of his mouth.

It never hit the floor. His shirt was soaking it up, not getting any blacker from it.

Pretty soon the decal there would be drowned.

Because his face was his face, I followed the blood, instead. It's instinctual for the predators we once were; motion means food, and food means life.

In this case, it led me the opposite way: to the shirt's emblem.

It was the logo of the music act that had filled that first hotel.

"You," I said, my skin crawling in a way I'd never documented in my early studies.

He lifted his arm as if to caress my face, and his elbow squealed with the sound of gurney wheels.

"I'm sorry," I said, my voice cracking at last, and when the lamp flickered again, I felt the atmospheric pressure in the room shift the smallest bit, too small a fraction for any but the finest neck hair to ever register.

Someone was joining us.

I barricaded my head with my arms and barreled back out into the hall, running blind now, not even enough breath to scream like my body was telling me to.

When the elevator wouldn't come no matter how much I hit the button, I fell into the stairway, but this was the maintenance stairwell that always got cocked open for the smokers. It only went up.

I took it anyway, crashed up onto the roof, the night air chilling the sweat I was coated in.

I laughed, fell to my knees.

I'd made it.

The dead had already taken their one life, the sacrifice they needed.

I was sorry it had to be Julia, but—but I had to publish what I knew, didn't I? In honor of her, now. As her memoriam.

I sat down out of the wind for the tears I knew were coming, that I already wasn't proud of, that I felt I owed her—science is never cheap—but, patting my pockets for a cocktail napkin, I came up instead with a pen stamped with the hotel name, the pen I'd assumed she'd knocked off the nightstand to roll under the bed, start its cycle anew.

It was coated in blood, this pen.

The blood would be Julia's.

I dropped it, watched its tacky barrel collect the smaller of the asphalt gravel to its shaft.

"They're trying to discredit me," I said, in wonder, and then looked all around, peeled out of my jacket and ran to the edge of the roof, let the jacket go, had to shake my hand when the sleeve caught on my shirt. And then, because the dead had to have secreted more damning evidence on me, I stripped out of the rest of my clothes, let them flutter down as well, drape over trees and streetlights, collect on windshields and in window planters.

"Now what are you going to do!" I screamed to them, trapped below, walking the halls for eternity.

Except Shay Matheson had said nothing about that.

I turned, this time sure it was going to be to a sea of hungry faces gathered in the moonlight. Because they had nowhere else to go.

I was still alone. And, now, naked. On top of the city.

"What do you want?" I said to my idea of them, my voice cracking. I felt back with my bare feet until I had to step up onto the narrow brick ledge, my heels hanging over a hundred feet of open air, my toes gripping down in response.

I wavered my arms, my chest hollowing out, and I would have gone over, except a hand grasped my wrist.

It was Julia.

There was no kindness in her eyes, though. There were no eyes at all.

"I didn't mean—not for you . . . " I said, trying to cover her hand with my other one, but she was already gone.

Not for you, I heard like an echo, and I knew it meant that this world wasn't for me. Not anymore. Not now that I knew its secrets.

"But my research," I pleaded, balancing back and forth, and then I saw there was blood on my hand. From the pen. From the balding man I had to admit I'd killed. From Mary, whom I'd always known I'd killed, even before I knew she was dead. From Julia, wherever I'd stabbed her: neck, eyes, base of the skull. In the crook of the groin, that ballpoint nosing around for the femoral artery. I could almost even remember the effort.

I didn't have any pants to wipe the blood on, so I brought it to my mouth.

It tasted right, so I left my fingers there.

Across the street a woman in the window of an apartment building was watching me, the light from her television set making one side of her glow rancid blue. Twentieth-century blue.

She shook her head *no* twice, suggesting maybe I shouldn't do this, and when she turned to look suspiciously behind her, her hair swept around. No, it cascaded down her back, it spilled down her back, it tumbled down her back in something a lot like slow motion, from where I was standing.

Mary?

"But I have to," I told her—she of all people would understand—"my research, see?" and then I looked down nine stories, into why I'd been left no option but the roof: because this proved my theory.

My notes were all down on the desk.

All the world needed now was my body.

I would get a tickertape parade, for what this would prove.

"It's science," I said across to the woman like the best secret ever, and then I looked past her, to her shadow self standing against her apartment wall, her murdered twin who threw no shadow, and she saw me looking, bared her teeth in a way that I had to turn away from. Because she had too many. Because her mouth was too wide. Because there was no explanation.

Where I turned was to the safety of the empty roof, except it was empty no more. Julia was thirty feet off. Murdered, dead Julia, thirty feet off, bare feet on the gravel, some of it sticking to the side of her feet, her own hair lifting with the wind. Not because it had to, but because it remembered. Because it wanted to lift.

It gave my chest a hollow feeling, like falling.

"I don't think she heard," she said with her impossible mouth, and I started to look back to that window across the way but stopped, came back.

Julia was rushing towards me on all fours, her twisted oval well of a mouth open, to swallow my soul.

"Science," I said again, weaker than I meant to say it, and she dove into me, to take us both over the edge, to prove my theory. If I couldn't have the tickertape parade, then I could get a tickertape funeral procession, anyway.

But, like I'd told Mary: the dead are immaterial.

Julia passed right into me, didn't come out the other side, and I fell forward into the black gravel, gasping, sure now of only one thing, a thing Mary should have warned me about all those years ago, what she'd learned from having eaten her own twin in the womb: that I could live like she had, or I could join the ranks of the dead, become a walker.

Killing isn't free, as it turns out.

I could feel it in the pit of my stomach, now. I could see it between my hands, directly under my eyes: Julia's toes. They were black, decaying, frostbitten from walking on the other side.

She was waiting for me to decide.

"Nobody will believe me if I don't—if I don't . . . " I said, my foolish tears collecting on the end of my nose.

I was trying to convince her of my own suicide. I was asking her permission. For one last kindness, one last withdrawal from her account.

"When I saw you on the bus that night—" I started, but then the gravel crunched again, and again, and all around. In my peripheral vision, there were discolored feet and shins in every direction, an army of the dead. Tattered pant legs, skirts trailing their own hems. Skin slicked with blood, toes crusted with hoarfrost and cracking open, the darkness within blooming.

They'd all come. To be seen.

I shook my head no, finally.

It was a promise. To not publish this in a peer-reviewed journal, as hard-earned findings, but in the usual places, if at all.

Turn the page to find out about Bigfoot, yes. For the incontrovertible truth about aliens.

And then I collapsed into the black gravel, hid my face, my naked back ready for their cold teeth, and when I woke that black gravel was pocked into my face.

Julia helped me up, guided me back to the land of the living, and here I remain, a shell of a man, a ghost of a human, playing out each day, each act of each moment, as if I'm alone, as if the darkness of a shallow closet or a kitchenette doesn't make me look away. And if some nights I spin a certain record in the privacy of my room in these lonely, crowded hotels and close my eyes to soak it in, please allow me this smallest of pleasures.

I'm not Elvis, no. But I've been in his room.

It was Hell.

Stephen Graham Jones is the author of fifteen novels and six short story collections. The most recent are *Not for Nothing*, *After the People Lights Have Gone Off*, and, with Paul Tremblay, *Floating Boy and the Girl Who Couldn't Fly*.

Jones has more than two hundred stories published, many reprinted in best of the year annuals. He's won the Texas Institute of Letters Award for fiction, the Independent Publishers Award for Multicultural Fiction, and an NEA fellowship in fiction. He teaches in the MFA programs at CU Boulder and UCR–Palm Desert.

He lives in Boulder, Colorado, with his wife and kids. For more information: demontheory.net or @SGJ72.

Cats have secrets rooted in antiquity and spanning worlds,
secret histories known to very few living men and women . . .

THE CATS OF RIVER STREET (1925)

Caitlín R. Kiernan

1.

Essie Babson lies awake, listening to the soft, soft murmur of the Manuxet flowing by, on its way down to the harbor and the sea beyond. Unable to find sleep, or unable to be found by sleep, she listens to the voice of the river and thinks about the long trip the waters have made, all the way from the confluence of the Pemigewasset and the Winnipesaukee, and before that, the headwaters at Franconia Notch and faraway Profile Lake in the White Mountains of New Hampshire. The waters have traveled hundreds of miles just to keep her company in the stillness of this too-warm last night of July. Or so she briefly chooses to pretend. Of course, the waters of the river, like all the rest of the wide world, neither know nor care about this sleepless spinster woman, but it's a pretty thought, all the same, and she holds tightly to it.

Some insomniacs count sheep; Essie traces the courses of rivers.

"You're still awake?" asks her sister, Emiline.

"I thought you were asleep," Essie sighs and turns over onto her right side, rolling over to face Emiline.

"No, no, it's too hot to sleep," Emiline replies. "I'm so tired, but it's really much too hot. I'm sweating on my sheets. They're soaked right through with sweat."

"Me, too," says Essie. "Mine, too."

There's only a single window in the second-story bedroom, and both storm shutters are open and the sash is raised. But the night is so still there's no breeze to bring relief, to stir the stagnant air trapped inside the room with the two women.

"Think about the river," Essie tells her sister. "Shut your eyes and think about the river and how cool it must be, out there in the night. Think about the harbor and the bay."

"No, I won't do that," Emiline says. "You know I won't do that. Why would you even suggest such a thing, when you know I won't."

Essie shuts her eyes. The room smells of perspiration and dust, talcum powder, tea rose perfume, and the potpourri they order from a shop in Boston. The latter sits in a bowl on the chifforobe: a salmagundi of allspice, marjoram leaves, rose hips, lavender, juniper and cinnamon bark, with a little mugwort thrown in to help keep the moths at bay. Emiline insists on having a bowl of the potpourri in every room in the high old house on River Street. She dislikes the smell of the Manuxet and the fishy, low-tide smells of the bay, whenever the wind blows from the east, and also the muddy odor of the salt marshes, whenever the wind blows from the west or south or north. Essie has never minded these smells, and sometimes they even comfort her, the way the sound of the river sometimes comforts her. But she also rarely minds the scent of the potpourri. Tonight, though, the potpourri is cloying and unwelcome, and it almost seems as if it could smother her, as if it means to seep up her nostrils and drown her.

Emiline is deathly afraid of drowning, which, of course, is why it was foolishness to suggest that thinking of the river might help her to sleep.

Essie rolls onto her back once more, and the box springs squeak like a bucket of angry mice.

"I'm going to buy a new mattress," she says.

And, again, Emiline says, "It's much too hot to sleep." Then she adds, "It's very silly, lying here, not sleeping, when there's work to be done."

"Yes, in the autumn, I think I will definitely buy a new mattress."

"There's really nothing wrong with the mattress you have," says Emiline.

"You don't know," Essie replies. "You don't have to sleep on it. Sometimes I think there are stones sewn up inside it."

"I should get up," whispers Emiline, and Essie isn't sure if her sister is speaking to her or speaking to herself. "I could get some baking done. A pie, some biscuits. It'll be too hot to bake after sunrise."

"Em, it's to hot to bake now. Try to sleep."

Then the door creaks open, just enough to admit their striped ginger tom Horace to the bedroom, and Essie listens to the not-quite inaudible padding of velvet paws against the white-pine floorboards. Horace reaches the space between the women's beds, and he pauses there a moment, deciding which sister he's in the mood to curl up with. The moonlight coming in through the open window is bright, and Essie can plainly see the cat, sitting back on its haunches, watching her.

"Well, where have you been?" she asks the ginger tom. "Making certain we're safe from marauding rodents?"

The cat glances her way, then turns its head towards Emiline.

Emiline calls Horace their "tough old gentleman." His ears are tattered, and there are ugly scars crisscrossing his broad nose and marring his flanks and shoulders, souvenirs of the battles he's won and lost. The sisters have had him for almost seventeen years now, since he was a tiny kitten, since they were both still young women. They found him one afternoon in the alley out back of the Gilman House, hiding behind an empty produce crate, and Emiline named him Horace, after Horace Greeley. It seemed an odd choice to Essie, but she's never asked her sister to explain herself. It isn't a bad name for a cat, and the kitten seemed to grow into it.

"Well, make up your mind," Essie says. "Don't take all night."

"Don't rush him," Emiline tells her. "What's the hurry. It's not as if we're going anywhere."

Downstairs, the grandfather clock in the front parlor chimes midnight.

And then Horace chooses Emiline. He jumps—a little stiffly—up onto her bed and, after sniffing about the quilt and sheets for a bit, lies down near her knees. Essie feels slightly disappointed, but then the cat has always preferred her sister. She sighs and stares up at the fine cracks in the ceiling plaster, concentrating once again on the soft, wet sound of the Manuxet flowing between River and Paine streets.

Across from her, Horace purrs himself and Emiline to sleep. After another hour or so, Essie also drifts off to sleep, and she dreams of tall ships and the sea.

2.

The brass bell hung over the shop door jingles, and Bertrand Cowlishaw—proprietor of River Street Grocery and Dry Goods—looks up from his newspaper just long enough to note that it's the elder Miss Babson who has come in. He nods to the woman as she eases the door shut behind her. Though the shades are drawn against the noonday heat, and despite the slowly spinning electric ceiling fan, it's stifling inside the dusty, dimly lit shop.

"And how are you today, Miss Babson," he says, then turns his attention back to the front page of a two-week old edition of the *Gloucester Daily Times*. Bertrand is old enough to remember when it wasn't so hard to get newspapers from Gloucester and Newburyport, and even as far away as Boston, in a timely fashion. He's old enough to remember when the offices of the *Innsmouth Courier* were still in business, and also he remembers when it quietly folded amid rumors of threats from elders of the Esoteric Order, of which it had frequently been openly critical.

"A bit out of sorts, Bert," she replies. "Emiline and me, we're having trouble sleeping again. It's the heat, I suppose. You'd think it would rain, wouldn't you? I can't recall such a dry summer." And then she picks up a can of peaches in heavy syrup and stares at the label a moment before setting in back on the shelf.

"Hot as Hades," Bertrand agrees, "and dry as a bone, to boot. You got a list there, Miss Babson?"

She tells him yes, she certainly does, and takes her neatly penned grocery list from a pocket of her gingham dress. It's written on the back of a letter from a cousin who moved away to Gary, Indiana, several years ago. Essie goes to the counter, stepping around a barrel of apples piled so high it's a marvel they haven't spilled out across the floor, and she gives the envelope to Bertrand.

"I confess, we haven't had much of an appetite," she tells the grocer. "And neither of us wants to cook, the house being as terribly hot as it is."

While Bertrand examines the list, Essie steals a glance at his newspaper, reading it upside down. The headline declares SCOPES FOUND GUILTY OF TEACHING EVOLUTION, and there's a photograph of William Jennings Bryan, smug and smiling for the press. Farther down the page, there's an article on a coal strike in West Virginia and another on the great-grandnephew of Napoleon Bonaparte. Essie Babson tends to avoid news of the world outside of Innsmouth, as it never seems to be anything but unpleasant. In all her forty years, she's not traveled farther from home than Ipswich and Hamilton, neither more than six miles away, as the crow flies . . .

"Let's see," says Bertrand, as he gathers the items from her shopping list and places them in a cardboard box. "Condensed milk, icing sugar, one can of lime juice, baking powder, raspberry jam, a dozen eggs, a can of lima beans. We do have some nice fresh blueberries, as it happens, if you and—"

"No, no," she tells him. "Just what's on the list, please."

"Very well, Miss Babson. Just thought I'd mention the blueberries. They're quite nice, for baking and canning."

"It's really much too hot for either."

"Can't argue with you there."

"You'd think," she says, glancing again at the July twenty-*second Gloucester Daily Times*, "people would want to be properly educated, in this day and age.

Even in Tennessee, you'd think people wouldn't put up such a ridiculous fuss over a man just trying to teach his students science."

"Folks can be peculiar," he says, reaching for a box of elbow macaroni. "And I when it comes down to religion, people get pigheaded and don't seem to mind how ignorant they might look to the rest of the world. Five cans of sardines, yes?"

"Yes, five cans. Emiline and I enjoy them for our luncheon. And soda crackers, please. Mother and Father, they were Presbyterians, you know. But they prided themselves on being enlightened people."

"Folks can be very peculiar," he says again, adding an orange tin of Y & S licorice wafers to the cardboard box. "And we are talking about Tennessee, after all."

"Still," says Essie Babson.

Just then, Bertrand Cowlishaw's fat calico cat—whose name is Terrapin leaps from the shadows onto the counter, landing silently next to the cash register.

Terrapin isn't as old as Horace, but she isn't a youngster, either. Bertrand has been known to boast that she's the best mouser in all of Essex County. Whether or not that was strictly true, there's no denying she's a fine cat.

"And what about you, Turtle," says Essie Babson. "Has the weather got you out of sorts, as well?" She always calls the cat Turtle, because she can never remember its name is actually Terrapin.

The cat crosses the counter to Essie, walking over Bertrand's paper and the smug newsprint portrait of William Jennings Bryan. Terrapin purrs loudly and gently butts Essie in the arm with its head.

"Well, then I'm glad to see you, too."

"Molasses? I don't see it on the list, but—"

"Oh, yes please. I must have forgotten to write it down."

Essie scratches behind Terrapin's ears, and the cat purrs even louder. Then, apparently tired of the woman's affection, she retreats to the register and begins washing her front paws.

"Horace," says Essie, "has been acting a little odd."

"Maybe it's the full moon coming on," replies Bertrand. "The Hay Moon's tonight. The tide'll be high."

"Maybe."

"Animals, you know, they're more sensitive to the moon and the tides and whatnot than we are."

"Maybe," Essie says again, watching the cat as it fastidiously grooms itself.

"Well, I'm pretty sure I have everything you needed. If you're absolutely certain I can't interest you in a pint or two of these blueberries."

"No, that's all, thank you."

Bertrand Cowlishaw brings the box to the counter, and Essie checks it over, checking it against her list to be certain nothing's been overlooked. The cat meows at Bertrand, and he strokes its back and waits patiently until Essie is satisfied.

"I'll have Matthew bring these around to you just as soon as he gets back," the grocer tells her. "He had a delivery over on Lafayette, but he shouldn't be long." Matthew Cowlishaw is Bertrand's only son. Next year, he goes away to college in Arkham to study mathematics, astronomy, and physics, which has always been the boy's dream, and Bertrand has reluctantly given up his own dream that Matthew would one day take over the store when his father retired. His son is much too bright, Bertrand knows, to spend his life selling groceries in a withering North Shore seaport.

"When it's cooler," Essie Babson says, "I'll bake some sugar cookies and bring some around to you. I will, or I'll have Emiline do it. She needs to get out more often. But it's much too hot to bake in this heat. It surely won't last much longer."

"One can only hope," replies Bertrand. He licks the tip of his pencil, tallies up her bill, and writes it down in his ledger book. He rarely ever uses the fancy new nickel-plated machine he bought last year from the National Cash Register Company in Dayton, Ohio. It is noisy, and the keys make his fingers ache.

Essie gives Terrapin a parting scratch beneath the chin, and the cat shuts its eyes and looks as content as any cat ever has.

"You take care," says Bertrand Cowlishaw.

"Just hope we get a break in this weather," she says, then leaves the shop, and the brass bell jingles as the door opens and swings shut behind her. Bertrand goes back to his newspaper, and Terrapin, having gotten her fill of humans for the time being, leaps off the counter to prowl among the aisles and barrels and bushel baskets.

3.

Frank Buckles sits in his rocking chair on the front porch of his narrow yellow house on River Street, sweating and smoking hand-rolled cigarettes and drinking the bootlegged Canadian whisky he buys down on the docks near the jetty. He stares at the green-black river flowing between then grey walls of the granite-and-mortar quay walls built half a century ago to contain it and keep the water flowing straight down to the harbor, a bulwark against spring floods. The river glistens brightly beneath the summer sun. He dislikes the river and often thinks of selling the house his grandfather built and getting a place set farther back from the Manuxet. Or, better yet, moving away from Innsmouth altogether, maybe all the way up to Portland or Bangor. Sometimes, he thinks he wouldn't stop until he was safely in the Maritimes, where no one had ever heard of Innsmouth or Obed Marsh or the Esoteric fucking Order of Dagon. But he isn't going anywhere, because he lacks the resolve, and what few tenuous roots he has, they're here, in this rotting town the outside world has done an admirable job of forgetting.

Lucky them, thinks Frank Buckles, as he shakes out a fresh line of Prince Albert, then licks the paper and twists it closed. He lights the cigarette with a kitchen match struck on the side of his chair, and for a few merciful seconds the smell of sulfur masks the musky stink of the river. It isn't so bad up above the falls, back in the marshes towards Choate and Corn and Dilly Islands, where the waters are broad and still. When he was young, he and his brother Joe would often spend their days in those marshes, digging for quahogs and fishing for white perch, steelhead, and shad.

Back there, away from the sewers that spill into the Manuxet below the falls, it was easy to pretend Innsmouth was only a bad dream.

In April of '18, both he and his brother were drafted, and they were sent off to the French trenches to fight the Huns. Joe died less than five months later in the Meuse-Argonne Offensive, blown limb from limb by a mortar round. The very next week, at the Battle of Blanc Mont Ridge, Frank lost his left foot and his right eye, and they shipped what was left of him back home to Massachusetts. Joe's remains were buried in Lorraine, in the American cemetery at Romagne-sous-Montfaucon, in a grave that Frank has never seen and never expects to see. That his brother was killed and he was mangled only weeks before the end of the war to end all wars is a horrible irony that isn't lost on Frank. And now, seven years have gone by, and both his mother and father have passed, and Frank spends his days sitting on the porch, drinking himself numb, watching the filthy river roll by. He spends his nights tossing and turning, lying awake or dreaming of murdered men tangled in barbed wire and of skies burning red as blood and roses. Sometimes, he sits with a shotgun pressed to his forehead or his mouth around the muzzle, but he hasn't got that much courage left anywhere in him. He wonders if there would be time to smell the cordite before his soul winked out, if he would taste it, how much pain there would be in the split second before this brains were sprayed across the wall. He has a stingy inheritance that might or might not be enough to see him through however many years he's left to suffer, and he has the narrow yellow house on River Street. Sometimes, he sobers up enough to do odd jobs about town.

Frank exhales a steel-gray cloud of smoke, and the breeze off the river immediately picks it apart. The breeze smells oily, of dead fish and human waste; it smells of rot.

This is Hell, he thinks. *I'm alive, and this is Hell.* It's an old thought, worn smooth as the cobbles along the breakwater.

"Is it better to be a living coward,
Or thrice a hero dead?"
"It's better to go to sleep, my lad,"
The Colour Sergeant said.

One of the three tortoiseshell kittens—two female, one male—that have recently taken up residence beneath his porch scrambles clumsily up the steps and mews at him. It can't be more than a couple or three months old. He has no idea where the kittens came from, whether they were abandoned by their mother, or if the mother were killed. She might have gotten a belly full of poison left out for the rats. She might have perished under the wheels of an automobile. It could have been a hungry dog, or she might have run afoul of the tribes of half-feral boys that roam the streets and alleys and the wharves, happy for any opportunity to do mischief or cruelty that comes their way. It might simply have been her time. But it hardly matters. Now, the kittens live beneath the porch of his narrow yellow house.

The first is followed by a second, and then the third, the brother, comes scrambling up. The trio is thin and crawling with fleas. The little tom has already lost an eye to some infection or parasite. To Frank, that makes him a sort of comrade in the great shitstorm of the world. Frank has been told that a male tortoiseshell is a rare thing.

"What's it you three want, eh?" he asks them, and they loudly mewl in tandem. "That so?" he replies. "Well, people in Hell want ice water, or so I've heard." One of the tortoiseshell girls parks herself between his boots, and she begins playing with the tattered laces. When the kittens first showed up, he seriously considered herding them all into an empty burlap potato sack from the pantry, putting a few stones in there to keep them company and weight it down, then dropping the sack into the river. It's what his father would have done with the strays. But the thought passed almost as soon as it had come.

Frank Buckles knows he's a sorry son of a bitch, but he's not so heartless that he'd send anything to its death in those foul waters.

He scratches at the stubble on the chin he hasn't bothered to shave in days and stares down at the kitten. Ash falls from his cigarette, but it misses the cat.

"Yeah, okay," he says. "How about you moochers just give me a goddamn minute." Then he gets up and goes inside the dark house. The kittens all line up at the screen door, waiting and watching for Frank's return. After only five minutes or so he comes back with a third of a tin of Holly-brand canned salmon and a chipped china saucer. He empties what's left into the dish and gives it to the hungry kittens.

They fall upon it with as much ferocity as any cat has ever shown a fish, living or dead. In only a few moments the saucer is licked clean.

"Greedy little shits," Frank mutters, tossing the empty tin at the Manuxet before sitting back down in the rocker. The chair was built by his paternal grandfather, as a gift to his grandmother, before he signed up with the 8th Massachusetts Volunteer Militia, left his pregnant wife behind, and marched off to die at the hands of a pro-succession mob in Baltimore, on the nineteenth day of April, 1861. His great-grandfather made many chairs and cabinets and tables, and sometimes Frank Buckle wonders where they've all gone, how many have survived the sixty-four years since the man's untimely death.

The kittens, their hunger sated for the time being, have all disappeared back beneath the porch, to the cool shadows below.

"Yeah," Frank mutters, "beat it. The lot of you. Stuff your faces and leave me here holding an empty can. Lotta gratitude that is, you bums."

Lithe and supple lads they were
Marching merrily away—
Was it only yesterday?

Frank Buckle, he sips his illegal whiskey, and he rocks in his grandmother's chair, and he watches the demon sun shining bright as diamonds off the greasy river. He reminds himself that there's always the shotgun he keeps beside his bed, and he tries not to think about where that burning river leads.

4.

She was only fourteen years of age when Annie Phelps took a keen interest in the things that wash up along the sands and shingle beaches of Innsmouth Harbor, the breakwater, and the marshy shorelines to the north and south of the port. The strandings and junk, the flotsam and jetsam of commerce and mishap, the remains of dead and dying creatures, fronds and branches of the kelp and algae forests that grow below the waves. As a child, her parents didn't exactly encourage her boyish fascinations, but neither did they discourage them. When she was eighteen, she would have gone away to study natural history and anatomy and chemistry at a university in Arkham, maybe, or Boston, or even Providence. But there wasn't the money for her tuition. So, she stayed at home, instead, and cared for her ailing mother and father.

Annie didn't marry, preferring always the company of women to that of men.

There is talk that she enjoys much more than their platonic company. However, in a shadowed and ill-starred place like Innsmouth, there are always far darker rumors than whispers of Sapphic passion to provide the grist for clothesline gossips. She was twenty- eight years when the influenza of '18 claimed Charles and Beulah Phelps, and afterwards she sold their listing Georgian house on Hancock Street and took up residence in three adjoining rooms in Hephzibah Peabody's boarding house on River Street. Her study and bedroom both have excellent views of the gurgling Manuxet.

Annie Phelps makes a modest living as a seamstress and a typist, keeping back most of the income from the sales of the house on Hancock for that proverbial rainy day. But her passion has remained for those treasures she finds on the shore, and hardly three days pass that she doesn't find time to make her way down to the fish markets or past the waterfront, where few women dare to venture alone, to see what the boats or the tides or a fortuitous storm have hauled in to arouse her curiosity. Most of the fishermen and fishmongers, the sailors, boatwrights, deckhands, and dockworkers, knew her by sight and left her be.

This day, this sweltering late Monday afternoon in July, she sits at her father's old roll-top desk, in her study, a small room lined with shelves loaded down with books and jars of biological specimens she's pickled in solutions of formaldehyde.

There are squid and sea cucumbers, eels and baby dogfish. Among the books and jars, there are also the bones of whales and dolphins, the jaws of a Great White shark, the skull and shell of a loggerhead sea turtle. There are also fossils and minerals sent to her by correspondents—of which she has many—from as far away as Montana, California, and Mexico. The pride of her collection is an enormous petrified whale vertebra from the Eocene of Alabama, fully two feet long. She pays Mrs. Peabody a little extra to allow her to keep this cabinet of oddities, but that doesn't prevent the old woman from regularly grousing about Annie's peculiar collection or the unpleasant odors that sometimes leak from beneath her door.

Annie Phelps has four cats: a black-and-white tom she's named Huxley; a fat gray tom with one yellow eye and one blue eye, whom she's named Darwin; a perpetually thin calico lady, Mary Anning; and, finally, the skittish young girl she christened Rowena after a Saxon woman in *Ivanhoe*. When she's not entertaining a friend or a lover, the cats are all the companionship she needs, even if the apartment is rather too small for all five of them, and even though they claw her mother's already threadbare heirlooms and leave the rooms smelling of piss. The cats are another thing she pays Mrs. Peabody extra to overlook. Were it not for the fact that it's getting harder and harder to find lodgers, the landlady likely would not be willing to make these concessions to Annie's eccentricities.

On this afternoon, she sits drinking a lukewarm glass of lemonade, spiked with a dash of Jamaican ginger, the jake she gets from a pharmacist over on Federal.

Annie is very careful how often she imbibes, because she's well aware of the cases of paralysis and even death that have resulted from excessive use of the extract.

Darwin and Huxley are both perched on the back of the roll-top. Darwin has scaled a stack of monographs on malacology and the hydromedusae of coastal New England. Meanwhile, Huxley has wedged himself between one of her compound microscopes and a copy of Lyell's *Geological Evidences of the Antiquity of Man*. Both cats are purring loudly and watching as she composes a letter to Dr. Osborn at the American Museum. Occasionally, she'll send him a few of her more intriguing specimens and is proud that some have become permanent additions to the museum's collections in Manhattan.

"What will he think of this piece, Mr. Darwin?" she asks the cat. "Frankly, I think it may be the most fascinating and curious object I've sent him yet." Darwin shuts his yellow-green eyes.

"Yes, well, what do you know, you chubby old fool?"

Annie stops writing and stares at the jawbone in its cardboard box, cradled in wads of excelsior. It's a bit worn from having been rolled about in the surf, but is unbroken and still has all its teeth. At first glance, she took it for the jaw of a man or woman, some unfortunate soul drowned in the harbor or the cold sea beyond the Water Street jetty. But that impression was fleeting, lasting hardly longer than the time it took her to pick the bone up off the sand. It's much too elongate and slender to be the jaw of any normal human being, and both the condyle and the coronoid process all but absent. The mental protuberance of the mandibular symphysis is almost blade-like. But the teeth are the strangest of all the strange jawbone's features.

Instead of the normal adult human compliment of four incisors, two canines, and eight molars, the teeth are homodont—completely undifferentiated—and more closely resemble the fangs of a garpike than those of any mammal.

Standing at the edge of the murky harbor, low waves sloshing insistently against the shore, Annie Phelps was briefly gripped by an almost irresistible urge to toss the strange bone away from her, to give it back to the sea from whence it had come. To be rid of it. She squinted through the mist, out past the lines of ruined and decaying wharves, at the low dark line of rock that the people of Innsmouth call Devil Reef. Growing up, she heard all the tales about the reef, yarns of pirate gold, sirens, and sea demons, and she knows, too, of the locals who compete in swimming races out to the granite ridge on moonlit nights, a sport sponsored by the Esoteric Order, a religious sect who long ago took over the Masonic Hall at New Church Green.

But she didn't throw the bone away. She carefully wrapped it in newspaper and added it to her basket with the other day's finds.

Annie Phelps is a rational woman of the twentieth century, a woman of science and reason, even if her circumstances mean that she will never be more than an amateur naturalist. She is not bound by the fearful, superstitious ways of so many of the people of the town, all those citizens of Innsmouth who mistake the effects of inbreeding, disease, and poor nutrition among the Marshes, Eliots, Gilmans, Waites, and other old families of the town for some metaphysical transformation brought about by the secretive rites and rituals of the Order of Dagon—as certainly a witch-cult as any described in the scholarly works of Margaret Murray. Growing up, she heard all that bushwa, and she sometimes feels anger and embarrassment at the way so many of her neighbors live in terror of whatever goes on inside the dilapidated, pillared hall.

"It certainly isn't a fossil," she says to Huxley, ignoring the less-than-useful Mr. Darwin. "There's no sign whatsoever of permineralization. It's no sort of reptile, and I don't believe it's a fish, neither cartilaginous or osteichthyan. But I can't believe it's a mammal, either."

If the cat has an opinion, he keeps it to himself.

Annie writes a few more lines of her letter—

I am very grateful for the copy of your description of Hesperopithicus, though I must confess it still looks to me very like a pig's tooth.

—and then she glances at the jawbone again.

"The water gets deep out past the reef," she says to Huxley and Darwin, "and who knows what might be swimming around out there."

The cats purr, and Huxley begins vigorously cleaning his ears.

The enclosed specimen has entirely confounded all my best attempts at classification. Beyond the self-evident fact that it resides somewhere within the Vertebrata, I'm entirely at a loss.

Sometimes, Annie dares to imagine she will one day find something entirely new to science, and Dr. Osborn—or someone else—will name the new animal or plant after her. She stares at the jaw and considers a number of appropriate Latin binomina, if it should prove to be something novel, finally settling on Deinognathus phelpsae, Phelp's terrible jaw. She likes that. She likes that very much.

But then she feels the prickling at the back of her neck and along her forearms, and the sinking, anxious feeling she first experienced the day she found the bone, and she quickly looks away and tries to focus on finishing the day's correspondence:

. . . and at any rate, I hope this letter finds you well.

Outside, there's a sudden commotion, a loud splashing from the river, and Annie sets her pen aside and goes to the window to see what it might have been. But there's nothing, just the waters of the Manuxet swirling past the boarding house, dark and secret as the coming night.

"Someday," she says to the cats, "I'm gonna pack up and leave this place. You just watch me. Someday, we're gonna get out of here."

5.

Ephraim Asher Peaslee closes his wrinkled eyelids, sixty-one years old and thin as vellum paper, sinking into the sweet rush and warm folds of the heroin coursing through his veins. All the world bleeds to white, and he could well be staring into the noonday sun, patiently waiting to go mercifully blind, so bright does the darkness around him blaze. But it doesn't blind him. It doesn't ever blind him, and neither does it burn him. He lies cradled in the worn cranberry velvet of the chaise lounge in the parlor of his house at the corner of River and Fish streets, directly across from the shattered arch of the Fish Street Bridge. The heavy drapes are drawn, like his eyelids, against the last dregs of twilight, against the rising Hay Moon, Corn Moon, Red Moon, goddamn Grain Moon, whichever folk name suits your fancy. None suit his. The moon is a cruel cyclopean eye, lidless, watchful, prying, and this night it will drag the sea so far inland, swelling the harbor and tidal river all the way back to the lower falls. It won't be the kindly, obscuring white of his opiate high, but will lie orange and bloated, low on the horizon. It will scrape its cratered belly against the sea, hemorrhaging for all the bloodthirsty mouths that lie in wait, always, just below the waves. Oh, Ephraim Asher Peaslee has seen so *many* of those slithering, spiny things, has drowned again and again in their serpent coils. He's been kissed by every undertow and riptide, dragged down screaming to bear witness to abyssal lands no human man ever was meant to see. Right now, this evening, he pushes back against those thoughts, awakened by the rising moon. He tries to cling to nothing but the heroin, the forever-white expanse laid out before him after the needle kiss. The radio's on, "I'll Build a Stairway to Paradise," and the music makes love to his waking alabaster dream. *It's madness to be always sitting around in sadness, when you could be learning the steps of gladness.* He folds his bony hands in supplication, in prayer to Saint Gershwin and the ghost of Guglielmo Marconi and the Crosley Model 51, that they have graced him with this balm, a sacred ward against the memories and the nightmares and the long hours to come before dawn. God bless, and take your choice of gods, but surely, please, bless the pharmaceutical manufacturers in faraway eastern Europe, in Turkey and Bulgaria, god bless the Chinese farmers and poppy fields, where moralizing tyrants have not yet obliterated his ragged soul's deliverance from the abominations of Innsmouth. Pray a rosary for the white powder that ferries him away to Arctic wastes, Antarctic plains, where water is stone and nothing can swim through those crystalline rivers. *I won't open my eyes,* thinks Ephraim Asher Peaslee. *I won't open my eyes until morning, and maybe not even then. Maybe I will never again open my eyes, but fall eternally, perpetually, into the saving grace of the heroin light.* Then he hears the rising moon, a sound like the sky being torn open, like steam engines and furnaces, and he turns his face into a brocade pillow, wishing he were able to smother himself, but knowing better. He's a failed suicide, several times over, a coward with straight razor and noose. And trying not to hear the moon or the sluice of the rising tide, trying only to drown in white and ancient snow and the fissured glaciers that course down the basalt flanks of Erebus, there is another sound, past the radio—*Dance with Maud the countess, or just plain Lizzy. Dance until you're blue in the face and dizzy. When you've learn'd to dance in your sleep, you're sure to win out*—past crooning and tinny strings, there is the thunder, earthquake, sundering purr of Bill Bailey, his gigantic Maine Coon, twenty-five pounds if he's an ounce. Bill Bailey, raised up from a kitten, and now he comes heroic, thinks the heroin addict hopefully, to pull *my sledge up the crags of a dead and frozen volcano in the South Polar climes, Mr. Poe's Mount Yaanek, where the filthy, unhallowed Manuxet never, never will do them mischief on this hot August night. Risking so many things—his shredded sanity not the least of all—Ephraim Asher Peaslee opens his eyes, letting the world back in, releasing his desperate hold on the white. He rolls over, and Bill Bailey stands not far from the cranberry chaise, watching him, waiting cat-patient, those amber eyes secret filled. "You hear it, too, don't you? We ought to have run. We ought to have packed our bags and taken that rattletrap bus away to Newburyport. They'd have let us go. They have no use for the likes of us. They'd be glad to be rid of us." The cat merely blinks, then sets about licking its shaggy chocolate coat, grooming paws and chest. "You *do* hear it, I *know* you do." And then, close to tears and disappointed by the cat's apparent lack of concern, by Bill Bailey's usual pacific demeanor, the old man once more turns away and presses his face into the cushion. Sure, what has a cat to fear from the evils of an encroaching, salty sea? A holy temple child of Ubaste, privy to immemorial knowledge forever set beyond the kin of loping apes fallen from African trees and the grace of Jehovah. Bill Bailey purrs and bathes and does not move from his appointed station by the chaise. And Ephraim Asher Peaslee tries to give himself back to the white place, but finds that, in the scant handful of seconds it took him to converse with the cat, the luminous White Lands have deserted him. Left him to his own meager devices, none of which are a match for the monsters the mad and unholy men and women of the Esoteric Order see fit to call forth on nights when the moon sprawls so obscenely large in the Massachusetts heavens. Their oblations and devotions that rot and gradually discard their human forms, sending those lost souls tumbling backwards, descending the rungs of the evolutionary ladder toward steamy Devonian and Carboniferous yesteryears, muddy swamp pools, silty lagoons, dim memories held in bone and blood and cells of morphologies devised and then abandoned two hundred and fifty, three hundred million ago. Ephraim Asher Peaslee of No. 7 River Street shuts his eyes more tightly than, he would say, he ever has shut his eyes before, skating his hypodermic fix down, down, *down*, but not down to the sanctuary of his white realms. Some door slammed and bolted shut against him, and, instead, he has only clamoring, fish-stinking recollections of the waterfront, the docks where beings no longer human cast suspicious, swollen eyes towards interlopers. Grotesque faces half glimpsed in doorways and peering out windows. Shadows and murmurs. The squirming green-black mass he once caught a fleeting sight of before it slipped over the edge of a pier and, with a plop, was swallowed up by the bay. The chanting and hullabaloo that pours from the old Masonic Hall. All of this and a hundred other images, sounds, and smells burned indelibly into his mind's eye. Shuffling hulks. Naked dancers on New Church Green, seen on stormy, starless nights, whirling devil dervishes. All you preachers who delight in panning the dancing teachers, let me tell you there are a lot of features of the dance that carry you through the gates of Heaven! So many other citizens might turn their heads and convince themselves they've seen nothing, and anyway, what business is it of theirs, the pagan rites of the debased followers of Father Dagon and Mother Hydra? Oh, old Ephraim Asher Peaslee, he knows those names, because he can't seem to shut out the voices that ride between the crests and troughs. Out there, as night comes on and the last scrap of sunset fades, he prays to his own heathen deities, the narcotic molecules in his veins, the radio, to keep him insensible for all the hours between now and dawn. And Bill Bailey stands guard, and listens, and waits.

6.

When even the solar system was young, a fledgling, Pre-Archean Earth was kissed by errant Theia, daughter of Selene, and four and a half billion years ago all the cooling crust of the world became once more a molten hell. Theia was obliterated for her reckless show of affection and reborn as a cold, dead sphere damned always to orbit her intended paramour; she a planet no more, but only a satellite never again permitted to touch the Earth. And so it is that the moon, spurned, scarred, diminished, has always haunted the sky, gazing spitefully across more than a million miles of near vacuum, hating silently—but not entirely powerless.

She has the tides.

A dance for three—sun, moon, and earth.

She can pull the seas, twice daily, and twice monthly her pull is vicious.

And so she has formed an alliance with those things within the briny waters of the world that would gain a greater foothold upon the land or would merely reach out and take what the ocean desires as her own.

For the ocean, like the moon, is a wicked, jealous thing.

Hold that thought.

Cats, too, have secrets rooted in antiquity and spanning worlds, secret histories known to very few living men and women, most of whom have only read books or heard tales in dreams and nightmares; far fewer have for themselves beheld the truth of the lives of cats, whether in the present day or in times so long past there are only crumbling monuments to mark the passage of those ages. The Pharaoh Hedjkheperre Setepenre Shoshenq's city of Bubastis, dedicated to the cult of Bast and Sekhmet, where holy cats swarmed the temples and were mummified, as attested by the writings of Herodotus. And the reverence for the *Tamra Maew* shown by Buddhist monks, the breeds sacred to the Courts of Siam; the *Wichien-maat, Sisawat, Suphalak, Khaomanee,* and *Ninlarat.* In the Dream Lands, the celebrated cats of Ulthar, whom no man may kill on pain of death, and, too, the great battle the cats fought against the loathsome, rodent-like zoogs on the dark side of the moon.

Cats upon the moon,

Star-eyed guardians whose power and glory has been forgotten, by and large, by humanity, which has come to look upon them as nothing more than pets.

The stage has been set.

Here's the scene:

All the cats of Innsmouth have assembled on this muggy night, coming together at a designated place within the shadowed, dying seaport at the mouth of Essex Bay, south of Plum Island Sound, and west of the winking lighthouses of Cape Ann. The sun is finally down, and that swollen moon has cleared the Atlantic horizon to shine so bright and violent over the harbor and the wharves, over fishing boats, the meeting hall of the Esoteric Order of Dagon, and over all the gables, balustrades, hipped Georgian and slate-shingled gambrel rooftops, the cupolas and chimneys and widow's walks, the high steeples of shuttered churches. The cats takes their positions along the low stone arch of Banker's Bridge, connecting River Street with Paine Street, just below the lower falls of the Manuxet. They've slipped out through windows left open, through attic crannies and basement crevices, all the egresses known to cats whose "owners" believe they control the comings and goings of their feline charges.

The cats of Innsmouth town have come together to hold the line. They've come, as they've done twice monthly since the sailing ships of Captain Obed Marsh returned a hundred years ago with his strange cargoes from the islands of New Guinea, Sumatra, and Malaysia. Strange cargoes and stranger rituals that set the seaport on a new and terrible path, as the converts to Marsh's transplanted South Sea's cult of Cthulhu called out to the inhabitants of the drowned cities beyond Devil Reef and far out beyond the wide plateau of Essex Bay. They sang for the deep ones and all the other abominations of that unplumbed submarine canyon and the halls of Y'ha-nthlei and Yoharneth-Lahai. And their songs were answered. Their blasphemies and blood sacrifices were rewarded.

Evolution spun backward for those who chose that road.

And even as the faithful went down, so did the deep ones rise.

On these nights, when the spiteful moon hefts the sea to cover the cobble beaches and slop against the edges of the tallest piers, threatening to overtop the Water Street jetty, on these nights do the beings called forth by the rites of the Esoteric Order seek the slip past the falls and gain the wetlands and the rivers beyond Innsmouth, to spread inland like a contagion. On *these* nights, the Manuxet swells and, usually, is contained by the quays erected when the city was still young. But during *especially* strong spring tides, such as this one of the first night of August 1925, the comingled sea and river may flood the streets flanking the Manuxet. And things may crawl out.

But the cats have come to hold the line.

None among them—not even the very young or the infirm or the very old shirk this duty.

Essie and Emiline Babson's tom Horace is here, as is shopkeeper Bertrand Cowlishaw's plump calico Terrapin. The three tortoiseshell kittens have scrambled out from beneath Frank Buckle's front porch to join the ranks. All four of Annie Phelps' cats—Darwin and Huxley, Mary Anning and Rowena— are here, and a place of honor has been accorded Mister Bill Bailey, the heroin addict Ephraim Asher Peaslee's enormous Maine Coon. Bill Bailey has led the cats of Innsmouth since his seventh year and will lead them until his death, when the burden will pass to another. *All* these have come to the bridge, and five score more, besides. The pampered and the stray, the beloved and the neglected and forgotten.

By the whim of gravity, the three bodies have aligned, sun, moon, and earth all caught now in the invisible tension of syzygy, and within an hour the Manuxet writhes with scaled and slimy shapes eager and hopeful that this is the eventide that will see them spill out into the wider world of men. The waters froth and splash as the deep ones, hideous frog-fish parodies of human beings, clamber over the squirming mass of great eels long as Swampscott dories and the arms of giant squid and cuttlefish that might easily crush a man in their grip. There are sharks and toothsome fish no ichthyologist has ever seen, and there are armored placoderms with razor jaws, believed by science to have vanished from the world æons ago.

Other Paleozoic anachronisms, neither quite fish or quite amphibians, beat at the quay with stubby, half-formed limbs.

The conspiring moon is lost briefly behind a sliver of cloud, but then that obstructing cataract passes from her eye and pale, borrowed light spills down and across the Belgian-block paving running the length of River and Paine, across all those rooftops and trickling down into alleyways. And there are those few, in this hour, who dare to peek between curtains pulled shut against the dark, and among them is Annie Phelps, distracted from her reading by some noise or another. She sees nothing more than the water growing perilously high between the quays, and she's grateful she has nothing of value stored in the basement, not after the flood of '18, when she lost her entire collection of snails and mermaids' purses, which she'd unwisely stored below street level. But she sees nothing more than the possibility of a flood, and she reminds herself again how she should move to some village where there would be crews with sandbags out on nights like this. She closes the curtain and goes back to her books.

Two doors down, Mr. Buckles sits near the bottom of the stairs, his 12-gauge, pump-action Browning across his lap. He carried the gun in France, and if it was good enough to kill Huns in the muddy trenches it ought to do just damn fine against anything slithering out of the muck to come calling at his door. The shotgun is cocked, both barrels loaded; he drinks from his bottle of bourbon and keeps his eyes open. Even in the house he can smell the stench from the river, worse times ten than it ever is during even the hottest, stillest days.

On Banker's Bridge, Bill Bailey glares with amber eyes at the interlopers, as they surge forward, borne by the tide.

Farther up the street, Essie Babson looks down at the river, and she sees nothing at all out of the ordinary, despite what she plainly *hears*.

"Come back to bed," says Emiline.

"You didn't hear that?" she asks her sister.

"I didn't hear anything at all. Come back to bed. You're keeping me awake."

"The heat's keeping you awake," mutters Essie.

"Have you seen Horace?" Emiline wants to know. "I couldn't find him. He didn't come for his dinner."

"No, Emiline. I haven't seen Horace," says Essie, and she squints into the night. "I'm sure he'll be along later."

Bill Bailey's ears are flat against the side of his head. The eyes of all the other cats of Innsmouth are, in this moment, upon him.

Above his store, Bertrand Cowlishaw lies in his bed, exhausted from a long, hot afternoon in the shop, by all the orders filled and the shelves he restocked himself because Matthew was in and out all day, making deliveries. Bertrand drifts uneasily in that liminal space between waking and sleep. And he half dreams about a city beneath the sea, and he half hears the clamor below the arch of Banker's Bridge.

Bill Bailey tenses, and all the other cats follow his lead.

Something hulking and only resembling a woman in the vaguest of ways lurches free of the roiling, slippery horde, rising to her full height, coming eye to eye with the chocolate Maine Coon.

Its eyes are black as holes punched in a midnight sky.

Ephraim Asher Peaslee floats, coddled in the gentle, protective arms of Madame Héroïne; after a long hour of pleading, he's been permitted to reenter the White Lands, where neither the sea nor the moon nor their demons may ever come. He isn't aware that Bill Bailey no longer sits near the cranberry velvet chaise lounge.

And the radio is like wind through the branches of distant trees, wind through a forest in a place he but half recalls, He is blissfully ignorant of the rising river and. the tide and the coming of the deep ones and all their retinue.

The scaled thing with bottomless pits for eyes opens its mouth, revealing teeth that Annie Phelps would no doubt recognize from the jaw she found on the shingle. Dripping with ooze and kelp fronds, its hide scabbed with barnacles and sea lice, the monster howls and rushes the bridge.

And the cats of Innsmouth town do what they have always done.

They hold the line.

They cheat the bitter moon, with claws and teeth, with the indomitable will of all cats, with iridescent eyeshine and with a perfect hatred for the invaders. Some of them are slain, dragged down and swallowed whole, or crushed between fangs and gnashing beaks, or borne down the riverbed and drowned. But most of them will live to fight at the next battle during New Moon spring tide.

Bill Bailey opens the throat of the black-eyed beast that once was a woman who lived in the town and cared for cats of her own.

Mary Anning is devoured, and Annie Phelps will spend a week searching for her.

One of the kittens from beneath Frank Buckles' front porch is crushed, its small body broken by flailing tentacles.

But there have been worse fights, and there will be worse fights again.

And when it is done and the soldiers of Y'ha-nthlei and Dagon and Mother Hydra have all been routed, retreating to the depths beyond the harbor, beyond the bay, when the cats have won, the survivors carry away the fallen and lay them in the reeds along the shore of Choate Island.

When the sun rises, there is left hardly any sign of the invasion, or of the bravery and sacrifice of the cats. Some will note dying crabs and drying strands of seaweed washed up along River and Paine streets, but most will not even see that much.

The day is hot again, but by evening rain clouds sweep in from the west, and from the windows of the Old Masonic lodge on New Church Green the watchers watch and curse. They say their prayers to forgotten gods, and they bide their time, patient as any cat.

The *New York Times* recently hailed **Caitlín R. Kiernan** as "one of our essential writers of dark fiction." Her novels include *The Red Tree* (nominated for the Shirley Jackson and World Fantasy awards) and *The Drowning Girl: A Memoir* (winner of the James Tiptree, Jr. Award and the Bram Stoker Award, nominated for the Nebula, Locus, Shirley Jackson, World Fantasy, British Fantasy, and Mythopoeic awards). In 2014 she was honored with the Locus Award for short fiction ("The Road of Needles"), the World Fantasy Award for Best Short Story 2014 ("The Prayer of Ninety Cats"), and a second World Fantasy Award for Best Collection 2014 (*The Ape's Wife and Other Stories*). To date, her short fiction has been collected in thirteen volumes. *Beneath an Oil-Dark Sea: The Best of Caitlin R. Kiernan (Volume Two)* is forthcoming in 2015. Currently, she's writing the graphic novel series Alabaster for Dark Horse.

It was nothing to brood upon, this slow doom that the earth or fate or the God he did not believe in had inflicted upon them . . .

THE END OF THE END OF EVERYTHING

═══◆═══

Dale Bailey

The last time Ben and Lois Devine saw Veronica Glass, the noted mutilation artist, was at a suicide party in Cerulean Cliffs, an artists colony far beyond their means. That they happened to be there at all was a simple matter of chance. Stan Miles, for whom Ben had twice served as best man, had invited them to his beach house to see things through with his new wife, MacKenzie, and her nine-year-old daughter Cecilia. Though the Devines had no great enthusiasm for the new wife—Stan had traded up, was how Lois put it—they still loved Stan and had resolved to put the best face on the thing. Besides, the prospect of watching ruin engulf the world among such glittering company was, for Ben at least, irresistible. He made his living on the college circuit as a poet, albeit a minor one, so when Stan said they would fit right in, his statement was not entirely without truth.

They drove down on a Sunday, to the muted strains of a Mozart piano concerto on the surround sound. Ruin had lately devoured most of the city and it encroached on either side of the abandoned interstate: derelict cars rusting back to the elements, skeletal trees stark against a gray horizon, an ashen, baked-looking landscape, though no fire had burned there. In some places the road was all but impassable. They made poor time. It was late when they finally pulled into the beach house's weedy gravel driveway and climbed out, stretching.

This was a still-living place. They could hear the distant sigh of breakers beyond the house, an enormous edifice of stacked stone with single-story wings sweeping back to either side of the driveway. The sharp tang of the ocean leavened the air. Gulls screamed in the distance and it was summer and it was evening, and in the cool dusk the declining sun made red splashes on the narrow windows of the house.

"I thought you'd never get here," Stan bellowed from the porch as they retrieved their luggage. "Come up here and let me give you a kiss, you two!" Stan—bearded, stout, hirsute as a bear—was as good as his promise. He delivered to each of them a scratchy wet smooch square on the lips, pounded Ben's back, and relieved Lois of her suitcase with one blunt-fingered hand. Ghostlike in the gloom, and surprisingly graceful for such a large man, he swept them inside on a tide of loose flowing white silk, his shirt unbuttoned at the neck to reveal corkscrews of gray hair.

He dumped their baggage in an untidy pile just inside the door, and ushered them into a blazing three-story glass atrium. It leaned rakishly over the dark, heaving water, more sensed than seen, and Ben, as always, felt a brief wave of vertigo, a premonition that the whole house might any moment slide over the cliff and plummet to the rocky white beach below. Ceiling fans whispered far above them. Two Oscars for Production Design stood on the mantle, over a fireplace big enough to roast a boar.

Stan collapsed into a low white sofa, and waved them into adjoining seats. "So the last days are upon us," he announced jovially. "I'm glad you've come."

"We're glad to be here," Ben said.

"Any word from Abby?" Stan asked.

Abby was Stan's ex-wife—Ben's first stint as best man—and just hearing her name sent a spasm through Ben's heart. When the dust from the divorce settled, Stan had gotten the beach house. Abby had ended up with the house in the city. But the last of the city was succumbing to ruin even as they spoke. A gust of sorrow shook Ben. He didn't like to think of Abby.

"Ruined," Lois said. "She's ruined."

"Ah, I knew it. I'm sorry." Stan sighed. "It's just a matter of time, isn't it?" Stan shook his head. "I am glad you decided to come. Really. I've missed you both."

"And how's MacKenzie?" Lois asked.

"She'll be down any minute. She and Cecy are upstairs getting ready for the party."

"Party?"

"Every night there's a party. You'll enjoy it, you'll see."

A moment later, MacKenzie—that was the only name she had, or admitted to—descended the backless risers that curved down from an upstairs gallery. She was a lithe blonde, high breasted, her face as pale and cool and unexpressive as a marble bust. She wore the same shimmering silks as her husband; and nine-year-old Cecy, trailing behind her, lovely beyond her years, wore them as well.

Ben got to his feet.

Lois pulled her shawl tight around her shoulders as she stood. "MacKenzie," she said, "it's been too long."

"It's so good to see you both again," MacKenzie said.

She brushed glossy lips against Ben's cheek.

Lois submitted to a brief embrace. Afterward, she knelt to draw Cecy into her arms. "How are you, dear?" she asked, and Ben, though he despised cliché, uttered the first thing that came into his head.

"My how you've grown," he said.

Yet his life had in some respects been a cliché. His poetry, while not without merit, had broken no new ground—though perhaps there was no new ground to break, as he sometimes told audiences at the small colleges that sought his services. Poetry was an exhausted art, readers a dying breed in a dying age, and he'd never broken through anyway. His verse was the stifled prosody of the little magazine, his life the incestuous circuit of the MFA program, and he had occasionally succumbed to the vices such an existence proffered: the passing infidelity, the weakness for drink and drug.

His marriage had weathered storms of its own. If Ben did not entirely approve of Stan's decision—he had loved Abby, and missed her—he could understand the allure of novelty, and he was not immune to the appeal of MacKenzie's beauty. Perhaps this accounted for the tension in their suite as he and Lois dressed for the party, and when they departed, descending the cliff-side steps to the beach, sensing her discontent, Ben reached out to take her hand.

Down here, that salty tang was stronger and a cool wind poured in off the water. The sea gleamed like the rippling hide of some living behemoth in the moonlight. The sand seemed to glow beneath their feet. Everything was precious, lovely in its impermanence, for what was not now imperiled? And an image came to Ben of the gray towers in the once-bustling city, of men and women in their millions but blackened effigies, shedding ashen debris in the unforgiving wind.

Yet it was nothing to brood upon, this slow doom that the earth or fate or the God Ben did not believe in had inflicted upon them. Not now anyway, not with another set of precipitous steps to ascend or another house of glass set back a hundred yards from the brink of cliff-side annihilation, great windows printing flickering panels of light upon the still-succulent grass, and pouring forth the dissonant, tremulous notes then in fashion. Inside, in the darkness, the intersecting beams of digital projectors cast violent images upon every available surface—upon walls and windows and the faces of the people who danced and drank there. "This is Bruno Vinnizi's place—you know, the director," Stan shouted over the music, passing Ben a drink, but he needn't have said anything at all. The movies spoke for themselves, half a dozen stylized art-house sensations that Ben had seen in the last decade and a half.

Somehow, in the chaos, Ben lost Lois—he caught glimpses of her now and then through the crowd—and found himself talking drunkenly to Vinnizi himself. A blisteringly bloody gunfight unfolded across Vinnizi's fashionably stubbled cheeks. "I have been making movies about ruin for years," Vinnizi pronounced. "Even before there was a ruin, no?" and Ben saw how true it was. "So you are a poet," Vinnizi said, and Ben answered something, he didn't know what, and then, without transition, he found himself in the bathroom with Gabrielle Abbruzzese, the sonic sculptor, chewing jagged crystals of prime. After that the party took on a hectic, impressionistic quality. A kind of wild exhilaration seized him. He saw Lois across the room, sipping wine and talking to the front man of some slam band or other—Ben had seen him on television—and stumbled once again into Stan's ursine embrace. "Having fun yet?" the big man yelled—and then, abruptly, Ben was squiring Cecy giggling across the dance floor.

Finally, exhausted, he reeled outside to piss. He unzipped, sighed, and let flow a long arc. A husky, female voice, deeply amused, said, "Something wrong with the bathrooms?"

Ben stepped back in dismay, tucking himself away.

A tall angular woman with razor-edged cheekbones and a cap of close-shorn blond hair stood in the shadows. She was smoking a joint. He could smell its faint sweetish scent. When she passed it to him he felt the effects of the prime recede a little.

"I know you," he said.

"Do you?"

"You're the artist—"

She took a hit off the joint. Exhaling, she said, "This place is lousy with artists."

"No"—slurring his words—"the humiliation artist. Victoria—Victoria—"

In a stray reflection from the house, a car screeched across one of those exquisite cheekbones.

"Victoria Glass," he announced, but she was already gone.

The party climaxed at dawn, when the rising sun revealed how closely ruin had encroached upon the house, and Vinnizi hurled himself over the cliff onto the rocks below.

It was accounted a triumph by all.

• • •

They slept late and joined Stan and MacKenzie on the verandah for drinks at eleven. Piano and saxophone burbled over the sound system. Stan paced, sucking down mimosas like water. MacKenzie reclined in an Adirondack chair, her long legs flung out before her. She sipped her drink, watching Cecy at some solitary game she'd improvised with a half-deflated soccer ball.

"Did you have a good time at the party?" Mackenzie asked.

"Of course they had a good time," Stan said, clapping Ben on the shoulder, and Ben supposed he had, but the night itself came back to him only in flashes: blue smoke adrift in the intersecting beams of the projectors; the taste of prime sour on his tongue; the tall angular woman who'd caught him cock in hand outside the house. Her name came to him, he'd seen a piece on her in The New Yorker—Veronica Glass, the mutilation artist—and he felt mortified for reasons that he could only vaguely recall. All this and more: the headachy regret that comes after any bacchanal; the image of Vinnizi leaping off the cliff onto the jagged rocks below. No sight for a little girl, he thought, and he recalled swinging Cecy drunkenly across the dance floor.

Lois must have been thinking the same thing. "Do you really want Cecy to see things like that?" she asked MacKenzie, and Ben could sense her struggling to reserve judgment, or anyway the appearance of judgment.

MacKenzie waved a languid hand.

"What does it matter anymore?" Stan said, and Ben thought of Abby, built like a fireplug, with none of MacKenzie's lissome beauty. Abby wouldn't have approved, but then she wouldn't have approved of MacKenzie either, even if the other woman hadn't stolen away her husband on the set of a failed summer blockbuster where her blank mien actually played to her advantage. Skill was a handicap in such a role; MacKenzie'd been little more than eye-candy on the arm of the star, an aging action hero long since ruined himself.

A wind off the ocean lifted Ben's hair. He leaned over to peer through the telescope mounted on the railing. Near at hand, white-capped breakers rolled toward shore. Farther out—he adjusted the focus—the waves gave way to the cracked, black mirror of dead water. Moldering fish turned their ashen bellies to the sky.

"How long, you think?" he asked Stan.

"Not long now."

"It doesn't matter. No child should have to see a man throw himself over a cliff," Lois said.

"She's not your child," MacKenzie responded drily, and Ben straightened up in time to see Lois shoot him a look of disgust—with MacKenzie and with Stan for marrying her, and with Ben most of all, for standing beside the groom and collaborating in the disposal of Abby like a used tissue, and this after more than twenty years of marriage.

But what was he to do? He and Stan had been friends since their freshman year at Columbia, when they'd been thrown together by the vagaries of admissions counselors on the basis of a vapid form with questions like: "Do you sleep late or get up early?" He slept late and so did Stan. And they'd had the same taste for girls (as many as possible, as often as possible, and no need to be choosy) and for drugs (ditto). It had been a match made in heaven. Sometimes Ben wondered why Lois had ever been attracted to him in the first place. He supposed she'd wanted to save him. The same was probably true of Abby and Stan. But old habits die hard and in his peripatetic days, reading indifferent poems to indifferent audiences, Ben had fallen into his former ways: banging nubile English majors and chewing prime. At home one man, on the road another: Jekyll and Hyde. Last night Hyde had been in the ascension. And why not? Nero fiddled as Rome burned, but what else could he do, break out impotent buckets against the conflagration?

All this in the space of an instant.

"Here," he said to Lois, "why don't you have a look?"

"I've seen all I want to see," she said, but she strode over and gazed through the telescope all the same. She'd thickened in middle age, and Ben found himself studying MacKenzie, suddenly envious of Stan, who'd had the courage to throw it all aside. A sudden hunger for MacKenzie's raw sexuality—she seemed to glow with lascivious potential—possessed him. What had Stan said, when he'd called to tell Ben that he and Abby were done? "She's a fucking tiger in the sack, Ben."

Stan shoved another drink into his hand—they'd moved to chilled vodka, it seemed—and Ben felt his headache retreat before the onslaught of the alcohol.

MacKenzie lit a cigarette. He could smell its acrid bite.

"Mom!"

"It's not like I'm going to die of lung cancer, sweetie," MacKenzie called, and Ben thought, no, none of us is going to die of lung cancer.

"You mind if I have one of those?" he said.

MacKenzie held the pack silently over her shoulder. Ben shook one out and struck it alight, inhaled deeply. Smoke drifted in twin blue streams through his nostrils. He'd smoked in college, but Lois had convinced him to give it up; it had become another vice of the road, indulged in frenetic after-reading parties. Playing the role of the dissolute poet, he used to think. That's what they wanted to see. Yet he wondered who he really was—if the persona hadn't become the person or if the persona hadn't been the person all along.

Lois looked up from the telescope. "It's terrifying," she said.

Stan shrugged. "It just is, that's all."

"It's terrifying all the same."

She set her unfinished mimosa on the railing. "I'm going in to make a sandwich. Anyone else want one?"

"Sure," Stan said.

And Ben, "Why not?"

She didn't bother asking MacKenzie, who, by the look of her, hadn't had a sandwich—or maybe any food—in years, if ever. The door clapped shut behind her.

Ben ground out his cigarette in MacKenzie's ashtray. "I've always wondered," he said. "What's your real name?

Stan laughed without humor and downed his drink.

"MacKenzie," MacKenzie said.

"No. I mean the name you were born with. I thought you'd adopted MacKenzie as a stage name. You know, like Bono, or Madonna."

"My name is MacKenzie," she said without looking at him.

Stan laughed again.

"Her name is Melissa Baranski," he said.

"My name is MacKenzie," her voice flat, without emotion.

Wishing he'd never asked, Ben descended to the lawn. "Throw me the ball," he called to Cecy, and for a while they played together by some rules Ben could never quite decipher. "Stand here," Cecy would say, or "Throw me the ball," and between sips from his drink, he would stand there or toss her the ball.

"I win," she announced suddenly.

"Sure, you win," he said, ruffling her hair.

They climbed the steps to the verandah together. By then Lois had returned with a tray of sandwiches for everyone.

Later, he and Lois made love in their suite. Before he came, Ben closed his eyes. A blur of faces passed through his mind: the features of an especially memorable undergraduate, and then MacKenzie's affectless face, and the woman on the lawn last of all, Veronica Glass, the mutilation artist, kneeling before him to take him into her mouth. He felt something break and release inside him. He cried out and drew Lois to him, whispering "I love you, I love you," uncertain whom he was speaking to, or why, and afterward, as she pillowed her head on his shoulder, that headachy sense of regret once again swept through him.

Later, they walked by the sea, waves foaming far down the beach. At high tide, the water would hurl its force against the stony cliff itself, undercutting it in a million timeless surges. It leaned over them like doom, unveiling the faint blue tinge that gave the colony its name.

He took Lois's hand and drew her into an embrace. "It's beautiful here, isn't it?" he said, as if by the force of language itself he could redeem the fallen world. But Ben had long since lost his faith in poetry. Words were but paltry things, frail hedges against the night. Ruin would consume them.

And it was to ruin that they came at last. They stopped at its edge, a ragged frontier where the beach turned as black and barren as burned-over soil, baked into a thousand jagged cracks, and the surf grew still, swallowed up by the same ashen surface. Digging their toes in the sand, they stood in the shadow of Bruno Vinnizi's ruined beach stair and gazed out across the devastation. Vinnizi's shattered corpse lay among the rocks, arms outflung, one charred hand lifted in mute supplication to the sky. As they stood there, the wind picked up and his outstretched fingers crumbled into dust and blew away, and the sea, where it still washed the shore, retreated down the naked shingles of the world.

As ruin spread, Cerulean Cliffs retreated. On the second night, Ben stood on the verandah and counted lights like a strand of Christmas bulbs strung along the coastline; in the days that followed they began to wink out. One afternoon, he and Stan hiked inland to the edge of the destruction: half a mile down the gravel driveway, and two more miles after that, along the narrow two-lane state road until it intersected with the expressway. In the distance, a soaring overpass had given way, its support pylons jutting from the earth like broken teeth. The pavement Ben and Lois had driven in upon was cracked and heaved, as if it had endured the ice of a thousand years. Businesses that had been thriving mere days ago had decayed into rubble. The arms of corroding gas pumps snaked across blistered asphalt. The roof of the Bar-B-Cue Diner had buckled, and the shards of its plate glass windows threw back their sooty reflections.

"Abby and I celebrated our fourteenth anniversary there," Stan said.

"We used to go there every time we came down," Ben said. "Best barbecue I ever had."

"It was shitty barbeque, and you know it. The company made it great."

Laughing, Stan unclipped a flask of bourbon from his belt. He took a long pull and handed it to Ben. The liquor suffused Ben with warmth, and he recalled his first liquor drunk—he'd been with a girl, he couldn't remember her name, only that she'd held his head as he puked into the toilet at some high school revel. After that, he'd vowed never to drink whiskey again. You had to learn to love your vices.

As they turned and started back, he snorted, thinking of Cecy and her soccer ball and her mysterious games upon the grass.

"What?" Stan said.

"Cecilia."

"She's a good kid."

"The best," Ben said, taking another swig of whiskey. He handed the flask back to Stan. They passed it back and forth as they walked. The blasted land fell behind them. The day brightened. The sky arced over them, fathomless and blue. Ben took out a cigarette and lit it and blew a stream of smoke into the clear air.

"You ever wish you'd had children?" he asked.

"I have Cecilia."

"You know what I mean."

"I had a career."

"What about Abby?"

"What about her?" Stan said.

"Did she want children?"

Stan was silent for a time.

"Ah, it was my fault," he said at last.

"What?"

"You know. The whole goddamn mess." He took a slug of whiskey. "We had a miscarriage once. I never told you. After that—" He shrugged. "She never forgave me you know."

"For a miscarriage? Stan, she couldn't have blamed you—"

"Not that. Cecilia, I mean. She could forgive the infidelity. God knows she had in the past. She never forgave me Cecilia." He looked up. "She always thought that was driving the whole thing: MacKenzie had the child she could never have."

"And was it?"

"No." Stan laughed. "It was lust, that's all. Simple lust." He shook his head in dismal self-regard. "I envy you, you know. Holding things together the way you have."

They turned into the driveway. Ben kicked a stone. A wind came down to comb the weeds. Somewhere in the trees a bird burst into song. The faint sound of the ocean came to him. Envy was a blade that cut two ways.

"What about you?" Stan said.

"What about me?"

"Kids?"

Ben finished his cigarette.

"It never crossed my mind," he lied. "I wish it had."

They'd reached the house by then. Ben went to his suite and lay down to sleep off the whiskey before the party. When he woke, the sun was red in his window, and Lois was reading in the chair by the side of the bed. They walked out onto the balcony and gazed at the ocean. The dead water had crept closer. He'd lost track of time. It all blurred together, the liquor and the prime and the multi-hued tabs of ecstasy spilled helter-skelter across the butcher block of a financier who'd filled her house with priceless paintings. Her taste had run toward the baroque—Bosch, Goya—and over the course of the party she'd slashed them to ribbons one by one. At dawn she'd walked out onto the lawn, doused herself with gasoline, and set herself on fire.

"Did you know Abby had a miscarriage?" Ben asked.

"Of course, I did," Lois said, and they stood there in silence until the first faint stars broke out in the dark void where ruin had not yet eaten up the sky.

The parties were Ben's solace and his consolation: the photographer whose prints adorned the walls of her house, the painter whose canvases did not, the novelist who'd won a Pulitzer. Ben had met her once before, a lean scarecrow of a woman with a thatch of pink hair and a heart-shaped pinkie ring on her left hand: a brief introduction by a friend of a friend at a Book Expo party. "What are you working on?" he'd asked as she paused. "I subscribe to the tea-kettle theory of art," she'd responded. "Open the valve and the energy escapes."

Ben had nodded, taking a long drink of his gin and tonic. He leaned against the wall, trying to pretend he wasn't alone. He'd come for the free drinks— he always did—but he knew that nothing was ever free; you paid the price in the coin of humiliation. And that reminded him of his fleeting encounter with Veronica Glass, the "humiliation artist," as he'd called her. He'd seen her flitting through the crowds occasionally, tall and gamine with her cap of blond hair, but mostly she lingered in corners. If it bothered her to be alone, Ben could not discern it. She observed everything with an air of bemused fascination, the expression of an anthropologist faced with a curious custom she had not seen before.

Once or twice, they'd even talked briefly.

"Hello, again," he'd said, as he squeezed past her in the scrum around the bar, and briefly he felt her taut body glide against his sagging middle aged one.

Another time, she appeared ghostlike at his side, and handed him a joint. "I've had my eye on you," she said.

"You have?" he said.

"Are you surprised?"

"A little."

She smiled, remote and amused, the way you'd smile at a child. "Outsiders interest me."

"What do you mean?"

"In Cerulean Cliffs, you're either a rich artist, or you're just plain rich."

Ben thought of the financier who'd torched herself on her lawn, staggering about in screaming agony until she collapsed and the flames consumed her.

"You don't seem to be either," Veronica Glass said.

"I'm a poet," he said.

"But not a successful one."

"I make a living. That's more than most poets can say."

"But is it a good living? Does anyone know your name?"

"It offers me a certain freedom."

The freedom to write mediocre verse, he thought.

"Is that enough?" she said, "I mean for you," and of course it wasn't. He coveted the trappings of fame: the *New Yorker* profile, the Oscars on Stan's mantel, the trophy wives. In the night, as Lois slept at his side, he thought of Stan, stout and hairy, running his thick fingers down MacKenzie's long body.

He couldn't say these things to Veronica Glass, couldn't say them to anyone at all if you got to the heart of the matter, so he settled for, "It's what I have."

And then the lights blinked twice. Veronica Glass—that was how Ben thought of her—laughed and pinched off the joint. She handed it to him as the novelist announced that there would be an hour of readings—twenty minutes of her novel in progress (so much for the tea-kettle theory, Ben thought), followed by a young woman much admired for her jewel-like short stories, and a poet last of all. The poet, when he took the mic looked the part. He had a head of dark hair that swept back to his collarbones in perfectly sculpted waves, a voice that rang out across the crowd, a National Book Award. He was twenty-seven.

The lights came up.

"Do you envy him?" Veronica Glass asked.

"A little."

"Poetry makes nothing happen," she said.

"Does mutilation?"

"Art pour l'art."

"Art moves me," he said.

And again she asked, "Is that enough?"

"Tell me," he said, "where do you get the subjects for your art?"

"They volunteer. I have more volunteers than I can possibly use." She gave him an appraising look. "Are you interested?"

Before he could answer, he saw Lois across the room.

"Is that your wife?"

"Yes."

"What does she do?"

"She was an accountant in the unruined age," he did not say. He did not say that she read good books—books that moved her and said something true about the world—and that she loved him and forgave him his trespasses, which were many, and that that was enough. He merely smiled at her through the thump of music, the crush on the dance floor, the smell of sweat in the air. Veronica Glass lifted a hand to her in some kind of ambiguous greeting, but she was gone before Lois could wend her way to them through the crowd.

"That was Veronica Glass, the mutilation artist," he said. "You've read about her."

"I know who it was," she said.

Ben wanted to ask her to dance but they were too old for the bass pounding from the speakers; they'd lost their way. Sometime in the deepest trench of the night, a cry arose from the master bathroom. The music died. They all trooped up to look at the novelist. She was dead in the blood-splashed tub, naked, her arms flung out, slit from wrist to elbow as neatly as a pair of whitened gills. Her sagging breasts seemed deflated somehow, empty of life. Her pale face was at peace.

MacKenzie laughed hysterically, her knuckles to her mouth, her eyes bright with an almost sexual excitement. Cecy began to cry and Lois took her into her arms and hurried her home. Ben lingered as the party wound down. He watched the sun rise with Stan and MacKenzie. Afterward, they looked out over the wretched ruin that had already begun to engulf the writer's grounds. It crept toward them, turning the soil to ash. Flowers withered to dust. The guesthouse sagged. They descended to the beach and walked home.

Cecy was sleeping. Lois had waited up.

Stan and MacKenzie went off to their bedroom. Ben and Lois heard

MacKenzie cry out after a time. They wandered outside and sat on the edge of the verandah, legs dangling. Ben dug out the crumpled joint and lit it, and they looked out over the sea and smoked it together. Ben spoke of Veronica Glass, and Lois held a finger to his lips.

"I don't want to hear about her, okay?" she said.

They went into their dim bedroom. The sun cast narrow bars of light through the blinds as they made love. When Ben finished he thought of Veronica Glass; when he slept, he dreamed of her.

He dreamed of her awake and sleeping both. One more party, two, another passing encounter. She didn't always show up. He asked Stan about her. "She lives six houses down," Stan said, gesturing. "Crazy bitch."

"Crazy?"

"The things she does. You call that art?"

The last picture Stan had worked on had been a slasher flick. The usual: a bunch of kids at some summer camp, screwing and smoking dope; a crazed killer; various implements of destruction, the more imaginative the better. The virtuous survived. There would be no Oscars for this formulaic trash, Ben reminded him. And didn't it trade upon our worst impulses?

"It trades upon imagination," Stan said. "There's a difference between special effects and the genuine item."

He was right, of course, demonstrably so, yet—

Maybe not, Ben thought. Maybe special effects were worse. People thrilled to the mayhem on screen; they identified with the killers, turned them into folk heroes. No one thrilled to the work of Veronica Glass. Horror and fascination, sure—how could you do such things to a human being, and why? What had she said? "I have more volunteers than I could possibly use." And worse yet: "Are you interested?"

And he was. The whole phenomenon interested him.

"Beauty is truth, truth beauty," Keats had said.

Was there some terrible beauty here? Or worse yet, some terrible truth?

Or maybe Veronica had been right. How had she put it? Art pour l'art.

Art for art's sake.

Perhaps it was these questions that led Ben to stray down the beach one day toward her house. Perhaps it was the woman herself—that blond hair, those high cheekbones. Perhaps it was chance. (It was not chance.) Yet that's what he told himself as he mounted the stair to her house—a house like every other house along the cliff side: gray-stained shingles and acres of windows that threw back the afternoon light, blinding him, and suddenly he didn't know what he was doing there, what was his intent?

Ben started to turn away—might have done so had a voice not hailed him from the verandah. "The poet takes courage," she called, and now he saw her, leaning toward him, elbows on the railing. "Come up."

He crossed the lawn, climbed a set of winding stairs. She had turned to greet him, her back to the railing, clad in a sheer white dress. She held a clear glass with a lime wedge floating among the ice, and she laughed when she saw him. She brushed her lips first against one cheek and then another; they were moist and cool from the drink.

"So we meet by daylight, Ben Devine."

"How did you know my name?"

"It's no great mystery, is it? You're a guest of Stan Miles—and MacKenzie, of course. Dear, poor MacKenzie, and that lost child of hers. Who doesn't know you, those of us who remain, a weed sprung up among the roses?"

"Is that how you think of me, a weed?"

"Is that how you think of yourself?"

How was he to answer that question? How indeed did he perceive himself among the glittering multitude of Cerulean Cliffs? Stan had said they would fit right in—he and Lois—but did they? Ben had his doubts.

He opted for silence.

If Veronica—and when had that shift occurred exactly, when had she come to be Veronica in his mind?—expected an answer she did not say. Nor did she ask him if he wanted a drink. She simply put one together for him at a bar tucked discreetly into the shadows. He brought it to his lips: the tickle of tonic, the woodsy bite of juniper and lime. At first he thought that she didn't care about his response to her question, but then—

"Do you think the poet who read the other night—the one with the beautiful hair—was any better than you are?"

"He has the National Book Award to prove it."

"Is that the measure of success?"

"So it would seem. Here in Cerulean Cliffs anyway."

"What do you believe, Ben?"

"What's an artist without an audience?"

"I have an audience. They mostly despise me, but they can't look away. I have a raft of awards. Does that make me an artist?"

"I don't know. I don't know what you are."

"And yet you're drawn to me."

"Am I?"

"You show up at my home without invitation."

"It was you who spoke to me first."

Ben turned and rested his elbows on the railing. He finished his drink and studied the horizon. Ruin had crept still closer, ashen and gray, enveloping the sea. For some reason, tears sprang to his eyes. For the first time in months, he found himself wanting to write, to set down lines in tribute to the lost world—yet even this aspiration exceeded his meager talent, and he grieved that, too: that the poems in his mind slipped through his fingers like rain. He grieved the hollowness at the heart of the enterprise. Nothing lasted. Not marble, nor the gilded monuments of princes, shall outlive this powerful rhyme. Except that the rhyme too came to ruin in the end.

Veronica handed him another drink.

"It won't be much longer now, will it?" she said.

"No."

"What spectacular suicide have you devised?"

"None. I suppose I'll see it through."

"Perhaps suicide too is an art."

"That's the premise of your work, isn't it?"

"Art pour l'art."

"Do you believe that?"

"I don't know. I suppose there is truth in what I do. The truth of ruin and death."

"You sound like Vinnizi."

"Is that what he told you? Poor Vinnizi. He was a fool. He made films about gunfights and car chases, that's all. The most artistic thing he ever did was hurl himself over that cliff." She paused. "Have you seen my work?"

"Photographs."

"Then you have not seen it."

"I'm not sure I want to."

Yet he did. In some secret chamber of his heart he yearned for nothing more, and when she turned away from him and started into the house, Ben followed, all too aware of the lines of her body beneath her dress. She turned to smile at him.

The door swung shut at his back. The air smelled of lavender. A whisper of air conditioning caressed his skin. The floor plan was open, airy, the sparse furniture upholstered in white leather, and he was struck suddenly by the similarity to Stan's house—the similarity to all the ruined houses he had fled in the light of dawn. Only here and there stood white pedestals, and on the pedestals—Ben felt his stomach clench—Veronica Glass's art. A woman's arm, severed at the shoulder and bent at the elbow, segmented into thin discs laid in order, an inch between, as though the wounds had never been inflicted, the hand alone still whole, palm up, like Vinnizi's, in supplication. The flesh had been preserved somehow, encased in a thin clear coat of silicone; he could see the white bone, the pinkish muscle, the neatly sundered nexus of artery and vein. A detail from the *New Yorker* profile came to him: how she strapped her subjects down and worked her way up to the final amputation, sans anesthesia, applying the first thin layer of silicone at every cut to keep the volunteer from bleeding out. A collaboration, she called her work, and the horror of it came to him afresh: in the leg flayed and tacked open from hip to toe to reveal the long muscles within; the severed penis, quartered from head to scrotum, and pinned back like a terrible flower; and, dear God, the ultimate volunteer, the shaven head mounted on a waist-high pedestal, a once-handsome man, lips sewn shut with heavy black cord, small spikes driven into his eyes.

The room seemed suddenly appalling.

Ben flung himself away and staggered outside to the verandah. Downing his drink, he stared out at the sea and the encroaching ruin, and saw for himself the absurdity of Vinnizi's claim that all along he'd been making films about the end of everything. This was ruin and horror, this the art of final things. Then she touched his shoulder and Ben turned and she pressed her lips to his and dear God, his cock was like a spike he was so hard—

Ben thrust her away and stumbled down the spiral stair to the lawn. When he turned at cliff side to look back, she was still there, standing against the railing, watching him. Her sheer dress blew back in some vagary of the wind, exposing her body so that he could see the weight of her breasts and the dark triangle of her sex. Another jolt of desire convulsed him and once again he turned away. He clambered down the stair to the beach, tore off his clothes and waded into the ocean, but no matter how long he scrubbed himself in the clear water that had not yet succumbed to ruin, he could not wash himself clean.

He told Stan of it; he told Lois.

His cigarette trembled as he described it. He drank off two glasses of Scotch as he spoke and poured another. The bottle chattered against the rim of the glass. He had known the nature of her work, had seen the photos, had read the profile. Yet nothing had prepared him for the way its cold reality shook him.

What had Dickinson written? "I like a look of agony because I know it's true." And had any poet in his ken written a poem so true as Veronica Glass's work— so icy that it shivered him, so fiery that it burned? Was this not art, and did not his own work—the work of any poet or novelist, sculptor or composer—pale in comparison?

Ruin closed inexorably upon them. The parties became ever more frenetic. Suicides came in clusters now. One night, flying on heroin and prime, Gabrielle Abbruzzese slit her own throat at the stroke of midnight. The vast house rang with her otherworldly sonic landscapes, and she twirled as she died, her white ball gown blooming around her. Blood sprayed the revelers. Finally she collapsed, one leg folding under her like a broken doll's. Someone else seized the blade from her still warm hand, and then another, and another until the floor was littered with corpses. Ben and Lois watched from the gallery above. Looking up from the slaughter, Ben locked gazes with Veronica Glass, on the other side of the great circular balcony. She gave him an enigmatic smile and vanished into the crowd. The revel continued until dawn. Dancers twirled among the bloody corpses until ruin withered the privet and shattered the lawn; they made their escape as the land burned black behind them.

So passed the nights. The days passed in a haze of sun and sleep and alcohol. One boozy afternoon, Ben found himself alone with MacKenzie, watching Cecy in the yard. He made MacKenzie a vodka tonic and slumped beside her in her Adirondack chair.

"Have you given up poetry?" she asked.

"Yes," he said, and he thought of his impulse to set down some record of the dying world in lines, knowing how useless it was, how it too would come to ruin, and no one would survive to read it. He admired her body. She wore a bikini, and he could not help imagining the tan lines as Stan stripped it away and carried her off to bed.

"Why bother?" he said. "Who will survive to read it?"

"Perhaps the value of it is in the doing of the thing itself."

"Is it? Then why did you give up acting?"

"I was never really an actor," she said. "I'm not delusional."

She had been the star of a popular sitcom before her single disastrous attempt to break into film: the fading action star, the failed movie.

"I never really made it," she said. "Or if I did, I never was up to the challenge of real acting. I posed for the camera. The money didn't matter, not as a measure of artistry anyway. I was a poseur."

"That's more than I ever achieved. I was a poseur, too."

MacKenzie looked at him for the first time, really looked at him, and he saw a bright intelligence in her eyes, a self-knowledge that he had not known was there. It had been there all along, of course, but he'd been too blind to see it.

"I never read your poetry," she said.

"Who did?"

They laughed, and he felt that desire for her quicken within him.

Cecy cried out on the lawn. Her ball had plunged over the cliff. Ben retrieved it. When he returned, MacKenzie had moved to a towel. She lay on her stomach. She had undone the back of her bikini top, and he could see the swell of her breast.

"Why do you let Cecy attend the parties?" he said.

"I'm not a bad parent," she told him. "Her father—he was a bad parent."

"But you didn't answer the question."

She propped herself on her elbows, and he could see her entire breast in profile, the areola of one brown nipple. She looked at him, and he wrenched his gaze away. He met her eyes.

"I will not hide the truth from her."

"And in ruin is truth?"

"You know there is."

She lay back down, and he looked out to the sea, and even that was not eternal. "Do you want another drink?" he said.

"I'm positively parched," she said. So he made them drinks, and they drank until his face grew not unpleasantly numb and they watched Cecilia in the splendor of the grass.

Stan joined them as the shadows grew long and fell across the yard. Then Lois. The four of them drank in companionable silence through the afternoon. MacKenzie said again, "I'm not a bad parent. She has to face it the same as we do."

Lois nodded. "Perhaps you're right."

At the party that night—a sculptor's—Ben spoke with Veronica Glass.

"Are you ready yet?" she asked.

"I will never be ready."

"We'll see," she said, and drifted off into the crowd. Afterwards he sought out Lois, and they watched together as the sculptor put a sawed-off shotgun in his mouth and blew out the back of his head. A spray of blood and brain and bone adorned the wall behind him; if you stared at it long enough, you could discern a meaning that was not there.

They walked home at dawn.

Stan drifted ahead along the rocky white beach with Lois and Cecilia. Ben and MacKenzie fell back.

"Let's swim," she said.

"The water's icy," Ben said, but she slipped out of her clothes all the same. With a twinge in his breast, he watched the muscular flex of her ass as she ran into the water. She swam far out to the edge of ruin—he feared for her—before she flipped like a seal and returned. When she emerged from the foaming breakers, crystalline bubbles clung to her pubic hair. Her brown nipples were erect. She leaned into him.

"I'm so cold," she said. She turned her face to his and they kissed for a long time. He broke away at last and they walked home along the beach. By the time they reached the house and MacKenzie had showered and Cecilia had been seen safely to bed, Stan had laid out lines of cocaine on the kitchen table. The drug blasted out the cobwebs in Ben's brain. He felt a bright light pervade him, energy and clarity and a sense of absolute invulnerability. Somewhere in the conversation that followed, Stan proposed a change of partners.

"Yes, let's," Lois said, and that cool longing for MacKenzie possessed Ben. Then he thought of Veronica Glass, and he said, "I don't think I can do that, Stan." They went off to bed soon after. Lois had never seemed so desirable or his stamina so prolonged, and when he made love to her in their bright morning bedroom, he made love to her alone.

One by one, the Christmas lights along the coastline blinked out. The revelers dwindled, the parties became more intimate. Ben spoke with the poet, and they agreed that poetry was a dead art. Yet Ben was flattered when he learned that the younger man had read his work.

"You're just being kind," he said.

"No," the poet—his name was Rosenthal—said, reeling off the titles of Ben's three books. They had been published by university presses—small university presses, at that—but Rosenthal, who had been published by Little, Brown before Little, Brown decayed into rubble and his editor was ruined, quoted back a line or two of Ben's. Ben forgave him the National Book Award and his perfect hair, as well. It was all ruined now anyway, meaningless. Maybe it always had been.

That's what Rosenthal said anyway, and whether he meant it or not, it was true: as meaningless as Stan's Oscars or the dead novelist's Pulitzer or any other prize or accolade.

"And do you still write?"

"Every day," Rosenthal said.

Ben thought of Veronica Glass's dictum: art for art's sake. He proposed the tautology, knowing as he did so that even she did not believe it—that her's was the aesthetic of ruination and destruction and final things.

Rosenthal looked at him askance. "I write the truth as I see and understand it."

"And will you continue to write?"

"To the very end," Rosenthal said.

But the end was closer than he perhaps thought: the very next night, he and five others slipped into the black waves and under a full moon swam out to the ruin and ruin took them. As they pulled themselves onto the surface of the dead water, where the moldering fish had blackened into nothing, they became burned effigies of themselves, ashen. Over the next day or so the wind would disintegrate them too into nothing.

That was the night Ben saw Lois slip away into a spare bedroom with the front man of the slam band, and whether she did it for revenge or out of despair or for some reason beyond his knowing, he could not say—only that he too had had his infidelities, and his was not to judge.

"And what will you do now that she has betrayed you?" Veronica Glass said at his shoulder. "Are you ready?"

"She has not betrayed me," he said. He said, "I am not ready, nor will I ever be."

They leaned against the bar, sipping Scotch. She slipped him a handful of prime and they smoked a joint together, and the party degenerated into strobic flashes of wanton frenzy: he stumbled into an unlocked bathroom and saw MacKenzie going down on the architect who'd designed the Sony tower in Tokyo, long since ruined. He shot up with Stan in the kitchen. He found himself alone with Veronica on the verandah, looking out at the ruined ocean.

"Did you ever want a family?" he said.

She said, "Hostages to fortune," and he tried to explain that Bacon had meant something entirely different than what she was trying to say.

"No, that's what I mean exactly," she told him, and then he was lying on his back in the grass with Cecy, pointing out the constellations that ruin had not yet devoured. A great wave of grief swept over him, grief for her and grief for all lost things, and as he watched Rosenthal and his companions swim out to meet their ruin, he grieved for them, as well.

Afterwards, Ben threw up on the beach. Someone lay a cool hand upon his neck. He looked up and it was MacKenzie. No, it was Veronica Glass. No, it was Lois. He scraped sand over his vomit, staggered into the icy waves, and fell to his knees, lifting cupped handfuls of water to rinse his mouth until it felt clean and salty. He did not remember coming home, but Lois was in bed beside him when awareness returned. He whispered her awake. They wandered out into the vast glassed-in rooms, in search of drinks and cigarettes.

Stan and MacKenzie still slept.

Ben mixed gimlets and they sat out in the Adirondack chairs, their eyes closed, nursing their hangovers. Their lives had by then become an endless round of revelry and recovery, midnight suicides and daylight drinks on the verandah, grilled steaks, liquor and iced beer in the long afternoons, sex, drugs. Cecilia joined them for a while and then wandered off to the other end of the verandah to play some game of her own invention. She had the virtues and the vices of the only child—she was both intensely independent, playing solo games of her own devising, and profoundly dependent. She had been too early inducted into the mysteries of adult life and she had not yet the emotional maturity to understand them. She was prone to tantrums, and for inexplicable reasons, Ben alone had the ability to soothe her.

But today she was calm.

Ben turned his face to the sunlight. He held a sip of gimlet in his mouth and wondered when he'd last been completely sober—or when Lois had last been sober, for that matter. She'd gradually slipped into the world he lived in on the road, whether out of despair or some other more complex reasons of her own, he did not know. And regardless of what he'd said to Veronica, he did feel in some degree betrayed. But his feelings were more complicated than that. He felt too a renewed sense of physical desire for her. If she did not possess the beauty of MacKenzie—or Veronica Glass's aura of sexual intensity—she possessed the virtue of familiarity: he knew how to please her; she knew how to please him. Yes, and love, love most of all.

He reached out for her.

"Did you ever want children?" he asked.

She squeezed his hand. "It's sweet of you to ask. I used to, but—"

"But I wasn't the best candidate for fatherhood."

"No, you weren't. But you're a good man, Ben. I always believed that. I knew it, but it's a little late now, don't you think?"

"Stan and I were talking about it, that day we walked inland."

"And what did you see?"

"Ruin," he said. "Ruin and devastation."

"Yes. And any child we'd had, she would be ruined by now." Lois looked the length of the verandah. Cecy pushed along a miniature truck. She sang softly to herself. "That sweet child will be ruined soon enough. And think of the things she has seen."

"Sometimes—sometimes I think she's more equipped to see them than we are. It's part of her reality, that's all. She barely knows the world before."

"Do you think we're the last ones, Ben?"

"Does it matter? Someone somewhere will be. It's only a matter of time."

"And nothing will survive."

"Nothing."

"No, I think I'm glad we've been childless. We are sufficient unto ourselves. We always have been."

Ben heaved himself to his feet, went to the bar, and made them fresh drinks.

He stood at the rail and lit a cigarette. He recalled MacKenzie running naked into the moon-washed water and felt once again a surge of desire. The flesh forever betrayed you. He felt headachy and regretful and even now he could recall the shape of her body in almost pornographic detail. Yes, and Lois, too, slipping into the empty bedroom with the tattooed front man of the slam band—Roadkill, that had been its name, and it too was ruined. And her hand upon his neck.

"Last night—"

"I'm sorry, Ben."

"No. I wanted you to know that I'm not jealous. I want to be. I should be. But the rules seem to have changed somehow."

He drew on the cigarette, sipped his drink.

"Yes, the rules have changed," she said. "There's a kind of terrible freedom to it, isn't there?"

"Your hand upon my neck. It felt so cool." He turned to look at her. "How did I make it home?"

"Stan and I practically carried you."

"And the stairs?"

"The stairs, my love, were an absolute bitch."

He laughed humorlessly.

"I remember opening a bathroom door to see MacKenzie—"

"You needn't bother. Last night became something of an orgy, I'm afraid."

"New rules," he said.

"Or perhaps no rules at all."

No rules at all. And what did that mean but ruin?

He thought of Rosenthal, writing every day, imposing a discipline of his own upon the world until even that collapsed into despair. Was not his own resistance of MacKenzie—or of Veronica Glass—a kind of discipline, a kind of personal rule, newly instituted. Maybe that was all you had in the end: the autonomy of the individual will.

"No," he said, "I have my rules still. Maybe for the first time I have them."

He ground out his cigarette in MacKenzie's ashtray.

"Is that why you wouldn't trade spouses with Stan the other night?"

"I don't know, I haven't thought it through. It just seemed wrong, that's all."

"Surely you want MacKenzie. I saw you kissing her."

He laughed. "I've wanted MacKenzie since the day I met her."

"Then why not take the opportunity? I wouldn't have minded."

"Maybe that's it. You wouldn't have minded. There was a time you would have."

She stood and came to him and cupped his face in both hands. She gazed into his eyes, and for the first time in years, he noticed how deeply green hers were, and kind.

"What a sweet man you've become, Ben Devine."

"I only love you," he said.

"And I you," she said. She said, "I'm sorry about last night. I didn't know."

"Didn't know what?" Stan said, pushing his way out onto the verandah. MacKenzie followed.

"What a capacity for drink you had, you old fool," Lois said with a sparkling laugh.

Stan dropped into a chair with a thud. He groaned and pressed a beer to his forehead. "Bullshit," he said. "You've known that as long as you've known me." He shot them a glance and shook his head. "Lovebirds, you."

"Lovebirds are entirely monogamous," MacKenzie said from the bar.

"Then you are no lovebird."

"Nor you, my dear."

"Nor any of us," said Lois, "except for Ben, monogamous in ruin."

"What's wrong with you, Ben?" Stan said.

Ben said, "I've always been monogamous in my heart."

"Your heart's not where it matters," Stan said.

"It's the only place that matters," Lois said. They were silent after that. Wind came in off the water. The last gulls screamed, and the red sun dropped behind the roofline of the great house. "Come play with me, Mommy," Cecy called from the grass. MacKenzie went down. They played a complex game involving the shrunken soccer ball. Ben could never decipher the rules, if there were any, but their laughter lifted into the air like birdsong, and that was enough. Waves washed the rocky shore; the sound of them was music. Stan broke out a joint and the three of them shared it as the summer day drew toward dusk. The air tasted more sweet then, and the beauty of all things grew sharper and more clear in its transience.

"So what shall we do tonight?" MacKenzie said when she joined them.

"Tonight Veronica Glass is our hostess," Stan said.

Carpe diem, thought Ben. He wondered what beautiful and grotesque death Veronica Glass had concocted for herself, and he took Lois's hand and held it tight. There was so little time left to seize.

As they climbed to Veronica Glass's cliff-side home that evening, they could hear the steady thump of music. The great windows pulsed with light and shadow. Wheeling scalpels of purple and red carved the dark. Reluctantly, Ben followed the others inside. He blundered through the crowd in revulsion, trying not to see the white pedestals with their grisly human freight. But he could not avoid them: colored lasers slashed the dance floor, and each bloodless piece had been illuminated by a blaze of clear light that exposed every detail in stunning clarity—every white knob of bone and gristle, every tendon, every severed artery, root-like and blue. The supplicating hand might have been begging him for mercy, the amputated head might have been his own.

Yet Ben felt something else as well, an almost sexual arousal that he could neither deny nor sate. He stumbled into the kitchen with Stan, where they snorted lines of coke and heroin that had been laid out on the counter-top. He poured himself a slug of eighteen-year-old Macallan and drank it off like water; he smoked a flash-laced joint with a short, heavy-set woman he had not seen before, a memory sculptor whose work had gone for millions before ruin took it all. Back in the enormous glassed-in atrium, he looked for Lois—for Stan or MacKenzie or even Cecy—but they'd all disappeared into the mob. He opened a door in search of the toilet, to find himself in a dim bedroom. Two couples—no three—writhed inside, on the bed, on the floor, against the wall. Someone—was it Stan?—held out an inviting hand. Ben reeled away instead, stumbled blindly through the orgiastic throng, and slammed outside.

He staggered down to the yard and stood cliff side, looking at the ocean.

Veronica Glass said, "It's quite the party, isn't it?"

"It's that all right. What madness have you prepared for tonight?"

"You started this, Ben," she said. "We chanced to meet on Vinnizi's lawn, nothing more. You're the one who wanted to talk about my work. You're the one who showed up uninvited at my door."

The wheeling lasers painted her face in shifting arcs of green and red. They illuminated the sheer material of her dress, exposing the shadows of her hips and breasts. Against his will, he found himself aroused all over again, by her or by her work, he could not say for sure. Probably both, and as if to deny this truth about himself—and what else was art to do if it didn't strip away our masks and expose us raw and naked to the world?—as if to deny this truth, he took a step toward her.

"It's anatomy, nothing more," he said. "It's cruelty."

"The world is a cruel place," she said. "Perhaps you've noticed."

An image of the sectioned arm possessed him, its imploring hand lifted in adjuration like Vinnizi's hand. An image of the flayed leg, the head on its pedestal, its mouth sewn shut against a scream. An image, most of all, of the ruined and dying world.

His hand lashed out against his will. The blow rocked her. She wiped blood from her lip and held it up for him to see. "You prove my thesis," she said. And turning, "You could have had me, Ben. You saw the truth and you could have possessed it. It was within your grasp. Beauty is truth, truth beauty. Isn't that what you believe? Let me show you the beauty that lies at the heart of ugliness. Let me show you the heart of ruin. Let me show you truth."

She didn't wait to see if he would follow. But he did, helpless not to. Up the stairs. Across the verandah. Into the great glassed-in room. She touched a switch. The music died. The lasers ceased to sculpt the dark. The lights came up.

"It's time," she announced to the silent crowd.

She led them murmuring through a cleverly disguised door, and down a broad stairway. A cold amphitheater lay at the bottom. Enormous flat-panel screens had been mounted overhead, at an angle facing the audience. On the floor below them, gently sloping toward a central drain, Veronica had readied the tools of her trade: an X-shaped surgical table, upholstered in black; bone saws and scalpels and anatomical needles for pinning back flesh; rolls of clear silicon.

Even as Veronica began to speak, Ben knew with a sick certainty what she planned to do. "The body is my canvas," she said, "the scalpel my brush." Her audience mesmerized looked on. "I sculpt the living human flesh in ways that unveil to the unseeing eye both our fragility and our strength, our capacity for love and our capacity for cruelty. As ruin closes in upon us, let my art unfold on the canvas of your flesh: the glorious art of death—prolonged, painful, beautiful to behold."

She paused.

"I have a friend"—and here she fixed Ben, in the third row from the bottom, with her gaze—"I have a friend who equates beauty with truth, who believes that art serves something other than its own ends. I did not always countenance this, but my friend convinced me otherwise. For there is beauty in pain and in our capacity, our courage, to bear it. There is beauty in death, and in that beauty lies a truth, as well—the truth of the ruin that every day engulfs us, that has awaited us from the moment we came screaming from the womb, when we were hurled into a world indifferent to our suffering. In these, the last days of Cerulean Cliffs, we have seen our little assays in the art of death. I propose that you transcend these small attempts. We are all artists here. I challenge you to pass from this world as you have lived in it, to make your death itself your final masterpiece."

She paused.

Silence fell over the amphitheater, an undersea silence fathoms deep, the silence of breath suspended, of heartbeats held in abeyance. Ben scanned the crowd, searching for Lois—for Stan and MacKenzie, for Cecy—Cecy who had been born into a world of ruin and death. There. There. There and there. He feared for them every one, but he feared for Cecy most of all.

Someone stirred and coughed. A chorus of murmurs echoed in the chamber. A man shifted, braced his hands upon his armrests, and subsided into his seat. Veronica Glass stood silent and unmoved. Another moment passed, and then, because Cerulean Cliffs had long since plunged into desperation and despair, and most of all perhaps because ruination and devastation would soon overwhelm them every one, a woman—lean and hungry and mad—stood abruptly and said, "I will stand your challenge."

She walked down to the arena floor. Her heels rang hollow in the silence. When she reached Veronica Glass, they exchanged words too quiet to make out, like the wings of moths whispering in the corners of the room. The woman disrobed, letting her clothes fall untended around her feet. Her flesh was blue and pale in the chill air, her breasts flat, her shanks thin and flaccid. Silent tears coursed down her narrow face as she turned to face them. Veronica strapped her to the table, winching the bands cruelly tight: at wrist and elbow, ankle and knee; across her shoulders and the mound of her sex. Her head she harnessed in a mask of leather straps, fastened snugly under the headrest.

"What you do here, you do of your own will," Veronica said.

"Yes."

"And once begun, you resolve not to turn back."

"Yes," the woman said. "I want to die."

The screens lit up with an image of the woman strapped to the table. Veronica turned to face the audience. She donned gloves and goggles, a white leather apron—and began. Using a scalpel, she drew a thin bead of blood between the woman's breasts, from sternum to pubis, and then, with a delicate intersecting X, she pulled back each quarter of flesh—there was an agonizing tearing sound—to unveil the pink musculature beneath. The woman arched her back, moaning, and Cecy—Cecy who had known nothing but ruin in her short life—Cecy screamed.

Ben, startled from a kind of entranced horror, held Veronica Glass's gaze for a moment. What he saw there was madness and in the madness something worse: a kind of truth. And then he tore himself away. Lurching to his feet, he shoved his way through the seated masses to scoop Cecy up. He clutched her against his breast, soothing her into a snarl of hiccupping sobs. Together, his arms aching, they stumbled to the aisle.

"You have to walk now," he said, setting her on her feet. "You have to walk." Cecy took his hand and together they began to climb the steps of the arena.

There was a rustle of movement in the stands. Ben looked around.

MacKenzie, weeping, had begun to make her way to join them, Lois too, and Stan.

They were almost to the cliff side when the screaming began.

So ended the last suicide party at Cerulean Cliffs—or at least the last such party attended by Ben and his companions. Over the next few days they gradually shifted back to a diurnal schedule. Stan dug up an old bicycle pump to inflate Cecy's soccer ball, and they spent most afternoons on the lawn, playing her incomprehensible games. There was no more talk of trading partners. Their drinking and drug use dwindled: a beer or two after dinner, the occasional joint as twilight lengthened its blue shadows over the grass.

Late one morning, Ben and Stan made another pilgrimage inland. They traded off carrying a small cooler and when they reached the edge of the devastation—they didn't have far to go—they stretched out against the trunk of a fallen tree and drank beer. Ruin had made deep inroads into the driveway by then. The weeds on the shoulders of the rutted lane had crumbled, and the gravel had melted into slag. Scorched-looking trees had turned into charred spikes, shedding their denuded branches in slow streamers of dust. Ben finished his beer and pitched his bottle out onto the baked and fractured earth. Ruin took it. It blackened and cracked as if he'd hurled it into a fire and began to dissolve into ash.

"It won't be long now," Stan said.

"It will be long enough," Ben said, twisting open a fresh beer.

They toasted one another in silence, and walked home along the winding sun-dappled road under trees that would not see another autumn. Ben and Lois made slow, languorous love when he got back, and as he drowsed afterward, Ben found himself thinking of Veronica Glass and whether she had fallen to ruin at last. And he found himself thinking too of the poet, Rosenthal, who'd chosen ruin over discipline in the end, who'd surrendered up his art to death. "I write the truth as I see it," he'd said, or something like that, and if there was no ultimate truth here in the twilight of all things—or if there never had been—there were at least small truths: small moments worthy of preservation in rhyme, even if it too would fall to ruin, and soon: Cecy's cries of joy; and the sound of breakers on a dying beach and the gentle touch of another human's skin. Art for art's sake, after all.

"Maybe I've been wasting my time," he told Lois.

"Of course you have," she said, and that afternoon he sat at a sunlit table in the kitchen, licked the tip of his pencil, and began.

Dale Bailey lives in North Carolina with his family, and has published three novels, *The Fallen*, *House of Bones*, and *Sleeping Policemen* (with Jack Slay, Jr.). His short fiction has been a three-time finalist for the International Horror Guild Award, a two-time finalist for the Nebula Award, and a finalist for the Shirley Jackson and the Bram Stoker Awards. His International Horror Guild Award-winning novelette "Death and Suffrage" was adapted by director Joe Dante as part of Showtime Television's anthology series, *Masters of Horror*. His collection, *The End of the End of Everything: Stories*, came out in the spring. A novel, *The Subterranean Season*, will be out this fall.

Their meandering path formed a pattern
that spoke to me and me alone . . .

FRAGMENTS FROM THE NOTES
OF A DEAD MYCOLOGIST

Jeff VanderMeer

[Composed of individual note cards found in disarray and then arranged into a "best approximation" of the original order of composition.]

i.

Have you ever dreamed, like I have, of something coming up through the ground—a camera, a periscope, a conduit? Something so mundane maybe you didn't even think of it in that way. Maybe you didn't even see them, even though they have always been there. When you do notice them, you don't think of networks, you don't think of connections. But they are—connected; I've seen it. Sentinel towers communicating under the soil.

ii.

They can look almost delicate and exposed, vulnerable, and be misleading that way. You can forget that they exist in a perpetual landscape of decay and dissolution. Until you encounter one that sits there, toadlike and muscular, tough as nails. Something in the stance and the positioning that defies an easy answer. That makes you think of something neither plant nor animal, with a perception of the world entirely alien to your own.

iii.

You can lose yourself in them, these beacons no one notices. Follow them wherever they lead, if you're willing. Say, a trail leading from a newly added gravestone. A trail of red-and-white fruiting bodies that only I could see because only I was looking, just a month after the funeral and the macabre thought: perhaps they came from the grave itself, although that contradicts the point of their invisible omnipresence. And following them in that state of mind? Fragile as their gills and stems? It leads to places not shown on any map.

iv.

Some try to mimic orchids or lilies to undercut your defenses, to make you believe everything has returned to normal even though it's not okay, not even close. Some get caught in mid-step, in mid-journey, on their way to distant battles of spore and climate, colonizing as they go. Foot-soldiers that freeze as you look at them because your senses are inadequate to grasp the movement there. Although the distraction of trying brings a kind of calm.

v.

A few of their journeys reach an unexpected ending, like the trail from the gravestone, and you encounter squalid inbred colonies far from the humming, ever-living discourse of decay. From high in the dead branches of deformed pine trees, they whisper down into the mulch . . . and standing there is this place where no wind reaches and the fruiting bodies seem to have gone awry. It all seems to make mockery of any grieving part of me. This quest, this need to follow wherever it might take you. No matter what has gone missing from your life.

vi.

I know I can't have him back, but it is cruel for nature to make me think that it might be possible. He's gone. He's gone.

vii.

Others exist only to mimic both the living and the dead, recreating the memory of skulls from ages of spore memory. They give those who witness them a shudder of horrible recognition. They know that they are continually dying only to rise again, and that they are emissaries of the immortal. They bring messages of fatal importance: that we are fruiting bodies unmoored from any anchor deep beneath the soil. When we are chosen before our time or after, there is no new growth to sustain us, to make us whole again. They wear the masks of the missing, and yet we find this fascinating rather than repugnant.

viii.

The message I received came to me from a tunnel, hidden under the hill atop which lay the graveyard. I followed those fruiting bodies with their milk-white stems and red-fringed gills through the bramble and the thicket, crawling vines and storm-strewn branches. The ground had a spongy bounce to it and the air around a decrepit stream crawled with the stench of chemical run-off. But their meandering path formed a pattern that spoke to me and me alone. I found a tunnel hidden under the hill, within an abandoned circle of concrete that had once been part of a construction project. There, still following the red-and-white, within the coolness and curve of concrete, I found a door that leads down. Into the earth.

ix.

Then there are the shy loners who watch from the side, who you only meet if you approach them. These shy ones lie hidden among the bright, superficial ones that call attention to themselves, obscure the lie within them. You can miss these quiet ones if you aren't careful. You can miss out on something that is vitally important. The rare and beautiful curve of the thick neck, the line of the throat, so delicate, leading to the thick cap. Something hidden in the ground now. Stolen without reason.

x.

Perhaps it wasn't a tunnel the fruiting bodies had led me to but a conduit. Perhaps it wasn't a corridor but a refuge. The staircase spiraled down, narrow, difficult to navigate, built for someone smaller. The trail of mushroom faded away to a thready, inconsistent line, and to either side a thick moss appeared from which rose a vague phosphorescence. The moss brushed against my shoulders, my arms, my neck. A smell like something that had died and been resurrected, mingling sweet with bitter, and underneath it a hint of some other, far more familiar scent. The fading of the trail matched a fading of my interest, but even as I turned back, I knew I would return.

xi.

Great shelves of cities rise in the aftermath of rain on that hill. Vast, complex communities of microorganisms, ants, lichen, and lizards having taken refuge under that many-tiered aegis. How much goes on beneath that we never recognize? How blind are we? How solitary in our company? Does a gravestone not epitomize that loneliness? Sitting there before the rough stone, this fruiting body that has a laughable permanence. So much more truthful if it were to rot away in a single day, be replaced by another, perhaps utterly different. Take all of these flowers and pebbles and photographs and dissolve them in the soil, reveal their meaninglessness.

xii.

I returned to that place, descended further in a kind of trance, and words came spiraling up out of the dark before the gleam of the flashlight. They hit me like a rockslide, brought a tightness into my chest. Dear Jack: "His tender mercies lie across all his works, swallowing up death in resurrection." I cannot believe that, but I know you do. Written at shoulder-height, rising from amid the moss, in a riotous profusion of green-gold fruiting bodies. A generous cursive script to be so cruel. The words continued on into the darkness and my imagination went with them. A network. A conduit. Language as living beings. Have you ever been ready for something and yet not ready at all? I wanted to follow, but I couldn't. Too much of me remained on the surface. And they were my own words.

xiv.

In the darkness of deep mulch—in public parks, in back alleys, at the base of hills—the elders, falling apart, rotted to pulp-rust, and almost senseless, dissolve into particles that each reveal a self-perpetuating story. The oldest of all, past memory and past recall, communicate with no one and nothing, not even the wind. Nothing can dissolve them. Nothing can destroy them. They are already destroyed.

xv.

You can be drawn in by spores, by mushrooms, by trails of things that seem to lead nowhere and yet lead everywhere. You can find yourself deep underground staring at a wall with writing on it that you recognize intimately. They were my own words, quoted from the text he worshiped that remained meaningless to me except in that it was not meaningless to him. This I saw when I went back, to walk in the darkness that was not dark. The words glowed and I did not need my flashlight. "Death has no sting; sorrow not for those who are gone, for they reside happily in the other realm." I'd like to believe that, but I don't have it in me. It feels like a failure, or maybe it just feels like the remnants of love. The walls that carry this message I have already seen appear to breathe, and in amongst these words so spore-writ, I can see creatures living. A heartbeat wells up from deep below and thrums through the steps and into me. These are my words confronting me; I wrote them to him in a letter, and I placed it atop the coffin before they lowered it into the ground. But here they have been transformed, as if into a message just for me. Nothing can dissolve them. Nothing can destroy them.

xvi.

A few outliers extend all-knowing spies above ground, bringing in information through senses we cannot imagine, the great bulk hidden in the soil, waiting for the moment to rise and re-make the world. That which travels through them they know only as a rising brightness, a fullness that is soon gone, leaving them empty again, and searching.

xvii.

Some fruiting bodies can absorb the world entire, and in them you will see the bones of a mouse or the rust of iron filings. In an uncanny yet incomplete mimicry they become whatever surrounds them. But words? My own words? My analysis fails me. My reliance on samples fails me. My intuition . . . fails me. But the words keep unraveling along the wall and I cannot escape the hope of them, no matter where they lead. The heartbeat like a cathedral bell. The slow, sonorous breathing. The sway of the tendrils of moss around the words . . . I would like "joy and gladness" now, I would like "sorrow and sighing to flee away," but it can't and it doesn't. I haunt these places we once walked together and I feel as if I am not really here . . . in the dark, under the earth, held here snugly. Not safe, but somehow comforted.

xviii.

You know the fleshy feel of a large mushroom, the way it resists puncture at first, not like rubber but like skin. The walls so close now, the brushings against the moss that is not moss, the brushing up against my own, living words. The eruption of ejected spores filling the air with golden dust. The sound of silent wings now, inside of my mouth. The need for light, for food, and even though you know all of these things and what they might mean, also there is a need to find an end to the words. I feel now as if we were cut off in mid-sentence. As if I turned away for just a moment and when I looked again you were gone. This feeling lives in the stomach and the chest and lungs . . . and it never goes away.

xix.

Moistness and trickles of water and the clean, smooth delight you feel at finding a newly formed fruiting body—not yet picked at by animals, trod upon, ruined by the passage of time. There is no death visible in such manifestations, no matter how it pulls at them mere hours later, no matter how it becomes the point of their journey. Now I know—I must really know—that someone below is writing these words of mine. "There shall be no more death, neither sorrow, nor crying, neither shall there be any more pain: for the former things are passed away." But it's not the pain that hurts: It's the interruption, it's the not knowing."

xx.

Some contain a vibration within them, as if a music waits to be released, even if it is only in the form of spores. These words now vibrate, and the path forward is heavy with friction and heat and the sounds of industry, the heartbeat bleeding in my ears. The way back has been blocked by the moss, which has grown out from both sides of the wall to form an impenetrable mass. Downward to the end of the word, to the impossible, is all that is left to me. "Fear not, for I am with thee; I will strengthen thee; I will uphold thee." But I don't need God to strengthen me; I need you to do that.

xxi.

Nothing hides from it in its task, and all orbit it. Nothing can be said to exist now without it. The words on the wall are in my throat, thrusting up and thrusting down. It burns in floating motes and still it writes inside of me. The silhouette of everything I have ever sought to see again lies around the curve of the stairs, but if I look upon it, will it be what I need? Above, the moss that is moss still pushes down. I am terrified. I am terrified that after all of this I will not be strong enough to look upon him again, here, in this place. You'll be near the park where we came to sit and read on Sunday afternoons. I think that you will be at peace here. It will be hard to say goodbye, and it is worse to come here knowing the park is so near, but I'd prefer that to forgetting.

xxii.

Some, too, will trap with misdirection and with stealth, adapt by leading others into oblivion. That is the way of something both so aware and so oblivious. You cannot blame them, for they do only what they must. No guile exists in the honest red of their gills—no guilt, no love, no loss, no need, no want . . . only the all-consuming song of a life cycle honed and perfected and adapted over eons. But there's nothing that cannot be misunderstood by the human mind. "Comfort us in tribulation." It's not that I can't appreciate the words—I understand them now more than ever before. I just want to hear them spoken by you.

xxiii.

Dispersal
Immersion
Integration
Immolation
Dissolution
There are no words left.
There are too many [words].
You were always so beautiful.

xiv.

Nothing seems to move. Nothing seems to breathe. But everything moves. Everything breathes. You just don't know it yet, not the way I know it.

[Notecards found in the pants pocket of a body discovered in a graveyard atop a hill. The body was badly decomposed, with an unidentified green powder pouring from the mouth and nose. Face unrecognizable. Expression ecstatic. After further investigation, searchers could find no tunnel at the bottom of the hill.]

Jeff VanderMeer's most recent fiction is the *New York Times*-bestselling Southern Reach trilogy (*Annihilation*, *Authority*, and *Acceptance*), all released in 2014 by Farrar, Straus and Giroux. The series has been acquired by publishers in twenty-three other countries. Paramount Pictures/Scott Rudin Productions have acquired the movie rights. His nonfiction has appeared in the *New York Times*, the *Guardian*, the *Washington Post*, *Atlantic.com*, and the *Los Angeles Times*. A three-time World Fantasy Award winner, VanderMeer has edited or coedited many iconic fiction anthologies. He lives in Tallahassee, Florida, with his wife, the noted editor Ann VanderMeer.

The Terrible Seven . . . incredibly powerful creatures responsible for every sort of human misery, invisible and unutterably malign . . .

A WISH FROM A BONE

Gemma Files

War zone archaeology is the best kind, Hynde liked to say, when drunk—and Goss couldn't disagree, at least in terms of ratings. The danger, the constant threat, was a clarifying influence, lending everything they did an extra meaty heft. Better yet, it was the world's best excuse for having to wrap real quick and pull out ahead of the tanks, regardless of whether or not they'd actually found anything.

The site for their latest TV special was miles out from anywhere else, far enough from the border between Eritrea and the Sudan that the first surveys missed it—first, second, third, fifteenth, until updated satellite surveillance finally revealed minute differences between what local experts could only assume was some sort of temple and all the similarly colored detritus surrounding it. It didn't help that it was only a few clicks (comparatively) away from the Meroitic pyramid find in Gebel Barkal, which had naturally kept most "real" archaeologists too busy to check out what the fuck that low-lying, hill-like building lurking in the middle distance might or might not be.

Yet on closer examination, of course, it turned out somebody already *had* stumbled over it, a couple of different times; the soldiers who'd set up initial camp inside in order to avoid a dust storm had found two separate batches of bodies, fresh-ish enough that their shreds of clothing and artifacts could be dated back to the 1930s on the one hand, the 1890s on the other. Gentlemen explorers, native guides, mercenaries. Same as today, pretty much, without the "gentlemen" part.

Partially ruined, and rudimentary, to say the least. It was laid out somewhat like El-Marraqua, or the temples of Lake Nasser: a roughly half-circular building with the rectangular section facing outwards like a big, blank wall centered by a single, permanently open doorway, twelve feet high by five feet wide. No windows, though the roof remained surprisingly intact.

"This whole area was under water, a million years ago," Hynde told Goss. "See these rocks? All sedimentary. Chalk, fossils, bone-bed silica and radiolarite—amazing any of it's still here, given the wind. Must've formed in a channel or a basin . . . but no, that doesn't make sense either, because the *inside* of the place is stable, no matter how much the outside erodes."

"So they quarried stone from somewhere else, brought it here, shored it up."

"Do you know how long that would've taken? Nearest hard-rock deposits are like—five hundred miles thataway. Besides, that's not even vaguely how it looks. It's more . . . unformed, like somebody set up channels while a lava-flow was going on and shepherded it into a hexagonal pattern, then waited for it to cool enough that the up-thrust slabs fit together like walls, blending at the seams."

"What's the roof made of?"

"Interlocking bricks of mud, weed, and gravel fix-baked in the sun, then fitted together and fired afterwards, from the outside in; must've piled flammable stuff on top of it, set it alight, let it cook. The glue for the gravel was bone-dust and chunks, marinated in vinegar."

"Seriously," Goss said, perking up. "Human? This a necropolis, or what?"

"We don't know, to either."

Outside, that new chick—Camberwell? The one who'd replaced that massive Eurasian guy they'd all just called *Gojira*, rumored to have finally screwed himself to death between projects—was wrangling their trucks into camp formation, angled to provide a combination of look-out, cover, and wind-brake. Moving inside, meanwhile, Goss began taking light-meter readings and setting up his initial shots, while Hynde showed him around this particular iteration of the Oh God Can Such Things Be traveling road-show.

"Watch your step," Hynde told him, all but leading him by the sleeve. "The floor slopes down, a series of shallow shelves . . . it's an old trick, designed to force perspective, move you farther in. To develop a sense of awe."

Goss nodded, allowing Hynde to draw him towards what at first looked like one back wall, but quickly proved to be a clever illusion—two slightly overlapping partial walls, slim as theatrical flats, set up to hide a sharply zigzagging passage beyond. This, in turn, gave access to a tunnel curling downwards into a sort of cavern underneath the temple floor, through which Hynde was all too happy to conduct Goss, filming as they went.

"Take a gander at all the mosaics," Hynde told him. "Get in close. See those hieroglyphs?"

"Is that what those are? They look sort of . . . organic, almost."

"They should; they were, once. Fossils."

Goss focused his lens closer, and grinned so wide his cheeks hurt. Because yes yes fucking YES, they were: rows on rows of skeletal little pressed-flat, stonified shrimp, fish, sea-ferns, and other assorted what-the-fuck-evers, painstakingly selected, sorted, and slotted into patterns that started at calf-level and rose almost to the equally creepy baked-bone brick roof, blending into darkness.

"Jesus," he said, out loud. "This is *gold*, man, even if it turns out you can't read 'em. This is an Emmy, right here."

Hynde nodded, grinning too now, though maybe not as wide. And told him: "Wait till you see the well."

The cistern in question, hand-dug down through rock and paved inside with slimy sandstone, had a roughly twenty-foot diameter and a depth that proved unsound-able even with the party's longest reel of rope, which put it at something over sixty-one metres. Whatever had once been inside it appeared to have dried up long since, though a certain liquid quality to the echoes it produced gave indications that there might still be the remains of a water table—poisoned or pure, no way to tell—lingering at its bottom. There was a weird saline quality to the crust inside its lip, a sort of whitish, gypsumesque candle-wax-dripping formation that looked as though it was just on the verge of blooming into stalactites.

Far more interesting, however, was the design scheme its excavators had chosen to decorate the well's exterior with—a mosaic, also assembled from fossils, though in this case the rocks themselves had been pulverized before use, reduced to fragments so that they could be recombined into surreally alien patterns: fish-eyed, weed-legged, shell-winged monstrosities, cut here and there with what might be fins or wings or insect torsos halved, quartered, chimerically repurposed and slapped together to form even larger, more complex figures of which these initial grotesques were only the pointillist building blocks. Step back far enough, and they coalesced into seven figures looking off into almost every possible direction save for where the southeast compass point should go. That spot was completely blank.

"I'm thinking the well-chamber was constructed first," Hynde explained, "here, under the ground—possibly around an already-existing cave, hollowed out by water that no longer exists, through limestone that shouldn't exist. After which the entire temple would've been built overtop, to hide and protect it . . . protect them."

"The statues." Hynde nodded. "Are those angels?" Goss asked, knowing they couldn't be.

"Do they *look* like angels?"

"Hey, there are some pretty fucked-up looking angels, is what I hear. Like— rings of eyes covered in wings, or those four-headed ones from *The X-Files*."

"Or the ones that look like Christopher Walken."

"Gabriel, in *The Prophecy*. Viggo Mortensen played Satan." Goss squinted. "But these sort of look like . . . Pazuzu."

Hynde nodded, pleased. "Good call: four wings, like a moth—definitely Sumerian. This one has clawed feet; this one's head is turned backwards, or maybe upside-down. This one looks like it's got no lower jaw. *This* one has a tail and no legs at all, like a snake . . . "

"Dude, do you actually know what they are, or are you just fucking with me?"

"How much do you know about the Terrible Seven?"

"Nothing."

"Excellent. That means our viewers won't, either."

They set up in front of the door, before they lost the sun. A tight shot on Hynde, hands thrown out in what Goss had come to call his classic Profsplaining pose; Goss shot from below, framing him in the temple's gaping maw, while 'Lij the sound guy checked his levels and everybody else shut the fuck up. From the corner of one eye, Goss could just glimpse Camberwell leaning back against the point truck's wheel with her distractingly curvy legs crossed, arms braced like she was about to start doing reverse triceps push-ups. Though it was hard to tell from behind those massive sun-goggles, she didn't seem too impressed.

"The Terrible Seven were mankind's first boogeymen," Hynde told whoever would eventually be up at three in the morning, or whenever the History Channel chose to run this. "To call them demons would be too . . . Christian. To the people who feared them most, the Sumerians, they were simply a group of incredibly powerful creatures responsible for every sort of human misery, invisible and unutterably malign—literally unnameable, since to name them was, inevitably, to invite their attention. According to experts, the only way to fend them off was with the so-called 'Maskim Chant,' a prayer for protection collected by E. Campbell Thompson in his book *The Devils and Evil Spirits Of Babylonia, Volumes One and Two* . . . and even that was no sure guarantee of safety, depending just how annoyed one—or all—of the Seven might be feeling, any given day of the week . . . "

Straightening slightly, he raised one hand in mock supplication, reciting:

"They are Seven! They are Seven!
Seven in the depths of the ocean, Seven in the Heavens above,
Those who are neither male nor female, those who stretch themselves out
like chains . . .
Terrible beyond description.
Those who are Nameless. Those who must not be named.
The enemies! The enemies! Bitter poison sent by the Gods.
Seven are they! Seven!"

Nice, Goss thought, and went to cut Hynde off. But there was more, apparently—a lot of it, and Hynde seemed intent on getting it all out. Good for inserts, Goss guessed, 'specially when cut together with the spooky shit from inside . . .

"In heaven they are unknown. On earth they are not understood.
They neither stand nor sit, nor eat nor drink.
Spirits that minish the earth, that minish the land, of giant strength
and giant tread—"

("Minish"?)

"Demons like raging bulls, great ghosts,
Ghosts that break through all the houses, demons that have no shame,
seven are they!
Knowing no care, they grind the land like corn.
Knowing no mercy, they rage against mankind.
They are demons full of violence, ceaselessly devouring blood.
Seven are they! Seven are they! Seven!
They are Seven! They are Seven! They are twice Seven! They are Seven
times seven!"

Camberwell was sitting up now, almost standing, while the rest of the crew made faces at each other. Goss had been sawing a finger across his throat since *knowing no care*, but Hynde just kept on going, hair crested, complexion purpling; he looked unhealthily sweat-shiny, spraying spit. Was that froth on his lower lip?

"The wicked Arralu *and* Allatu, *who wander alone in the wilderness,*
covering man like a garment,
The wicked Namtaru, *who seizes by the throat.*

The wicked Asakku, *who envelops the skull like a fever.*
The wicked Utukku, *who slays man alive on the plain.*
The wicked Lammyatu, *who causes disease in every portion.*
The wicked Ekimmu, *who draws out the bowels.*
The wicked Gallu *and* Alu, *who bind the hands and body . . . "*

By this point even 'Lij was looking up, visibly worried. Hynde began to shake, eyes stutter-lidded, and fell sidelong even as Goss moved to catch him, only to find himself blocked—Camberwell was there already, folding Hynde into a brisk paramedic's hold.

"A rag, *something*," she ordered 'Lij, who whipped his shirt off so fast his 'phones went bouncing, rolling it flat enough it'd fit between Hynde's teeth; Goss didn't feel like being in the way, so he drew back, kept rolling. As they laid Hynde back, limbs flailing hard enough to make dust angels, Goss could just make out more words seeping out half through the cloth stopper and half through Hynde's bleeding nose, quick and dry: rhythmic, nasal, ancient. Another chant he could only assume, this time left entirely untranslated, though words here and there popped as familiar from the preceding bunch of rabid mystic bullshit—

Arralu-Allatu Namtaru Maskim
Asakku Utukku Lammyatu Maskim
Ekimmu Gallu-Alu Maskim
Maskim Maskim Maskim

Voices to his right, his left, while his lens-sight steadily narrowed and dimmed: *Go get Doc Journee, man! The fuck's head office pay her for, exactly?* 'Lij and Camberwell kneeling in the dirt, holding Hynde down, trying their best to make sure he didn't hurt himself till the only person on-site with an actual medical license got there. And all the while that same babble rising, louder and ever more throb-buzz deformed, like the guy had a swarm of bees stuck in his clogged and swelling throat . . .

ArralAllatNamtarAssakUtukkLammyatEkimmGalluAlu
MaskimMaskimMaskim
(Maskim)

The dust storm kicked up while Journee was still attending to Hynde, getting him safely laid down in a corner of the temple's outer chamber and doing her best to stabilize him even as he resolved down into some shallow-breathing species of coma.

"Any one of these fuckers flips, they'll take out a fuckin' wall!" Camberwell yelled, as the other two drivers scrambled to get the trucks as stable as possible, digging out 'round the wheels and anchoring them with rocks, applying locks to axles and steering wheels. Goss, for his own part, was already busy helping hustle the supplies inside, stacking ration-packs around Hynde like sandbags; a crash from the door made his head jerk up, just in time to see that chick Lao and her friend-who-was-a-boy Katz (both from craft services) staring at each other over a mess of broken plastic, floor between them suddenly half-turned to mud.

Katz: "What the *shit*, man!"

Lao: "I don't know, Christ! Those bottles aren't s'posed to break—"

The well, something dry and small "said" at the back of Goss's head, barely a voice at all—more a touch, in passing, in the dark.

And: "There's a well," he heard himself say, before he could think better of it. "Down through there, behind the walls."

Katz looked at Lao, shrugged. "Better check it out, then," he suggested— started to, anyhow. Until Camberwell somehow turned up between them, half stepping sidelong and half like she'd just materialized, the rotating storm her personal wormhole.

"I'll do that," she said, firmly. "Still two gallon cans in the back of Truck Two, for weight; cut a path, make sure we can get to 'em. I'll tell you if what's down there's viable."

"Deal," Lao agreed, visibly grateful—and Camberwell was gone a second later, down into the passage, a shadow into shadow. While at almost the same time, from Goss's elbow, 'Lij suddenly asked (of no one in particular, given *he* was the resident expert): "Sat-phones aren't supposed to just stop working, right?"

Katz: "Nope."

"Could be we're in a dead zone, I guess . . . or the storm . . . "

"Yeah, good luck on that, buddy."

Across the room, the rest of the party were congregating in a clot, huddled 'round a cracked packet of glow-sticks because nobody wanted to break out the lanterns, not in this weather. Journee had opened Hynde's shirt to give him CPR, but left off when he stopped seizing. Now she sat crouched above him, peering down at his chest like she was trying to play connect-the-dots with moles, hair, and nipples.

"Got a weird rash forming here," she told Goss, when he squatted down beside her. "Allergy? Or photosensitive, maybe, if he's prone to that, 'cause . . . it really does seem to turn darker the closer you move the flashlight."

"He uses a lot of sunscreen."

"Don't we all. Seriously, look for yourself."

He did. Thinking: *Optical illusion, has to be* . . . but wondering, all the same. Because—it was just so clear, so defined, rucking Hynde's skin as though something was raising it up from inside. Like a letter from some completely alien alphabet; a symbol, unrecognizable, unreadable.

(**A sigil**, the same tiny voice corrected. And Goss felt the hairs on his back ruffle, sudden-slick with cold, foul sweat.)

It took a few minutes more for 'Lij to give up on the sat-phone, tossing it aside so hard it bounced. "Try the radio mikes," Goss heard him tell himself, "see what kinda bandwidth we can . . . back to Gebel, might be somebody listening. But not the border, nope, gotta keep off *that* squawk-channel, for sure. Don't want the military gettin' wind, on either side . . . "

By then, Camberwell had been gone for almost ten minutes, so Goss felt free to leave Hynde in Journee's care and follow, at his own pace—through the passage and into the tunnel, feeling along the wall, trying to be quiet. But two painful stumbles later, halfway down the tunnel's curve, he had to flip open his phone just to see; the stone-bone walls gave off a faint, ill light, vaguely slick, a dead jellyfish luminescence.

He drew within just enough range to hear Camberwell's boots rasp on the downward slope, then pause—saw her glance over one shoulder, eyes weirdly bright through a dim fall of hair gust-popped from her severe, sweat-soaked working gal's braid. Asking, as she did: "Want me to wait while you catch up?"

Boss, other people might've appended, almost automatically, but never her. Then again, Goss had to admit, he wouldn't have really believed that shit coming from Camberwell, even if she had.

He straightened up, sighing, and joined her—standing pretty much exactly where he thought she'd've ended up, right next to the well, though keeping a careful distance between herself and its creepy-coated sides. "Try sending down a cup yet, or what?"

"Why? Oh, right . . . no, no point; that's why I volunteered, so those dumbasses *wouldn't* try. Don't want to be drinking *any* of the shit comes out of there, believe you me."

"Oh, I do, and that's—kinda interesting, given. Rings a bit like you obviously know more about this than you're letting on."

She arched a brow, denial reflex-quick, though not particularly convincing. "Hey, who was it sent Lao and what's-his-name down here, in the first place? I'm motor pool, man. Cryptoarchaeology is you and coma-boy's gig."

"Says the chick who knows the correct terminology."

"Look who I work for."

Goss sighed. "Okay, I'll bite. What's in the well?"

"What's *on* the well? Should give you some idea. Or, better yet—"

She held out her hand for his phone, the little glowing screen, with its pathetic rectangular light. After a moment, he gave it over and watched her cast it 'round, outlining the chamber's canted, circular floor: seen face on, those ridges he'd felt under his feet when Hynde first brought him in here and dismissed without a first glance, let alone a second, proved to be in-spiraling channels stained black from centuries of use: run-off ditches once used for drainage, aimed at drawing some sort of liquid—layered and faded now into muck and dust, a resinous stew clogged with dead insects—away from (what else) seven separate niches set into the surrounding walls, inset so sharply they only became apparent when you observed them at an angle.

In front of each niche, one of the mosaicked figures, with a funneling spout set at ditch-level under the creature in question's feet, or lack thereof. Inside each niche, meanwhile, a quartet of hooked spikes set vertically, maybe five feet apart: two up top, possibly for hands or wrists, depending if you were doing things Roman- or Renaissance-style; two down below, suitable for lashing somebody's ankles to. And now Goss looked closer, something else as well, in each of those upright stone coffins . . .

(Ivory scraps, shattered yellow-brown shards, broken down by time and gravity alike, and painted to match their surroundings by lack of light. Bones, piled where they fell.)

"What the fuck *was* this place?" Goss asked, out loud. But mainly because he wanted confirmation, more than anything else.

Camberwell shrugged, yet again—her default setting, he guessed. "A trap," she answered. "And you fell in it, but don't feel bad—you weren't to know, right?"

"We found it, though. Hynde, and me . . . "

"If not you, somebody else. Some places are already empty, already ruined—they just wait, long as it takes. They don't ever go away. 'Cause they *want* to be found."

Goss felt his stomach roil, fresh sweat springing up even colder, so rank he could smell it. "A trap," he repeated, biting down, as Camberwell nodded. Then: "For us?"

But here she shook her head, pointing back at the well, with its seven watchful guardians. Saying, as she did—

"Naw, man. For *them*."

• • •

She laid her hand on his, half its size but twice as strong, and walked him through it—puppeted his numb and clumsy finger-pads bodily over the clumps of fossil chunks in turn, allowing him time to recognize what was hidden inside the mosaic's design more by touch than by sight: a symbol (**sigil**) for every figure, tumor-blooming and weirdly organic, each one just ever-so-slightly different from the next. He found the thing Hynde's rash most reminded him of on number four, and stopped dead; Camberwell's gaze flicked down to confirm, her mouth moving slightly, shaping words. *Ah*, one looked like—*ah, I see. Or maybe I see you.*

"What?" he demanded, for what seemed like the tenth time in quick succession. Thinking: *I sound like a damn parrot.*

Camberwell didn't seem to mind, though. "Ashreel," she replied, not looking up. "That's what I said. The Terrible Ashreel, who wears us like clothing."

"Allatu, you mean. The wicked, who covers man like a garment—"

"Whatever, Mister G. If you prefer."

"It's just—I mean, that's nothing like what Hynde said, up there—"

"Yeah sure, 'cause that shit was what the Sumerians and Babylonians called 'em, from that book Hynde was quoting." She knocked knuckles against Hynde's brand, then the ones on either side—three sharp little raps, invisible cross-nails. "These are their actual names. Like . . . what they call themselves."

"How the fuck would you know that? Camberwell, what the hell."

Straightening, shrugging yet again, like she was throwing off flies. "There's a book, okay? The *Liber Carne*—'Book of Meat.' And all's it has is just a list of names with these symbols carved alongside, so you'll know which one you're looking at, when they're—embodied. In the flesh."

"In the—you mean *bodies*, like possession? Like that's what's happening to Hynde?" At her nod: "Well . . . makes sense, I guess, in context; he already said they were demons."

"Oh, that's a misnomer, actually. 'Terrible' used to mean 'awe-inspiring, more whatever than any other whatever,' like Tsar Ivan of all the Russias. So the Seven, the *Terrible* Seven, what they really are is angels, just like you thought."

"Fallen angels."

"Nope, those are Goetim, like you call the ones who stayed up top Elohim—*these* are Maskim, same as the Chant. Arralu-Allatu, Namtaru, Asakku, Utukku, Gallu-Alu, Ekimmu, Lammyatu; Ashreel, Yphemaal, Zemyel, Eshphoriel, Immoel, Coiab, Ushephekad. Angel of Confusion, the

Mender Angel, Angel of Severance, Angel of Whispers, Angel of Translation, Angel of Ripening, Angel of the Empty . . . "

All these half-foreign words spilling from her mouth, impossibly glib, ringing in Goss's head like popped blood vessels. But: "Wait," he threw back, struggling. "A 'trap' . . . I thought this place was supposed to be a temple. Like the people who built it worshipped these things."

"Okay, then play that out. Given how Hynde described 'em, what sort of people would *worship* the Seven, you think?"

" . . . terrible people?"

"You got it. Sad people, weird people, crazy people. People who get off on power, good, bad, or indifferent. People who hate the world they got so damn bad they don't really care what they swap it for, as long as it's *something else*."

"And they expect—the Seven—to do that for them."

"It's what they were made for."

Straight through cryptoarchaeology and out the other side, into a version of the Creation so literally Apocryphal it would've gotten them both burnt at the stake just a few hundred years earlier. Because to hear Camberwell tell it, sometimes, when a Creator got very, verrry lonely, It decided to make Itself some friends—after which, needing someplace to put them, It contracted the making of such a place out to creatures themselves made to order: fragments of its own reflected glory haphazardly hammered into vaguely humanesque form, perfectly suited to this one colossal task, and almost nothing else.

"They made the world, in other words," Goss said. "All seven of them."

"Yeah. 'Cept back then they were still one angel in seven parts—the Voltron angel, I call it. Splitting apart came later on, after the schism."

"Lucifer, war in heaven, cast down into hell and yadda yadda. All that. So this is all, what . . . some sort of metaphysical labor dispute?"

"They wouldn't think of it that way."

"How do they think of it?"

"*Differently*, like every other thing. Look, once the shit hit the cosmic fan, the Seven didn't stay with God, but they didn't go with the devil, either—they just went, forced themselves from outside space and time into the universe they'd made, and never looked back. And that was because they wanted something angels are uniquely unqualified for: free will. They wanted to be us."

Back to the fast-forward, then, the bend and the warp, till her ridiculously plausible-seeming exposition-dump seemed to come at him from everywhere at once, a perfect storm. Because: *misery's their meat, see—the honey that draws flies, by-product of every worst moment of all our brief lives, when people will*

cry out for anything who'll listen. That's when one of the Seven usually shows up,
offering help—except the kind of help they come up with is usually nothing very
helpful at all, considering how they just don't really get the way things work for us,
even now. And it's always just one of them at first, 'cause they each blame the other
for having made the decision to run, stranding themselves in the here and now, so
they don't want to be anywhere near each other . . . but if you can get 'em all in
one place—someplace like here, say, with seven bleeding, suffering vessels left all
ready and waiting for 'em—then they'll be automatically drawn back together,
like gravity, a black hole event horizon. They'll form a vector, and at the middle of
that cyclone they'll become a single angel once again, ready to tear everything they
built up right the fuck on back down.

Words words words, every one more painful than the last. Goss looked at
Camberwell as she spoke, straight on, the way he didn't think he'd ever actually
done, previously. She was short and stacked, skin tanned and plentiful, eyes
darkish brown shot with a sort of creamier shade, like petrified wood. A barely
visible scar quirked through one eyebrow, threading down over the cheekbone
beneath to intersect with another at the corner of her mouth, keloid raised in
their wake like a negative-image beauty mark, a reversed dimple.

Examined this way, at close quarters, he found he liked the look of her,
suddenly and sharply—and for some reason, that mainly made him angry.

"This is a fairy tale," he heard himself tell her, with what seemed like over-
the-top emphasis. "I'm sitting here in the dark, letting you spout some . . .
Catholic campfire story about angel-traps, free will, fuckin' misery vectors . . . "
A quick head-shake, firm enough to hurt. "None of it's true."

"Yeah, okay, you want to play it that way."

"If I *want*—?"

Here she turned on *him*, abruptly equal-fierce, clearing her throat to hork
a contemptuous wad out on the ground between them, like she was making a
point. "Look, you think I give a runny jackshit if you believe me or not? *I know*
what I know. It's just that things are gonna start to move fast from now on, so
you need to know that; *somebody* in this crap-pit does, aside from me. And I
guess—" Stopping and hissing, annoyed with herself, before adding, quieter:
"I guess I wanted to just say it, too—out loud, for once. For all the good it'll
probably do either of us."

They stood there a second, listening, Goss didn't know for what—nothing
but muffled wind, people murmuring scared out beyond the passage, a general
scrape and drip. Till he asked: "What about Hynde? Can we, like, *do* anything?"

"Not much. Why? You guys friends?"

Yes, dammit, Goss wanted to snap, but he was pretty sure she had lie-dar to go with her Seven-dar. "There's . . . not really a show, without him," was all he said, finally.

"All right, well—he's pretty good and got, at this point, so I'd keep him sedated, restrained if I could, and wait, see who else shows up: there's six more to go, after all."

"What happens if they all show up?"

"All Seven? Then we're fucked, basically, as a species. Stuck back together, the Maskim are a load-bearing boss the likes of which this world was not designed to contain, and the vector they form in proximity, well—it's like putting too much weight on a sheet of . . . something. Do it long enough, it rips wide open."

"*What* rips?"

"The crap you think? Everything."

There was a sort of a jump-cut, and Goss found himself tagging along beside her as Camberwell strode back up the passageway, listening to her tell him: "Important point about Hynde, as of right now, is to make sure he doesn't start doin' stuff to himself."

" . . . like?"

"Well—"

As she said it, though, there came a scream-led general uproar up in front, making them both break into a run. They tumbled back into the light-sticks' circular glow to find Journee contorted on the ground with her heels drumming, chewing at her own lips—everybody else had already shrunk back, eyes and mouths covered like it was catching, save for big, stupid 'Lij, who was trying his level best to pry her jaws apart and thrust his folding pocket spork in between. Goss darted forward to grab one arm, Camberwell the other, but Journee used the leverage to flip back up onto her feet, throwing them both off against the walls.

She looked straight at Camberwell, spit blood and grinned wide, as though she recognized her: *Oh, it's you. How do, buddy? Welcome to the main event.*

Then reached back into her own sides, fingers plunging straight down through flesh to grip bone—ripped her red ribs wide, whole back opening up like that meat-book Camberwell had mentioned and both lungs flopping out, way too large for comfort: two dirty gray-pink balloons breathing and growing, already disgustingly over-swollen yet inflating even further, like mammoth water wings.

The pain of it made her roar and jackknife, vomiting on her own feet. And when Journee looked up once more, horrid grin trailing yellow sick-strings, Goss saw she now had a sigil of her own embossed on her forehead, fresh as some stomped-in bone-bruise.

"Asakku, the Terrible Zemyel," Camberwell said, to no one in particular. "Who desecrates the faithful."

And: "God!" Somebody else—Lao?—could be heard to sob, behind them.

"Fuck Him," Journee rasped back, throwing the tarp pinned 'cross the permanently open doorway wide and taking impossibly off up into the storm with a single flap, blood splattering everywhere, a foul red spindrift.

'Lij slapped both hands up to seal his mouth, retching loudly; Katz fell on his ass, skull colliding with the wall's sharp surface, so hard he knocked himself out. Lao continued to sob-pray on, mindless, while everybody else just stared. And Goss found himself looking over at Camberwell, automatically, only to catch her nodding—just once, like she'd seen it coming.

"—like *that*, basically," she concluded, without a shred of surprise.

Five minutes at most, but it felt like an hour: things narrowed, got treacly, in that accident-in-progress way. Outside, the dust had thickened into its own artificial night; they could hear the thing inside Journee swooping high above it, laughing like a loon, yelling raucous insults at the sky. The other two drivers had never come back inside, lost in the storm. Katz stayed slumped where he'd fallen; Lao wept and wept. 'Lij came feeling towards Camberwell and Goss as the glow-sticks dimmed, almost clambering over Hynde, whose breathing had sunk so low his chest barely seemed to move. "Gotta *do* something, man," he told them, like he was the first one ever to have that particular thought. "*Something.* Y'know? Before it's too late."

"It was too late when we got here," Goss heard himself reply—again, not what he'd thought he was going to say, when he'd opened his mouth. His tongue felt suddenly hot, inside of his mouth gone all itchy, swollen tight; strep? Tonsillitis? Jesus, if he could only reach back in there and *scratch* . . .

And Camberwell was looking at him sidelong now, with interest, though 'Lij just continued on blissfully unaware of anything, aside from his own worries. "Look, fuck *that* shit," he said, before asking her: "Can we get to the trucks?"

She shook her head. "No driving in this weather, even if we did. You ever raise anybody, or did the mikes crap out too?"

"Uh, I don't think so; caught somebody talkin' in Arabic one time, close-ish, but it sounded military, so I rung off real quick. Something about containment protocol."

Goss: *"What?"*

"Well, I thought maybe that was 'cause they were doing minefield sweeps, or whatever—"

"When *was* this?"

" . . . fifteen minutes ago, when you guys were still down there, 'bout the time the storm went mega. Why?"

Goss opened his mouth again, but Camberwell was already bolting up, grabbing both Katz and Hynde at once by their shirt-collars, ready to heave and drag. The wind's whistle had taken on a weird, sharp edge, an atonal descending keen, so loud Goss could barely hear her—though he sure as hell saw her lips move, read them with widening, horrified eyes, at almost the same split-second he found himself turning, already in mid-leap towards the descending passage—

"—INCOMING, get the shit downstairs, before those sons of bitches bring this whole fuckin' place down around our goddamn—"

(ears)

Three hits, Goss thought, or maybe two and a half; it was hard to tell, when your head wouldn't stop ringing. What he could only assume was at least two of the trucks had gone up right as the walls came down, or perhaps a shade before. Now the top half of the temple was flattened, once more indistinguishable from the mountainside above and around it, a deadfall of shattered lava-rock, bone-bricks and fossils. No more missiles fell, which was good, yet—so far as they could tell, pinned beneath slabs and sediment—the storm above still raged on. And now they were all down in the well-room, trapped, with only a flickering congregation of phones to raise against the dark.

"Did you have any kind of *plan* when you came here, exactly?" Goss asked Camberwell, hoarsely. "I mean, aside from 'find Seven congregation site—question mark—profit'?"

To which she simply sighed, and replied—"Yeah, sort of. But you're not gonna like it."

"Try me."

Reluctantly: "The last couple times I did this, there was a physical copy of the *Liber Carne* in play, so getting rid of that helped—but there's no copy here, which makes us the *Liber Carne*, the human pages being Inscribed." He could hear the big I on that last word, and it scared him. "And when people are being Inscribed, well . . . the *best* plan is usually to just start killing those who aren't possessed until you've got less than seven left, because then why bother?"

"Uh huh . . . "

"Getting to know you people well enough to *like* you, that was my mistake, obviously," she continued, partly under her breath, like she was talking to herself. Then added, louder: "Anyhow. What we're dealing with right now is two people definitely Inscribed and possessed, four potential Inscriptions, and one halfway gone . . . "

"Halfway? Who?"

She shot him that look, yet one more time—softer, almost sympathetic. "Open your mouth, Goss."

"Why? What f—oh, you gotta be kidding."

No change, just a slightly raised eyebrow, as if to say: *Do I look it, motherfucker?* Which, he was forced to admit, she very much did not.

Nothing to do but obey, then. Or scream, and keep on screaming.

Goss felt his jaw slacken, pop out and down like an unhinged jewel-box, revealing all its secrets. His tongue's itch was approaching some sort of critical mass. And then, right then, was when he felt it—fully and completely, without even trying. Some kind of raised area on his own soft palate, yearning down as sharply as the rest of his mouth's sensitive insides yearned up, straining to map its impossibly angled curves. His eyes skittered to the well's rim, where he knew he would find its twin, if he only searched long enough.

"Uck ee," he got out, consonants drowned away in a mixture of hot spit and cold sweat. "Oh it, uck *ee*."

A small, sad nod. "The Terrible Eshphoriel," Camberwell confirmed. "Who whispers in the empty places."

Goss closed his mouth, then spat like he was trying to clear it, for all he knew that wouldn't work. Then asked, hoarsely, stumbling slightly over the words he found increasingly difficult to form: "How mush . . . time I got?"

"Not much, probably."

"'S what I fought." He looked down, then back up at her, eyes sharpening. "How you geh those scars uh yers, Cammerwell?"

"Knowing's not gonna help you, Goss." But since he didn't look away, she sighed, and replied. "Hunting accident. Okay?"

"Hmh, 'kay. Then . . . thing we need uh . . . new plan, mebbe. You 'gree?"

She nodded, twisting her lips; he could see her thinking, literally, cross-referencing what had to be a thousand scribbled notes from the margins of her mental grand grimoire. Time slowed to an excruciating crawl, within which Goss began to hear that still, small voice begin to mount up again, no doubt aware it no longer had to be particularly subtle about things anymore:

Eshphoriel Maskim, sometimes called Utukku, Angel of Whispers . . . and yes, I can hear you, little fleshbag, as you hear me; feel you, in all your incipient flowering and decay, your time-anchored freedom. We are all the same in this way, and yes, we mostly hate you for it, which only makes your pain all the sweeter, in context—though not quite so much, at this point, as we imitation-of-passionately strive to hate each other.

You guys stand outside space and time, though, right? he longed to demand, as he felt the constant background chatter of what he'd always thought of as "him" start to dim. *Laid the foundations of the Earth—you're megaton bombs, and we're like . . . viruses. So why the hell would you want to be* anything *like us? To lower yourselves that way?*

A small pause came in this last idea's wake, not quite present, yet too much there to be absent, somehow: a breath, perhaps, or the concept of one, drawn from the non-throat of something far infinitely larger. The feather's shadow, floating above the Word of God.

It does make you wonder, does it not? the small voice "said." **I know I do, and have, since before your first cells split.**

Because they want to defile the creation they set in place, yet have no real part in, Goss's mind—*his* mind, yes, he was *almost* sure—chimed in. *Because they long to insert themselves where they have no cause to be and let it shiver apart all around them, to run counter to everything, a curse on Heaven. To make themselves the worm in the cosmic apple, rotting everything they touch . . .*

The breath returned, drawn harder this time in a semi-insulted way, a universal "tch!" But at the same time, something else presented itself—just as likely, or un-. Valid as anything else, in a world touched by the Seven.

(Or because . . . maybe, this is all there is. Maybe, this is as good as it gets.)

That's all.

"I have an idea," Camberwell said, at last, from somewhere nearby. And Goss opened his mouth to answer only to hear the angel's still, small voice issue from between his teeth, replying, mildly—

"Do you, huntress? Then please, say on."

This, then, was how they all finally came to be arrayed 'round the well's rim, the seven of them who were left, standing—or propped up/lying, in Hynde and Katz's cases—in front of those awful wall-orifices, staring into the multifaceted mosaic-eyes of God's former *Flip My Universe* crew. 'Lij stood at the empty southeastern point, looking nervous, for which neither Goss nor the creature inhabiting his brain-pan could possibly blame him. While Camberwell busied herself moving from person to person, sketching quick and dirty version of the sigils on them with the point of a flick-knife she'd produced from one of her boots. Lao opened her mouth like she was gonna start crying even harder when she first saw it, but Camberwell just shot her the fearsomest glare yet—Medusa-grade, for sure—and watched her shut the fuck up, with a hitchy little gasp.

"This will bring us together sooner rather than later, you must realize," Eshphoriel told Camberwell, who nodded. Replying: "That's the idea."

"Ah. That seems somewhat . . . antithetical, knowing our works, as you claim to."

"Maybe so. But you tell me—what's better? Stay down here in the dark waiting for the air to run out only to have you celestial tapeworms soul-rape us all at last minute anyways, when we're too weak to put up a fight? Or force an end now, while we're all semi-fresh, and see what happens?"

"Fine tactics, yes—very born-again barbarian. Your own pocket Ragnarok, with all that the term implies."

"Yeah, yeah: clam up, Legion, if you don't have anything useful to contribute." To 'Lij: "You ready, sound-boy?"

"Uhhhh . . . "

"I'll take that as a 'yes.' "

Done with Katz, she swapped places with 'Lij, handing him the knife as she went, and tapping the relevant sigil. "Like that," she said. "Try to do it all in one motion, if you can—it'll hurt less."

'Lij looked dubious. **"One can't fail to notice you aren't volunteering for impromptu body-modification,"** Eshphoriel noted, through Goss's lips, while Camberwell met the comment with a tiny, bitter smile.

Replying, as she hiked her shirt up to demonstrate—"That'd be 'cause I've already got one."

Cocking a hip to display the thing in question where it nestled in the hollow at the base of her spine, more a scab than a scar, edges blurred like some infinitely fucked-up tramp stamp. And as she did, Goss saw *something* come fluttering up behind her skin, a parallel-dimension full-body ripple, the barest glowing shadow of a disproportionately huge tentacle-tip still up-thrust through Camberwell's whole being, as though everything she was, had been and would ever come to be was nothing more than some indistinct no-creature's fleshy finger-puppet.

One cream-brown eye flushed with livid color, green on yellow, while the other stayed exactly the same—human, weary, bitter to its soul's bones. And Camberwell opened her mouth to let her tongue protrude, pink and healthy except for an odd whitish strip that ran ragged down its center from tip to—not exactly *tail*, Goss assumed, since the tongue was fairly huge, or so he seemed to recall. But definitely almost to the uvula, and: oh God, oh shit, was it actually splitting as he watched, bisecting itself not-so-neatly into two separate semi-points, like a child's snaky scribble?

Camberwell gave it a flourish, swallowed the resultant spit-mouthful, then said, without much affect: "Yeah, that's right—'Gallu-Alu, the Terrible Immoel, who speaks with a dead tongue . . . '" Camberwell fluttered the organ in question at what had taken control of Goss, showing its central scars long-healed, extending the smile into a wide, entirely unamused grin. "So say hey, assfuck. Remember me now?"

"You were its vessel, then, once before," Goss heard his lips reply. **"And . . . yes, yes, I do recall it. Apologies, huntress; I cannot say, with the best will in all this world, that any of you look so very different, to me."**

Camberwell snapped her fingers. "Aw, gee." To 'Lij, sharper: "I tell you to stop cutting?"

Goss felt "his" eyes slide to poor 'Lij, caught and wavering (his face a sickly gray-green, chest heaving slightly, like he didn't know whether to run or puke), then watched him shake his head, and bow back down to it. The knife went in shallow, blunter than the job called for—he had to drag it, hooking up underneath his own hide, to make the meat part as cleanly as the job required. While Camberwell kept a sure and steady watch on the other well-riders, all of whom were beginning to look equally disturbed, even those who were supposedly unconscious. Goss felt his own lips curve, far more genuinely amused, even as an alien emotion-tangle wound itself invasively throughout his chest: half proprietorially expectant, half vaguely annoyed.

"We are coming," he heard himself say. **"All of us. Meaning you may have miscalculated, somewhat . . . what a sad state of affairs indeed, when the prospective welfare of your entire species depends on you not doing so."**

That same interior ripple ran 'round the well's perimeter as 'Lij pulled the knife past "his" sigil's final slashing loop and yanked it free, splattering the frieze in front of him; in response, the very stones seemed to arch hungrily, that composite mouth gaping, eager for blood. Above, even through the heavy-pressing rubble-mound which must be all that was left of the temple proper, Goss could hear Journee-Zemyel swooping and cawing in the updraft, swirled on endless waves of storm; from his eye's corner he saw Hynde-whoever

(Arralu-Allatu, the Terrible Ashreel, Eshphoriel supplied, helpfully) open one similarly parti-colored eye and lever himself up, clumsy-clambering to his feet. Katz's head fell back, spine suddenly hooping so heels struck shoulderblades with a wetly awful crack, and began to lift off, levitating gently, turning in the air like some horrible ornament. Meanwhile, Lao continued to grind her fisted knuckles into both eyes at once, bruising lids but hopefully held back from pulping the balls themselves, at least so long as her sockets held fast. . . .

(Ekimmu, the Terrible Coaib, who seeds without regard. Lamyatu, the Terrible Ushephekad, who opens the ground beneath us.)

From the well, dusty mortar popped forth between every suture, and the thing as a whole gave one great shrug, shivering itself apart—began caving in and expanding at the same time, becoming a nothing-column for its parts to revolve around, an incipient reality fabric-tear. And in turn, the urge to rotate likewise—just let go of gravity's pull, throw physical law to the winds, and see where that might lead—cored through Goss, ass to cranium, Vlad Tepes style, a phantom impalement pole spearing every neural pathway. Simultaneously gone limp and stiff, he didn't have to look down to know his crotch must be darkening, or over to 'Lij to confirm how the same invisible angel-driven marionette hooks were now pulling at his muscles, making his knife-hand grip and flex, sharp enough the handle almost broke free of his sweaty palm entirely—

(Namtaru, the Terrible Yphemaal, who stitches what was rent asunder)

"And now we are Seven, without a doubt," Goss heard that voice in his throat note, its disappointment audible. **"For all your bravado, perhaps you are not as well-educated as you believe."**

Camberwell shrugged yet one more time, slow but distinct; her possessed eye widened slightly, as though in surprise. And in that instant, it occurred to Goss how much of herself she still retained, even in the Immoel-thing's grip, which seemed far—slipperier, in her case, than with everybody else. Because maybe coming pre-Inscribed built up a certain pad of scar tissue in the soul, in situations like these; maybe that's what she'd been gambling on, amongst other things. Having just enough slack on her lead to allow her to do stuff like (for example) reach down into her other boot, the way she was even as they "spoke," and—

Holy crap, just how many knives does this chick walk around with, exactly?

—bringing up the second of a matched pair, trigger already thumbed, blade halfway from its socket. Tucking it beneath her jaw, point tapping at her jugular, and saying, as she did—

"Never claimed to be, but I do know *this* much: Sam Raimi got it wrong. You guys don't like wearing nothin' *dead*."

And: *That's your plan?* Goss wanted to yell, right in the face of her martyr-stupid, *fuck all y'all snarl*. Except that that was when the thing inside 'Lij (Yphemaal, its name is Yphemaal) turned him, bodily—two great twitches, a child "walking" a doll. Its purple eyes fell on Camberwell in mid-move, and narrowed; Goss heard something rush up and out in every direction, rustle-ruffling as it went: some massive and indistinct pair of wings, mostly elsewhere, only a few pinions intruding to lash the blade from Camberwell's throat before the cut could complete itself, leaving a shallow red trail in its wake.

(Another "hunting" trophy, Goss guessed, eventually. Not that she'd probably notice.)

"No," 'Lij-Yphemaal told the room at large, all its hovering sibling-selves, in a voice colder than orbit-bound satellite-skin. **"Enough."**

"We are Seven," Eshphoriel Maskim replied, with Goss's flayed mouth. **"The huntress has the right of it: remove one vessel, break the quorum, before we reassemble. If she wants to sacrifice herself, who are we to interfere?"**

"Who *were* we to, ever, every time we have? But there is another way."

The sigils flowed each to each, Goss recalled having noticed at this freak-show's outset, albeit only subconsciously—one basic design exponentially added upon, a fresh new (literal) twist summoning Two out of One, Three out of Two, Four out of Three, etcetera. Which left Immoel and Yphemaal separated by both a pair of places and a triad of contortionate squiggle-slashes; far more work to imitate than 'Lij could possibly do under pressure with his semi-blunt knife, his wholly inadequate human hands and brain.

But Yphemaal wasn't 'Lij. Hell, this very second, *'Lij* wasn't even 'Lij.

The Mender-angel was at least merciful enough to let him scream as it remade its sigil into Immoel's with three quick cuts, then slipped forth, blowing away up through the well's centre-spoke like a backwards lightning rod. Two niches on, Katz lit back to earth with a cartilaginous creak, while Lao let go just in time to avoid tearing her own corneas; Hynde's head whipped up, face gone trauma-slack but finally recognizable, abruptly vacated. And Immoel Maskim spurted forth from Camberwell in a gross black cloud from mouth, nose, the corner of the eyes, its passage dimming her yellow-green eye back to brown, then buzzed angrily back and forth between two equally useless prospective vessels until seeming to give up in disgust.

Seemed even angels couldn't be in two places at once. Who knew?

Not inside time and space, no. And unfortunately—

That's where we live, Goss realized.

Yes.

Goss saw the bulk of the Immoel-stuff blend into the well room's wall, sucked away like blotted ink. Then fell to his knees, as though prompted, only to see the well collapse in upon its own shaft, ruined forever—its final cosmic strut removed, solved away like some video game's culminative challenge.

Beneath, the ground shook, like jelly. Above, a thunderclap whoosh sucked all the dust away, darkness boiling up, peeling itself away like an onion till only the sun remained, pale and high and bright. And straight through the hole in the "roof" dropped all that was left of Journee-turned-Zemyel—face-down, from a twenty-plus-foot height, horrible thunk of impact driving her features right back into her skull, leaving nothing behind but a smashed-flat, raw meat mask.

Goss watched those wing-lungs of hers deflate, thinking: *she couldn't've survived.* And felt Eshphoriel, still lingering, clawed to his brain's pathways even in the face of utter defeat, interiorly agree that: **It does seem unlikely. But then, my sister loves to leave no toy unbroken, if only to spit in your— and our—Maker's absent eye.**

Uh huh, Goss thought back, suddenly far too tired for fear, or even sorrow. *So maybe it's time to get the fuck out too, huh, while the going's good? "Minish" yourself, like the old chant goes . . .*

Perhaps, yes. For now.

He looked to Camberwell, who stood there shaking slightly, caught off-guard for once—amazed to be alive, it was fairly obvious, part-cut throat and all. Asking 'Lij, as she dabbed at the blood: "What did you *do*, dude?"

To which 'Lij only shook his head, equally freaked. "I . . . yeah, dunno, really. I don't—even think that was me."

"No, 'course not: Yphemaal, right? Who sews crooked seams straight . . . " She shook her head, cracked her neck back and forth. "Only one of 'em still *building* stuff, these days, instead of tearing down or undermining, so maybe it's the only one of 'em who really *doesn't* want to go back, 'cause it knows what'll happen next."

"Maaaaybe," 'Lij said, dubious—then grabbed his wound, like something'd just reminded him it was there. "Oh, *shit*, that hurts!"

"You'll be fine, ya big baby—magic shit heals fast, like you wouldn't believe. Makes for a great conversation piece, too."

"Okay, sure. Hey . . . I saved your life."

Camberwell snorted. "Yeah, well—I would've saved yours, you hadn't beat me to it. Which makes us even."

'Lij opened his mouth at that, perhaps to object, but was interrupted by Hynde, his voice creaky with disuse. Demanding, of Goss directly—"Hey, Arthur, what . . . the hell *happened*, here? Last thing I remember was doing pick-ups, outside, and then—" His eyes fell on Journee, widening. "—then I, oh Christ, is that—who is that?"

Goss sighed, equally hoarse. "Long story."

By the time he was done, they were all outside—even poor Journee, who 'Lij had badgered Katz and Lao into helping roll up in a tarp, stowing her for transport in the back of the one blessedly still-operative truck Camberwell had managed to excavate from the missile-strike's wreckage. Better yet, it ensued that 'Lij's backup sat-phone was now once again functional; once contacted, the production office informed them that border skirmishes had definitely spilled over into undeclared war, thus necessitating a quick retreat to the airstrip they'd rented near Karima town. Camberwell reckoned they could make it if they started now, though the last mile or so might be mainly on fumes.

"Better saddle up," she told Goss, briskly, as she brushed past, headed for the truck's cab. Adding, to a visibly gobsmacked Hynde: "Yo, Professor: you gonna be okay? 'Cause the fact is, we kinda can't stop to let you process."

Hynde shook his head, wincing; one hand went to his chest, probably just as raw as Goss's mouth-roof. "No, I'll . . . be okay. Eventually."

"Mmm. Won't we all."

Lao opened the truck's back door and beckoned, face wan—all cried out, at least for the nonce. Prayed too, probably.

Goss clambered in first, offering his hand. "Did we at least get enough footage to make a show?" Hynde had the insufferable balls to ask him, taking it.

"Just get in the fucking truck, Lyman."

Weeks after, Goss came awake with a full-body slam, tangled in his sleeping bag and coated with cold sweat, as though having just been ejected from his dreams like a cannonball. They were in the Falklands by then, investigating a weird earthwork discovered in and amongst the 1982 war's detritus—it wound like a harrow, a potential subterranean grinding room for squishy human corn, but thankfully, nothing they'd discovered inside seemed (thus far) to indicate any sort of connection to the Seven, either directly or metaphorically.

In the interim since the Sudan, Katz had quit, for which Goss could hardly blame him—but Camberwell was still with them, which didn't make either

Goss or Hynde exactly comfortable, though neither felt like calling her on it. When pressed, she'd admitted to 'Lij that her hunting "methods" involved a fair deal of intuition-surfing, moving hither and yon at the call of her own angel voice-tainted subconscious, letting her post-Immoelization hangover do the psychic driving. Which did all seem to imply they were stuck with her, at least until the tides told her to move elsewhere . . .

She is a woman of fate, your huntress, the still, small voice of Eshphoriel Maskim told him, in the darkness of his tent. **Thus, where we go, she follows—and vice versa.**

Goss took a breath, tasting his own fear-stink. *Are you here for me?* he made himself wonder, though the possible answer terrified him even more.

Oh, I am not here at all, meat-sack. I suppose I am . . . bored, you might say, and find you a welcome distraction. For there is so much misery everywhere here, in this world of yours, and so very little I am allowed to do with it.

Having frankly no idea what to say to that, Goss simply hugged his knees and struggled to keep his breathing regular, his pulse calm and steady. His mouth prickled with gooseflesh, as though something were feeling its way around his tongue: the Whisper-angel, exploring his soul's ill-kept boundaries with unsympathetic care, from somewhere entirely Other.

I thought you were—done, is all. With me.

Did you? Yet the universe is far too complicated a place for that. And so it is that you are none of you ever so alone as you fear, nor as you hope. A pause. **Nonetheless, I am . . . glad to see you well, I find, or as much as I can be. Her too, for all her inconvenience.**

Here, however, Goss felt fear give way to anger, a welcome palate-cleanser. Because it seemed like maybe he'd finally developed an allergy to bullshit, at least when it came to the Maskim—or this Maskim, to be exact—and their fucked-up version of what passed for a celestial-to-human pep-talk.

Would've been perfectly content to let Camberwell cut her own throat, though, wouldn't you? he pointed out, shoulders rucking, hair rising like quills. *If that—brother-sister-whatever of yours hadn't made 'Lij interfere . . .*

Indubitably, yes. Did you expect anything else?

Yes! What kind of angels are you, goddammit?

The God-damned kind, Eshphoriel Maskim replied, without a shred of irony.

You damned yourselves, is what I hear, Goss snapped back—then froze, appalled by his own hubris. But no bolt of lightning fell; the ground stayed firm, the night around him quiet, aside from lapping waves. Outside, someone turned in their sleep, moaning. And beyond it all, the earthwork's narrow descending groove stood open to the stars, ready to receive whatever might arrive, as Heaven dictated.

. . . there is that, too, the still, small voice admitted, so low Goss could feel more than hear it, tolling like a dim bone bell.

(But then again—what is free will for, in the end, except to let us make our own mistakes?)

Even quieter still, that last part. So much so that, in the end—no matter how long, or hard, he considered it—Goss eventually realized it was impossible to tell if it had been meant to be the angel's thought, or his own.

Doesn't matter, he thought, closing his eyes. And went back to sleep.

Former film critic and teacher turned horror author **Gemma Files** is best known for her Weird Western Hexslinger series (*A Book of Tongues, A Ropes of Thorns,* and *A Tree of Bones*, all from ChiZine Publications). In 1999, her story "The Emperor's Old Bones" won an International Horror Guild Best Short Fiction award, while *A Book of Tongues* won the 2010 DarkScribe Magazine Black Quill Award for Small Press Chill, in both the Editors' and Readers' Choice categories. She has also written two chapbooks of speculative poetry, two story collections and a story cycle, *We Will All Go Down Together: Stories of the Five-Family Coven.* Her latest novel, *Experimental Film,* will be available from CZP by November, 2015.

She took a photo of the spell with her phone, and immediately texted it to them without explanation, confident the symbols were so powerful they would tentacle through screens and into their hearts . . .

MOTHERS, LOCK UP YOUR DAUGHTERS BECAUSE THEY ARE TERRIFYING

Alice Sola Kim

At midnight we parked by a Staples and tried some *seriously dark fucking magic*. We had been discussing it for weeks and could have stayed in that *Wouldn't it be funny if* groove forever, zipping between *Yes, we should* and *No, we shouldn't* until it became a joke so dumb that we would never. But that night Mini had said, "If we don't do it right now, I'm going to be so mad at you guys, and I'll know from now on that all you chickenheads can do is talk and not do," and the whole way she ranted at us like that, even though we were already doing and not talking, or at least about to. (We always let her do that, get all shirty and sharp with us, because she had the car, but perhaps we should have said something. Perhaps once everyone had cars, Mini would have to figure out how to live in the world as *not* a total bitch, and she would be leagues behind everyone else.)

The parking lot at night looked like the ocean, the black Atlantic, as we imagined it, and in Mini's car we brought up the spell on our phones and Caroline read it first. She always had to be first to do anything, because she had the most to prove, being scared of everything. We couldn't help but tease her about that, even though we knew it wasn't her fault—her parents made her that way, but then again, if someone didn't get told off for being a pill just because we could trace said pill-ness back to their parents, then where would it ever end?

We had an X-Acto knife and a lighter and antibacterial ointment and lard and a fat red candle still shrink-wrapped. A chipped saucer from Ronnie's dad's grandmother's wedding set, made of china that glowed even in dim light and sang when you rubbed your thumb along it, which she took because it was chipped and thought they wouldn't miss it, but we thought that was dumb because they would definitely miss the chipped one. The different one. We could have wrapped it all up and sold it as a Satanism starter kit.

Those were the things. What we did with them *we'll never tell.*

For a moment, it seemed like it would work. The moment stayed the same, even though it should have changed. A real staring contest of a moment: Ronnie's face shining in the lunar light of her phone, the slow tick of the blood into the saucer, like a radiator settling. But Mini ruined it. "Do you feel anything?" asked Mini, too soon and too loudly.

We glanced at one another, dismayed. We thought, *Perhaps if she had just waited a little longer*—"I don't think so," said Ronnie.

"I knew this was a dumb idea," said Mini. "Let's clean up this blood before it gets all over my car. So if one of you got murdered, they wouldn't blame me." Caroline handed out the Band-Aids. She put hers on and saw the blood well up instantly against the Band-Aid, not red or black or any color in particular, only a dark splotch like a shape under ice.

So much for that, everyone thought, wrong.

Mini dropped Caroline off first, even though she lived closer to Mini, then Ronnie after. It had been this way always. At first Caroline had been hurt by this, had imagined that we were talking about her in the fifteen extra minutes of alone time that we shared. The truth was both a relief and an even greater insult. There was nothing to say about Caroline, no shit we would talk that wasn't right to her face. We loved Caroline, but her best jokes were unintentional. We loved Caroline, but she didn't know how to pretend to be cool and at home in strange places like we did; she was the one who always seemed like a pie-faced country girleen wearing a straw hat and holding a suitcase, asking obvious questions, like, "Wait, which hand do you want to stamp?" or "Is that illegal?" Not that the answers were always obvious to us, but we knew what not to ask about. We knew how to be cool, so why didn't Caroline?

Usually, we liked to take a moment at the end of the night without Caroline, to discuss the events of the night without someone to remind us how young we were and how little we knew. But tonight we didn't really talk. We didn't talk about how we believed, and how our belief had been shattered. We didn't talk about the next time we would hang out. Ronnie snuck into her house. Her brother, Alex, had left the window open for her. Caroline was already in bed, wearing an ugly quilted headband that kept her bangs off her face so she wouldn't get forehead zits. Mini's mom wasn't home yet, so she microwaved some egg rolls. She put her feet up on the kitchen table, next to her homework, which had been completed hours ago. The egg rolls exploded tiny scalding droplets of water when she bit into them. She soothed her seared lips on a beer. *This is the life*, Mini thought.

We didn't go to the same school, and we wouldn't have been friends if we had. We met at an event for Korean adoptees, a party at a low-ceilinged community center catered with the stinkiest food possible. *Koreans*, amirite?! That's how we/they roll.

     Mini and Caroline were having fun. Ronnie was not having fun. Mini's fun was different from Caroline's fun, being a fake-jolly fun in which she was imagining telling her *real* friends about this doofus loser event later, although due to the fact that she was reminding them that she was adopted, they would either squirm with discomfort or stay very still and serious and stare her in the pupils with great intensity, nodding all the while. Caroline was having fun—the pure uncut stuff, nothing ironic about it. She liked talking earnestly with people her age about basic biographical details, because there was a safety in conversational topics that no one cared about all that much. Talking about which high school you go to? Great! Which activities you did at aforementioned school? Raaaad. Talking about the neighborhood where you live? How was it possible that they weren't all dead of fun! Caroline already knew and liked the K-pop sound-tracking the evening, the taste of the marinated beef and the clear noodles, dishes that her family re-created on a regular basis.

     Ronnie rooted herself by a giant cut-glass bowl full of kimchi, which looked exactly like a big wet pile of fresh guts. She soon realized that (1) the area by the kimchi was very high traffic and (2) the kimchi emitted a powerful vinegar-poop-death stench. As Ronnie edged away from the food table, Mini and Caroline were walking toward it. Caroline saw a lost and lonely soul and immediately said, "Hi! Is this your first time at a meet-up?"

     At this Ronnie experienced split consciousness, feeling annoyed that she was about to be sucked into wearying small talk *in addition to* a nearly sacramental sense of gratitude about being saved from standing alone at a gathering. You could even say that Ronnie was experiencing quadruple consciousness if you counted the fact that she was both judging and admiring Mini and Caroline— Mini for being the kind of girl who tries to look ugly on purpose and thinks it looks so great (*ooh, except it did look kinda great*), her torn sneakers and one thousand silver earrings and chewed-up hair, and Caroline of the sweetly tilted eyes and cashmere sweater dress and ballet flats like she was some pampered cat turned human.

Mini had a stainless-steel water bottle full of ice and vodka cut with the minimal amount of orange juice. She shared it with Ronnie and Caroline. And Caroline drank it. Caroline ate and drank like she was a laughing two-dimensional cutout and everything she consumed just went through her face and evaporated behind her, affecting her not at all.

Ronnie could not stop staring at Caroline, who was a one-woman band of laughing and drinking and ferrying food to her mouth and nodding and asking skin-rippingly boring questions that nevertheless got them talking. Ronnie went from laughing at Caroline to being incredibly envious of her. People got drunk just to be like Caroline!

Crap, Ronnie thought. Social graces are actually worth something.

But Caroline was getting drunk, and since she was already Caroline, she went too far with the whole being-Caroline thing and asked if she could tell us a joke. Only if we promised not to get offended!

Mini threw her head back, smiled condescendingly at an imaginary person to her left, and said, "Of course." She frowned to hide a burp that was, if not exactly a solid, still alarmingly substantial, and passed the water bottle to Ronnie.

Caroline wound up. This had the potential to be long. "So, you know how— oh wait, no, okay, this is how it starts. Okay, so white people play the violin like this." She made some movements. "Black people play it like this." She made some more movements. "And then *Korean* people play it like th—" and she began to bend at the waist but suddenly farted so loudly that it was like the fart had bent her, had then jet-packed her into the air and crumpled her to the ground.

She tried to talk over it, but Ronnie and Mini were ended by their laughter. They fell out of themselves. They were puking laughter, the laughter was a thick brambly painful rope being pulled out of their faces, but they couldn't stop it, and finally Caroline stopped trying to finish the joke and we were all laughing.

Consequences: For days after, we would think that we had exhausted the joke and sanded off all the funniness rubbing it so often with our sweaty fingers, but then we would remember again and, whoa, there we went again, off to the races.

Consequences: Summer arrived. Decoupled from school, we were free to see one another, to feel happy misfitting with one another because we knew we were peas from different pods—we delighted in being such different kinds of girls from one another.

Consequences: For weeks after, we'd end sentences with, "Korean people do it like *ppppbbbbbbbbtttth*."

There are so many ways to miss your mother. Your real mother—the one who looks like you, the one who has to love you because she grew you from her own body, the one who hates you so much that she dumped you in the garbage for white people to pick up and dust off. In Mini's case, it manifested as some weird gothy shit. She had been engaging in a shady flirtation with a clerk at an antiquarian bookshop. We did not approve. We thought this clerk wore thick-rimmed hipster glasses to hide his crow's feet and hoodies to hide his man boobs so that weird high-school chicks would still want to flirt with him. We hoped that Mini mostly liked him only because he was willing to trade clammy glances with her and go no further. Unlike us, Mini was not a fan of going far. When the manager wasn't around, this guy let her go into the room with the padlock on it, where all of the really expensive stuff was. That's where she found the book with the spell. That's were she took a photo of the spell with her phone. That's where she immediately texted it to us without any explanation attached, confident that the symbols were so powerful they would tentacle through our screens and into our hearts, and that we would know it for what it was.

Each of us had had that same moment where we saw ourselves in a photo, caught one of those wonky glances in the mirror that tricks you into thinking that you're seeing someone else, and it's electric. *Kapow boom sizzle*, you got slapped upside the head with the Korean wand, and now you feel weird at family gatherings that veer blond, you feel weird when your friends replace their Facebook profile photos with pictures of the celebrities they look like and all you have is, say, Mulan or Jackie Chan, ha-ha-ha, hahahahaha.

You feel like you could do one thing wrong, one stupid thing, and the sight of you would become a terrible taste in your parents' mouths.

"I'll tell you this," Mini had said. "None of us actually knows what happened to our mothers. None of our parents tell us anything. We don't have the cool parents who'll tell us about our backgrounds and shit like that."

For Mini, this extended to everything else. When her parents decided to get a divorce, Mini felt like she had a hive of bees in her head (her brain was both the bees and the brain that the bees were stinging). She searched online for articles about adoptees with divorced parents. The gist of the articles was that she would be going through an awfully hard time, as in, chick already felt kind of weird and dislocated when it came to family and belonging and now it was just going to be worse. *Internet, you asshole*, thought Mini. *I already knew that.* The articles for the parents told them to reassure their children. Make them feel secure and safe. She waited for the parents to try so she could flame-throw scorn all over them. They did not try. She waited longer.

And she had given up on them long before Mom finally arrived.

We were hanging out in Mini's room, not talking about our unsuccessful attempt at magic. Caroline was painting Ronnie's nails with a color called Balsamic.

"I love this color," said Caroline. "I wish my parents would let me wear it."

"Why wouldn't they?"

"I can't wear dark nail polish until I'm eighteen."

"Wait—they really said that?"

"How many things have they promised you when you turn eighteen?"

"You know they're just going to change the terms of the agreement when you actually turn eighteen, and then you'll be forty and still wearing clear nail polish and taking ballet and not being able to date."

"And not being able to have posters up in your room. Although I guess you won't need posters when you're forty."

"Fuck that! No one's taking away my posters when I get old."

Caroline didn't say anything. She shrugged, keeping her eyes on Ronnie's nails. When we first started hanging out with Caroline, we wondered if we shouldn't shit-talk Caroline's parents, because she never joined in, but we realized that she liked it. It helped her, and it helped her to not have to say anything. "You're all set. Just let it dry."

"I don't know," said Ronnie. "It doesn't go with anything. It just looks random on me."

Mini said, "Well." She squinted and cocked her head back until she had a double chin, taking all of Ronnie in. "You kind of look like you're in prison and you traded a pack of cigarettes for nail polish because you wanted to feel glamorous again."

"Wow, thanks!"

"No, come on. You know what I mean. It's great. You look tough. You look like a normal girl, but you still look tough. Look at me. I'll never look tough."

And she so wanted to, we knew. "I'd have to get a face tattoo, like a face tattoo of someone else's face over my face. Maybe I should get your face."

"Makeover montage," said Caroline.

"Koreans do makeovers like *pppppbbbbbbth*," we said.

Caroline laughed and the nail polish brush veered and swiped Ronnie's knuckle. We saw Ronnie get a little pissed. She didn't like physical insults. Once she wouldn't speak to us for an hour when Mini flicked her in the face with water in a movie theater bathroom.

"Sorry," Caroline said. She coughed. Something had gone down wrong. She coughed some more and started to retch, and we were stuck between looking away politely and staring at her with our hands held out in this Jesus-looking way, figuring out how to help. There was a wet burr to her coughing that became a growl, and the growl rose and rose until it became a voice, a fluted voice, like silver flutes, like flutes of bubbly champagne, a beautiful voice full of rich-people things.

MY DAUGHTERS

MY GIRLS

MY MY MINE MINE

Mom skipped around. When she spoke, she didn't move our mouths. We felt only the vibration of her voice rumbling through us.

"Did you come to us because we called for you?" asked Mini.

Mom liked to jump into the mouth of the person asking the question. Mini's mouth popped open. Her eyes darted down, to the side, like she was trying to get a glimpse of herself talking.

I HEARD YOU, MY DAUGHTERS

"You speak really good English," Caroline said.

I LEARNED IT WHEN I WAS DEAD

We wanted to talk to one another but it felt rude with Mom in the room. If Mom was still in the room.

LOOK AT YOU SO BEAUTIFUL

THE MOST BEAUTIFUL GIRL IN THE WORLD

Who was beautiful? Which one of us was she talking about? We asked and she did not answer directly. She only said that we were all beautiful, and any mother would be proud to have us. We thought we might work it out later.

OH, I LEFT YOU

AND OH

I'LL NEVER DO IT AGAIN

• • •

At first we found Mom highly scary. At first we were scared of her voice and the way she used our faces to speak her words, and we were scared about how she loved us already and found us beautiful without knowing a thing about us. That is what parents are supposed to do, and we found it incredibly stressful and a little bit creepy. *Our parents love us*, thought Caroline and Mini. They do, they do, they do, but every so often we cannot help but feel that we have to earn our places in our homes. Caroline did it by being perfect and PG-rated, though her mind boiled with filthy, outrageous thoughts, though she often got so frustrated at meals with her family during her performances of perfection that she wanted to bite the dining room table in half. *I'm not the way you think I am, and you're dumb to be so fooled.* Mini did it by never asking for anything. Never complaining. Though she could sulk and stew at the Olympic level. Girl's got to have an outlet.

Mom took turns with us, and in this way we got used to her. A few days after Mom's first appearance, Caroline woke herself up singing softly, a song she had never before heard. It sounded a little like *baaaaaachudaaaaa/ neeeeedeowadaaaa.* Peaceful, droning. She sang it again, and then Mom said:

THIS IS A SONG MY MOTHER SANG TO ME WHEN I DIDN'T WANT TO WAKE UP FOR SCHOOL. IT CALLS THE VINES DOWN TO LIFT YOU UP AND—

"Mom?" said Caroline.

YES, SWEETIE

"Could you speak more quietly? It gets pretty loud in my head."

Oh, Of Course. Yes. This Song Is What My Mother Sang In The Mornings. And Her Hands Were Vines And She Would Lift Lift Lift Me Up, Mom said.

Caroline's stomach muscles stiffened as she sat up by degrees, like a mummy. Caroline's entire body ached, from her toenails to her temples, but that wasn't Mom's fault. It was her other mom's fault. Summers were almost worse for Caroline than the school year was. There was more ballet, for one thing, including a pointe-intensive that made her feet twinge like loose teeth, and this really cheesed her off most of all, because her parents didn't even like ballet. They were bored into microsleeps by it, their heads drifting forward, their heads jumping back. What they liked was the idea of a daughter who did ballet, and who would therefore be skinny and not a lesbian. She volunteered at their church and attended youth group, where everyone mostly played foosball. She worked a few shifts at a chocolate shop, where she got to try every kind of chocolate they sold once and then never again. *But what if she forgot how they tasted?* She was tutored in calculus and biology, not because she needed any help with those subjects, but because her parents didn't want to wait to find out whether she was the best or not at them—they wanted best and *they wanted it now.*

Once Ronnie said, "Caroline, your parents are like Asian parents," and Mini said, "Sucks to be you," and Caroline answered, "That's not what you're going to say in a few years when you're bagging my groceries," which sounded mean, but we knew she really said it only because she was confident that we wouldn't be bagging her groceries. Except for Ronnie, actually. We were worried about Ronnie, who wasn't academically motivated like Caroline or even *C'mon, c'mon, c'mon, what's next* motivated like Mini.

That first day Caroline enjoyed ballet class as she never had before, and she knew it was because Mom was there. She felt her chin tipped upward by Mom, arranging her daughter like a flower, a sleek and sinuous flower that would be admired until it died and even afterward. Mom had learned to speak quietly, and she murmured to Caroline to stand taller and suck in her stomach and become grace itself. The ballet teacher nodded her approval.

Though You Are A Little Bit Too Fat For Ballet, Mom murmured. Caroline cringed. She said, "Yeah, but Mom, I'm not going to be a ballerina." But Mom told her that it was important to try her best at everything and not be motivated by pure careerism only.

Mom told us we were beautiful and special and loved, but that is not to say that she was afraid to criticize the fuck out of us. Once Caroline tried to sing the song about getting up in the morning to please Mom, and Mom just laughed. *Ha-Ha-Ha-Ha-Ha-Ha, Oh Sweetie Ha-Ha-Ha-Ha-Ha-Ha!*

"Mom," said Caroline. "I know the words."

You Don't Speak Korean, Mom told Caroline. *You Will Never Speak Real Korean.*

"You speak real English, though. How come you get both?"

I Told You. I'm Your Mother And I Know A Lot More Than You And I'm Dead.

It was true, though, about Caroline. The words came out of Caroline's mouth all sideways and awkward, like someone pushing a couch through a hallway. Worst of all, she didn't sound like someone speaking Korean—she sounded like someone making fun of it.

But if we knew Caroline, we knew that this was also what she wanted. Because she wanted to be perfect, so she also wanted to be told about the ways in which she was imperfect.

• • •

Mini was the first to actually see Mom. She made herself Jell-O for dinner, which was taking too long because she kept opening the refrigerator door to poke at it. Mini's brain: *C'mon, c'mon, c'mon, c'mon.* She walked around the dining room table. She tried to read the *New Yorker* that her mother had been neglecting, but it was all tiny-print listings of events that happened about five months ago anywhere but where she was. She came back to the fridge to check on the Jell-O. Its condition seemed improved from the last time she checked, and anyhow she was getting hungrier, and it wasn't like Jell-O soup was the worst thing she'd ever eaten since her mom stopped cooking after the divorce. She looked down at the Jell-O, as any of us would do before breaking that perfect jeweled surface with the spoon, and saw reflected upon it the face of another. The face was on Mini, made up of the Mini material but everything tweaked and adjusted, made longer and thinner and sadder. Mini was awed. "Is that what you look like?" Mini asked. When she spoke she realized how loose her jaw felt. "Ouch," she said. Mom said, *Oh, Honey, I Apologize. I Just Wanted You To See What Mom Looks Like. I'll Stop Now.*

"It's okay," said Mini.

Mom thought that Mini should be eating healthier food, and what do you know, Mini agreed. She told us about the dinner that Mom had Mini make. "I ate vegetables, you guys, and I kind of liked it." She did not tell us that her mother came home near the end of preparations, and Mini told her that she could not have any of it. She did not tell us that she frightened her mother with her cold, slack expression and the way she laughed at nothing in particular as she went up to her room.

Caroline would have said: *I can't believe your mom had the nerve to ask if she could!*

Ronnie would have thought: There's being butt-hurt about your parents' divorce, and then there's being epically, unfairly butt-hurt about your parents' divorce, and you are veering toward the latter, Mini my friend. But what did Ronnie know? She was still scared of Mom. She probably hated her family more than any of us—we knew something was wrong but not what was wrong—but she wouldn't let Mom come too close either.

"Have you been hanging out with Mom?"

"Yeah. We went shopping yesterday."

"I haven't seen her in a long time."

"Caroline, that's not fair! You had her first."

"I just miss her."

"Don't be jealous."

We would wake up with braids in our hair, complicated little tiny braids that we didn't know how to do. We would find ourselves making food that we didn't know how to make, stews and porridges and little sweet hotcakes. Ronnie pulled the braids out. Ronnie did not eat the food. We knew that Mom didn't like that. We knew Mom would want to have a serious talk with Ronnie soon.

We knew and we allowed ourselves to forget that we already had people in our lives who wanted to parent us, who had already been parenting us for years. But we found it impossible to accept them as our parents, now that our real mother was back. Someone's real mother. Sometimes we were sisters. Sometimes we were competitors.

Our parents didn't know us anymore. They couldn't do anything right, if they ever had in the first place. This is one problem with having another set of parents. *A dotted outline of parents.* For every time your parents forget to pick you up from soccer practice, there is the other set that would have picked you up. They—she—would have been perfect at all of it.

Ronnie was washing the dishes when a terrible pain gripped her head. She shouted and fell to her knees. Water ran over the broken glass in the sink.

Honey, said Mom, *You Won't Let Me Get To Know You. Ronnie, Don't You Love Me? Don't You Like The Food I Make For You? Don't You Miss Your Mother?*

Ronnie shook her head.

Ronnie, I Am Going To Knock First—

Someone was putting hot, tiny little fingers in her head like her head was a glove, up her nose, in her eyes, against the roof of her mouth. And then they squeezed. Ronnie started crying.

—And Then I'm Coming In.

She didn't want this; she didn't want for Mom to know her like Mom had gotten to know Caroline and Mini; she didn't want to become these weird monosyllabic love-zombies like them, them with their wonderful families— how dare they complain so much, how dare they abandon them for this creature? And perhaps Ronnie was just stronger and more skeptical, but she had another reason for wanting to keep Mom away. She was ashamed. The truth was that there was already someone inside her head. It was her brother, Alex. He was the tumor that rolled and pressed on her brain to shift her moods between dreamy and horrified.

Ronnie first became infected with the wrong kind of love for Alex on a school-day morning, when she stood in front of the bathroom mirror brushing her teeth. He had stood there not a minute before her, shaving. On school-day mornings, they were on the same schedule, nearly on top of each other. His hot footprints pressed up into hers. And then he was pressing up against her, and it was confusing, and she forgot now whose idea all of this was in the first place, but there was no mistake about the fact that she instigated everything now. Everything she did and felt, Alex returned, and this troubled Ronnie, that he never started it anymore, so that she was definitely the sole foreign element and corrupting influence in this household of Scandinavian blonds.

("Do you want to do this?") ("Okay. Then I want to do this too.")

Ronnie hated it and liked it when they did stuff in the bathroom. Having the mirror there was horrible. She didn't need to see all that to know it was wrong. Having the mirror there helped. It reassured her to see how different they looked—everything opposed and chiaroscuro—no laws were being broken and triggering alarms from deep inside their DNA.

Sometimes Alex told her that they could get married. Or if not married, they could just leave the state or the country and be together in some nameless elsewhere. The thought filled Ronnie with a vicious horror. If the Halversons weren't her parents, if Mrs. Halverson wasn't her mother, then *who was to be her mother?* Alex would still have his family. He wasn't the adopted one, after all. Ronnie would be alone in the world, with only fake companions—a blond husband who used to be her brother, and a ghost who would rest its hands on Ronnie's shoulders until the weight was unbearable, a ghost that couldn't even tell different Asian girls apart to recognize its own daughter.

Mom was silent. Ronnie stayed on the floor. She collected her limbs to herself and laced her fingers behind her neck. She felt it: something terrible approached. It was too far away to see or hear or feel, but when it finally arrived, it would shake her hard enough to break her in half. Freeing a hand, Ronnie pulled out her phone and called Mini. She told her to come quickly and to bring Caroline and it was about Mom, and before she could finish, Mom squeezed the phone and slammed Ronnie's hand hard against the kitchen cabinet.

YOU ARE A DIRTY GIRL
NEVER
HAVE I
EVER
SLUT SLUT
FILTHY SLUT

Ronnie's ears rang. Mom was crying now too. *You Do This To These People Who Took You In And Care For You*, Mom sobbed. *I Don't Know You At All. I Don't Know Any Of You.*
YOU'RE NOT NICE GIRLS
NO DAUGHTERS OF MINE

When Mini and Caroline came into the kitchen, Ronnie was sitting on the floor. Her hand was bleeding and swollen, but otherwise she was fine, her face calm, her back straight. She looked up at us. "We have to go reverse the spell. We have to send her back. I made her hate us. I'm sorry. She's going to kill us."

"Oh no," said Caroline.

Mini's head turned to look at Caroline, then the rest of her body followed. She slapped Caroline neatly across the face. *You I Don't Like So Much Either*, Mom said, using Mini's mouth to speak. *I Know What You Think About At Night, During The Day, All Day. You Can't Fool Me. I Tried And Tried—*

Mini covered her mouth, and then Mom switched to Caroline. *—And Tried To Make You Good. But Ronnie Showed Me It Was All Useless. You Are All Worthless.* Caroline shook her head until Mom left, and we pulled Ronnie up and ran out to the car together, gripping one another's hands the whole way.

We drove, or just Mini drove, but we were rearing forward in our seats, and it was as though we were all driving, strenuously, horsewhippingly, like there was an away to get to, as if what we were trying to escape was behind us and not inside of us. We were screaming and shouting louder and louder until Mini was suddenly seized again. We saw it and we waited. Mini's jaw unhinged, and we didn't scream only because this had happened many times—certainly we didn't like it when it happened to us, but that way at least we didn't have to look at it, the way that it was only skin holding the moving parts of her skull together, skin become liquid like glass in heat, and then her mouth opened beyond everything we knew to be possible, and the words that came out—oh, the words. Mini began to speak and then we did, we did scream, even though we should have been used to it by now.

DRIVE SAFE
DRIVE SAFE
DO YOU WANT TO DIE BEFORE I TEACH YOU EVERYTHING THERE IS TO KNOW

The car veered, a tree loomed, and we were garlanded in glass, and a branch insinuated itself into Mini's ribs and encircled her heart, and Ronnie sprang forth and broke against the tree, and in the backseat Caroline was marveling at how her brain became unmoored and seesawed forward into the jagged coastline of the front of her skull and back again, until she was no longer herself, and it was all so mortifying that we could have just died, and we did, we did die, we watched every second of it happen until we realized that we were back on the road, driving, and all of the preceding was just a little movie that Mom had played inside of our heads.

"Stop," said Ronnie. "Stop the car."

"No way," said Mini. "That's what she wants."

Mom's sobs again. *I Killed Myself For Love. I Killed Myself For You*, she said. *I Came Back For Girls Who Wanted Parents But You Already Had Parents.*

"Mini, listen to me," said Ronnie. "I said it because it seemed like a thing to say, and it would have been nice to have, but there is no way to reverse the spell, is there?"

"We can try it. We can go back to the parking lot and do everything, but backward."

"We can change the words. We have to try," Caroline said.

"Mom," said Ronnie, "if you're still here, I want to tell you that I want you. I'm the one who needs a mother. You saw."

"Ronnie," said Caroline, "what are you talking about?"

From Mini, Mom said, *You Girls Lie To One Another. All The Things You Don't Tell Your Friends.* Ronnie thought she already sounded less angry. Just sad and a little petulant. Maybe showing all of them their deaths by car crash had gotten it out of her system.

"The thing I'm doing," said Ronnie, "that's a thing they would kick me out of the family for doing. I need my real family. I need you." She didn't want to say the rest out loud, so she waited. She felt Mom open up her head, take one cautious step inside with one foot and then the other. Ronnie knew that she didn't want to be this way or do those things anymore. Ronnie knew that she couldn't find a way to stop or escape Alex's gaze from across the room when everyone else was watching TV. *Stop looking at me. If you could stop looking at me for just one second, then I could stop too.*

Mom, while we're speaking honestly, I don't think you're any of our mothers. I don't think you're Korean. I don't even think you come from any country on this planet.

(Don't tell me either way.)

But I don't care. I need your help, Mom. Please, are you still there? I'll be your daughter. I love your strength. I'm not scared anymore. You can sleep inside my bone marrow, and you can eat my thoughts for dinner, and I promise, I promise I'll always listen to you. Just make me good.

They didn't see Ronnie for a few months. Mini did see Alex at a concert pretty soon after everything that happened. He had a black eye and his arm in a sling. She hid behind a pillar until he passed out of sight. Mini, at least, had sort of figured it out. First she wondered why Ronnie had never told them, but then, immediately, she wondered how Ronnie could do such a thing. She wondered how Alex could do such a thing. Her thoughts shuttled back and forth between both of those stations and would not rest on one, so she made herself stop thinking about it.

As for Mini and Caroline, their hair grew out or they got haircuts, and everything was different, and Caroline's parents had allowed her to quit ballet and Mini's parents were still leaving her alone too much but she grew to like it. And when they were around, they weren't so bad. These days they could even be in the same room without screaming at each other.

There was another meet-up for Korean adoptees. They decided to go. School had started up again, and Mini and Caroline were on the wane. Mini and Caroline thought that maybe bringing it all back full circle would help. But they knew it wouldn't be the same without Ronnie.

Mini and Caroline saw us first before we saw them. They saw us emerge from a crowd of people, people that even Caroline hadn't befriended already. They saw our skin and hair, skin and eyes, hair and teeth. The way we seemed to exist in more dimensions than other people did. How something was going on with us—something was shakin' it—on the fourth, fifth, and possibly sixth dimensions. Space and time and space-time and skin and hair and teeth. You can't say "pretty" to describe us. You can't say "beautiful." You can, however, look upon us and know true terror. The Halversons know. All of our friends and admirers know.

Who are we? We are Ronnie and someone standing behind her, with hands on her shoulders, a voice in her ear, and sometimes we are someone standing inside her, with feet in her shoes, moving her around. We are Ronnie and we are her mom and we are every magazine clipping on how to charm and beautify, the tickle of a mascara wand on a tear duct, the burn of a waxed armpit.

We watched Mini and Caroline, observed how shocked they were. Afraid, too. Ronnie could tell that they would not come up to her first. *No?* she said to her mother. *No*, we said. For a moment Ronnie considered rebellion. She rejected the idea. Those girls were from the bad old days. Look at her now. She would never go back. Mom was pushing us away from them. She was telling Ronnie to let them go.

Ronnie watched Mini and Caroline recede. The tables, the tables of food and the chairs on either side of them, rushed toward us as their two skinny figures pinned and blurred. We both felt a moment of regret. She once loved them too, you know. Then her mother turned our head and we walked away.

Alice Sola Kim lives in New York. Her fiction has recently been published or is forthcoming in *Tin House, Monstrous Affections: An Anthology of Beastly Tales, McSweeney's Literary Quarterly*, and *The Magazine of Fantasy & Science Fiction*.

Family comes before everything. Someone wrongs one of yours, you bring misery to whoever offended. That's what your blood demands of you . . .

CHILDREN OF THE FANG

John Langan

1. In the Basement (Now): Secret Doors and Mole-Men

The smells of the basement: dust, mildew, and the faint, plastic stink of the synthetic rug Grandpa had spread down here two decades ago. The round, astringent odor of mothballs stuffed in the pockets of the clothes hung in the closet. A distant, damp earthiness, the soil on the other side of the cinderblock walls. The barest trace of cinnamon mixed with vanilla; underneath them, brine.

The sounds of the basement: the furnace, first humming expectantly than switching on with a dull roar. The rug scraping under her sneakers. What Rachel insisted was the ring of water in the water tank, though her father swore there was no way she could be hearing that. The house above, its timbers creaking as the air in its rooms warmed.

The feel of the basement: openness, as if the space that she knew was not as large as the house overhead was somehow bigger than it. When they were kids, Josh had convinced her that there were secret doors concealed in the walls, through which she might stumble while making her way along one of them. If she did, she would find herself in a huge, black, underground cavern full of mole-men. The prospect of utter darkness had not troubled her as much as her younger brother had intended, but the mole-men and the endless caves to which he promised they would drag her had more than made up for that. Even now, at what she liked to think of as a self-possessed twenty-five, the sensation of spaciousness raised the skin of her arms in gooseflesh.

The look of the basement: the same dark blur that occulted all but the farthest edges of her visual field. Out of habit, she switched her cane from right hand to left and flipped the light switch at the bottom of the stairs.

The resulting glow registered as only the slightest lightening in her vision. It didn't matter: she hardly needed the cane to navigate the boxed toys and clothes stacked around the basement floor, to where Grandpa's huge old freezer squatted in the corner opposite her. For what she had come to do, it was probably better that she couldn't see.

2. The Tape (1): Iram

Around her and Josh, the attic, hushed as a church. Off to one side, their grandfather's trunk, whose lack of a lock Josh, bold and nosy at sixteen as he'd ever been, had taken as an invitation to look inside it. Buried beneath old clothes, he'd found the tape recorder and cassettes. Rachel slid her index finger left over three worn, plastic buttons, pressed down on the fourth, and the tape recorder started talking. A snap and a clatter, a hiss like soda fizzing, and a voice, a man—a young man's, someone in his teens, rendered tinny and high by time and the age of the cassette: "Okay," he said, "you were saying, Dad?"

Now a second speaker, Grandpa, the nasal complaint of the accent that had followed him north to New York state from Kentucky accentuated by the recording. "It was Jerry had found the map and figured it showed some place in the Quarter, but it was me worked out where, exactly, we needed to head."

"That's Grandpa," Josh said, "And . . . Dad?"

"It isn't Dad," Rachel said.

"Then who is it?"

"I'm not sure," she said. "I think it might be Uncle Jim."

"Uncle Jim?"

"James," she said, "Dad's younger brother."

"But he ran away."

"Obviously, this was made before," she said, and shushed him.

"—the company would have been happy to have the two of you just take off," Uncle Jim was saying.

"Well," Grandpa was saying, "there was time between the end of work on one site and the beginning of work on the next. It's true, though: we couldn't wander off for a week. If we said there was a spot we wanted to investigate, the head man was willing to give us a day or two, but that was because he thought we meant something to do with oil."

"Not the Atlantis of the Sands," Jim said.

"Iram," Grandpa said. "Iram of the Pillars, *Iram dāt al-`imād*."

"Right," Jim said, "Iram. So I guess the sixty-four thousand dollar question is: did you find it?"

Their grandfather did not answer.

"Dad?" Jim said.

"Oh, we found it, all right," Grandpa said, his voice thick.

3. The Freezer (1): Early Investigations

Enamel-smooth, the surface of the freezer was no colder than anything else in the basement. Once he understood this, at the age of nine, Josh declared it evidence that the appliance was malfunctioning. Rachel corrected him. "If it was cold," she said, "it would mean it wasn't properly insulated." She softened her tone. "I know it sounds weird, but it's supposed to feel like this." She had tested the freezer with her cane, drawing the tip along the side of it and knocking every six inches. "There's something in it," she announced. She set the cane on the floor and pressed her ear to the appliance. She could hear ice sighing and shifting. When the motor clicked to life and she placed her hands on the lid, the metal trembled under her fingertips.

Six feet long by three high by three wide, the freezer served her and Josh as a prop when they were young, and a topic of conversation as they aged. She would lie, first on top of, then beside the metal box with one ear against it, trying to decipher the sounds within, while Josh ran his fingers along the rubber seam that marked the meeting of lid and container. Both of them studied the trio of padlocked latches that guaranteed Grandpa's insistence that the freezer's contents were off-limits. Josh inspected the bolts which fastened the locks to the freezer, the makes of the padlocks, their keyholes; she felt for gaps between the heads of bolts and the latches, between the latches and the freezer, tugged on the padlocks to test the strength of their hold. After speculating about diamonds, or some kind of rare artifact, or a meteor, she and Josh had decided the freezer most likely housed something connected to their grandfather's old job. Grandpa had made his money helping to establish the oil fields in Saudi Arabia, in what was known as the Empty Quarter. As he never tired of reminding them, it was among the most inhospitable places on the planet. It was, however, a desert, whose daily temperature regularly crossed the three-digit mark. What he could have brought back from such a land that would require an industrial freezer remained a mystery.

Interlude: Grandpa (1): The Hippie Wars

The house in which Rachel and her brother were raised was among the largest in Wiltwyck. However, its second story belonged entirely to their grandfather. Within the house, it was accessed by a staircase which rose from the front hall to a door at which you were required to knock for entry; outside the house, a set of stairs that clung to the southern wall brought you to a small platform and another door on which you were obliged to rap your knuckles. There was no guarantee of entry at either door; even if she and Josh had heard Grandpa clomping across his floor in the heavy work-shoes he favored, he might and frequently did choose to ignore their request for admission.

When he opened the door to them, they confronted a gallery of closed rooms against whose doors her cane knocked. Should either of them touch one of the cut-glass doorknobs, Grandpa's "You let that alone," was swift and sharp. To her, Josh complained that Grandpa's part of the house smelled funny, a description with which Rachel did not disagree. It was the odor that weighted the air after their father performed his weekly scrub of the bathroom, the chlorine slap of bleach. Heaviest in the hallways, it was slightly better in the sitting room to which Grandpa led them. There, the couch on which she and Josh positioned themselves was saturated with a sweet scent spiced with traces of nutmeg, residue of the smoke that had spilled from the bowl of Grandpa's pipe for who knew how long. Once he had settled himself opposite them, in a wooden chair whose sharp creaks seemed to give warning of its imminent collapse, he conducted what amounted to a brief interview with each of them. How was school? What had they learned today? What was one thing they'd learned this past week they could explain to him? In general, she and her brother were happy to submit to the process, because it ended with a reward of hard candy, usually lemon-drops that made her cheeks pucker, but sometimes cherry Life Savers or Atomic Fireballs.

Once in a while, the questioning did not go as smoothly. As time passed, Rachel would understand that this was due to her grandfather's moods— generally neutral if not pleasant—which could take sudden swings in a hostile, and nasty, direction. Should she and Josh find themselves in front of him during one of these shifts, the hard candies would be replaced by a lecture on how the two of them were squandering the opportunities they hadn't deserved in the first place, and were going to end up as nothing but hippies. That last word, he charged with such venom that Rachel assumed it must be among the words she was not permitted to say. If Josh had done something particularly annoying, she might use it on him, and vice-versa. Long after her parents had clarified the term's meaning, it retained something of the opprobrium with which Grandpa had infused it—so much so that, when Josh, aged twelve, answered the old man's use of it by declaring that he didn't get what the big deal about hippies was, Rachel flinched, as if her brother had shouted, "Motherfucker!" at him.

Given Grandpa's reaction, he might as well have. Already sour, his voice chilled. "Oh you don't, do you?" he said.

Josh maintained his position. "No," he said. "I mean, they were kind of weird looking, I guess, but the hippies were into peace and love. Isn't that what everyone's always telling us is important, peace and love? So," he concluded, a lawyer finishing his closing argument, "hippies don't sound all that bad, to me."

"I see," Grandpa said, his phrasing given a slight slur as he bit down on the stem of his pipe. "I take it you are an expert on the Hippie Wars."

The name was so ridiculous she almost burst out laughing. Josh managed to channel his amusement into a question. "The Hippie Wars?"

"Didn't think so," Grandpa said. "Happened back in 1968. Damned country was tearing itself apart. Group of hippies decided to leave civilization behind and live off the land, return to the nation's agrarian roots. Bunch of college drop-outs, from New Jersey, New York City. Place they selected for this enterprise was a stretch of back woods belonged to a man named Josiah Sparks. He and his family had shared a fence with our people for nigh on fifty years. Good man, who didn't mind these strangers had settled themselves on his land without so much as a by-your-leave. 'Soil's poor,' he said. 'Snakes in the leaves, bear in the caves. If they can make a go of it, might be they can teach me something.' All through the spring and summer after they arrived, he left them to their own devices. But once fall started to pave the way for winter, Josiah began to speak about his guests. 'Kids'll never make a winter out there,' he said. Good, folks said, it'll send them back where they came from. Josiah, though—it was as if he wanted them to succeed. Not what you would've expected from a marine who'd survived the Chosin Reservoir. One especially cold day, Josiah decided it was past time he went up and introduced himself to his tenants, found out what assistance he could offer them.

"Turned out, they didn't need his help. Could be, they had in the weeks right after they'd arrived. In the time since, they'd figured out a crop they could tend that would keep them in money: marijuana. When Josiah went walking into their camp, that was what he found, row upon row of the plants, set amongst the trees to conceal them. He hadn't spoken two words to them before one fellow ran up from behind and brought a shovel down on Josiah's head. Killed him straight away. Hippies panicked, decided they had to get rid of his body. They had a couple of axes to hand, so they set to chopping Josiah to pieces. Once their butchery was finished, they dumped his remains into a metal barrel along with some kindling, doused the lot with gasoline, and dropped a match on it. Their plan was to mix the ashes in with their fertilizer and spread them over their plants. Anything the fire didn't take, they'd bury.

"Could be their scheme would've worked, but a couple of Josiah's nephews decided their uncle had been gone long enough and went searching for him. They arrived to what smelled like a pork roast. Hippies ambushed them, too, but one of the brothers saw the fellow coming and laid him out. After that, the rest of the camp went for them. They fought their way clear, but it cost an ear and a few fingers between them.

"By the time Josiah's nephews returned with the rest of their menfolk and what friends they could muster, the camp had improved its armament to firearms, mostly pistols, a few shotguns. I figure they were supplied by whoever had partnered in their little enterprise. For the next week, your peace and love crew proved they could put a bullet in a man with the best of them. They favored sneak-attacks—sent a handful of men to the hospital.

"So you'll appreciate why I do not share your view of the hippie, and you'll understand my views, unlike yours, are based in fact."

Neither Rachel nor Josh questioned that their visit was over. She picked up her cane. As they stood to leave, however, Josh said, "Grandpa?"

"Hmm?"

"Weren't you already living up here with Grandma in 1968?"

"I was."

"Then how did you know about the Hippie Wars?"

Grandpa's chair creaked as he leaned forward. "You think I'm telling stories?"

"No sir," Josh said. "I was just wondering who told you."

"My cousin, Samuel, called me."

"Oh, okay, thank you," Josh said. "Did you go to Kentucky to help them?"

Grandpa paused. "I did," he said. His voice almost light, he added, "Brought those hippies a surprise."

"What?" Josh said. "What was it?"

But their grandfather would say no more.

4. The Tape (2): Down the Well

"—the shore of a dried-up lake," Grandpa was saying. "Looked like an old well, but if you'd dropped a bucket into it, you'd have come up empty. Ventilation shaft, though Jerry thought it might've helped light the place, too. He lowered me down, on account of he was a foot taller and a hundred pounds heavier than I was. Played football at Harvard, was strong as any of the roughnecks. The shaft sunk about fifty feet, then opened out. I switched on my light, and found myself dangling near the roof of a huge cavern. It was another seventy-five feet to the floor, and I couldn't tell how far away the walls were. The rock looked volcanic, which set me to wondering if this wasn't an old volcano, or at least, a series of lava tubes."

"Was it?" Uncle Jim asked.

"Don't know," Grandpa said. "I was so concerned with what we found in that place, I never managed a proper geological survey of it. I'd stake money, though, that it was the remains of a small volcano."

"Okay," Jim said. "Can you talk about what you found there?"

"It was a city," Grandpa said, "or a sizable settlement, anyway. Maybe two-thirds of the cavern had collapsed, but you could see from what was left how the ceiling swept up to openings like the one I'd been lowered through, which gave the impression of enormous tents, rising to their tent poles. Huge pillars that joined ceiling to floor added to the sensation of being under a great, black tent. Iram had also been called the city of the tent poles, and standing there shining my light around it, I could see why."

"But how did you know it was a city, and not just a cave?"

"For one thing, the entrance I'd used. We took that as a pretty clear indication that someone had known about the place and used it for something. Could've been a garbage dump, though—right? We found proof. Around the perimeter of the cavern, smaller caves had been turned into dwelling-places. There were clay jars, metal pots, folded pieces of cloth that fell apart when we touched them. A few of the caves led to even smaller caves, like bedrooms. There was evidence of fires having been kept in all of them. Plus, most of the walls had been written on. I didn't know enough about such things to identify it, but Jerry said it resembled some of what he'd seen on digs down in Dhofar."

"You must have been pretty excited," Jim said. "I mean, this was a historic find."

"It was," Grandpa said, "but we weren't thinking about that. Well, maybe a little bit. May have been some talk about an endowed chair at Columbia for Jerry, a big promotion for me. Mostly, we were interested in the tunnels we saw leading out of the cavern."

5. Family History

Officially, Grandpa had been retired from the oil company since shortly before Rachel's birth, when a series of shrewd investments had vaulted him several rungs up the economic ladder. His money had covered whatever portion of Rachel's appointments with a succession of retinal specialists her father's teachers insurance did not, and he had paid for all of the specialized schooling and instruction she had required to navigate life with minimal vision. To Rachel's mother, in particular, her grandfather was a benefactor of whose largesse she was in constant need of reminding. To Rachel, he was a sharp voice which had retained most of the accent it had acquired growing up among the eastern Kentucky knobs, when a talent for math and science had allowed him to escape first to the university, then to the world beyond, working as a geologist for the American oil companies opening the oil fields of Saudi Arabia. The edge with which he spoke matched what he said, which consisted in almost equal parts of complaint and criticism—a rare compliment thrown in, as her father put it, to keep them on their toes.

According to Dad, his father had tended to the dour as far back as he could remember, but the tendency had been locked into place after Uncle Jim had run away from home at the end of his junior year in high school. Jim had been the brains of the brothers, a prodigy in math and science like his father before him. He tried not to show it, Dad said, but Grandpa favored his younger son, seemed genuinely excited by Jim, by his abilities, kept saying that, once Jim was old enough, there were things he was going to show him . . . When they realized Jim had left home without a note or anything, the family was devastated. The police had conducted a lengthy investigation, which had included multiple interviews with each member of the family, but which had led nowhere. Grandma was heartbroken. Dad had no doubt the pain of Jim's departure lay at the root of the heart attack that killed her the following year. Grandpa was overtaken by bitterness, which his wife's death only deepened. Dad had already been away at college, and so had missed a lot of the day-to-day pain his parents had suffered, but for a long time, he said, he had been angry at his missing brother. Jim had given no hint of anything in his life so wrong as to require him abandoning it, and them, entirely. Later, especially after he'd met Mom, Dad's anger had softened. Who knew what Jim had been going through? Still waters run deep and all that.

Jim's disappearance, combined with Grandma's death—not to mention, the blossoming of his stock portfolio—had set Grandpa on the path to retirement, a destination he had reached in the months before his first grandchild appeared. As far as Dad could tell, it had been years since the old man had been happy with his job. Every other week, it seemed, he was complaining about the idiots he worked with, their failure to recognize the need for bold action. Dad had never been much interested in his father's problems at work, and while Jim had been more (and genuinely) sympathetic, Grandpa had said he couldn't explain it to his second son, he was too young. Dad supposed it was a wonder his father had stayed at his job as long as he had, but the pay was good, and he had responsibilities. After his principle obligation shrank from three members to one, however, he was free to play out the scenario he'd probably imagined a thousand times, and tender his resignation.

Grandpa's retirement had been an unusually active one. Several times a year, sometimes as often as once a month, he hired a car to take him and several large cases down to one of the metropolitan airports, JFK or LaGuardia or Newark, from which he boarded flights whose destinations were a survey of global geography: Argentina, China, Iceland, Morocco, Vietnam. Asked the purpose of his latest trip by either of his grandchildren, he would answer that he'd been called on to do a little consulting work, and if they were good while he was gone, he'd bring them back something nice. Any attempts at further questions were met by him shooing them out of whatever room they were in, telling them to go play. He was usually away for a week to ten days, although once he was gone for a month on a trip to Antarctica. While he was abroad, Rachel missed his presence in the house, but her missing him had more to do with her sense of a familiar element absent than any strong emotion. Neither her father nor her brother seemed much affected by his absence, and her mother was clearly relieved.

6. The Tape (3): The Tunnels

"—two kinds," Grandpa was saying. "There were four tunnels leading out of the main chamber. Big enough for one, maybe two folks to walk along side-by-side. They led off to smaller caves, from which further tunnels branched to more caves. Jerry was for investigating these, trying to map out as much of the place as time would allow."

"But you wanted to look at the other tunnels?" Uncle Jim said.

"There were two of them," Grandpa said, "one next to the other. Each about half as tall as the first set: three and a half, four feet. Much wider: eight, maybe nine feet. More smoothly cut. The walls of the taller tunnels were rough, covered in tool marks. The walls of the shorter tunnels were polished, smooth as glass. To me, that made them all sorts of interesting. While Jerry sketched the layout of the main cavern, I got down on my hands and knees and checked the opening of the short tunnel on my right. Straight away, when I passed my light over it, I saw it was covered in writing. That brought Jerry running. The characters were like nothing either of us had seen before, and Jerry, in particular, had seen a lot. Had the tunnel's surface not been so even, you might have mistaken the writing for the after-effect of a natural process, one of those times Mother Nature tries to fool you into believing there's intent where there isn't. The figures were composed of individual curved lines, each one like a comma, but slightly longer. These curves were put together in combinations that looked halfway between pictures and equations. We checked the tunnel on the left, and it was full of writing, too, the same script—though whatever it spelled out seemed to differ from tunnel to tunnel.

"Thing was," Grandpa went on, "while the shorter tunnels had the appearance of more recent construction, they had the feel of being much older than their counterparts. Sounds strange, I guess, but you do enough of this work, you develop a sense for these things. To Jerry and me, it was obvious that some amount of time had passed between the carving of the two sets of tunnels, and whichever came first, we were sure a long time separated it from the second. What we had was a site that had been occupied by two different— two very different groups of people. We crept into each of the shorter tunnels about ten feet, and right away, felt the floor sloping downwards. The tunnel on the right veered off to the right; the tunnel on the left headed left. I think it was that decided us on exploring these tunnels, first. The taller tunnels appeared to be carved on approximately the same level. The shorter ones promised a whole new layer, maybe more. We flipped a coin, and decided to start with the one on the right.

"We didn't get very far. No more than fifty feet in, the tunnel had collapsed. If it had been our only option, we might have searched for a way around it. As it was, we had another tunnel to try, so we crawled out the way we'd come and entered the tunnel on the left.

"Our luck with this one was better. We followed the passage down and to the left for a good couple of hundred feet. Wasn't the most pleasant trip either of us had taken. The rock was hard on our hands and knees, and it had been a spell since we'd done much in the way of crawling. We had our lights, but they didn't seem that much in the face of the darkness before and behind us, the rock hanging above us. I'm not usually one for the jitters, but I was happy enough to see the end of the tunnel ahead. Jerry was, too.

"The room we emerged into was round, shaped like a giant cylinder. From one side to the other, it was easily a hundred feet. Dome ceiling, twenty feet overhead. Across from where we'd entered was another tunnel, same dimensions as the one that had brought us here. I was all for finding out where that led, but Jerry stopped to linger a moment. He wanted to have a look at the walls, at the carvings on them.'"

Interlude: Grandpa (2): Cousin Julius and the Charolais

As a rule, Grandpa did not interfere with their parents' disciplining of them. Any decision with which he disagreed would be addressed via an incident from his own experience which he would narrate to Rachel and Josh the next time he had them upstairs. For Rachel, the most dramatic instance of this occurred when she was twelve. Seemingly overnight, a trio of neighborhood girls her age, previously friendly to her, decided that her lack of vision merited near-constant mockery. While she had been able to conceal the upset their teasing caused her from her parents, Josh had witnessed an instance of it in front of their house and immediately decided upon revenge. Rather than attacking the girls then and there, he had waited a few days, until he could catch one of them on her own. He had leapt from the bushes in which he'd been concealed and swung his heavy bookbag at the side of her head. The girl had not seen him, which had allowed him to escape and attempt the same tactic with another of the girls the following day. After what had happened to her friend, though, this girl was prepared for Josh. She raised her shoulder to take the brunt of his swing, then pivoted into a punch that dropped him to the sidewalk. As black spots were dancing in front of his vision, the girl seized him by the hair and dragged him into her house, where she turned him over to her shocked mother. During the ensuing rounds of phone calls and parental meetings, the girls' cruelty to Rachel was acknowledged and reprimanded, but the heaviest punishment descended upon Josh, who was grounded for an entire month.

In the aftermath of this incident, the mixture of embarrassment, anger, and gratitude that suffused Rachel received a generous addition of anxiety the next afternoon, when Grandpa descended to the first floor to request her and Josh's presence in his sitting room. The two of them expected a continuation of the lectures they had been on the receiving end of for the last twenty-four hours—as, Rachel guessed, did their parents, who released them into their grandfather's care with grim satisfaction. Despite her belief that Josh hadn't done anything that bad—and that there was no reason at all for her to be involved in any of this—the prospect of a reprimand from Grandpa, who had a talent for finding the words that would wound most acutely, made her stomach hurt. If only she could leave Josh to face the old man himself— but her brother, stupid as he was, had acted on her behalf, and she owed him, however grudgingly, her solidarity. Swinging her cane side-to-side, she followed Josh up the stairs to the second floor and passed along the halls with their faint smell of bleach to Grandpa's sitting room and the smoky couch. She collapsed her cane and sat beside Josh. Maybe Grandpa would finish what he had to say and turn them loose quickly.

She recognized the tinkle of glass on glass that came from one of the six-packs of old-fashioned root beer that their grandfather sometimes shared with them. The pop and sigh of a cap twisting loose confirmed her intuition that he was going to sit in front of them and drink one of the sodas as he lectured. The second pop and sigh, and the third, confused her. Was he planning to consume all three of their root beers? The floor creaked, and cold glass pressed against the fingertips of her right hand. She took the bottle, its treacly sweetness bubbling up to her nostrils, but did not lift it to her mouth, in case this was some sort of test.

Grandpa seated himself, and said, "The two of you are in a heap of trouble. It's your parents' right to raise you as they see fit, and there's naught anyone can say or do about it. It's how I was with my boys, and I won't grant your Dad any less with you. Joshua, they don't take too kindly to you walloping this one girl and trying for the other, and Rachel, they're tarring you with some of the same brush in case you had anything to do with putting your brother up to it. These days, folks tend to take a dim view of one youngster raising his hand against another. Especially if it's a girl—your Dad would say I'm wrong, times've changed, but rest assured: if those had been two boys you'd gone after, the tone of the recent discussions you've been involved in would have been different.

"I can't intervene with your parents, but there's nothing that says I can't have a few words with you. So. When I was a tad older than the two of you, I went everywhere and did everything with my cousin, Julius Augustus. Some name, I know. It was the smartest thing about him. I expect your folks would call him 'developmentally delayed' or somesuch. We said he was slow. He was four years older, but he sat through ninth grade with me. It was his third time, after two tries at the grade before. He'd wanted to quit school and find a job, maybe on his uncle's farm, but Julius's dad fancied himself an educated man—which I guess you might have guessed from the names he loaded on his son—and he could not believe a child of his would not possess the same aptitude for learning as himself. Once I'd moved on to tenth grade and Julius had been invited to give ninth another try, his father relented, and allowed him to ask his uncle about that job.

"Julius's dad, Roy, was my uncle by marriage. His family owned a farm a couple of miles up the road from where I lived. Had a big house set atop a knob, from which they looked down on the rest of us. They'd been fairly scandalized when Roy took a liking to Aunt Allison, who was my mom's middle sister, but Roy had proved more stubborn than the rest of his family, and in the end, his father had granted Roy and Allison a piece of land which ran along one bank of the stream that swung around the foot of the hill. Julius Augustus was their only child who lived, and if folks judged it ironic that a man of Roy's intellectual pretensions found himself with a boy who had trouble with the Sunday funnies, none of them denied the sweetness of Julius's temperament. You could say or do nigh on anything to him, and the most it would provoke was a frown.

"It let him get along at his uncle's, which had been his grandfather's until the old man's heart had burst. The grandfather hadn't been what you'd call kind to his laborers, but he had been fair. His elder son, Roy's brother, Rick, was less consistent. Not long after his father's death, Rick had sunk a fair portion of the farm's money into a project he'd been talking up for years. He bought a small herd of French cattle—Charolais, the breed was called. He'd seen them while he was serving in France, in what we still called the Great War. Bigger cattle, heavier, more meat on them. Cream-colored. Rick had a notion they would give him an advantage over the local competition, so he returned to France, found some animals he liked and a farmer willing to sell them, and arranged to have his white cattle shipped across the Atlantic. This was no easy task, not least because the Great Depression still had the country in its claws. More than few palms wanted crossing with silver, and then a couple of the cows sickened and died on the journey. The Charolais that arrived took to the farm well enough, but Rick had imagined that, as soon as they were grazing his fields, everything was going to happen overnight, which, of course, it didn't. The great sea of white cattle he pictured needed time to establish itself. I guess some folks, including Roy, tried telling him this, but Rick would not, maybe could not, accept it. After another pair of the Charolais died their first summer, Rick decided it was because they hadn't been eating the best grass. Anyone could see that the grass all over the farm, and all around the farm, was pretty much the same. But Rick got it in his head that the grazing would make his herd prosper lay on the far side of the stream that snaked around the base of their family's hill—where Roy, Allison, and Julius had their home. Had he asked Roy to allow the cattle to feed on his land, his brother might've agreed. Rick demanded, though, said it was his right as elder son and heir to the farm to do what was best for it. Roy didn't argue his authority over what happened on the farm. But, he said, his property was his property, granted him fair and square by their father, and the first one of those white cows he caught on his side of the stream was going to get shot, as were any subsequent trespassers. As you might expect, this did not go down so well with Rick.

"Despite the bad blood between his father and uncle, Julius was offered and accepted a job on the farm. Consisted mostly of helping with whatever labor needed done, from repairing a fence to painting the barn to baling hay. I suppose I found it unusual that Uncle Roy would permit his son to cross the stream to the farm, but there wasn't much else I could picture Julius doing, except digging coal, which was a prospect none of our parents was eager for us to explore. Anyway, Julius let me tell him how to spend what portion of his wages his parents allowed him to keep. Usually, this was on candy or soda pop; though sometimes, I'd promise him that, if he bought me a certain funnybook I especially wanted, I'd read to him from it. I would, too, at least until I was tired of explaining what all the big words meant. I reckon I wasn't always as kind to my big cousin as I should've been, and I reckon I knew it at the time, too. He was a great, strapping fellow, taller, stronger than me. Long as he was near, the boys who teased and occasionally pushed and tripped me kept their distance. Julius never let on that he didn't like spending time with me, so I didn't worry about the rest of it too much.

"Did I mention that Rick had a daughter? He had three of them, and a pair of sons, besides, but the one I'm speaking of was the second youngest, a girl name of Eileen. Plain, quiet. Don't know that anyone paid her much mind until her daddy showed up at Roy's house with her on one side of him and the sheriff on the other. Eileen, Rick said, was going to have a baby. Julius, he also said, was the baby's father. I don't know what-all your folks have told you about such matters, but a man can force a baby on a woman. This was what Rick said Julius had done to his Eileen. Julius denied the accusation, but it was Eileen's word against his, and given he wasn't the sharpest knife in the drawer, her yes carried more weight than his no. The charge was a serious one, enough to have brought the sheriff to the door; though you can be sure Rick's house on top of that knob helped guarantee his presence. The way the sheriff told it, he already possessed sufficient evidence to put Julius under lock and key, at least until a trial. And, Rick chimed in, did his younger brother know what would happen to Julius once the other prisoners learned what he was awaiting trial for? Messing around with a young girl—it would not go well for him. Julius might not reach his day in court, and that wasn't even mentioning the cost of hiring a lawyer to defend him . . .

"In a matter of ten, fifteen minutes, Rick and the sheriff maneuvered Roy and Allison into believing that all they held dear was about to be taken from them. They were frantic. You can be sure Roy had some notion there was more going on here than his brother was letting on, but he couldn't ignore the situation at hand, either. Rick let Roy and Allison sweat just long enough, then sprung his trap. Of course, he said, there might be another way out of this for all of them. He wasn't saying there was, mind you, only that there might be. Everyone knew Julius wasn't equipped with the same faculties as those around him. There were places that would take care of such folk, ensure they would not be a danger to anyone else. In fact, there was a fine one outside of Harrodsburg, small, private, where Julius could expect to be well-looked-after. Wasn't cheap, no, though Rick supposed it was less than they might lay out for a decent lawyer, especially if the trial dragged out, or if Julius was convicted and they needed to appeal. Not to mention, it would avoid the talk about Julius that was sure to spread as a result of his imprisonment. Thing about that kind of talk was, it got folks riled up, thinking they needed to get together and take matters into their own hands. There wasn't much the sheriff and his boys would be able to do if a mob of angry men marched up to the jail and demanded his prisoner, was there?

"By the end of an hour, Rick had everything he needed. To pay for the asylum to which their son was to be shipped in lieu of criminal charges and time in jail, Roy and Allison agreed to sign over their property to him. Within a couple of days, Julius's bags were packed and he was on his way to Harrodsburg. I saw him before he left, and he wasn't upset—mostly, he seemed confused by everything. Soon after he left, his parents went, too, to be closer to him. A school hired Roy as a janitor, and Allison took in washing.

"I saw Julius once, not long after he'd entered the asylum. Nice enough place, I guess, an old mansion that'd seen better days. But Julius was different. Among the conditions of his entering this place was that he not pose a danger to any of the women who worked or were patients there. Shortly after he arrived, he was given an operation to prevent him forcing babies on anyone else. When I called on him, he hadn't fully healed. They'd dressed him in a white shirt and pants, to make him easy to track down in case he went to leave. There was a patch of damp blood down one leg of his trousers. He couldn't understand what had been done to him, and they had him on some kind of pain medicine that made things worse. He kept asking me to explain what had happened to him, and when I couldn't, tried to show me his wound to help. I don't imagine my visit made things any clearer for him.

"All the ride home, I kept thinking about those white cattle. Our family had talked about the situation. Wasn't anyone doubted it had been a way for Rick to get where he wanted to go. Question was, had the road presented itself to him, or had he paved it, himself? No one could credit the charge that had been brought against Julius. On the other hand, whatever his intelligence, his body was a man's, subject to all a man's urges. With only a boy's understanding to guide him, who could say what he might have done, had his blood been up? The women, in particular, would have liked a word with Eileen, but she was gone, sent off to a cousin in Memphis the day after her daddy had reached his agreement with her uncle.

"I knew. I knew that my cousin was innocent and that a terrible crime had been committed against him and his family. Sitting with him in the asylum had made me certain. For a brief time, I hoped the other members of my family might take action, avenge the wrong done Julius, but the furthest they would go was talking about it. One of my uncles proposed shooting Rick's special cattle, but the rest of the family rejected the plan. Rick would guess who'd done it right away, they said, and he'd already proved beyond any doubt he had the law snug in his pocket. God would take care of Rick in His time, my Aunt Sharon said. We had to be patient.

"While I didn't put much stock in Divine Justice overtaking Rick, I saw my aunt was right about the necessity of waiting. Such a man as Rick couldn't help making enemies. He collected them the way a long-haired dog does ticks. The secret was to wait until he had gathered so many enemies as to move our name well down a list of potential suspects. This meant another six years, till I was halfway done with the university. Julius was dead—had died not many months after I'd seen him. The wound from his operation had never closed properly. Infection set in, and though he fought it for a good long time, this was in the days before penicillin. I was at his funeral. Rick insisted he have a place in the family plot. As much as anything, what he intended as a magnanimous gesture settled me against him. If a man had done to your daughter what Rick had accused Julius of, there was no way you'd make room for him alongside the rest of your kin. Had he been your patsy, you might try to soothe any twinges of conscience by permitting him the privilege of a burial amongst the elect of your line. I swear to you, it was all I could do not to walk over to where Rick and his wife stood beside Roy and Allison and spit in his face. Not then, though, not then. Years had to pass, Julius's grave receive a fancy headstone, the grass grow thick over it. Roy and Allison had to leave for a fresh start in Chicago, where the family lost touch with them.

"At last, the time came around. It was a rainy night, the tail end of storm that had hung about for a couple of days. I wanted it raining so no one would think twice of my wearing a raincoat and hat, gloves, and boots. There was a fellow at the university who owed me a considerable favor. He owned a car. I proposed to him that, should he drive me a couple of hours to a location with which I would provide him, wait there no more than an hour, and return me to campus, we would be square. He agreed. I had him take me to a crossroads a mile or so up the road from Rick's farm, where the stream that circled the bottom of his hill swerved close to the road. The stream was swollen with the rain, but not so much that I couldn't wade it to the spot where Roy and Allison's house had stood. Rick had torn it down, had a kind of lean-to built for his cattle to shelter under. This was where I found the lot of them, crowded in together. Their huge white bodies glowed in what little light there was. I dug around in my coat pocket, and came out with my buck knife. I didn't know if the cattle would spook, so I opened it slowly. The ones on the open side of the lean-to shifted their feet, but made no move to run. Speaking softly, smoothly, the kind of nonsense you coo to a baby, I approached. I put my free hand on the cow to my right, to steady her. Then I leaned behind and drew my knife across the backs of her knees. She didn't scream, just gave a little grunt as her hamstrings split and her back end collapsed. That knife was sharp as a smile. I doubt she felt much of anything. I did the same to her forelegs, and moved on to the cow in front of her. Once I had the cattle on the open side done, and the way out of the lean-to blocked, I relaxed. The rest of Rick's Charolais put up no more resistance, though a couple called in protest. I was quick and I was thorough, and when I was done, I retraced my steps to the stream and walked it to where my friend sat waiting for me. The rain and the stream had washed most of the blood and mud from me. All the same, he kept his eyes fixed straight ahead. I told him we could go, and we did.

"You can be sure, I spent the next few days wondering what had been reported by the local press. It was all I could do not to rush out and buy the papers. Problem was, as a rule, I didn't pay much attention to newspapers; plus, I was in the middle of exams. I wasn't sure at what stage the investigation into what I'd done to Rick's cattle was. I didn't want to do anything, however trivial, that might cast suspicion on me later. I didn't really need to read a reporter's account of what had taken place after I'd left. I could picture it well enough. Early the next morning, whoever Rick had put in charge of tending the cattle would've wandered over to check on them. He'd have discovered the herd under the lean-to, unable to move, blood watering the mud. He'd have run for Rick, who might've sent someone to fetch the veterinarian. The precise details weren't important. What was, was there was nothing could be done for the animals. To a one, they would have to be destroyed, the meat sold for whatever Rick could get for it. I couldn't decide if he'd have what it took to load the rifle and do what had to be done himself, or if he'd direct a couple of his men to it. I preferred the former scenario, but either possibility would suffice, because whoever's finger was on the trigger, he'd hear the gunshots, each and every one of them.

"For a couple of months afterwards, I half-expected a visit from one lawman or another. Over the Christmas holidays, I kept a low profile. Rumor was, Rick's suspicion had lighted on a fellow out towards Springfield with whom he'd had a dispute about money the man claimed Rick owed him. Naturally, everyone in my family had an opinion as to who was responsible, but none of them so much as glanced in my direction. I was at the university; I was the last person who would commit such an act and jeopardize his future. The exception was Aunt Sharon, who, as she decreed that God's wrath had descended on His enemy, let her eyes fall on me long enough for me to know it.

"Obviously, what I did on behalf of Julius, I got away with. Even if I hadn't, though—even if the police had broken down my door and dragged me off to prison—it was the right thing to do. Family comes before everything. Someone wrongs one of yours, you do not let that go unanswered. You may have to bide your time, but you always redress an injury to your own. And when you do, you make certain it's in a way that will bring misery to whoever offended. That's what your blood demands of you.

"So anybody who stood up for his big sister to a trio of girls who deserve to have their lips sewn shut, I'd not only give him a bottle of pop, I'd hoist mine in salute to him."

Rachel followed her grandfather's direction and lifted her soda in Josh's direction. The time it had spent in her hand had taken the chill from it, but it was still sweet, and she drank it down eagerly.

7. The Freezer (2): Opened

One time Grandpa was away, he left the freezer unlocked. As they always did after he was safely gone from the house, Rachel and Josh descended the basement stairs; although she, for one, had done so without much enthusiasm, as if she were going through the motions of a ritual grown stale and meaningless. At least in part, that was due to her being seventeen, and more concerned with college applications and the senior prom than with a riddle whose solution never came any closer, and was probably not all that exciting, anyway. But Josh had insisted she come, the moodiness that had erupted with his fifteenth birthday temporarily calmed by the reappearance of their familiar game. He had been working on his lock-picking skills, he said—for reasons she did not wish to consider—and was eager to exercise them on the freezer's locks. Rachel couldn't remember the last time she'd spared any thought for the freezer, but the change in Josh was welcome and substantial enough for her to want to prolong it, so she had accompanied him.

As it turned out, her brother would have to find another test for his burgeoning criminal skills. For a moment, she thought the trickling she heard as she swept her cane from basement stair to basement stair was water running through the brass pipes concealed by the basement's ceiling tiles. Except no, there was none of the metallic echo that passage made. This was water chuckling into open air. At almost the same time, the smells mixing in the basement reached her. The typically faint odors of cinnamon and vanilla, with the barest trace of brine, flooded her nostrils, the cinnamon filling the end of her nose with its powdery fragrance, the vanilla pushing that aside with its almost oily sweetness, the brine suddenly higher in her nose. There was another smell, too, stale water. In comparison, the basement's usual odors of synthetic carpet, dust, and damp were hardly noticeable.

Josh's, "Holy shit," was not a surprise; nor, really, were his next words: "It's open. Grandpa left the fucking thing wide open." The sound, the smells, had told her as much. She said, "He's defrosting it."

He was. He had pushed the freezer a couple of feet to the left, until the spigot that projected from its lower left side was hanging over the edge of the drywell. He unplugged and unlocked the freezer, turned the lever on the spigot, and who knew how many years' worth of ice was trickling down into the ground. Late-afternoon sunlight was warming the basement, but Josh flipped on the light. Rachel would have predicted her brother would run across to inspect the freezer, but he hesitated, and she swatted his leg with her cane. "Hey," she said.

"Sorry," he said. "What?"

"This is kind of weird."

"No weirder than having the goddamned thing here in the first place."

"Do you think he knows—you know?"

"That we've been fixated on it since we were kids?" she said. "Yeah, I'm pretty sure he's figured that one out by now."

"Could it be some kind of, I don't know, like a trap or something?"

"A trap? What the fuck are you talking about? This is Grandpa."

"Right," Josh said, "it is. Are you telling me he'd pass up a chance to teach us a lesson, especially about minding our own business?"

"You're being paranoid." She shoved past him and made her way across the basement. Her cane clacked against the freezer. When her hand had closed on the edge of it, she said, "You want to come over here and tell me what's in front of me?"

With the exasperated sigh that had become the trademark of his adolescence, he did. "Move over," he said, pushing her with his hip. She shuffled to her left. Standing over the open freezer, she found the cinnamon-vanilla-brine combination strong enough to make her cough. "I know," Josh said, "pretty intense, huh?"

"What do you see?"

"Ice, mostly. I mean, there's a lot of ice in here, a shitload of it. I'd say Grandpa had this thing about two-thirds full of ice."

"Well, it is a freezer."

"Ha-fucking-ha."

"The question is, what has he been using it for?"

"Storage."

"Obviously. Any sign of what, exactly, was being stored?"

"I—wait."

She felt him lean forward, heard ice shifting. "What the fuck?" he breathed.

"What is it?"

"I don't know. It's like, paper or something."

"Let me—" she held out her hand.

"Here." He placed a piece of what might have been heavy tissue paper in her palm. She leaned her cane against the freezer and ran her other hand over the substance. Its texture was almost pebbled. It crinkled and bunched under her fingertips. Josh said, "It's translucent—has a kind of greenish tint. At one edge, it's brown—light brown."

"It's skin," she said. "It could be from a plant, I guess, but I think it's a piece of skin." She brought it to her face. The cinnamon-vanilla-brine mix made her temples throb.

"Skin?" Josh said.

"Like from a snake," she said, "or a lizard."

"What the fuck?" Josh said.

Rachel had no answer.

8. The Tape (4): The Carvings

"—ten disks," Grandpa was saying, "evenly spaced around the room. Each was a good six feet or so across. They were hung low, only about a foot off the floor. I'm not one for art, but I reckon I could find my way around a museum. The style of these things wasn't like anything I'd run across before. What was pictured tended more in the direction of abstract shapes—cylinders, spheres, cubes, blocks—than of specific details. The scenes had been carved in something like bas-relief, and incised with the same writing we'd found at the tunnel mouths. I couldn't decide if it was vandalism, or part of the original design. The letters seemed too regular, too evenly placed to be graffiti, but I'm hardly the expert in such things.

"Jerry had brought his camera. He'd used up most of his film shooting the main cavern, but had enough left for the disks, so he photographed them."

"What did they show?" Uncle Jim asked.

"Half of them, I couldn't make heads nor tails of. Maybe if I'd had another few hours to study them, I might've been able to decipher them. The hands on our watches were moving on, though, and there was that other tunnel to consider."

"How about the ones you could figure out?"

"There was a picture of a city," Grandpa said, "although no such city as I'd ever seen, in or out of a book. Great buildings that curved to points, nary a straight line amongst them, like fangs of all different sizes. Another showed that same city—I'm pretty sure it was—destroyed, shattered by an enormous sphere crashing down into it. Third was of a long line of what I took for people, crossing a wide plane full of bones. There was one of another catastrophe, a large group of whoever this had been being trampled by a herd of animals— actually, this disk was a bit confusing, too. The animals were at the lead edge of a mass of triangular shapes that I took to be waves, but whether the animals were supposed to represent a flood, or vice-versa, wasn't clear to me.

"The picture that was most interesting was the one set over the tunnel out of the room. At its center, there was a person—or, what was supposed to be a person—and, at all four points of the compass surrounding him, there was another, smaller person, maybe half his size. Seemed to me there was more writing on this disk than the others, concentrated between the fellow in the middle and his four satellites. Jerry said it might be a representation of their gods, or their ancestors, or their caste system—which was to say, just about anything."

"Did you explore the other tunnel?" Jim said. "Of course you did. Did you find anything?"

Grandpa laughed. "I guess you know your old man, don't you? Jerry would've been happy to return, said we'd already found plenty. We had, and I wasn't too sure of our lights, but by God did I want to find out what lay at the end of that other tunnel. Told Jerry I'd go, myself, which I would've; though I was betting on him not wanting to be left alone. He didn't, but he made me promise we'd turn around the second our lights started to go.

"The tunnel out of the chamber was the exact copy of the one that brought us to it. For another couple hundred feet, it slanted down and to the left. The darkness wasn't any darker here than it had been at any point since we'd started our descent, but I found myself estimating how far below the surface we'd come, and that number seemed to make the blackness thicker.

"We issued into a room that was pretty much identical in size and shape to the one we'd left. Only difference was the tombs along the walls."

9. A Familiar Debate

"Suppose everything Grandpa told Uncle Jim on that tape—suppose it's true."

"What?" Rachel said. Her bed shifted and complained as Josh lowered himself onto it. She closed the textbook her fingers had been trailing across. "Are you high again? Because if you are, I have the LSAT to prepare for."

"No," Josh said, the pungent, leafy odor he'd brought with him a clear contradiction of his denial. "I mean, I might've had a little grass to chill me out, but this is serious. What if he was telling the truth?"

With a sigh, Rachel placed her book on the bed. "Do I have to do this? Are you really going to make me run through all the problems with what's on that tape?"

"They were in the Empty Quarter," Josh said, "the *Rub' al Khali*. There's all kinds of crazy shit's supposed to be out there."

"Actually," she said, "that point, I can almost believe. Apparently, there are some famous caves not too far from where they were, so why couldn't they have discovered another? And why couldn't it have been inhabited? If there was a cave-in, and the desert came pouring through the ceiling, there's your Atlantis of the sands legend."

"So—"

"But. This would have been an archaeological find of historic significance.

It would have made his friend Jerry's career. He would have been famous, too. You don't think two young guys wouldn't have publicized the shit out of something like this?"

"Ah," Josh said, "but you're thinking in twenty-first century terms. They couldn't snap a picture with their phones and upload it to Facebook, while verifying their coordinates with their personal GPS's. They had to do things the old-fashioned way, which meant returning for additional photos and a survey of the location."

"By which time," she said, "there had been not one, but two week-long sandstorms, and the terrain had been entirely changed."

"It's the desert. There are sandstorms all the time."

"I'm sure there are, which begs the question: how did they find a map to guide them there, in the first place?"

"Maybe it was a star map."

"Then why couldn't they find their way back?"

"Okay, so it was dumb luck they found the place. There are still the pictures they did take."

"Most of which," she said, "were ruined by some kind of mysterious radiation they're supposed to have encountered underground. What could be developed is—apparently—so generic it could be anyplace."

Josh paused. "What about the egg?"

"Seriously?"

"Why not?"

"Why—because extraordinary claims require extraordinary proof."

"There's the freezer," Josh said, "and its locks."

"That's hardly—"

"Remember the piece of skin we found in it?"

"You don't think that was Grandpa fucking with us?"

"We hadn't found Jim's tape in the attic, then. What would have been the point?"

"I said: to fuck with us."

"I don't know," Josh said.

"I do," Rachel said. "Our grandfather is not keeping a pet monster in the freezer in the basement."

"Not a monster," Josh said, "a new species."

"An intelligent dinosaur?"

"It's not—that's like calling us thinking monkeys. It's what the dinosaurs developed into."

"Again—and this is ignoring a ton of other problems with your scenario— what you're describing would have been—I mean, can you imagine? A living example of another, completely different, rational creature? Grandpa and Jerry would have been beyond famous. Yet we're supposed to believe Grandpa raised it, himself?"

"They wanted to study it. They thought it would be better for them to observe and document its development."

"Which neither of them had any training for," Rachel said. "And, once more, where's the data they're supposed to have accumulated?"

"Presumably, Jerry lost it, sometime before his heart attack."

"How incredibly convenient, on both counts."

"Anyway, from what I can figure, it isn't as if the thing is all that smart."

"Does it matter? You do not keep an earth-shaking scientific find on ice in the cellar of your house in upstate New York. Shit," she added, "why are we even having this conversation?"

"It's Uncle Jim," Josh said.

"What about him?"

"I've been thinking about him running away—the timing of it. Near as I can tell, he and Grandpa sat down to record that tape about a month before Jim split."

"And?"

"Well—do they sound like they aren't getting along?"

"No," Rachel said, "but that doesn't mean anything. This could have been the calm before the storm."

"Not according to Dad. The way he tells it, everything was fine between Uncle Jim and Grandpa and Grandma right until he left."

"You have to take what Dad says about Uncle Jim with a chunk of salt. It's safe to say he was a little jealous of his baby brother."

"What I'm getting at," Josh said, "is maybe Uncle Jim saw what was in the freezer. And maybe he didn't like it. Maybe he freaked out."

"So he ran away?"

"Could be. Could also be, he never left the house."

"What—the thing ate him?"

"Maybe it was an accident," Josh said. "He figured out how to unlock the freezer while Grandpa wasn't there. Or Grandpa was there, but Jim got too close. Or—what about this?—Grandpa turned the thing loose on Jim because he was threatening to tell people about it, go public."

"That's pretty fucked-up," Rachel said. "Grandpa's an asshole who's committed some acts that are, to put it mildly, of questionable morality, but that doesn't mean he'd sic his pet monster on his child."

"It would explain why Jim disappeared so completely, why he's never been found."

"As would a less-elaborate—and –ridiculous—narrative. Not to mention, weren't you sitting beside me during his family-comes-first lectures? Remember cousin Julius Augustus, the terrible things you do for your kin?"

"Family loyalty cuts both ways. If Jim set himself against the family, then he'd be liable for the consequences."

"Seriously? Are you sure this paranoid fantasy isn't about Grandpa and you?"

"Don't laugh. You honestly believe that, if Grandpa thought I was harming the family, he wouldn't take action?"

" 'Take action:' will you listen to yourself? He's an old man."

"With a very powerful weapon at his command. You don't need to be too strong to fire a gun."

"Jesus—okay, this conversation is over. I have to get back to studying." As Josh raised himself from the bed, Rachel added, "Occam's razor, Josh: the simplest answer is generally the right one."

"If I'm right about what's in that freezer," he said, "then this *is* the simplest answer."

Interlude: Dad and Mom

Neither of Rachel's parents cared to discuss her grandfather at any length. In her father's case, this was the residue of an adolescence complicated by the loss of his brother and mother, and an adulthood spent in a career for which his father showed a bemused tolerance, at best. In her mother's case, it was due to her father-in-law's decades-long refusal to be won over by her efforts to achieve anything more than a tepid formality. Mom had been enough of a hippie in her youth for Rachel to have a sense of the root of Grandpa's coldness to her; on a couple of occasions, however, she had hinted to Rachel that her uneasiness around her husband's father had to do with more than his disdain for her lifestyle. There was something she thought she had seen— but it was probably all her imagination. Rachel wasn't to say anything to her grandfather, or he'd accuse Mom of having had a flashback, or worse, of having been tripping. Rachel tried to coax her mother into describing what she had seen, but she refused to be drawn.

• • •

10. The Tape (5): Visions of the Lost World

"—eight sarcophagi," Grandpa was saying. "That was what it looked like, at first. Huge stone boxes, ten feet long by four high by four deep. Cut from the same stone as the tunnels and the chambers. Six of them set around one side of the room, the remaining two opposite. It appeared the tombs had been turned over, because the front of each was open. Full of what we took for rocks, smooth, oblong stones the length of a man's hand, all a speckled material I didn't recognize. We circled the room, and it seemed every last one of the stones was cracked, most from end to end. I picked up one to inspect. Lighter than its size, almost delicate. Surface was tacky. I aimed my light into the crack, and saw it was hollow. I replaced it, and chose another one. It was empty, too, as were the others I checked. I moved onto the next stone box, and the one after that, and all the stones I examined were the same, fragile shells that stuck to my fingers. Not until I lifted a rock that hadn't split all the way—and which was heavier than the others—and shone my light into it did the penny finally drop. These weren't stones. They were eggs. The stone containers weren't sarcophagi. They were incubators. This wasn't a mausoleum. It was a nursery."

"What?" Uncle Jim said. "What was in there? What did you see?"

"Broke the shell, myself," Grandpa said. "Shouldn't have, wasn't anything like proper procedure, but what was inside that egg . . . "

"What?" Jim said. "What was it?"

"Conditions in the chamber had preserved the creature it contained well enough for me to make out the pattern on its skin. It was dried out, more like paper than flesh and bone. Guess you could say I found a mummy, after all. Curled up in the half-shell I was holding, it put me in mind of an alligator, or a crocodile. The body and tail did, anyway. Head was something else. For the size of the skull, the eye was huge, round, like what you find in some species of gecko. Its brow, snout, flowed together into a thick horn that jutted beyond the end of its lower jaw. Damnedest looking thing, and when I studied its forelimbs more closely, I noticed the paws were closer to hands, the toes fingers."

"No way," Jim said.

"Boy, have you ever known me to lie to you?" A warning edge sharpened Grandpa's question.

"No sir," Jim said. "So what was it? Some kind of pet lizard?"

"Not by a long shot," Grandpa said. "I was holding in my palm the withered remains of one of the beings who had carved out the very room in which we were standing." During the pause that followed Grandpa's revelation, Rachel could feel her vanished uncle's distant desire to call her grandfather on his bullshit vibrating the silence; apparently, however, Uncle Jim had decided to water his valor with discretion. Grandpa went on, "Of course, I didn't know this at the time. I assumed the thing I'd found was another lizard, if a strange one. There were a couple more mummified creatures in amongst the eggs in this box, and something even more important: a single, unopened egg, its outside sticky with a coat of the gel that had been left on the others. I wrapped the unbroken egg with the utmost care, and placed it in the bottom of the rucksack I'd worn. Beside it, I packed the three dried-out creatures, along with a sampling of a half-dozen empty eggs. Wasn't anything else we could take as proof we'd been here, but I figured this was better than nothing.

"The trip back to the main cavern, then to the surface, then to the camp, was uneventful. Jerry and I talked about what we'd found, what it might portend for us. We agreed not to say anything to anyone until he'd developed the pictures he'd taken and we'd found someone we could trust to examine the things in my rucksack. Neither seemed as if it would take long—a week or two at the outside—and once we were in possession of evidence we could show someone, we didn't think we'd have any difficulty locating a sponsor who would reward us generously for leading a second, larger and better-equipped, expedition to Iram.

"What we didn't count on was the rolls of film Jerry had shot being almost completely ruined, most likely by some variety of radiation we encountered underground. The couple of photos you could distinguish in any detail showed cave structures that could've been anywhere. On top of that, within twelve hours of our return, I developed a rash on my hands that raced up my arms to my chest and head, bringing with it a raging fever and a coma. Camp doctor'd never seen the like, said it was as if I'd had an allergic reaction to some kind of animal bite."

"The eggs," Jim said, "the stuff that was on them. Was it poisonous?"

"Delivery system," Grandpa said, "for a virus—several, each hitched to a cartload of information. Imagine if you could infect someone with knowledge, deliver whatever he needed to know directly to the brain. Was what was supposed to happen to the creatures when they hatched. On the way out of their eggs, they'd contract what learning they required to assume their role in their civilization. I assume the process was more benign than what I, the descendant of a different evolutionary branch, went through. Prior to this, had you asked me what I thought a coma was like, I would have predicted a deep sleep. It's what the word means, right? Not once did it occur to me such a sleep might be filled with dreams—nightmares. Now, I understand what I saw while unconscious as my brain's effort to reckon with the foreign data being inserted into it. At the time, I felt as if I was losing my mind. Even after I came out of the coma, it was weeks till I could manage a day without some pretty strong medicine, or a night in anything close to peace."

"What did you see?" Jim said.

"Lot of it was in fragments," Grandpa said, "whether because the viruses had decayed over time, or my brain chemistry was too different, I'm not sure. Maybe both. I saw a city standing on the shore of a long, low sea. Made up of tall, triangular structures that curved to one side or another, like the teeth of a vast, buried beast. Their surfaces were ridged, like the bark of a plane tree, and I understood this was because they hadn't been built so much as grown. They were of a piece with the forest that surrounded the place. Herds of what looked like a cross between a bird and a lizard, their feet armed with a single, outsized claw, patrolled the forest lanes, chasing off the larger animals that wandered into them from time to time. These bird-lizards had been grown much the same way as the city, what was already there shaped to the ends of the place's inhabitants. That was what the creatures had raised it did, took what the world around them gave and altered it to fit their purposes. They'd done so for an unimaginable length of years, while the stars rearranged into dozens of sets of constellations. They did it to themselves, steering their biology down certain paths, until they'd split into four . . . you might call them castes, I suppose. They were distinct enough from one another to be almost separate species. Soldier class was at the bottom; next came the farmers, then the scientists, and finally the leaders. They'd fixed it so they developed from infant to adult in about three years.

"Some kind of disaster brought the whole thing tumbling down. I couldn't tell exactly what. I glimpsed a wall of fire reaching all the way to the sky, but that was it. There weren't many of the creatures to begin with. Their civilization had been in decline for tens of thousands of years, pulling back to the location I'd seen, the original city. Had it not been for some of them working underground, the things would've been burned away, entirely. As it was, there were only a few thousand survivors, left with a landscape that had been charcoaled, bunched up like a blanket. Overhead, the sky was black clouds. A few of the creatures proposed throwing in the towel, joining their brethren in oblivion, but they were outvoted by the rest of the survivors, who decided to search for a new spot to call home. Dissenters didn't have much choice in the matter: their leaders had the ability to force their actions with their minds. So the lot of them left on a journey which would consume decades. Everywhere they went, things were the same, the earth and pretty much everything that had lived on it seared to ash. Once, they came to an ocean, and it was choked with carcasses out to the horizon. The air chilled. Clouds churned above, spilling dirty snow by the foot. Half the creatures died over the course of their travels. In the end, the leaders decided their best hope was hibernation. There were places—the sites of cities long-abandoned— where they could find sufficient facilities left to put themselves into a long, deep sleep, from which they might awaken when the planet had recovered itself. They found one such location in the far south, on the other side of what would be called Antarctica. As best they could, they secured the site, and settled down to sleep.

"And sleep they did, for fifty thousand, a hundred thousand years at a stretch. The world's wounds scarred over. New plants and trees appeared, spread across the land, were joined by new and strange animals. The creatures had lived during the great age of the dinosaurs—were its crowning achievement. They'd witnessed families of beasts like small mountains ambling across the grasslands; they'd fought feathered monsters with teeth like knives in the forests. Now, when they sent scouts to inspect their surroundings, they heard tales of smaller animals, covered in hair. As they woke from rests that lasted millennia, those animals grew larger, until it was if the wildlife they'd known in their former existence was being recast in other flesh. Nor was the rise of these beasts the only change in their environment. The continents were shifting, sliding towards the positions we know. Antarctica was cooling, ice and snow spreading across it. Never ones to act in haste when they didn't have to, the creatures chose to wait. Eventually, they did abandon that location. I can't say when, or why.

"The rest was even more fractured. They left Antarctica in search of a spot closer to the equator. That might have been what we called Iram, or it might have been another spot before it. For a little while, they did all right. Population increased, to the point a group set out west, to find another of the old sites. The two settlements kept up contact with one another. After more time than you or I could comprehend, it appeared the creatures might be on the rebound.

"There was one problem for them, one fly doing the backstroke in the ointment: us, humans. They'd been aware of us as we'd risen from four legs to two and started our long climb up the evolutionary staircase, but it was only as another instance of the weird fauna that had overtaken the world. In what must have seemed the blink of an eye, we were on our way to becoming the dominant lifeform on the planet. To make matters worse, we were hostile to them from the get-go, aggressively so. If a human encountered one of them, he fled screaming in the other direction. If a group of humans ran into one of them, they would do their level best to kill it. The creatures had the advantage in terms of firepower. Each of their soldiers had been crafted to be all the weapon it would need against foes much worse than a handful of hairless apes. We had the advantage in terms of numbers—not to mention, we had an ability to make leaps in our reasoning that was completely alien to them. We could surprise the creatures in ways they couldn't us. So began a war that spanned a good deal of man's prehistory. By and large, it was fought by small groups from either side, sometimes individual warriors. There was a point when the creatures who'd settled in the west came out in force against the human kingdom that had arisen near them. Fought all the way into its capital city, to have it swept by a mighty wave that drowned both sides alike. Creatures never recovered from that. They ceded more and more of what territory they'd held to humans. In the end, they opted for the only route left open them: another long sleep. As they had before, they fortified their retreat as best they could, and let slumber take them."

There was a moment's pause, Uncle Jim allowing his father to pick up the thread of his narrative. When it was clear that was not about to happen, Jim said, "Then what?"

"That was it," Grandpa said. "Wasn't anything else. Believe you me, what had been stuffed between my ears was more than enough. You know how full your brain feels after you've pulled an all-nighter prepping for a big test? This was like all the cramming you'd ever done for every test you've ever taken, present at the same time. After I'd climbed out of the coma, the doctor and nurses thought I was delirious. Wasn't that. It was a library's worth of new information trying to squeeze itself into my neurons. Gradually, over a span of weeks, I came to terms with the knowledge I'd gained. By the time I was walking out of that room, though, there was more for me to reckon with. For one thing, after sweating whether anyone would blame him for the sickness that had overwhelmed me, Jerry had gone off in search of Iram, alone. But the entire region had been swept by sandstorms that had reconfigured the landscape beyond his ability to accommodate. For another thing, our team had been moved to a new site, fifty miles east of where we'd been. Fortunately, Jerry had kept my rucksack close and unopened. Absent his photographs and unable to retrace the path to Iram, he doubted anyone would credit him with finding anything but a cache of lizard eggs.

"They were more than that—much, much more. I'd an idea we might locate a scientist to show the eggs to. Wasn't sure if we'd be better with a paleontologist, or a zoologist. I also figured a biochemist might be interested in the substance that had coated the eggs, what it contained. Hadn't paid much mind to the single unhatched egg I'd found; guess I assumed its contents would be useful for purposes of comparison. I certainly was not expecting it to hatch."

11. Thanksgiving

Thanksgiving was the kitchen summer-hot, humid with dishes simmering and steaming on the stove. It was the tomato-smell of the ketchup and soy-sauce glaze her mother had applied to the turkey in the oven; the rough skins of the potatoes Mom had set at one end of the table for Rachel to peel, a tradition that reached back seventeen years, to when her seven-year-old self had insisted on being involved in the preparation of the meal, and her mother had sat her down with a peeler and a handful of potatoes and allowed her to feel her way through removing the tubers' skins. Mom usually bought potatoes whose surfaces were covered in ridges and bumps, and there had been moments Rachel fancied she could almost pick out letters and parts of words encoded on them. She had advanced well beyond those first four potatoes; now, she was responsible for peeling and chopping all the necessary vegetables. For a brief time in his late teens, Josh had insisted on helping her; mostly, she had thought, to improve his standing with their parents. The last few years, he had abandoned the kitchen in favor of the living room, where their father and grandfather passed the hours prior to dinner watching whatever football games were on the television. Dad wasn't a big football fan, not in the same way as Grandpa, who took an almost visceral delight in the players' collisions. But he had grown up with his father's passion for the sport, and had learned enough about it to discuss the plays onscreen with the old man. It wasn't something they did that often—the Super Bowl was the only other instance she could think of—but it seemed to fulfill a need both men felt to demonstrate their bond as father and son. Rachel hadn't been surprised when Josh, despite his almost complete ignorance of anything sports-related, had wanted to join their fraternity. She judged it a demonstration of the event's ongoing importance to him that he had raised himself from the bed into which he'd collapsed at who-knew-when this morning, and, still reeking of stale cigarette smoke and watery beer, shuffled in to join them, stopping in the kitchen long enough to pour himself a glass of orange juice. Their father had greeted him with typical irony—"Hail! The conquering hero graces us with his presence!"—their grandfather with his typical grunt.

Afterwards, Rachel would think that she hadn't been expecting any trouble, today. Then she would correct herself, as she realized that she had been anticipating a disruption of the holiday, and had tied it to Josh. What she had been prepared for was her brother disappearing for ten minutes right as they were about to sit down to eat, and returning reeking of pot. Mom would say, "Josh," the tone of her voice a reproach not so much of the act—she and Dad had done (and continued to do, Rachel thought) their share of grass—as of his total lack of discretion. Grandpa wouldn't say anything, but his end of the table would practically crackle with barely-suppressed rage. Dad would hurry to ask Rachel, who would be attempting to recall a sufficiently lengthy and distracting anecdote, how Albany Law was going. Scenarios approximating this one had played out over the last several Thanksgiving and Christmas dinners, since Josh had discovered the joys of mood- and mind-altering substances. To the best of her knowledge, his proclivities hadn't interfered with his studies as an undergraduate or graduate student, which Rachel guessed was the reason their parents hadn't come down on him with more force than they had. But it angered Grandpa to no end, which, Rachel increasingly believed, constituted a good part of the reason her brother did it.

But the argument that erupted this day: no way she could have predicted it. It began with something her grandfather said to her father, something that registered as background noise because she was answering her mother's question about where she was planning on going after she passed the bar. Clear as a bell, Josh's voice rang out: "Hey, Grandpa, why don't you give Dad a break, okay?"

"Josh!" their father said.

"All I'm saying is, he should take it easy on you," Josh said.

"That's enough," Dad said. "We're watching the game."

"That were my boy," Grandpa said, "he'd speak to his elders with a bit more respect."

"Dad," their father said.

"That were my son," Josh said, "I wouldn't treat him like a piece of shit all the time, especially after what I did to his brother."

"Josh!" Dad said. "What the hell is wrong with you?"

Grandpa said nothing.

"I'm fine," Josh said. "Not like poor Uncle Jim. Right, Grandpa?"

"What the hell are you going on about?" Dad said. "Are you high?"

"No I am not," Josh said. "If I were, it wouldn't have any bearing on what we're talking about, would it, Grandpa?"

"Stop it," Dad said. "I don't know what you're talking about, but give it a rest, okay?"

"What I can't work out," Josh said, "is whether it was an accident, or deliberate. Did things slip out of control, or did you turn that thing on your son? And if you did loose it on him, what can he possibly have done to drive you to do so? Oh, and one more thing: how can you stand yourself?"

"Leave," Dad said. "Just leave. Get out of here."

"Boy," Grandpa said, "you've gone beyond the thin ice to the open water."

"Which means what? That I can expect a visit from your friend in the freezer?"

"Josh," Dad said, his easy-chair creaking as he sat forward in it, "I'm not kidding. You need to leave."

"All right," Josh said, "I'll go. If there's anything you want to show me, Grandpa, you know where to find me." The couch springs groaned as he stood. Rachel half-expected him to pause in the kitchen on his way to his room, or for her mother to call his name, but neither happened. When his footsteps had finished their tromp along the hall, their father said, "Dad, I am so sorry for that. I don't know what got into him. Are you all right?"

"Game's on," Grandpa said.

12. The Second Tape

The second tape had been damaged, to the extent that the portion of Uncle Jim's conversation with Grandpa it recorded had been reduced to a stream of garble to whose surface select words and phrases bobbed up. The majority of them ("room," "go," "space") were sufficiently generic to be of little aid in inferring the contents of Grandpa's speech; although a few ("scared," "raw meat," "soldier") seemed to point in a more specific direction. From the first listen, Josh insisted that their Grandfather had been describing how the creature which crawled out of the egg had been frightened, until he had fed it the uncooked flesh of some animal or another, probably winning its trust. Later on, Grandpa had identified the creature as belonging to the soldier class he'd learned about during his coma. While she conceded that Josh's interpretation was reasonable, Rachel refused to commit to it, which Josh claimed was just her being a pain in the ass. Given what they'd already listened to, what better construction did she have to offer?

None, she was forced to admit, nor did the three longer passages they found on the tape provide any help. The first came five minutes in; the babble unsnarled and Grandpa was saying, "—like when you come down with the flu. High temperature, head swimming, every square inch of skin like a mob of angry men beat it with sticks. Maybe it would have had the same effect on the creatures, but I doubt it. Has to do with the difference in biology, is my guess. Doesn't help that the thing fights you. Especially if there's blood in the air, it's like trying to wrestle a strong man to the ground and keep him there. Sometimes, there's no choice but to let it go, a little bit. Why I use the freezer. Long as it's in there, it's dormant. After you take it out, if you're careful and don't overdo things, there's no problem keeping it under control almost the entire time. I—" and his words ran together.

Twenty-four minutes after that passage, long after they had given up hope of encountering another and left the tape playing so they could tell themselves they had listened to all of it, the garble gave way to Grandpa saying, "After that, I received a visit from a couple of fellows whose matching crew cuts, sunglasses, and black suits were as much ID as what they flashed in their wallets. I'd caught sight of such characters before. Every now and again, they would show up at the camp, ask to speak to one of the experts about something. Wasn't too strange, when you thought about it. Here we were, working in a foreign land, where we might notice a detail about the place or people that would be useful for these boys. Cold War was in full swing, and the lessons of the last big one were fresh in everyone's mind, especially the strategic advantage of a plentiful supply of fuel. Our work was tied up with national security, so it wasn't a surprise that the fellows who concerned themselves with it should keep an eye on us. Tell the truth, I was curious to find out what they'd driven all this way to ask me about. Naïve as it sounds, not once did it cross my mind that they might be here to inquire about my other activities. Not that the company would have had any remorse over what they'd had me do to the competition: I just assumed they wouldn't want me revealing such a valuable secret. Never did learn if someone had blabbed, or if the G-men had sweated it out of them. No matter. These boys cut straight to the point. Said they knew I'd been up to some extra-curricular activities, and were going to provide me the opportunity to put those activities to work for my country. Which was to say—" a paraphrase that was swallowed in a mess of sound.

Before the third and final section, the tape spat out the phrase, "children of the fang." Three minutes after that, at the very end of the second side of the second tape, the nonsense came to an end and was replaced by silence. As Rachel was running her finger across the tape recorder's buttons, Grandpa's voice said, "What we never could work out was whether the viruses floating around my blood had changed me permanently. Could I pass along my control of the creature to my child, or was it confined to me? How could we know, right? I hadn't met your ma, hadn't settled down and started a family, yet."

Uncle Jim said, "What do you think, now?"

"I think we might find out," Grandpa said, and the tape recorder snapped off.

Interlude: Grandpa (3): Knife Wants to Cut

Whether birthday, Christmas, or other celebration such as graduation, the gift Rachel or her brother could expect from Grandpa was predictable: money, a generous amount of it tucked into a card whose saccharine sentimentality it was difficult to credit their grandfather sharing. When they were younger, the bills that slid out of their cards from Grandpa had been a source of puzzlement and occasional frustration to her and Josh. Why couldn't their grandfather have given them whatever present they'd requested of him, instead of money? In a relatively short time, their complaints were replaced by gratitude, as Grandpa's beneficence enabled Rachel and Josh to afford extravagances their parents had refused them.

The exception to this practice occurred on Josh's thirteenth birthday. After he had unwrapped his gifts from his parents and Rachel, but before he had moved on to their cards, Grandpa said, "Here." A box scratched across the table's surface.

"Grandpa?" Josh said. Whatever was inside the box thwacked against its side as Josh picked it up. Something heavy, Rachel thought, probably metal. A watch? "Buck knife," Josh read. "Really?"

"Open it and find out," Grandpa said.

Rachel could feel the look her father and mother exchanged.

The cardboard made a popping sound as Josh tore into it. "Coooooooooool," he said. Plastic crinkled against his fingers.

Their father said, "Dad."

Grandpa said, "Boy your age should have a knife—a good one."

The blade snicked as Josh unfolded it into place. "Whoa," he said.

Their father said, "Josh."

Grandpa said, "It's not a toy. It's a tool. A tool's only as good as your control of it, you understand? Your control slips—you get sloppy—and you'll slice your skin wide open. Someone's next to you, you'll slice them open. That is not something you want. Knife wants to cut: it's what it's made for. You keep that in mind every time you reach for it, and you'll be fine."

Their mother said, "Josh, what do you say?"

"Thank you, Grandpa," Josh said, "thank you thank you thank you!"

Within a week, the knife would be gone, confiscated by Josh's homeroom teacher when she caught him showing it off to his friends. After a lengthy conference with Mrs. Kleinbaum, their father retrieved the knife, which he insisted on holding onto until the school year was out, his penalty for Josh's error in judgment. By the time summer arrived, Josh had pretty much forgotten about his grandfather's present, and if he remembered to mention it to their father, it was not in Rachel's hearing.

Before all of this, though, Josh let her hold the gift. The knife was heavy, dense in the way that metal was. Longer than her palm, the handle was smooth on either end, slightly rougher between. "That's where the wood panels are," Josh said. On one side of the handle, a dip near one of the ends exposed the top edge of the blade. By digging her nail into a groove in it, she could lever the blade out. As it clicked into place, a tremor ran up the handle. Rachel slid her finger along the knife's dull spine. About a third of the way from its end, the metal angled down to the tip. "Like a scimitar," Josh said. She dimpled her skin on the point. "Careful," Josh said.

"Shut up," she said, "I am being careful." Ready to part her flesh, the blade's edge passed under her touch. In her best approximation of Grandpa's voice, she said, "Knife wants to cut." She folded the knife closed, and handed it back to Josh.

He laughed. "Knife wants to cut," he said.

13. In the Basement (Now): The Thing in the Ice

Because of Grandpa's stroke Christmas Eve, neither Rachel nor her parents paid much attention to what they assumed at the time was Josh's refusal to appear for Christmas. Granted, it had been a few years since he'd last missed a family holiday, but he had spent most of his Thanksgiving visit complaining about the workload required by his doctoral classes (the stress of which their parents had diagnosed as the cause of his blowup with Grandpa). He had a trio of long papers due immediately before Christmas break—not the most work he'd ever faced, but on a couple of occasions on the day before Thanksgiving, he'd alluded to Rachel about a mid-semester affair with a guy from Maine that had crashed and burned in spectacular fashion, leaving him dramatically behind in all his classes. She had offered his backlog of assignments to her mother as the reason for his abrupt departure Saturday afternoon, while Rachel and her parents were braving the crowds at the Wiltwyck mall. His assignments were probably the reason that none of them had heard from Josh the last few weeks, either.

And if she and her parents were to be honest with one another, it was likely as well that Josh had opted to give Christmas a pass. After Mom heard the thump and crash on the front stairs and went to investigate, and found Grandpa sprawled halfway down, his breathing labored, the left side of his face slack, his left arm and leg so much dead lumber, the focus had shifted from holiday preparations (which included planning for a possible Round Two between Josh and Grandpa) to whether the old man would survive the next twenty-four hours. Even after the doctors had pronounced Grandpa's condition stable, and expressed a cautious optimism that subsequent days would bear out, he remained the center of attention, as Rachel and her parents talked through what needed doing at home to accommodate his changed condition, and set about making the necessary calls to arrange the place for him. She left a couple of messages on Josh's phone, the first telling him to call her, the second, a few days later, informing him of Grandpa's stroke, and though she was annoyed at his failure to respond, especially once he knew the situation, she didn't miss the inevitable torrent of self-reproach with which he would have greeted the news—and which certainly would have been worse had he been there with them.

By Valentine's Day, what Rachel referred to as her brother's radio-silence had become a source of worry for their mother. "Do you think he's still upset about Thanksgiving?" she asked during one of their daily calls. Rachel could not believe that Josh would sulk for this long; although there had been a couple of occasions during his undergraduate years when a particularly intense relationship had caused him to drop off the face of the earth for a couple of months. She phoned his cell, but her, "It's me. Listen: Mom's worried. Call her, okay?" betrayed more pique than she intended. But she could not credit the edge to her voice for Josh's continuing failure to phone their mother. And, despite his assurances that Josh was probably caught up in some project or another, Dad's voice when she spoke with him revealed his own anxiety. Only Grandpa, his speech slowed and distorted by the stroke, seemed untroubled by Josh's silence. Both her parents were desperate to drive up to Josh's apartment, but feared that appearing unannounced would aggravate whatever the situation with him was. Rachel bowed to their none-too-subtle hints, and offered to do so for them.

Before she could take a taxi to the other side of the city, however, one of Josh's fellow students at SUNY Albany called her to ask if everything was okay with her brother, whom, he said, he hadn't seen since he'd left for Thanksgiving vacation the previous semester. He'd left messages on Josh's cell, but had heard nothing in reply. He'd remembered Josh mentioning a sister at Albany Law, so he'd looked up her number, which he'd been meaning to call for a while, now. He didn't want to be intrusive. He just wanted to be sure Josh was okay and knew his friends were asking for him. That conversation was the first of a chain that led to several of Josh's other friends, then their parents, then the police. By the end of the day, her mother had left her father to watch Grandpa and raced up the Thruway to pick up Rachel and drive to Josh's apartment, where they were met by Detective Calasso of the Albany PD and a pair of uniform officers. Both Rachel and her mother had keys to the door. Her heart was beating so fast it was painful, not because of what she was afraid they were going to find, but because of what she was certain they were not. The moment the door swung in, the smell that rolled out, dry, cool dust, confirmed her suspicion. During their search of Josh's small living quarters, the detective and his colleagues discovered two bags of pot, a smaller one in the top drawer of the bedroom dresser, and a larger one sunk inside the toilet's cistern. Once they'd found the second bag, the tenor of the detective's questions underwent a distinct change, as Josh went from graduate student in philosophy to small-time drug-dealer. Rachel could hear the narrative Calasso's line of inquiry was assembling, one in which her brother's criminal activities had brought him into jeopardy from a client, competitor, or supplier. Best case, Josh had gone into hiding; worst, he'd never had the chance. From the detective's perspective, she could understand: it was an attractive explanation, that had the virtue of neatly accounting for all the evidence confronting him. Her and her mother's protests that this wasn't Josh were to be expected. How often, in such situations, could family members admit that their loved ones were so markedly different from what they'd known? Detective Calasso assured them the police would do everything in their power to locate Josh, but by the time her mother was dropping her back at her apartment, she was reasonably sure the detective deemed the case essentially solved.

That she would entertain Josh's claims about Grandpa and what he had locked away in his basement freezer was at first an index of her frustration after four weeks of regular calls to Detective Calasso, during which he never failed to insist that he and his men were working tirelessly to ascertain her brother's whereabouts. Approximately every third conversation, he would inform Rachel that they were pursuing a number of promising leads, but when she asked him what those leads were, he appealed to the sensitivity of the information. She hardly required a lifetime spent mastering the nuances of spoken expression to recognize that he was bullshitting her. She could believe that Calasso had queried what criminal informants he knew for information on her brother, as she could that his failure to turn up anything substantive would have done little to change his theory of the case. Compared to the plot in which her brother had been assassinated by a rival drug dealer and his weighted corpse dumped in the Hudson, the prospect that the accusations he'd lobbed at their grandfather at Thanksgiving had prompted the old man to some terrible act had the benefit of familiarity.

In the space of a week, however, the Grandpa's-monster-theory, as she christened it, went from absurd to slightly-less-than-absurd, which, while not a huge change, was testament to the amount of time she'd spent turning it over in her mind, playing devil's advocate with herself, arguing Josh's position for him. Her dismissal of the story Grandpa had told Uncle Jim was based in her assumption that he and his friend, Jerry, would have been sufficiently competent to take full advantage of the opportunities with which their supposed discoveries presented them. What if they hadn't been? What if they hadn't known how to exploit their findings? After all, why should they have? Especially if they couldn't trace their way back to the place? And say, for the sake of argument, that Grandpa had come into care of . . . something, something fantastic. Who was to say he would have turned it over to a zoo, or university? It wouldn't have been the most sensible course of action, but, as her favorite professor did not tire of reminding her, logical, self-consistent behavior was the province of bad fiction. Actual people tended to move in ways that, while in keeping with the peculiarities of their psychology, resembled more the sudden shifts in course typical of the soap opera.

Which meant, of course, that her younger brother could have had a secret life as a drug dealer. And that their grandfather could have been keeping an unimaginable creature in enforced hibernation in the basement. The impossibility of what she was considering did not stop her from making a couple of discrete inquiries among her closer friends as to the possibility of acquiring a set of lock picks and being instructed in their use. This proved remarkably easy. One of those friends had a friend who earned extra cash as a stage magician whose skill set included a facility with opening locks. For the price of a couple of dinners, the magician was happy to procure for Rachel her own set of tools and to teach her how to employ them. She wasn't certain if she was one hundred percent serious about what she appeared to be planning, or if it was a temporary obsession that had to work itself out. The entirety of the bus ride to Wiltwyck, she told herself that she was not yet positive she would descend to the basement. That her parents were away for the afternoon and Grandpa still of limited mobility meant no more than it meant. She managed to keep that train of thought running for the taxi ride from the bus station to her parents' house. But once she had let herself in the front door, hung up her coat, and slid the soft bag with the lock picks in it from her pocketbook, it seemed pointless to continue pretending there was any doubt of her intentions. She listened for Grandpa, his home health aide, and when she was satisfied there was no one else on the first floor, set off sweeping her cane from side to side down the front hall, towards the basement door.

In no time at all, she was resting the cane against the freezer. How many times had she been here, sliding her hands along the appliance's edge until they encountered each of Grandpa's locks? Always with Josh maintaining a steady stream of chatter beside her. Now, the only sound was the low hiss of her palms over the freezer's surface, the click of metal on metal as she found a lock and tilted it up. How long ago had Grandpa switched entirely to padlocks? It made what she was about to do easier. She placed the lockpick bag on top of the freezer, rolled it open, selected her tools, and set to work.

The locks unclasped so easily, it was almost anticlimactic. Half-anticipating an additional security measure she'd missed, Rachel searched the freezer lid. Nothing. She put the opened locks on the floor, returned her tools to their bag and put it beside the locks, and braced her hands against the lid. After all these years, to be . . . There was no point delaying. She pushed upwards, and with the pop of its rubber seal parting, the lid released.

A cloud of cinnamon, vanilla, and brine enveloped her. She choked, coughed, stepped away from the freezer. Her eyes were streaming, her nose and tongue numb. She bent forward, unable to control the coughs that shook her lungs. So much for secrecy: if Grandpa had been unaware of her presence in the house previously, she'd just advertised it. Still coughing, she returned to the freezer and plunged her hands into it.

Ice cubes heaped almost to its tops rattled as her fingers parted their frozen geometry. She moved her hands back and forth, ice chattering and rattling. There was a click, and the freezer's motor whirred to life. When had Grandpa loaded all this ice in here? Funny to think that not once had she and Josh asked that question.

Her fingertips brushed something that wasn't ice. She gasped, overcome with sudden terror that she had found her brother, that Grandpa had flipped out, murdered him, and used the freezer to hide the body. Even as her heart leapt in her chest, her not-completely-numb fingers were telling her that this wasn't Josh. It was an arm, but it was shorter than her brother's, the skin weird, pebbled. She followed it to one end, and found a hand with three thick fingers and a thumb set back towards the wrist. A claw sharp as a fresh razor protruded from each of the fingers.

Nausea roiled her stomach. She withdrew her hands from the ice and sat down hard on the basement floor. Her head was pounding. She pressed her cold palms to either side of it. Somewhere in the recesses of her brain, Josh crowed, "See? I told you!" Her pulse was racing. She felt hot, feverish. The floor seemed to tilt under her, and she was lying on it. She could not draw in enough breath. Her body was light, almost hollow. She was moving away from it, into darkness that gave the sensation of movement, as if passing through a tunnel. She

14. Affiliation

opened her eyes to light. Brilliance flooded her vision. She gasped, and heard it at a distance. She jerked her hands to her face, but found her arms weighted with something that rattled and rustled as she tried to move them. Her entire body was covered in the stuff. Panic surged through her. She thrashed from side to side, up and down, the medium that held her snapping and cracking as it shifted around her. There was something wrong with her arms and legs. They were sluggish, clumsy. The brightness before her eyes resolved into shapes, triangles, diamonds, blocks, jumbling against one another. With a crash, her right arm broke free of its confinement. Her hand flailed on the rough surface of the material. She braced her forearm against it, and pushed her head and shoulders into the air.

She was in a large box, filled, she realized, with ice. That she could see this was no less remarkable than the circumstance itself. Her head had emerged near one side of the container. If she stretched her neck, she could take in more of the space around her. The figure lying beside the box startled her. She gasped again—and heard it from the woman's lips. In a rush, she took in the sweater and faded jeans, the hair in its shoulder-length cut, the round, freckled face, its eyes wide and unfocused *(and the colors, God, was this what color was?)*—

—and she was looking at a dark blur that kept all except the outermost limits of her vision from her. Above, something moved in Grandpa's freezer, shoving ice from side to side, spilling it on the carpet. She went to sit up—

—and was in the box, her head hanging over the side. Her hands clutched the metal of the box. Below her, the woman on the floor shivered. Her face was flushed, her breathing rapid. She reached a hand to her, and what already had registered peripherally—the pebbled skin, patterned with dark swirls, the three fingers, each taloned, the thumb almost too far back to be practical, armed with its own claw, longer and more curved—shouted itself at her, bringing with it a thunderclap of understanding. A fresh wave of nausea swept her, but it was the woman on the floor who coughed and vomited. For a moment, less—

—she was spitting out the remains of a partially-digested Danish—

—and then she had heaved herself out of the box (*Grandpa's freezer*) and went stumbling across the basement floor, pieces of ice dropping from her on the way. Her legs were different—out of proportion in a way she couldn't assimilate. Some of the bones had been shortened, some lengthened, the angles of her joints changed. Her balance was shot. If she stood straight, she felt as if she was about to tip over onto her back. Not to mention, the sight of everything around her, which kept tugging her head this way and that, further unbalancing her. She had developed a fair estimate of the basement's appearance, but it was as if, after having encountered water a handful at a time, she had been dropped into the ocean. All of it was so *vivid*, from the swirling grain of the paneling on the walls to the spiky texture of the carpet, from the squat bulk of the freezer to the sharp edges of the cardboard boxes stacked around the floor. On top of that, the rest of her senses were dulled, practically to nonexistence. She struck the wall at the foot of the basement stairs, and realized that she hadn't felt the collision as painfully as she should. *Grandpa,* she thought, and half-pulled herself, half-climbed towards the door at the top of the stairs.

As she pushed through into the kitchen, an image burst across her mind's eye: a man, looking over his shoulder at her, his eyes widening with the shock that had stunned the rest of his face. He appeared to be wearing a gray suit jacket, but there wasn't time for her to be sure, because he was replaced by another man, this one dressed in a white robe and a white headdress, his mouth open in a shout that she heard (*"Ya Allah!"*), his eyes hidden behind sunglasses in the lenses of which something awful was reflected as it bore down on him, claws outstretched. She caromed across the kitchen, slamming into the breakfast bar at its center. The tall, glass cylinders in which Mom kept the cereal toppled onto the floor, where they detonated like so many bombs, spraying glass and corn flakes across the tiles. She stepped away from the breakfast bar, and was staring down at a man whose eyes were rolling up as blood bubbled from his lips, over his scraggly beard, and the claws of her right hand slid deeper into his jaw. The next man she saw was dressed in a tuxedo, the white shirt of which was turning dark from the wave of blood spilling down from the slash to his throat. She lurched out of the kitchen, down the hallway to the stairs to the second floor. The sightless eyes of a fair-haired boy (*Jim?*) whose throat and chest were a ruin of meat and bone stared at her while a man's voice wailed somewhere out of sight (*Grandpa?*). A lab-coated man held out his hands in front of him as he retreated from her. She shouldered aside the door to her grandfather's portion of the house, and saw the terrified expression of a young man whose round, freckled face and curly hair marked him as Josh, while her grandfather's voice screamed something (*"Is this what you wanted? Is it?"*).

The door to Grandpa's bedroom had been left ajar by the home health aide. She shoved it open and crossed the threshold.

Despite the unbridled insanity in which she was caught up, a small part of her thought, *So this is what his room looks like.* It was larger than she would have anticipated, the far corner filled by a king-sized bed draped with a plaid comforter. Next to it, a nightstand held a lamp that could be bent to direct its light. On the other side of it, her grandfather sat dozing in a recliner. A coarsely knitted blanket covered his legs and lap; under it, a thick, heavy robe wrapped his chest and arms. His face was as she'd imagined it: the flesh sparse on the bone, the mouth downturned at the corners, the nose blunt as a hatchet, the eyes sunken, shadowed by the brows. Lines like the beds of dried rivers crossed his skin, which had not lost the tan his years in the sun had burned into it. The stroke's damage was visible in the sag of the left half of his face, which lent it an almost comically morose appearance. The ghost of her and Josh's mocking mimicry of him flitted through her memory. She leaned closer to him.

He opened his eyes, and she leapt back, thumping into a wall as she did. Although his eyelids raised ever-so-slightly, his voice remained level. Nodding, he said, "Wondered if it might be . . . you." His tongue slid over his lips. "Tried with . . . Jim." He shook his head. "Couldn't . . . leave remains. Beast needed . . . to eat . . . " He shrugged. "Lost . . . Joshua . . . "

Had he attempted the same experiment with Josh? Did it matter? Like a swell of lava rising over the lip of a volcano, anger rolled through her, carrying her deeper into the thing she was inhabiting. She crouched forward to steady herself. She could feel the claws jutting from her fingertips, the fangs filling her mouth. Anger swelled within her, incinerating everything in its path. She drew back her lips, and hissed, a long, sibilant vent of rage that summoned her grandfather's attention from whatever memory had distracted him.

He saw her teeth bared, her claws rising. Something like satisfaction crossed his face. "That's . . . my girl," he said.

•

"They have the power of calling snakes, and feel great pleasure in playing with and handling them. Their own bite becomes poisonous to people not inoculated in the same manner. Thus a part of the serpent's nature appears to be transfused into them."

—Nathaniel Hawthorne, *American Notebooks*

John Langan is the author of two collections of short fiction: *The Wide, Carnivorous Sky and Other Monstrous Geographies* (Hippocampus, 2013), and *Mr. Gaunt and Other Uneasy Encounters* (Prime 2008); a third, *Sefira and Other Betrayals,* is forthcoming. He has written a novel, *House of Windows* (Night Shade, 2009), and with Paul Tremblay, has co-edited *Creatures: Thirty Years of Monsters* (Prime, 2011). He lives in upstate New York with his wife and younger son.

The Big Arena is a savage place, run for the very rich and full of the superfluous young. People get desperate for attention . . .

SLEEP WALKING NOW AND THEN

Richard Bowes

Rosalin Quay, the set and costume designer, stood in a bankrupt Brooklyn warehouse staring at the rewards of a long quest. Inside a dusty storage space were manikins. Stiff limbed, sexless ones from the early twentieth century stood alongside figures with abstract sexuality (which is how some described Rosalin) from the early twenty-first.

But the prime treasure of this discovery was dummies from a critical moment of change. Manikins circa 1970 were fluid in their poses, slightly androgynous but still recognizably male or female. The look would be iconic in the immersive stage design she had been hired to assemble.

The warehouse manager, Sonya, was tall, strong, and desperate. Rosalin, who had an eye for these things, placed her on the wrong side of thirty but with a bit of grace in her movements. Sonya brought up computer records on the palm of her hand. The owner of the manikins had stopped paying rent during the crash of 2053. The warehouse would shut down in two days and was unloading abandoned stock at going-out-of-business prices.

A pretty good guess on Rosalin's part was that Sonya came to New York intending to be a dancer/actor, had no luck, and was about to be unemployed: a common tale in the city everyone called the Big Arena.

"These pieces are for my current project," Rosalin said, and sent her an address. "I consider finding you and the manikins at the same moment an interesting coincidence. It would be to your advantage to deliver them personally."

She believed she saw a bit of what was called espontáneo *in the younger woman.*

One

Jacoby Cass awoke a few days later in the penthouse of a notorious hotel. The Angouleme, built in 1890, had stood in the old Manhattan neighborhood of

Kips Bay for a hundred and seventy years. Its back was to the East River and sunlight bounced off the water and through the uncurtained windows.

Cass rose and watched tides from the Atlantic swirl upstream. Water spilled over the seawall and got pumped into drainage ditches. In 2060, every coastline on earth that could afford floodwalls had them. The rest either pumped or treaded water.

Like many New Yorkers, Jacoby Cass saw the rising waters as a warning of impending doom but, like most of them, Cass had bigger worries. None are as superstitious as the actor, the director, or the playwright in the rehearsals of a new show. And for his drama *Sleep Walking Now and Then*, which was to be put on in this very building, Jacoby Cass was all three.

Weeks before, his most recent marriage had dissolved. She kept the co-op while he slept on a futon in the defunct hotel. Most of his clothes were still in the suitcases in which he'd brought them.

All was barren in the room except for a rack holding a velvet-collared frock coat, an evening jacket, silk vests, starched white shirts and collars, opera pumps, striped trousers, arm and sock garters, a high silk hat, and pairs of dress shoes sturdy as ships. He was going to play Edwin Lowery Nance, the man who had built this hotel. And this was his wardrobe for *Sleep Walking*.

Cass's palm implant vibrated. Messages flashed: Security told him a city elevator inspector was in the building. His ex-wife announced she was closing their safe-deposit box. A painting crew for the lower floors was delayed. His eyes skimmed this unpleasant list as he tapped out a demand for coffee.

An image of the lobby of The Angouleme popped up. The lobby looked as it had when he'd run through a scene there the week before. Relentless sunlight showed the cracks in the dark wood paneling, the peeling paint and sagging chandeliers. The place was bare of furniture and rugs.

Then an elevator door opened and Cass saw himself step out with two other actors. The man and the woman wore their own contemporary street clothes and carried scripts. Cass, though, wore bits of his 1890s costume—a high hat, a loosely tied cravat. He was Edwin Lowery Nance showing wealthy friends the palace he'd just built, where he would die so mysteriously.

"My good sir and lovely madam," he heard himself say, "I intend this place to be a magnet, attracting a clientele which aspires to your elegance." They played out the scene as he'd written it, in that shoddy space devoid of any magic. The other two actors were still learning their lines. But Cass found his own rendition of the lines he'd written flat and ridiculous.

Irritated, wondering why this had been sent to him, Cass was about to close his fist and erase the messages when he heard Rosalin's voice, with its traces of an indefinable (and some said phony) European accent.

"Not an impressive outing. But I believe if you try again this evening, you will find everything transformed."

Rosalin and Jacoby Cass had worked together over the years without ever becoming more than acquaintances. But Cass found a ray of hope in the message and decided to grasp it.

His coffee was delivered by the new production assistant, a tall and tense young lady. Cass noted her legs in pants down to the shoe tops, though autumn fashion had decreed bare legs for women and long pants for men. Quite a reverse of the styles of the last few years.

He could imagine her life in the Big Arena with multiple aspiring artists/roommates all scraping by in a deteriorating high-rise. This was Rosalin's protégé. He thought her name was Sonya but wasn't positive. At the outset of his career, almost forty years before, he had learned to be nice to the assistants, because one never knew which of them would end as a huge name. So he smiled the smile that had made him a star and took the coffee into the bathroom.

Water pressure wasn't good, and the pipes were rusty, but like the building itself, the pipes and wiring pretty much worked. Twenty minutes later, shaved, showered, purged, and scented, he donned modern underwear then got dressed from the costume rack: a starched shirt minus the collar, trousers held up with suspenders, an unbuttoned vest, and slippers.

A palm message told him the elevator inspector was waiting. He opened his bedroom door and walked into the big skylighted room that had once been the office/den of Edwin Lowery Nance, whose unproven murder haunted the Angouleme Hotel.

In Nance's lair all was old wood and brass and it had not aged well. For scores of years The Angouleme had followed a downward path before being seized by the city. Bright sun streamed down and highlighted the scarred desk and worn rugs. After dark and in the low glow of early electricity, all would have to appear mysterious, rich, and rotten. Everything depended on that.

Down a very short corridor lay the bedchamber of Evangeline, daughter of Edwin Lowery Nance, and more famous in her time than Lizzie Borden. Through the open door Cass could see the curtains on the canopied bed parted to display a beautifully dressed Parisian doll. Legend demanded it. Just as Lizzie will always be the harridan with the axe, Evangeline Nance was the sleep-walking child with a doll under her arm.

Jacoby Cass's career had high points which many in this city remembered.

His *Hamlet* was set in an abandoned seminary where audience members could pick flowers with Ophelia, help dig graves or secretly poison swords.

The Downton Abbey he staged in the Frick Museum was a week-long twenty-four-hour-a-day drama built around an antique television show. Customers took tea with aristocrats, spied on lovers, searched closets and dresser drawers for clues and scandal. It ran for years and rescued the bankrupt museum for a time.

Once, Cass was spoken of as a theatrical giant: Barrymore and Ziegfeld combined. But at the moment he was coming off flops on stage, screen, and net. He'd recently been approached to take the film role of a hammy older actor. He'd turned it down. But the backers of *Sleep Walking Now and Then* were not a patient crew, and in his bad moments he wondered if he'd regret not taking the part. This show would click fast or die fast.

Cass inhaled deeply and stepped out of Nance's sanctuary: *His* sanctuary he reminded himself, as he stood straight and walked down the hall to the private elevator. The public elevators had all been upgraded many times over the years. But this one stood with its door half-open. The original machinery had been replaced, but the car with its golden cage and faded eighteenth century silhouetted couples in wigs and finery still remained.

Cass intended this to be a central motif of his drama. It was here that the first death had blackened the Angouleme's name and begun its legend.

The story was well known. Deep in the night of April 12, 1895, Nance—drunk, distracted, or both—thought he was stepping into the elevator. Instead he went through the open door and fell nine stories to his death at the bottom of the elevator shaft. Rumor had it he was in pursuit of his daughter. Most accounts now considered it a murder.

The city inspector, a small, neatly dressed man, was in the elevator car examining the control panel. As Cass approached he caught the eye of Ms. Jackson, head of security for *Sleep Walking*. She gave an almost invisible nod and he understood that Inspector Jason Chen had accepted a green handshake.

By reputation Chen was honest and would stay bribed. But he was also smart enough to be quite wary of a major scandal wiping out his career. "Let's talk," he said, and Cass led the way back to the lair.

They sat in Nance's old office with Cass's lawyer linked to both. The inspector said, "Jackson tells me that twice a night you're going to have that door open and the cage downstairs."

Cass smiled and explained, "The car will only be a few feet below the floor so as to be out of the audience's sight. Other than that it will just have regular usage."

"I want Ms. Jackson and her people here every minute the door is open and the car is in that condition. And I want it locked every minute it's not in use by your production while there are customers in the building. We will send observers."

"I'm playing Nance," Cass told him. "I'm the only one who'll go through the door with the car not in place. And at my age I don't take risks."

The inspector shook his head. "It's not you I'm worried about. I'm concerned about some spectators who have so little in their lives that they decide to become part of the show. We all know about them! My wife's Spanish. She talks about *espontáneos*—the ones who used to jump into the ring during bullfights and get maimed or killed but became famous for a little while. People get desperate for attention. Like that one who torched himself at the *Firebird* ballet!

"Something like that happens with the elevator and they fire me, shut you down forever, and we're up to our necks in indictments. Now let's take a look at your insurance and permits."

As he authorized documents with eye photos, Cass remembered an old show business joke: "A play is an original dramatic construction *that has something wrong with the second act.*" His second act was the murder of the designer/performer Jacky Mac on these very premises. It happened seventy-five years after Nance's death and was even more dramatic. What his play still needed was a third act.

Chen departed; the lawyer broke contact. Cass, half in costume, sat behind the huge, battered desk Rosalin had found somewhere. His New York was the Big Arena, a tough city with a sharp divide between rich and poor, between a cruel, easily bored audience and the desperate artists. It seemed more like 1895 than not.

Cass felt he was looking for a main chance again, just as he had forty years and many roles before. He told himself that Edwin Lowery Nance, an entrepreneur in his fifties afloat with his daughter in the tumultuous late nineteenth century, must have had moments like this.

Like an echo of the thought, a child's voice said, "Daddy! Thank you! I shall call her Mirabella!"

Startled, Cass/Nance looked up and found Evangeline Nance, with her long golden-honey hair and the nineteenth-century Parisian fashion doll she had named Mirabella tucked under her arm. Her eyes were shut and she didn't appear to sleep walk so much as to float toward the door amid the smoke-blue silks of a flowing dress and sea of petticoats. Her satin slippers hardly seemed to touch the floor.

In character, Jacoby Cass picked up a pair of gold-rimmed pince-nez from the desk, put them on his nose and peered silently at his daughter

At the door Evangeline stopped, turned and nodded, satisfied she had his full attention. "We're scheduled to do a run-through of the elevator chase. Remember, Mr. Nance?" she asked in a voice that was all New York actress. And suddenly Evangeline was Keri Mayne, a woman in her endlessly extended late thirties.

Keri had a history with Jacoby Cass—Ophelia to his Hamlet, a refuge fifteen years before when his third marriage broke down. The two had discussed Evangeline Nance. Her mother died when she was six. Over the twenty years before Evangeline became an orphan she remained a child and a sleep walker.

Keri Mayne's Evangeline threw open the door to the outer hallway and Jacoby Cass arose ready to be Edwin Lowery Nance. Researching his play Cass found no one solid account of the night of April 12, 1895. It seemed very likely that Evangeline sleep walked her way out of the apartment and the father followed. Servants had seen this happen before. No witnesses were available to testify about that April night.

In Cass's script and performance, Nance rushed out of his office after her, calling, "Evangeline!" in a voice he felt would sound like cigar smoke and Scotch. "My child, where do you think you're going?" he cried as Keri/Evangeline sailed down the hall. Cass wore more of Nance's wardrobe: a vest, shoes that hurt his feet but somehow enhanced his performance.

Whispered rumor held that Evangeline had fled her bedroom with him in pursuit. And there was servants' testimony that this had happened before.

Almost all tellings agreed that Nance, in the dim light thought Evangeline had gone to the elevator and stepped through the open door. He followed and found not Evangeline but a nine-story drop. How the elevator car happened not to be there was a matter of mystery and dispute.

With all that in mind, after an hour and a half of rehearsals, Cass/Nance called out "Evangeline!" for the tenth time. All this took place with late September light streaming through the windows. But Cass channeling Nance began to see it happening by moonlight and primitive bulbs. He had to dodge assistants and understudies who had been instructed to stand in his way, walk across his path just as the theatergoers would.

He actually lost sight of Keri/Evangeline before he reached the elevator. The faded gold door was wide open and she had to be inside the car. Nance hurried forward, stepped inside, and fell nine stories into the cellar. It was only three feet and the padding was well placed. But he screamed "EVANGELINE" and made it seem to fade as if coming out of Nance as he hurtled nine stories down.

Jackson and a burly assistant moved forward and would have blocked the line of sight had there been any audience.

Lying face down on the padding, Cass's palm tingled and he read a message from Rosalin telling him that at 6:00 p.m. the Angouleme Hotel's lobby would be ready and awaiting his approval. Rolling over, he looked up at Keri and Jackson staring down and made arrangements for a run-through of the lobby scene at 6:30.

Taking a director/playwright's privilege, he wrote Evangeline into the scene. When the elevator door opened at 6:30 the lobby was all in shadows, low wattage light caught remnants of gold filigree on the walls. The three-story-high ceiling loomed above them with its mural of the European discovery of Manhattan still showing traces of grandeur.

The lobby was a collage of a hundred and seventy years of history. Singly and in groups, manikins lingered in corners and stairs. A sexual spectrum, enigmatic and sinister, they were dressed in 1970s miniskirts, flared pants, and psychedelic T-shirts, in 1890s bustles and floor-length gowns, in World War I doughboy uniforms. Some of their eyes seemed to reflect the light. One with dark hair, a red silk kerchief around his neck, and a leather jacket appeared to move slightly.

With his lovely daughter on his arm and the pair of wealthy customers alongside him, Cass/Nance surveyed them as if he saw the cream of New York society. When he said, "My good sir and lovely madam" and the rest of his opening lines, Cass had fully mastered his Nance voice, throaty and a bit choked with good living.

The actors playing the couple had their lines down. "But," said the man, "what of the location here, almost on the docks and in a neighborhood of factories?"

"The anteroom of the Mighty Atlantic, sir! We shall steal the Hudson River's thunder. This is meant to be a palace for my lovely princess, my daughter." His daughter looked up at him, adoring but somehow lost.

The man frowned but the woman smiled and said, "How enchanting!"

"Come and partake of the Angouleme's humble fare," said Cass/Nance, and the quartet moved toward what had once been a famous hotel dining room and soon would be the *Sleep Walking* snack bar.

As they moved, Cass glanced at the front doors and saw them fly open right on cue. A long-haired figure in gold-rimmed dark glasses, an impeccably fitted velvet jacket and slacks strode across the empty lobby.

The young actor, Jeremy Knight—a rising star in the Big Arena—was Jacky Mac, dubbed the Kit Marlowe of late 1960s New York, whose murder was the Angouleme's second famous death.

Before Jeremy Knight got any further, Cass stepped out of character and into the center of the space. He addressed the company, human and manikin alike: "Our city loves scandals. When current misconduct is too drab the city seeks out its past, desires old relics. This lobby reflects that perfectly." Catching sight of her in the shadows, he bowed. "Thank you, Rosalin! But let's remember that it's only two weeks to opening night and there's so much to be done."

Everyone, cast and crew, applauded. He noticed that Keri Mayne, the charmer, and Jeremy Knight, the young lion, were talking together.

Rosalin led forward the production assistant who'd brought his coffee. "Sonya went out of her way to be helpful when I was acquiring props, saved us a lot of money. She has theatrical experience. There's the silent part of the maid for which we were going to use one of Jackson's people. She can do that and I could use her assistance."

Cass looked at this tense young woman from deep in the artist underclass and wondered about Rosalin's motives. But he was sure of her loyalty to this production into which she'd put so much invaluable work, if not to him. Sonya would come cheap and might be of use. So he nodded, smiled, and agreed with what was proposed.

When she and Sonya were alone Rosalin said, "I came to this city when it was first being called the Big Arena. Thirty years ago I was where you are now." Rosalin had learned that Sonya had no family she could go to, no close friends outside the city. "I had nobody in this world and nothing but my work."

Two

Thursday night, at the 8:00 p.m. show two weeks into the run, Keri Mayne leaned against the wall of Evangeline's bedroom. In full costume, the flowing skirts made sitting both difficult and unwise.

She listened to Cass/Nance outside, saw his image on her palm—cameras were everywhere—heard him say, "Of course, J. P.," into the wall telephone. Nance spoke loudly because he didn't trust the instrument and because an audience needed to hear.

In the play it was well after midnight in the midst of the financial crisis of 1895 and J. P. Morgan had just called. "Of course I will stand with you, Mr. Morgan. Tomorrow at ten? I will be there, sir."

Keri/Evangeline watched Sonya, in a European maid's uniform, standing at the bedroom door and listening. In the intricately jealous context of a theater company Keri mistrusted and feared her.

Outside Nance said, "Of course, sir, I too know the loneliness of losing a wife." His voice became muffled as he turned away. But those in the room could hear the great financier describe a need a discreet hotelkeeper might satisfy. Nance had left behind him some nasty rumors and Cass had used all of them.

Keri/Evangeline heard the others in the room move closer to Nance, trying to catch the conversation. This was the moment. She nodded; Sonya threw open the door and Evangeline floated out of her room and into her father's den.

Evangeline, light as a package of feathers, was wrapped in silk. Shimmering hair flowed down to Evangeline's waist. Her eyes were half open, as if she was in a trance. She had Mirabella in her left arm. The gold slippers glided across the floor.

Half a dozen audience members were in the room. Women wore short skirts; men's legs were concealed in trousers. These were the rich and *Sleep Walking* was a game as much as a play. Devices that enabled communication, blocked insects and rain, illuminated, cooled, or heated the area around one as the moment dictated were turned off. Mostly.

By clustering around Nance in the corner, the playgoers opened the way to the outer hall door, which Sonya opened, revealing a crowd of eavesdroppers. She plowed through them. Seemingly unaware of all this Keri/Evangeline floated over the threshold, and maid and mistress passed down a dim-lit hall.

Most of the windowpanes were blackened and heavily curtained. But an occasional one seemed to look onto the outside world. Playgoers on this floor could gaze out upon a nineteenth century night. Hologram pedestrians and horse-dawn vehicles traveled on the avenue, lanterns on ships bobbed on East River piers. Some figures in lighted windows across the way spoke intently to each other by lamplight while others seemed to grope naked in the dark.

"Evangeline!" she heard Nance cry as he came out the office door. Playgoers followed him. Figures in nineteenth century clothes discreetly got in their way. Audience members accidently blocked him. "My child, where are you going?" Nance cried to his daughter, who gave no sign she was aware of him.

Playgoers were supposed to be absolutely silent. But a man whispered, "She's a bit taller than I would have thought." And a woman responded, "Looks like a child and at the same time older." Sonya kept them away.

Though their conversation irritated Keri, she did prize her ability to alternate between radiant child and disturbed adult. All was shadows and misdirection at the end of the hall. Evangeline floated toward the open elevator door.

Nance, in a voice that was authoritarian and pleading at the same time, shouted, "Young lady, you must obey me. Stop!" His heavy shoes banged on the floor as he began to run.

For a moment everyone looked his way. When they looked back to the elevator, Evangeline and her maid had disappeared.

Edwin Lowery Nance, who managed to appear to hurry while not really moving quickly, came down the hall. He ran through the open doorway and his shout turned into a scream. His voice faded as he fell nine stories into the cellar.

Jackson and her equally big cohort, dressed in 1890s street clothes, were suddenly there blocking the audience members' view. She and her partner looked into the pit. The partner screamed. "Someone get a doctor! Call the police!" Ms. Jackson shook her head sadly and pulled the elevator door closed.

"I saw him, his body was all bloody and smashed," a theatergoer cried.

Keri—standing inside the door that led to the servants' stairs—listened, amused by this. Someone was always getting caught up in the drama. She imagined Cass/Nance lying on the padding, looking up at the faded fleur-de-lis design on the elevator car's roof and, like her, taking the cry as a kind of applause. When reviews called the show "Just a Halloween entertainment," Cass told her, "That gets us through the next month. After that we'll find something else." She hoped he was right.

Her costume made stairs difficult and the maid reached out to help her. Sonya spoke, voice low and intense: "Just after Nance fell they thought it was a tragic accident. Then rumors started that I was seen near the elevator machinery in the cellar. I disappeared before I could be questioned about the events and was never seen again."

At moments when Sonya identified with the part of Evangeline's maid like this Keri wondered why Rosalin, who took care of so many things, had arranged for this person to be alone with her in two performances a night, six nights a week. She hoped Sonya was aware how vital to the production her Evangeline was. Surveillance cams were everywhere but she wondered if they didn't just offer a greater chance for immortality.

So she gazed at Sonya with admiration and delight (and none could look with as much admiration and delight as she). "I'm amazed at the amount of research you've done. You have the makings of an actor," she said.

Then, as Evangeline, she motioned Sonya to go first, and said in a breathless child voice, "After Nance's death rumors got in the papers. One of my dolls was supposedly found in the elevator with his corpse. It's when the term 'Angouleme Murder' began being used. Servants testified that Nance had always taken an unnatural interest in his daughter." Here Evangeline covered her eyes for a moment. But Keri managed to catch Sonya's expression of both horror and sympathy.

Their destination was the sixth floor. On the landing, they paused, heard a 1920s Gershwin tune played by a jazz pianist. Privately, Keri was certain Evangeline had killed her old man, who in every way deserved it. Life with him and after him had made her a manipulative crazy person. It was what Keri loved about the part.

But she looked at Sonya and said with great sincerity, "I try to remember what that poor child-woman went through and put that into my performance."

Sonya held a light and a mirror like this was a sacred ritual. Evangeline's haunted face—just a trifle worn—appeared. Keri Mayne did a couple of makeup adjustments, held the doll to her chest, and braced herself.

Sonya opened the door and followed as Evangeline half floated into a hallway with distant, slightly flickering lights. Keri paused, listened for a moment, then wafted toward the music.

Playgoers, drinks in hand, stared out a window into a hologram of a lamp-lit street scene. A big square-built convertible rolled by with its top down and men and women in fur coats waving glasses over their heads, while a cop made a point of not looking. Flappers in cloche hats and tight skirts scurried to avoid getting run down. They gained the sidewalk and disappeared into the Angouleme's main door downstairs.

On the sixth floor it was 1929.

It took a few moments for the well-upholstered crowd to notice the sleep walker and the woman in a maid's uniform who guided her.

Keri heard their whispered conversations:

" . . . maybe down here trying to avoid her father?"

" . . . a little older, this is long afterwards, when he's dead and she's still living here."

"We missed his big moment."

" . . . looks like she's been on opium for years."

"Morphine, actually."

"Creepy, just like the Angouleme!"

"But delicious!"

" . . . like a ghost in her own hotel for decades after the murder."

The illicit, low-level whispering was the audience telling each other the story they'd seen and heard online. Cass had wanted that. "Makes it like opera or Shakespeare, where the audience knows the plot but not how it'll be twisted this time."

On the sixth floor Keri was Evangeline in the long years after her father's death and before she died in 1932 addicted, isolated. Even before the First World War the Angouleme was called "louche" when that was the word used by people too nice to mention any specific decadence.

"She looks like she's hurt!" murmured a playgoer in a lavish, shimmering suit as he moved toward Evangeline. Keri lurched the other way, Sonya got between them.

Always in these audiences were ones like this who wanted to be part of the drama. If there were a long run, their faces would appear again and again. Certain people would start going out in public dressed like characters in the play. Great publicity, but a warning that no one should get too immersed in a part.

"Oh, who are all these ghosts, Marie?" Evangeline asked her maid in a whispery child voice and looked around at the faces staring at her. "People like these weren't allowed in the Angouleme when Father was here." She held up the doll. "Mirabella was his last gift to me."

She could hear the crowd murmur at this, felt them closing in. And in that moment, the character Jacoby Cass's script simply called "The Killer" came down the hall. This young man wore a leather jacket and a red silk kerchief tied around his neck. The butt of a revolver was visible in a pocket. The actor looked at Evangeline and the rest of the crowd with a cold, dead-eyed stare.

"How did he get in here?" a man whispered. "Where's security?"

This amused his partner. "More than likely he's a fugitive from the Jacky Mac Studio downstairs," she said. "We must pay a visit."

For a moment all attention focused on The Killer. Evangeline wobbling slightly, continued to the jazz piano.

By the 1920s, a louche, scandalous hotel had become attractive to certain people. Artists stayed at the Angouleme and entertained there: French Surrealists and their mistresses, wealthy bohemians poets from Greenwich Village, Broadway composers looking for someplace out of the way but not too far.

Something between a party and a cabaret went on in the living room of Gershwin's suite. Around the door, slender, elegant flappers leaned towards smiling men in evening clothes. The lights were soft; it usually took a couple of glances before someone would recognize them as manikins. But then the silvery figure, you were sure was a statue, would turn slightly and a pair of dark eyes would hold yours for a moment.

Inside the room a musician who looked not unlike Gershwin sat at a baby grand and played the sketches that would become *An American in Paris*.

The suite was set up as a speakeasy where audience members bought drinks, leaned on furniture, listened but also watched. Evangeline shimmered before them, exchanged a long kiss with the silver flapper. All eyes were on the two and Gershwin played a slow fox trot. As they danced he turned from the piano, looked to the audience as though asking if they saw what he did.

When theatergoers from the hall began to crowd into the room, Evangeline floated through a bedroom door and her maid closed it. When people opened it to follow her, they found the room was empty and the door on the opposite wall was locked.

Some at that point would realize that the sixth floor was a diversion, a place to spend money and waste time that would have been better spent up in the penthouse or downstairs where a murder was brewing.

Sonya brought Keri/Evangeline down to the third floor where her next scene would be. The maid character didn't appear again in *Sleep Walking*. "I feel like I should stay with you," she said, and opened the door.

Keri grasped her arm, looked into her eyes and said, "You've done enough. You're wonderful."

The next day Sonya was setting up antique wooden folding chairs in Studio Mac on the third floor. She said, "I wish my part was bigger. I want to be in every minute of this play. I know that's how actors feel."

Rosalin believed the intensity could possibly be of use. "The Big Arena is a savage place, run for the very rich and full of the superfluous young. Most of them will never find something larger than themselves as you are doing. It takes a certain kind of personal sacrifice to fully achieve this. But it will live in others' memories."

Three

In New York it was shortly before midnight of Halloween 2060. Over the years, this holiday had surpassed New Year's Eve as the city's expression of its identity. Especially at times like this when the legendary metropolis was short of cash and looking for some new idea to carry it forward.

In the Angouleme it was time for a special midnight show. Playgoers entered *Sleep Walking* through the lobby. From there they either went up the stairs, waited for the elevators, or just looked for a place to sit while getting acclimated. Rosalin had managed to exploit the lobby's disreputable, fallen majesty. It was a place made for loitering. Upstairs each floor was set in a different decade. The lobby celebrated the entire sordid past. Here, a cluster of 1960s rent boys lingered in the shadows next to the main staircase and several

1900s ladies of the evening in big hats and bustles stood near the ever-vacant concierge desk.

Jeremy Knight waited in a side doorway of the building. At exactly five minutes after the final stroke of twelve he got the one-minute signal, walked a few feet down the sidewalk to the front of the hotel, and was flanked by security.

They threw open the doors and Knight/Jacky entered the lobby: tall and wire-thin, his eyes hidden behind dark glasses, his blond hair in a ponytail down almost to his ass.

Knight was irritated as he always was at this moment by the sight of Jacoby Cass, who, with his speech about the God-given nineteenth century being finished, was making a grand exit with his party. A few patrons tried to follow but found themselves blocked by Jackson and company.

Jeremy Knight marveled at the number of scene-stealing opportunities Cass, the shameless ham, had managed to insert into the script.

Knight surveyed the crowd. The show was booked solid for the Halloween weekend. Advance sales were another matter and his guts turned cold whenever that crossed his mind. So he didn't think about it.

In fact, Cass's distraction allowed Knight to be through the crowd before they were aware of him. He turned then to face them and they saw Jacky Mac—couturier, poet, playwright—in a classic outfit of his own design: V-shaped, slim-waisted jacket; bell-bottom trousers; a wide tie with bright pop art flowers that looked like faces. Jacky Mac had been known to wear miniskirts and silver knee boots, but not on this occasion.

On cue, the public elevator's doors opened. Customers hesitated as always about getting on board because of the legends surrounding the place.

Of Jeremy Knight it had been written, "He was born to wear a costume; put him in anything from a 1940 RAF uniform to a pink tutu and he is transformed." He despised the description but had found that in roles like this an actor grabbed inspiration wherever it could be found.

Without missing a beat, Jacky Mac stepped backwards into an elevator and seemed amused by the audience's fear. "Oh, it's safe!" He somehow murmured and shouted in the same breath. "And if it begins to fall, just do as I do: flap your arms and fly!"

From the elevator doorway, Mac gazed at the manikins in the corner, saw something, and nodded. The audience watched fascinated as one of the figures, dressed in leather and a blood red kerchief stepped out of the shadows and walked unsmiling into the car. "I was crucified just now by his glance," Jacky announced as The Killer joined him and the door closed.

Alone, without an audience to overhear them, Jeremy and Remo, the young actor who played The Killer, didn't exchange a word. Each got off on a different floor, and over the next hour made rehearsed appearances in dark halls and bright interiors.

Forty minutes into the play, Jeremy Knight/Jacky Mac listened to Gershwin's piano and heard Nance's death scream. Ten minutes after that he did a huge double take when he passed the ghost of Evangeline on the tiresome seventh floor where it was always 2010 and the well-lighted halls were lined with display windows offering overpriced *Sleep Walking* souvenirs. Coming down the servants' stairs five minutes later, he passed Sonya trudging up carrying costumes. He smiled and she looked at him as wide-eyed as any fan.

Halloween week was great. Capacity crowds were willing and able to laugh and scream at every performance. On the third floor of the Angouleme two weeks later, at about an hour and twenty minutes into *Sleep Walking*, Knight/Jacky climbed onto the small stage in the Mac Studio and felt the difference.

The Studio included a large performance space with sixty chairs set up. At the Halloween midnight show all seats had been taken and many more patrons stood or sat on the floor. Halloween had been a triumph. But it's in the weeks between holidays that hit shows are revealed and flops begin to die.

Jeremy Knight had that in mind as he pirouetted on the stage. He estimated thirty people in the seats. And this included The Killer, always the first to arrive. Remo was also Jeremy Knight's understudy. He sat down front with his legs stuck out so far his booted feet rested on the stage. A little knowledge of history and one would be reminded of Jacky Mac's fatal tastes.

The under-capacity crowd bothered Knight. But he told himself that any audience of any size was fated to be his. And the people at these performances who sat on antique wooden folding chairs were willing extras.

They were drawn to the Studio by the sounds and the lights flashing through the open double doors. Or they were told not to miss this by friends who had seen Knight/Jacky perform this monologue, one-man play, stand-up routine, whatever you wanted to call it. Jacky Mac's writing was out of copyright and Cass had lifted big chunks of it for a play within a play called *A Death Made for Speculation*.

Jacky leaned over the front of the stage, hummed a few bars of music, and said in a husky voice, "I'd thought of coming out in an evening gown and doing a Dietrich medley. But I've seen the way women look at me when I do drag. It's the look Negroes get when a white person sings the blues. So I'm here to fulfill a secret dream. I'm playing a guy."

Rosalin had taken liberties with the decor but 1970 was a hard moment to exaggerate. Jacky's loft had been described and shown in articles, books, and documentary footage. Like Warhol's Factory, it was iconic. On the walls and above mantelpieces were mirrors, which at certain angles turned into windows looking into other rooms. In those rooms doll automata played cards, a mechanical rogue and his partner cavorted, and one or both might look your way, indicate you were next.

"When I was young," Jacky Mac said, "I tried to make myself look beautiful. Later I tried to make myself look young. Now I'm satisfied with making myself look different."

In the lawless 1960s, the Angouleme Hotel was almost as famous as the Chelsea across town. When it was sold as co-op apartments and lofts Jacky bought most of the third floor of the building with the proceeds of his clothing line and his performance art. Jacky Mac was not, of course, his real name, which was boring and provincial Donald Sprang.

For Jeremy Knight the task was making something as ordinary as homosexuality feel as mysterious, hysterical, and dangerous as Jacky had found his life to be. A brief film clip existed of Jacky Mac working out some of this material in the Studio, performing for an audience of friends in just this manner.

Jeremy caught the odd, fluid near-dance of Jacky Mac, which he'd learned from old videos. On the walls Hendrix, Joplin, and DayGlo acrylic nude boys and girls melted into a landscape of red and blue trees. A light show played intermittently on the ceiling. Deep yellow blobs turned into crisp light green snakes, which drowned in orange, quivering jelly. The color spectrum dazed the eye.

Knight/Jacky leaned forward to show a once-angelic face now touched with lines and makeup and asked, "Why do men over thirty with long hair always look like their mothers?"

On cue, The Killer down front swallowed a few pills, stood up, pulled a bottle from his back pocket, spat out, "Faggot" at Jacky and walked toward the door while taking a long slug. In the old-fashioned manner, Jacky Mac liked his partners rough. It would be the death of him.

The audience watched the long, slow exit. Wrist limp, Jacky Mac gestured after him. "We have the perfect relationship. I pretend he doesn't exist and he pretends that he does."

It wasn't just the costume; Jeremy Knight had absorbed every bit of the lost manner and voice of someone society hated for what he was. Ninety years later it was hard to convey. For a few years in his teens Jeremy had been Jenna

Knight, making the change because boys in school got neglected and there was an advantage to being a boy with the mind of a girl.

Each day Knight felt closer to Jacky's alienation. Saw it intertwine with his own fear of falling off a very small pedestal and back into the vast, penniless crowd in the Big Arena.

The Killer stopped at the door and yelled, "IT'S YOUR TURN NOW, BITCH!" at somebody no one could see.

Jacky glanced his way, turned back to the seats and found everyone staring wide-eyed. "Dear me, are the snakes growing out of my head again? That Medusa look was so popular once upon a time!" He peered at the crowd and remarked half to himself, "Judging by your faces, I've turned you all to stone. Forgive me. My mother always said . . . "

But few were listening. All eyes were on a figure in silks floating past the stage humming "Beautiful Dreamer" under her breath, while the audience whispered her name.

Cass had invented a liaison in this hotel between a self-destructive artist and the ghost of a legendary suspected murderess. The character Jacky was haunted by Evangeline decades after she had died of an overdose.

Once he caught sight of her he seemed to forget the audience completely and followed her out of the room. When audience members came after them, they found a locked door.

But the room into which the two had gone was Jacky's legendary mirrored bedroom. The ceiling, an entire wall, even the floor in places reflected the room and its outsize bed. One wall was a two-way mirror. Jacky was always aware of this, as were some of his bedmates.

The *Sleep Walking* audience flocked around the glass, saw silhouettes dance in semi-darkness as Jacky tried to trap Evangeline or she ensnared him. One shadow seemed to pass through another. One or the other always had a back to the audience and both whispered so none outside could hear.

"How's the gate tonight?" she asked.

"Seventy percent for this show, about the same for the midnight show," he said.

"Shit," she said. "It's going to fold."

"Needs a third act," he said. "I have my eye out for especially unstable repeat patrons."

"A third victim," she said. "Rosalin's got one but Sonya scares me."

He shook his head. "She's harmless."

"A suicide might do," Keri said.

"I volunteer my understudy, Remo."

"Silly, understudies don't want to die; they want to kill the leads."

Through the glass the two heard, "Where are you, faggot? Fucking the ghost girl?" The Killer had returned.

Jeremy Knight took a deep breath and walked out of the bedroom. "Let's talk, one faggot to another. I'm the terrible secret: the herpes sore on the ten-inch cock, the skunk at the tea dance, the troll without the decency to hide under the bridge. I'm the one who's here to call you sister, to tell you . . . "

In *Sleep Walking* The Killer emptied the pistol into him just as had happened in real life. Audience members screamed. Keri always stayed for this and always had to stop herself from crying. Then she'd slip out for her big scene with Nance.

Only after his death was Jacky Mac described as "The Kit Marlowe of this bedraggled city." The press didn't get into the details of his life. The murderer was never identified, never caught.

Business did pick up for Christmas/New Year. But January brought bad weather and bad box office. On the last performance that month Rosalin stood several steps above Sonya, looking down at her as she said, *"This show needed something that would get the Big Arena talking about us and not the thousand other entertainments available. That never happened. We're posting closing notices next week. All my work wasted. I hope you enjoyed your brief time on stage."*

Sonya's eyes glistened. Rosalin recognized tears. They had talked about suicide. But heights bothered the stupid girl, guns were a mystery. Rosalin had thought to bring a knife.

Finale

The show's final scene was actors playing detectives, questioning the audience members as they filed out of the Studio after Jacky Mac's death.

And down the hall, Edwin Lowery and Evangeline Nance went at each other in hoarse ghost whispers. "Oh finally, my daughter, you will have no more to do with that sodomite!" Anger is never hard for actors to achieve in a failing production.

Keri was scared and irritated. Sonya, like a rat deserting a sinking ship, hadn't shown up that evening to get her through the dwindling crowd. She screeched, "So unlike the midnight visits to my room when I was still a child! Let us talk about pederasty and hypocrisy!"

Playgoers, still a bit ensnared by the drama they'd just witnessed, kept pointing them out to the actors/police who would look but be unable to see the ghosts.

"And that reminds me, dear Father . . . " Evangeline started to say, when there was a long, piercing and—Keri realized—quite heartfelt scream.

"That sounds very authentic!" said Jacoby Cass in his own voice and with a look of hope in his eyes.

Actor/cops and audience members stared down the hall. The Killer was running toward them with tears in his eyes and the prop gun still in his hand, babbling. " . . . in the elevator . . . opened the door . . . blood . . . "

Jeremy Knight/Jacky Mac arose from the floor of the Studio to discover what the commotion outside was about and was stunned when Remo/The Killer threw himself sobbing into his arms.

City police found Sonya holding open the faded gold door of the elevator. She'd knocked Rosalin down and stabbed her multiple times. The surveillance tape showed it all. She'd even looked up and waved.

When they hustled her out of the hotel and into a police car, Sonya yelled to the crowd, "She wanted me to die, wanted somebody else to die. But her work was over and the play must go on!"

A reporter asked Cass, "City officials think the production can open again in another few days. Do you believe it's safe for theatergoers?"

Jacoby Cass had heard from Inspector Chen that the authorities regarded this as a murder that could have taken place anywhere. The elevator, though, would need to be thoroughly inspected and his supervisors would accompany him.

Cass anticipated a flurry of green handshakes but knew *Sleep Walking Now and Then* was booked solid for at least the next six months. He told the reporter, "Yes. Notice that at no time was the life of any patron threatened!"

"Is the place haunted?" Keri Mayne was constantly asked.

Leaving the building the night of the murder, she had felt Rosalin's presence in the lobby and wondered if her death was her greatest piece of theatrical design. Until then Keri hadn't thought much about spirits. "Yes," she always said. "And I'm dedicating each of my future performances to the ghosts."

Seeing Jeremy Knight and Remo arrive at a party as a couple, a social blogger asked, "Does this feel like your on-stage relationship?"

Remo shook his head. Jeremy stopped smiling for a moment and said, "Yes."

As a foreign correspondent put it, "The Big Arena was made for moments like this."

Richard Bowes is nominated for a 2015 Nebula Award. His most recent novel, *Dust Devil On a Quiet Street* was on the 2014 World Fantasy and Lambda Awards short lists. He has published six novels, four story collections, over seventy short stories and has won two World Fantasy Awards, as well as Lambda, Million Writers, and IHG awards. Recent and forthcoming appearances include stories for *The Doll Collection, Tor.com, XIII, Farrago's Wainscot, The Magazine of Fantasy & Science Fiction, Uncanny, Interfictions,* and *In the Shadow of the Towers: Speculative Fiction in the Post-9/11 World.*

It's not a coincidence that the knight has a gun
the way the queen has a scepter . . .

COMBUSTION HOUR

Yoon Ha Lee

This story is about the eschatology of shadow puppets.

You've been a long time away from home with its vast, pale stage of textured silk and the queen's everywhere garden. There is only a binary of colors in your existence, just as you are supposed to narrow everything into the binary of target and not-target. Nevertheless, your language has words for colors. They are not red or ochre or azure. They are not even white or black, the logical defaults. But there is a word for the color of a string just as it is slit. Another for the color of the queen's favorite flowers, which coil so promisingly from each doorway. One for the color of fire. That last is rarely spoken, especially in the queen's presence.

Your uniform is the same color as the queen's gloves; it is defined that way. The queen's hands, they say of her knights. And now you've come back to the court with its thorn-collared tigers, its hawk-headed courtiers, its endlessly thwarted geodesics. The summons didn't give a reason why your return was so urgent, but you can guess.

The world-tapestry's weave is replete with imperfections: stains scrubbed out, clots of thread, small tears subtly mended. Like the queen's court entire, you glide frictionlessly across the tapestry's surface. But you are always aware that there is a world beyond the tapestry, in three dimensions of space rather than two, and, perhaps, the pitiless audience; you are always aware of the faraway lanterns.

The queen's court measures time by her smiles. Lately she has smiled less and less frequently. For the distinction between light and dark has been diminishing little by little, a phenomenon your soldiers observed even in the Knotted Reaches. And that means that the lanterns, little by little, are going out.

People quiet as you pass by them, lengthening and shortening in accordance to the laws of geometry, your position relative to the light sources. They have a name for you: the Knight of Pyres. It is not, despite the rumors, a reference to the nations you've torched, or even to the smoke like Cantor dust that drifts endlessly from your gun. You have never seen any point in telling them where the name comes from. After all, the queen would disapprove. Even in an airless world, a shadow-queen's disapproval can suffocate.

You approach the throne. The queen is flanked by her guards, and her poets, and her bearers-of-flowers. The last scatter petals of grave's-breath at your approach. They have a fragrance like sickle nights and slivered moons. You lay your gun before the queen, kneel, and wait.

It's not a long wait, just enough to make the point that she commands your loyalty still. You have never liked the queen, but you concede her efficiency. Besides, you don't have to like her to do her will. She made that clear to you a long time ago.

"I did not wish to recall you from a campaign where you were enjoying such success," the queen says. Her voice is low, and sharp the way that ice is sharp. At least there is no rebuke in it. "I have another mission for you."

Your lieutenant is competent enough. You have no doubt that she can finish the current war of subjugation to the queen's satisfaction. There's little left to do in any case. You could recite the figures readily enough. The houses slashed to tessellated debris, the number of knives, the dimensionless weight of ashes. But the queen has not asked about any of this, so you hold your silence.

"The lanterns are becoming exhausted," the queen says. The courtiers stir like a tremor in the tapestry: she has spoken the unspeakable after all. "You know what happens when all the lights go out." One of the tame tigers yawns; a poet mutters half a verse-of-warding in hexameter flattened to a scrap of desperation. The queen's head turns slightly. The poet shivers and subsides.

The lights have gone out before, but they have always come back on. On those occasions she made use of you and your gun, too. You remember the last such nightplunge. In the darkness your face had no boundaries. You were unable to discern the scars in your history or the contours of your future. When the lights came back on, you had to rebuild yourself from ligatures of shadow and shapes whose names you had to mine out of convolute dreams. You started with your gun. The queen, it is said, started with her scepter. You remind yourself of this every so often, because it's important to understand your adversaries, especially when you have something in common.

"You have only to command me," you say, which is not quite the case. She's not incapable of giving an unwise order.

The lanterns are an outside phenomenon, but it's not entirely true that your people have no influence over the world beyond. You are the proof of that.

The queen's smile in her oval face is a gash of light. "Then my command is this," she says. "Travel to the eastern border and bring back the Jewel of Mirrors. You will have to fight the eastern philosopher-king for it. But if the lanterns are failing us, if the world beyond is starved of mornings, then we will have to feed the lanterns ourselves. A foreign jewel is a small enough sacrifice."

It's not the solution you had expected. In times past you have gone hunting in the world beyond. But the supply of prey is finite, and you are not surprised that she knows what to do after it is exhausted.

East, right, away from the gates-ever-gaping; it's a matter of cartographic convention, but the dawn-voyaging symbolism counts for something. What the queen isn't saying is that the philosopher-king will have his armies, and his citizens, and his libraries of tomes inscribed in shadow-script as tiny and perfect as insects. What she isn't saying is that she wants you to reduce his land to a rubble of pixels.

"Your will is mine," you say, the old bitter formula. At least nothing more is expected of you.

The flower-bearers scatter petals of birds-ascending, so called because the flowers in full bloom resemble firebirds caught in the incandescent act of transporting themselves off the tapestry and into the impossible z-axis sky. You hide your cynicism; long practice.

The queen nods, and you take up your gun. "You will leave tomorrow," she says, and you wish she had given you permission to quit her presence straightaway. But instead you bow, and linger in the court for appearance's sake, never comfortable amid the shadow-edges of spear and vine and people who know better than to come too close to the queen's unchancy favorite.

At this point, it may be fruitful to review facts of stellar evolution. Stars like our sun effloresce into red giants, then shrink into white dwarfs, and eventually cool; in an older universe, the resulting black dwarfs would lurk in the vast reaches like carrion husks. More massive stars singe the darkness with heavy elements as they crumple into neutron stars. More massive still, and stars swallow themselves, leaving only black holes.

What's notable is not just the coruscating variety of colors, but the fact that each of these trajectories, while dependent on mass, eventually ends in darkness.

• • •

You know a lot of stories about the Jewel of Mirrors. None of them help you.

The Jewel of Mirrors is a necklace guarded by a bird that has been bricked up in a tower since the hour of its birth, and whose song can reduce shadow to the transparency of dew. To slay the bird, you must reflect its voice upon itself so that it boils away into formlessness. It is not known whether the bird would welcome this release.

The Jewel of Mirrors is a lock of twisting logic upon a starship's carcass. If you remove the lock, the starship will rouse, and with it all its nine-and-twenty cannons, one for each bitter star in your world's home constellation. The difficulty is not the lock, it's preserving the astrology of oppression.

The Jewel of Mirrors is a painting upon glass by the only artist to retrieve colors from outside the world-tapestry. Colors like crimson and bronze and viridian. Its virtue is that you can look into the painting and find a portrait of yourself. Its curse is that you can never unsee what you have seen there.

You would much rather be studying intelligence on the philosopher-king than some gaudy gem wrapped up in folklore. But all you know is that he has given tribute dutifully year by year to keep the queen's rapacious eye from turning in his direction. Indeed, some of those treasures decorate the queen's throne room. Frogs composed of gears imperfectly meshed, who sing dolorous songs of ruination. Banners upon which eddies and curves of light depict thunderstorms, cyclones, the occasional stray dragon. Once, a lily with eyes blinking stutteringly in its petals. This one was not entirely successful: the queen liked the idea, but suspected the eyes of belonging to the philosopher-king's sages or spymasters. Even now no one is certain how she disposed of the thing.

Before this day you knew the philosopher-king owned the Jewel of Mirrors, or at least, you knew that everyone said he did. You hadn't expected the story to be put to the test. And for that matter, how is a necklace or a starship unlocked or a painting supposed to address the problem of the lanterns?

Although you could ask the queen, it's unlikely that she would answer. It's more likely that you will find out when everyone else does.

Logistics becomes easy when everything from tinned dehydrated meals to space suits collapses into darkness, and can be reconstituted as neatly as an ancient theorem. For this mission the queen has assigned you the greatest of her warships, the starscourge *Stormrose*. All the queen's ships are named after flowers.

For most of her wars the queen accedes to her soldiers' sensibilities and sends them out by foot, or sometimes in chariots drawn by horse or swan or slow-blinking lizard. This way they can breathe, in the way of shadow moving through an atmosphere of light. And this way they need not endure the starships' claustrophobic nightcage.

The *Stormrose*, concocted of feral triangles and claw-projections, overgrown with guns, gives no hint as to its contents. No holes have been cut into it for people to look out of. It's a single connected silhouette, representing massacre in the semiotics of inkblots.

The queen has come to the starport to see you off. There is a black arc above you both, and cut into it are diamonds, stars, ringed planets, the occasional prismatic flicker of meteorites flashing by. The tiger at the queen's side sits back on its haunches and regards one of the diamonds as though it were prey for winter nights.

"My liege," you say as you bow before the queen.

Her smile, you imagine, is every bit as sardonic as the one that you hide inside your heart. "I know that I cannot command you as I do the others," she says, "no matter how disagreeable you find my presence. Nevertheless, good service is good service, and should be recognized as such. I expect nothing less of you now."

The queen taps your shoulder with the scepter. Long practice: you don't shudder as your shape is joined to hers, shadows merging for a moment. You don't need the reminder, but the ritual has to be observed, even if you are the one person who has nothing to fear from the scepter. "Go," she says. "Bring the jewel back to me."

It won't be the only thing you bring. Neither of you needs to say it, though.

A law of etiquette in the world of puppets: You may gesture, you may intimate, but you do not touch. You do not intersect shadow upon shadow, especially when the shadow is a person. Even lovers exchange their caresses through some intermediary: handkerchiefs of filigree lace, tangram poetry, perfectly useless masks. To touch is to become conjoined. It is not something you do where you can be seen, and everything on the world-tapestry can be seen.

The queen with her scepter is one exception. Not only does she touch people with it, she also commands them. It is not entirely accurate to call it a scepter. Rather, it is a rod of puppet-strings, condensed to hungry facets. You have never seen your string, but you can feel it like a flickering ember even when you are far from the queen's presence. Doubtless her other subjects experience something similar.

The other exception is travel in conveyances: carriages that admit no windows, submarines scarred by battles with gnashing kraken, starships like the one that you will command against the philosopher-king. Leisurely journeys, foregoing such vehicles, are fashionable for a reason.

Another law of etiquette in the world of puppets: you do not speak of the ligatures fraying, of the paper shedding its fibers and the limbs worn thin, of the scalloped edges after encounters with water. (After fire, water is the element that puppets fear most. Glue is not well-regarded, either.) You do not speak of the fact that the queen's favorite tiger smells incongruously of tangerines and cloves and amber after a mishap with a perfume bottle, or the stiffness of the queen's hands, which she makes no attempt to disguise, and which no one is foolish enough to remark on. Everything is smoothed over by shadow.

This is probably the only reason nobody asks how it is that you are char-marked, fire-scarred, and whole of form; how you survived.

We are the *Stormrose*. Within this warship's boundary crenellations, we are one weapon and one will. A single burnt knight stands apart; but the knight's mission is ours, and in any case it is not for us to question the queen's dictate.

In times unwritten, we have punched holes like arpeggiated quavers into crowds that flee, but never fast enough. We have called down fire as sudden as cardiac failure upon citadels new-crowded with ghosts. We have cultivated flowers whose radiations exhale calligraphy-splashes onto the threadbare cloth.

In times unwritten, there were no graves and no pyres, no corpses and no epitaphs, only bland expanses of background fabric where shadows once moved. Our orders this time are different. So the queen said. So the knight says now.

The ship breathes with one breath, strikes with one hand. At some later time we may disembark and become individuals again. We will not concern ourselves with this until it becomes necessary.

We do not know what the knight thinks of this, except that this is a familiar story to it, possibly unworthy of special attention. We do not ask.

It's not a coincidence that the knight has a gun the way the queen has a scepter.

On the last day that his capital stands, the philosopher-king sets free his flocks of origami birds, crane and goose and extravagant peacock. He sends all his servants home, and persuades the courtiers and guards and alchemists to follow them. The guards, like the soldiers, may keep their weapons, but he makes it plain, without words, that those weapons are unlikely to bring them any profit. The great towers of the palace fold in upon themselves so that the band of sky with its cloudscatter and raindrift can be seen without obstruction. The *Stormrose*, too, can be seen as it eclipses the cut-out sun in its descent.

Then the philosopher-king sits in his study and writes. He writes upon a shadow-book with shadow-pages, incising words of light like the bite marks of didactic snakes. For years he has been adding oddments of lore, fragments of story: everything he has heard about the Jewel of Mirrors, including a few divertissements of his own.

On this last day, your soldiers march through the streets with their thorn-swords and bramble-nets to collect the philosopher-king's former subjects for removal. In the meantime, you walk unimpeded through the mazy passages of his palace and come upon him, still sitting, still writing. You wait patiently while he finishes the page that he is working on.

"I had expected you to fight," you say. The queen had said he would. Instead, he has done anything but.

The philosopher-king laughs softly. "I am unlike your queen in most matters," he says, "but like her, I know the name of your gun. If I saw some escape for my people, I would have taken it. But I have read the signs in the sky, the world-tapestry's inexorable dimming. It's one death or another, however you figure it."

He closes the book and holds it out to you. You eye it askance. "This is the Jewel of Mirrors," he says. "A collection of fables. I imagine your queen will find it entertaining bedtime reading for the sleep she never indulges in. Go on, you may as well ask the obvious question."

"If you wish," you say. No harm in accommodating a man whose realm you have so thoroughly ruined, especially when you can sieve him dead at any moment. In the distance you hear silence baked upon silence as your soldiers staple their captives' mouths shut. The queen despises screaming and lamentations. "Where do the fables come from?"

"The same place any riddle comes from," the philosopher-king says. "I have spent a lifetime collecting them. Not enough of a lifetime finding answers. It appears my turn is done and your queen may have much joy of this endeavor. Call it a final gift."

"You don't expect to be spared," you say, because you have to be sure.

"Of course not."

"Why bother?" you ask. "If she appreciates the gift, it will be to lock it up in a cage of shelves, to be admired but not perused." She has received you in her library before. Sometimes she studies the intricate spiraling designs stamped across the books' covers, but it is rare that you catch her reading.

The philosopher-king shrugs. "Oh, I'm not concerned with her. I am, however, pleased to have this small opportunity to talk to you."

His calm makes you wary. This entire conversation could be a trap. Still, surely he realizes that the queen has other knights, and that her soldiers will carry out their orders whether or not you're there to supervise them? "One captive more or less will make no difference to the queen," you say. Indeed, she made it explicit that she has no particular need for the philosopher-king's carcass. "You cannot hope to dissuade me. I have no heart to appeal to." One more thing the queen made certain of.

He stirs slightly at that, as if he had begun to smile. "In that you are mistaken," he says. "I have no doubt that your queen knows the truth, even if she has misled you. A heart isn't what you have. It's what you do."

Not just the palace but the capital entire is cloaked in strata of silence. The only sounds now are the words that pass between you and the doomed king. You listen for heartbeat drums and hear nothing. Even your soldiers are escorting the captives back to the *Stormrose* without sound.

"Take the book," the philosopher-king says. "As a souvenir if nothing else." And then he tells you something unexpected: "Try not to think too harshly of your queen. She is something of an expert on difficult choices."

You accept the gift, tucking it into folds of shadow. The snakebite words pass into you; you ignore the scour of stories freeze-dried. "It's your turn now," you say, and raise your gun.

The queen's people know your gun as Candor. The queen's idea of a joke, a gift to someone who rarely has the opportunity to speak freely.

You and the queen know the gun's true name. It is called Combustion.

As a point of fact, the gun's incomparable lethality is only tangentially related to the vulnerabilities of paper or cloth.

The *Stormrose* bears you and the soldiers and the prisoners back to the queen's starport. You are the first to disembark. The queen awaits you with her customary tiger. "What have you brought for me?" she asks. "The smoke-skeleton of a bird? A scintillant circuit? A mirror of undesired insights?"

"A book," you say as you salute her, attempting to not express your doubts about the whole endeavor. You produce it for her inspection.

The queen laughs and returns your salute with a mocking wave. "Of course. He always did believe that everyone could be educated. It isn't the worst fallacy I've ever encountered." She takes the book from you and sets it before the tiger. The tiger bats at it experimentally. Probably just as dubious as you are.

"The disposition of the prisoners?" you ask. What was the point of ferrying them all back here, anyway? The queen has occasionally taken interest in gladiatorial amusements, but she is unlikely to be frivolous at a time like this.

"In your absence I have prepared a dungeon," the queen says. She gestures, and you see it in the distance: an obtrusion you had mistaken for some recent fantasia of topiary. "The prisoners can reside there for the moment."

You give the necessary orders, and the soldiers and their freight of unspeaking captives begin to march toward the dungeon. "I don't understand what use you have for these people," you say.

She doesn't smile. "Book, jewel, bird, it's immaterial," she says. "The people were the point of this exercise in numbers."

You should have figured it out earlier. She was never interested in refueling the lanterns through some treasure contrived of riddles, although in a land where starships coexist with chimeras, it wasn't impossible that such a treasure would perform as specified. No: she means to use the captives as fuel.

"You have never approved of me," the queen says dryly, "but then, I have never required your approval. It has only been enough that what I do is for the preservation of the realm; any ruler's duty."

"You're going to run out of prisoners," you say. "The supply of foreigners is finite. And after that, what then—your own people? Incompetent chefs? Birds that sing too early in the morning? Overly demanding consorts?"

"I almost wish you'd lose your temper more often," she muses. "You're not incapable of wit." Her regard narrows. "But the world is dimming, and I have need of you yet."

The world beyond has lanterns, which are called stars. Nuclei strike each other, overcome the forces that would repel them from each other, and form new nuclei. Just as shadows can be crushed together, so can particles, and in the process they dance a fury of light. Yet no star burns forever, and no universe warms its inhabitants forever, either.

This process, while it lasts, is known as fusion. A form of combustion, if you like.

You don't like the queen, yet she has this virtue: she has always looked out for the best interests of her realm. If the rest of the world has to burn for her people's welfare, so be it. It is this knifing purity of purpose that has kept you by her side all this time.

"A lesson for you, if you will," the queen says. She sounds quietly exhausted, and that faint vulnerability alarms you. You do not wish to see weakness in her. It implies weakness in yourself, to the extent that you are her instrument. "There is no convenient isomorphism between the physics of the world beyond and the laws by which we live here. People are shadows, and shadows are souls. Unlike nuclei, they will burn forever: the perfect fuel. Even so, I sought to spare people—not just our people, but our enemies as well—as long as possible.

"Look up—not toward the cut-out shapes of star and crescent, but up out of the plane of the world-tapestry, up along the perpendicular. All the stars out there have burned out. Everything is cooling. We have denuded a universe of lanterns for our own survival. The only ones left to us are those we nourish ourselves."

You are learning to ask questions too late. You look up, then back at the queen. "There weren't just lanterns in that universe," you say.

Civilizations come to terms with the heat death of the universe in various ways, if they do at all. A small selection of possibilities:

Some of them attempt to rewrite the laws of entropy, as though statistical mechanics were amenable to postmodern narrative techniques.

Some of them research ways to punch through into other universes, anthropic principle notwithstanding. It is rarely the case that other universes are more hospitable than the current one.

Some of them build monuments of the rarest materials that they can devise, even knowing that everything will be pulverized to the same singularity punctuation. Not all of the art thus created is particularly worthy of the effort put into it, but neither will there be anyone left to judge.

And some of them simply commit mass suicide, on the grounds that they would prefer to choose the manner of their passing. At this end of time, weapons of incandescent destruction are commonplace. We may assume that a sufficiently determined civilization can contrive to obtain some.

Each of these trajectories ends in darkness.

"You want the captives to burn forever," you say. "Then, as a corollary, the people you put into those lanterns will never escape through death."

"You're learning about consequences," the queen says. "Yes. That's exactly what I'm saying."

You know why the queen chose you for this task, and not some other, although it's not inconceivable that there are backups. She cut you from the paper of a lantern, sacrificing its light forever. You remember being raked by fire, and the shearing scissors. You remember being constructed without a heart.

Knight of Pyres. Combustion. She needs you to light the lanterns for her.

A heart isn't what you have. It's what you do, the philosopher-king had said. You wonder what would have happened if someone had said it to you a lifetime ago. It's unlikely that you would have listened. Only now, as you behold a universe comprehensively dissipated, do you realize what service you have rendered all this time.

"I can't do this for you," you say.

"So you are no longer content to be a knight," the queen says, unnervingly composed. The queen's hands. "I advise you to consider your decision carefully. Once you start making choices of your own, you move into the realm of consequence, and in most matters you cannot erase mistakes, or responsibility. Are you certain this is what you want? Our world slowly waning to a forever black?" Her mouth curves as you hesitate.

You raise your gun.

She raises the scepter.

You're faster. And you don't shoot her, anyway. You shoot the scepter. It goes up in a hellscream of fire and smoke and uncoiled volition.

The queen doesn't let go, and the fire spreads to her hand. "In the darkness you will be outnumbered," she says, raising her voice over the crackling. "People will attempt to relight the lanterns themselves. They will seek weapons deadlier than Combustion. They will come to you and beg in words like broken wings for any pittance of light. You will have to stand vigil alone in the forever night, listening, in case someone in the mass of shadow is clever enough to undo what you have done and start the furnace of souls."

"Drop the scepter," you cry. The gun is specific in its effect. This is an airless world and all fire is, in a sense, artificially sustained. She could survive a little while yet, one-armed.

"The realm of consequence," she says remindingly.

Time does not pass here as it does in the world beyond, but it passes quickly enough when it cares to. The queen burns up like a candle, like a torch, like a star of guttering ambitions.

The queen's people haven't yet figured out what has transpired, but they will know soon enough.

You settle back, gun smoking endlessly, and wait as the darkness settles over the world by smothering degrees. You have a long vigil ahead of you: time to begin.

There is nothing left of this story but a whispering condensate of shadow, and a single unknight standing apart.

Yoon Ha Lee's fiction has appeared in *Tor.com*, *Beneath Ceaseless Skies*, *Clarkesworld*, *The Magazine of Fantasy & Science Fiction*, and other venues. His first short story collection, *Conservation of Shadows,* was published in 2013. He lives in Louisiana with his family and has not yet been eaten by gators.

There are no sides. Only love and hate . . .

RESURRECTION POINTS

Usman T. Malik

I was thirteen when I dissected my first corpse. It was a fetid, soggy teenager Baba dragged home from Clifton Beach and threw in the shed. The ceiling leaked in places, so he told me to drape the dead boy with tarpaulin so that the monsoon water wouldn't get at him.

When I went to the shed, DeadBoy had stunk the place up. I pinched my nostrils, gently removed the sea-blackened aluminum crucifix from around his neck, pulled the tarp across his chest. The tarp was a bit short—Ma had cut some for the chicken coop after heavy rainfall killed a hen—and I had to tuck it beneath DeadBoy's chin so it seemed he were sleeping. Then I saw that the fish had eaten most of his lips and part of his nose and my stomach heaved and I began to retch.

After a while I felt better and went inside the house.

"How's he look?" said Baba.

"Fine, I guess," I said.

Baba looked at me curiously. "You all right?"

"Yes." I looked at Ma rolling dough peras in the kitchen for dinner, her face red and sweaty from heat, and leaned into the smell of mint leaves and chopped onions. "Half his face is gone, Baba."

He nodded. "Yes. Water and flesh don't go well together and the fish get the rest. You see his teeth?"

"No."

"Go look at his teeth and tell me what you see."

I went back to the shed and peeled the pale raw lip-flesh back with my fingers. His front teeth were almost entirely gone, sockets blackened with blood, and the snaillike uvula at the back of the throat was half-missing. I peered into his gaping mouth, tried to feel the uvula's edge with my finger. It was smooth and covered with clots, and I knew what had happened to this boy.

"So?" Baba said when I got back.

"Someone tortured him," I said. Behind Baba, Mama sucked a breath in and fanned the manure oven urgently, billowing the smoke away from us toward the open door.

"How do you know?" Baba said.

"They slashed his uvula with a razor while he was alive, and when he tried to bite down they knocked out his teeth with a hammer."

Baba nodded. "How can you tell?"

"Clean cut. It was sliced with a blade. And there are no teeth chips at the back of the throat or stuck to the palate to indicate bullet trauma."

"Good." Baba looked pleased. He tapped his chin with a spoon and glanced at Mama. "You think he's ready?"

Mama tried to lift the steaming pot, hissed with pain, let it go and grabbed a rough cotton rag to hold the edges. "Now?"

"Sure. I was his age when I did my first." He looked at me. "You're old enough. Eat your dinner. Later tonight I'll show you how to work them."

We sat on the floor and Ma brought lentil soup, vegetable curry, raw onion rings, and corn flour roti. We ate in silence on the meal mat. When we were done we thanked Allah for his blessings. Ma began to clear the dinner remains, her bony elbows jutting out as she scraped crumbs and wiped the mat. She looked unhappy and didn't look up when Baba and I went out to work on DeadBoy.

DeadBoy's armpits reeked. I asked Baba if I could stuff my nostrils with scented cotton. He said no.

We put on plastic gloves made from shopping bags. Baba lay the boy on the tools table, situating his palms upward in the traditional anatomical position. I turned on the shed's naked bulb and it swung from its chain above the cadaver, like a hanged animal.

"Now," Baba said, handing me the scalpel, "locate the following structures." He named superficial landmarks: jugular notch, sternal body, xiphoid process, others familiar to me from my study of his work and his textbooks. Once I had located them, he handed me the scalpel and said: "Cut."

I made a midline horizontal and two parallel incisions in DeadBoy's chest. Baba watched me, shaking his head and frowning, as I fumbled my way through the dissection. "No. More laterally" and "Yes, that's the one. Now reflect the skin back, peel it slowly. Remove the superficial fascia," and "Repeat on the other side."

DeadBoy's skin was wet and slippery from water damage and much of the fat was putrefied. His pectoral and abdominal musculature was dark and soft. I scraped the congealed blood away and removed the fascia, and as I worked muscles and tendons slowly emerged and glistened in the yellow light, displaying neurovascular bundles weaving between their edges. It took me three hours but finally I was done. I stood, surrounded by DeadBoy's odor, trembling with excitement, peering at my handiwork.

Baba nodded. "Not bad. Now show me where the resurrection points are." When I hesitated, he raised his eyebrows. "Don't be scared. You know what to do."

I took a glove off and placed it on DeadBoy's thigh. I tentatively touched the right pec major, groping around its edges. The sternal head was firm and spongy. When I felt a small cord in the medial corner with my fingers, I tapped it lightly. The pec didn't twitch.

I looked at Baba. He smiled but his eyes were black and serious. I licked my lips, took the nerve cord between my fingers, closed my eyes, and discharged.

The jolt thrummed up my fingers into my shoulder. Instantly the pec contracted and DeadBoy's right arm jerked. I shot the biocurrent again, feeling the recoil tear through my flesh, and this time DeadBoy's arm jumped and flopped onto his chest.

"Something, isn't it," Baba said. "Well done."

I didn't reply. My heart raced, my skin was feverish and crawling. My nostrils were filled with the smell of electricity.

"First time's hard, no denying it. But it's gotta be done. Only way you'll learn to control it."

I was on fire. We had talked about it before, but this wasn't anything like I had expected. When Baba did it, he could smile and make conversation as the deadboys spasmed and danced on his fingertips. Their flesh turned into calligraphy in his hands.

"That felt like something exploded inside me, Baba," I said, hearing the tremble in my voice. "What happens if I can't control it?"

He shrugged. "You will. It just takes time and practice, that's all. Our elders have done it for generations." He leaned forward, lifted DeadBoy's hand, and returned it to supine position. "Want to try the smaller muscles? They need finer control and the nerves are thinner. Would be wise to use your fingertips."

And thus we practiced my first danse macabre. Sought out the nerve bundles, made them pop and sizzle, watched the cadaver spider its way across the table. With each discharge, the pain lessened, but soon my fingers began to go numb and Baba made me halt. Carefully he draped DeadBoy.

"Baba, are there others?" I asked as we walked back to the house.

"Like us?" He nodded. "The Prophet Isa is said to have returned men to life. When Martha of Bethany asked him how he would bring her brother Lazarus back to life, Hazrat Isa said, 'I am the Resurrection and the life. He who believes in me will live, even though he dies.'"

We were in the backyard; the light of our home shone out bright and comforting. Baba turned and smiled at me. "But he was a healer first. Like our beloved Prophet Muhammad Peace-Be-Upon-Him. Do you understand?"

"I guess," I said. DeadBoy's face swam in front of my eyes. "Baba, who do you think killed him?"

His smile disappeared. "Animals." He didn't look at me when he said, "How's your friend Sadiq these days? I haven't seen him in a while." His tone was casual, and he tilted his jaw and stared into the distance as if looking for something.

"Fine," I said. "He's just been busy, I think."

Baba rubbed his cheek with a hairy knuckle and we began walking again. "Decent start," he said. "Tomorrow will be harder, though." I looked at him; he spread his arms and smiled, and I realized what he meant.

"So soon?" I said, horrified. "But I need more practice."

"Sure, you do, but it's not that different. You did well back there."

"But—"

"You will do fine, Daoud," he said gently, and would say no more.

Ma watched us approach the front door, her face silvered by moonlight. Baba didn't meet her eyes as we entered, but his hand rose and rubbed against his khaddar shirt, as if wiping dirt away.

Ma said nothing, but later, huddled in the charpoy, staring through the skylight window at the expansive darkness, I heard them arguing. At one point, I thought she said, "Worry about the damn house," and he tried to shush her, but she said something hot and angry and Baba got up and left. There was silence and then there was sobbing, and I lay there, filled with sorrow and excitement, listening to her grief, thinking if only there was a way to reconcile the two.

The dead foot leaped when I touched the resurrection point. Mr. Kurmully yelped.

"Sorry," I said, jerking my fingers away. "Did that hurt?"

"No." He massaged the foot with his hand. "I was . . . surprised. I haven't had any feeling in this for years. Just a dry burning around the shin. But when you touched it there," he gestured at the inner part of his left ankle, "I *felt* it. I felt you touching me."

He looked at me with awe, then at Baba, who stood by the door, hands laced behind his back, looking pleased. "He's good," Mr. Kurmully said.

"Yes," Baba said.

"So when are you retiring, Jamshed?"

Baba laughed. "Not for a while, I hope. Anyway, let's get on with it. Daoud," he said to me, "can you find the pain point in his ankle?"

I spent the next thirty minutes probing and prodding Mr. Kurmully's diabetic foot, feeling between his tendons for nerves. It wasn't easy. Over the years, Mr. Kurmully had lost two toes and the stumps had shriveled, distorting the anatomy. Eventually I found two points, braced myself, and gently shot them.

"Feel better?" I said, as Mr. Kurmully withdrew his foot and stepped on it tentatively.

"He won't know until tomorrow," Baba said. "Sometimes instant effect may occur, but our true goal is nocturnal relief when the neuropathy is worst. Am I right, Habib?"

"Yes." Mr. Kurmully nodded and flexed his foot this way and that. "The boy's gifted. I had some burning when I came. It's gone now. His first time?"

"Yes."

"Good God." Mr. Kurmully shook his head wonderingly. "He will go far." He came toward me and patted me on the head. "Your father's been a boon to our community for twenty years, boy. Always be gentle, like him, you hear me? Be humble. It's the branch laden with fruit that bends the most." He smiled at me and turned to Baba. "Let me pay you this once, Jamshed."

Baba waved a hand. "Just tip the Edhi driver when he takes the cadaver. One of their volunteers has agreed to bury it for free."

"They are good to you, aren't they."

Baba beamed. He opened his mouth to speak, but there was sudden commotion at the front of the clinic and a tall, gangly man with a squirrel tail mustache strode in, followed by the sulky-faced Edhi driver looking angry and unhappy.

Baba's gaze went from one to another and settled on the gangly stranger. "Salam, brother," Baba said pleasantly. "How can I help you?"

The gangly man pulled out a sheath of papers and handed it to Baba. He had gleaming rat eyes that narrowed like cracks in cement when he spoke. He sounded as if he had a cold. "Doctor Sahib, you know why I'm here."

"I'm not sure I do. Why don't you tell me? Would you like to take a seat?"

"Just read the papers, sahib," he said in his soft, nasal voice.

"Oh?" Baba looked at the Edhi driver. He was a gloomy, chubby boy fond of charas and ganja and often rolled joints one-handed on his fat belly when waiting at red lights. I had ridden with him a couple of times and once he showed me his weird jutting navel. Everted since birth, he told me proudly.

"Zamir, what's going on?" Baba said.

"Sahib, they're giving us trouble with the burial," Zamir said. "This man is from the local *Defend The Sharia* office. They have a written fatwa stating that since the dead boy was Christian he cannot be buried in a Muslim cemetery."

Baba turned back to the gangly man. "Is that true, brother?"

Gangly Man thrust the papers into Baba's hands. "This is from Imam Barani. Take a look."

Baba took the roll, but didn't open it. "This boy," Baba said, "was tortured by someone."

Gangly Man's shoulders stiffened.

"He was beaten badly. His teeth knocked out with a hammer. Someone took a razor to his mouth. When he was near dead, they threw him in the river."

Gangly Man's lips pressed into a thin, white line.

"He was sixteen. He had a scar on his stomach from a childhood surgery, probably appendectomy. He wore a tawiz charm on his forearm his mother likely got from a Muslim saint. You know how illiterate these poor Christians are. Can't tell the difference between one holy man and another, and—"

"Doctor Sahib." Gangly Man leaned forward and whispered conspiratorially, "He and his filthy religion can ride my dick. My orders are simple. He will not be buried in the Muslim cemetery, and if I were you I wouldn't push it." He grinned and shook his head as if talking to a child.

Baba's face changed color. He looked around and for the first time I saw how angry and tired he was. He looked like he hadn't slept in days. Maybe he hadn't. It was hard to know. He and Ma were talking less to each other lately.

"If you make it difficult for us, well, things could go many ways, couldn't they? Sometimes clinics run by quacks can be shut down by provincial governments until NOCs are obtained. I don't even see a diploma on your wall. Surely, you went to medical school?" Still smiling, he toed the foot of the threadbare couch, the only piece of furniture in the room. "Besides, you might be Muslim but blasphemy is blasphemy, brother, and punishable under the Hadood Ordinance. The boy is Christian. That cemetery is not."

The Edhi driver took Baba's arm and led him aside. They talked. Zamir gestured furiously. Baba's shoulders rose and sagged. They came back.

"We will take the body to Aga Khan Medical College and donate it to their anatomy lab," cried Zamir.

"But he has already been—" Baba began

"I'm sure they will find more to do with it," Zamir said, nodding and smiling.

Gangly Man took the front of his own shirt with a tarantula-like hand and began to shake it, fanning his chest. "Very wise. How they will appreciate you!"

Baba remained silent, but a heavy ice block appeared in my belly and settled there. I turned and ran from the clinic, ran all the way to our house three streets down. I burst into the shed and went to DeadBoy and wrenched away the tarp. His insides were tucked in with thin stitches. I yanked the stitches out, peeled back his skin, and pressed my gloveless fingers into his muscles. I discharged the biocurrent again and again until his limbs twirled and snapped, a lifeless dervish whirling around his own axis. I let the electricity flow through my fingertips like a raging torrent, until the room sizzled with charge and my nostrils filled with the odor of burnt flesh.

After a while I stepped back. My cheeks burned and the corners of my eyes tickled. Even though it was close to noon, the shed was dark from a low-hanging monsoon ceiling. Interstices of sunlight fell on DeadBoy's half-face, revealing the blackness of his absent teeth and his mutilated lips.

"Sorry, DeadBoy," I said.

He twitched his shoulder.

The movement was so unexpected that I jerked and fell over the toolbox on the floor. I sat on the sodden ground, gazing at DeadBoy, my heart pounding in my chest. He was still. Had I imagined it? That movement—it was impossible. The deadboys couldn't move without stimulus.

I got up and went to him. His disfigured flesh was placid and motionless.

"Hey," I whispered, feeling foolish and nervous. "Can you hear me?"

The shadows in the room deepened. Somewhere outside a swallow cheeped. DeadBoy never said a word.

After the Edhi driver hauled DeadBoy away, I walked around for a while. Soon it began to drizzle, the kind of sprinkle that makes you feel hot and damp but never really cool, so I took off my shirt, tucked it into my armpit, and ran bare-chested to Sadiq's house.

He lived in the Christian muhallah near Kala Pul, a couple kilometers away. His two-room tin-and-timber house was next to a dirty canal swollen with rainwater, plastic bags, and lifeless rodents, and the rotten smell filled the street.

His mother opened the door. Khala Apee was a young-old woman. Her cheeks were often bruised. Her right eye was swollen shut today.

"He's at the Master sahib's," she told me in a hoarse voice. She smoked cigarettes when her husband was not home, Sadiq had told me. "He'll be back in an hour. Want a soda?"

They couldn't afford sodas. It was probably leftover sherbat from last Ramadan. But what was Sadiq doing at Master sahib's? Summer vacation wouldn't be over for another month. "Thank you, but no, Khala Apee. I'll wait under the elm outside."

She nodded and tried to smile. "Let me know if you want something. And if you can, do stay for dinner."

Plain roti with sliced onions. No gravy. "I'll try, Khala Apee. May I borrow a plastic bag?"

She brought me one. I went to the charpoy under the elm where we sometimes sat and made fun of our families. Rain pattered on the elm leaves and hissed on the ground, and as I sat there with my plastic-draped head on the steeple of my fingers I thought about Baba and Ma and how they had been arguing for months. Ma was worried about the house, she wanted Baba to start charging patients. Baba refused. His father and grandfather had never charged a fee, he said. They lived on food and gifts people gave them.

Ma laughed bitterly. Those were different times, you fool. So different. And the house, what about the house, Jamshed? We are in debt. So much debt. What will you do when they come to take our home? If you cared as much about your family as you do about your goddamn corpse-learning, we could live like normal people, like normal human beings.

But we're *not* normal, Baba protested. This is a good way to blend in, to be part of this world. Be part of the community—

Blend in? Mama said. We will never blend in if you keep antagonizing them. What was the point of arguing with that mullah? You know they are dangerous people. You keep going like this, we will never be part of the community. How could we be? We are . . .

Sadiq was shaking me awake. "Hey, Daoud, hey. Wake up."

I opened my eyes. "Hey, how was . . . *what?*" I said when I saw his face.

Sadiq was a small boy with mousy features and at the moment they were chiseled with worry.

"You've got to leave, Daoud," said Sadiq, glancing around. "Now."

"What's going on? Everything okay?"

"Yes. Master sahib had heard some rumors and he wanted to warn us. He . . ." Sadiq gnawed at his lip, his fingers still tugging at my arm. "Go home. We'll talk tomorrow."

"Why?" But he was already leading me away from the elm and toward the canal. The drizzle had stopped and the canal water eddied gently. I put on my shirt and watched as Sadiq took a tin box from his pocket and tied a brick around it with jute twine and twice-doubled rubber band. He waded into the shallow canal and deposited the box at a spot two feet from the bank.

"What are you doing?" I said when he climbed back up the embankment.

"Nothing," he said, but his voice was strange. "Run back home now. I'll come by in a couple days if I can."

I went up the canal road, occasionally looking back, trying to make sense of what had just happened. Sadiq stood there, hands in the pockets of his shorts, a skinny, brown boy with a sad face and a fake-silver cross gleaming around his neck. Sometimes even now I see that cross in my dreams, throwing silver shadows across my path as I trudge down alleys filled with heartache and rotting bodies.

As I glanced back one last time, Sadiq took off the cross and slipped it into his pocket.

Baba was waiting for me.

"Where were you?" he said, his eyes hard and red. "I was worried sick."

"At Sadiq's. I wanted to—"

"Foolish boy," he said. "Don't you know how dangerous that was? Don't you realize?" I stared at him, feeling my head throb. He saw my incomprehension and his voice softened. "Someone vandalized a church in Lahore yesterday. Someone else found feces strewn in a mosque in Quetta. As a result, two people are dead and tens more injured in riots around the country. These tensions have been building for a while. You saw what that *Defend The Sharia* asshole did this morning. This will only get worse. You cannot visit Sadiq until things settle down."

"But what does Sadiq have to do with that?"

Baba gazed at me with pity. "Everything."

I met his eyes and whatever was in them frightened me so much that my hands began to shake. I couldn't stand facing him anymore. Quickly I walked past him and went to my room, where I sat on my rickety charpoy and watched the dusk through the skylight. In the other room, Ma prayed loudly on the musallah. She might have been crying, I couldn't tell. I tried to read a medical textbook Baba gave me for my last birthday, but my mind was too restless, so I gave up and went to the kitchen where Ma had arranged unwashed raw chicken breasts on a chopping board.

I lay my hands on the meat. I thought about Sadiq and his tin box, and softly let the current flow. The chicken breast jumped and thudded on the wood. I discharged again, this time with more force, removed my hands, stepped back, and watched as for a whole minute the meat slapped up and down, squirting blood that puddled on the wooden board, making curious dark shapes.

That should have been impossible but clearly wasn't.

In school during physics class our teacher had explained capacitors to us. Strange ideas came to me now. Words that Baba taught me from his textbooks: cell membranes, calcium-gates, egg-shaped mitochondria, and polarized ionic channels. Could *they* act as capacitors at times and hold charge so the flesh would stay alive even after I removed my fingertips?

The boy is gifted, someone said in my head.

I should have felt better. Instead I felt angry and miserable. I went to Ma's room and opened the door.

She was sitting on her haunches in front of the only pretty piece of furniture in the room, a mahogany dresser Baba's mother gave her as a wedding present. Ma had been fiddling with a half-open drawer, a jewelry box glittering in her hand. When I entered, she plunged the drawer into place. "Are you so ill-mannered now that you won't knock?"

"Sorry, Ma. I wasn't thinking."

"Idiot boy," she said quietly. Her gaze drifted back down to the box she held, fingers sliding up and down its metallic edges. The space beneath her eyes was dark and wet. "Next time mind your manners."

I thought it prudent to remain silent. Ma lifted the lid and gazed within and her eyes turned inward. The effect was so intense that for a moment she looked dead, her lifeless eyes watching something in the box, or behind it. Uneasy, I took a step forward and glanced inside. A picture of a naked man nailed to a cross, surrounded by wailing people; then Ma was snapping the lid back into place so violently that I jerked and fell back.

Ma's hands shook and she said something that didn't make sense, "Never wanted to come here. Your father made me. I never wanted to leave my people," and she glared at me hatefully. It was a brief moment, but nothing in my life since has made me feel so ashamed. So lonely and self-loathing; a mutant child broken and hated forever.

I turned and ran from the room, blinded by anger or tears or both, while my mother watched me from the darkness of her room, the jewelry box still in her callused hands.

Later they told us it was an accident, that a wooden shanty caught fire and set the muhallah ablaze, but we all knew better.

It was the tail end of monsoon season and the rains had petered out which worsened the conflagration. Fifty Christian houses burned down that night; the flames and smoke ceiling could be seen from as far as Gulshan Iqbal, we were told. Twenty people died; Sadiq's father (who survived tuberculosis and, later, the 1999 Kargil War) was among them. Their corpses were pulled out from the wreckage, burnt and twisted. Sadiq's mother recognized him only by the hare-shaped mole on his left foot.

When I went to see Sadiq, he sobbed on my shoulder.

"They took everything," he wept. "My house, our belongings. My father," he added as an afterthought. "They burnt the house down. My cousin saw them, I swear to God."

"Which God?" I said. My right arm was around him. My left hand dug so hard into the flesh of my thigh I popped the blood blister a biocurrent discharge had raised on my finger. "*Which* God?"

He stared at me with bloodshot eyes, threw his head back, and cried some more; while his mother sat stone-like in the charpoy under the elm, rocking back and forth, her face blank. One hand tapped the bruises on her cheek. The other hid her lips.

I held Sadiq for as long as I could, then I went home, where Ma sat knitting a cotton sweater. Winter would come in two months, and we couldn't afford to buy new clothes. Baba was out—he'd been delayed at the clinic—so I sat at Ma's feet and counted her toes. Ten.

She watched me through the emptiness between her needles and said, "I'm sorry."

"Yes."

"It was horrible, wasn't it?"

"Yes."

"Tell you what. Why don't we take Sadiq and his mother some naans and beef korma tomorrow? I'm sure his mother is too upset to cook right now."

I recalled Khala Apee's vacuous stare, the hand covering her mouth, and nodded.

Ma placed her knitting needles aside, lowered herself to the floor, and hugged me.

"The world is a bad place," she whispered. "We're in danger all the time. People who are different like you, like us . . . can sometimes seem like a threat to others."

I listened. Outside, thunder cracked. The skylight window rippled with water as the night opened.

"You use your gift to heal others, you hear me?" she said. "Don't get involved with anger or hatred or sides. There are no sides. Only love and hate."

Behind me the door banged open. My left eye twitched, the vision in it dimmed transiently, and cleared. Ma sprang to her feet.

"Zamir?" she said. "What is it?"

"Your husband," someone said. I turned. It was the Edhi driver. His hair was dark from rain. His cotton shirt was soaked and I could see his abnormal navel protrude through it like a hernia.

"What about him?" Ma's voice was full of fear. "What happened?"

Zamir had a look on his face I had never seen before. His lips trembled. "There was an incident at the clinic."

Ma stared at him, eyes wide and unbelieving, then comprehension dawned in them and she screamed. It was a sudden noise, sharp and unfamiliar, and it wrenched the air out of me. I shrank back and clutched the end of Ma's couch, and the knitting needles slipped and fell to the floor, forming a steel cross.

"No, God, no," Ma said. Her hair was in her eyes. She clawed it away, looked at the ends, screamed again. "Please don't let it be true. I told him to be careful. I *told* him."

Zamir's face was ashen. He said nothing.

I scrabbled blindly on the dirty floor. The steel cross glinted at me. Pinching the skin of my thighs, I hauled myself up, feeling the world flicker and recede. Zamir was holding Ma's hand and speaking gently. Your husband went to the Police, he was saying. He reported the Christian boy's mutilated body. The mullahs didn't like that. Then someone somewhere discovered an old marriage certificate with *your* maiden name on it.

Ma yanked her hand away from Zamir's. "I killed him," she whispered. Her fists flew to her chest and beat it once, then again and again. She rushed to the door, she shrieked at the rain, but the night was moonless.

Bewildered and crying, I thought about the tin box Sadiq hid in the canal when he realized they would be attacked. I thought about dead bodies and festering secrets; of limbs thrashing on a healer's fingertips; of the young Christian boy who was tortured to death. I thought of how "Daoud" could have been "David" in a different world, such a strange idea, that. Most of all I thought about the way the chicken breast thrummed under the influence of my will, how it kept jerking long after I took my hands away. Would Baba whirl if I touched him, would he dance a final dance for me?

I wiped my tears. From the crevasse of the night rain blood-black gushed and pawed at my eyes. Then we went in Zamir's rickshaw to pick up my father's corpse.

Someone once told me dust has no religion.

Perhaps it was the maulvi sahib who taught me my first Arabic words; a balding kind, quiet man with a voice meant to chant godly secrets and a white beard that flowed like a river of Allah's nur. The gravedigger who was now shoveling and turning the soil five feet away looked a bit like him, except when he panted. His string vest was drenched with sweat, even though the ground was soft and muddy from the downpour.

Perhaps it was Ma. She stood next to me before this widening hole, leaning on Khala Apee as if she were an axed tree about to fall. Her lips moved silently all the time. Whether she prayed or talked to Baba's ghost, I don't know.

Or perhaps it was Baba who lay draped in white on the charpoy bier under the pipal tree. The best cotton shroud we could afford rippled when the graveyard wind gusted. It was still wet from his last bath. Before they log-rolled him onto his back, the men of our neighborhood had asked me if I wanted to help wash him.

I said no. My eyes never brimmed.

Now I let a fistful of this forgiving dust exhaust itself between my fingers. It whispered through, a gentle earthskin shedding off me and upon Baba's face. It would carry the scent of my flesh, let him inhale my presence. I leaned down and touched my father's lips, so white, so cold, and a ghastly image came to me: Baba juddering on my fingertips as I reach inside his mouth, shock his tongue, and watch it jump and thrash like a bloodied carp. Tell me who murdered you, I tell my father's tongue. Talk to me, speak to me. For I am Resurrection and whoso believes in me will live again.

But his tongue doesn't quiver. It says nothing.

Someone touched my shoulder and drew me back. It was Ma. Her mouth was a pale scar in her face. She gripped my fingers tightly. I looked down, saw that she had colored her hand with henna, and dropped it.

A shiny flaming orange heart, lanced in the middle, glistened on her palm.

It was dark enough to feel invisible. I left Ma praying in her room and went to Kala Pul.

Lights flickered in the streets and on chowrangis. Sad-faced vendors sold fake perfumes and plastic toys at traffic signals. Women with hollow eyes offered jasmine motia bracelets and necklaces and the flower's scent filled my nose, removing Baba's smell in death. Children fished for paan leaves and cigarette stubs in puddles, and I walked past them all.

Something dark lay in the middle of the road under a bright fluorescent median light. I raised a hand to block the glare and bent to look at it. An alley cat, a starved, mangy creature with a crushed back. Tread marks were imprinted on its fur; clots glistened between them. A chipped fang hung from one of whiskers.

I didn't know my right hand was on it until I saw my fingertips curve. They pressed into the carcass like metal probes seeking, seeking. I didn't even need to feel for a point. In death, the creature's entire body was an enormous potential ready to be evoked.

I met the cat's gaze. Lifeless eyes reflected the traffic light changing from green to red. I discharged.

A smell like charred meat, like sparks from metal screeching against metal, rust on old bicycle wheels. The creature arched its spine, its four legs locking together, so much tension in its muscles they thrummed like electric wires. Creaking, making a frothing sound, the alley cat flopped over to its paws and tried to stand.

It lives, I thought and felt no joy or satisfaction.

Blood trickled from the creature's right eye. It tried to blink and the left eye wouldn't open. It was glued shut with postmortem secretions.

My hand was hurting. I shook it, brought it before my eyes, looked at it. A large bulla had formed in the middle of the palm, blue-red and warm. Rubbing it gently, I got up and left, leaving the newly risen feline tottering around the traffic median, strange sounds emitting from its throat as if it were trying to remember how to mewl.

Deep inside the Christian muhallah I waded through rubble, piles of blackened bricks, and charred wood. I stood atop the destruction and imagined the fire consuming rows upon rows of these tiny shacks. Teetering chairs, plywood tables, meal mats, dung stoves, patchworked clothes—all set ablaze. Bricks fell, embers popped, and shadow fingers danced in the flames.

I shivered and turned to leave. Moonlight dappled the debris, shadows twisted, and as I made my way through the wreckage I nearly tripped over something poking from beneath a corrugated tin sheet.

I stooped to examine the object. It was a heavy, callused human hand, knuckles bruised and hairy like my father's. Blood had clotted at the wrist and formed a puddle below the sharp edge of the tin.

A darkness turned inside my chest; rivers of blood pounded in the veins of my neck and forehead. I don't know how long I sat in the gloom, in that sacred silence. Head bowed, fingers curled around the crushed man's, I crouched with my eyes closed and groped for the meat of the city with my other hand's fingertips. I felt for its faint pulse, I looked for its resurrection point; and when the dirt shivered and a sound like ocean surf surged into my ears, I thought I had found it.

I stiffened my shoulders, touched the dead man's palm, and let the current flow.

The hand jerked, the fingers splayed. A sigh went through the shantytown. Somewhere in the dark bricks shifted. The ruins were stirring.

Something plopped on the tin sheet. I looked down. Fat drops of blood bulged from between my clenched knuckles. I let the dead hand go (it skittered to a side and began to thrash). I opened both of my fists and raised them to the sky.

A crop of raised, engorged bullas on my palms. One amidst the right cluster had popped and was bleeding. The pain was a steady ache, almost pleasant in its tingling. As I watched, blisters on the left palm burst as well and began to gush. Dark red pulsed and quivered its way down my wrists.

Trembling, I crouched on my haunches and grasped the dead man's convulsing limb with both hands. I closed my eyes and jolted the Christian muhallah back to life. Then I sat back, rocking on my heels, and waited.

They came. Dragging their limbs off sparkling morgue tables, slicing through mounds of blessed dirt, wrenching free of rain-soaked grass, my derelict innocents seized and twitched their way across the city. I rose to my feet when they arrived, trailing a metallic tang behind them that drowned the smell of the jasmine. Metal rattled and clanged as my last finally managed to crawl out from under the tin sheet and joined the ranks of the faithful.

I looked at them one last time, my people, faces shining with blood and fervor. Their shredded limbs dangled. Autopsy incisions crisscrossed the naked flesh of some. Blackened men, women and children swaying in rows, waiting for me. How unafraid, joyous, and visible they were.

I raised my chin high and led my living thus on their final pilgrimage through this land of the dead.

Usman T. Malik is a Pakistani writer resident in Florida. He reads Sufi poetry, likes long walks, and occasionally strums naats on the guitar. His fiction has been nominated for the Nebula and Bram Stoker awards. His work has appeared in *The Year's Best Dark Fantasy and Horror*, *The Year's Best YA Speculative Fiction*, *The Best Science Fiction and Fantasy of the Year*, *Year's Best Weird Fiction*, *Tor.com*, and *The Apex Book of World SF* among other venues. In December 2014, Malik led Pakistan's first speculative fiction workshop in Lahore in conjunction with Desi Writers Lounge and Liberty Books.

There was always movement in the Nursery Corner; more so at night when the floor flickered with shadow as if there were candles, but there were none . . .

THE NURSERY CORNER

Kaaron Warren

Now that I am old myself, with grandchildren, one dead husband and a lover of twenty years, I feel odd twinges of pain that cannot be explained by anyone but myself. I know that somewhere in the Nursery Corner Mario Laudati is playing a game with a part of me I will never get back.

It was no secret that my father died violently.

"He was under the table and it was like a fountain," I told everyone at school. "Blood gushing up and banging under the table and coming back on top of him. He was so covered in blood, he kept slipping out of the ambulance men's hands."

I squeezed my hands together. The other kids all thought I was fascinating, anyway. I lived in a bigger house than any of them, and my mum worked in the old people's home there, and I always had stories to tell. I was popular because I took them stuff from the home, like little sugars and soaps. I took them hand lotion and packets of biscuits. They didn't mind the old-people's home stink, but I tired of it, and I kept clothes at a friend's place, wanting the smell of the place off me, out of my hair. I used a highly perfumed shampoo my mother didn't approve of, *it's so bloody expensive, just use the home stuff*, my mother said, because everything we had was taken from the home. Shampoo, soap, biscuits. Chips, sometimes, frozen meals, medicine, plates, glasses. I hated the supply cupboard, though. The old people would corner me and try to hug me, they'd make me hold their teeth, they'd make me hold their dry, weak hands.

I didn't miss my father. He'd been away a lot, mining (and yes, I had a nice collection of rocks but I didn't know what any of them were) and when he was home he was nasty to be around. Falling asleep, drunk, under the kitchen table. I'd sit there, eating my cereal before school, his snores shaking my bowl, his stink making me ill. Only the cat sitting on his chest, enjoying the rise and fall, could make me smile.

He wanted us to move to Far North Queensland, so he didn't have to fly in fly out. He wanted us to be with him, up among the dust and rocks, where women and children stayed home unless they went to the movies on Saturday night or sometimes shopping.

Mum talked to the patients, not really thinking they'd understand, needing someone to vent to. "He really expects me to pack this in? Move up north, live in a tin shed? What's Jessie supposed to do? She needs good schooling, lots of friends," her voice strong, full of courage.

"God's country, this," one of the old men said, but many Australians say that about their hometown. Our quiet Sydney suburb was pleasant enough, but God's country? That was pushing it.

Dad didn't like what he overheard, and I slept with my pillow over my ears and my cat curled up against my cheek because I hated the shouting.

Mum was cheery the next day, with bruises up her arms, one on her chin, one on her throat, and it was the same every time he came home.

We smiled through it, and I hardly ever saw her cry, but even at six years old I knew this was not how things should be.

She had a job to do though; looking after them and me and she did it so well we all adored her.

The *compos mentis* old people gossiped together. I learnt most of what I know from listening in. The old men were the ones who decided. You wouldn't think they could manage it, and no one else believed it, but it was them. He was weak and pathetic, snoring under the table like he did, bottle spilt out beside him and it was a simple matter, they told me, to slit the bastard's throat. They left the knife in his hand and it would have taken a family member to push for a real inquiry, and that didn't happen.

These men had been to war. They'd killed before. They told me all this from the age of six, competing to horrify me with stories, giving me nightmares about the enemy begging for mercy, and watching souls rise like steam.

They saved us from my father, and I was always kind to old men because of it.

After Dad was buried, Mum signed a four-year contract to manage the home, and there was a little party to celebrate. The gossipers said she got it because the owners felt sorry for her, but no one seemed to care what the reason was. I was happy. I liked it there most of the time, with the old people being kind to me when they remembered who I was and when I was too fast for their grab hands, and where my mother felt confident and safe.

She set up special places for me here and there. A windowshelf with knickknacks, like a snowdome from Darwin, which made us all laugh because snow in Darwin! And puzzles carved from rainforest wood. And there was a bookshelf with a secret stash of lollies. And a place she called the Nursery Corner, which had a soft blanket, toys and some of my pictures pinned to the wall. It was a dull place, really, and none of the children who came to visit sat there. Mostly they hunched near the exit, trying not to look at the residents.

Things happened I would never tell a soul about. The bodily fluids that seemed to appear out of nowhere, and the evil things they'd say, some of them. Bile spewing out of their mouths, telling me awful things a child shouldn't know. We took the people other places rejected. Reform School for the Elderly, my mother joked.

She started to bring in entertainers for the patients, and I could invite friends along and often the room would be filled with children sitting on the floor, the buzz of them making the place so much brighter, so much further from death.

Mostly the entertainment was awful. The old people didn't mind it except Aunt Em, who hated everything.

"You can call me Aunt Em," she said when she first moved in, as if hoping a friendly name would soften her edges. Nasty woman with pursed lips disapproving all the time as if she thought life doled her out something wrong, as if everyone around her was wrong. She liked me most of the time, though.

I avoided the entertainment when I could. Elderly magicians. Singers, dancers. There was nothing wrong with being old, but these people had always been crap.

The musicians in particular were tragic. They played slow music, the old people clapping out of time, vague memories lapping at them of what it used to be like to listen to music. To dance. To be moved by the notes. Some wept and instantly forgot why they had wet cheeks.

Doesn't it take you back, they said. Listening to songs from fifty years ago. *Doesn't it just! Remember that as clear as a movie.*

Some remembered nothing, or were stuck in a single moment in time.

"Wasn't that marvellous?" the residents would say afterwards, as if they'd seen the Bolshoi Ballet.

All the entertainers flirted with my mother. "Look at Matron blushing," because they wanted more work and she was charming. Even as a kid I knew that, and she was at last free of Dad's rules, his disapproval and his desire she be nothing but a cipher for him.

Mum rarely got someone back twice.

That changed when I was about twelve and Mario Laudati appeared, with a magic chest of goodies, bright clear eyes, a warm, strong handshake. He had one earring; a flashing LED light.

He said, "I'm an all-rounder. Take a tape measure and you'll see. One hundred centimeters all the way around. Can't get much rounder than that!"

They loved him, including Mum. He was a bit older than she was. *Save me a chair*, he said, *I'll be moving in here before long*, clapping his hands, bright and breezy, and they all chuckled because clearly he would never be old enough to sit with them, unmoving for hours. He was so lively, hopping from toe to toe.

He made me nervous, thinking he wouldn't like me. He asked odd questions, as some adults do, trying to disconcert me.

"Is this place haunted? Any nasty ghosts I should know about?" he asked me.

I nodded. Thinking on the spot, I said, "It's haunted by all the people they've killed."

He laughed. "Are there many?"

I counted on my fingers, holding them up like a child in kindergarten showing how old she is. I looked sideways to see if he found me funny and he was smiling, a big, genuine grin I wanted to see all the time.

He set me up in the front row to be his assistant. It was all about light and dark.

Somehow he seemed to have control over our electricity because the power went out, leaving him in the dark, standing with a swinging lantern. The old people were quiet; was it the first time ever? He walked around us, telling a story I can't remember, making cats appear in the shadows, and children playing with a hoop. "There I am!" Aunt Em said. "That's me with my hoop!" and others clamored to be the one.

If it wasn't hypnotism, it came very close.

For a moment, between the flickering lights, I saw him with a different face. He looked like a teenager, like one of the boys I admired at school, perhaps. The ones on the train my mother would tug me close to avoid. She seemed to think teenagers were the worst things on earth and would have kept me locked up if it would stop me becoming one. She didn't accept that some of the old people she looked after were worse. Mr. Adams, with his hysterical scratching. Martha Jones, who could shift from a quiet mouse to a woman so filled with fury she tore the throat open of a patient one time. These were not the only ones.

When their attention wandered Mario drew them back with a sharp clap of his hands.

When the lights came on people had shifted around. Some had lost their socks, others found a rose on their lap. For them it was mostly meaningless because they were used to the disconnect of change. They were used to appearing at the breakfast table and having no idea how they got there.

"Isn't it magic?" the residents said. "Isn't he wonderful?"

I had seen that other face, though, and I couldn't look at him in the light. I went to the corner where Mum kept my box of rocks, and I ran my fingers through them, thinking of my father before he died, when he would show me the rocks and tell me their long-forgotten names.

"What's that you've got there? A boxarox? I know a lot about rocks."

Mario picked up a pale blue one. "This one is called a poo pellet." I giggled. This was silly. He went through my box, naming them all. He was so rude, so outrageous, that I wept with laughter and the old people, those who could move, came to watch.

This was the moment, I think, that they came to consider him a suitable boyfriend for Mum.

She kept a lot of secrets. I remained unaware of their changing relationship, even as he came to perform again and again.

He had yellowed fingers but told me he hadn't smoked for a long time. He lit a cigarette, "Don't smoke," he said, "Don't you ever," and he held it up. "I love the smell and the burn," he said. "That glowing red tip." He touched it to a patient's hair, which flared brightly before fizzling out. It was our secret.

I started taking my friends on private tours of the place when I was fifteen. Like most kids, we were obsessed with ghosts and killers, with creepy people and disgusting things; we loved to be scared. I'd lead them through the hallways, making up stories about what the residents had done. Showing them where my father had died, lifting the table to show them his blood. I asked the old people to lend me a dollar and you should have seen them, searching for wallets or purses they no longer owned or, if they still had one, opening it again and again and again, looking for money that wasn't there. My mother didn't notice until the man who called himself John John moved in.

John John would cut himself with anything. Plastic forks, the edge of the drink trolley, a sugar spoon. It was a challenge for him and it was terrifying for my friends to watch him. If you took his weapon away he'd scream like a hyena. He'd attack the nurses or anyone who got close, so we stood far away.

Until one of my friends snuck up to him, wanting a closer look at all his scars. John John roared, stabbed the boy with a key he'd stolen. The boy was fine but it meant Mum finally found out.

Jesus, when Mum found out. It was her disappointment that got me more than anything else. "I can't believe you could treat them this way. Such disrespect," she said, her voice flat, depressed, as if I made her very tired. She laid her head on Mario's shoulder. We sat in her office with the door shut, the old people shuffling outside, wanting to come in.

Mario said, "Jessie has the greatest respect. She's allowing them to entertain, one of life's great privileges." He was on my side; he understood me. He'd comforted me when one of them threw shit at me. He'd said, "It's okay to be upset, but I know you want to be strong for your mum. You don't want to freak her out." He'd brought me shampoo, a secret supply, stuff that didn't smell like the home. He really did understand.

The old people scrabbled at the door, and my mother had to call for backup to get them all settled down.

Once they were all drugged and asleep, Mario said, "I've been thinking of something for a while now, something that might work here. Let me play with the Nursery Corner. I've done it before. I'll make it a place for calm reflection. You'll see. It might help with people like John John."

"It's Jessie's corner. Your time. It's up to you two."

"What do you think, Jessie? Do you mind if I mess your corner up?"

I didn't mind for a second.

He was back a couple of days later, laden with a carpet, a chair, other stuff. He stacked all my toys from the Nursery Corner into a box and handed it to me. "Bin it if you like," he said. The residents started to gather as they often did when he was around. The drugs made them slow, made them flap their gums, suck on their teeth. The sound of it made me ill.

Mario moved around among them, talking, building his corner.

"Keep watching!" he said, and it seemed to me as if the residents stiffened, lost control of their ability to move.

First, he rolled out the carpet. It was bright yellow, like a sun, with purple edges and a large dark stain in the center. "I was born on this carpet," he said, "right there, so it symbolizes the beauty and the miracle of birth. The beginning."

They barely reacted, except Aunt Em, who had no children yet loved to judge those who did.

"I can still see the bloodstain."

"It's possible I top it up every now and then. For the sake of a good story."

He placed the rocking chair on the carpet. It looked rugged, unpolished. There was a crocheted cushion cover, filled with a thin cushion, and a white fluffy blanket.

"I've traveled the world with this chair," he said. "It's all that is left of the place I was happiest in all my life. School." Some of them shifted in their seats. Others were asleep. One ground his finger into the back of the woman in front of him; she acted as if it wasn't happening.

"Imagine a time," Mario said, "before we had light at the flick of a switch. He remembers, he was there!" pointing at Jerry Everard who, at ninety-eight, remembered very little.

Some chuckled. I sat on a chair with my knees tucked under my chin until a nurse told me *down*. They usually used single syllable words with me, as if I was a dog. They mostly didn't like me there; they thought I was a distraction, that I upset the patients. It wasn't true; the patients liked me. The staff were jealous, more like.

He set a bowl of jelly beans down on a small table beside the rocking chair. I did not ever see that bowl empty.

"That's when my school was built. It was a place for the lost, the lonely. It was the place we could go when our families didn't want us and nobody could teach us. It sat out in the bush, bright, with impossible gardens around it."

Were they listening? It was hard to tell. Jerry smiled, but that was his default expression. "It was full of lost children. All of us being given a future. And then . . . it burnt down."

There was no more reaction to this than to anything else he said. "How did it burn down?" I asked.

He closed his eyes and tears squeezed down his cheeks. "A horrible bloody accident." He swung his lantern. "No one's fault." He didn't try to make it funny; he'd stopped entertaining.

"But you survived."

"I did. I was the only one who came out alive."

He gave the rocking chair a push. "Who would like to be first? Who wants to experience the pure calm of the Nursery Corner?"

I did. "Me first!" I said. He glanced at my mother, who nodded indulgently.

He said, "Not yet for you. Not yet. You're happy, and innocent, and have a life to live. There is nothing to calm in you."

John John, up the hall in his room, screamed as he did every five minutes or ten, often enough to make me want to scream myself.

"Let's start with him," Mario said. He wriggled his fingers like a puppet master. Two of the nurses wheeled John John down the hallway, his arms strapped to the chair but his fingers reaching for them as if they could stretch beyond their means and scratch eyeballs out.

Four nurses lifted him into the chair in the Nursery Corner, one for each limb to keep him still. Mario set it rocking as they held him down. The rhythm of it did calm him, and one by one, the nurses tentatively let go. John John sat quietly, eyes closed, rocking, rocking, finding muscles he hadn't used in months.

This seemed to quiet all of the residents, and they mimicked his movement back and forth, back and forth.

"How long does he get to stay there?" Aunt Em said. She'd elbowed others out of the way to stand in front.

"As long as he likes."

It was over an hour before the man stirred and lifted his head. His face seemed gentler, and there had been silence from the moment he sat in the chair.

"He's happier now," Mario said. "Now, who is good at sharing? Sharing is Caring!"

The Nursery Corner worked on all of them. If they started to throw a tantrum, if they screamed, became violent, if they attacked a staff member, they were placed in the Nursery Corner and they would come out softer, quieter. It was a godsend, my mother said, and she said that Mario was a godsend as well.

I didn't like it. To me, it was like they became puppets. Diminished.

"Where did you go?" I asked when they came out. "What did you see?"

Many forgot instantly, their eyes clouding over. Others remembered long enough to say, "The air was fresh," or "I saw my father there," before memory was gone. I didn't keep a record, but I reckon many of them gave up the ghost not long after a visit to the Nursery Corner. As if they'd seen heaven and no longer feared it.

One night, I heard a creaking sound. I crept out to have a look at the Nursery Corner. The hallway was lit only by the floor lights set to guide the staff in the dark.

The Nursery Corner seemed to glow, but I knew that wasn't possible. It made me think of when the circus was in town, set up in the school's playing field. From home, at night, the lights of the circus set a halo of light around the school, and this is how the Nursery Corner seemed, as if there was something bright and exciting beyond it.

I heard *creak creak*. It was Aunt Em, gently rocking. She clutched the soft white blanket and her mouth drooled.

There was a noise behind me and it was Mr. Simons, completely naked, pulling at his penis in a way I have never seen since, stretching it almost to his mouth. I was enthralled, and that's where my mother found me, staring, open mouthed, and Aunt Em, rocking and drooling, and Mr. Simons, tugging and tugging.

She bundled me up and put me to bed. She stayed and talked with me for an hour. My sleepiness, and the shock, and her quietness as I was talking led me to say more than I should have about the things I saw and heard.

"I hadn't quite realized. I'd forgotten how young you are," she said.

"It's okay, Mum. It doesn't bother me," but still she spoke to my teachers, and to the nurses, and between them they decided the home was not a good place for me, at least until I was older. Mario said he was jealous I was going to boarding school; best years of his life, bar none.

"Until it burnt down," I said.

"You be careful. No smoking in the cupboards," he said, and I shook my head, because I knew what smoking did and that I'd never do it. He was a private school boy and Mum was too. Fancy schools, they both went to. My father went to the nasty local, my mother said, and she always said it in that way of knowing.

"You'll make connections for life at these schools," Mario said, but he appeared to have no friends from childhood at all.

I had time to say goodbye to all my substitute grandparents, but none of them really noticed. Aunt Em complained that her arms hurt. She held them out, weeping, and the nurse, in attendance said, "There is nothing wrong," like the doctors told her to say, but gave Aunt Em pain relief nonetheless.

So many of these old people felt pain others saw no reason for.

My cat was old and slow and I couldn't consider taking her. Besides, she loved it there; so many laps. So many hands to stroke her. And she knew, she had learnt, when a person was about to turn nasty.

She knew when it was time to get off a lap.

Boarding school was not all that, but it was okay. It was boring compared to the old people and what they told me. Those secrets and outrageous stories.

My mother's letters grew increasingly bizarre, listing all the deaths, first up, before anything else. Then it was all about Mario and how wonderfully the Nursery Corner worked to calm people down.

She spoke of aches and pains her patients suffered that the doctors couldn't identify. *The doctors never listen, is the problem. They think these people are making it up, but none of them have the imagination any more. Mr. Simons left us the watch collection he was always talking about. Turns out it was worth money after all.*

At first, I visited every term break; less often as I got older. Mario looked after Mum and he wanted me to understand that, to the extent that he kept his hand firmly on her arse, as if to let me know the story, in case there was any doubt. Mum looked happier every time, less severe, more full of genuine laughter. She worried over her patients, always, but she somehow seemed to believe they were safer now.

"He's a wonder," everyone told me. "What he does for these people," and truly, the place was far quieter. They all sat in their chairs, smiles on their faces. Some played with toys, holding them weakly in their laps. Others gazed at the TV, especially if a singing show was on.

When school was done I moved back home. After starring in the drama productions for two years I thought my path was set, but finding work as an actor proved to be soul-destroying ("Lose some weight and get back to us") and not what I thought it would be. I moved back to help Mum out and bide my time, waiting for Hollywood to call.

"How's my favorite audience member? My favorite movie star?" Mario said most mornings, winking at me. He knew I was worldly wise, now, not the innocent I once was.

I wondered what he got out of it all. What he gained. Was it just the adulation? The love of a good woman like my mother? He still traveled, giving shows around town and sometimes further afar, but he was always there for her, he always called if he was late.

The staff still rolled residents into the nursery corner if they got a bit Bolshie. The nasty ones, the whining ones, they'd get sat there every few days, because after an hour, they'd come out child-like. Happier. More willing to work at the repetitive tasks and activities that were supposed to help them. Vaguely useful things, like making lavender bags or packing candles. Sometimes they tied bows for funeral homes, black ribbons needed in the hundreds. Cruel but they have to face it, Mum said. She didn't think you should pretend death isn't going to happen. It wasn't like other places, where people simply "went away," as if they moved to a pleasant place we'd never visit. Here, we had wakes.

We had a lot of wakes.

There was always movement in the Nursery Corner. A trick of the light, the nurses said (the doctors were never there long enough) more so at night when the whole floor flickered with shadow as if there were candles but there were none.

Sometimes I watched it like a movie, straining my eyes to identify shapes.

Sometimes my old cat curled up on the chair, emerging hours later with fur ruffled and a wild look in her eye.

No visitor wanted to stand in the Nursery Corner. Sometimes it happened by mistake and they'd shiver, look up and down for a draught, a fan, an explanation. But there was also a sense of comfort. Of well-being. Like the good days of childhood. Warm summer holiday mornings. Nights when dinner was your favorite meal. A birthday when you liked every present so didn't have to lie. Those moments when your mother was her real self, laughing like a young girl. This is what they told me; I never stood there myself. The breeze of the corner, and the scent I smelled there put me off. Sometimes it was new books. Sometimes it was boiled cabbage.

Grandchildren and great-grandchildren brought in to visit were sent to the Nursery Corner as if it was a treat.

They sat on the edge of the rug, bunched up. "Go on, have a rock in the chair," but you couldn't get many of them to step into the corner or sit in the chair. Those who did would come out quiet, very quiet. What would a child see, if an adult saw childhood? Past lives?

I heard the chair rocking late some nights and wondered who was in it. I'd find out the next day; the one who was the most vacant.

I thought they sank into dementia with greater speed and less resistance once they'd been in the Nursery Corner.

"What do they see?" I asked Mario.

"Lots of friendly people; you've never felt so welcome."

"Have you ever been?"

He said he hadn't, but I knew he had. I'd seen him rocking there at night, especially on nights my mother was out shopping, or visiting her sister. Not often.

"Are there other places like this one? Other Nursery Corners?" He still traveled to perform, but rarely spent more than a night away.

"A few. I like to help where I can." He listed them and there were more than a few. He had Nursery Corners set up wherever he visited.

Mario told me that, depending on the sort of person you are, you'll find peace or sorrow in the Nursery Corner. "You might see battered children, lost to a parent's fury. Or tiny babies, sucked from life like metal filings to a magnet. Or a train filled with laughing families, or a table laden with sweets. Each of us sees something new in there, something different. You, I think you will see a thing of great beauty. You will feel more loved and needed than you have ever felt before. You will be at the very center of the universe. A star. Like *moi*."

I'd missed out on a dozen auditions ("lose some weight") and was beginning to think I was kidding myself, so this fantasy of his resonated with me.

I never bothered Mum with my audition woes. Tried to help out where I could. We attended to Mrs. T, who had stripped naked and was attempting to climb onto the table.

"Come on, now, into the Nursery Corner. Let's have a nice sit."

Mrs. T sat in there, folded into a blanket, rocking, tears coursing. "They're good tears," Mum said. "Best to have something to remember with sadness than to have no memory, no sorrow at all." She looked me straight in the eye as she said this. She thought I needed to get a life, or I'd have nothing to cry about when I was that age. "You're twenty-four, Jessie. What have you experienced? Who have you loved? You need to take chances."

I thought, *I'm going to see what I see when I sit there. See how I feel.* I wasn't sure if she was right or not. Had I lived, yet? Was Mario right, and I'd feel fulfilled after sitting in the corner? Would I come out knowing what to do with my life?

I'd wanted to try for a long time, had been tempted to send my friends in when we were younger, just to freak them out. But it had never happened.

I sat down on the chair in the Nursery Corner and began to rock.

Within moments, I heard music, but so faint it was like an echo. The smell of soap, age and toilets lifted and it was dusty, mostly, outside road dust, pollen and, I thought, frying bacon. We had bacon twice a year at the home, on Mothers' Day and Fathers' Day. It made them cry every time. "It's like the old days, going back," one told me, "it's as if all the rest of my life hasn't passed yet."

I could still feel the press of wood against my arms, the scratch of wool from the blanket on my leg, the soft give of the cushion, but what I saw was far different.

Lit by bright sunlight, shaded by ancient oak trees, the two buildings sat low and long in lush, green lawn. One painted red, the other yellow, even at a distance I could see they were well maintained.

My feet were bare and as I walked towards the buildings (because where else would I go?) the softness of the lawn tickled my soles and I began to run, filled with a sense of pure joy the like of which I had never felt before. The sun was so bright my eyes teared up.

The sound of laughter, and voices chanting, the smell of baking bread and of rich, red roses led me on. Children played on swings and slides and as I watched a boy fell off and sat in the dirt, dusting himself off. One girl seemed to hurt her arm badly and if I hadn't seen the other children helping her, would have run over.

I reached the red building. A sign by the door said, *St. Lucia's School* with the motto beneath: *There is a Light at the End of the Tunnel* and I thought, *This is the school I would have loved to go to.*

I pushed the door open.

"There you are, Jessie!" It was a girl I didn't know but who seemed familiar. She had clear blue eyes and her cheeks were flushed. "Come on, come and play. We have to do Maths soon, yuck, but we can play for a while."

She took my hand and led me to a vast playroom. Many other children were there, and they all looked up at me and smiled. "It's Jessie!" they said, as if I was a long-lost friend. They seemed happy but, on closer inspection, some had marks around their wrists, bruising around their eyes. All of them looked tired.

My new friend led me to sit among the toys. Robots, hoops, pirate costumes. *Sharing Is Caring* a handwritten sign said.

I wondered why the children would welcome me, an adult, so delightedly, then realized that I, too, was a child. Was I eight? Six? My father was alive, then, and I wondered if I could find a phone and call him, just to hear his voice, see if he was sorry.

There were no phones, though. No television, no computers.

In the corner sat a large beanbag, jellybean print. The small table beside it had a box of jellybeans and some tweezers next to it. I wanted one of those jellybeans, wanted to have the taste of sugar, the memory of home. My friend stopped me. "That's Mario's. He'll give you one if you wait till he gets here."

Time passed. I don't know how long. I slept. I ate. There was custard, hot dogs, there were cheese sticks and there were beautiful peaches. I watched the others playing and sometimes joined in. Sometimes they would stand in one place for hours as if waiting. Or they played skip rope for hour after hour after hour, tears running down their cheeks as their arms tired. They didn't respond when I told them they should stop, have a rest. My cat was there, young again, chasing butterflies and purring so loudly you could hear her in the other room. She didn't know me, though. She wouldn't sit on my lap.

Sometimes I would rock on my heels and remember; there is another place. Not this one. I knew that in that place, people had to be shaken awake, physically carried out of the Nursery Corner, and I wondered if anyone would do it for me.

They did, at last. My own mother, giving me a poke in the Nursery Corner.

On my lap was the banana I had been holding when I sat in the chair and it was rotten, after being a perfect piece of fruit. "You've had a good nap!" Mum said, as if I'd been gone only moments. "You look so peaceful I barely wanted to wake you. But I need to sit Mrs. Allan down. She's a bit agitated."

Mrs. Allan winked at me. "See you there," she said.

I stepped away, feeling shaky, but with a deep sense of peace.

"Did you like my school?" Mario asked. He sat closer to me than he normally would, as if our relationship had changed.

"I had a pretty weird dream."

"Not a dream. Ask all of them." He waved at the room, all the old people and, I thought, the wall of the dead, all the photos of long-gone and recently departed. I walked along the wall until I found her, my new friend. A woman who'd lived with us for only two months before she died of an infection. I remembered her as being a great lover of the Nursery Corner. I remembered her clear blue eyes.

There were others, too; they played as children, fell, sang, learned, ate as children in that other place.

"A little piece of you with me forever," Mario said. "In my place, waiting for me, with all the others. I don't take it all. Just a glimmer, an echo, a hint."

He was a hypnotist, and he had finally managed to crack me. I backed away from him, my eyes downcast. I knew I could clear my head of him, and of that place, that I would not be diminished by it.

I also knew I wanted my mother to get rid of him. That he shouldn't be among these people.

"You didn't say if you liked my school. It's an exact replica of the one that burnt down."

"It was fine. Quite lovely, actually. No sign of flames, or burning."

He had tears in his eyes. "Thank you. Thank you. None of them ever remember."

I thought of the patients, how much emptier they seemed. He thought he stole very little but I thought he stole the last of them. He took any dreams they had of their own heaven and made them vanish completely.

Mum wouldn't get rid of him. She said he made her happy and this was true; he adored her, treated her like a princess. He adored her so much, he never asked her to sit in the Nursery Corner. He never tried to take that part of her.

She'd stand there sometimes, saying, "Sit! When do I have time to sit?" and he'd say, "On the toilet!" and she'd screech with laughter at this.

I asked him what he was creating that place for; what was the point. "Filling it up again salves my conscience."

Because children had died in the fire; I'd looked that up. The lights had failed and they had stumbled in the darkness. Handprints were found; you could see them online. Tiny handprints, some of them, along a hallway leading to a storage cupboard. A dead end. "And I will live there forever, one day. When the place is full."

"It *is* full," I said, although I knew perfectly well the walls rang with silence and that there was room for hundreds more. "Seriously, you couldn't fit anyone else in there and have it still be nice to live there."

"Did they talk about me when you were there? Ask about me? Because when I'm there . . . well. You see how people are with me here. You see how much people love me."

At that moment, he lost all that made him loveable; his humor, his cleverness, his confidence. He exuded a desperate lonely neediness I hated to be around.

In the Nursery Corner, the whole world revolved around him. "Yes," I said. "They talked about you a lot. Laughing, you know, like people do here when they mention your name, because you're funny."

My neck hurt when I awoke the next day. I rubbed it as I walked the ward, and the residents nodded at me. "Sore neck? Sore neck? There will be more."

In the end, he rocked himself to death. He left a note, saying he was ill and not able to cope with the pain, and he said he was sorry, and that he loved us all.

I wondered if the old men had stepped in to defend us again; if they had killed another predator for me. But I had to accept that this was not the case, that Mario Laudati had chosen to go and therefore had won.

After Mario died, the residents tried sitting in the Nursery Corner and it made them angry. They got nothing out of it, rocking rocking rocking with no transformation, no good feeling. I thought, *Good. I'll burn it all, the carpet, the chair, cushion, blanket. Then his school will burn again, and we'll be free of him.*

• • •

My bonfire achieved nothing.

Over the years the Nursery Corner sat empty. It lost its glow and all feeling. Mum did, too. She turned the age many of them were when they went in, and she knew, she was absolutely sure she did not want to be among them. I took her to live with me and my family; this was inevitable and worked well for all of us.

I never told her about the sudden pains, the aches, the unexplained twinges. I never told her it meant that Mario was playing with me, in the school, that he was making me skip rope, or eat chili, or climb a tree, that he was wanting more from me that I would ever have given him here, on the other side. She had no aches and pains of her own, not really, until she caught pneumonia at ninety-two. She went quickly after that.

I will not go quickly. I'm in no hurry. Because I know where I'm going.

Back to school.

<hr>

Bram Stoker nominee and Shirley Jackson Award-winner **Kaaron Warren** has lived in Melbourne, Sydney, Canberra, and Fiji. She's sold almost two hundred short stories, three novels (the multi-award-winning *Slights*, *Walking the Tree*, and *Mistification*) and five short story collections including the multi-award-winning *Through Splintered Walls*. Her latest short story collection is *The Gate Theory*. Kaaron is a Current Fellow at The Museum of Australian Democracy at Old Parliament House, where she is researching Robert Menzies, Sir William Ashton, and the Granny Killer, John Wayne Glover. The resulting crime novel should see print in 2016. You can find her at kaaronwarren.wordpress.com/ and she Tweets @KaaronWarren

<hr>

Magic versus metal, mindless beast versus cunning hunter,
masked enemy versus bold warrior . . .

WATER IN SPRINGTIME

—◆—

Kali Wallace

I woke in the darkness. My mother was leaning over me.

"We have to leave," she said. Her breath was warm on my face.

The scent of dried flowers and wood-smoke drifted after her. She had spent the night by the fire, singing for a young mother and her sickly child. The child had not survived. Few did, in winter. Its skin was veined with rust-dark lines, its eyes hot with fever. There was nothing my mother could do but ease its pain. It would not be wise for us to linger.

We wrapped ourselves in stolen furs and filled our packs with stolen food. It was not the first time we had slunk in the night.

The ground was frozen and uneven, treacherous beneath the snow. There were no stars. Low, dark clouds had been hanging over the valley for days. The trees were laced with ice, but in that hollow, at least, they were still alive. The dead infant with its rust-veined skin was the only sign the blight had reached this far, but scouts who ventured south, darting into the mountains like nervous birds, claimed it was overtaking the forests.

I did not speak until we were well away from the camp. "Where are we going?"

My mother stopped but did not look at me. She removed a glove from one hand and reached for the trunk of a tree. The swarm burst from her fingertips in a shower of blue, clinging to her hand as marsh flies to cattle.

We had traveled the length of the continent, from the sea in the north to these southern mountains, across deserts and swamps, through forests with trees so tall entire villages swayed in the branches, and everywhere we went, my mother's swarm was a novelty. People called her a witch, but quietly, when they thought she would not hear. She always laughed. It was never a kind laugh.

Some were awed; some were frightened. Children were always delighted. They tried to catch the bright specks in their hands, giggling at the cool tickle on their skin, begging my mother to show them what her magic could do.

My mother closed her hand. The swarm vanished.

"South," she said. "Into the mountains."

We followed a road so ancient it was a wound in the forest floor. The crumbling embankment was as high as my shoulder, and the exposed roots were tainted with red-orange rust. The scouts had not lied. The blight was spreading. In places sharp blades of metal and chunks of broken rock jutted from the black soil, mere suggestions of what the iron skeletons had been before they fell: wolves with teeth like daggers, birds with too many wings and too long claws, hulking bulls with curved horns. They might have been monstrous once, malformed nightmares raging in battle, but now they were sorry old things caught in root cages and rotting away to dust.

There were no doubt human bones in the ground as well, but I saw none. It had been a very long time since the invaders and their metal beasts had swept north over the mountains. They were little more than legends now, stories shared by old women around campfires while children huddled at their feet. In the best stories, the oldest and grandest adventures, the mountain clans had repelled the invaders with the help of mysterious sorcerers who cast spells of befuddlement on the armies. They had tricked the metal beasts into attacking themselves and forced the hidden invaders to reveal their true forms. Recreating those great battles was a favorite game among the clan children. Magic versus metal, mindless beast versus cunning hunter, masked enemy versus bold warrior. It was as much fun to play the invaders—lurching, ill-formed, insect-like in their awkwardness—as it was to play the defenders.

On the third day of our journey, I spotted delicate white flowers blooming from the eyes of an iron skull. Frosthands, the clansmen called them, for they had small, fat petals like a child's fingers. In the stories, a single frosthand petal ground into tea was enough to poison any impostor from the south. The first sip, said the old women, would strip away the invader's disguise, and the second would close his throat and stop his heart.

That was another favorite game of the clan children: to pluck a petal and place it on your tongue, to cough and gag and laugh as your friends raced away shrieking.

"Mother," I said. She was, as always, several paces ahead. "Frosthands. It's nearly spring."

My mother did not look back. "It happens every year. Stop wasting time."

I plucked a flower from the skull and rolled the soft green stem between my fingers. It was this way wherever we traveled, whatever the season. Long roads carried us from blight to plague to fever, whispered rumors leading us across the world, and always my mother was silent as a frozen lake when we were alone. She was formal but polite with strangers; they thought her stiff and strange and foreign. When asked about her homeland, she smiled thinly and agreed to whatever they chose to believe. Sometimes she changed her face to match their expectations, darkened her skin or made herself pale, became tall or short or fat or thin with a subtle twitch of her hand and a pass of the swarm. More often she didn't bother. In truth nobody cared where she came from. The healing songs she traded for food and shelter were valuable and rare, and the quick blue swarm was a wonder.

"You needn't worry," the old women said to me, when they noticed me at all. There were old women everywhere we went, their faces lined with the same creases, their eyes lit with the same laughter, their gray hair twisted in the same plaits beneath the same scarves. As a child I had coveted their smiles, empty but still more than my mother offered, but I found no comfort in their tolerance as I grew. "You haven't a bit of her strangeness in you," said the old women, and they meant it kindly.

It was more true than the old women knew. I could not alter my face or the color of my skin. I could not make my hair curl or my arms lengthen. I was as pale as sand and slight as a child. I had small hands, small feet, no breasts, and my hair was a dirt-brown bird's nest tangle. I could not sing or heal. I could not dress wounds and I did not know which herbs to mix into which medicines. Strangers mistook me for a boy. My mother rarely corrected them.

Worst of all, I could not draw a swarm from my fingertips, no matter how often I lay awake in the darkness, hidden beneath my blanket, rubbing my fingers together and yearning.

I dropped the frosthand blossom and ran to catch up.

We followed the battlefield road until dusk. Weak snow turned to rain, and the ground churned into a sticking, sucking mud. As the sun set behind the clouds, we scrambled up the embankment, using a cage of iron ribs as a ladder, and turned into a forest of sweet-scented pines and chalky aspens. There was no trail. My mother's swarm, pale and restful, ringed her like a crown in the twilight. Without it I would have been lost.

Somewhere nearby, hidden by the towering trees, a river flowed. Its roar was muffled, but I felt it in my throat and the tips of my fingers.

We made camp in a cradle of blight-reddened roots. The pines were large but sickly, flecked with shards of metal and veins of rust, branches weakened and cracking. Aside from the rumble of the river, the forest was silent. There were more felled metal beasts beneath the soil than there were living creatures in the underbrush.

I dug into my pack to find a water skin, but my mother stopped me. "No. You stay here."

"I was only going for water."

My mother's eyes were pale and unblinking. She flicked her tongue between her lips, snake-like and quick. Whatever she tasted in the air made her frown. "Your sisters were never this stupid. Stay away from the water. Tonight of all nights, Alis, do as you're told."

She left, boots kicking up the moldering remains of fallen needles.

I was too stunned to call after her. My mother used my name rarely and spoke of my sisters even less. They were dead, all of them. I didn't even know their names.

My mother's pack was lying at the base of the tree. I folded it open to find our food. We had been traveling too quickly to hunt, but our supply of stolen meat and bread would soon be gone. I set aside three knives tucked in leather sheaths, a twist of thin rope, a handful of metal arrowheads. The food was at the bottom, and with it a bundle of dirty cloth I had never seen before.

I pulled the odd bundle from the pack. It rattled and shifted as I unrolled it. I looked into the woods, into the shadows, but my mother was still away. I drew back the last folds.

On the threadbare cloth lay the skeleton of a human child. Its skull was the size of a fist, its bones as white as fresh-fallen snow but except the fine lines of rust. There was no clinging flesh, no shriveled skin. It had been scoured clean.

I had seen my mother strip the carcasses of rabbits and birds. When we had taken what we could eat and it was unwise to leave remains behind, she would loose the hungry swarm and watch as the specks crawled like maggots over the limp dead thing and gorged themselves, blue fading to purple, purple to red, swelling and finally popping like blood-fat mosquitoes as the last flesh fell away in charred curls.

My hands shook as I wrapped the bones into their shroud and hid it again. I retreated to the far side of the camp, hugged my knees to my chest and waited.

My mother returned only moments later, as though she had been watching from the forest. She said nothing. We did not speak for the rest of the night. After we ate, she sat by the fire and sharpened her knives one by one, a narrow shadow with flat pale eyes. The hiss of her blades on the whetstone drew shivers across my skin.

In the morning my mother gave me a knife. It was a sturdy blade on a wooden haft, too large for my hand, undecorated but stained with smudges that might have been oil, might have been blood. The blade was black, free of rust, sharp enough to sting my fingertips at the lightest touch.

I spread my fingers to match the stains, held it against my palm and tested its weight. It was the first gift my mother had ever given to me. I did not know if I should thank her.

"Stop wasting time," said my mother, as I turned the blade. "We're going to the river."

The clouds had broken during the night. Above the imperfect cathedral of pines the sky was brightening, but the aching cold lingered. We followed a creek into a steep ravine. Sunlight touched the hilltops, but the river was in shadow and blanketed in mist. All of the color the snow and rain had leached from the world was returning: the deep green of the pine boughs, the white and pink rocks, the blue sky. Even the rich brown trees twisted with blight were beautiful in the rising morning, with streaks of red and orange lacing the wood like a caravan matriarch's jewelry.

Beautiful, but frightening as well. As the weather warmed the infestation would spread, and by the end of the summer this hillside, this valley, this pretty green lean of pines and oaks crawling down to the river would be dead.

At the river, my mother led me onto a flat boulder. Water curled in eddies and gulped beneath rocks, and thin ice crackled along the banks.

My mother leaned close to speak over the river's roar: "Your boots. Take them off."

I obeyed. The cold granite burned, and edges of knobby white crystals bit into my bare feet.

My mother held out one arm and rolled up her sleeve. "Like this," she said.

I did the same, shivering.

"Your knife," said my mother, her lips moving against the shell of my ear. I looked at her, and she snapped, "Take out your knife."

She jerked the knife from its sheath and pressed the hilt into my hand, closed my fingers over the stained wood. With her other hand she grabbed my free wrist. She was wrapped around me, pressed warm against my back. We had not been so close since we had slept together on cold nights when I was young.

"Like this," she said. "Not too shallow. You have to bleed."

She sliced the blade across my arm. Blood welled from the wound and slid over my skin. I tried to pull free, but my mother shoved me forward until I stepped into the water. The shock of cold made me gasp and kick, but my mother was immovable at my back.

"Not over the stone, stupid girl!"

The first drop struck the water.

There was a sickening lurch in my gut and a black flood engulfed me. I was upright still, on wobbling legs and knees, my feet going numb, but it made no difference to the mindless panic overtaking my mind. I coughed and choked and kicked. My mother's arm was strong across my chest, her hand an iron cuff around my wrist. I fought until my strength failed and every breath filled my lungs with freezing water. The river stripped away my skin, my twitching muscles and pumping blood, scouring down to the bone, then took the bones as well.

The world beneath was slick, shifting and dark, and the current caught me. The surface above shimmered: trees and cliffs whipping by, boulders bending the water this way and that, logs and tangles of branches and sodden grass. I tumbled to the riverbed. Grit scraped my face, stones bruised my chin, my cheeks, my knees. A bridge flashed overhead, fish danced quick and silver, and still I flowed faster, faster, until a great weight overtook me, tugging me down and down and down, and the last sunlight winked away.

I opened my eyes.

I was lying on my back beside the river. For a moment, I felt nothing but the granite beneath me, then I choked and rolled onto my side. I coughed and retched and did not stop until my throat ached and my body shuddered. My hair was not wet, nor my clothes, nor any part of me save my feet, blue with cold.

My mother stood over me, a silhouette against the morning sky.

She said, "Did you feel that?"

I wiped my mouth and could not speak.

"Did it frighten you?"

A stiff nod.

"That's what will happen if you don't learn to control it."

Her mouth was thin as a knife, but she was smiling.

The valley narrowed to a gash as we climbed into the mountains. There was rarely more than a faint deer trail to follow. The days lengthened as spring approached, but the nights were cold and snow fell often.

My mother did not make me bleed into the river itself again, but every time we crossed a spring or tributary stream, she stopped and said, "Your knife."

And every time I returned, gasping and quaking, she asked me what I had discovered and told me what I had done wrong. She delivered each lesson like the lash of a whip: Sit down before you fall down. Don't bleed on soil or stone. Don't linger where people might see. Don't stay away more than half a day. Don't follow more than one route. Don't forget what you are. Remember to eat. Remember to sleep. Clean and wrap the wounds. Find the cracks, find the seams, find the flaws. Everything is weak against water and patience.

My arms were soon crisscrossed with new red cuts and tender scabs. My mother refused to use the swarm to heal them. I kept the blade sharp and clean.

Ankle-deep in the water, eyes closed tight and blood dripping from my arm, I rode a dozen streams into the mountain river. I explored their turns and stones, their logjams and bending reeds. I tasted the water as it wound through overhanging roots and high grass, seeped into impossible cracks and worked stones loose in their muddy banks. I smelled elk and bears where they stopped to drink, the nests of birds in quiet ponds, the ash of human campfires.

I grew bolder. I let myself venture into the northern lowlands, where spring was giving way to summer. It did not matter how swiftly or how slowly the water moved; if it flowed to a place, I could go there. I tasted sweet fields freshly plowed and felt bridges thrumming with hooves and boots. I watched women burdened with baskets wading in the shallows, farmers leading mules and carts through fords, and barefoot children skipping rocks on quiet river bends.

Sometimes, if I lurked too long, comfortably nested in a lazy eddy or deep pool, I might catch a child studying the water so intently I was certain she could see me. I imagined myself as a shivering, bleeding specter, a reflection of a reflection, wavering and thin.

Sometimes I looked back before flowing away again.

"You are a coward," said my mother.

She was whittling arrow shafts. The swarm followed her blade, smoothing the wood with every stroke. It was evening and the day had been dreary. High in the mountains, the few creeks we crossed were icy trickles, and the trees were gnarled, twisted knots so rusted with blight they rattled like chimes in the wind.

"I'm not," I said. I dug my fingers into what little soft earth I could find and watched stars wake in the purple sky. I focused with every breath on pulling the thousand slippery pieces of myself back into the barrier of my skin.

That afternoon I had followed the river all the way to the coast. It was a journey of several months' time by foot, but for me it had flashed by in moments. I had stopped before I entered the sea itself. It was endless and strange and dark, and I did not know if I could ever find my way back.

I had been to the city as a child and I remembered the smell of it, refuse and smoke and the green stink of low tide, but it was different in the water. In the water I could crawl along the canals and explore sunken boats and drowned ruins. I could creep through cracks in walls and see what was meant to be hidden. I saw a man cut a soldier's throat in a cellar and seal the body in a barrel of wine. I saw a laughing woman lead a laughing man into a pantry and lift her skirts while he fumbled with his belt. I saw sickly blank-eyed children huddling in a garret with a locked door, sailors bartering colorful caged birds and black snakes on the docks, men in red robes with red-stained eyes boarding a ship with red sails. I saw mud-splattered masons building a wall of stone between the city and the sea, trowels in hand, warily watching the tide.

They never saw me, slipping as I did through the cracks and gutters, dripping down walls and draining through floors, testing the strength of every seam and wondering what would survive if the wall failed and the sea swallowed the city. It was so easy to slip through gaps unseen, to open paths where no water had flowed before, to weaken the mortar with a slow damp seep.

"I'm not," I said again.

My mother whittled and was silent.

"They're building a new seawall," I said. We had walked the old one when I was a child, early in the morning to watch gulls diving and children with nets fishing at low tide. "The masons don't think it will hold through next winter's storms."

"Find a beaver dam first," said my mother. Her knife snicked cleanly as she sliced bark from wood. Her eyes were bright with silent laughter; her amusement made me uneasy. "They're easier to take apart."

"I'm not going to destroy the seawall," I said, aghast.

My mother snorted. "As if you could. Don't be stupid. Start with a beaver dam."

The next morning, I bled into the same creek and explored the mountain waterways until I found a quiet beaver pond. I examined the dam and the lodge, flowing in circles through the grass at the bottom, surprising the sleepy creatures in their musk-scented den. I slipped into the piled branches and tested the bend of waterlogged wood. Fish darted around me, slick, nervous. Once or twice I felt a branch shift, but the dam was strong.

I tried for three days to topple the dam, and each time I opened my eyes my mother said, "You'll do it tomorrow."

"I don't know what you want," I said after my third failure. I was lying on my back and catching my breath. "They're only animals."

"You won't learn if you're too frightened," said my mother, and her voice turned mocking. "Are you scared? What do you have to fear? They're only animals."

I rolled onto my side to look at her.

"Did you bring my sisters here?" I asked. The sisters I imagined were small and thin like me, but they had no faces. "Did you teach them too?"

My mother's hands stilled. She was crouched by the fire, roasting a marmot she had caught during the day. We had left the trees behind two days ago; the shrubs that dotted the rocky slopes were squat and thorny. We had not seen another person since we had left the clan's winter camp. I wondered how far away my mother had ventured to set the snare, if during the day she had left me here alone, insensible by the water, my body limp and useless.

"Were they better than me?" I asked. "Did they learn faster? Was it easy for them? Did they—"

"Alis."

My name, as always, a foreign word on her tongue.

"You'll do it tomorrow," she said. "Come to the fire. You have to eat."

I didn't ask her anything else that night. I decided, when our meal was finished and the fire burning low, I didn't want to know if my sisters had been here before me, if they had bled into this same river, traced the same scars on their pale childlike arms. I didn't want to know if they had cut too deep and bled too fast and been lost, one by one, swept away while my mother whittled by the empty shells of their bodies.

Two days later I found a weakness in the beaver dam. The logs collapsed and I rode the torrent down and down, out of the valley and onto a broad, sunny plain.

When I opened my eyes, the sun was still climbing toward noon.

"Well?" my mother asked.

"I destroyed it," I said.

She was not whittling or shaping arrows or sharpening her knives. She was sitting very close to me; her shadow fell over my face. I did not want to look at her.

"That was well done," she said. "You learn more quickly than they did."

I could not recall if my mother had ever praised me before. The words were like the gift of the knife, ill-fitting and sharp.

We crested the mountains at a high pass of stone and snow. What little water we found was frozen in shallow tarns, useless to me, and I grew restless. Walking was so slow, so plodding, and the ache of my feet so tiresome. I scratched at my wounds in idle moments, dropped my hands when I caught my mother watching.

The south-flowing streams joined a silty river that tasted of iron and mud. The land was quiet, barren, infected with blight. The trees still struggled to grow, but the wood was laced with rust and leaves scraped and screeched in the wind.

I passed through towns as I explored the river, but they were all empty. Sand drifted through doorways and roofs gaped with holes. Buried on the muddy bottom of the river were countless skeletons: horses and cattle and oxen, mostly, but people too, their bones traced with rust, skulls sunk in the muck. The bridges were crumbling and weak with neglect, but they were still harder to tease apart than the beaver dam. Stone by stone, crack by crack, I pushed my way in and worked the blocks free.

The first time I brought a bridge down, I pulled out in shock, shaken, and my mother laughed. She laughed so rarely the sound was alien and startling.

"They won't all be as easy as that," my mother said. She was sitting on her scarf, holding the swarm in the palm of her hand. The blue specks weren't doing anything, not even humming. "Go farther. You'll see."

I withdrew my feet from the water and sat up. I rubbed my hand over my face to remind myself of the shape of my body.

"Where are the people?"

"Who could live in such a place?" said my mother.

"The invaders," I said, as much a question as an answer. I had never asked what they called themselves or what had happened to them after their invasion failed. The stories the old women shared never followed the iron armies back to where they had come from.

"There's no one there to hurt, if that's what worries you," my mother said.

"Would you care if there were?"

I watched for the same spark of hunger I had seen when I told her how the seawall shivered before pounding waves. But she was not looking at me. She was watching the dark clouds gathering over the mountains.

"Go farther," she said again.

"I have gone farther. There's nothing. There's barely anything alive at all."

"Venom spreads from a single bite," said my mother. She closed her fingers; the blue swarm blinked out. "Even if the snake is stupid enough to bite its own tail. We should keep going. I don't want to be above timberline when that storm arrives.

Late in the day the trail led us out of the spiny mountain shrubs and into a proper forest. The trees were no healthier than the high country snarls had been, but if I breathed deeply, I could smell pine sap beneath the sharp tang of iron. Thunder rumbled distantly and the sky was dark, but the only suggestion of rain was a smear blotting out the highest peaks.

My mother left to set snares, and I took my knife to a delicate stream. The water was shallow and choked by yellow grass. I sunk my feet into a tepid pool. I flicked away the scab and opened the same cut I had made that morning.

I raced along the creek, impatient with its playful course, and joined the river in an exhilarating rush. The forest fell away as a stutter of shadows, replaced by rusted fields and empty villages. I passed the wreckage of my bridge. It was still daylight on the plains. Sunlight danced in oily rings on the river's surface.

Go farther, my mother had said. She knew what I would find across the wasteland.

The city erupted on the horizon like a cancer, and in a blink I was upon it. The river split into a stone maze, a drunken spider's web of crisscrossing circles and spokes, and countless canals wound through the ruins of fine houses and market squares and palaces protected by high walls. The buildings had once been white, their slate roofs green and blue, but many were crooked and unfinished, angles skewed, dimensions distorted, windows broken and tiles fallen away. Armies of marble statues stood as silent sentries along every tree-lined road, every stagnant garden pond. The statues were as misshapen as the buildings: too many limbs or too few, knees bent backwards, faces twisted the wrong way around.

I had never seen a city so massive and so sprawling. Such places existed only in legends.

All of it, every broken building, every deformed bust, was cloaked in corroded vines and washed with the colors of late autumn, hints of red and orange now rotted away to brown, not a breath of green anywhere to be seen.

I believed the city dead, long abandoned. I disobeyed one of my mother's sternest rules and divided myself to explore numerous stone channels. I spread through the city as an army of ants would cover a forest floor, pulling farther and farther apart.

The first living thing I saw startled me so much I nearly snapped out of the water.

It was at first glance only a shadow over the water. A barren tree, leafless branches, that was all I could see from my underwater vantage, but it moved. Long spindly legs unfolded and thin arms reached, and I saw its head, round as a seed, and two large unblinking eyes. It reminded me of the stick insects I had seen in distant forests, but it was as tall as a man, and when it rose to its feet, it ran upright on two legs, swift and surprisingly graceful.

Now that I knew what to look for, I saw others like it in every corner of the city. Odd crouching bodies and unblinking eyes perched atop stone walls, in blighted trees, in broken windows. Most did not react to my presence even when I studied them. The few who did startled and clattered away on long stick legs.

The fourth or fifth time this happened, I followed, and that was how I found the tower.

It stood at the center of the city, a crooked black slash of metal, slanted like a blade driven into the ground or an arrowhead punched from within. Around its base was a deep, dirty moat spanned by a dozen failing bridges. I gathered myself from all corners of the city and circled the tower curiously, slowly, skating just beneath the surface. The structure was crooked and split; it had been breaking apart for a very long time. It was marked all along its length by windows smeared with soot and oil to prevent those outside from seeing in, or those inside from looking out.

Around the lowest of those blacked-out windows, where the edges dipped into the filthy lapping water, a scattering of pale blue sparks clung to the frames, snaking through seams in the metal and circling each sunken bolt. They pulsed, those shimmering veins of light, and I felt it; they trembled, and I trembled with them. They pushed and squeezed into the cracks at the base of the tower, and I felt the same pressure and grind they felt.

I had never known before what I looked like from the outside.

One of the stick-creatures ran across a bridge and scrambled along the tower's scarred surface. It climbed toward the top but changed its course midway and turned, scurried down the warped gray metal. It lowered its face to the water and I knew, knew it as surely as I felt the gritty water and the rough metal, as sharply as I tasted the blight-rust, that its flat pale eyes were looking right at me.

I flinched, and blinked, and retreated from the city.

• • •

I withdrew my feet from the stream. My heart slowed and my breath quieted. My skin felt bruised all over, tender to the touch. The dizziness passed, but my head was a heavy block on an aching neck.

"It's nearly summer," my mother said.

She was sitting on a stone on the other side of the water. She held the swarm in the palm of her hand; the blue dust danced around her fingers. Fragile pink flowers blossomed along the creek, and in the swaying grass green blades shone among the yellow and red. A breeze tugged at my hair and rustled the leaves in gentle chimes.

"Did it rain last night?" I asked. My voice was rough, grating as the drag of footsteps in mud. I licked my lips, but my tongue offered scant moisture. I wanted to soothe my throat but dared not touch the water.

"It rained four days ago. Did you go to the city?"

"Four days?" I had never stayed away so long. My stomach clenched with hunger.

"Did you go to the city?"

The questions I wanted to ask tangled and tumbled in my mind, like a knot of snakes after first thaw. "How long have they been there?"

"You know what the old women say," said my mother. "Longer than memory. Longer than time. They've been invading the world since there was a world to invade, if the stories can be believed. They—"

"Not them," I said. "Not those things."

My mother's fingers twitched. The swarm hummed.

"My sisters. How long have they been there?"

"Nearly as long," said my mother. She would not meet my eyes. Her voice was fragile with hope. "I did not know if they had survived. You saw them?"

"I found a tower."

"How does it look?"

"Old," I said. "Weak. It's falling over."

"Ah." My mother closed her eyes and I imagined, for a moment, that she had spent the past four days sitting exactly where she was now, never moving, never stirring, doing nothing but waiting. "That's something, at least. At least they've managed that."

We sat in silence for a time. I listened to the bell-like music of the blighted bushes.

"How do you know it will make any difference?" I asked.

There were men in the northern swamplands who would treat a snakebite by first killing the snake, then amputating the hand, then the forearm, the elbow, all the flesh up to the shoulder as the dying boy screamed around a leather strap. I had seen them do it. I had been hiding behind my hands, too horrified to watch, and mother had scowled at their blades and blood-splattered faces before telling them it was too late.

"Mother? How do you know?"

She stood slowly, unsteadily, joints snapping and legs unfolding beneath her as though she had forgotten how they worked. She said, "You must be hungry. I'll check the traps."

She disappeared into the forest. I laid down on the rock again, feet tucked safely away from the water. Wisps of clouds drifted overhead. I felt I was floating above the land, but at any moment I might fall and splash to the ground like a dropped bucket of water, scatter into rivulets before seeping into the earth.

My mother had taken my knife while I was in the city. She kept it as we descended into the rolling foothills. I settled into my body again, that frail prison of skin and bone, so clumsy and slow and hungry. The nights had lost their chill while I was away. Each day was hotter than the last, the hours of sunlight harder to endure.

After noon on the second day we came to a meadow. The river spilled from the trees and into broad open bowl. Without thinking I brushed my hand over the swaying grass and withdrew with a gasp of pain. The meadow grass was sharp enough to open a fan of tiny cuts across my fingers and palm.

"Alis, wait."

I looked over my shoulder. My mother stood at the edge of the forest, safely in the shadows.

"I'm only going for water," I said.

"Not here," said my mother. She stepped forward, hesitated. "Come back to the shade. Please."

I had never heard my mother plead before.

I turned away from the meadow and followed her into the forest again. A few paces from the trail she brushed orange leaves from a log and sat down. The sunlight dappled her shoulders and the crown of her head. I sat beside her.

"We'll wait for evening," my mother said.

I took the water skin from my pack and tilted the last drops into my mouth. Sunset seemed an age in the future. I imagined my lips and tongue drying like summer mud, pink flesh splitting along cracks, all the spit and blood evaporating away. I shifted into a firmer patch of shade, but it did nothing to alleviate the heat. My mother passed her water to me.

"What were their names?" I asked.

I expected her to tell me not to ask questions, not to be stupid. I did not expect an answer.

"I never gave them names," said my mother. "I never named you either. You chose your name for yourself. Do you remember? We were in one of the desert forts. There was an old woman leading a caravan. You tried to run away with her. She said she wouldn't take you unless you had a name. You made one up, and she brought you back to me." My mother looked at me. "You don't remember?"

I remembered hiding in a pile of blankets that stank of camel and falling asleep to the grind of cartwheels on sand.

"All old women are the same to me," I said, and my mother laughed.

The sunlight deepened the lines around her eyes and sharpened the angles of her face. She would not pass for a mountain clanswoman now, nor a desert wanderer, nor an island adventuress. Should we cross the mountains again, my mother wearing that thin face and those golden eyes, she would be a stranger everywhere. Children would dare each other to slip frosthand blossoms into her tea and hide behind tent flaps to watch her choke.

"We still have a chance," she said. My mother plucked a handful of grass from the ground near her feet, crushed the brittle blades in her palm. Blood rose in beads across her skin. The swarm flowed from her fingertips, ate through the grass and stitched the wounds closed. "If most of them are still hiding away in the ark, we still have a chance."

She stood and strode into the forest. I listened until her footsteps faded, then slid to the ground and closed my eyes. There was nothing to hunt and we had not eaten in days. I drifted into a restless slumber.

When evening came and the heat released its chokehold on the day, I returned to the meadow of knife-sharp grass. The mountains still shone with light, but the river was in shadow. I found my mother kneeling in a fresh clearing. The swarm hummed around her in, cutting the grass blade by blade. It slowed when I approached, quivered uncertainly, sped along.

There was a pile of dirt on the ground before her, oblong, the length of her forearm. She dribbled water from the skin and stirred it with her hands. Beside her lay the bundle she had carried from the nomad's camp: clean white bones in a tattered shawl.

My mother drew my knife from its sheath and drove it into the ground, jerked it free and stabbed again, and again, churning up dirt, grass, sand. She mixed in more water and worked it with both hands until it she had a sticky, gritty mud. She unwrapped the bundle, and one by one she picked the bones from the pile. The skull first, the knobs of the spine, the shoulders and ribs, arms and legs, the twin curves of the pelvis, the impossibly tiny fingers and toes. The swarm gathered to watch. The last daylight vanished from the highest peaks and the first stars emerged.

With my knife, my mother opened a long cut down her forearm. She smeared blood onto every bone and scooped handfuls of mud to shape two legs, two stubby arms, a small head and a round body. She smoothed the shawl over the child-to-be.

"You have more water in you than your sisters did," my mother said. She was looking at the lump on the ground. The swarm spiraled and danced, twining through her fingers, and disappeared beneath the bloody cloth. "I used to think it was a mistake. They never tried join a caravan or sneak aboard a trading ship."

The shroud shifted as though caught in a breeze.

My mother held up my knife. I stepped forward to claim it.

"I won't tell you what to do," she said. "You can go back over the mountains if you want. You'll have to decide. I'll let you go now."

Something like a laugh teased the back of my throat, but the sound I made was closer to a sob. She wanted me to decide. She had woken me from a warm sleep in the nomads' camp, led me through the ancient battlefield and the winter forest, spilled my blood into a wild river. She had brought me over the mountains to this dying land, and she wanted me to decide. Here, where the grass cut like knives and trees rattled in the wind and we hadn't spotted a bird or a squirrel for days. Here, beside this lonely river that tasted of iron and fed into the heart of a grotesque city, and there was nothing to see out to every horizon but what would become of the forests and farms and cities and swamps, to the entire world, if the blight spread unchecked.

Here, where she had made me from sand and bones and blood, she was letting me go.

"Will you give her a name?" I asked.

My mother tugged at a corner of the shawl, touched her hand to the round belly of mud. I turned away and pushed through the biting grass until I found the trail again.

"Alis," said my mother.

I stopped, and my heart thudded with faint hope, but I did not turn.

"I'll choose a good name for her," she said.

Her voice was so low it breathed with the murmur of the river. When she fell silent the night swallowed her whole.

I walked to the edge of the river. Perhaps it was the same beach where my sisters had once stood, trusting and docile, before my mother asked for their knives and led them into the water. The river ran swift and smooth. I unlaced my boots. I waded into the water and squeezed the shifting sand between my toes. Beneath the stars, the meadow and the forest might almost be mistaken for alive.

I pressed my knife to the inside of my arm.

There was a chance, my mother had said.

The first drop fell. I ran with the current out of the foothills and onto the plain. The shifting riverbank beneath my feet, the water lapping my legs, the night air teasing the hair around my face, the burn of thirst and dull ache of hunger, the rattle of wind through dying grass, all of it slipped away, and there was nothing left but rust and silt and the cool dark river.

Kali Wallace studied geology and geophysics before she realized she enjoyed inventing imaginary worlds more than she liked researching the real one. Her short fiction has appeared in *Clarkesworld, The Magazine of Fantasy & Science Fiction, Asimov's, Lightspeed,* and *Tor.com.* Her first novel, a young adult horror story titled *Shallow Graves,* will be published by Katherine Tegen Books in 2016.

*Even though Giang worked in a shoe factory, she preferred to
go barefoot as much as she could . . .*

RUNNING SHOES

Ken Liu

"You're under quota again!" Foreman Vuong shouted. "Why are you so slow?"

Fourteen-year-old Giang's face flushed with shame. She stared at the angry veins on the foreman's sweaty neck, pulsing like fat slugs on a ripe tomato. She hated Vuong even more than she hated the shoe factory's Taiwanese owners and managers. One expected the foreigners to treat the Vietnamese badly, but Vuong was from right here in Yên Châu District.

"Sixteen hours is a long shift," Giang mumbled. She lowered her eyes. "I get tired."

"You're lazy!" Vuong went on to spew a stream of curses.

Giang flinched, anticipating a flurry of strikes and blows. She tried desperately to look contrite.

Vuong considered her, his lips curling up in a cruel smile. "I'll have to make you stronger through punishment. Run five laps around the factory, right now, and you'll stay as long as you have to tonight to make up your quota."

Giang was thankful. It was a hot and humid day, but running was a mild punishment compared to being beaten. Besides, it allowed her to stay out of the factory a bit longer, where the buffeting noise never ceased, and the big machines frightened her with their brutal and careless strength.

The first lap around the compound was easy. Her bare feet pounded lightly, rhythmically against the packed dirt. Vuong shouted as she passed. "Faster!"

Even though Giang worked in a shoe factory, she preferred to go barefoot as much as she could, like she used to when her family still lived in the countryside. Back then she had loved to run along the soft muddy trails next to the rice paddies, wiggling her toes in the earth, and looked forward to a sweet fried *bánh rán* sticky rice ball that her father might buy for her at the end of the month.

But then her father had decided to move to the city, where he thought he could make more money as a laborer and give his family a better life. Here, the air was thick, the rooms were crowded, and the streets were full of broken glass and nails so that she had to wear cheap plastic sandals.

Halfway through the second lap, she started to feel lightheaded. It was now like breathing under water. Her shirt stuck to her skin, and black spots danced before her eyes. Her calves and lungs burned.

"Faster! Pick up your pace or you'll have to do an extra lap."

Giang wished that she could run away from Vuong and the factory. She imagined herself wearing the shoes that she made: sneakers that felt as light as air but were as strong as steel boots. She often admired them, thought they would protect her feet against the roughest ground, but of course she couldn't afford such shoes.

Running in them probably feels like flying, she thought. *Wouldn't it be nice to run all the way into the sky and become friends with birds?*

But Vuong's foul curses brought her back to earth, back to the present.

It was getting harder and harder to lift her legs. Her feet hurt as they struck against the ground. She couldn't catch her breath. The sun was so hot and bright.

"If you don't run faster, you can leave right now and never come back. And don't ever expect to find any work in any other factory in this town either. I know all the foremen."

Giang was ready to give up. She wanted to stop and just walk away. She wanted to go home, where she would be able to cry in the warm embrace of her mother and fall asleep against her shoulders.

But then she imagined the scene around the bedroom after she would have fallen asleep. There would be her father, confined to his bed after he lost the use of his legs because of that construction accident. He would stare hopelessly at the ceiling, biting his lips and trying not to moan from the pain. Next to him would be her mother, who would have to get up before the sun was out to walk to the shirt factory on the other side of the city. The money she earned there paid for her father's medicine. It was Giang's wages that paid for their food, and allowed her brother to continue in high school at the provincial capital. But now, with Giang fired, what would they do?

Her mother would only hug her tighter, of course, but Giang remembered that she was no longer a little girl.

She forced herself to run faster.

• • •

A few girls looked up as an exhausted Giang stumbled back into the factory, but most ignored her because they were too busy. Vuong impressed the owners by running the machines so fast that the girls could barely keep up.

The cavernous hall was filled with noise: the constant staccato *dik-dik-dik* from the stitching stations, the *whoosh-slam* of the stamping and die cutting machines, the hissing from the workbenches with the rubber molds and hot glue.

Giang made her way back to the die cutter, and tried to keep up with the frantic routine of feeding sheets of plastic to the hungry blades of the machine. She was thirsty and hot. The dust and fumes—chemicals, glue, plastic—made her cough and gag. Tears blurred her eyes. She wiped them away roughly, angrily.

She tried to comfort herself by thinking of the end of the shift. She would get to go home, where her mother would be ready with a pot of hot tea even though she was even more tired than Giang.

"Faster!" Her partner Nhung interrupted her daydream. "You've already made me fall behind. I don't want to be punished!"

Giang's legs were so sore that she could not stand up straight. The room seemed to spin around her. But she tried, really tried to speed up. She threw her weight forward, hoping to use the momentum of the stack of uppers she carried to move faster.

Her foot caught something on the ground. She dropped her load and barely avoided banging her head against the machine in front of her by grabbing onto it with her hands. The girls had often complained about how dangerous it was to leave broken machine parts around the factory floor, but Vuong just said they were careless.

I'll just take a little break, she thought.

Time seemed to slow down, each moment lingering in her consciousness like a memory of childhood.

She felt the pressure on her fingers, and a brief moment of unbelievable pain as the cutter blades sliced through.

Nhung's shouts and screams seemed to come from a great distance. *Sorry,* Giang thought, *I didn't mean to get you in more trouble.*

As she fell, she saw a broken, rusty spike at the foot of the machine rushing up at her face. She closed her eyes.

Shadows gathered around her. More shouting. The loudest voice belonged to Vuong: "Back to work! Back to work!"

Yes, Giang thought. *I have to get back to work. I'll get up in just a second, Mama.*

But she could no longer feel her hands, her legs, her body. She felt herself soaking into the stack of uncut uppers under her. She willed herself to grab onto the fibers, to entwine herself into the soft material. She couldn't just fade away. She had work to do.

"Why throw these away?" She heard Vuong speaking impatiently to someone. "They're perfectly usable! Just a little blood. You want me to take it out of your wages?"

And then she felt herself lifted onto the conveyer belt, sensed the sharp blades of the die cutter slicing around her, endured the metallic, heavy punch of the pneumatic press, bore the sting of needle and thread, and tasted the bitter flavor of hot glue. She wanted to scream, but could not.

I'm sorry, Mama.

Enclosed in a dark box, Giang remembered little of her journey across the Pacific, over the highways of this new continent, into the warehouse of the shoe store. By the time she finally woke up, she had been taken to a new home in this suburban house in Massachusetts, where she was wrapped in shiny paper and placed under a tree with many other wrapped packages.

She didn't understand the language spoken in the house. But she did understand the happiness on the boy's face as she was unwrapped and taken out of her box. He flexed her and put her on his feet, and bounded around the house.

She also understood the look on the faces of the parents as they looked on: Giang's father used to smile at her just like that as he handed her the sweet *bánh rán*.

With time, she learned that the boy's name was Bobby, and that he wanted to run fast and long.

Every morning, Bobby took her running. She loved running in the crisp, cold air. It was so quiet here, different from her home back in Vietnam. Bobby ran at an even, effortless pace, and she liked the graceful, rhythmic pounding sound she made against the pavement. Sometimes she imagined that she was flying, skimming, dipping over the ground, like a pair of fluttering sparrows.

The pounding also allowed her to speak. *Thwack, thwack, thwack*, she sang to the dew-speckled grass and sun-warmed sidewalk. *Crunch, crunch, crunch*, she greeted the gravel in the driveways and the pebbles lining the road shoulders. She observed the comfortable, large houses around her, the clean streets, and the wide, open spaces. She listened to Bobby's breathing, even and deep, as though he and she could run forever.

Giang tried to not feel sorry for herself. Sure, she was no longer a person, but a thing. But in her old life at the factory, she had often felt that she was little more than an extension of the machines, a lever or belt made of flesh and bone instead of metal and rubber. Cradling Bobby's feet as he ran made her feel almost more real, more alive by comparison.

She did miss her mother, and often wished that she could get a message to her: *Mama, I'm fine; I don't worry any more about money, food, quotas, pain.* She hoped that her father was feeling better, and that they found a way to keep her brother in school.

Spring turned to summer, then to fall and winter. Giang liked the challenge of finding her footing in the ice, but running in the snow was hard on her body. Cracks appeared in her, and water seeped in. She could feel that she was losing traction, her grip on the ground.

It was spring. Bobby opened a box and took out a new pair of shoes.

Giang looked at the newcomers with dread. As Bobby kicked her across the floor, squeaking, she whispered to the new shoes, but they were not like her, not alive. Bobby laced the new shoes on his feet, and hopped around to try them out.

Then he bent down and picked up Giang, lacing the two parts of her together. Her heart leapt. Bobby didn't forget about her. She wasn't being replaced. They would go on running together.

Being draped around Bobby's neck as he ran was a different sensation. She liked being high up, being able to see things. It was a bit like when she was little, when she rode on her father's shoulders to watch the parades at the festivals.

Giang wanted to sing an old song that her mother used to sing. She wished she still had her voice. She wanted to tell Bobby her story, about the dusty, noisy factory, the chattering girls, the sweet-smelling tea at home, her mother's calming voice. Bobby would be interested, wouldn't he? In a way, hadn't his desire for good and cheap running shoes called her across the Pacific into this new life?

Bobby stopped by the side of the road. Dark electric wires stretched overhead.

And then she really was flying, high into the air. She reached the apex of her arc and began to fall, but her laces were caught on the wires, and she dangled high over the road, empty as far as she could see in both directions.

Bobby was already disappearing down the shoulder of the road. He didn't look back.

Giang sighed and settled down. She imagined the years ahead, the rain, the sleet, the snow and the sun. She imagined herself growing old and falling apart.

But a powerful gust of wind tossed her about, whistled through the holes in her sides and the cracks in her soles. Up here, the wind was strong.

"Hello," Giang tried out her new voice and startled the sparrows dozing on the wire. She was now loud, louder than she had ever been.

I've finally run into the sky, she thought. *I'll become friends with the birds.*

As the wind continued to howl and groan through her decaying body, she began to sing her story.

Ken Liu (kenliu.name) is an author and translator of speculative fiction, as well as a lawyer and programmer. A winner of the Nebula, Hugo, and World Fantasy Awards, he has been published in *The Magazine of Fantasy & Science Fiction, Asimov's, Analog, Clarkesworld, Lightspeed,* and *Strange Horizons,* among other places. He lives with his family near Boston, Massachusetts.

Ken's debut novel, *The Grace of Kings*, the first in a silkpunk epic fantasy series, will be published by Saga Press, Simon & Schuster's new genre fiction imprint, in April 2015. Saga will also publish a collection of his short stories, *The Paper Menagerie and Other Stories,* in November 2015.

For years, his job has shown him how easily people can fall apart—
friendships, relationships, even all alone. Humans are fragile . . .

AND THE CARNIVAL LEAVES TOWN

A. C. Wise

The first piece of evidence appears on Walter Eckert's desk in a locked office to which he has the only key. It is wrapped in brown paper, neatly labeled with his name, no return address. He unwraps it with wary hands.

Cheap plywood, as if from a construction site wall, pasted with a handbill-sized poster. It could be advertising any event around town—a rock band no one has ever heard of, an avant-garde art exhibition no one will ever see—but it appears to advertise nothing at all.

The paper is grayed. Darkened by soot, slush, city smog. Carved into the bottom righthand corner of the wood is a date—October 17, 1973—a date currently forty one years, one month, and fourteen days in Walter's past.

The image: A clown in whiteface, black crosses over his eyes, tilted slightly so they resemble X's. A conical hat. Pompoms in black against the whiteness of his baggy uniform. The clown cradles an infant's skeleton in his arms.

The skull is human, but subtly wrong, enlarged. There is a hair-thin fracture, widening and darkening as it runs back toward where the skull meets the spine. Out of the camera's view, one can only imagine the clot of darkness where the fissure disappears, the fragments of bone, caved in beneath a terrible blow. The ribcage appears human as well, but unnaturally small in comparison to the skull.

Below the waist, the skeletal remains are not remotely human.

Walter Eckert has investigated almost everything in his time—domestic violence, cheating partners, insurance fraud, arson, petty theft, and even murder. He has never encountered anything quite like this before. Cold case. Two parents, one child. House, abandoned. Cups half-filled with coffee. Beds, immaculately made. Clothing, neatly hung. Refrigerator, humming and full. Television, left on.

The house remains; the evidence of daily life remains. The Miller family is simply gone.

Walter isn't certain what motivated him to look up the case. It wasn't even his, back when he was on the force; he inherited the file from his partner, Don. Walter should be actively pursuing new clients, sleazily patrolling social media for rumors of infidelity and foul play. But there's something about the poster, something about the date. They remind him of something, two seemingly disparate events that lodge in his mind and refuse to let go. So instead of seeking new business, Walter chases down the cold trail of business over forty years old.

A carnival enters town in the fall of 1973. The Millers are a seemingly happy family, living the American dream. The carnival leaves town, and the Millers are gone.

Their house is left in perfect condition. The only remarkable thing is thirteen-year-old Charlie Miller's room. The posters of his favorite baseball players have been turned to face the wall; his baseball cards have been removed from their plastic sleeves and dealt out across his bed, facedown. In his closet, his stuffed animals—artifacts of a younger age—have all had their eyes removed.

Three days after the Millers disappear, a group of kids gathers in an empty lot to play. Midway through the game of tag, the dust in the lot blows slightly to the west and uncovers the remains of two complete adult skeletons. The bones are aged, colored faintly as though with years buried under desert sands. The remains, lying side by side, holding hands, are eventually identified through dental records as Jasper and Anita Miller.

Charlie Miller is never found.

The second piece of evidence comes into Walter Eckert's possession much as the first; appearing in his locked office, part of his life as though it has always been there. It is a flat, gray canister, holding an old reel of film. Walter is at a loss until he remembers the storage locker in the basement of the building. He finds the key in his desk, descends into the chilly, ill-lit space, and digs out the old film projector left behind by his former partner, Don. The man never threw anything away, and it seems Walter has picked up his habit.

The film is black and white, jittery, and popping in the way old movies do. The camera fixes on an empty room, which contains only a surgical operating table. A man enters the room, walking from the left side of the frame toward the right. He strips out of his clothes, folds them neatly upon the floor, and lies on the table, face up. He wipes his palms against his legs, licks his lips, and blinks.

His fingers twitch restlessly at his sides; his eyes are open, staring at the ceiling. He never looks at the camera. The film continues to skip and pop, phantoms skating through the scene, flaws in the medium or deliberate splices, Walter can't tell.

Another man enters from the left of the frame and stops in front of the table. He looks at the camera full on and smiles. He wears a white surgeon's robe, but no mask or gloves. His motions are jerky and exaggerated, like any actor in a silent film. He reaches to his left, just beyond the frame. His arm returns with a scalpel held in his hand. He shows it to the camera, letting the blade glint as much as it can in black and white. This done, he makes a single, precise incision in the chest of the man on the table. He draws a line, in stark black against gray-white, from the man's clavicle to his pelvic bone. And so the surgery begins.

For the next fifteen minutes of film, the surgeon dissects the man upon the table, who appears conscious the whole time. His fingers twitch once more, drumming the table before he clenches them still, and with their stillness, holds his whole body rigid. The cords of his neck strain, his mouth set in what might be agony, or a wild, delirious grin, but he makes no attempt to leave. The surgeon slits open the man's arms, his legs, his cheeks, and each one of his ten fingers and toes. The movement of the blade is straight and true every time. Blood is wiped away meticulously after each pass of the knife. The skin is peeled back, pinned. The surgeon's eyes gleam and the crook of his mouth never wavers. There is no soundtrack, but one can imagine the movements set to a jolly tune.

When there is only bone left, the skin and muscle vanishing by degrees between the lapses in the film, the surgeon once more reaches to the left of the camera frame, and returns with a silver mallet. This too gleams in the lack of light. The bones of the man lying upon the table are systematically and utterly shattered, one by one.

The surgeon leaves the frame, but perhaps not the room. It is impossible to tell. Perhaps he waits, breathing, just out of the camera's view.

Another minute passes with the camera fixed securely upon the ruins of what was once a man.

After that minute is done, the surgeon re-enters the frame backward. From there, the film proceeds as though it is being run in reverse, though when Walter checks, the projector—also inherited from Don—is still running as it should. The surgeon raises the mallet and the bones are restored; he runs the knife up from pelvis to clavicle and the skin is healed.

At the end of the film, the dead man stands up from the table. He does not reclaim his clothes, but he takes the surgeon's hand. Together, one smiling, one shaking, they face the camera and bow. Still holding hands, they exit the frame.

The camera remains steady on the empty room for an additional thirty seconds. Within the last five seconds of film, a date flashes across the screen: December 14, 2015—a date three months and seven days in the future of Walter Eckert, who watches the scene over and over in a small, poorly lit room smelling of stale coffee and cigarettes, smelling of noir cliché and whiskey, smelling of, above all, fear.

The pieces of evidence don't match. Walter isn't even certain they are evidence yet. Only Walter's mother insists they are and they do.

Walter's mother is psychic, or claims to be. She even had her own 1-800 number once upon a time. His childhood memories are littered with phone calls landing like exotic birds at all hours of the night, lost souls seeking counsel and hope, weeping and giddy, desperate to be told exactly what they want to hear.

Holding his breath so it wouldn't be heard, Walter listened to his mother listen to Jeannie from Paramus asking about her job. He listened to John from Denver worrying about his health, Kirk from Sault Saint Marie wanting to know if he'd ever find true love, and Tina from Havertown who played the lottery every day and was willing to pay his mother $2.99 per minute for lucky numbers.

December 14, 2015 is still two months and twenty-seven days in Walter Eckert's future when his mother calls from her nursing home to tell him the pieces of evidence, the film and the photograph, are connected. There are two things Walter never discusses with his mother—his work and his dreams, which are usually about *Twin Peaks* and who really killed Laura Palmer.

Walter has never entirely believed in his mother's psychic powers, but when she calls him as he's staring at the photograph of Charlie Miller paper-clipped to the cold case file, a shiver traces his spine.

He hasn't told her anything about the Miller family or the cold case file currently sitting open on his desk. He hasn't said one word about the two pieces of evidence, not even that they exist, but she knows and she tells him they are connected anyway.

Just before he hangs up, she says, "There's more. Lemuel Mason. The name came to me in a dream. Find him."

After he hangs up, Walter slips the Miller file into his briefcase. He puts the picture of the clown, pasted to the section of plywood, and the reel of film into his briefcase, as well. Following what he would call a hunch and his mother would call a prediction, Walter ventures out into the blustery September weather and goes to the local library to do some serious and irrational searching.

Virginia Mason, a resident of Pottstown, Pennsylvania from 1863 to 1887, wife of the Reverend Lemuel Mason, was generally known to be a pious woman. She aided her husband in his ministerial duties, and was much-loved in their town, known for organizing women's charity drives and bake sales with all the proceeds going to support Mr. Clement and his one-room school house. The great tragedy of her life, as far as the town was concerned, is that she never bore the reverend a child.

So the stories say.

So some stories say.

But there are other stories, too.

There are stories of a certain tree where the devil was said to appear, and of Virginia, walking at night, restless and unable to sleep. Stories of Virginia growing large although her husband was away, conducting missionary work in Peru. Stories, contrary to the tutting of the townsfolk over the Masons' childless life, that Virginia was indeed delivered of a babe. But what babe? Was it born sad, mad, twisted, and deformed, as rumors claimed? And who was its sire?

Other tales say Reverend Lemuel Mason was never a missionary and, devoted husband that he was, rarely left his wife's side.

What can be confirmed by public records is Virginia Mason died at a young age. Or, at least, that a stone exists sits on the outmost edge of the churchyard, indicating she was given a Christian burial. Her cause of death is unknown. Some terrible, wasting illness is suspected, as Virginia was little seen by anyone but her husband in her final days.

Lemuel Mason mourned deeply. Some good folk of his town, when they came upon him unexpected, heard him talking to Virginia, even after she died. On occasion, he was also heard talking to a child, rocking it in his empty arms and singing lullabies.

Some rumors suggest the desecration of Virginia Mason's grave. But they are only rumors.

There are wilder stories still, of Virginia Mason's body found in a tree, with only scraps of cloth clinging to its bones, and wisps of hair adhering to its skull. The body was found wedged in a crook of the tree, arms and knees raised to wrap around a conspicuous absence, just the size of a child. The remains were discovered three days after Virginia Mason was supposedly buried—not long enough for her to decompose to such a state, if those were indeed her bones.

Two months after the stone was raised in the churchyard bearing Virginia Mason's name, words in white chalk appeared upon the tree where the bones were found: *Who put Ginnie in the tree?*

Whatever the truth, this is a publicly recorded matter as well, appearing in the local Pottstown newspaper: Three months after Virginia Mason died, Lemuel Mason vanished.

No trace of his fate was ever discovered. He was never seen again.

A day before he vanished, the carnival entered town. The day after his absence was noticed, the carnival left town again.

It's impossible to tell whether the grainy, black and white image of Lemuel Mason accompanying the news story of his disappearance shows the same man depicted in the black-and-white image of the clown cradling a child's deformed bones. The greasepaint is too thick. It could be anyone lost in all that whiteness, with black crosses over their eyes.

Who would even think to compare the pictures? Walter would not, unless his mother had called him to say the name *Lemuel Mason*, which came to her in a dream. He would not if the paper reporting Lemuel Mason's disappearance had not also contained a note regarding the "funfair" leaving town.

The pieces of evidence are connected, Walter thinks. *It is not an advertisement; it's an invitation.*

"It's coming back," a voice just behind Walter says.

He twists around in his chair to hide his startled jump. "What is?"

The librarian is slender, nervous, like a young colt. Her hands flutter in the direction of the newspapers spread in front him—stories of carnivals, *the* carnival, as Walter has come to think of it, coming to town and leaving town. The librarian's hands settle, falling to clasp and twist in front of her.

"The carnival," she says. "I'm sure I saw it somewhere."

She lifts the top paper from Walter's pile, the local paper from today, and scans it briefly, frowning, before replacing it.

"Maybe I imagined it." The librarian shrugs, but her frown lingers. Her expression is one of someone who has misplaced an object they were holding just a moment ago, an object they could swear they never set down.

The same finger of dread that touched Walter when his mother called touches him again. He resists the urge to grab the librarian by the shoulders, shake her, and demand she tell him everything she knows about the carnival.

As evenly as he can, trying on his most disarming smile, Walter Eckert meets the librarian's eyes and asks, "Would you like to have dinner with me?"

The third piece of evidence is the oldest thus far. It is not a piece of evidence yet, but as he digs deeper, following tenuous connections and unexplained coincidences, Walter will encounter a glossy, full-color reproduction in a museum catalog, and file it as such.

The original is under glass at the University of Pennsylvania Museum. It is a shirt found among the grave goods of a nomadic steppe warrior, believed to have lived in the early 1200s, during the time of Ogedei Khan. It is remarkably well preserved. There are words stitched into the fabric, in a jumble of languages, as though each part was stitched by a different hand.

The words tell a fairy tale about a tame flock of crows and a girl who trained them to do tricks and follow simple commands. Like all good fairy tales, it is laced with darkness of the most brutal kind. The girl, who is only known as *the daughter* and never given a name, asks the birds to do something for her after she has taught them all the tricks she knows. She asks them to pick the flesh from her mother and stepfather's living bones.

The crows obey.

And, hungry, wicked birds that crows are, once they are done, they devour the nameless girl's eyes, too. It is not clear whether they do this as punishment, or an act of mercy. After all, who would want to walk around with the image of their parents' flesh-stripped bones fixed in their skull for the rest of their days? None but the most heartless of creatures, carrying feathers where their hearts should be.

After the crows swallow the girl's eyes and everything she has seen, they lead her away. It is never specified where. The story only says that for the rest of her days, the girl made her way through the world by following the sound of her tame birds' wings.

No other versions of this fairy tale have ever been found, despite the natural tendency of stories to travel far and wide, much like crows. How it came to be stitched onto the shirt of a steppe warrior, no one can say.

At the end of the fairy tale there is a date, unfathomably far in the steppe nomad's future—June 17, 1985.

• • •

"It's not the same carnival, of course," the librarian, whose parents named her Marian, thus guaranteeing her future career, says.

She toys with her salad fork as she speaks. She's shy, Walter has learned, but he's also learned the second glass of wine, currently warming her cheeks with a delicate glow, has given her more of an inclination to talk.

"It's *a* carnival. I went to it . . . *one* . . . when I was little. My father took me, after my mother left."

Marian hesitates, and Walter feels as though he should say something, but he doesn't know what. After a beat, Marian goes on.

"I don't remember any of the shows. I must have been really young. All I remember is holding my father's hand and being convinced we would find my mother at the carnival, and bring her back home."

Marian blushes. It's the most she's said all night. Walter breathes out, and only then does he realize he's been holding his breath. He finds himself leaning forward, as though his proximity will draw out more words, but it has the opposite effect. Marian reaches for a breadstick. Breaks it into pieces, but doesn't put a single one in her mouth.

Walter leans back, trying not to let his disappointment show. The next thing out of his mouth surprises him.

"My mother is a psychic," he says.

His fingers twitch, and he hides the motion by reaching for his glass. He can't remember the last time he told anyone, and it's not what he meant to say. The cynical part of him wonders if he's manipulating Marian, giving her a piece of himself in order to keep her talking. But why? It's too late for Charlie Miller and Lemuel Mason. He's never been one to obsess over unexplained mysteries. Some things simply are, and cold cases don't pay the bills.

But December 14, 2015 is still in the future, and there's a possibility, maybe even a hope that it is in *his* future. So he has to know.

Marian raises her head, her expression wary as though she suspects Walter is making fun of her.

"I'm sorry." Walter shakes his head.

Marian's expression softens.

"Don't be."

Then, in another move that surprises them both, she reaches across the table and touches his hand. It's a gentle thing, brief, just a tap of her fingers along his bones, there and just as quickly gone.

Guilt comes like a knife. A rift opens in Marian, and Walter sees a wanting in her that goes all the way through. Suddenly, he doesn't care about the carnival.

Suddenly, Walter wants to tell Marian about holding his breath, pressing the phone to his ear and listening as his mother dispensed fortunes. He wants to tell her a true thing, an apology for a deception he's not even sure he's made. The need wells up in him, bringing memories so sharp he is there again.

Rain pats against the window, steaming down and making odd shadows on the wall. Walter clutches the phone, holding his breath, wrapped in a communion his ten year-old mind doesn't have the language to understand. But he knows, deep in his bones, that he and his mother and his mother's client are all connected. The rain and the telephone lines make a barrier, separating them from the world. He is *essential* in a way he can't explain. If he breaks the connection, if he breathes out and lets on that he's there, his mother's prophecies will never come true.

The sensation is so real and overwhelming, Walter can scarcely breathe. Here and now, he is still holding his breath, listening to the whisper of words down the line. It terrifies him. He swallows deep from his glass, washing the memories away. They're too big. He tamps the impulse to speak down, far, farther, until it is gone.

He will not ask Marian about her father, or the hitch in her breath when she said the word *mother*. He will not tell her about his own life. And with this decision, a new impulse wells up in Walter, one he knows he will not be able to resist. Before the night is through, he will show Marian something terrible; he will make her afraid.

Because he is afraid.

For years, his job has shown him how easily people can fall apart— friendships, relationships, even all alone. Humans are fragile. If he opens himself to Marian, if she opens herself to him, they will become responsible for each other, and that isn't something Walter wants or needs. And, paradoxically, he is afraid precisely because he isn't responsible for anyone and no one is responsible for him. December 14, 2015 is in the future, but what if it isn't in *his* future? What if he isn't essential and never was, only an observer, trapped on the outside?

Marian looks at him strangely and Walter realizes his hand is shaking. He sets his glass down, regrettably empty, and reaches for his water instead, swallowing and swallowing again. Even so, his throat his still parched when he speaks.

"Do you know anything about the Miller family? They lived in this area back in the 70s. They disappeared."

As he says it, Walter knows it is the wrong thing to say. Something indefinable changes, a thread snaps. Marian tucks her hands back in her lap. Her shoulders tighten.

"My neighbor, Mrs. Pheebig, knew them." Marian looks at her hands, her voice edged. "She's ninety-one."

"Does she have any theories about what happened to them?"

"No." Marian has barely touched her pasta, twirling and twirling the noodles around her fork. Her plate is a minefield of pasta-nests, cradling chunks of seafood, surrounded by rivers of sauce.

"Mrs. Pheebig told me everyone in the neighborhood suspected the parents were abusive, but no one said anything because people just didn't talk about that sort of thing back then. I don't understand how anyone could stay quiet about something like that."

Marian finally lifts her head, and it's almost like an accusation. In the rawness of her gaze, Walter finds it difficult to breathe. The terrible thing coming for him, for both of them, is almost here. Walter's head pounds. He looks at Marian, and she's nothing human.

She's running ahead of him. Her eyes are inkwells. Her skin the finest kind of paper. The whorls of her fingerprints smell of the dust particular to libraries, the spines of books, the rarely touched yet time-stained cards of the archaic catalog, bearing the immaculately typed numbers of the Dewey decimal system. She is a prophet, an oracle. Somewhere, buried deep in her bones, are the answers to all his questions.

Because it had to be one or the other, kindness or cruelty, Walter reaches out to catch Marian before it's too late.

"Can I show you something?"

Marian puts her head to one side, considering. For a moment, Walter has the sense of her looking right through him, knowing he's dangerous, and weighing risk against reward.

"All right." Marian reaches for her purse.

The bill settled, they walk two blocks to Walter's office. He flicks the lights off, switches the projector on, and watches Marian watching the film. Walter doesn't know what he expects, what he wants—a companion, someone to share the burden? Confirmation that he isn't mad, someone to say, yes, I see it too? His pulse trips, watching the play of light reflected in Marian's eyes. Despite the horror on the screen, her expression doesn't change. She says nothing. Only her fingers curl, tightening where she leans against Walter's desk. But even as her fingers tighten, she leans forward slightly, waiting.

This is it, Walter thinks, without ever knowing what *it* might be. The air shifts, and for just a moment the scent is salty-sweet, popcorn and candy apples, and it tastes like lightning.

Whatever it is sweeps past him, leaving the after-taste of electricity on his tongue. The date flashes across the screen, and Marian's expression finally changes. Her mouth makes an O, and she raises a hand to cover it.

"What . . . ?" Walter says. And "No." He reaches for her, but it's too late. When Marian brushed his knuckles, that was the moment to take her hand.

"Wait," he says.

Marian is past him, her shoulder striking his so he's off-balance. He follows just in time to see the cab door slam.

There are puddles on the street, reflecting stoplights and neon and the night smells of freshly departed rain. The cab pulls away in a cloud of exhaust and ruby-burning headlights. The faint sigh of a calliope hangs in the air. Walter raises his hand, but the cab doesn't slow. What was he thinking? What has he done?

Walter returns to the library the next day. He asks after Marian, and the young man at the desk presses his lips into a thin line before telling Walter Marian isn't here today. But he cuts his eyes toward the frosted glass office door without meaning to as he says it, so Walter scribbles a note on the back of an old circulation card, before shoving it into the young man's hands.

"Just give her this for me, will you?"

It's only two words: *I'm sorry.* Walter stations himself at a table, surrounding himself with books and drifts of paper. After twenty-three minutes, Marian emerges. She is polite, but closed. She brings him books, helps him find articles buried deep in the archives room, but doesn't linger. He watches her, but the wild creature of paper skin and inkwell eyes has vanished. Slipped around a corner. Disappeared. Gone.

Perhaps he imagined it all. Perhaps he's made a fool of himself and hurt a woman who wanted nothing more than a friend.

"Marian. About last night . . . " he says, as she lays a heavy tome of town records beside him.

"There's nothing to talk about." Marian's lips press into a thin line identical to the one worn by the young man behind the desk when Walter asked after Marian. Is there a school that teaches librarians that expression?

Walter's hand hovers in the space between them. He lets it drop even before Marian turns. The subject is closed.

Confused, uncertain, Walter retreats behind his own wall. Stories of the disappeared and unexplained surround him like birds coming to roost, like carnival tents rising from the ground.

There is the story of three men and seven women vanishing from their retirement home, leaving in their wake doctors and nurses who can only speak backward from that moment on.

There is the story of an opera, performed only once, telling of the beheading of St. John at the request of Salome. The lead singer walked off the stage halfway through the final act and was never seen again. The lighting rig above the orchestra pit detached while the baffled audience was still trying to sort out whether the departure was part of the show, and the conductor was instantly killed.

There is a bone pit in Pig Hill, Maryland. An ossuary in Springfield, New Hampshire. The entire town of Salt Lick, Indiana, which, in 1757, simply disappeared.

Walter studies. He combs news articles, conspiracy websites, birth and death records. He consults any and every source he can. He doesn't know whether he's chasing something, fleeing something, or trying to hold something back.

Walter dreams, and sometimes he's trying to catch Marian, sometimes he's trying to outpace her, and sometimes, he's running scared.

This is what Walter Eckert knows from the research he's done: There are never any advertisements of the carnival coming to town. There are only stories reporting where it once was before it vanished, packed up, moved on.

This is what Walter Eckert knows deep in his bones: If you are not invited, you cannot attend. You will not be invited unless you would give up anything, *everything*, to have the carnival steal you away.

This is what Walter Eckert doesn't know: Does he want it badly enough?

From January 1983 to May 1985, Melissa Anderson, one of the top accountants at Beckman, Deniller & Wright, quietly embezzled nearly two million dollars from her employers and their clients. On the sixteenth of June 1985, Beckman, Deniller & Wright received notice of an impending IRS audit.

On the seventeenth of June, Melissa took the elevator to the thirty-fourth floor of her office building, and climbed the fire stairs to the roof. She removed her jacket and folded it neatly by the door. She slipped off her shoes and placed them beside her jacket. In her stocking feet, she climbed onto the building's ledge. The wind tugged her blouse and hair. She looked down at the traffic on Market Street below.

In that moment, she could conceive only of the fall. Her muscles forgot how to turn around, walk to the door, descend the stairs. Elevators didn't exist. If she wanted to get back down, she'd have to jump. And she was terribly afraid.

She told the wind, "I don't want to die today."

Perhaps the distant notes of a calliope reached her. Perhaps it was simply the way the birds turned, a scattered flock of pigeons appearing much larger and more sinister as they banked away. Or it was the scent of popcorn. Candy apples. Sawdust. The flicker of lights lining a fairway.

Whatever it was, Melissa remembered how to turn around. She climbed from the ledge and tore the delicate soles of her stockings as she crossed the roof to reclaim her shoes. She put her jacket back on, rode the elevator to the ground floor, and instead of returning to her desk, she walked three blocks to the university museum.

Melissa Anderson did not return to work the next day. Or the day after.

On the twentieth of June, the car carrying the IRS auditors to the firm of Beckman, Deniller & Wright was struck by a city bus. The driver and all three passengers were killed.

The next day, the carnival left town.

How long does it take to fall in love? Seven minutes? Five hours? Two months, fourteen minutes, twenty-six days?

Walter catches his gaze drifting to Marian as he reads of the lost and disappeared and it gets harder and harder to look away.

Maybe it isn't love. Maybe it's only that he missed her when she was sitting across from him, so distant he couldn't bear to take her hand.

Maybe it's only that he knows he lost her the moment he asked about the Miller family instead of her telling her about the hushed, connected world of held breath, psychic predictions, telephone lines, and rain.

The fourth piece of evidence . . . Well, no one's really counting anymore, are they? There is a standing stone in Ireland, carved with Russian characters. There is a body frozen into a chunk of ice, forensic evidence dating it from the 1760s though its brow is sloped like a Neanderthal's. There are documents written in code on devices that haven't been invented yet. There's a set of coordinates leading to a planet no one has yet discovered. All delivered in nondescript envelopes, no return address, bearing Walter's name.

Whatever the evidence, it is always the same. The carnival enters town, the carnival leaves town. People disappear.

• • •

As the clock ticks over from December 13 to December 14, 2015, Walter Eckert wakes in a panic. It's Marian. Marian is gone. Of course she's gone. Because the invitation was never meant for him.

Frantic, he drives to her apartment—an address he shouldn't have, because she didn't give it to him, but which wasn't particularly hard to find. He told himself "just in case" at the time. In case what? This, he thinks, hunched forward, windshield wipers struggling to keep up with the rain. He parks catty-corner to the curb, leaves the car door hanging open, takes the stairs two at a time. He pounds on Marian's door, not expecting an answer, and eventually he kicks it in.

The windows are open. Rain blows in and dampens the sill. The air smells faintly of mildew, as though it's been raining in Marian's apartment for a very long time. She could be out, visiting friends, on vacation, at a Christmas party, but Walter knows she isn't. He goes through Marian's apartment, room by room.

The clothes in her closet and her drawers, the towels in her bathroom, the bed sheets, the curtains—every bit of fabric in Marian's apartment has been carefully knotted and left in place.

Under the scent of mildew is the lingering odor of lightning and popcorn.

And Marian is gone.

On New Year's Eve a stray firework ignites a blaze that burns the library to the ground.

"Follow her." Walter's mother calls him in the middle of the worst ice storm in memory.

It's New Year's Day plus one. His mother's voice is slurred. It's dark, and Walter can't work out whether it's from ice coating the windows or the time of day. His bare feet kick empty bottles as he fumbles toward the bedside clock and its ruby light.

"Mom? I can barely hear you." Walter's tongue feels thick, as though he's trying to shape words in a dream. Maybe the dwarf will show up soon and tell him how Laura Palmer really died.

"Go after her," his mother says. Walter grips the phone.

"I don't know how. Mom?"

There's a hush like static. Like a secret world of rain. Like ice freezing on the telephone line sealing up his words. His world.

"Go." His mother's ghost-voice is buried under a fall of not-snow. The line dies. As it does, instead of a dial tone, Walter hears the murmur of a calliope.

• • •

It is January 4, 2016, and Walter awakes from a dream.

It must be a dream.

It *is* a dream because he enters the carnival with no invitation, only the evidence in his hands—the poster, the shirt, the film. He is allowed in. Even though none of the invitations are for him. They are for Charlie Miller and Melissa Anderson. They are for Lemuel Mason and Marian. But not him.

Unless, taken all together, they are. Evidence numbers one through To Be Determined—case files, half-vocalized conversations, newspaper articles, microfilm, archives, cigarettes smoked, and alcohol consumed. Perhaps these are Walter Eckert's invitation to step right up, come on in.

It hurts. And Walter will never admit this.

What has he been chasing?

It *has* to be a dream.

Walter passes through the turnstile, evidence clutched in his hands—the photograph, the film reel, a reproduction of the shirt, the standing stone, the Neanderthal man. He holds them out to a blank-eyed boy at the ticket booth who waves his hand and makes the gate standing between Walter and the carnival disappear.

Walter steps inside.

The boy, no longer blank-eyed, runs ahead of him. Walter follows, hurrying to keep him in sight. No older than thirteen, the boy is naked, loping on hands and knees between tents staked into the dusty ground. Skinny. Faint bruises trace the ladder of his ribs, the knobs of his spine. Walter almost remembers the boy's name. But every time he opens his mouth to speak, it slips away.

Down narrow ways. Between tents pulsing with breath, buzzing with the sound of tattoo needles, humming with the burr of electricity and the importance of a honey-producing hive. Walter is utterly disoriented.

There!

When Walter catches sight of him again, the boy wears a wolf's head in place of his own—muzzle frozen in a snarl, glass eyes reflecting the glow of the pale fairway lights.

Fried crickets served here. Ten for a dollar, all skewered up neat and crunchy in a row.

Skin of mice. So nice. Peeled fresh and heaped with shaved ice. Drizzled with any flavor syrup you want.

Try your luck, Ma'am-Sir. Prizes no worse than your heart's desire! Careful what you wish for. At-any-cost is a steep price to pay.

Walter almost loses sight of the boy again; he ducks into a tent. Walter follows.

Seats rise in concentric circles from the center ring. A spotlight, dusty-dim, pins the boy, who throws his head back and howls. The sound is muffled inside the echo chamber of the wolf's skull.

In the spotlight there is no mistaking the bruises, dark purple scars that will not fade numbering his ivory bones.

The boy crouches and the light snaps off. Wolves, real wolves, who bear no human skin, creep between the seats, which are full now. The rabbit-masked audience holds collective breath, leans forward. The wolves ignore them, dripping slow between the seats. Trickling down. The boy curls in the middle of the ring. Skinny, scarred arms wrap around the taxidermied wolf's head. He waits.

Walter can't bear to watch.

He flees.

And stumbles into another tent with a single man, a clown, spotlit in the center of the ring.

The clown stands behind a table, stitching. His eyes are downcast, covered in crosses. He works with infinite care, unpicking seams and re-doing them, crooning softly all the while. A lullaby. The needle goes in, the needle comes out. The thread is a form of weeping, one that won't smear his makeup, joining rust-colored bone to gleaming fish scale. The child's skull is exaggerated, swollen. A hairline crack runs from brow back to somewhere Walter can't see.

There are other tents, other exhibits. A woman rides a bicycle. Her legs churn the pedals, turn them insistently. Blood flows. Walter traces it from the wheels to her heart, to her legs, to her arms, and back again. Her skin is translucent. The bicycle, too.

A flock of crows follows her around the ring. If she slows, the blood will stop moving. If she slows, the birds swallow her eyes.

Walter runs, on and on. Faster through the carnival, through the fortune teller's tent where tarot cards chase his heels like fallen leaves, past the world's strongest man, the living skeleton, the ring toss game. He is looking for something, someone. A woman whose eyes are inkwells, whose spine is a card catalog, whose skin holds the tales of a thousand library books lost and burned. He needs to tell her he's sorry; he needs to take hold of her hand.

But all he finds is a snake woman—half-mechanical, half flesh-and-blood, selling lies for twenty-five cents a go in sawdust-filled ring. All he finds is a surgeon with a silver mallet and a scalpel in his hand. A band of seven old women and three old men, playing flute and drum, xylophone and horn, with each other's bones.

The exhibits are endless. They smell of popcorn. Cotton candy. Lightning. Eternity. Walter keeps running, but he never arrives anywhere. There is always another corner, some trick and fold of the carnival, keeping him close but at bay. After all, if there's no audience, no one there to observe just outside the ring, how can the show ever go on?

It is a dream. It must be a dream. It doesn't matter that his boots are sitting beside his bed in the morning, caked with dust when he left them neat and clean on the mat beside the door before going to sleep. It doesn't matter that his hair smells of greasepaint. It doesn't matter that his palm remembers the touch of a librarian he didn't have the courage to reach for across a table spanning the gulf of a thousand years.

Once invited, once the invitation is turned down, it will never come again. It has to be a dream.

Because right now, Walter's entire world is made of wanting. If he really went to the carnival, he would still be there, wouldn't he? If they invited him in, asked him to stay, dear god, why didn't he?

And more importantly: How will he ever get back there again?

A. C. Wise is the author of numerous short stories appearing in publications such as *Apex, Clarkesworld, Shimmer,* and *Year's Best Weird Fiction: Volume One*. Her first collection, *The Ultra Fabulous Glitter Squadron Saves the World Again*, will be published by Lethe Press in 2015. In addition to her fiction, she co-edits *Unlikely Story*, and contributes a monthly *Women to Read: Where to Start* column to *SF Signal*. Find her online at acwise.net.

Oona, this gorgeous eccentric, charming enough to sideswipe the fact that she's professionally a scholar of creepiness . . . There's a thin line between out of control and spectacular . . .

WHO IS YOUR EXECUTIONER?

Maria Dahvana Headley

Five

Since we were little, Oona's collected Victorian photographs. A certain subset of people love them, but I got a library book of them once, just before I met her, and I've never not been appalled. I don't know what a book like that was doing lost in our local library. It's exactly the kind of thing that would normally have been removed by a logical parent. The book was death images, yes, but worse than that. These were all dead children and babies dressed in their best clothes and propped up for the last family photo. Held in their parents' arms, posed with their pets and toys, staring at the camera. It was like some sort of Egyptian funerary ritual, except much more hardcore. The thing about them was that everyone in them had to pose for a long time to make it through the film exposure. There's lots of accidental motion, lots of blur, and so the families look like ghosts. The dead children are the only ones who look alive.

"Did you hear about Oona? Because if you did, and you didn't call me, I don't know who you are anymore," the voice on the other end of the line says.

The same rattle Trevor's had in his voice since we were seven, a sound like tin cans tied to the back of a wedding day junker. It's been a while since we've spoken. Since I've spoken to anyone, really. I tried to start over with new people, but I was still the same person and it never works the way you think it will.

Trev and I faded out in a record shop a few years back, arguing over Kate Bush for reasons that are now difficult to recall. Kate Bush wasn't really the problem. The problem was the way friendship can tilt into more than friendship for one person, and less than friendship for the other. Trevor and I have a history of cheater's matinees in crappy un-airconditioned theaters. Back then, we watched superhero movies together, the three-dollar shows where no one we knew would be hanging out. Sometimes I reached over and put my hand in his lap, and sometimes he put his in mine. We were having an affair, but neither of us could commit to a bedroom. Instead, it was his fingers inside me, and my hand on him, both of us watching the latest incarnation of Spider-Man like nothing was happening below our waists.

We were trying, as we'd been trying for years, to not be in love with Oona.

"What about her?" She and I have history too, but not the history I wanted. Probably she's gotten married or is happy or had a baby or something. I'm expecting a *New York Times* announcement, her with something handsome beside her, a grinning, sports-playing something, and Oona, her yellow eyes and long red hair. She looks—has always looked—like a tree on fire. She's six foot two and covered with freckles. One time she and I were naked, and I drew the constellations on her with a Sharpie. All there. Next time I tried it, they were gone. There were new configurations but not the ones I'd mapped.

It's getting to be time again for weddings and babies. This is the second round after the first marriages. Trevor's been divorced a couple years now, and I'm single again too after trying to settle for a woman in Georgia who got pregnant by sperm donor and then said, witheringly, "You always act like you're so smart, but you're not as smart as you think you are. You're fucked up. You're in love with her, and you should stop lying about it."

She was four months pregnant and I hadn't noticed. I didn't know she wanted to have kids with me, and she didn't, it turned out. She wanted to have kids without me. Now I'm back in the city, avoiding my roommate. My life, what there was of it, has dissolved like Kool-Aid in a cup.

We're all thirty-seven, Trevor and Oona and me, and we've known each other since second grade. I haven't talked to Oona in years. Every time I see her name in my inbox, I delete it. After the last time I saw her, I'm better off alone. She messes with my head.

"She's dead," says Trevor, sounding astonished. "Oona finally died."

He says it like Oona's gone to India. I'm used to mishearing things like this. Every time I pick up the phone I think someone's going to announce a tragedy. I've been writing a lot of condolences, everyone of my parents' generation fizzling out, and a fair number of mine too, suicides and cancers, car wrecks.

"She did what? Who did what?" In my head, I'm looking frantically at a slideshow of the Taj Mahal.

"Oona," he says. "What the fuck? Oona died. Where are you?"

I take a moment to try to be this person, in this world, where Oona isn't. "On my way wherever you are," I say.

"Around the corner from your place, in that bar. The shit one."

I didn't know he knew where I lived. "Are you drunk yet?"

"I ordered for you. Your ice is melting."

I walk in, and there he is. His hair long and dark, his face gaunt. Goatee pointing off his chin like he's a cave ceiling. He's got on a T-shirt that I recognize, an anatomical drawing from the 1700s, a memento mori, a face pared down to the skull on one side, handsome and bearded on the other. Trevor has the whole bottle on the table, and when I look at it, he shrugs.

"To Oona," he says and raises the bottle at me.

"To Oona," I say and pour my own bourbon down my throat. For a minute, we sit in silence. But then:

"You know what I'm going to say."

I'd rather he didn't.

"Is she really dead?" Trevor insists. "Where is she, if she's not? Is she back there?"

"I don't know," I say. "How would I know? We don't even know where *there* is, not really, Trev. What do we know? Nothing."

"Because," Trevor says. "You know why I'm wondering." And he sings it, against the rules, the first time I've heard it in years. "*Dead girl, dead girl, come alive.*"

"Christ, Trev. Fucking don't," I say. My skin is covered in buzz. I feel like I'm full of tiny brainless insects, my body a sack of wings and antennae. My stomach lurches painfully, like something inside me's trying to get out.

"How?" I ask him.

"Obit didn't say," he says. "I called. Her mom wouldn't tell me. She was in Indonesia somewhere, collecting beetles. She got some kind of weird entomology job. Fuck," Trevor says, and sighs. "The last time I saw her, something bad happened."

"Don't," I say, again. "Please. I don't need to know any more stories about Oona. I know what she was like when she was weird."

But Trevor can't help himself. "I was sitting at a bar," he says. "Six o'clock on a Tuesday. Bar was empty except me and the bartender. I heard this sound."

"Stop it," I say. "I don't want to talk about Oona anymore."

Trevor looks at me. "I tried to tell Bridget about it, and you should have heard her. 'Always been in love with Oona,' she said. 'You think that woman's mouth is magic. You want a witch, Trevor,' she said."

I look at Trevor. He blushes.

"She wasn't wrong. So, I hear this noise, and I'm trying to figure it out, when something crawls over my foot. Big black bug. Like, huge. Size of my middle finger. And more of them coming. A whole row of them. Each one of them perfectly in line with the next."

"You always did like dive bars," I say, trying to shut him up.

His fingers corkscrew awkwardly into mine. I can feel the clammy creeping from me to him and from him back to me.

"I bend over, and she's under the bar, crouched down. Oona. Not Oona now. Oona then. She looks up at me, and she makes this face, this so-Oona face. And I'm freaking out, and the bartender's freaking out on me because he can't see the bugs, and he can't see her either. The last thing I see as he kicks me out into the street is Oona, her braids, the corner of her mouth, and then she turns her head and she's gone."

"What do you mean, gone?"

"Like she folded up."

"She didn't fold up. Oona was still around. I got emails."

"Did you open them?"

I shake my head.

"They weren't from Oona. They'd be spam, win a vacation to somewhere, free car, lend money to the lost. Jumbles of numbers, lists of lines from things."

"But she was around," I insist. "Her mom talked to my mom. She grew up. You know she did. Come on. We both slept with Oona."

"She was like an animal," Trevor says. I wonder how much he's been drinking. "An animal that might bite your face off."

He fumbles in his jacket. "I brought something," he says. "I know you don't want to see it."

We used to be special. Now we're grown-ups, and this is what you learn. Special children turn into fucked up adults. You can't even use the word magic now. Back then, we said it all the time, like we'd fallen into something amazing, like what had happened when we were seven could only be a good thing.

"Something went wrong. I don't know if it's ever going to be right."

He brings a snapshot out of his pocket. Faded, from the 80s. I don't have to look. The three of us the day we met. Oona's in the middle of the photo. She'd lost a front tooth. Yellow dress. I'm in a dirty T-shirt printed with a buffalo, and Trev's shirtless. We're on the steps of the trailer my mom lived in back then. It was the first day of summer, and we'd met at the swimming pool line, but they wouldn't let Trevor in because he didn't have a suit. Oona, who was already in her swimsuit, took it off and stood there naked. She said, "I don't have a suit either." It took about two seconds for us all to get kicked out, including me, because I'd seen Oona, and so I took my suit off too.

In the picture, both Trevor and I are blurred. We were jumping.

"Look at her, Zell," Trevor says, and there's something in his voice that makes me want to shut my eyes. "Look at the picture. Tell me I'm not crazy."

I look over Trevor's shoulder instead, out the door of the bar, from the dark and into the cold, bright January street. I see a girl walking past. Pale yellow sundress. Long red hair. A hitch in her step that I know. Except that this girl isn't thirty-seven. And as she passes, she presses her fingers to the glass and looks in at me.

"Trev," I say. "Trevor."

"This is the only one she was in, and now she's gone," Trevor says, shaking the photo at me. "So maybe she's really dead."

The window explodes inward.

Four

"Kagome, Kagome?" Oona asks me and laughs. "All kid's games started as adult games. That's not more creepy than the normal ones."

"I think it's creepy," I say. "Who Is My Executioner isn't an adult game. It's not a fucking game at all. Why would you need to know who your executioner is? You need to know what your crime is. You need to know who accused you. The executioner isn't the point."

"Maybe you want to know who's capable of actually killing you," Oona says, sitting twist-legged in front of me in a blue bustier and a pair of ridiculously short cut-offs. "Like, maybe they're your lover, Zellie. Maybe you know their secrets."

We're twenty-seven, and I'm sleeping with her for another round of probable heartbreak. She's midway through a dissertation on children's games, and everything about it makes me miserable. Oona knows all my secrets. I don't know hers. I only know she has them. She's been mostly normal lately, mostly Oona, this gorgeous eccentric, charming enough to sideswipe the fact that she's professionally a scholar of creepiness. This has always been true. She can do better than pass, most of the time. There's a thin line between out of control and spectacular.

I'm in love again, considering tattoos of Oona's name because here she is, her hair in long copper braids, each one interspersed with black lilies she's bought somewhere. She's not goth. The flowers are alive. We're in a coffee shop she likes, a place hung with bad art and someone in charge of the playlists who chooses Alan Lomax recordings of field songs. I hate it. Slave songs played over a backdrop of cappuccino steaming. Oona's always been like this. It makes everyone else skeeved out.

Oona collects horrible things. I regret ever introducing her to the pictures of the dead, but that ship's sailed. Her walls are covered in them now, all beautifully framed. It's only when you look closely that you wish you hadn't. There's one she's had blown up. Black beetle on a little blond girl's face, right at the corner of her open eye, like a tear.

"It's about a beheading, maybe, or about a woman in a cage. Anyway, it's Japanese," Oona says. "And it might not be creepy. It might just be sweet. Translators disagree and so does everyone else."

She shows me the game, even though I should know better than to play with Oona. She doesn't play fair. "You're the oni," she says. "The demon who gets killed."

She blindfolds me in the park with a long red scarf she's uncoiled from around her neck. She recruits a bunch of kids, and the group runs around me, Oona singing in Japanese:

> *"Kagome, kagome*
> *Kago no naka no tori wa*
> *Itsu itsu deyaru*
> *Yoake no ban ni*
> *Tsuru to kame ga subetta.*
> *Ushiro no shoumen daare."*

I don't know the words to the song and can't see the kids. I don't want to do any of this. Old history. Bad history. The kids don't mind. It's blind man's bluff combined with ring around the rosy, except no one falls down. When—through some silent signal—Oona ceases the ring running around me, I'm supposed to stand up. After that, she hasn't given any instruction.

"I'm standing up now," I say, but I don't hear anything. Not even laughing. It's daylight, and we're in public, this day in July, but I feel like I'm lying face down on cold ceramic tile. "I'm standing up."

"Who's behind you?" I hear Oona ask. I can't tell where her voice is coming from. "Who's your executioner?"

I feel breath on my neck, and I feel something else, something I've never been able to describe, other than that there's a sudden weight in my hands and a lightness in my skull. A spinning feeling. I see, for a second, myself as a tiny child, and then my same self, ancient. I see my head falling from my shoulders and into a basket.

I'm gagging, choking, and I tear off the blindfold only to find all the children gone. Oona's always had a way with kids. I spin around. No one's there. The park's empty.

Oona's always insisted she doesn't remember what happened when we were little.

"It was just a normal day," Oona always says, her eyes flashing gold. "Whatever you think happened, it didn't. I don't know why you always bring it up."

Now Oona laughs from above me. High in a tree, she sits on a branch, her bare feet dangling down.

> *"Kagome, kagome,"* she sings.
> *"The bird in the basket-cage.*
> *When, oh when will it come out, in the night of dawn,*
> *The crane and turtle slipped,*
> *Who is it in front of behind?"*

I look up at her. I'm sweating, like I've played another childhood game, a dizzying prelude to a blinded hunt. Her boyish body, her long white throat, her thighs in her cut-offs. Oona's head is blazed out by the sun behind her, and for a moment it's like it's gone. The way I'm seeing her is not the angle I should be seeing her from. I feel like I'm looking up from too low, and from behind myself. I feel like I'm on the ground, and I start to turn to see what's there.

The next moment, I'm down on my hands and knees, puking in the grass.

"You're so sensitive," Oona says, holding back my hair, her fingers on the back of my neck, and I shiver. She got down from that tree faster than she should have. I didn't hear her land.

There's something boiling inside her, a kettle left on the fire. I raise my head to look at Oona, and what I see is not Oona but something else.

"Who's your executioner?" Oona says. "Come on. It's just a game." She runs her fingers along my thigh, and it's like I'm being flayed. The air is full of black dots, a swarm of beetles, then gone.

I take off running out of the park, my feet bleeding, and I don't stop running 'til I get to my mom's extra bedroom, where I stay for the next three weeks, losing my job, falling apart, dropping out of the grad school I sold my soul to get into.

That's the last time I see Oona.

Three

We're seventeen. We're at the prom. I don't do prom. I'm wearing fishnets that I ripped with safety scissors and then sealed with nail polish. I didn't want them to disintegrate. They're my only pair. Otherwise I'm inappropriately dressed. I should have tried to look pretty. I already don't belong here. Me and Trevor are the only people of any color at this school, unless you count white as a color. My family came from Veracruz. His came from China. His people believe in ghosts and so do mine, and every time Oona comes around, my mom is like: *Out.* But that's partially because Oona's a high-end drug dealer's daughter with a fancy house and all the cars anyone could want. My mom thinks they look like a funeral procession.

Oona's in magenta, and it doesn't suit her. Her red hair clashes, and she looks strangely old. Her mother took her to a salon and got her hair done into a high topknot full of bobby pins and hairspray and fluffy silk flowers. Her neck is like a too-thin stalk for a peony, and her head keeps sagging. She's got vodka in her water bottle. Periodically she looks at me and grins, her eyes lined in silver. She's been not okay lately.

"She's gonna puke," says Trev.

"No, she's not," I say. Oona is known for her iron tolerance.

Trev and I are the least of her interests tonight. We're watching from the edge of the dance floor as Oona leads the dance. She's the prom queen, of course. Oona is everything at once, and the daily Oona is nearly perfect. It's only that sometimes things slip. People have short memories. Oona is mostly sweet. Mostly charming. Mostly beautiful. When she's not, people think it's them who've gone nuts, not her.

She neglected to bring a date, and so she's supposed to get a king out of the crowd. Somehow no one got elected. I don't get it. Neither does Trev, though I look at him, and he looks at me and shrugs, and I think I might know something about where the ballots went. Every boy in the room is circling her.

"Walk around me 'til I choose one of you," she tells them. "I guess we need a king if we're doing this stupid thing."

Oona's kneeling. She puts her head in her hands and sings.

> *"Poor Jenny is a-weeping,*
> *A-weeping, a-weeping,*
> *Poor Jenny is a-weeping*
> *On a bright summer's day."*

I don't even know where she learned that, but this is classic choose-a-husband stuff, so I hate it. I'd rather do something involving jump rope. At least that would mean the husband needed a skill. She's shut the DJ up, and we have no Nirvana, no "Smells Like Teen Spirit." Just Oona.

She does the next verse herself, standing up and looking down at the place she was. Boys shuffle nervously in their stupid-looking tuxedoes. I have a wrist corsage provided by Trevor. It's made of weeds. He has a matching one. We both hate ourselves.

> *"Why are you weeping,*
> *Weeping, weeping,*
> *Why are you weeping,*
> *On a bright summer's day?"*

She kneels down again and puts her head in her hands. Her hair's stiff, a crest of red bone standing up from the back of her neck. I hate her. I don't.

"Come on," says the DJ. "What kind of prom plays fucking madrigals?" He makes a nervous attempt at something else, but the something else is Alanis Morrisette, and so it gets shouted down.

> *"I'm weeping for a loved one,*
> *A loved one, a loved one,*
> *I'm weeping for a loved one,*
> *On a bright summer's day."*

"Shut up, Oona," Trev says mournfully as Oona starts spinning, her eyes shut, her topknot swaying like she's going to break her own head off.

> *"Stand up and choose your loved one,*
> *Your loved one, your loved one,*
> *Stand up and choose your loved one,*
> *On a bright summer's day."*

I see something moving out of the corner of my eye near the doorway of the gymnasium, near the photo backdrops. We got our picture Polaroided there earlier, me and Trev and Oona, looking all wrong together, a trio of suspicious class hierarchy, the popular girl being nice to the weirdos, the weirdos embracing the popular girl, and even as we got shot, I knew it was a trick. Oona was the weirdo, not us. Trevor and I were tag-a-longs, as always.

"That's strange," said that photographer, squinting at Oona, who smiled at her.

"What's strange?"

"The pretty one," said the photographer. "You're not showing up very well."

"Am I not?" said Oona as though this wasn't something she knew already.

"Maybe it's the glitter," said the photographer, looking bewildered. "We'll do the real one. That's twenty bucks for the wallet prints."

The wallet prints won't turn out.

Oona, her eyes shut, reaches out her hands and grabs a kid named Steven. He's tall and gawky, taller even than Oona is.

"Hey," he says.

"I guess you're the king," she says.

"I can't believe you picked me."

"It wasn't me," she says. "I was spinning. The spinning picked you. That's how the game works. It's like spin the bottle, but I'm the bottle."

"Are we going to kiss, then?" asks Steven and manages a grin. He's out of his league beyond belief.

Oona takes a paper crown from one of her attendants, and puts it on his head. He looks knighted. He stands taller. The foil shines, and it's horrible for a second. I see Trevor cringe too. Blade, I'm thinking, but then it's just a crown made of craft paper and staples.

Oona takes a step back from Steven and looks at him quizzically for a moment.

"Pretty," she says and then takes his hands in hers and dances as she sings.

> *"Shake hands before you leave 'er,*
> *You leave 'er, you leave 'er,*
> *Shake hands before you leave 'er,*
> *On a bright summer's day."*

She lets go of Steven's hands, and I feel Trevor flinch. Something's moving over by the photo backdrop. Something small and fast, a flash of yellow, long red braids. Holding hands with someone else, this person tall and slender, same hair, but this hair caught up in white-streaked snarls. The somethings are spinning, running, flying around the edge of the room.

I look back in time to see Oona kiss Steven very properly, very gently, on the mouth, and him, dazzled, kiss her back.

"Oh no," says Steven. He lifts his hand to his mouth. His eyes widen.

Steven starts coughing, and Oona leans toward him. He doubles over. A crowd around him. He coughs harder. People are closing in on him now, worried, patting him on the back, and he begins to choke something up. People start screaming and backing away, a chorus of *Oh my gods* and swearing, the music the DJ's put on ringing over the whole thing, a crazy chorus of beat and bass as Steven falls to his knees.

"Somebody call an ambulance!" someone yells.

Steven's coughing up black beetles, a torrent of them, all wings and legs. Thousands of them, legs tearing and twitching at each other, chitinous crunches underfoot as people freak out and climb onto the chairs, run from the room in their high heels.

Oona's right beside him, but Steven's not looking at her. They're swarming out of his nose and mouth. Oona's scared. She looks around frantically, and as she does, we all see it, Steven stops breathing.

Nobody's breathing. The people left in the room are all just frozen, staring, me and Trev included.

"Help!" Oona yells, but no one moves.

He falls forward, and the crown tilts off his head and crumples on the ground.

At the corner of my vision, I see the redheaded girl and the white-haired woman shift back into the bouncing gleam coming off the disco ball, and all the beetles are gone with them, the floor covered in black confetti.

Someone laughs nervously, and Steven stands up looking stunned, and Oona's there beside him, her spine straight, herself again.

"King and Queen," she says, and maybe only Trev and I can hear her voice wobbling. "There you have it, ladies and gentlemen."

"Are you okay?" I ask her, even though she looks like she is. She looks fine.

"Nothing happened," she says.

I watch a beetle crawl from the inside of her fist, very slowly, up her arm and into her dress. She reapplies her lipgloss. Her hands shake.

On the photo wall as we leave the prom, there's a fully developed Polaroid of me and of Trev, with Oona between us looking like a smudge of light, and inside that the faintest outlines of a little girl looking straight at the camera, her eyes glowing.

Trevor and I each take her hands and we go out to Trevor's car, borrowed from his grandfather. We ignore the sweetish smoky smell. Oona's fingers lace into ours.

"What was that?" I ask her.

"That was nothing," she says. Her eyes reflect headlights, and then she gets out of the car and takes off running down the highway, five miles from anywhere. We follow her. Her magenta dress, her corsage, her heels, one by one, her bra, her underwear, center of the road. She gets home. I call. Her mom answers. Oona's sleeping.

I'll sleep, eventually. All of high school is a process of forgiving Oona for moments like this, but we're not even sure it's Oona who's the problem. Maybe me and Trev are the problem. Maybe we just love someone who's crazy. That happens. Me and Trev sit in the car listening to Nine Inch Nails, a pile of Oona's clothes in the passenger seat.

"I hope this gets better sometime," says Trev.

"Which 'this' do you mean?" I ask him.

"All this."

"Everything?"

"It's never getting better, is it?"

"It might."

We look at Oona's clothes. They're still there, even if Oona is gone. Later they tell us that somebody slipped LSD in the punch, but they never figure out who it was.

Two

We're seven. Oona's on the ground in the middle of the trailer park, surrounded by window blinds not usually opened. The trailers face inwards around a central core where there's nothing planted. I sometimes find bits of old toys here, little things in the ground. There's not much to recommend it beyond the fact that it's an open space no one wants to deal with, and so it's available. We play here like crazy. This is where I learned to do a backflip. This is where my neighbor taught me to square dance, and where I learned to identify birdcalls. It's a piece of dirt but it's my dirt.

I brought Trevor and Oona here, showing off my powers. Oona's not allowed to do anything. Her parents live in a different part of town where there are driveways. My mom, when Oona says her last name, is impressed and also not. "I've heard about your dad," she says.

Oona's yellow dress is spread on the ground. She doesn't care about it, and I'm desperate to be like her. She already trampled it at the swimming pool. It's still wet. My own T-shirt is nothing nice. It came from Salvation Army, but the thought that dirt on it might become permanent is always a thing in my household, my mom crying over stains. Oona's dress seems to ask for the dirt of the world. This dirt especially likes it. It's all over her in a minute.

We're playing a game. I learned it from my friend who has a trampoline at her house. Not a friend, really, but a birthday party I got invited to because everyone did. Someone's mom had rules. In the original version, a person sits curled in a ball, eyes shut in the center of the trampoline, and the rest of the party bounces around her, chanting the words to the game.

Deadgirl, deadgirl come alive, come alive at the count of five. One, two, three, four, five.

The dead girl bounces up and keeps her eyes shut while she jumps around trying to grab someone. You try to keep the dead girl from getting you.

We eat cheese sandwiches, and I teach the game to Trevor and Oona. No trampoline here, but it can be done in dirt. I'm dead first. I curl up, and Oona and Trev run in circles around me, singing out the words to the game. I'm smelling the ground, hot and dry, and under that something chemical that burns my nose. I stand up blind, and start hunting for them. It only takes me a second to grab Trevor because he can't stop giggling.

"Dead girl," he says weakly because he's laughing too hard to talk.

"You must be bad at hide and seek," says Oona.

Then Trevor's dead, and he can't get either of us because we're better at it than he is. Oona's moving fast and I keep looking at her, and finally I'm looking at her so hard she turns around and says, "What?" and then stumbles and cuts her knee on something.

I see something, a firefly, maybe, a bright flare, and then it's gone, right into the wound, but it disappears. Maybe it wasn't there. She dabs at her knee, which is bloody.

"Ow," she says. "Sharp."

I catch a glimpse of something that looks like an old knife and feel the dirt where she fell for whatever cut her, but there's nothing.

Trevor grabs her. "Dead Girl," he shouts, triumphant.

I see a glint just for a second, the firefly, maybe, but not from outside Oona. Her eyes are almost all black, and then they aren't. I see them glow, a brightness, and then black again. I could yell for a grown-up but they're not home.

She licks her finger. She shuts her eyes and curls up. "I'm dead," she says. "So now you get to be alive."

She might need a Band-Aid. From where I'm standing, I'm seeing blood soaking into the dirt, but Oona waves her hand. Her eyes are still shut.

"Run around," she insists.

We do. I keep looking at that blood. The dirt is wet. I feel like I see something crawling up out of it. I feel like I see the firefly under Oona's skin, making its way somewhere. Oona seems pale, but she also seems like it doesn't hurt. There's a clacking sound, and I don't know where it's coming from. Like wings rattling against one another. I look up. Nothing.

We circle her, and Trevor starts chanting. "Dead girl, dead girl, come alive."

I join him. "Come alive at the count of five."

Now together: "One." Oona's face is turned toward the ground, and her shoulders are hunched inside her yellow dress.

"Two," and the sky has thunderheads. Oona's totally still. I want to start laughing, but I don't.

"Three," and a dog's barking. The last light's on Oona now from the sun coming down, and I hear a screen door slap itself against a doorframe like a mosquito killed on a thigh.

"Four," and Trevor's jigging high-kneed behind Oona and then around in front of her. She's still as a statue, and for a second that's what she is, a marble girl, hard-skinned and smooth and waxy as a plum. There's a smell, an oven smell, and then a cold smell, a dark blue-green smell, and I feel my bladder give.

Trevor doesn't notice. He's swooping and bouncing and Oona doesn't notice either, because she's getting up.

"Five," Trevor shouts, but Oona's already off the ground. Not Oona. Someone else, unfolding like a newborn calf, awkward arms and knees all folded up. Red hair to her waist. Ragged yellow dress. Pale speckled skin and wide eyes. I look at the ground. Oona's gone.

"Dead girl," the lady says, and looks at me. Her lips are parched. She's filthy. She raises her hand to her mouth and coughs, and I'm stuck in front of her as she gags on bugs. The whole world's full of bugs suddenly, all kinds, and I don't know where they're coming from, but I can see them coming out of the sky and up from the dirt too, all in rows and then in a rush as quick and glittering as water. Beetles and moths and lightning.

"Where's Oona?" I ask the lady, but she doesn't answer me. In the sky around us, something's ripping like nylon stockings, running down from the center of the dark. Brightness rolling casually from behind the black. Holes all around us. Lightning bugs disappearing into them, a blink, a blink.

I feel her hands on me, on my shoulders, and she's looking down at me as her head rips off her shoulders and falls. I'm a basket. I'm a hoop. I put my hands up to cover my face, and I catch her crown of braids. One of my fingers sticks in her mouth and I feel her teeth in my skin. Another in the corner of her eye, and I feel it give, swishing wet, a ripeness.

"Oona!" I'm screaming, and I'm holding this dead thing, and I move my hands, trying to drop it, but I can feel her skull. I can feel her jawbone and the sockets of her eyes, and she's dead.

I look at the ground and it's covered in a carpet of dying lightning bugs.

The head in my hands says something, but she can't even talk. Her tongue is thick and garbled, and my hand is in her mouth, and when she looks up at me, I see one of her eyes is missing. I can't move. I can't scream anymore. The sky is ripping open. I see ambulance lights and someone on a motorcycle. I see a fishhook gleaming. I see a pile of bodies. I'm seeing all these things and also I see my own skinned knees in front of me, and my mom is nowhere.

A dark hole in a pale face, a mouth around my hand, bugs crawling out the corners, dirt everywhere, and blood, and then it's done. There's a flash of light brighter than the bugs.

Trevor's standing behind me with a flashlight, and all the screen doors are opening, and Oona's on the ground in front of me, a flickering image at first, fetal position, dress torn, and all around her this woman, a bigger version, who looks at me, her eyes screaming, glowing, and then she's gone.

"Don't," she says, but she's not saying it to me. The sky zips itself like the back of a dress.

Oona sits up. She looks at us and at my mom and at all the parents in the circle, who wonder why I screamed. I look down at my hand. I wipe it on my T-shirt.

"Do I come alive now?" she says and laughs. "You look weird."

There's a stripe of red on my buffalo T-shirt. There are teeth marks in my finger. When I go to bed, I find dead lightning bugs in my shoes. Everyone says we have a big imagination. Oona doesn't say anything.

We didn't really know her, and now we don't really know her more. We're invited to her birthday. She turns another age. We're invited to all her birthdays. Her dad doesn't notice us. We ride in fancy cars. We get bikes. We eat hamburgers. Oona never shows up in school pictures. Oona never shows up on videos. Sometimes I see the lady outside the school, waiting, but if I look at her, she's gone.

Sometimes I pull the book from under my bed, the one full of dead girls, pictures of them in their fancy silk dresses, but I don't look at it. I just pull out the library check-out card, and then I put it back in. My name isn't even on it. Nobody knows I have it. Nobody knows anything.

I don't think it was my fault.

I think it was my fault.

One

The window explodes behind Trevor, and I watch it happen. A swarm of insects filling the bar so there's nothing to it but wings, and all of them on fire, glowing with captured sunlight.

The little girl steps over the sill. The bottoms of her feet are black. She's been walking dead for thirty years, and beside her I see another Oona, and another still, this one old, all of them walking through that window.

Trevor turns. I look at his neck. There's a piece of glass in his skin. I lift my hand, wondering at the piece of glass in my arm, and blood around it, pulsing out calmly to a beat. I see myself from the wrong angle, and then I see Trev from the wrong angle. I see dirt below me, me pitching into it, downward.

We're surrounded. All the Oonas are in the bar with us, and there's something about them, the way their hair is braided, the way they hang for a moment by their necks and then tilt forward under the blade, the way we're everywhere at once, an execution on a hillside somewhere, Oona's head shaved, a basket to catch it, and an execution in a prison somewhere, Oona's head hooded, and an execution on a street somewhere, a little Oona and a car slamming its brakes on, a grave full of beetles, a little Oona in a Victorian dress, a little Oona made of light, her whole body glowing and then dark, glowing and then dark.

Trev and I are on the floor in a landscape of glass and both of us on our knees.

"Who'd we bring back?" I ask him, because we tangled time back then, thirty years ago, and the Oona that was with us that day is not the Oona we've ever seen again. I've known it and Trev's known it too, and now we're going to die knowing it. We've seen her sometimes, glimpses of the original, but she's wired together with something else, an Oona full of centuries worth of dead girls, all held in one body, all moving at once. I've tried to puzzle it out: thirty years of antennae and wings, thirty years of insects crossing centuries, flying fast. No one would listen to me when I tried to talk about it. I stopped trying. I thought I might end up shouting, trying to tell strangers. No one ever believed that something came up out of the dirt. No one ever believed she was a nest full of spirits, and I tried not to believe it either.

I try to be ready to go. I try to be ready to skip back in time, to die over and over, to be whatever it is Oona needs me to be.

Trev's looking over my shoulder at her.

"Who's your executioner?" says Oona from behind me. "You catch your own head in a basket and spend the rest of time carrying it around with you. You get murdered in Mexico and dropped into the dirt and no one ever finds you. You get beheaded for being a witch in Massachusetts. You walk through a jungle with a basket on your head. You fill a basket with bugs. You die in a pit in Indonesia, shot for selling them to the highest bidder because the beetles all contained god and you blackmarketed them." She pauses. "I did that one time. Maybe that's how this started."

She leans over me. "You shake hands with your lover before you leave her. How about you, Zellie? You used to love me. Do you still love me?"

She coughs. A lightning bug on her tongue.

This Oona's not the little girl Oona, but the ancient Oona, her body full of bright, her eyes dark.

"Where is she?" I ask. Trev's choking and a little bit of blood is coming out of the corner of his mouth.

"There's no Oona left," she says. "We filled her up."

But there's a flash in those eyes, a thirty-year-old circle of dirt. The ancient Oona looks at me, her head tilted, black wings running down her cheeks. The thirty-seven-year-old Oona looks at me too, and at Trev. She leans forward and picks him up. She blows into his mouth, and in her breath appears a black butterfly. Trev gulps.

"Oona?" Trev asks. "Are you in there? I'll take the rest of them."

"Let's go home, Oona," I say. "Dead girl, dead girl," I say, and I struggle to my feet. "Come alive."

There's a blurry motion and for a bending moment, there are nine of us in the room, three children, three adults, three old people tilting to our graves.

I grab Trev's hand, and Trev grabs mine, and another mine, and another Trev takes another me. We ring around the Oonas and the room fills with light, with glowing and dark, with blurring motion.

Trevor leans in. He's a broken man in bad shape and he doesn't give a fuck about fear. He kisses Oona, and the room bends. I lean in. I kiss another Oona, the old Oona before me, and the floor tilts. The little ones stand together in the center of us all, children, smaller than I remember being. We're both kissing blurs.

"Dead girl, dead girl, come alive," I say into the ancient Oona's mouth.

"Five, four, three, two . . . " Trev says into the little Oona's ear. We are both the dead in the picture, but we've been good as dead since we fell in love with someone who wasn't living. We have nothing to lose.

"One," we say together.

I see my executioner, and I see us all weeping for a loved one. I see a basket, and I see myself in it, my own head, my own hands. I see an Oona, naked and dead, and beneath her body a litter of shining insects carrying her over the forest floor, moving their treasure to a mound of dirt. I see an Oona swarmed by tiny gods, all with their wings humming, their mandibles clacking. I see a living, breathing Oona in our arms.

Someone flies into me, and someone flies into Trevor, filling us with the dead. Our bellies, our bodies. We carry the lost. We share the burden.

But on the floor, there's a circle of dirt. And curled in it is Oona, asleep, like a volcano erupting, like a yellow iris blooming, her hands full of old knives, rusted with centuries of exposure to the elements.

She opens her eyes.

"When did we get so old?" she says, and outside it's bright, and gold, and summer.

Maria Dahvana Headley is the author of the young adult fantasy novel *Magonia*, the dark fantasy/alt-history novel *Queen of Kings*, and the internationally bestselling memoir *The Year of Yes*. She co-edited the *New York Times*-bestselling anthology *Unnatural Creatures*, benefitting 826DC, with Neil Gaiman. With Kat Howard, she is the author of the novella *The End of the Sentence*—one of NPR's Best Books of 2014. Her Nebula and Shirley Jackson Award-nominated short fiction has recently appeared in *Lightspeed*, *Uncanny*, *Nightmare*, *Tor.com*, *Shimmer*, *Apex*, *The Journal of Unlikely Entomology*, *Subterranean Online*, *The Toast*, and more. She is anthologized in *Wastelands 2*, *Glitter & Mayhem*, *The Lowest Heaven*, *The Book of the Dead*, and several "year's best" compilations. Her nonfiction has been published and covered in places ranging from the *New York Times* to Harvard's *Nieman Storyboard*.

Death is like a movie star: he can't just tell you his real name.
He has to go incognito . . .

DEATH AND THE GIRL FROM PI DELTA ZETA

Helen Marshall

Carissa first sees Death at the Panhellenic Graffiti mixer where he is circled by the guys from Sigma Rho. They can't seem to help crowding him even though they clearly don't want to be near him. She has gone with several of the Sig-Rho boys. All of them have. But she has never gone with anyone like Death before.

Death is wearing a black track jacket, with a black T-shirt on beneath and faded black jeans. Carissa, like all the other girls, is wearing a pink cashmere sweater with the letters Pi Delta Zeta embroidered in darker pink and a white cotton tank top. She is also carrying a marker. The boys from Sig-Rho have already begun to make use of the marker to write things around her breasts and stomach and neck, things like *Sig-Rho 4Evr* and *Love your body* and *Kevin likes it with mittens on.*

The guy with the black T-shirt and black jeans doesn't call himself Death though. This is what he says:

"Hi," says Death. "My name is David."

"Hi," says Carissa. She wants to say more but Logan Frees has grabbed her in a big, meaty, underarm embrace so that he can write *Occupy my crotch* on the small of her back, except he is drunk so it comes out as *Occupy my crouch*, which doesn't make any sense.

It is only later that Marelaine points him out to her.

"There," says Marelaine. "On the couch. That's Death."

"Oh," says Carissa. "He said his name was David. How do you know that's really Death?"

"Death is like a movie star: he can't just tell you his real name. He has to go incognito. But you can tell anyway." Marelaine punctuates this with a sniff. Marelaine is the former Miss Texas Polestar. Her talents include trick-shooting, world change through bake sales, and getting what she wants. She has mastered the sniff. She has also mastered the pony-tail flip, the high-gloss lipstick pout, and the cross-body cleavage thrust. Only Sydney, from the third floor, has a better cross-body cleave thrust.

Carissa is concentrating on the pitch and execution of Marelaine's sniff. She misses what she is saying.

"What?" asks Carissa.

"You know, when that Phi Lamb girl died last term. Staci. Or Traci. Or Christy. Whatever. He was there. When you've seen him once, you always recognize him. He's Death."

"I think he's kind of cute," says Carissa.

"If you like that type," says Marelaine. This time, her sniff is deadly.

Death's face is smooth and white as marble. His eyes are the color of pigeon feathers. His smile has many teeth to it and some of them are baby teeth, which are less frightening, and some of them are shark's teeth, which are more frightening.

This is what Death looks like, except Death looks nothing like this at all.

His hair is cowlicked, brown with flecks of gold at the temples. His chin has a stylishly faint shadow of stubble. His cheeks curve into dimples when he smiles, which he does often, and it is not frightening at all.

Marelaine is watching as Carissa approaches Death, and Carissa knows that Marelaine is watching. She wonders if she should attempt the three-ounce vodka flounce or try for something more subtle. She has an apple-flavored cooler beading droplets of water in one hand. She taps Death on the shoulder with the other.

"Have we met?" asks Carissa.

"Not the way you mean," says Death. He is smiling at her with that dimpled smile. "I don't come out to these things very much."

"Why is that?" asks Carissa.

"People make me nervous," Death answers. "I'm only here for work." He laughs at this, and his laughter is not what she expects it to be. It is cool and soft. It has the texture of velvet. It is intelligent laughter, and Carissa feels charmed by it, by its simplicity, its brevity, the way it sounds nothing like church gates yawning, the way it doesn't smack of eternity. She decides she likes talking to someone as famous as Death.

"That's a pity," says Carissa, and her fingers brush her pink cashmere sweater, pulling it tighter around her breasts. "Would you like to give it a go?" She hands him the marker.

"What do you want me to write?"

"Write me a magic word," says Carissa.

Death's writing is easy and graceful. There are many loops to it. He chooses a place somewhere near her left shoulder blade, and when he bends over to do it Carissa can feel the warmth of him, even though his skin is so white it is bloodless. He writes, *Abracadabra* first, and then *Open up* and then *I know you're in there* and signs it with a *D*.

Carissa smiles at him.

Later they play Spin the Bottle and every time Death sends the vodka twenty-sixer whirling it points at Carissa. Carissa wonders if she should try the closed-mouth kiss, the single-lip kiss, or the tongue-flick kiss. She knows she is best at the tongue-flick kiss, or at least that is what she has been told by the Sig-Rho boys. She tries the tongue-flick kiss but finds, unexpectedly, that she has transitioned first into a bottom-lip nibble and next into the deeper and more complex one-inch tongue glide.

At the end, Carissa smiles at Death, and Death smiles back at Carissa.

"Don't eat the lemon squares," he whispers with a wink. And then he carefully writes his number on the hem of her tank top.

Carissa thinks Marelaine would be proud of her for this, but then, reconsidering, thinks she probably wouldn't be after all. Soon she stops thinking about Marelaine, and instead thinks about the feel of Death's teeth, both the smoothed, tiny pearls and the sharp, jagged ones.

Carissa waits a week after Sydney's funeral before she gets up the nerve to call.

Death takes Carissa to a fancy restaurant, somewhere where they serve French food and French wine and all the entrees have French names that she can't pronounce. Death has a certain celebrity status, and they are shown to the table immediately.

At one point one of the other diners comes to their table. Carissa is eating the *poulet à la provençale*, which is delicious, and Death is most of the way through his *filet de boeuf sauce au poivre*.

"It's you, isn't it?" The man is sweating. Damp patches have bloomed at his armpits.

"Yes," says Death.

"I bet you don't remember, but you were there when my wife died." The man pauses. "I just wanted to say thank you. Thank you so much. She was in such pain." He plucks at his mustache nervously. "Could I get an autograph?"

Death is gracious. He signs the napkin in large, looping letters.

"Thank you," the man says. "Thank you for taking such good care of her."

Death smiles.

Afterwards, Death walks Carissa back to the house, and they laugh about it. "Does that really happen all the time?"

"All the time," Death says, and he slips his arm around her.

Carissa wonders what Death's Johnson will look like. Does Death have a Johnson? Will he put it inside her, and what will happen when he does? Does Death have a mother? Does he call her on Sundays and on her birthday, or is he too busy with being famous and being Death to remember the people who were there before he was Death?

As it turns out Death does have a Johnson after all.

He is a gentle lover unlike the many lovers Carissa has had in the past, most of whom tasted of stale beer; most of whom smelled like old socks. But Death is sweet and attentive and polite.

He brings her flowers first. These flowers are not ironic. They are not lilies. They are not roses with petals dyed to black velvet. They are not grave myrtle, cut-finger, vervain, deadnettle or sorcerer's violets. They are not death camus or flower-of-death. Death hates irony.

Instead, Death brings her a bouquet of yellow and deep orange celandines, which he says are named after the Greek word for swallow, and will bring her pleasant dreams.

Marelaine and the other Pi Delta Zeta girls are jealous of the flowers, and they slip into Carissa's room when she has gone to class and cut away some of the blossoms for themselves. In the morning at the breakfast table they talk in hushed whispers about their dreams.

They dream of Death, but the death they dream of is the death of sorority girls: they dream of killers with long, hooked knives and fraying ski masks; they dream of sizzling in superhot tanning beds; they dream endless shower scenes in which they discover their names written in fogged mirrors and their blood on the white porcelain tiling.

But when Carissa breathes in the blossoms, she dreams about Knick-knack, the shepherd mutt she got when she was eight. Knick-knack who waited patiently for her to come home for Christmas break before he collapsed that first evening home on her bedroom carpet unable to move his legs, waiting noiseless, not a whimper, until she woke up and held him. Carissa dreams that Knick-knack is a puppy, and she holds his velveteen muzzle close to her cheek while his tail ricochets back and forth like a live wire. She dreams about him nuzzling her under the blankets with his cold, wet nose.

Their wedding is the September following graduation, and it is a surprise to everyone.

"You're so young," her mother coos.

"Will he be able to support you?" her father demands.

Carissa sends out invitations to all the girls from Pi Delta Zeta: *You are cordially invited to witness the union of Carissa and Death.* They have not included last names because Death does not have a last name. All the girls send their RSVPs immediately. Marelaine is her maid of honor.

It is a celebrity wedding. Carissa wears a beautiful wedding dress with a chapel train and the bridesmaids wear taffeta. Death wears black.

Carissa and Death have decided on a simple double-lip graze and peck kiss for the ceremony because Carissa's parents are both religious. Even though it is not entirely proper she ends up halfway into a tongue glide anyway, but she remembers where she is and what she is doing. When they pull away from each other, they are both a bit embarrassed, but nevertheless they smile as if they have both gotten away with something.

Later, as they are standing in the receiving line, Death introduces his brother, Dennis. Death has never mentioned that he has a brother, and so there is some initial awkwardness, but Carissa is a Pi Delta Zeta and so she is good at recovering. She takes his hand, and it is warm and slightly damp. There are fine golden hairs on his fingers, and he has long eyelashes. He looks the way that Death sometimes looks when he is not being Death.

"I'm so pleased to meet you, Dennis," Carissa says. "Death talks about you all the time." Carissa wonders why he doesn't.

Dennis smiles, and he has the same dimples that Death has. He holds her hand for too long. She lets go first.

"Welcome to the family," he says.

Later, after the cake has been cut, Marelaine pulls Carissa aside.

"Who's he?" she asks. She is pointing at Dennis, who is trying to teach her mother how to foxtrot.

"That's Dennis," Carissa says. "Death's brother."

"Oh," says Marelaine. "He's quite a looker, isn't he? I mean, he's not Death. But."

In a year, she receives an invitation that says *You are cordially invited to the union of Marelaine and Dennis.* She wonders if she should RSVP.

They lived happily ever after.

When Death dies it is very sudden.

Neither of them planned for this, and so Carissa is caught off-guard when she hears the news. She thought they would have more time. She thought she would die first, and Death would be there for it, to help her through.

At the funeral Carissa wears black. Death is also wearing black. Death is lying in a coffin, and makeup has been applied to his skin to give it a deep, bronze tan that makes him into a stranger.

Carissa secretly hopes that Death will attend the funeral, and she is disappointed when he does not. She wants to see him one last time.

Marelaine hosts the post-funeral reception. At first Carissa thinks she has gotten fat, but then Carissa realizes she has gotten pregnant. Dennis is there as well. He pats her hand, and he fetches her cocktail shrimp, which Carissa doesn't even like.

"How are you holding up?" Dennis asks. He smiles, and his cheeks are still dimpled.

"Don't ask her that," says Marelaine. "How do you think she's holding up? Just look at her."

Carissa finds herself thinking that Death must have been so mindlessly bored if this was what he did all day at work.

Carissa is lonely.

She tries Ouija boards, but she can never get anyone on the other line.

Sometimes Dennis comes over.

At first he is purely solicitous. He brings over frozen lasagnas that Marelaine has prepared meticulously. He brings over casseroles. He brings over pies. And then he collects the baking pans, and the casserole dishes, and the pie plates, only so that he and Marelaine can fill them all over again.

After the first month Carissa wonders if she is pregnant, but then she realizes she is only getting fat.

One time when Dennis comes over, his hand accidentally grazes against her ass as he washes a two-quart dish that previously contained a tuna casserole.

"Oops," he says, smiling. His hands are dripping water and soap onto the kitchen floor. Carissa doesn't say anything.

The next time he comes over, he brings a bottle of cabernet sauvignon along with a black cherry pie that Marelaine just baked this morning. She has crisscrossed the top with strips of dough with scalloped edges the way that pies always look when they are on television.

"How are you getting on today?" Dennis asks, and his voice sounds to Carissa like a famous person's voice. It is smooth and cool and easy to listen to, but it is not Death's voice.

"I'm fine," she says, and she takes a sip of her wine. It tastes better than the pie. "I'm fine," she says again.

They finish the bottle of wine quickly. Carissa suggests that they play Ouija because there are two of them, and Dennis agrees. Carissa has lost the pointer so they use an ace of hearts instead, and it circles and circles and circles but it only ever stops on the picture of the crescent moon. Dennis suggests that they play Spin the Bottle, and Carissa feels like it's only polite so she agrees.

The bottle spins and spins and spins, but there are only the two of them so no matter where it ends up pointing, she still has to kiss Dennis. His teeth are entirely smooth.

Carissa wakes in the middle of the night, and Dennis is still beside her. The sheets are all askew and somehow she has ended up on the wrong side of the bed. From this side, the bedroom seems strange, like it could be another place. Like she could be another person sleeping in it.

Dennis is beautiful. She cannot tell whether his hair is blond or gray in the moonlight, and so she decides that it must be both at the same time. She decides she likes to look at him while he is sleeping.

She takes the marker from the bedside table and she writes on Dennis' perfect, moon-white skin.

Abracadabra, she writes.

Open up, she writes.

I know you're in there.

"Did he tell you he was going to die?" asks Carissa.

"I never asked him," Dennis answers. "We didn't talk that much. He was Death."

Carissa is quiet for a while.

"Do you want to run away with me?" Carissa asks.

"Yes," says Dennis.

• • •

Dennis decides that they must tell Marelaine in person. Carissa wonders if she is nervous, but she decides that, in the end, she isn't. But when Dennis opens the door, Death is sitting at the table with Marelaine.

"Darling," says Dennis.

"I knew it," says Marelaine. "And with her too. I knew it would be with her."

"No," says Dennis. "It's not like that. We're in love."

"We're not in love," says Carissa. "I don't love you."

They both look at her.

"I knew it," says Marelaine once more, and she rushes out of the room. Dennis follows after her. Carissa wonders if she is supposed to go as well, but decides that she probably shouldn't. Sometimes it seems as if real life is exactly like sorority life.

"Why didn't you ever come to see me?" asks Carissa.

"That's not how it works," Death says at last. "I'm Death. I couldn't be David forever."

"I've missed you," says Carissa.

Death says nothing. He is still handsome, although Carissa can see the glint of a few threads of silver near his temples. He looks older. He looks tired. She wonders what she must look like to him.

"What are you doing here?" Carissa asks at last.

"Triple homicide," says Death.

BANG goes Marelaine's gun somewhere upstairs. And BANG again. There is a sound as bodies hit the floor.

"Oh," says Carissa. She considers this. "Oh."

They sit together in silence, and, for the first time since the funeral, Carissa feels happy again. She decides that Death does not look that old. He looks good. Death is supposed to have some gray to him. It makes him look distinguished.

"That was only two gunshots," she says.

"I know," Death says. After a moment, he says, "It was arsenic in the pies. You know. Marelaine always was such a bitch." He pauses, and pours a glass of wine for her. "I think we'll both have to wait for a bit."

"It's good to see you," Carissa says.

"I've been waiting for such a long time," says Death. "I've brought you flowers." He removes a single, yellow celandine blossom from his jacket pocket. Carissa smiles. She takes it from him gently, afraid to crush the petals. Their fingers touch, and his hand is warm, familiar.

"Where are we going?" she asks.

"You'll see," Death says. "Don't worry, Darling. We'll go together."

She breathes in the scent.

When she dreams it is of Death, and she is happy.

Helen Marshall is a critically acclaimed author, editor, and doctor of medieval studies. Her debut collection of short stories, *Hair Side, Flesh Side* (ChiZine Publications, 2012), won the 2013 British Fantasy Award for Best Newcomer. Her second collection, *Gifts for the One Who Comes After*, was released in September, 2014. She lives in Oxford, England where she spends her time staring at old books.

They were everyone and anyone, and after that night in August,
they were no more . . .

THE FLOATING GIRLS: A DOCUMENTARY

Damien Angelica Walters

The floating girls are all but forgotten now; it's easier to pretend they didn't exist, to pretend it didn't happen. But there are parents who still keep bedrooms captured in time, complete with clothes folded in bureau drawers and diaries tucked beneath pillows, everything in its place, waiting, and there are friends who still gaze at the sky, wondering how far the girls floated and if they ever fell.

Some of us haven't forgotten. Some of us never will.

Twelve years ago, three hours after the sun set on the second of August, nearly three hundred thousand girls between the ages of eleven and seventeen vanished. Eyewitness reports state that the girls floated away, yet even now, many of those eyewitnesses have recanted their stories or simply refuse to talk about it at all.

The girls lived in cities, in the suburbs, in the country. They lived in first world and third world countries. They were only children; they were one of many siblings; they were of all ethnicities and religious backgrounds. They were everyone and anyone, and after that night in August, they were no more.

I've found plenty of evidence decrying the phenomenon, but there are lists, lists of the girls who disappeared. Those who claim it's all bullshit provide other lists, girls who vanished and were found years later: the runaways; the girls involved in ugly custody battles, who were spirited away by either custodial or non-custodial parents; the girls whose decomposing bodies were recovered from forests, old drainpipes, beneath concrete patios.

But none of those girls were floating girls, only gone girls; the reports always conveniently leave that out.

I wonder about the evidence I haven't found, that doesn't exist; it seems like there should be so much more. And how many girls who vanished were never reported? And why just girls? Why just *these* girls?

As far as I can tell, very few scientists or statisticians studied the phenomenon itself. No one counseled the families; no one dug through the chaos to find the facts. Like certain religious or political scandals, everyone wanted to brush it under the rug.

Maybe it made a strange sort of sense at the time. I don't know.

Jessie and I grew up next-door in a tiny corner of suburbia. You know the sort: backyard cookouts, running through the sprinklers, drinking water from the hose, playing tag. Perfectly charming. The sort of childhood that screams ideal. The sort of childhood that could take place anywhere, in any town, not just our little corner of Baltimore, Maryland.

Our backyards were separated by a row of hedges with spaces in between perfectly sized for someone to walk through. We would flit from yard to yard— mine had the swing set and the sprinkler; hers the sandbox and hammock— and house to house, nearly inseparable, spinning circles and holding hands while we chanted Jessie and Tracy, best friends forever.

My strongest memory is how she and I spent countless hours catching fireflies. We'd keep them inside glass jars with holes poked in the lids so they wouldn't die, and we'd invent stories that the fireflies were princesses trapped in the bodies and the lights were their way of calling for help because they couldn't speak. And every night, we'd let them go, watching until they blinked out of sight, pretending they were off to find their mothers, their princes, the witches who'd cursed them.

I think you only truly make those sort of friendships in childhood; when you get older, you know better than to let people in. You know they'll only disappoint you in the end.

Video interview with Karen Michaels of Monmouth, Oregon, March 17, 2010:

[A woman is sitting in a cramped, dingy kitchen, a lit cigarette clutched tightly between two fingers, an overflowing ashtray by her side. She grimaces at the camera and looks down at her cigarette. Her face is worn and heavily lined, her shoulders hunched forward.]

"Thank you for agreeing to talk to me, Mrs. Michaels. I know this is difficult."

[Mrs. Michaels takes a drag from her cigarette. Exhales the smoke loudly.]

"Call me Karen, okay?"

"Okay, Karen. I know it's been a long time, but can you tell me what happened that night, August second—"

[She waves the hand holding the cigarette.]

"I know what night you're talking about."

[Another inhale from her cigarette. Another exhale.]

"Nina had problems with sleepwalking when she was a kid. Used to drive me crazy. For a couple years, I had to lock her bedroom door from the outside to keep her in the house. You got kids?"

"No—"

"That's right. You already told me you didn't. Who knows, maybe you're lucky. Anyway, that night, the night Nina floated, it had been years since she walked in her sleep. I heard her go down the steps, and I followed her. She went out the front door and stood on the lawn, staring down at her feet, like this."

[Mrs. Michaels stubs out her cigarette and stands with her arms straight and her head down, her hands held out a few inches from her body.]

"I thought she was sleepwalking again, that's all, so I stayed on the front porch. I was getting ready to go get her, grab her arm, and take her back in because I had to get up early in the morning. But then she went up, just up, like a balloon. I, I—"

[Video cuts off. Returns. Mrs. Michaels is wiping her eyes.]

"Are you sure you're okay?"

"Yeah, sure, I'm fine. I . . . so she went up, and I thought . . . I don't know what I thought. I ran and tried to grab her, but she was already up too far. I touched the side of her foot, but I guess, I guess I was just too late."

[She grabs another cigarette and lights it. Her voice is barely audible when she speaks again.]

"I let her go. I didn't know what else to do, so I let her go."

[Her head snaps up. She looks straight into the camera.]

"Everyone told me not to talk about it. It's like she never existed at all. But she did. She did. No one cared that she was gone. No one. Do you really think this thing, your project, will help?"

"I'd like to think it will, yes."

[She makes a sound low in her throat.]

"Will you tell me what Nina was like?"

"She was like every other kid. Listened to her music too loud, left her dirty clothes on the floor, griped about her chores, but she didn't run around wild or anything like that. She didn't drink or do drugs."

"And what was your relationship with Nina like?"

"Normal. I mean, we had fights, but nothing really serious. She was always in her room, reading or listening to music."

"What about with her siblings, her father?"

"Everyone was fine. Everything was fine."

[There's a long pause, and she looks away with tears in her eyes. Video ends.]

Jessie's father died the year we turned eight. I remember black clothing, tears, confusion, and the smell of flowers. At some point, she and I snuck out into her backyard and played in the sandbox. I don't remember what we talked about or if we talked about anything at all, but I remember how we slipped out of our dress shoes and wriggled our toes through the warm top layer of sand to the cool beneath. I remember the scent of honeysuckle thick in the air.

Recording of a telephone interview, July 28, 2012:

"You're not going to use my name, right? I don't want you to use my name."

"No, I won't."

"Good. Okay."

"Tell me what you think happened on the night of August second."

"All I can tell you is what I saw. The kid was hanging in the air in her backyard, looking like some kind of angel, only not the kind you can see through. I mean, she wasn't wearing anything like an angel would. I think she had on some kind of dress, but nothing like you see in pictures of angels or anything like that. Then she went straight up. Craziest damn thing I ever saw. I kept thinking it was the beer. I only had a couple, maybe three, but . . . "

"Did you do anything?"

"What could I do? Hell, by the time I figured out my eyes wasn't playing tricks, she was high up. I mean really high up."

"And you told the authorities what you saw?"

"Yeah, I told them. Lot of good that did me. They said I was crazy. Or drunk. People can't float. But I know what I saw, and that girl just floated up and away."

"Did you know anything about her?"

"No, she was just the kid who lived next door. She kept to herself, the whole family did. I mean they were nice enough, just not real friendly."

"Is there anything else you'd like to say?"

"You're not going to use my name for this thing, right? I don't want my name used."

"No, sir. As I said before, I won't use your name."

• • •

Jessie and I started to drift apart the summer she turned eleven, about a year after her mom remarried. I'd ask her to come over and catch fireflies, and she'd say no. I'd invite her to spend the night. She'd say no. I spent countless nights crying, trying to figure out what I'd done wrong, because best friends didn't stop talking to each other unless something was wrong.

My mother said, "Tracy, honey, that's what happens with friends sometimes. Don't worry. Maybe she's just going through a phase. You are becoming young women, you know."

I know she was only trying to help, but I wanted everything to go back to the way it had been, not the way it was.

Video footage, dated August 2, 2002:

Video opens with a scene of a backyard, complete with a hot tub, a fire pit, and tables and chairs setup for a party. There's a break in the video; when it returns, the sky is full-dark and a party is in full swing. No children are present. The camera captures several people saying hello to the cameraman, there's a break in the filming, and when it returns, the camera is stationary, capturing a wide-view of the partygoers.

5 minutes, 06 seconds: A pale blotch can be seen in the far left corner, above a row of well-trimmed hedges.

5 minutes, 08 seconds: The pale blotch is larger, the shape completely visible over the hedge.

5 minutes, 10 seconds: While the partygoers continue to drink and laugh, the blotch continues to rise.

Video editing enhancement of the last few seconds before the blotch disappears from the film clearly shows a young girl in her early teens, her face solemn, rising up through the air.

[Note: Records state the video was taken by Jack Stevenson of Denver, Colorado. Repeated attempts to contact Mr. Stevenson have been unsuccessful.]

By the time I was twelve, the drift between Jessie and I had become a crevasse. We weren't even on speaking terms. She was just a girl I used to know. As kids do, I'd made new friends and sure, her rejection of our friendship hurt and sometimes I'd look over the fence to see if she was outside, but I was a kid, just a stupid kid.

How was I supposed to know?

• • •

Photograph A: Photo shows a baobab tree and a girl beside it. On closer inspection, the girl's feet are hovering about a foot from the ground. The girl is looking away from the camera. The back of the photograph reads August 2, Shurugwi, Zimbabwe.

[Note: Photograph provided by one of the girl's family members, who asked to remain anonymous. For that reason, the name of the girl is also withheld.]

Photograph B: The central image is the Eiffel Tower in Paris, France. On the far right of the photo, a girl is suspended in the air, her arms held in the distinct way described by many others, her face serene. Using the tower as a point of measure, she is approximately 1,050 feet in the air.

[Note: Image found on a website claiming it was manipulated digitally, however, no evidence of alteration can be found in the image itself. The girl in the photograph has not yet been identified.]

Photograph C: Photo of Trakai Castle, south of Vilnius, Lithuania, taken by Algimantas Serunis of Chicago, Illinois, while on vacation. A girl's head and shoulders are visible above the westernmost tower of the castle.

[Note: The girl has been tentatively identified as Ruta Gremaila. Attempts to contact her family have been unsuccessful.]

When I was fourteen, Jessie showed up at the backdoor one night. I was blaring music and eating the last of the mint chocolate chip ice cream, knowing my dad would pretend to make a big deal about the empty container and my mom would roll her eyes at the both of us. My parents weren't home, and yes, I've wondered more than once if it would've made a difference.

"Yeah?" I remember saying.

"I was wondering if maybe you'd want to hang out for a little bit?" she asked, her voice whisper-thin, her eyes all red, like she'd been crying. Behind the red, though, there was a strange emptiness, a hollow where laughter had once lived.

I remember being surprised, more at her request than her eyes. Although I'd made new friends, she hadn't. She skulked through the halls at school like a ghost. She sat alone in the cafeteria at lunchtime and with her shoulders hunched in class. She wore baggy clothing and kept her head down so her hair almost covered her face. After school, she walked home alone.

"I can't, sorry. I have a math test tomorrow I have to study for."

"Oh, okay." She stood for a minute, toeing the doormat with the tip of her shoe. "See you around then?"

"Sure."

But I lied. There was no math test. I just didn't want to talk to her.

Video footage of interview with Sheriff Joseph Miller, Brookhaven, Pennsylvania, September 9, 2008:

"No, none of it's true. I have no idea why you'd even want to talk about it."

"So why do you think everyone reported the same thing?"

"I don't have an answer to that."

"Maybe it's because it really happened."

[He glares into the camera.]

"Look, it didn't happen. A bunch of kids ran away, a bunch more people got upset and invented some story about floating."

"But didn't three girls from your own town vanish?"

[His expression changes, and he crosses his arms over his chest.]

"Yeah."

"Don't you think that's suspect?"

"Sometimes kids, especially girls, run away together. It happens."

"And what if I told you those girls weren't even friends, didn't even go to the same schools?"

[He sighs heavily, looks at some spot in the distance, and shakes his head in dismissal.]

"We're done here. Some of us have real work to do."

On August 2, 2002, the summer Jessie and I were fifteen, I was in the backyard on a blanket, staring at the stars, waiting for one to fall so I could make a wish. My parents were out at the movies, and other than the crickets chirping, the neighborhood was quiet.

Jessie's kitchen door opened—it had a funny little squeak that all the oil in the world wouldn't fix—and Jessie walked out into the yard. All the lights in her house were off, and she was little more than a shadow flitting across the grass.

I hunched down on the blanket and watched through the hedges. She stood still in the middle of her yard for several minutes with her head down, her hands fisted at her sides. I thought about calling her name—I know I did— but then her hands relaxed, her arms extended slightly, and she lifted her chin to stare straight ahead. And then she lifted off the ground.

She was a foot in the air before I realized it wasn't an illusion, before I was able to do anything other than blink. I scrambled to my feet, told her to stop, and raced through the hedges, scratching my upper arms all to hell in the process. I shouted her name and called out for my parents, for her parents, for anyone.

Jessie never looked down, not once. I stood right underneath her, waving my arms and yelling at her to come back, until my legs couldn't hold me up anymore and my throat was too thick to speak.

My parents found me in the backyard when they got home. I was on the blanket, sitting with my grass-stained knees up to my chin, crying. I told them how Jessie just floated and kept floating until I couldn't see her anymore, until she was gone.

I saw the disbelief in their eyes. My father went over to Jessie's house, knocked on the door, and came back shrugging his shoulders after no one answered. My mom pressed her hand against my forehead, proclaimed I had a fever, and sent me to bed. I stayed there for three days.

Jessie's parents told the police she ran away.

Video footage of an attempted interview on August 18, 2011 with John Gelvin from Brawley, California, whose daughter, Rosie, age thirteen, is still listed as missing. Documents show she was reported as a floating girl. Other documents show that Child Protective Services had been called on at least one occasion before Rosie's disappearance, but no further action from CPS can be found.

"Sir, you said you saw Rosie float."

"No. I didn't. Sorry. You're the one who's mistaken. She ran away."

"But I have a report here, a police report, that says—"

"Leave me alone. Just leave me alone."

I tried to tell people the truth. My parents continued to blame the fever. When I told Jessie's parents, her mother's eyes filled with tears, the silent, terrifying kind; her stepfather told me to leave their house and never come back. They moved away a few months later and didn't tell anyone where they were going.

People at school thought I was crazy, even after the other reports came out. Jessie was just another troubled kid who ran away. It happened every day. No big deal.

If I'd been an adult, if I hadn't see Jessie float away, I wonder if I would've been as dismissive. Possibly. Probably.

I tried to tell the truth so many times, but no one would listen.

Graffiti on the side of a building in Rapid City, South Dakota, June 8, 2013, in the section of the city known as Art Alley:

SILENCE IS ITS OWN FORM OF HELIUM

[Note: According to a local artist, who asked not to be named, the graffiti was originally written on the building in September of 2002, and she's been repainting it as needed ever since. When asked if she knew the identity of the original artist or thought that the statement was related to the floating girls, she declined to answer.]

Eventually I stopped talking about it, about Jessie. I didn't forget her, but it was too hard to keep trying to explain what I saw to people who refused to believe it. I finished high school, moved out of state for college, dropped out in my second year, and came back home.

When my parents decided to sell their house and move to Florida, I found a box of photos in the attic, pictures of me and Jessie when we were young, pictures of us holding our firefly jars, grinning crazy kid smiles, those smiles that scream innocence. Our eyes were filled with laughter and happiness and hope.

And I remembered her eyes the night she came over, the night I turned her away. We all have a secret spot, a tiny light, inside us, and it doesn't take much to make that light go out. It doesn't take much to extinguish that light forever.

As I carried the photos out to my car, I decided to do something. I'm not sure if I decided to do it for Jessie or for the others or for me, but I don't think it matters.

I'm not a fifteen-year-old girl anymore, and I've spent years digging for proof, searching for the truth. Maybe now people will listen, and maybe they'll start talking.

Excerpt from "A Study into the Phenomenon of the Floating Girls", dated November 2002, author not cited:

Given a lack of concrete evidence to the phenomenon, and with evidence that a percentage of the girls were from troubled homes and had a history of running away, we can only conclude there was no phenomenon, only a strange set of coincidental circumstances.

It is also noted that there was a heavy incident of fog in the northwestern states, which may explain the visual oddities noted there.

Reports from other countries are sketchy at best with most being reported well after the disappearances in the United States, leading this researcher to determine that they were copying the phenomenon, perhaps in hope of cashing in on the notoriety. More research is needed.

[Note: There is no evidence that any further research was conducted.]

• • •

I live twenty minutes away from the house I grew up in. Kids still play in sandboxes, they still catch fireflies and run through sprinklers. At night, I stare at the sky and wonder if the girls are still floating. I think they are, and we just can't see them.

I tell Jessie I'm sorry, but the words seem so fucking inadequate. I should've been there for her. I should've listened. And after, I should've kept talking. Hell, I should've screamed and shouted. But I didn't.

No one did.

Damien Angelica Walters' short fiction has appeared or is forthcoming in various anthologies and magazines, including *Year's Best Weird Fiction: Volume One*, *The Mammoth Book of Cthulhu: New Lovecraftian Fiction*, *Cassilda's Song*, *Nightmare*, *Black Static*, and *Apex*. *Sing Me Your Scars*, a collection of her short fiction, is out now from Apex Publications, and *Paper Tigers*, a novel, is forthcoming from Dark House Press. You can find her on Twitter @ DamienAWalters or damienangelicawalters.com

According to Aristotle—and Mr. Hill—tragedy must involve a flawed, but noble, hero who suffers a change of fortune and gains knowledge . . .

MR. HILL'S DEATH

S. L. Gilbow

Mr. Hill's death is posted on YouTube. You can't actually see him. Just the back of his sunflower yellow convertible, top up, cruising along a two-lane road. The fifty-second clip, taken from a dash cam in a following car, seems rather ordinary at first, and you might think you were watching a typical drive through a wooded countryside. That is if the clip weren't titled "Tragic Car Wreck."

Emily Williams, a stack of notecards cupped in her right hand, slouches in front of a whiteboard presenting her end-of-term Tone Project.

"Tragic, an adjective," says Emily, sounding mildly uncertain.

The Tone Project is Mr. Hill's way of giving his eleventh-grade English students one last chance to boost their grades and review key terms prior to the final exam. Mr. Hill sits at a chair-desk combo in the back of the room grading the presentations. He's not dead yet.

"Pertaining to tragedy." Emily glances at her notecards then looks at Nate and Janet and Mr. Hill, making eye contact with each one, just like Mr. Hill taught her. "Associated with death and great sorrow."

"Acceptable," Mr. Hill writes in the definition block of the grading rubric. Emily's definition is accurate, but Mr. Hill had hoped for more depth, more insight. "May not fully understand tragedy," he writes.

Emily pulls a strand of blond hair back behind her shoulder, clears her throat, and reads a passage from *Macbeth*:

> *Tomorrow, and tomorrow, and tomorrow,*
> *Creeps in this petty pace from day to day*
> *To the last syllable of recorded time;*

> *And all our yesterdays have lighted fools*
> *The way to dusty death. Out, out, brief candle!*

Emily puts down her notecards and walks around the classroom displaying a diorama she made of a decapitation scene from *Cut to a Scream*, a recent horror film she highly recommends.

"These things have a tragic tone," says Emily, returning to the front of the classroom. "People suffer and die and that is tragedy."

What makes someone's story a tragedy? Mr. Hill wrote an essay on tragedy his senior year in college. The paper earned him an A, and he has considered himself an expert on tragedy ever since.

Mr. Hill leans toward the classical definition. Tragic hero. Noble stature. *Hubris*. Self-knowledge. Reversal of fortune. All the ingredients from Aristotle's *Poetics*.

According to Aristotle, and Mr. Hill, the tragic hero must be of noble stature. Mr. Hill has given that some thought, and sometimes wonders if he is noble enough to be a tragic hero. He's a teacher, certainly an important profession, but not noble by the classical standard. He's not a king. Not the principal. Not even one of the assistant principals. He's been working at Meritville High School for eight years and hasn't even made English department head yet.

Sure, he might rise to the level of Willy Loman from *Death of a Salesman* if you're inclined to go with the more modern interpretation of the tragic hero. But he's no Macbeth. Not even a Jay Gatsby. Mr. Hill doesn't come close to the classical standard by a long shot, and he knows that.

Emily ends her presentation with a video clip of a yellow convertible driving down a road.

"Is that your car, Mr. Hill?" asks Jessie.

"I don't own the only yellow convertible in the world," says Mr. Hill.

"I'm getting a car like that," says Janet. She's sending a text and thinks Mr. Hill hasn't noticed. Janet, like many of Mr. Hill's students, has recently earned her driver's license. She tends to send texts to her friends during class offering to take them home after school.

The class watches the convertible with anticipation until it fishtails to the left and then to the right, then swerves off the road, smashing into a tree, transforming into a yellow smear of crushed metal which quickly disappears off the right side of the screen.

"Cool," says Nate.

But it's not cool. Not cool at all. Mr. Hill has just watched a car, and presumably its driver, get ripped to shreds.

"Go back," says Janet, putting away her cell phone. "I didn't see it."

"Once is enough," says Mr. Hill. "More than enough." The class moans in disappointment.

"And that is my presentation of 'tragic,'" says Emily.

"Well, I guess that's tragic in a sense," says Mr. Hill, standing up.

"In a sense?" says Nate. "The guy hit a tree going at least sixty."

Seizing the opportunity to teach, Mr. Hill strides to the front of the room as Emily steps back and tries to blend in with the whiteboard. "Tragedy is more complicated than that," says Mr. Hill. "It's more than just someone hitting a tree."

"I bet you wouldn't say that if you were in that car," says Nate.

After Mr. Hill dismisses his last class for the day at three o'clock, he sits down at his computer and enters the grades for the tone presentations. As he closes the grading program and turns away from his computer, he sees something flash on his desktop. He's not quite sure what he saw. Just a flash. A flicker. He hopes there's nothing wrong with his computer. He hates dealing with tech support. He studies his computer screen and it looks all right. Then he notices something he hadn't seen before. There on his desktop is an icon labeled "Tragic Car Wreck." Mr. Hill wasn't even aware Emily had loaded the file onto his computer. He thought she had played it off her flash drive, but there it is on his desktop.

Mr. Hill takes his mouse, clicks on the video clip, and watches it again, stopping the video just before the car smashes into the tree. He watches the video clip over and over again. Not the last ten seconds. But he watches the convertible roll down the road, and he thinks about what Jessie said. The car does look a lot like his. Right color. Right model. No bumper stickers. No visible dents. Mr. Hill pauses the video and zooms in, trying to make out the rear license plate. The letters and numbers seem to be the right color and size, but they're no more than an indecipherable blur.

According to Aristotle, and Mr. Hill, the tragic hero's tragic flaw is usually *hubris* or pride.

When he wrote his essay in college, Mr. Hill wondered what his tragic flaw would be. He didn't think it was pride. He figured if he had a tragic flaw it would probably be obsession. The need to fixate on one thing to the exclusion of all others. Once it was Faulkner novels. Once it was a girl named Cindy. Once it was jogging. Now it is a video clip of a car wreck.

Mr. Hill leans in close to the screen as he watches the clip. He can't stop watching it, can't stop thinking about it, can't get those last ten seconds out of his head. He can't unsee what he has seen.

Mr. Hill closes the video file and leans back in his chair. Logically, he knows the convertible isn't his car. How could it be? But now, as the other teachers filter out of the school, he has no desire to get in his car and drive home. He finally packs some ungraded assignments into his backpack and shuffles out to the parking lot. He looks his car over carefully, hoping to spot some feature that would distinguish it from the car in the video, but he doesn't find one.

Once he's on the freeway, headed north, he drives cautiously in the right lane, looking repeatedly into his rearview mirror, making sure no one gets too close. A truck in front of him slows, and he hits his breaks hard, startling himself. When he finally takes the cut-off home, he creeps along, driving like the people he has always complained about, thinking of the accident in that damned video clip.

As the term draws to a close and the winter break nears, Mr. Hill's students finish their tone presentations. Mr. Hill grades Nate's "accusatory," Janet's "haughty," Jamie's " jovial," and Sara's "sardonic." Nothing he sees, however, sticks with him like Emily's "tragic."

Every afternoon, Mr. Hill enters the scores for the students' presentations for the day. Then he clicks on Emily's video and watches it. He now watches the entire thing. All fifty seconds. Half a dozen times every day. And as he watches the video he wonders if he will ever be able to get the image of the sports car slamming into the tree out of his head.

On the first Saturday of the winter break, Mr. Hill drives to Dusty's Auto World on Main Street, haggles with Dusty himself for half an hour, and trades in his sunflower convertible for a black, four-door sedan.

Mr. Hill spends the winter break at home putting together his unit plan for the next term. He decides to start off the year by teaching *Macbeth*, so he reads the play again and reviews some of his study notes from college. He rereads Aristotle's Poetics and thinks deeply about tragedy and how to help his students really understand what makes something tragic. What he doesn't think about anymore is the yellow convertible hitting the tree.

In early January, Mr. Hill's first class of the new term wanders in, grumbling about having to come back to school. Mr. Hill lets the students talk while he hands out paperback copies of *Macbeth*. When he gets to Emily's desk, she holds up her cell phone.

"Look familiar?" she asks, showing Mr. Hill a picture of her standing beside a yellow convertible at Dusty's Auto World.

"That's my car," says Mr. Hill.

"Not anymore," says Nate. "She bought it."

"Her dad bought it for her," says Janet.

"I love your car, Mr. Hill." Emily smiles, looking younger than Mr. Hill thought she ever could.

During his lunch break, Mr. Hill sits in his classroom all alone eating a turkey sandwich and watching "Tragic Car Wreck " over and over. But this time he is looking for something different. He hadn't been able to identify the driver before, but now he is trying to see if he can tell if the driver is male or female. All he needs is one quick glimpse of the back of the driver's head. All he needs is one single flash of sunlight off of blond hair. There is no flash. There is no glimpse. There is no clue.

Mr. Hill closes the file, deletes it off his desktop, and walks to the restroom down the hall to wash his hands. When he returns, the file is back on his desktop. He changes the name of the file to "Fuzzy Kittens" to get the words "Tragic Car Wreck " off his desktop. After a few seconds, the name changes back. Mr. Hill right clicks on the desktop icon and checks the file properties. Everything seems normal enough except for the creation date of the file. It's dated this year, but February 2—a month from today.

According to Aristotle, and Mr. Hill, the tragic hero must gain self-knowledge. Mr. Hill does learn something important about himself. He learns he is an asshole. He also believes now, with an unsettling certainty, that the car is his. No, not his. The car is Emily's.

He had stopped thinking about the car after he traded it in. Now, he sits back in his chair staring at the words "Tragic Car Wreck " on his desktop. He knows that he won't die in that car. He solved that problem when he sold it. He won't be in it when it hits the tree. But somebody will. And he thinks he knows who.

Macbeth's future is foretold by three witches. Mr. Hill's is foretold by a video clip off of YouTube.

Mr. Hill isn't sure how much time he has left. According to the file, the video will be downloaded off of YouTube in less than a month. He's not quite sure how it will be downloaded or who will do it, but he knows it will happen. He also knows he doesn't have much time left.

After school, Mr. Hill goes home, eats a burger, and chases it down with a dark ale. Then he drives to Emily's house.

"Everything okay?" asks Mr. Williams opening the front door.

Mr. Hill had met Mr. Williams at a parent/teacher conference at the beginning of the school year. He was a large, soft-spoken man who talked about how important it was to him that Emily learn to read and write well. He had such hopes for her and wanted her to get into a good college.

"Everything is fine," says Mr. Hill. "Emily is doing wonderfully in class," he adds, following Mr. Williams into the living room.

"You know, I helped her on that project," says Mr. Williams. "I helped her pick the passage from *Macbeth*. That's okay, isn't it?"

"That's fine," says Mr. Hill.

"So, what brings you here?" asks Mr. Williams.

It takes Mr. Hill a while to convince Emily's father to sell him the car. Mr. Hill explains that he hadn't realized how much the car meant to him when he sold it. He tells Mr. Williams that he was short on cash, but had come into some money recently. He tells him the car is as important to him as life itself.

Mr. Williams nods in understanding and finally calls Emily into the room.

"Mr. Hill would like his car back," says Emily's father.

"Really?" says Emily, her voice not much more than a whisper.

"Afraid so," says her father.

"But he sold it," says Emily. "He didn't want it anymore. I do."

"It would mean a lot to me," says Mr. Hill.

"Mr. Hill." She is pleading now. "I love that car."

"I understand," says Mr. Hill. "I didn't realize what I was doing when I sold it. I didn't realize the mistake I was making."

Mr. Hill looks at Emily and looks at her hard, studying her blond hair and soft features, picturing her lying dead in the wreckage of a yellow sports car, her face mangled, her hair bloody. No, he can't stop Emily from dying. She is going to die. She is going to die someday. But he doesn't want any part of it. It can't be his fault. "Emily," he says, "I made a mistake. A big mistake."

Mr. Hill ends up paying more for the car then he got for it when he traded it in. It doesn't matter though. He has enough in the bank to cover the cost, and he doesn't think he will be needing much money in the future.

• • •

Mr. Hill doesn't die for another two weeks. During those two weeks Emily's class is pretty difficult.

When he starts class one morning by asking everyone to think about what is really important to them in life, Emily responds, "My car."

The next day, Mr. Hill asks Nate what he is going to do after high school. He says he is going to get a job so he can earn enough money to buy a car. Then he is going to hide it from Mr. Hill.

"A yellow convertible," becomes the standard answer to every question Mr. Hill asks.

One afternoon on Mr. Hill's way home, there is a wreck on the highway. Traffic backs up, so he gets off and takes a detour home. As long as he has lived here, he doesn't think he has taken this road more than a couple of times. But it now seems very familiar to him. It seems as if he has driven it a hundred times. It is the road in the video clip. Mr. Hill looks in his rearview mirror and sees a car following him. He can't tell if it has a dash cam, but he's guessing it does. He should slow down. He knows that. But he doesn't. He just hits the gas and drives faster and faster.

There's not much question on the reversal of fortune part. Macbeth dies. Jay Gatsby dies. Willy Loman dies. Mr. Hill dies.

Most of Mr. Hill's students come to his funeral. They file into Plot 841 in Solemn Nights Cemetery where Mr. Hill's casket is perched over his open grave. It is a closed casket ceremony.

Janet is crying. Nate, for once, is silent. Emily is there with her father.

"Did you see the clip?" asks Sara. "I heard it was on YouTube."

Emily shakes her head. "I don't want to see it," she says. "It's just such a tragedy."

Mr. Hill would say, "No, it isn't." He would say that he isn't Macbeth or Jay Gatsby or Willie Loman. It doesn't really matter though. All that's left of Mr. Hill is a fifty-second drive he takes hundreds of times every day, always wondering how he got there, sometimes alone, sometimes with Aristotle sitting beside him, but always ending up the same way.

⟨⟨—⟩⟩

S. L. Gilbow is an active member of Science Fiction and Fantasy Writers of America and a 2011 graduate of Clarion West Writers Workshop. His stories have appeared in *The Magazine of Fantasy & Science Fiction, Lightspeed, Rose Red Review, The Dark,* and anthologies *Federations* and *Brave New Worlds.* Gilbow is a retired Air Force lieutenant colonel and navigator with over two thousand flying hours in the B-52. He currently teaches English at Thomas Nelson Community College in Hampton, Virginia.

Madam Damnable was here now and
she was going to take care of everything . . .

MADAM DAMNABLE'S SEWING CIRCLE

Elizabeth Bear

Seattle, Washington, 1899

You ain't gonna like what I have to tell you, but I'm gonna tell you anyway. See, my name is Karen Memery, like *memory* only spelt with an e, and I'm one of the girls what works in the Hôtel Mon Cherie. Hôtel has a little hat over the o like that. It's French, so Beatrice tells me.

Some call it the Cherry Hotel. But most just say it's Madam Damnable's Sewing Circle and have done. So I guess that makes me a seamstress, just like Beatrice and Miss Francina and Pollywog and Effie and all the other girls. I pay my sewing machine tax to the city, which is fifty dollar a week, and they don't care if your sewing machine's got a foot treadle, if you take my meaning.

Sure, fifty dollar'd be a year's wages back in Hay Camp for a real seamstress, and here in Seattle it'll barely buy you a dozen of eggs, a shot of whisky, and a couple pair of those new blue jeans that Mister Strauss is sewing. But here in Seattle a girl can pay fifty dollar a week and have enough to live on and put a little away besides, even after the house's cut.

You want to work for a house, if you're working. I mean . . . "sewing." Because Madam Damnable is a battleship, and she runs the Hôtel Mon Cherie tight, but nobody hits her girls, and we've got an Ancient and Honorable Guild of Seamstresses, and nobody's going to make us do anything we really don't want to unless it's by paying us so much we'll consider it in spite of ourselves. Not like in the cribs down in the mud beside the pier with the locked doors and no fireplaces, where they keep the Chinese and the Indian girls the sailors use.

I've never been down there, but I've been up along the pier, and you can't hear the girls except once in a while when one goes crazy, crying and screaming.

All you can hear up there is the sailors cursing and the dog teams barking in the kennels like they know they're going to be loaded on those deep-keel ships and sent up north to Alaska to probably freeze in the snow and die along with some Eastern idiot who's heard there's gold. Sometimes girls go north too—there's supposed to be good money from the men in the gold camps—but I ain't known but one who came back ever.

That was Madam Damnable, and when she came back she had enough to set herself up in business and keep her seamstresses dry and clean. She was also missing half her right foot from gangrene, and five or six teeth from scurvy, so I guess it's up to you to decide if you think that was worth it to her.

She seems pretty happy, and she walks all right with a cane, but it ain't half hard for her to get up and down the ladders to street level.

So anyway, about them ladders. Madam Damnable's is in the deep part of town where they ain't finished raising the streets yet. What I mean is when they started building up the roads a while back so the sound wouldn't flood up the downtown every spring tide, they couldn't very well close down all the shopping—and all the *sewing*—so they built these big old masonry walls and started filling in the streets between them up to the top level with just any old thing they had to throw in there. There's dead horses down there, dead men for all I know. Street signs and old couches and broken-up wagons and such.

They left the sidewalks down where they had been, and the front doors to the shops and such, so on each block there's this passage between the walls of the street and the walls of the buildings. And since horses can't climb ladders and wagons can't fly, they didn't connect the blocks. Well, I guess they could have built tunnels, but it's bad enough down there on the walkways at night as it is now and worth your life to go out without a couple of good big lantern bearers each with a cudgel.

At Madam Damnable's, we've got Crispin, who's our doorman and about as big as a house. He's the only man allowed to live in the hotel, as he doesn't care for humping with women. He hardly talks, and he's real calm and quiet, but you never feel not safe with him standing right behind you, even when you're strong-arming out a drunk or a deadbeat. Especially if Miss Francina is standing on the other side.

So all over downtown, from one block to the next you've got to climb a ladder—in your hoop skirts and corset and bustle, that ain't no small thing even if you've got two good feet in your boots to stand on—and in our part of town that's thirty-two feet from down on the walk up to street level.

When the water table's high, the walks still flood out, of course. Bet you guessed that without me.

They filled up the streets at the top of town first, because the rich folk live there—Colonel Marsh who owns the lumber mill and such. And Skid Row they didn't fill in at all, because they needed it steep on account of the logs, so there's staircases up from it to the new streets, where the new streets are finished and sometimes where they ain't. The better neighborhoods got steam lifts, too, all brass and shiny, so the rich ladies ain't got to show their bloomers to the whole world climbing ladders. Nobody cares if a soiled dove shows off her underthings, I guess, as long as the *underthings* is clean.

Up there some places the fill was only eight feet, and they've got the new sidewalks finished over top of the old already. What they did there was use deck prisms meant for ships, green and blue from the glass factory on the north end, set in metal gratings so that when there's light the light can shine down.

Down here we'll get wood plank, I expect, and like it. And then Madam Damnable will just keep those ruby lamps by the front door burning all the time.

The red light looks nice on the gilt, anyway.

Our business mostly ain't sailors but gold camp men coming or going to Anchorage, which is about the stupidest thing you ever could get to naming a harbor. I mean, why not just call it "Harbor," like it was the only one ever? So we get late nights, sure, but our trade's more late afternoon to, say, two or four, more like a saloon than like those poor girls down under the docks who work all night, five dollar a poke, when the neap tide keeps the ships locked in. Which means most nights 'cept Fridays and Saturdays by three we're down in the dining room while Miss Bethel serves us supper. She's the cook and barkeep. She don't work the parlor, but she feeds us better than we'd get at home and she keeps a sharp eye on the patrons.

Sundays, we close down for the Sabbath, and such girls as like can get their churching in.

I don't remember which day it was exactly that Merry Lee and Priya came staggering into the parlor a little before three in the morning, but I can tell you it wasn't a Friday or Saturday, because all the punters had gone home except one who'd paid Prudence for an all-night "alteration session" and was up in the Chinese Room with her getting his seams ripped, if you take my meaning. The rest of us—just the girls and Crispin, not Madam Damnable—were in our robes and slippers, faces scrubbed and hair down, sitting in the library when it happened. We don't use the parlor except for working. Beatrice, who's the only one at the hotel younger than me, was practicing reading out loud to the rest of us, her slim dark fingers bent back holding the big ivory-bound book of Grimm's fairy tales.

We'd just settled in with tea and biscuits when there was a crash down the ladder out front and the sound of somebody crying like her leg was broke. Given the sound of the thump, I reckoned that might not be too far from the truth of it.

Crispin and Miss Francina gave one another The Look, and while Beatrice put the ribbon in her book they both got up and moved toward the front door. Crispin I already said about, and the thing about Miss Francina is that Miss Francina's got a pecker under her dress. But that ain't nothing but God's rude joke. She's one of us girls every way else, and handy for a bouncer.

I followed along just behind them, and so did Effie. Though I'm young, we're the sturdiest girls, and Effie can shoot well enough that Madam Damnable lets her keep a gun in her room. Miss Bethel kept a pump shotgun under the bar, too, but she was upstairs in bed already, so while Crispin was unlocking the door I went over and got it, working the breech to make sure it was loaded. Beatrice grabbed Signor, the deaf white cat who lives in the parlor—he's got one blue eye and one yellow and he's loud as a ghost when he wants something— and pulled him back into the library with the rest of the girls.

When I got up behind Crispin, it was all silence outside. Not even anymore crying, though we all stood with our ears straining. Crispin pulled open the door and Miss Francina went striding out into that burning cold in her negligee and marabou slippers like she owned the night and the rest of us was just paying rent on it. I skin-flinched, just from nerves, but it was okay because I'd had the sense to keep my finger off the shotgun triggers.

And then Miss Francina said "Sweet child Christ!" in that breathy voice of hers and Crispin was through the door with his truncheon, bald head shining in the red lantern light. I heard him curse too, but it sounded worried rather than angry or fearful, so I let the shotgun muzzle droop and walked up to the doorway just in time to grab the arm of a pretty little Indian girl—Eastern Indian, not American Indian—who was half-naked and in hysterics. Her clothes had never been good, or warm enough for the night, though somewhere she'd gotten some lace-up boots and a man's coat too big for her. All she had on else was a ripped-up shift all stained across the bosom, and I could tell she weren't wearing nothing under it.

She was turned around, tugging something—another girl's arm, poking out frontward between Crispin and Miss Francina where they were half-dragging her. Once they got both girls inside in the light, Effie lunged forward and slammed the door.

"Here, Karen," Crispin said in his big slow molasses voice. "You take this little one. Bring her after. I'll get Miss Merry here upstairs to the sickroom."

Miss Francina stepped back and I could see that the girl between them was somebody I knew, at least by reputation. Not a girl, really. A woman, a Chinese woman.

"Aw, shit," Effie said. Not only can she shoot, but Effie's not real well-spoken. "That's Merry Lee."

Merry Lee, which was as close as most American tongues could get to her real name I guess, was half-conscious and half-fighting, batting at Crispin's hands while he swung her up into his arms. Miss Francina stuck her own hands in there to try to hold her still, where they looked very white against all the red on Merry Lee's face and arms.

Effie said, "She's gunshot. I guess all that running around Chinatown busting out crib whores finally done caught up with her. You know'd it was sooner or later going to."

"You hush about things you know nothing about," Miss Francina said, so Effie drew back chastened like and said, "I didn't mean nothing by it."

"Go and watch the door, Effie," Miss Francina said. I gave Effie the shotgun. Effie took it and did, not sulking at all. Effie talks without thinking sometimes, but she's a good girl. Madam Damnable don't tolerate them what ain't.

The girl in my arms wanted to get loose of me—she pulled away once and threw herself at Crispin, but Miss Francina caught her and gave her back, and honest she was mostly too light and skinny to put up a good fight once I had a grip on her. I tried to talk to her, tell her she was safe and we were going to take care of her and Merry Lee both. I didn't think then she understood a word of it, but I found out later her English was pretty good so I think it was mostly that she couldn't hardly have been more upset. But something got through to her, because after a minute of twisting her wrists and getting blood all over my good pink flannel she stood still, shivering, and let me bundle her up the stairs after Crispin and Merry Lee while Miss Francina went to fetch Miss Lizzie.

We followed them down the long rose-painted hall to the sickroom door. Crispin wanted to take Merry Lee in without the Indian girl, but the girl weren't having none of it. She leaned against my arms and keened through the doorway, and finally Crispin just looked at me helplessly and said, "Karen honey, you better bring that child in here before she cries down the roof."

She was better inside, sitting in a chair beside the bed while Crispin checked over Merry Lee for where she was hurt worst. Effie was right about her being gunshot, too—she had a graze through her long black hair showing bone, and that was where most of the blood was from, but there was a bullet in her back too and Crispin couldn't tell from looking if it had gone through to a lung. It wasn't in the spine, he said, or she wouldn't have been walking.

Just as he was stoking up the surgery machine—it hissed and clanked like a steam engine, which was never too reassuring when you just needed a boil lanced or something—Miss Lizzie came barreling up the stairs with an armload of towels and a bottle of clear corn liquor, and I knew it was time for me to be leaving. The girl wasn't going anywhere, but she didn't look like interfering anymore—she just leaned forward in the bedside chair moaning in her throat like a hurt kitten, both hands clenched on the cane arms.

Crispin could handle her if she did anything. And he could hold down Merry Lee if she woke up that much.

I slipped through the door while Miss Lizzie was cutting the dress off Merry Lee's back. I'd seen her and that machine pull a bullet before, and I didn't feel like puking.

I got downstairs just as somebody started trying to kick in the front door.

In all the fuss, Effie hadn't thrown the bolt, which should be second nature but you'd be surprised what you can forget when there's blood all over everywhere and people are handing you guns. The good thing was that I had handed her the gun, and when the front doors busted in on their hinges she had the presence of mind to raise up that gun and yell at the top of her little lungs, "Stop!"

They didn't, though. There were four of them, and they came boiling through the door like a confusion of scalded weasels, shouting and swearing. They checked just inside, staring from side to side and trading glances, and from halfway up the stairs I got a real fine look at all of them. It was Peter Bantle and three of his bully boys, all of them tricked out in gold watch-chains and brocade and carrying truncheons and chains along with their lanterns, and you never saw a crew more looking for a fight.

The edges of the big doors were splintered where they'd busted out the latch. So maybe they'd have broken out the bolt trying to get in anyway.

"I said *stop*," said Effie, all alone in her nightgown in the middle of the floor, that big gun on her shoulder looking like to tip her over.

Miss Francina wasn't anywhere to be seen, and I could tell from the sounds through the sickroom door that Crispin had his hands full of Merry Lee.

Madam Damnable, bless her heart, was half-deaf from working in dance halls; she might have gone up to bed and even if Miss Francina had headed up to fetch her it would take her a minute to find her cane and glasses, which meant a minute in which somebody had to do something.

I didn't think on it. I just jumped over the banister, flannel gown and quilted robe and slippers and all, exactly the way Miss Bethel was always after me about for it not being ladylike, and thumped down on the red velvet couch below the staircase.

I stepped off the couch, swept my robe up like skirts, and stuck my chin out. "Peter Bantle," I said, real loud, hoping wherever Miss Francina had got off to she would hear me and come running, "you wipe your damn muddy feet before you come into my parlor."

Now I ain't one of the smaller girls—like I said, I'm sturdy—and Peter Bantle is like his name—a banty and a peckerwood—which is probably why he struts so much. I'm plump too—the men like that—and I'm broad across the shoulders, and when I came marching up beside Effie he had to look up to meet my eyes. I saw him frown a little on the size I had on him.

The three in front of him were plenty big, though, and they didn't look impressed by two girls with a single pump shotgun between them. Bantle's men had all kinds of gear hung on them I didn't even recognize, technologics and contrivances with lenses and brass tubes and glossy black enamel. Bantle his own self had a kind of gauntlet on his left hand, stiff boiled leather segmented so the rubber underneath showed through, copper coils on each segment connected by bare wires.

I'd heard about that thing; I talked to a girl once he made piss herself with it. She had burns all up her arm where he'd grabbed her. But I didn't look at it, and I didn't let him see me shudder. You get to know a lot about men in my work, and men like Peter Bantle? They're all over seeing a woman shudder.

I don't take to men who like to hit. If he reached out at me with that gadget, I was afraid I'd like to kill him.

He didn't, though. He just ignored me, and looked over at Effie, who he could get eye to eye with. He sneered at her and through a curled lip said, "Where's Madam Damnable?"

"She's busy," I said. Only reason I didn't step in front of Effie was on account of she had the gun, but the urge to was that strong. "Me and Effie can help you. Or escort you out, if you'd rather."

Miss Bethel would have cringed at my grammar, too. But right then I couldn't afford to stammer over it to make it pretty.

Effie settled that gun on her shoulder a little better and lowered her eye to sight down the barrel. Bantle's men looked unimpressed so hard I could tell they was a little nervous. One hefted his black rubber truncheon.

"You got one of my whores in here, you little chit, and that thieving outlaw Merry Lee." Bantle's voice was all out of proportion with his weedy little body. Maybe he was wearing some kind of amplifier in that high flounced collar of his. "I aim to have them with me when I go. And if you're lucky and give them over nice and easy, my boys here won't bust up your face *or* your parlor."

Rightly, I didn't know what to say. It wasn't my house, after all; Madam Damnable gives us a lot of liberty but setting the rules of her parlor and offering sanctuary to someone else's girls ain't in it. But I knew she didn't like Peter Bantle, with his bruised-up, hungry crib whores and his saddle shoes, and since he had come crashing through the front door with three armed men and a world of insolence, I figured I had a little more scope than usual.

"You're going to leave this parlor now," I said. "And shut the door behind you. And Madam Damnable will send somebody around in the morning so you can settle up for the lock you busted."

"I know they came in here," Bantle said. "There's Chink whore blood all over your hands and the floor here."

Oh, I knew the answer to that one. I'd heard Madam Damnable say it often enough. "It's not the house's policy to discuss anyone who we may or may not be entertaining."

Then the thing happened that I ain't been able to make head nor tail of. My head went all sort of sticky fuzzy, like your mouth when you wake up, and I started feeling like maybe Bantle had a point. That *was* one of his girls upstairs, and Merry Lee *had* brought her here—or vice versa maybe—without asking. And didn't she owe him, that girl, for paying to have her brought over from India? And there was Effie pointing a gun at him.

Bantle was pointing that glove at me, finger and thumb cocked like he was making a "gun." I had another skin-flinch, this time as I wondered if Bantle could *shoot* electricity out of that thing. His eyes sort of . . . glittered, with the reflections moving across them. It was like what they say Mesmeric—I think Mr. Mesmer was the fellow's name?

"Do it," Bantle said, and God help me didn't I think it seemed like a good idea.

I was just about reaching over to grab the barrel of Effie's shotgun when the library door eased open off to my left. Through the crack I could see Beatrice's bright eyes peeping. Bantle saw her too, because he snarled, "Get that Negra whore out here," and one of his standover men started toward her.

I had just enough warning to snatch back my reaching hand and slap my palms over my ears before Effie jerked the gun up and sent a load of buckshot through the stained glass over the door panels that didn't never get no sun no more anyhow. The window burst out like a spray of glory and Bantle and his men all ducked and cringed like quirted hounds.

I just stood there, dumbfounded, useless, as full of shame for what I'd been thinking about doing to Effie and Madam Damnable as some folks think I ought to be for whoring.

"I got four more shells," Effie said. "Go on. *Go and get her.*"

The bully who'd started moving couldn't seem to make his feet work all of a sudden, like the floor'd got as sticky as my head had been. Without looking over at Beatrice, I said, "Bea sweetie, you take Pollywog and go run get the constable. It seems these gentlemen have lost their way and need directions."

When it was coming out of my mouth, I couldn't believe it. The words sounded calm and smooth, the opposite of the sticky fuzz I'd been feeling a moment before. I even saw one of the bully boys take a half-step back. It didn't impress Peter Bantle, though, because while the library door was closing across Beatrice's face he started forward. Effie worked the pump on the shotgun, but he looked right at her and sneered, "You don't have the *balls*," and then he was reaching for me with that awful glove and I didn't know yet if I was going to scream or run or try to hit him, or if Effie was really going to have to learn to shoot him.

But a big voice arrested him before I had to decide.

"Peter Bantle, just what the hell do you think you're doing in my house?"

Peter Bantle didn't have the sense to turn around and run when he heard the ferrule of Madam Damnable's cane clicking on the marble tile at the top of the stair. He did let his hand fall, though, and stepped back smartly. I heard Effie let her breath go. I looked over at her pale, sweaty face and saw her move her finger off the trigger.

She really had been gonna shoot him.

I stepped back and half-turned so I could watch Madam Damnable coming down the stairs, her cane in one hand, the other clenching on the banister with each step.

She was a great battleship of a woman, her black hair gone all steel-color at the temples. Her eyes hadn't had to go steel-color; they started off that way. Miss Francina was behind her on the one side and Miss Bethel on the other, and they didn't look like they was in any hurry nor in any mood for conversation.

"You got one of my girls in here, Alice," Peter Bantle said.

She reached the bottom of the stairs and Miss Bethel fanned off left to come take the shotgun from Effie.

"You speak with respect to Madam Damnable," Miss Francina said.

Bantle turned his head and spat on the fireplace rug. "I'll give a tart what respect she deserves. Now are you going to give me my whore back or not?"

Madam Damnable kept coming, slow and inexorable, like a steam locomotive rolling through the yard. She was in her robe and slippers, like the rest of us, and it didn't one wit make her less scary. "I'll give you your head back if you don't step outside my parlor. You may think you can own folks, Peter Bantle, but this here Seattle is a free city, and no letter of indenture signed overseas is going to hold water. The constable's on his way, and if you're not gone when he gets here I'm going to have him arrest you and your boys for trespass, breaking and entering, and malicious mischief. I pay more in taxes than you do, so you know how that's going to end." She gestured to the broken door and the busted-out window. "The evidence is right there."

"Your own girl shot out that window!" Outrage made his voice squeak.

I had to hide my laugh behind my hand. Effie squeezed the other one. She was shaking, but it was okay. Madam Damnable was here now and she was going to take care of everything.

Peter Bantle knew it, too. He had already taken a step back, and when you were faced with Madam Damnable, there was no coming back from that. He drew himself up in the doorway as his bully boys collapsed around him. Madam Damnable kept walking forward, and all four of them slid out the door like water running out a drain.

Their boots crunched in the glass outside. He couldn't resist a parting shot, but he called it over his shoulder, and it didn't so much as shift Madam Damnable's nighttime braid against her shoulders. "You ain't heard the last of this, Alice."

"For tonight, I think I have."

He took two more steps away. "And it's Hôtel *Ma* Cherie, you stupid slag!"

We heard the boots on the broken ladder before Madam Damnable breathed out, and let herself look around at us. "Well," she said cheerfully, "what a mess. Effie, fetch a bucket. Miss Bethel, put that gun away and find the broom, honey. Karen, you go tell Crispin when they're done with the Chinese girl he's to come down here and board up this window and sweep the glass up. He'll just have to sit by the door until we can get in a locksmith. Miss Francina, you go after Beatrice and Pollywog and tell them we won't need the constable."

Miss Francina bit her lip. "Are you sure, ma'am?"

Madam Damnable's hand glittered with diamonds and rubies when she flipped it. "I'm sure. Go on, sweeties, scoot." She paused. "Oh, and ladies? That was quick thinking. Well done."

When I came back up the grand stair with coffee in the china service, the sickroom door was still closed, but I didn't hear any screaming or any steam engine chugging through it which could only be a good sign. If Merry Lee was still under the knife, she would have been screaming and the machine would have been whining and wheezing away, and if she had died of it, I thought the girl would be screaming instead. So I rapped kind of light on the frame, on account of if Crispin or Miss Lizzie was busy in there I didn't want to startle them. It took me two tries to make my hand move, I was still that ashamed of myself from downstairs.

His voice floated back. "It's safe to come through." So I set the tray on my hip and turned the knob left-handed, slow in case there was somebody behind the door. The sickroom's different from our other bedrooms. There's no wallpaper and the sheets aren't fancy, and the bedstead and floor and all is just painted white. It makes it easy to just bleach or paint over again if there's a bad mess, and you'd rather paint stained wood than rip up carpet with puke or pus or crusted blood in it any day. The knife machine kind of hangs in one corner on a frame, like a shiny spider with all black rubber belts between the gears to make the limbs dance. It's one of only three or four in the city, and it needs somebody skilled as Miss Lizzie to run it, but it don't hesitate—which when you're cutting flesh, is a blessing—and it don't balk at some operations like other doctors might. And you always know its tools is clean, because Crispin boils 'em after every use.

When I stepped inside, that whole white room looked like it had been splashed about with red paint, and none too carefully. Crispin looked up from washing his hands in a pink-tinged basin with clotted blood floating like strings of tidepool slime around the edges. Merry Lee was laid sleeping or insensible in the bed on her side, clean sheets tucked around her waist and a man's white button shirt on her backwards so you could get to the dressings on her back. There was a mask over her face, and Crispin's other big enamel-knobbed brass machine that handles all those sickbed things that the steam-powered knife machine doesn't was kind of wheezing and whirring around her, its clockworks all wound up fresh and humming. The bloody sheets were heaped up in the basket, and the Indian girl was perched on the chair by the head of the bed, holding Merry's sallow hand clutched between her olive ones and rocking back and forth just a tiny bit, like she was trying with all her might to hold herself still.

I picked my way between smears of blood. Crispin looked up, grinning instead of grim, so I knew Merry Lee was going to be just fine unless the blood poisoning got her.

"Karen honey, you are a delivering angel." He nodded to the tray. "This here is Priya. She helped me change the sheets."

I got a good look at her and Merry Lee while I set the coffee on the cleanest bureau. Merry was a lot younger than I would have expected from the stories, fresh-faced and sweet as a babe in her sleep and maybe seventeen, eighteen—not more than a year or two older than me.

Given she's been a thorn in the side of Peter Bantle and Amrutar—who's like Bantle's older, meaner, richer, Indian twin—and the rest of those cribhouse pimps for longer than I've been working, she must have started pretty young. Which ain't no surprise, given some of Peter Bantle's girls—and boys too—ain't no older than your sister, and before she got away from Amrutar, Merry Lee is supposed to have been one of them.

The Indian girl had taken off that coat and Crispin or somebody must have given her a clean shift. Now I could see her arms and legs and neck, she was skinnier than anybody ought to be who wasn't starving to death. I sat there watching the knobs of her wrists and elbows stick out and the tendon strings move in the backs of her hands. I guess sailors and merchantmen don't care so much if the slatterns they visit are pretty so long as they're cheap, and it's dark in a whore's crib anyway; plus, I guess if Peter Bantle underfeeds his girls they're cheap keepers.

Still, as I sat there looking at her, her bloody tangled hair and her cheekbones all sharp under skin the color of an old, old brass statue's, it more and more griped me thinking on it. And it more and more griped me that I'd been going to let Bantle have her.

And what the hell had I been thinking? That wasn't like me at all.

There was plenty coffee in the pot, cream and sugar too, and I'd brought up cups for everybody. But it didn't look like the Indian girl—Priya—was going to let go of Merry Lee's hand and pour herself a cup.

So I did it for her, loaded it up with cream and sugar, and balanced all but one of the biscuits I'd brought along on the saucer when I carried it to her.

She looked up surprised when I touched her hand to put the saucer in it, like she might have pulled away. She wasn't any older than me either, and this close I could see all the bruises on her under the brown of her skin—layers of them.

There was red fresh scrapes that would blossom into something spectacular, that might have been from dragging Merry Lee bleeding across half of Seattle. There was black-purple ones with red mottles like pansy blossoms. And there was every shade of green and yellow, and you could pick out the hand and fingerprints among 'em. And the red skinned-off slick-looking burns from Peter Bantle's electric glove, too, which made me angry and sick in all sorts of ways I couldn't even find half the words to tell you.

She was a fighter, and it had cost her. My daddy was a horse-tamer, and he taught me. Some men don't know how to manage a woman or a horse or a dog. Where a good master earns trust and makes a partner of a smart wife or beast—acts the protector and gets all the benefit of those brains and that spirit—all the bad ones know is how to crush it out and make them cringing meek. There's a reason they call it "breaking."

The more spirit, the longer it takes to break them. And the strongest ones you can't break at all. They die on it, and my daddy used to say it was a damned tragic bloody loss.

He probably wouldn't think much of me working on my back, but what he taught me kept me safe anyway, and it wasn't like either of us asked him to go dying.

Priya looked up at me through all those bruises, and I could see in her eyes what I saw in some of my daddy's Spanish mustang ponies. You'd never break this one. You'd never even bend her. She'd die like Joan of Arc first, and spit blood on you through a smile.

My hand shook when I pushed the coffee at her.

"I can't take that," she said, and that was my second surprise. Her English wasn't no worse than mine, and maybe a little better. "You can't wait on me. You're a white lady."

"I'm a white tart," I said, and let her see me grin. "And you need it if you're going to sit up with Miss Lee here. You're skin over bones, and how far did you carry her tonight?"

I thought she'd look down, but she didn't. Her eyes—you'd call 'em black, but that was only if you didn't look too closely. Like people call coffee black. And her hair was the same; it wasn't not-black, if you take my meaning, but the highlights in it were chestnut-red. I knew I wasn't supposed to think so, but she was beautiful.

"She got shot coming out from under the pier," she said. "She told me where to run to."

Which was a half-mile off, and uphill the whole way. I poked the coffee at her again, and this time she let go of Merry Lee's hand with one of hers and lifted the cup off the saucer, which seemed like meeting me halfway. I leaned around her to put the saucer and the biscuits on the bedside stand. I could still hear Crispin moving around behind me and I was sure he was listening, but that was fine. I'd trust Crispin to birth my babies.

She swallowed. "I heard Mister Bantle shouting downstairs."

There was more she meant to say, but it wouldn't come out. Like it won't sometimes. I knew what she wanted to ask anyway, because it was the same I would have wanted if I was her. "Priya—did I say that right?"

She sipped the coffee and then looked at it funny, like she'd never tasted such a thing. "Priyadarshini," she said. "Priya is fine. This is sweet."

"I put sugar in it," I said. "You need it. In a minute here I'm going to head down to the kitchen and see if Miss Bethel can rustle up a plate of supper for you. But what I'm trying to say is Madam Damnable—this is Madam Damnable's house Merry Lee brought you to—she's not going to give you back to Bantle for him to beat on no more."

I'm not sure she believed me. But she looked down at her coffee and she nodded. I patted her shoulder where the shift covered it. "You eat your biscuits. I'll be back up with some food."

"And a bucket," Crispin said. When I turned, he was waving around at all that blood on rags and his forceps and on the floor.

"And a bucket," I agreed. I took one look back at Priya before I went, cup up over her face hiding her frown, eyes back on Merry.

And then and there I swore an oath that Peter Bantle was *damned* sure going to know what hit him.

On récolte ce que l'on sème. That's French. It means, "What goes around comes around." So Beatrice tells me.

Elizabeth Bear was born on the same day as Frodo and Bilbo Baggins, but in a different year. When coupled with a childhood tendency to read the dictionary for fun, this led her inevitably to penury, intransigence, and the writing of speculative fiction. She is the Hugo, Sturgeon, Locus, and Campbell Award winning author of twenty-seven novels (The most recent is *Karen Memory*, from Tor) and over a hundred short stories. Her dog lives in Massachusetts; her partner, writer Scott Lynch, lives in Wisconsin. She spends a lot of time on planes.

*All roads led to Goose Lake, and all of Goose Lake's dirt paths led
to the Witching Tree, the oak to seed and end the world . . .*

ONLY UNITY SAVES THE DAMNED

—◆—

Nadia Bulkin

"Dude, are you getting this?"

Rosslyn Taro, twenty-five, and Clark Dunkin, twenty-five, are standing in the woods. It's evening—the bald cypresses behind them are shadowed, and the light between the needles is the somber blue that follows sunsets—and they are wearing sweatshirts and holding stones.

"It's on," says the voice behind the camera. "To the winner go the spoils!"

They whip their arms back and start throwing stones. The camera pans to the right as the stones skip into the heart of Goose Lake. After a dozen rounds, the camera pans back to Rosslyn Taro and Clark Dunkin arguing over whose stone made the most skips, and then slowly returns to the right. Its focus settles on a large bur oak looming around the bend of the lake, forty yards away.

"Hey, isn't that the Witching Tree?"

Off camera, Clark Dunkin says, "What?" and Rosslyn Taro says, "Come on, seriously?"

"You know, Raggedy Annie's Witching Tree."

The girl sounds too shaky to be truly skeptical. "How do you know?"

"Remember the song? 'We hung her over water, from the mighty oak tree.' Well, there aren't any other lakes around here. And First Plymouth is on the other side of the lake." The camera zooms, searches for a white steeple across the still water, but the light is bad. " 'We hung her looking over at the cemetery.' "

The camera swings to Rosslyn Taro, because she is suddenly upset. She is walking to the camera, and, when she reaches it, shoves the cameraman. "Bay, shut up! I hate that stupid song. Let's just go, I'm getting cold. Come on, please." But Clark Dunkin is still staring at the tree. His hands are shaking. Rosslyn Taro calls his name: "Lark!"

The camera follows Clark Dunkin's gaze to the tree. There is a figure standing in front of it, dressed in a soiled white shift and a black execution hood. The figure reaches two pale, thin hands to the edge of the hood as if to reveal its face. And then the camera enters a topspin, all dirt and branches and violet sky, as the cameraman begins to run. Rosslyn Taro is heard screaming. Someone—the cameraman, or possibly Clark Dunkin—is whimpering, as if from very far away, "Oh, shit, oh, shit."

And then the video abruptly cuts to black.

They called themselves the LunaTicks. Like everything else, it was Bay's idea: he named them after an old British secret society, supposedly "the smartest men in Birmingham." There were ground rules not only for their operations, but for life as a whole: if one got caught, the rest would confess or expect to be ratted out; where one goes, the others must follow. Only unity saves the damned, Bay said.

Roz's father thought the boys were a terrible influence on her. These slouching undead fools had metastasized at his front door one day when Roz was in sixth grade, with their uncombed hair and unwashed skin and vulgar black T-shirts. He'd made the mistake of letting the vampires in. Under their watch, his daughter's mood swings escalated from mild distemper to a full-blown madness. The charcoal rings around her eyes got deeper; her silver skull necklaces got bigger. She was vandalizing the elementary school; she was shoplifting lipstick. He'd tell her he was locking the doors at midnight and in the morning he would find her sleeping, nearly frozen, on the porch—or worse, he wouldn't find her at all. So he excavated her room, vowing to take the Baileys and the Dunkins to court if he found a single pipe, a single syringe. He gave up when she failed to apply to community college. The screen door swung shut behind her and he thanked God that he also had a son.

He was not alone. Bay's parents hated Roz and Lark as well; their hatred of the two losers who hung like stones around Bay's neck was the only thing the former Mr. and Mrs. Bailey still shared. They tried, separately, to introduce Bay to different crowds: the jocks, the computer geeks, the 4-H Club. Bay said he hated them all (too dumb too weird too Christian), but the truth was that they had all rejected him. Eventually Bay's parents gave him an ultimatum: get rid of your friends, or we get rid of the car. So the responsibility of driving down bedraggled county roads—and all roads lead to Goose Lake, the old folks said—fell to Roz and Lark.

Lark's parents couldn't have named Roz or Bay if they had tried. "There's that raccoon girl," they'd say, or "It's that damn scarecrow boy again," before drifting back into a dreamless sleep.

None of the LunaTicks would have graduated high school without the other two.

The Goose Lake video went viral, and life started to change just like Bay predicted. They sent the video from Bay's phone to the local news and suddenly they weren't the LunaTicks or the "dumb-ass emo kids" anymore—they were crisp and poignant, three local youths who had captured shocking footage of their hometown spook. People on the street gave them second looks of fear and fascination. A couple reporters came out from Lincoln and Omaha, though their arrogance forbade them from understanding what this video meant to Whippoorwill. They were interviewed on a paranormal radio show, Unheard Of, based in Minneapolis. For the first time in their lives, they came with the warning label they'd always wanted. "The footage that you are about to see," dramatic pause, "may disturb you."

Bay had to keep from laughing whenever he watched the Goose Lake video, because of the absurdity of his perky little girlfriend pretending to be a dead witch—for Halloween last fall, Jessica had been a sexy strawberry. He was proud of her moxie, even though she'd whined afterwards that she smelled like a dead rat.

"When we make the real movie, I want a better costume," she said.

"We ought to hire a real actress for the real movie, babe," he replied.

The movie was his big plan for getting out of Whippoorwill. It was all that time spent working at the theater, selling tickets to the "sheeple." Said sheeple couldn't get enough of those found-footage mockumentaries. But really, they had a lot of ways out of Whippoorwill. There was working on a Dream America cruise, or hitchhiking, or Greenpeace. There were communes and oil rigs. The LunaTicks would lie on the asphalt watching jets pass overhead and dream up these exit ramps out of car exhaust. I can't wait to get out of here, they'd say, smiling wistfully—they'd been saying it for years.

Lark couldn't stop watching the Goose Lake video. He got the file on his own phone and then showed it off like a newborn baby to his retired neighbors, the gas station clerk, the town drunk who sat outside the grocery store with a whiskey bottle in a paper bag. Lark always asked what they saw, as if even he didn't know the answer. No matter what they said, he'd shake his head and mutter, "That's not it." Bay said he was taking the method-acting thing too seriously.

Roz couldn't watch the video at all. This played well during interviews because she seemed traumatized, but after the microphones were off she was angry all the time. She wasn't getting enough sleep, she said. The silver maple outside scratched at her window, as if asking to be let in.

The town bent around them like a car wrapping around a tree during a tornado. Suddenly all these Raggedy Annies—Raggedy Annie in my yard, Raggedy Annie in my attic, Raggedy Annie in the hospital when my husband passed away—came crawling out into the sunlight. The entire town had grown up with the same story about a witch who aborted babies back when the town was still being sculpted raw out of the rolling prairie, and they all knew the matching nursery rhyme as sure as they knew "Happy Birthday"—we hung her over water, from the mighty oak tree/we hung her looking over at the cemetery.

A girl from high school, an ex-cheerleader, chatted Lark up in the express lane at the grocery store where he worked. She was buying diapers, but she wasn't wearing a wedding ring. "Aren't you freaked out? God, I think I might have died if I had seen her." Lark said that wasn't part of the story. Raggedy Annie didn't kill on sight. The ex-cheerleader made a mock screaming sound and hissed, "Don't say her name!" She also said to meet her at The Pale Horse on Friday night, but she didn't show.

So Lark sat at the bar with Bay and Roz. The bartender said he'd always known that bitch Raggedy Annie was real. "Shit, man, every time I drive by Goose Lake, I get this weird feeling. I thought it was a magnetic field or something, like Mystery Quadrant up in South Dakota. But nah, man. Our fucking parents were right! She's our demon. She's our cross to bear, if you don't mind me saying. And the bitch can't let go of a grudge. There's just this one thing I don't get though . . . but why did she show herself to you? Of all the people who've been boating and camping out at Goose Lake, why you guys?"

What they knew he meant was why, out of all the great little people in this great little town, would Raggedy Annie choose these losers? Or was it like attracts like: yesterday's demon for today's devils?

On Monday Lark showed the video to a pack of shabby children in the candy aisle. Tears were shed; one kid pissed himself. As a furious mother hoisted her away, one girl pointed at Lark and shrieked, "Mommy, the tree!" Lark's coworkers would later say that they had never seen him look so freaked out, so cracked up. He started shouting—in desperation, everyone told the manager, not anger—"I know, it's the Witching Tree!"

The day after, Lark neither showed up for work nor answered his phone. He probably would have been fired anyway, given the children-in-the-candy-aisle incident, but Roz and Bay had to make certain he hadn't somehow died—a freak electrocution, carbon monoxide, anything seemed possible if Lark wasn't answering his phone—because where one goes, the others must follow. So Roz drove them to the Dunkins' house on the scraggly edge of town. No luck, no Lark. "I have no idea where he is," said Mrs. Dunkin, from the couch. It smelled more foul than usual. "But he isn't here, raccoon girl."

His parents had really let the yard go—the branches of a grotesque hackberry tree were grasping the roof of the little tin house, like the tentacles of a mummified octopus. They always kept the shades drawn, so maybe they hadn't noticed it. "Nice tree, Mrs. Dunkin," Bay said as they left, but she didn't respond.

Bay had the big ideas, but Lark was the smartest LunaTick. He slouched in the back of classrooms, mumbling answers only when forced. Most of his teachers dismissed his potential—as the twig's bent, so the tree inclines, they said. But there was no arguing with test scores. When the time came to shuffle the seventeen-year-olds out of gymnasiums and into the real world, Lark got the Four-Year-Colleges handout instead of Two-Year-Colleges or The-US-Armed-Forces. He stared at it for a week before quietly applying to the University of Nebraska-Lincoln. If he stayed he knew he would end up like Roger Malkin. Bay would eventually get a job at the Toyota dealership, and Roz would marry some tool with bad hair, but he'd take up the mantle of town drunk. He had the genes for it. Roger would slur, "You's a good kid," and that meant they understood each other, damn it.

He told the other LunaTicks that he'd gotten into UNL while Bay was driving them to Dairy Queen. Bay was so upset that he nearly drove the car off Dead Man's Bridge, and that moment of gut-flattening fear was the most alive any of them had felt in months. "Come with me," Lark begged, but Roz just chewed her hair while Bay ground his teeth. They looked like scared rats, backing into their holes.

After the university paperwork started coming in—Get Involved! See What's New!—Lark realized that his life in Whippoorwill was a mere shadow of real human experience. He saw himself in an inspirational poster: teetering alone on a cliff, muslin wings outstretched, DARE TO DREAM emblazoned across the bottom. In what should have been his final summer in his hometown, Whippoorwill shrank and withered until just driving down Jefferson Street made him itchy, claustrophobic. He'd stand in the shower stall with the centipedes for hours, drowning out the coughs of his narcoleptic parents, willing the water to wash off his mildewed skin. All this is ending, he would think. All this is dead to me.

When he loaded up his car in August, his parents pried themselves off the couch to see him off. "You won't get far," his mother whispered in his ear as she hugged him, bones digging into his back, and from the doorway his father said, "He'll come crawling back. They always do."

And he was right. After Lark came home for winter break, he never made the drive back east. Classes were hard. Dorm rooms were small. People were brusque, shallow, vulgar. Everyone had more money than he did. The jocks who'd made high school miserable were now living in frat houses behind the quad. He hadn't made any real friends—not friends like Roz and Bay, anyway. They were waiting for him at Dead Man's Bridge after the big December snow, smiling with outstretched wool gloves. "We knew you couldn't stay away," Roz said. For a moment Lark considered grabbing both their hands and jumping into the river of ice below.

Raggedy Annie stood at the end of the bed. It's Jessica, Roz thought. Jessica broke into my room and she's trying to scare me and she and Bay are going to laugh about this tomorrow. She tried to open her mouth and couldn't. She tried to pry her jaw open with her hand and couldn't lift her arm.

The thing at the end of the bed—Jessica, Jessica, Jessica—stretched two bone-white arms to the black hood. Roz tried to close her eyes, but before she could, the hood was gone, and the face of the ghoul was revealed. She didn't know what to expect, since Raggedy Annie never had a face in the story—but it was her mother. She was glowing blue-green, like fox fire in the woods, and if not for that glow, her face was so flat and her movements so jerky that she could have been an old film reel. Her mother—who should have been a mile away and six feet deep in First Plymouth—opened and closed her mouth as if trying to speak, though only a hoarse, coffin-cramped gasp escaped.

Roz was a mess the next day. She forgot about makeup and coffee and straightening her hair. She forgot to call the landscaping company about getting the silver maple tree, the one that knocked on her window every night, under control. It was almost as tall as the chimney now; it was overwhelming the house. The one thing I tell you to do, as her father would later say. You're just like your mother. Apple doesn't fall far from the tree, I guess. She also forgot about the performance review that would have determined whether she'd be made accessories sales supervisor at Clipmann's, and ended up spending most of the review trying to save her job. "Are you on drugs?" her manager asked, disappointed. He'd made it clear how important it was for women to look put-together on the sales floor. "You look terrible."

Old Lady Marigold, who had nothing to do now that her husband was dead except rifle through clearance racks, found her listlessly hanging hats upon the hat tree. It looked like a headhunter's tower. "You shouldn't have messed with Raggedy Annie, Rosslyn Taro."

Roz squeezed the cloche in her hand and took a deep breath that was meant to be calming. "We didn't do anything to her, we just . . . " The calming breath hitched in her throat—memories of smearing the white shift in damp dirt, saying hell no she wouldn't wear it, watching Jessica slip it on instead—"We were just hanging out at Goose Lake and happened to . . . "

"You must have done something!" Old Lady Marigold squinted as if to see through a curtain. "You must have been trying something, you must have invited . . . "

"You care so much about her now, but the town elders killed Raggedy Annie, didn't they? Isn't that the whole point of the stupid story? This town will literally kill you if you step out of line?"

Old Lady Marigold pursed her wrinkled, wine-stained lips but held her tongue for fifteen seconds longer than normal, so Roz knew she was right. Not that anyone needed Raggedy Annie to teach them that lesson—just live in Whippoorwill long enough for the walls to build up, either behind or beyond you. "It is not a stupid story. Good Lord, what did your mother teach you?"

She shoved the cloche into place. "My mother's dead."

"And you don't want to let her down, do you? Now Raggedy Annie was an evil woman, but her story is part of our story, Rosslyn Taro, and for that alone you ought to have some respect. You shouldn't have showed that tape to anyone. You shouldn't have paraded her around like a damn pageant queen."

Roz willed herself to say nothing. Bay had warned them about keeping quiet regarding Goose Lake, to make sure their stories matched. He was getting calls from famous television shows, Paranormal Detectives-type stuff. He kept saying this is it, but Roz couldn't help thinking that more publicity—more pageantry—would only make the haunting worse. Bay wasn't getting visits from anything pretending to be Raggedy Annie, so he probably didn't care. She'd asked him how they would explain Lark's absence, and he said, "Say he went insane, it'll sound creepier." She had never so much wanted to hit him.

"That friend of yours has been hanging out in Roger Malkin's trailer. What's his name, Lark?" Before he gave up the ghost several weeks ago, Mr. Malkin used to sit outside the grocery store next to the mechanical horses, drinking whiskey from a paper bag. Lark would be sent to shoo him away, but never had the heart to do it. "My hairdresser lives out in Gaslight Village, and she says you gotta get him out of there. The debt collectors are coming to get the trailer any day now."

She called Bay on her lunch break, to tell him that Lark had not in fact run off to Mexico, and ask him if Jessica still had the costume—her tongue no longer wanted to voice the hallowed, damned name of Raggedy Annie. "Because I think we should burn it."

Bay was in an awful mood, supposedly due to a severe toothache. "Don't flake out on me like Lark."

"I'm not flaking, I just think we fucked up! I think we shouldn't have done this!" She pulled back her hair, sunk into herself, felt the rapid beating of her heart. She thought she saw Raggedy Annie—Mom?—at the other end of the parking lot, but then a car passed and it was just a stop sign. Talk about this, and she'd sound crazy. Forget sounding crazy, she'd be crazy. Another loony. Just like Lark. She had to use language Bay understood. "We should get rid of the evidence before anybody ever finds it."

"Well, I have no idea where it is. I haven't talked to Jessica since Tuesday. She's being a bitch."

If Lark was here, he'd say no! all sarcastic and wry, and she'd let out her horselaugh, and Bay would get pissed because he was the only one allowed to diss Jessica, and she'd say, "What do you expect with some nineteen-year-old Hot Topic wannabe?"

"She's never got the time anymore. She's always working on her damn terrariums." She heard him scoff through the phone. "Here I thought she hated science."

The next day Roz called KLNW news and said she wanted to come clean about the Goose Lake video. "Our first mistake was making the film at all," she said on the six o'clock news. "Our second mistake was showing it to other people. I just want to say to the entire community that I'm so sorry for lying, and I'm so sorry for any disrespect we may have caused." To the nameless, unseen power behind the visitations, she added a silent prayer: Please forgive me. Please let me go.

The Bailey family tree lived in Aunt Vivian's upstairs closet. Once upon a time, when Bay was young and bored and his parents were having it out at home, Aunt Vivian had unrolled it and presented it to him on her kitchen table. It was his inheritance, she said. Just like his father's Smith & Wesson and his mother's bad teeth. Aunt Vivian's lacquered fingernails ran from name to name, jumping back and forth in time. "That's your great-great-grandpa Johnny, he enlisted after getting married and then went and died in the War," she said. "And that's Laura Jean, she's your cousin twice removed. She wanted to be a movie star, but she only sang backup in commercials."

"Why is it called a tree?" little Bay asked.

"Because we all grew from the same roots. Lots of people draw their family trees starting from their great-grandpas at the top, as if all your ancestors lived and died just so you could be born, you special little cupcake. But that doesn't make a damn bit of sense. You start with the roots—that's Herman and Sarah Bailey, when they moved here from Ohio. The rest of us are their twigs. We grew out of them."

The chart indeed looked like everyone since Herman and Sarah had grown out of their subterranean bones, children sprouting from their parents like spores.

"Does that mean we're stuck here?"

Aunt Vivian cocked her head. "And just what is wrong with here?"

His parents had met in elementary school; they grew into a big-haired Stairway to Heaven couple with matching letterman jackets. Whippoorwill born and bred, they cooed, as if that was anything to be proud of. They'd disproved their own manifesto by the time Bay was old enough to dial child services. For a while he was the only one who heard the plastic plates ricocheting off the dining room wall, the fuck yous and the just get outs, the station wagon scurrying out of the driveway and jumping the curb. He wondered how to put that shit in the family tree. Attention, the tree is currently on fire. After the divorce severed his parents' bond, he imagined his own name gliding away as if it had never been rooted to this gnarled monstrosity that began with Herman and Sarah. Yet nothing changed. He stayed tethered to the crown of the Bailey tree: a struggling, captive bird.

His father never liked it when he talked about New York, Vegas, Mexico. He would point a beer can at him and say, "You think you're better than this town? We're not good enough for you anymore?"

It seemed easier to say he was sick of "you fucking hillbillies" than to tell the truth. He knew that would get a response, probably a box in the ear for pissing on his surroundings. But what he really wanted to say was You were never good enough for me. You were never good enough for anyone.

Rumor had it that the weirdo living in Roger "Alkie" Malkin's trailer in Gaslight Village was an escaped convict. Tweaked-out gremlins in neon shirts sometimes snuck peeks through the windows, standing on their tiptoes in the muddy swamp grass that had swallowed most of the trailer's tires. The weirdo was usually sitting in the dark with a flashlight, watching something terrifying on his phone. The glow on his face was lunar. When he noticed them, he'd growl and scurry to the window and pull the curtains. The rumor adjusted— now he was a scientist from Area 51, on the run from the Feds.

But he was just a man—a boy, really—who had the misfortune of stumbling upon some hidden fold in the world that he couldn't explain, and knew of no other recourse than retreat. He was just Lark. When Roz knocked on the door of the trailer, distressed because she'd seen feet descend from the silver maple tree in her backyard, he opened the door. And when Bay banged upon the door an hour later, yelling that he knew they were in there, Lark again relented.

"The gang's back together," Lark whispered, trembling and huddling on the piss-stained carpet. He looked like death by then—he'd lost so much weight, so much color. But Roz and Bay were red-eyed too. They hadn't spoken to each other since her confession to KLNW news. He had tried to contact her at first—called twenty-three times and sent seven text messages, including Fuck you you fucking bitch—but, within forty-eight hours, he was the one on KLNW, and Roz was the unstable nut job with the ax to grind. He swore to the town of Whippoorwill that the video was one-hundred-percent authentic. "Only unity saves the damned."

"I just got fired," Bay said in the trailer. "My manager says she lost trust in me since my friend Rosslyn went on TV and said we faked the entire Goose Lake video." Roz was clenching her stomach, refusing to look at him. "So thank you, Rosslyn. Thank you so much."

"I was desperate!" she shouted. "You don't know what it's like! You turn every corner and you wonder—is she gonna be there? Is she watching me? Will anybody else see her? And even after I said sorry, she still didn't stop!" She knelt down beside Lark and cautiously tugged on the hems of the blanket he wore like a shawl around his head. "Lark, I know you've been seeing her too."

Lark stared blankly at her, and Bay clapped his hands over his head. "You're unbelievable. It's not Raggedy Annie, fuckwit, Raggedy Annie isn't real! Remember? We made her! She's Jessica!"

"Yeah? And where is your little girlfriend anyway? She's a part of this mess, she ought to be here too."

Bay nervously chewed on his fingernail as he stalked around Alkie's trailer. It was empty save for plastic bags and cigarette butts and half-eaten meals: evidence of a life undone. "Jessica's gone."

The other LunaTicks were silent, but Bay slammed his fist into a plastic cabinet and snapped an answer to a question he'd heard only in his head, "I don't know where! She's just gone, she hasn't been to work, her parents haven't seen her . . . they think she got mad at me and ran off. When they looked in her room all they found were those . . . damn terrariums." Suddenly exhausted, Bay slid to the carpet and pulled off his black beanie. "They're all the same too. Just one tiny tree in every one. Looks like a little oak tree." The tiniest sliver of a bittersweet smile cracked Bay's face. "Like a tiny Witching Tree."

"Bay's right," Lark mumbled. "It's not Raggedy Annie. It's the trees. Here, look at the video again." He held up his phone and their no-budget home movie began to play. Roz and Bay were so hollowed out by then that they didn't have the strength to object to watching their little experimental film another, final time. They watched themselves skip stones across Goose Lake, watched the camera find the Witching Tree. They watched themselves act out the script they'd written at Jessica's house the night before—"Let's just go, I'm getting cold"—and watched Jessica stand ominous and hooded in front of the Witching Tree. And finally, they watched the branches of the Witching Tree curl, like the fingers of some enormous dryad, toward Jessica.

"Do you see the tree?" Lark whispered, like he was coaching a baby to speak. The leaves of the tree stood on end, fluttering as if swept by a celestial wind, trembling as if awakening. "See it move?"

"I don't understand," Roz whined. "It's the breeze . . . "

"No, no, no! Listen, I've looked this up, and these beings exist across the world, in dozens of civilizations across time . . . there's Yggdrasil, there's Ashvattha, there's Vilçgfa, there's Kalpavrishka, and now there's . . . there's the Witching Tree." Bay was about to punch Lark in the face, and they all knew it, so he spoke faster. "These trees, they connect . . . all the planes of existence, the world of the living with the world of the dead. The Witching Tree is our Cosmic Tree."

Those words—Cosmic Tree—hung like smoke circles in Alkie's musty trailer. Jessica's terrariums. The trees that grew manic and hungry over their houses. The Witching Tree itself, eternal long-limbed sentinel of Goose Lake. And all roads led to Goose Lake . . .

Bay was the first to break the trance and grapple to his feet. He claimed not to understand what Lark was trying to say. He said he couldn't waste his time on this bullshit about trees, because what could a tree do to him? All he knew was that Lark and Roz had gone completely batshit, and now none of them were ever getting out of Whippoorwill, and was that what they wanted all along? Did they want to be stuck in this inbred town forever, maybe open a tree nursery if they were so obsessed with greenery?

"... dude, what are you doing to your teeth?"

Bay was picking at one of his bottom canine teeth, digging into the gum, trying to rip it out. "It's the root!" he shouted through his bloody fingers. "It's fucking killing me!"

Bay waited until he'd returned home to extract the tooth. He was so distracted by the electric pain that he failed to see that the dead cottonwood outside his mother's house, the one that had broken his arm as a child, was growing green again. He used a pair of pliers and the bathroom mirror—the pain was nothing compared to the horror of enduring another moment with the tooth's ruined root in his skull. Yet even as he stared at the ugly disembodied thing lying at the bottom of the sink, he could feel the roots of his other teeth rotting. He didn't know what had happened to them—his bad teeth, his mother's teeth—but he could feel their decay spreading into his jaws, his sinuses. The thought of those sick roots growing into his bones—he saw them jutting out of his chin like saber teeth, drilling down in search of soil—made him want to die ...

They all had to go. By the time his mother came in, he was lying delirious on the tiles, his teeth scattered around him like bloody seeds.

The day after Bay was committed to Teller Psychiatric, Roz drove alone to Jessica Grauner's house in the half-light. She went because only unity saves the damned, though she'd hated Jessica when she'd tagged along on the LunaTicks' vandalism operations and petty larceny sprees. Where one goes, the others must follow, and she neither wanted to follow Bay to Teller Psychiatric nor knew how to follow Lark into his rabbit hole. And she had the squirmy feeling that Jessica was still hanging around—like Raggedy Annie hung from the Witching Tree?—somewhere on the property.

Roz had been to this house twice—once for a grotesque house party while Jessica's parents were out of town, and once to prepare for the Goose Lake stunt. On neither occasion had there been a linden tree in the front yard, but now a full-grown specimen had broken through the earth to stand in proud, terrifying splendor before Jessica's window. Its roots bubbled across the lawn, disrupting her parents' carefully manicured ornamental ferns. A large, discolored knot peeked out from the linden's trunk—a malformed branch, right, a sleeping bud? But when Roz got close enough to touch it, she saw that it was a face: Jessica's face, her eyes clenched shut and her mouth stretched open in an anguished forever-scream. Roz ran her finger down one wooden eye, heard Jessica's nasal whine—I smell like a dead rat!—and quickly stuffed her hand back in her pocket, running back to her car.

Roz's mother died during the Great Storm. She died at home, of cancer, while the world raged around them. Electric lines sparked, cars slid off roads, walls fell in, and smaller trees were torn out of the earth, but their older, larger counterparts miraculously survived. It seemed like a condolence card from God: The world is filled with death, but Life endures.

There were strange things said at the funeral. "She's waiting for you, in heaven." "We will all meet again, by-and-by." Roz hated to admit it—because who wouldn't want to see their mother again?—but when these words floated up on desolate roads at midnight, she was frightened. She wanted to hear that her mother was at peace, in a better place, had moved on—not that she was waiting, lingering, hovering, skeletal hands outstretched to receive her daughter as soon as death delivered her—no. That was ugly.

Her mother loved trees. They were her favorite thing about Whippoorwill. Don't you love how tall they are, how old they are? These trees are older than all of us. She was a native, so she had grown up with them—climbed them, slept in their nooks, taken their shelter, carved her initials into their skin with the neighbor boy. Roz's father had agreed to move to Whippoorwill before they got married because it was supposedly a good place to raise a family— what with the safe streets and heritage fairs and seasonal festivals—but when he wanted to move to Lincoln for the sake of a higher salary, her mother had refused on account of the trees. But there are trees everywhere, he said. It's not the same, she said. These trees are my inheritance. They're the kids' inheritance.

She had a special bedtime story about the Witching Tree. It had nothing at all to do with Raggedy Annie. It was about the men and women who first built Whippoorwill, back when America was young. They built the jail and they built the church, they built the courthouse and they built the school. And then they planted the Witching Tree, so after their human bodies died they would stay close to their children, and live forever.

Her father listened in once, and got so upset that her mother never told it again, and Roz never heard it again from anyone else. At middle-school sleepovers—before the other girls decided she was just too weird—they only ever whispered about Raggedy Annie, the abortionist-witch. When she asked about that Witching Tree story they would indignantly snap, "That is the Witching Tree story, dummy!"

But one time in high school when they were all smoking pot in Bay's basement, Roz tried to retell her mother's version of the Witching Tree story, what little she could remember of it. It turned out Bay and Lark had heard similar shit from their parents, once or twice. Bay and Lark were, first and last and always, the only people she could count on not to lie to her. Lark said, "It's a creation myth. And an apocalypse myth, too. The end and the beginning, the beginning and the end."

Dawn came, and they never spoke of it again. The Witching Tree story—the real one, the one submerged beneath the arsenic-and-old-lace of Raggedy Annie—was only whispered in the ears of Whippoorwill babies, so the truth would soften like sugar cubes right into their unfinished brains. These babies grew up and forgot except when they were sleeping, usually, but sometimes when they looked at the massive, infallible trees of Whippoorwill for too long, that primordial story writhed like a worm and they would shiver, listening to the leaves rustling like ocean waves, wondering who was waiting for them.

Raggedy Annie stood, again, at the end of Roz's bed. Roz could almost hear her breathing.

"No," Roz mumbled to herself. "She's not real. Raggedy Annie is not real." And maybe she wasn't, but something stood there. Something had turned Bay into a pile of dirt in Teller Psychiatric. Oh, that wasn't in the official hospital report—the hospital said he somehow escaped, from the restraints and the room and the asylum, and the forest-fresh soil that had replaced him in the cot was—what—a practical joke? The LunaTicks knew all about those, but this was something else, something beyond. Roz closed her eyes, telling herself that once she opened them, it would be morning, and Raggedy Annie would be gone.

When she opened her eyes the figure was leaning over her, twitching. This time it wasn't her mother beneath the hood. This was the face that looked back at her in the mirror every morning, bleary-eyed and bloodless, sapped of life. It was her. Her doppelganger cocked its head to the side like a bird and stared at her with her own big black eyes—black, then blacker, in the face of the ghost. It was death looking down; she could feel that in her veins, because that wasn't blood roiling inside her anymore. It was sap. Slow like honey. Death leaned in, and Roz screamed herself awake.

It was midnight. Roz drove to Gaslight Village in a fugue, but Lark wasn't there. Alkie's trailer looked like it had been spat out by a tornado—it had been smashed nearly in half by a fallen tree. Branches had broken through the windows and now grew inside the trailer, as if they'd been searching for him. Her first thought was that the trailer had become his coffin, but after she scrambled to reach a broken window, cutting her hands on glass shards, she didn't see a body in the dark. No soil, either. There was only one place, unhappily, that he would have gone.

She could see the woods around Goose Lake stirring before she even got out of the car. For a second she sat behind the wheel, trying to delay the inevitable, hypnotized by the razor-sharp static that had overcome the radio, until she saw again the figure that she'd been running from since they made the video. Raggedy Annie was standing where the trees parted to make way for a little human path. The hooded ghost turned and disappeared down the trail, and Roz knew this would not end if she did not pursue. Where one goes the others must follow, and Raggedy Annie was one of them. The truth was she always had been. Raggedy Annie and her mother and father and brother and Lark's parents and Bay's parents and Jessica and Old Lady Marigold and Roger Malkin and everybody, everybody in this town: they were all in this together.

She willed her legs to move into the rippling chaos. As soon as she stepped foot on the dirt path the air pressure dropped, and her bones felt calcified in pain. She'd been hoping not to return to Goose Lake. She'd been hoping to leave Whippoorwill. She'd been hoping . . . well. Hope was just delusion that hadn't ripened yet. The forest didn't smell like pine or cedar or Christmas or anything else they could pack into an air freshener—it smelled like rot. A fleet of dead were howling overhead, and there was nowhere left to go but forward. Just like all roads led to Goose Lake, all of Goose Lake's dirt paths led to the Witching Tree, the oak to seed and end the world.

The Tree had grown since she last saw it. She felt the urge to kneel under its swaying, groaning shadow. Even as worms crawled out of cavities in its trunk, new twigs and leaves sprouted on its boughs. Lark was a dwarf beneath it, wildly swinging a rusty ax. Every strike was true, but he wasn't getting anywhere—not only was the oak enormous, but its bone-like bark yielded nothing except for a few brittle chips of wood. She could see this, even though she could not see stars through the foliage. What stars? The Witching Tree was everything in this world.

Lark looked up and tried to smile when he saw her through his sweat. He looked so weak and mortal, a mere weed next to the Witching Tree. "We can make it, Roz! You and me. Just you and me. You just gotta help me. Help me end this thing."

She shook her head. She could feel the Tree's roots moving like great pythons beneath the fertile earth. "I don't think we can, Lark . . . I don't think we're getting away."

Lark frowned and paused his work, catching the blade with his hand. "But if we cut it down, it ends," he said, and then cried out and dropped the ax. He was squeezing his left palm—he'd nicked it. Or it had nicked him, it was hard to tell. So the blade was sharp after all—just not sharp enough to slay the tower of space-time that was the Tree. He moaned and pressed his right hand into the wound. "Something's wrong," his voice warbled, holding out his hand. By the Tree's light, Roz could barely see it: dark amber where red should have been. It was sap. He was bleeding sap.

"Roz," Lark whimpered. He sounded like the eleven-year-old Clark Dunkin that she had happened to sit next to in sixth grade: sniveling and sullen but, still, full of a future. The years of dishevelment sloughed off in seconds, revealing the baby face below. Was this how the Tree could promise endless life, like her mother said? "Help me."

She blinked, and became faintly aware that she was crying. "Don't fight it."

Now roots were bursting out of his storm-worn sneakers, running wildly toward moist earth—they were trying to find some place to settle, to never let go. Lark was trying to shamble forward but he could only heave his chest, retching until he couldn't breathe. Tree bark tore through his jeans, and his arms finally straightened and seized and were destroyed—no, transformed. Only the human skin died. Lark arched his back and would have broken his vertebrae had they not turned to pliable wood; his mouth tore open and a dozen branches leapt from his wooden throat, sprouting blood blossoms. It was almost beautiful.

Roz was kneeling by then, in deference and fear. When Lark's screams finally stopped, she knew that it was her turn. Where others go, one must follow. She lifted her head and saw the great and gnarled Tree, glowing blue-green with something far stronger and far more alien than fox fire, achingly reach its branches toward her and then shrivel back. It was so jealous, so unsure of her loyalty. "Roz-zz-lyn," her mother said, from somewhere in the rush of leaves, "why d' you want to lee-eave us?"

Roz picked up the ax. A wail swept through the branches, but Roz only threw the weapon into the murky green waters of Goose Lake. "I'll never leave," she said, and began trudging homeward. "I promise."

It was not a warm embrace. The Tree's branches bit deep into her back as it entwined her, and she soon lost the ability to see anything but heartwood. Still, she melted into the Tree as easily and completely as if she had never been parted from it. Little by little, the walls came down: the walls of Whippoorwill, the walls of her skin. I'm scared, she thought as the flesh of her tongue dissolved into sap, and though the only response she heard was a deep and ancient drumbeat pulsing from far within the Witching Tree, she finally understood.

Nadia Bulkin writes scary stories about the scary world we live in. It took her two tries to leave Nebraska, but she has lived in Washington, D.C. for four years now, tending her garden of student debt sowed by two political science degrees. In 2015, you can find more of her stories in the *Aickman's Heirs*, *Cassilda's Song*, and *She Walks in Shadows* anthologies—or check out nadiabulkin.wordpress.com.

He could taste sorcery in the air, and he hated the flavor . . .

KUR-A-LEN

Lavie Tidhar

Part One: Expectations of a Funeral

The funeral, Gorel thought, went very well: and it was only partially marred by the deceased rising in his coffin with his arms outstretched, his mouth open in a scream that echoed amidst the silent gravestones.

In the event it was dealt with summarily. It had not, it seemed to Gorel, come entirely unexpected. The young man—the deceased's nephew, so Gorel understood—reached for a curved knife that hung his side and in a smooth, seemingly practiced movement plunged it into his uncle's chest. The deceased sank back in the coffin and ceased from all semblance of life. The proceeding service was tasteful, subdued, and accompanied with heart-felt sobs, but whether of grief or relief Gorel couldn't quite say. When it was over and the coffin, nailed tightly shut, had been lowered into the earth and covered thoroughly, the small party of mourners slowly dispersed.

"Here lies the body of Seraph Gadashtill, Ninth Caliph of Mindano Caliphate, last in the line of the necromancer-kings," the caretaker said in a singsong voice. Then she put a mark by the name on her list and turned away. She made a gesture with her hand and the Zambur servers hurried over in their shambling gait, spades and materials at the ready. "You know what to do," the caretaker said. She and Gorel stood and watched the Zambur begin to build the Last House of Rest above the former-caliph's grave. Around them similar structures spread out to the horizon and beyond. Mansions and palaces, castles and towers and manors, all built to miniature scale.

Amongst them the silent statues were dotted here and there, adding up to an immeasurable assembly of human and non-human figures. Far in the distance the Lake of the Drowned God glinted in the light of a dim sun, concealing inside its depths the buried remains of the sea-folk, the Merlangai; and away from it, and equally distant, were the giant Migdal trees whose canopies were decorated with what looked like hanging, pod-like nests, and which were, in reality, the last resting places of Avians.

"Everyone ends up here, sooner or later," the caretaker said, perhaps putting a slight accent on "ends" than was strictly necessary. "Care for a drink, Gorel of Goliris?"

Already the dim sun was low on the horizon, and the mists were gathering at the bases of statues and follies. "Why not?" Gorel said, and the two of them turned away from the caliph's new and final home and walked away, the sound of the working Zambur receding slowly behind them.

Gorel came to Kur-a-len, the Garden of Statues, on a night as cold as a dead woman's hands. Above his head the darkness was punctured with the white light of cold distant stars. Mist curled about him and his graal moved slowly, having been made lethargic by the weak daylight that prevailed in that region. Through the mist Gorel could see lights, far away, and he thought longingly of a drink. He hurried his graal, trying to avoid looking directly at the shapes the mist was forming around them, shapes that formed mouths and spoke without sound, reaching insubstantial hands in what could have been threat, or pleading, or both.

He could taste sorcery in the air, and he hated the flavor. His hand hovered by the gun at his side, but there was nothing to shoot, nothing there but the mist. As if sensing rest was close, the graal hurried its steps, its legs moving soundlessly on the hard ground, its carapace a deep, exhausted black. Then they were through the mist and there were indeed lights there, and voices, and a strange, small town, a single street bounded on both sides by low-lying houses.

Gorel rode down the street, registering details: no two buildings were the same. There was a construction of metal and glass, built at odd angles, seeming to reach up to the night sky; there was a small squat building of pure white stone, no lights shining inside; a wooden longhouse where the shadow-veiled faces of Nocturne women seemed to stare down at him, but it could have just been shadows; a colony of bamboo houses piled on top of each other where small, shambling figures seemed to converse without sound, turning bald, round heads to watch him as he passed—Zambur, he thought with a shudder, his hand once again going to his gun. Finally, however, a cheerful round building with lights in its windows, the sound of singing, and a sign that said *The Last Homily House*. Gorel climbed off the graal and the creature sank gratefully to the ground, its long arched tail folded above it, the sting at its end closed, ready to capture moisture, at last, from the mist.

Gorel stepped into the Last Homily. Inside: a wooden curving counter, a row of dusty bottles on shelves reaching up to the ceiling, resembling an apothecary's cabinet. Candles on the counter, spluttering with fat. The whole perception of the room was skewed: it seemed to swell and contract like a living thing. Tables in a semi-circle, occupied by shady figures—hard to tell in the faint light. No more singing—he had the sense of eyes studying him from the shadows. He fought the craving that swelled inside him the for the dark kiss, the goddess Shar's dying gift to him, her curse. He stepped toward the counter and conversation resumed around him and he said, "Give me a drink."

The thing behind the bar wasn't human. Peeling skin stretched over an elongated skull; green-black teeth spread out in a grin; sunken eyes, yellow, and long thin fingers mottled gray, handling a bottle, deftly. Gorel stared at the grave-wraith and the grave-wraith stared back. "What would you like?"

Gorel scanned the shelves. Ancient bottles, crusted with dirt. Grass Giant tear wine; rice whiskey from the banks of Tharat; Merlangai red, made with the sea-grapes from the deeps of the Drowned God's domain; pickled scorpion oil from the sands of Meskatel; Suicide Rum from far-off Waterfalling; even a small bottle of the tree-sprite blood, called draeken. Rare bottles, impossible vintages: they had the smell of the grave upon them. "What's the special?" Gorel said.

The bartender smiled. "Gravedigger's Punch," he said. "My own recipe. Heated up and guaranteed to fend off the cold."

Gorel nodded, and the grave-wraith went to the side of the bar, where coal fire was burning low in a metal brazier, returned with a steaming mug.

"Cut with just a hint of dust," the bartender said with a leer. "For the discerning gentleman of the road."

The craving rose inside Gorel again, and he put the mug to his mouth and drank, greedily, the hot liquid burning his lips. Yes. There was gods' dust there. His mind seemed to soar, to clear, return. The craving he had been suppressing eased at once. The grave-wraith leered harder, said, "Hey, Preacher. I think you got a customer."

Wood scraping stone: the sound of a chair being pushed slowly back. Gorel turned, one hand going for the gun. In the shadows, a figure standing up, wide-brimmed pulled-down hat, approaching with slow, heavy steps. A single eye stared into his face. The other was missing. There was no eye-patch. There was no wound. Smooth skin grew where the left eye should have been. He thought—sorcery, and his fingers itched on the butt of the gun.

The face regarded him serenely for a long moment. Then, "Where you from, stranger?"

The voice was melodious and rich. Gorel, taking another sip from the punch, said, "Not from here."

A single eye regarded him with some amusement. "No one is from here," the man said. "For most of us this is the final stop in a long and wearing journey."

"Just passing through," Gorel said. "Sorry to disappoint."

The man nodded, as if to himself. "Mind if I sit down?" he said. Not waiting for an answer he pulled a bar stool toward him and sat down. "I can tell," he said, "that you are a man of great faith. Pray, what church do you belong to?"

"The church of mind your own fucking business," Gorel said, and the man laughed. "A most ancient and venerable one, then."

In a round corner that was still a corner, a group of Zambur, glancing over: they looked like pale toadstools. The man shot them a glance and they looked away. He said, "But you are not without faith. Or have your stores been depleted?"

Gorel looked at him again: this time he looked closer.

Tall, the hair turning into the gray of old wood. The single eye bright and blue and clear as a pond. He glanced down: the hands were dark brown and scarred. He glanced up again. The man wore a coat. Now he let it open, just a little, showing Gorel a small black vial hanging on the inside lining. "You in the market?" the preacher said, glancing—too casually—at Gorel's arms, where the old tracks of needle marks from his time in Meskatel could still be seen. "Because, as it happens, I have the goods if you are."

Gorel smiled. The preacher smiled. Behind the counter, the grave-wraith's rotting teeth shone wet in the candlelight.

He spent his first night in Gardentown, as the small enclave of the living outside the Garden of Statues was called, in the Hotel of Nameless Gods that stood beside the Last Homily, and he spent it in blissful oblivion, the supply of gods' dust he had acquired from the preacher coursing through his blood and into his brain, setting him on a fire that was better than food, better than sex, better than being alive. As he slept, if he slept, it seemed to him for some time that he was walking on a vast plane, and above his head there were no stars, and he heard voices whisper to him, joining up into a multitude that became one sound, a howling like a great wind: but what it said he didn't know.

When morning arrived the sunlight was weak and murky, as if strained through a dirty glass. It was cold, a clammy, unpleasant chill that insinuated itself against the body, penetrating like questing fingers through the clothes. Mist lay in clumps and lazy eddies on the street. When he came out to check on it, the graal was motionless, its carapace dark, only the barest green showing through. As he walked down the one street Gorel saw a group of Duraali chieftains, the elaborate scars on their faces vivid, talking in hushed voices; and further down, as the town ended, a group of Ebong carrying a large round sarcophagus as black and impenetrable as their own heads. Funeral parties, he thought. He passed the last house and found himself outside the Garden of Statues.

He had heard of the place. A memory, far, painful: his adoptive father in the Lower Kidron, speaking. It was only a short while, perhaps a year after he was found, a boy exile from Goliris, cast off by sorcery and treachery across the World to this strange place. He was not yet fluent in the language . . .

Uncle Neshev had just died, an explosion in his workshop finally terminating the long and illustrious career of the old gunsmith. "We should have sent him to Kur-a-len," Gorel's father had said to his mother. Gorel, listening: "What is Kuralen?"

He had learned their language, after they had found him. The language of Lower Kidron was strange to him, so different to the rich tongue of Goliris, where words had the force of command, and a prince of Goliris could name and thus order all that was around him.

"*Kur* meaning garden," his adoptive father said patiently. "*A-len,* of statues, plural. It is a cemetery. The greatest cemetery in all the World."

"Uncle Neshev always spoke of going there, one day," his adoptive mother said. "The greatest gunsmith of all Lower Kidron, founder of our Foundry, is buried there. Mirkah the Gunmaker, who was once a sorcerer but had abandoned sorcery for the honesty of a gun."

"Why can't Uncle Neshev go?" the young Gorel had asked. His father sighed and shook his head. "It is far, far from here," he said. "For a man of the Lower Kidron to be buried in Kur-a-len he must set out while he is still young. No, Uncle Neshev must be satisfied here. A burned-down foundry is a decent enough grave for a gunsmith."

And now he was there. The cemetery spread out before him, the mist thinning where the graves began. It was not an entirely flat land. The cemetery seemed to slope down, forming small, uneven rolling hills and shallow dales, but all were occupied: a metropolis in miniature, houses of glass and metal and stone, enduring all, and amidst them the statues, denizens of this vast realm who seemed to have frozen in mid-stroll.

For a moment the sun seemed to shine brighter, its light casting away the gloom of the mist, and a thousand thousand graves gleamed as one, almost blinding him.

"Breathtaking, isn't it? I could look at them forever," a voice said softly behind him. Startled, Gorel turned.

She was wreathed in shadow. He could not see her face, could only glimpse hints of a full round figure, of bright eyes studying him from behind the darkness that was her veil. A Nocturne, he thought—but it was daylight, now. She seemed to read his mind. "Half-Nocturne," she said. "Half-Diurnal."

"I thought the two never met," Gorel said.

The figure behind the shadows seemed to smile. "There are stories of love in the liminal hours," she said in a singsong voice, as if reciting a well-worn-out poem. "In the times of dusk and dawn, brief stolen moments before the sun, after the moon. I," she added, "was a dusk child. But that was long ago, and far away from here, and the story of that love is not buried here."

They watched the garden then. It was a scene of decayed grandeur, and it seemed peaceful to Gorel. He thought then of his home, of the vast palace of Goliris where the shoreline met the jungle, where the seat of the great empire was, and he thought of the cemetery of Goliris, where his ancestors resided in the great palaces of the dead. Memory came floating into his mind:

Dusk, and his father held his hand in his. "Where are we going?" Gorel had asked, and the ruler of all Goliris said, "To a family council."

They had walked through the twisting corridors of the palace, deeper and deeper, and when they stepped outside it was at the gardens that met the deep dark forests, their smell overpowering in its mixture of rot and growth, and they followed a dark path and came at last to the houses of the dead.

They had been built in concentric circles. Each was a miniature of the grand palace of Goliris. There were halls and corridors inside those tombs, and the traps of Goliris were replicated inside them, the vast underground prisons and the foundries and laboratories and, in each, the throne room, and a full-sized throne. They walked amidst the palaces as the sky became the deep purple of a bruise and at last turned black. Standing inside the circle, with no light and the darkness pressing from all sides, Gorel was afraid, and held on tightly to his father's hand. "Gorel," his father had said, "The line of Goliris had never been broken. Not even death releases a prince of Goliris—" and the faces came out of the darkness, the same faces that would later visit him in his dreams and make him cry in the night—ancient, wizened faces, as bitter as coffee beans, and reached out pale, insubstantial hands to him, and said—

He shook himself awake, found himself craving dust again, and noticed the half-Nocturne was examining him. "Who are you?" he said.

She seemed to laugh. The sound was like night wind rushing through bamboo walls. "I'm just the caretaker," she said.

"Do you—" he said, and stopped, and said again, "Do you have dead here from Goliris?"

It was hard to tell, but it seemed to him that she was troubled. "The dead come here from everywhere in the World," she said.

"You must know," he said. She shook her head. "There are lists, maps of the cemetery, but . . . you must understand, sometimes they are inaccurate. And sometimes they just . . . change. It is dangerous to wander the avenues of the dead."

Gorel said, "I have a gun," and the caretaker laughed. "Who are you?" she said.

He said, "Gorel of Goliris."

"Goliris . . . " she said. "I have heard of it. Yes. It is said to be a great empire . . . "

"The greatest," Gorel said, "the World had ever known."

Veiled eyes regarded him. "There may be," she said. "Yes, there may be some who are buried here."

"I would like," Gorel said, "to find them."

Not even death releases a prince of Goliris . . . another memory was worrying at him, a story he had once been told . . . there had once been another exile of Goliris. The caretaker said, "Perhaps we could work out a deal."

Gorel stopped, watched her.

"I could do with some . . . help," the caretaker said. "On a temporary basis."

Gorel said, "What sort of help?"

Behind her shadows, the caretaker seemed to smile.

Most people, when they have finished with the business of living, are happy to remain dead. Death comes as a restful absence, an infinite nothingness in which one is free to not be, unshackled from existence. The wish to live is bound into every living thing: few welcome death, but most accept it, willingly or not. But to crave life, to desire and hunger for it beyond the grave itself, is to rail against nature, against the way of the World. There are those who hunger and crave and desire, yes. There are those who fight oblivion, seeking above all else to gain a semblance of life.

And there are . . . stages of undeath. There are levels.

And in Kur-a-len, the Garden of Statues, that mass burial ground, that vast necropolis, they were all, at some point, made manifest.

"Most of it is straightforward enough," the caretaker said. It was night. They were sitting at a quiet corner in the Last Homily. The caretaker's darkness seemed to grow as night fell, the shadows multiplying about her; and some of them seemed to wrap around Gorel as well, so that it felt to him as if they were sitting entirely on their own, on a vast and empty plane where no stars shone; and it made him suddenly uncomfortable, as if he had been there before, and had heard voices calling out to him; but he could not remember where or when that might have been.

"Straightforward how?" Gorel said.

"Grave robbing . . . " she said it with a slight apologetic note.

"Really?"

"You'd be surprised. The Garden's fame is widespread, patrolling the perimeter difficult. There are always bands of thieves attempting to find treasure—sometimes they succeed." She seemed to smile, without much humor. "Sometimes they even get to enjoy the spoils. For a while."

"Defenses?" Gorel said.

"An appropriate curse is put on each grave as it is dug and built. That," the caretaker said, "is part of the service. However—"

"They weaken with time?"

"Naturally. Also, some of the more enterprising robbers may employ a sorcerer."

"I have a cure for sorcery," Gorel said, opening his hand, spilling bullets on the table—he had been absentmindedly loading his gun under the table. "A handful of these usually does the trick."

"Indeed," the caretaker said, dryly.

Gorel shrugged and collected the bullets. The caretaker said, "The more . . . elaborate structures have their own defenses. Unfortunately, those are usually the ones robbers are most anxious to get into."

"Naturally," Gorel said. He thought about it for a moment. "Do you have sizeable treasure buried in the tombs?"

The darkness that was the caretaker seemed to shrug. "Probably."

"Hmmm."

"I'm not sure I like that sound," the caretaker said.

Gorel grinned. "Tell me more about the defenses," he said.

"Frankly," the caretaker said, "the biggest problem is not outside interference. The major . . . complications, shall we say? They usually arise internally."

"The dead," Gorel said. He was no longer smiling.

"Yes," the caretaker said. "And right now, I have the feeling of a particular complication of that shape approaching the Garden . . . "

A job was a job, Gorel thought. And a bullet cured most things. Truth to tell, he was tired: wearied by the events that took place in Falang-Et, by his endless journey across the World, searching, always searching for his distant home, for the truth of his exile from eternal Goliris.

It was then, as the caretaker began to outline the problem she—by dint of hard logic or numinous foreseeing, Gorel didn't know—was expecting, that they were interrupted by two curious individuals who had suddenly materialized by their table. "Madam Caretaker," the one on the left said. "Sorry to interrupt. We wish—"

"We wish," the one on the right said, "to petition you once more to allow us—"

"To commence the excavations in sector three—"

"For the purpose of our research—"

"Which is, I need not stress the point, of *material* importance—"

"Material importance."

It seemed to Gorel that the caretaker scowled. "Dr. Blud, Professor Deth—"

"*I'm* Blud," the one on the right said, reproachfully.

"And *I'm* Deth," the one on the left said.

"This gentleman is Gorel of Goliris," the caretaker finished. "And he's the man you need talk to from now on."

"What? Preposterous," Dr. Blud said.

"This man? What is his role?" Professor Deth said.

"He is the new sheriff," the caretaker said, and the shadows seemed to smile. "Just hired."

Gorel studied the two men as they spluttered indignation. First, Dr. Blud, on the right, who was tall and skeletal, a rare white-skin human in this world of dark-skinned men. In contrast, Professor Deth (on the left), was stumpy and fat, with skin darker than Gorel's but a face that seemed a vivid red.

"Gentlemen," the caretaker said, and rose gracefully from her seat, "I have work to do."

"Wait!" Dr. Blud said. "What does a cemetery need with a sheriff?"

Professor Deth, perhaps a little quicker on the uptake, said: "Does he have magical powers? Is he a necromancer, a wraith-herd, a spirit-lord?"

But the caretaker was no longer there.

"No, no, and no," Gorel said calmly. The gun jumped from its holster into his hand, a fine, handcrafted device with a grip of dark wood bearing the small, exquisitely wrought silver pattern of a seven-pointed star that was the ancient sign of Goliris. "But I have this."

The two men edged back from the table, just a fraction.

"It's only a *gun*," Dr. Blud said with an unconvincing laugh.

"A mere projectile weapon," Professor Deth said, sounding a touch more interested. He edged back toward the table. "Yes, indeed . . . a six-shot? Made in . . . " he bent closer to peer at the gun. "The Lower Kidron? I recognize the workmanship. Quite exquisite, I must say."

"I'm impressed," Gorel said, the gun dematerializing from his hand. "May we sit down?" Professor Deth said and then, with a slight hesitation—"Sheriff?"

"Sheriff . . . " Dr. Blud snorted. His companion shushed him with a wave of a short fat hand. Gorel shrugged. Like the two men, he was not entirely convinced by the title. However, he *had* made a deal. And the thought of finding the information he craved sustained him. "Please," he said, waving his hand. The two men, after another moment of hesitation, sat down opposite.

"Barkeep!" Dr. Blud shouted. "Bring us some drinks."

"What would you like, Dr. Blud?" the grave-wraith's voice was soft, but it carried. Dr. Blud shrugged in the gloom of the bar. "Beer," he said.

Beside him, Professor Deth looked suddenly alarmed. "Not the *beer*," he said.

Dr. Blud shook his head mournfully. "I told you I analyzed it," he said. "It's perfectly safe."

"He brews it in the *dragon* tomb," Professor Deth hissed.

"The bones," Dr. Blud said, unruffled, and Gorel suddenly realized that the tall, thin man was quite drunk, "when ground to powder and mixed in liquid, are known for their *potency*."

While they were squabbling the drinks arrived, and with them the slight, tangy odor of the grave-wraith. He put down their drinks and departed in silence. Gorel took a sip from his beer. It was surprisingly good. For a moment he was torn. Then he reached into a pocket, returned with a small packet, and emptied its contents into the drink before him. He mixed it in with his finger and drank again. Gods' dust coursed through him, and he let out a sigh.

"I . . . see," Professor Deth said. "A true believer. Interesting."

"Dust?" Dr. Blud said. Without asking he reached for the empty packet, rubbed his finger on it, brought the tip of the finger to his lips. "Indeed."

Gorel ignored them, took another sip from his beer, and another, and set the mug back down on the table. "Care to tell me what it is you want, exactly?" he said.

"Gorel of . . . Goliris?" Professor Deth said, looking at him keenly.

"Goliris?" Dr. Blud said. The two men exchanged glances.

Driven by a sense of sudden urgency, Gorel said, "Do you know of it?"

"Many," Professor Deth said after a moment's hesitation, "have heard of Goliris."

"Yet few have seen it," Dr. Blud said. "Or lived to tell the tale," Professor Deth said.

"Gorel of Goliris."

They exchanged another glance. Something unspoken seemed to pass between them, a message of some sort. The dust in Gorel's blood surged, making him feel light and insubstantial. "Gorel—" Dr. Blud said.

"Sheriff—" Professor Deth said. "We would like to introduce ourselves—"

"Properly, that is—"

"We are," Dr. Blud said, "scientists."

"Necroscientists, to be exact," Professor Deth said. "Students of mortality—"

"And post-mortality."

"I . . . see," Gorel said, and didn't. The two scientists exchanged guilty glances. "Though you must understand we did not set out *originally* to—"

"An accident of circumstances—" Dr. Blud said.

"A conjunction of coincidences—" Professor Deth said.

"I, for instance," Dr. Blud said, "began my academic work in the field of archaeology—"

"A wonderful field—" Professor Deth said.

"Focusing on the Zul-Ware'i—"

"Or Ware'i-Zul—" Professor Deth said, and his companion nodded quickly several times—"War. Of course. And since there had been no survivors—"

"No survivors," Professor Deth confirmed—"I began to divert my study—a product of pure necessity, you understand—"

"Necessity," Professor Deth said, his big round head bobbing like a fallen mushroom—"into the field of necrostudies. And, incidentally, armaments. Wonderful weapons they had, the Zul—"

"Wonderful."

"While my companion here, the esteemed Professor Deth—"

"That would be me," the professor said, and shrugged—"began in the field of the human mind—"

"Studying the *psyche*," Professor Deth said, with some pride. "—but unfortunately—"

"Most unfortunately—"

"At the city of Waterfalling—"

"Waterfalling—"

"Where the subjects tended to, um, *terminate* early on in the study—"

"Crushed," Professor Deth said sadly.

"Smashed," Dr. Blud said.

"Broken," Professor Deth said. "It is the fall, you see. Impossible to survive. Which is the whole point, of course. But—"

"Quite resolutely *dead*," Dr. Blud said.

"Yes," Professor Deth said.

"And so," Dr. Blud said. "Here we are."

"Here we are," Professor Deth said, and there was a short silence.

Gorel took another sip from his beer. Strangely, it was almost empty. He decided he needed to talk to the preacher again. Perhaps he could negotiate a law-enforcement discount on the dust. He said, "So what do you *want*?"

"What we want?"

"What we want . . . "

There was another short silence.

"It is our work, you see . . . " Professor Deth said, his voice a sad whisper.

"Crucial to it," Dr. Blud said, nervously.

"We need to excavate," Professor Deth said.

"In section three . . . "

Two pairs of mournful eyes gazed at Gorel from their differing vertical positions, already expecting the inevitable answer.

Gorel smiled and stood up. "Absolutely not," he said.

The necromancer-king's funeral was still a few days away, but the dead were restless. For Gorel, the days took on a surreal aspect: in his sleep, as the wan sun rose and fell, voices babbled at him in a thousand different dialects and tongues. They pleaded with him, threatened him, cried out to him. *Release us. Set us free.* The nights were ink-black, the sky studded with pale stars that gave off no useful light. When he rose at sunset he ate, sparingly, at the Last Homily, took his first dose of dust for the day, and went out on patrol.

Wandering through Kur-a-len in the bleak of night . . . the statues seemed to move then, beyond the walls of mist, slowly, almost imperceptibly—an arm here, a talon there, the minute movement of a head, the opening of previously shut eyes, so that the landscape he wandered through seemed to subtly change with each pass, and he had the sense of the dead laughing at him. Whispers in the dark . . . the sounds of earth shifting, of doors creaking, of unseen things digging in the dark . . . once, he surprised the grave-wraith from the Last Homily as he was emerging from a vast and dilapidated tomb.

"What are you doing here?" Gorel growled. The grave-wraith fidgeted. Behind him emerged a small wooden cart, piled high with barrels. "I have permission from the caretaker," he said, a little sullen. Gorel stared up at the mausoleum: it rose high above, an enormous stone head emerging through the strands of mist, and somewhere to either side of it, the tips of two enormous wings that had a curiously leathery feel . . . "The Dragon Tomb?" he said, and the grave-wraith shrugged. "The dead," he said flatly, "are dead. Whatever they once were."

Gorel let him go, but as time passed he became aware that other, living denizens of this mist-and-night, black-and-white world roamed the cemetery at night.

Once, for instance, in what almost felt like a dream . . . he had come upon a broken heap of masonry that must have once been a Last House of Rest. A little of the roof remained, and the shadows were deep, and he was about to go on his way when he heard a soft and painful moan arise from the shadows and, coming closer to investigate, saw one of the most curious creatures he had ever encountered.

The creature had not noticed him. It was squatting on the ground, its face twisted in pain. It was making little moaning noises.

The creature was a little like a miniature human. The skin was a deep red, the head bald save for a few tufts of reddish hair. It had a big, bulging belly and an equally large behind. It was naked save for two folds of leather around its waist, at the front and rear. As Gorel watched, the little creature gave a last, dispiriting moan, grasped its short knees with both hands, and rocked on the balls of its feet. A blast of foul air erupted from its rear—Gorel took a step back—and it was followed, a short moment later, by—

It was a large stone. Its colors were dazzling. It rolled for a moment and then lay still on the ground, adding to the strange illumination in that enclosed space. The small creature sat back with a sigh, its face relaxing. After a moment it began to hum.

Gorel stared, repelled and fascinated. The egg lay there, glinting in the light of the stars. Gorel holstered his gun slowly and said, "Would you like a cigar?"

The little creature jumped on its feet, emitting a scream. It looked wildly this way and that. Clearly, it had expected no intruders here, in this abandoned, ruined place. "I won't hurt you," Gorel said, speaking softly.

The little creature looked up at him. It had large, round eyes that seemed to soften as it regarded Gorel. Was it some type of distant cousin to the Zambur? Gorel wondered. Did it habitually make its habitat in cemeteries? He said, "I won't take your . . . " it was a moment before the word formed. "Stones. My name is Gorel. Gorel of Goliris. I . . . I guard the cemetery grounds." He thought about it. "Temporarily."

The little creature looked up at him. Then, surprising Gorel, it reached a long, thin hand up to him and said, "Jais!"

"Jais?"

The creature nodded its ugly head. Gorel reached out and gingerly held the creature's hand. "Are there others like you?" Gorel said. The hand felt like rough stone. The creature nodded. "Jais!" it said again.

"Many Jais?"

The creature looked uncertain. Then, as if startled by something unseen, it quickly withdrew its hand, emitted a high-pitched shriek and, picking up the stone, disappeared in a scuttle into the shadows. Gorel stood and waited a moment: he noticed several pairs of bright eyes regarding him from the shadows. He shrugged, and smiled, and nodded to them, and they blinked, and Gorel left them.

On the night before the necromancer's funeral party at last arrived, Gorel had crested a low hill and, looking toward the horizon, thought he saw (beyond the Lake of the Drowned God; far into the more sparsely populated border area of the grounds) a great metal pyramid rising, shining a sickly green in the starlight. He stared at it, drawn somehow by the sight of the thing, sensing great power, and the black kiss pulsed through him and roared into life, and he followed blindly through the twisting avenues of the dead, but could not find it. He had gone past the Lake, where ripples seemed to form unexpectedly, and one had the sense of ethereal, moving bodies underneath the surface, of pale dead eyes watching from the depths. He had gone further, into sector eight, but could see no trace of that mysterious pyramid, though the black kiss still burned inside him. And at last, as he wove a drunken path through the structures of sector eight, he heard stealthy footsteps and, hiding in wait, saw the preacher walk slowly toward him.

The preacher: his wide-brimmed hat was gone and his head was bare, his single eye staring ahead, His lips moved constantly, mumbling over and over something that might have been a prayer. His boots left faint marks in the ground, and his open coat flapped about him in an unseen wind. As the coat moved Gorel could see, revealed for just an instance, a row of gleaming vials hooked to the lining of the coat: gods' dust, and freshly procured.

Gorel stepped out of the shadows. "Preacher," he said. The preacher stopped, his eye gazing this way and that like a pendulum unable to settle on a precise rhythm. Finally, his lips stopped moving, his eye focused, and he regarded Gorel with the hint of a smile before saying, "Yes, sheriff?"

"What are you doing here?" Gorel said, and the preacher shrugged and said, "Taking a stroll."

"Is that a usual thing?"

The smile became mocking. "Almost every night. *Sheriff.*"

"Where do you get it?" Gorel found himself asking. The mocking smile grew wider. "What gods are there to track within a cemetery?"

"Ah," the preacher said, and the smile grew obscene. "There is your question and your answer right there, in one neat package. Good night, sheriff." And he made to turn away, but slowly, and there was something suggestive in the way he did it, a watching awareness that made the hairs on Gorel's arms stand on end and form a hardness in him . . . He had a sudden, overwhelming desire, but didn't know if it was to shoot the man, or fuck him.

The question and the answer in one neat package . . .

"I need to . . . " Gorel said, and his voice was hoarse.

"Yes, sheriff?"

"I need to search you."

"By all means," the preacher said, and then he was close. Gorel could smell the scent of him, a smell of sweat and gods' dust and power. He reached under the coat and patted the preacher, but did so slowly, his hands traveling across the man's powerful torso and then down, to the preacher's belt. "Is it dust you want," the preacher said, his voice soft—"or is it love? And can you even tell the difference, man of Goliris?"

Their bodies came together, and Gorel's hardness encountered the preacher's own. When they kissed the preacher tasted of alcohol and dust, and his bristles were against the skin of Gorel's palms. The preacher's tongue was in Gorel's mouth and then Gorel pushed the preacher to the ground, removing his coat, unbuckling his belt with slow, sure hands. They kissed again, and Gorel licked the flesh on the man's face where his eye should have been, tasting it with the tip of his tongue. Then, working his way down, he took the preacher's hardness in his mouth, tasting gods' dust even there—it was as if the preacher was a being made of the stuff, and Gorel found him irresistible. When the preacher began to moan Gorel eased off him and the preacher's hands found him and were rubbing him, forcing his own trousers down, and then he was pushing Gorel down to the ground, Gorel's face in the dirt as the preacher's hardness was against Gorel's cheeks, rubbing slowly in those twin mounds of flesh, and when he entered him his hand cupped Gorel from behind and rubbed him, and he cried out.

When it was done they had walked away from each other, as strange to each other as when they met. He did not encounter the preacher this way again and, mostly, the nights were quiet—at least until the burial of Seraph Gadashtill, Ninth Caliph of Mindano Caliphate, last in the line of the necromancer-kings . . .

Part Two: The Corpse Had No Face

She came to him in the dream. She had no face, no substance. She was all fog, and cold to the touch. Wraith-fingers touched his skin and made him shiver. Her voice was dead. She said, *Who are you?*

Gorel, he whispered.

Her voice grew insistent, the touch of her unbearable. *Where do you come from? Where do you belong?*

Golir—he began to say, and she screamed, the noise like an ice pick driven into his brain, and he woke, his heart pounding, into a silent night.

The funeral was over. The caliph had been laid to rest. That night darkness lay over the tombs like an old blanket. Nothing stirred. In the Last Homily last drinks had been served and the lights were killed. The ninth caliph's burial party had since retreated to their beds and to sleep, having spent the day in mourning, prayer, and drinking. All was silent.

Gorel prowled the cemetery. His head hurt. The traces of a dream lingered inside like wisps of cloth, cloying, frayed. A faceless woman who looked familiar despite the lack of form.

A scream tore through the night.

At first he thought the scream was in his head. An echo from his dream, still going.

The scream rose, cut through the graveyard air like a butcher's knife, fear primal and ugly in every note. Gorel felt his hands instinctively fall down to his guns. He left them there. Began to run.

The scream rose into a crescendo. Black birds rose in a cloud into the sky, startling him. The scream was cut short.

Running through the avenues of graves, birds silent above and around him, like an explosion caught in dark amber. All sound seemed to have stopped. He ran in the direction he thought the scream had come from, gun in hand, and saw a shadow fleeing ahead of him.

Not thinking, he pursued. The shadow fled faster, blending in and out of the outlines of giant graves. Running, the breath catching in his chest, the world in black and white but primarily black, echoes of the scream still in his head, dream or awakening he didn't know which.

Through black night and tombstones jutting from the ground, his feet soft on the earth, the shadow never slackening his pace. His breath was coming out burning, dragon's breath, the shadow slowed, turned to face him—

No face, nothing but shadow, and yet: he could sense it, feel it, a grin splitting up that mask of darkness, amused or manic or both—

Gorel raised his gun. His finger tightened on the trigger, yet he had only the sense of the watching shadow's grin growing wider still. He squeezed off a shot and, still running, stumbled into something heavy on the ground. The unexpected impact threw him, a second shot went wide, and he went down. When he rose a moment later the shadow he'd been pursuing was gone, and on the ground beside him was a dead woman.

"Kelini Pashtill," the caretaker said. She sighed, and the shadows rustled around her like garments that, for her, they perhaps were. "Third cousin to the former caliph and a member of the burial party."

"What was she doing out here on her own?" Gorel said, thinking—no wonder she isn't pleased. He said aloud, "People bring their dead to the Garden, they don't expect it to be the other way around."

"We'll offer a free burial," the caretaker said. "Of course. Still . . . "

A hunch: "Has this happened before?"

Silence. Finally, another shrug. "There are always complications . . . "

He wanted to answer, thought better of it, bent down to examine the body instead.

Kelini Pashtill could have been pretty once. It was impossible to tell with her face gone.

"But nothing recent."

Bending down, a faceless corpse staring back at him. Nothing else missing— the rest of the body in perfect shape. He said, "One of the dead?"

"It seems likely."

He searched through the woman's pockets. A small rolled pack-et—he palmed it on the way out. "The caliph?"

The caretaker shrugged. "He should be safely ensconced in his grave," she said.

Gorel remembered a past encounter with a necromancer. They did not die easy. He said, "This is murder."

The caretaker said, "Yes."

"And therefore bad for business?"

"Yes."

He stood up, nodded. Behind the caretaker a huddled group of Zambur, waiting. "Take her away," Gorel said.

Where do you come from, the ethereal voice said, the sound like crunched glass rattling in his skull. Longing in the voice, and hate—a strange mixture. Fingers like fog touching him, caressing him, the voice whispering, *Tell me*, again and again, Gorel frozen, trapped in the membrane of the dream world where the separation between the living and the dead was weakest. He braced himself for a scream but this time it wasn't there, which was somehow more frightening. He could sense hunger again, coming back strong, and desire and loathing, but all that happened was the voice repeating, again and again the words *Tell me*.

He fought to awaken. Her fog, her form, wrapped him like a shroud. Goliris, he said, and felt her slacken about him. Goliris. The word hurt her, and he wielded it like a knife, cutting away at her entrapment of him. Goliris. Goliris. She whispered, *No . . .* and let him go and he reached for her and took her face and turned it toward his own, expecting the blankness—and screamed, because where before there had been no face at all was now the countenance of the dead Kelini Pashtill.

"This is an outrage," Sorel Gadashtill said. He spoke flatly, without an intonation. There was no emotion in his voice, unless you counted cold as an emotion. Gorel said, "I quite understand—" and the caliph's nephew—fat, red-faced, with intelligent eyes that seemed to look through Gorel as if he were a graveyard worm, said, "Do you, sheriff?"

"Explain it to me, then," Gorel said, and the man sighed. "We brought our dear, dead caliph—" Gorel bit back on mentioning the caliph was not *quite* dead when he was brought back, if the frenzied scene at the funeral was any indication—"to this place because it is a place of *peace*. We *paid*—" the word seemed to pain him—"*paid* a not-insignificant sum of money to the caretaker of this place, to *ensure* my uncle's final rest. That, clearly, hasn't happened."

"I'm confused," Gorel said. He noted the rings on the fat man's fingers. Had Jericho Moon, his friend and some-time companion, been there, he would have quickly found the right time and place to relieve the caliph's nephew of those bulky, expensive items. It occurred to Gorel he would do well to do it himself. Nevertheless . . . he was being paid with knowledge this time, not money. Well . . . not *only* money. That there might be dead of Goliris at the Garden . . . he made a note to himself to chase the caretaker again for the information. She had seemed reluctant to part with it so far. "Are you suggesting it was the *caliph* responsible for the death?"

"The *murder*," Sorel Gadashtill said—with some relish, it seemed to Gorel. "Of course it is. You didn't know him."

Gorel listened. Sorel Gadashtill seemed to appreciate the audience. He said, "He was a monster." He said it the way one would ask for the salt to be passed. Gorel marked it, didn't comment. "He was a bloodthirsty, vicious, cruel, capricious ghoul." A small, affectionate smile lit up his face for a moment, transforming it completely: at that moment he looked younger and innocent, a nephew talking about a favorite uncle. Perversely, it reminded Gorel of his own younger self. "He was the best ruler the Gadashtill dynasty had seen in over four hundred years. His loss is a loss to us all."

"I'm not sure," Gorel said slowly, "that I entirely understand." Though he suspected that he did.

"Don't you?" the caliph's nephew said. "It seems perfectly obvious to me. The caliph had served his country diligently for far longer than the duration of a normal human's life. Again and again he came back from the dead to serve. It was enough. The man needed rest! And at vast expense, this was the place settled on. It was, in fact, the caliph's own explicit wish, to be buried here. The great Garden of Statues! A haven of the dead, a place *guaranteed* by tradition and money to hold its denizens. No wonder he is upset."

"*Upset?*" Gorel said, thinking again of the woman's faceless corpse.

"Don't you understand?" Sorel Gadashtill said. "*He cannot help returning.* It was why we had to—even at the funeral itself—most regrettable—" he actually looked embarrassed for a moment. Gorel flashed back to the caliph rising in his coffin, the nephew's knife rising in tandem, plunging into his uncle's chest, sending him back. Shaking himself back to the present, he said, "So you think your uncle is behind the death."

"It is his nature," Sorel Gadashtill said. "And besides, Kelini was always his favorite."

So far, so bad, Gorel thought. He had a corpse, and he had a suspect, only the suspect too was dead. Yet something rang false to him in the nephew's story, and he couldn't tell what it was. He shelved it, went to the Last Homily instead. Bartender grave-wraith behind the counter, members of the caliph's burial party drinking in a corner, scowling as he walked in. No sign of Blud or Deth, no sign of the preacher—by the window a party of new arrivals, talking in low voices. A huddle of Zambur drinking from smoking beakers—he didn't want to know.

He went up to the counter, sat down on a stool. The bartender eyeballed him. "What can I get you, sheriff?"

"Punch," Gorel said.

The grave-wraith leered. "Coming right up."

Gorel's hand on his wrist stopped him. The grave-wraith's flesh felt slimy, flecks of skin coming off in his grip. "And some information."

"That's extra," the grave-wraith said, and pulled his hand away. He was no longer smiling.

Gorel said, "The dead girl."

"What about her?"

"She was here last night."

The grave-wraith shrugged. "Where else is there to go?"

"You tell me."

"Let me get your drink," the grave-wraith said, and leered again. "Mix some dust in for you? That's also extra."

He poured the drink from a casket the shape of a closed coffin, mixed in dust from a vial. When he brought it over Gorel said, "Who do *you* think killed her?"

"I don't think," the grave-wraith said. His long fingers tapped a beat on the counter, skeletal sound making Gorel wince. Gorel plonked a bracelet on the counter—death money, part of the caretaker's idea of an expense account. The grave-wraith's eyes grew larger and his leer subsided. "What's that?" he said, trying for casual, and failing.

"Enchanted bracelet, gold inlaid with encased mermaids' eyes"—the eyes, preserved under the sea, like chunks of amber—"from the island-nation of Etern, second dynasty." He covered it with his hand, one frozen eye peeking out. "You like it?"

"Etern . . ." the grave-wraith said. "Section eight has a few Etern tombs . . . "

"You got family here?"

"What?" The grave-wraith took a step back from the counter. Slime oozed out of his left eye, yellow-green like pus.

Gorel said, "You might want to wipe that off."

Instead of an answer the grave-wraith reached under the counter, returned with a small glass jug, unstoppered it. He put his eye over the opening and squeezed—the viscous liquid falling down like tears. The grave-wraith stoppered the bottle, returned it to its place, and put his leer back on. There were tiny insects moving between his teeth. "Family. Relatives. However that works."

"I was *buried* here," the grave-wraith said. "I didn't live here."

"Other wraiths around?"

The bartender shrugged.

"You don't know, or you don't care?"

The shrug again. "You're not being very helpful," Gorel said. "Considering."

"Considering what, *sheriff*?"

"Considering what's bad for the Garden's business is bad for your business," Gorel said. "In the long term. If people don't trust the cemetery any more . . . "

"They'll keep coming," the grave-wraith said. "No one cares much for the affairs of the dead. It's why they put them here in the first place."

Gorel sighed, took a sip from his punch. Dust hit him like a fist, sent him flying. "You may not have much of a personality," Gorel said, "but you can mix a drink."

"I should probably say thank you," the grave-wraith said, "but fuck off will serve instead."

Gorel smiled, showing teeth. "Tell me about the girl," he said. He lifted the bracelet off the counter, dangled it in the air between them. The gold caught the light. The mermaids' dead eyes stared into nothing.

The bartender swallowed. "What do you want to know?" he said. His eyes were on the bracelet.

Gorel said: "Last night, she was here. Tell me."

The bartender reached for the bracelet. Gorel moved it away. "You like it?" he said.

"Fuck you," the bartender said, but without conviction.

"Tell," Gorel said. The bartender told.

She came to the Last Homily with the rest of the Mindano Caliphate mission. They sat on their own. The men had beer, apart from the caliph's nephew, who had Suicide Rum. The two ladies had draeken and Gravedigger's Punch, respectively. Kelini Pashtill had the punch.

"Dust?" Gorel said, interested. The bartender shrugged. "Not apart from what's in the punch, or not that I'd seen, at any rate."

"Anyone else?" Gorel said.

The bartender shook his head, no.

Gorel said, "Go on."

They were talking quietly. None of the regulars were around. "Isn't that a bit strange?" Gorel said.

The bartender shrugged. "Things to do," he said.

"Like what?"

The shrug again. It was beginning to irritate Gorel. "Do you know where they were?"

"You'll have to ask them that yourself," the grave-wraith said, but his eyes were locked on the bracelet and he didn't sound convinced.

Gorel said, "Want to try harder?"

"Blud and Deth came in earlier for a drink," the grave-wraith said. He looked like he'd come to a decision. "They left as the burial party came in. I heard Blud mention something about their dig. That's all I know—they've been spending a lot of time in the Garden recently."

"Do they have permission?" Gorel said.

The bartender began to shrug, took one look at Gorel's expression and thought better of it. "You'll have to ask the caretaker," he said. "But I think they do. You don't go messing around inside without some form of sanction."

"And the preacher?" Gorel said, changing tack.

"He wasn't . . . " the bartender began, then hesitated.

"Go on," Gorel said. Tense now. The bartender said, "Look, he wasn't here. But . . . "

Gorel waited, silence like a web waiting for a catch.

The bartender said, "I saw him outside. Before the burial party came in."

Gorel, a flash—"With Pashtill?"

"With the woman, yes. I figured she was buying, and didn't want to make it too public."

"She drank the punch."

"Sheriff," the grave-wraith said and leered, "she drank it like you do. She drank it like it was water and she was frying on the sands of Meskatel."

"Tell me about Blud and Deth," Gorel said. "They have any interaction with the Mindano people?"

"I told you, they left as the others arrived," the grave-wraith said. Behind Gorel the door banged open and he heard footsteps.

"Can we talk?" the caretaker said.

Gorel nodded, not turning around. "Why did they leave?" he said.

"I got the impression they didn't want to have to see the big guy," the grave-wraith said.

Gorel said: "Sorel Gadashtill? The nephew?"

"The fat one," the grave-wraith said. "If that's his name. They left through the back."

Gorel tossed him the bracelet. The grave-wraith made it disappear. Gorel said, "And you were here all night?"

"I'm here every night," the bartender said.

"What do you think?" the caretaker said.

"I think any one of them could have done it," Gorel said. "What I don't know is *why*."

"You think it was a flesh-and-blood killer, then?"

"As opposed to the former caliph? I don't know."

"But you have some ideas."

"I always have some ideas." They were walking through Gardentown toward the cemetery.

Already the light was waning, the short day winking out. Gorel said, "Blud and Deth."

"Yes?"

"What *are* they doing here?"

The caretaker shrugged. "Research. We get a surprising number of visiting scholars. Those two are just the latest. The . . . management is usually indifferent."

"The management?"

"The . . . interests I represent."

He noticed the hesitation, twice. "Who are they?" he said.

The caretaker shook her head and the shadows withdrew around her. "Just hope you never have occasion to meet them," she said.

Gorel let it pass. "What research?" he said. The caretaker said, "Officially? The study of undeath distribution patterns across sections one to five. That's—"

"All the things that don't quite stay dead?"

"Quite. It does help to have recorded migration patterns, you know. The last study was conducted by Deo the Third, of Sotrn'Ak, and that was several centuries ago."

"Who was the caretaker then?" Gorel said, playing a hunch.

"A distant relative," the caretaker said, a little cold.

"Did you find the information I was looking for?" Gorel said, changing tack again.

The caretaker seemed to hesitate. "Goliris . . . " she said. "Yes . . . "

"You said there may be some who are buried here."

"One," the caretaker said. The shadows congregated around her then. "There is one."

Gorel waited. The caretaker seemed deep in thought. Finally she said, "Yes. Tomorrow I will show you. Who knows, it might help . . . " She said no more, and he didn't push her. They turned and walked down the avenues of the dead.

All about them the great follies and Last Houses of Rest, the tombstones and headstones rose like an unoccupied city. Yet it was occupied: and as they walked, in silence now, Gorel could sense them all around him, the silent dead, generations upon generations, centuries upon centuries of beings who had once been alive and great, and were now reduced, diminished, kings and queens, sorcerers and senators, warriors and poets, merchants and killers, all brought here, at the end of their days, to be interred in the grandest dumping grounds of the dead, this necropolis of Kur-a-Len. He watched them now, these silent simulacra that stood like markers above their dead counterparts, faces chiseled in stone and metal and wood, and he asked himself whether it had made one little bit of difference to them, to the people they had once been, whether their grave was a palace or a sewer: to Gorel, dead was simply dead.

But not to some, he thought. Some fought death, railed against it, schemed and planned and plotted against the day. Some sought immortality, and no doubt found it, after a fashion. Even gods died, in the end. And some had died and were returned, living in the twilight, shaped from the material that formed the membrane between worlds. They were the creatures in between, refusing to depart, to end, to cease, and he respected that, while not quite sharing the sentiment. Beside him the caretaker seemed to shiver, and the shadows gathered round her, wrapping her in a cloak of night. They had come to her house. It had once been a grave.

Of course, to have called it a grave was to have done injustice to it. If it were once a grave then it was a palatial one. Even in such as place as the Garden, the caretaker's abode towered over plain mausoleums, mere castles and citadels. It was nothing short of a palace, with servants' quarters, a library, a dining room, even baths. The outside was done in Nocturne architectural style, all dark and brooding shadows, tall walls, forbidding turrets that seemed to capture the night. Gorel said, "I'm impressed."

Behind her shadows, the caretaker seemed to smile. "You should be," she said. "That was the intention."

"Is this converted?" he said, following her through a door of solid dark stone.

"In a manner of speaking."

"Who was buried here?"

She seemed to smile again, and didn't answer. There was something he didn't like about her silence, and at the same time, it excited him. He wanted to know the caretaker better, he realized. She was an enigma on par with the rest of the place, an unknown quantity. For a moment he considered her as the dark shadow he had chased, the stealer of a woman's face—a killer. It was a possibility.

"The library is through there," she said, pointing. Their feet, he noticed, made no sound on the black marble floor. "You wanted to look up Mindano Caliphate."

It was not said as a question. And he had, but didn't mention it. Interesting.

"I'll just go and . . . change," the caretaker said. She spoke with those odd hesitations, as if picking words a little too carefully, so that they never came out quite right. "Make yourself comfortable."

He decided he would. He followed her with his eyes as she glided away, wondering what hid behind the shadows, and felt desire flare inside him like a funeral pyre.

The library first: rows and rows of bookshelves made of hard black wood, warm to the touch, rising from floor to distant ceiling. He saw no coffins, no sarcophagi—and wondered. Who had this place been built for? And what had they expected death to bring? He felt depth below him, hidden caverns underneath his feet and the cold marble floor, yet a comfortable fire burned in the large fireplace. A silent Zambur brought over a glass of warm wine, and he didn't even need to taste it to know it had been laced most liberally with dust. Was that in his honor?

He watched the Zambur depart, the strange little creature making no sound. They were like the fungus that grows only in moonlight, only around graves. He was not even sure they were not some half-plant species, only partially flesh. He had only ever heard rumors before . . .

He looked up Mindano Caliphate: third cabinet, fifth shelf—Gorod &

Zdruss' *A Traveler's Guide to the Mindano, Gesheft and Torqan Principalities, with Commentaries on their Geography, Fauna and Flora, Politics and Customs, With Illustrations by Krodin the Second.*

He looked at the illustrations first. High mountains rising in the distance, the lands of Mindano and Gesheft in constant shade, bare country, snow high up in the mountains, eyes seeming to watch the artist from the shadows as he sketched—he drew them in, constantly. *Mindano, Caliphate of:* he skimmed the text, looking for salient points. "An inhospitable region dominated by the Ware'i-Zul mountains and by the consequences of its devastating war . . . The modern Caliphate was formed at the conclusion of the war . . . necessity for labor created the conditions for the rise of the modern line of necromancer-rulers, the line originally coming from . . . it is a condition of the monarchic rule that caliphs be buried as far away from the land as possible to prevent the possibility of civil war (see *Succession, War of, Third and Fourth Caliph, Period of*) . . ." A few pages on, woodcuts of dark dull-eyed birds, dead or alive he couldn't tell, a march of dead men clearing a road, a note—"*Reanimated Canaries, The:* Favorite pets originating in the deadwoods of Mindano Caliphate, known for their ability to sometimes sing the future. See also *Notable Exports.*" Images of the caliphs, all looking more or less the same. Few more pages: *Stories and Legends.* One at the bottom of a page caught his eye: *A Princess of Neverwas.* He read the story, looking for something, not sure why:

> *Once upon a time, in the dark final days as the Zul and the Ware'i fought and the mountains were devastated, when the First Caliph was yet a young boy, a princess came to Mindano. She came from a no-place and a no-when, a place and a time she called Neverwas. She was beautiful and strong, and had come over the mountain passes, in the midst of the final days of the war, yet was unscathed. It was said there was much magic in her, though she seldom displayed it. When asked about her home, she never spoke. There was a sadness about her, and an anger, and the young boy who was to become caliph saw his own sadness and anger reflected in her, and fell in love with her. It was said many, men and women, were in love with her that long, dark winter. At that time the Final Weapon of the Zul was deployed, and the mountains flared in a great light, and were then silent, and the Great Sickness came over the mountain as if following in the woman's footsteps, and a multitude joined the ranks of the dead. The people of Mindano were frightened, and blamed the princess, though she protested her innocence.*

The boy protected her, but at last, as the survivors surrounded the home
he by now shared with the princess, he brought her outside and, before
the watching people, put a knife through her heart.

Gorel looked at the woodcut depicting this scene. All he could see were
eyes in the shadows. He wondered what it was that Krodin the Second saw in
Mindano as he slowly went insane . . .

As she died, the young boy was transformed, and all knelt down before
him. He raised the bloodied knife to the skies and a flash of lightning
hit the metal, sending bright blue sparks into the air. Then the boy
went amongst the dead, and his eyes were cold and hard, and wherever
he pointed the blade the dead rose, and followed him, and the First
Regiment of the Dead was formed. That night the boy sent the princess
away in a coffin carried by reanimated corpses who were in thrall to
him, and where they went was never known.

Gorel put down the book. The memory of a memory niggled at him, as of
something he remembered he *should* remember. All he knew was that he was
glad never to have visited Mindano Caliphate, which sounded dismal, and
he suspected the food was bad there. It was a place founded on sorcery, and
Gorel hated sorcery, hated and despised it. He stood and stretched and left the
library, pushing thoughts of Mindano, necromancers, murder, and princesses
from his mind.

They dined in the caretaker's dining hall, which was a study in necromantic
elegance.

A mix of Diurnal and Nocturne . . . but mainly Nocturne, he thought.
Shadows hung from the walls like tapestries. Fat wax candles burned in silver
chandeliers. There were family portraits on the walls, or so he assumed: they
were all pure black, the painting of shadows. The caretaker followed his gaze,
said, "You can see them in a range of other light. Here—" she handed him a
curious device.

Gorel said, "What is it?"

"An invention of Blud and Deth," she said. "They took quite an interest in
the portraits. Put it on. Like this—" she demonstrated.

Gorel put the device over his eyes. Two metal cones telescoped down from
his eyes, a series of prisms nestled inside. He moved his head, seeing the world

as a sudden bright unnatural glow, blinking back tears. He turned to the caretaker but she was not there. Her voice came from behind him. "Look at the paintings."

"I'd rather look at you."

She laughed. The laughter was guttural and made Gorel shiver. He felt her hand on his shoulder, her thumb digging into the muscles of his back. He realized he desperately wanted to see her, beyond the veils of shade, and touch her too . . . He looked at the paintings instead.

They were radiant. The shades had fallen away like dropped clothing, revealing an illumination beyond that was hard to focus on. He detected delicate cheekbones, small elongated ears, almond-shaped eyes that seemed to focus on him as he stared, and lips that formed into mocking smiles . . . both her hands were now on his shoulders, massaging him, caressing him. He turned, catching her by surprise, got a glimpse of a face both beautiful and old. She put her hands on the lens, blocking his sight.

Impatient, he tore off the goggles. The candlelight danced in the holders. The caretaker was wrapped in shadows. She laughed and he rose and grabbed her, feeling warm, naked skin beyond the shadows. His hands were on her body. She danced into his arms and the shadows wrapped them both. "I am old," she whispered in his ear, her breath hot on his skin. "And surrounded by death on all sides . . . "

His hand found a breast, stayed. Her nipple grew in the space between his fingers. He could feel the blood coursing through her, the beating of her heart against his palm. His lips sought hers. She tasted of night flowers and slowly released heat. He said, "You feel alive to me . . . " and felt her smile against him. Then her tongue was in his mouth and his hand was on her neck, stroking it, and he pulled back and said, "And not that old . . . " He heard her laugh.

He eased his way down her, traveling blind, compensating for the lack of sight with touch and smell and taste. Her nipples were hard in his mouth, and tasted of the berries that only grow at night. She pushed him further down then, and he found the source of her heat and buried his head between her thighs as she rocked against him, grinding herself on his face. Her skin was smooth and very delicate. His tongue probed deep inside her and he heard her gasp.

He ran his hand down her backside, between her legs. She turned easily, eagerly, and his tongue ran between the mounds of her ass and found the dark well there. He took her from behind, a woman with no face, and all the while he was haunted by another. His hard stomach slapped against her and his erection was a black-sailed mast plowing a sunless sea. She cried when she came, and shook against him, but Gorel could find no respite, had to keep going, seeing a face that wasn't a face, a dead woman's mask stretched over a blankness. The caretaker pulled away, turned on her back, came back to him with hands and mouth, shadows coagulating. She stroked him, fondled, whispered, her lips kissing him, running up and down, swallowing him whole until at last he mastered release and exploded in her mouth. Then they were silent, entwined together, wrapped in Nocturnal darkness, as close to content as Gorel could ever come, which was some distance. He said, "Goliris."

"Tomorrow," she whispered. "I will show you the grave you're looking for."

He felt her fall asleep against him and thought about tomorrow, and the grave that might hold an answer from his far-off home. He felt himself falling too, sleep taking him, forcing him under the waves, and as he drowned he saw her, the faceless woman, staring at him, caressing him through the impenetrable night. Tomorrow, he said, or tried to say, and then he was gone, asleep in the place where no dreams came.

When he woke up it was tomorrow, but the caretaker was dead.

Part Three: Death Waits Underground

He woke up cold; he shivered in the gloom; it was very quiet. His skin felt sticky. He rolled, one arm flung over the sleeping woman beside him, tried to nestle into her warmth—but it was like cuddling up to a block of ice.

He opened his eyes and the corpse of the caretaker stared back at him. He pushed back a scream. He thrashed in the bed and it was a pool of dark liquid. As he stood he realized he was covered in blood. The caretaker was lying on the bed. There was a fist-sized hole in her chest, where her heart had been.

He realized then that he could see her. The shadows had fled from her in death and the corpse was quite ordinary, a woman neither old nor young. He examined her fingers, saw no sign of a struggle. Whoever—whatever—had killer had, had done so swiftly.

He was naked. He looked for his guns. They were on the floor with his clothes. He went for them and had the guns in his hands just as the first Zambur came through the door and emitted a high-tone shriek. Gorel said, "Fuck." The Zambur disappeared through the door.

There was a mirror on the wall and what it showed did not look good. Gorel, naked and covered in gore, guns in hand. On the bed, the caretaker, dead and missing a heart.

He thought—why the *heart*? There were cultures that believed the heart was the seat of emotion, but Gorel knew that wasn't true. It was a pump, keeping the blood flowing throughout the body. He had seen enough bodies, enough dying men—a few women, too, when it came to that.

There were shouts outside, human. He put on his clothes with one hand, the other holding a gun. Three Zambur came through the door simultaneously, holding a large metal pipe between them, its open mouth aimed at Gorel, and he said, "Fuck," again. "I didn't kill her!" The Zambur didn't seem to have heard. He heard a slow whining sound rising from inside the weapon. He tried to master some authority. "This is a crime scene," he said. "You need to leave, now."

The Zambur, small and pale, aimed the weapon and the whine grew louder and piercing. Gorel said, "Fuck it," and shot them. They fell like burst mushrooms, making no sound. The massive gun dropped to the floor. Gorel dropped with it, rolling sideways. When the gun hit the ground it discharged. A burst of blue light, Gorel still rolling away, the light hit the wall where he had stood and the wall disintegrated. Gorel rolled and dove for the gun, grabbing it, was surprised at how light it was. His clothes stuck to him with the caretaker's blood. He looked down, saw that now he was covered, in addition, in Zambur remains. They had a rotten smell, as of things that had been buried too long underground. The voices outside grew louder. He stepped through the door, still holding the Zambur gun.

They were coming for him. He walked through the caretaker's vast mausoleum, peered out of a window and took a step back.

Wave after wave of white-pale Zamburs, carrying torches, brandishing spades, coming through the cemetery toward him.

Humans: he thought he saw the preacher, hat pulled low over his eyes, watching in the shadows of a nearby tombstone, but couldn't be sure. He looked again but the figure was gone. It could have just been a member of the Mindano delegation. He realized then that he hadn't seen the preacher since . . . since before the first murder, and he wondered with some unease what it meant.

He scanned the crowd again, pushing the preacher from his thoughts. There. Somewhere the other side, half-hidden behind other Gardentown residents, tall, skeletal, pale: Dr. Blud.

Two watchers with an interest—a possible motive? Something Dr. Blud had said to him came back, suddenly: he had studied the Zul-Ware'i war, had come, therefore, from the vicinity of Mindano. And he was a necroscientist . . . which meant necromancer to Gorel, which meant sorcerer, which meant . . .

He didn't know what it meant. But he was going to find out.

At least, he thought, watching the Zambur converging on the tomb with their burning torches, he would if he could somehow manage to escaped . . .

But why try? she said. He turned to her. She hovered beside him, not flesh, not quite real: the woman from his dreams. She had a face now, the dead girl's face, but it was changing, shifting itself to fit her. *Stay and let them take you,* she said. *Join me. I am lonely. We could . . .*

"We could start by cutting out the shit," Gorel said, speaking aloud, and the specter beside him seemed to shimmer—in anger or amusement, he couldn't tell. Her naked body was flushed, a translucent cover that didn't hide the flow of blood inside, and the beating heart that wasn't there before. She smiled when she saw his eyes. *Soon I will be ready,* she said. *It has been so long . . .*

"You?" he said. Her body both repelled and attracted him. Outside the Zambur were advancing, but slowly. He had to find a way out. "You killed them?"

How could I? she said. *I am dead.*

"Not dead enough . . . " Gorel muttered, and she laughed. Gorel backed away from the window. He remembered his earlier thoughts—that there must have been something underneath this place. He stared at the mute portraits on the walls, but they were just blackened frames. "How do I get out of here?" he said. But the specter was no longer there.

Gorel cursed ghosts, women, murderers, and Zambur. Of the four, he reflected, the Zambur were the least palatable. And they were after him. He went back to the library, hoping to find an answer in books. Outside, the tomb was surrounded in a ring of flame.

He was not a reading man by nature. He used books the way he used his guns: to track and to gain. But he remembered a saying of his friend, the old wizard Champol: "A book near the heart can save your life." Champol would then pull out, with great ceremony, a small battered leather-bound volume, a neat hole drilled at its center, cutting almost clean through. "There's your proof," Champol would say, and wheeze a laugh. He hadn't seen the old bastard in years. He wondered what he was up to.

He scanned the bookshelves. Champol's book, if he remembered rightly, was some sort of religious tract. For some reason it seemed important to him at that moment to recall the exact title. Champol was not much for religion— neither was Gorel, until that encounter with the goddess Shar and her black kiss . . . he shuddered and wished he had more dust. He had put off seeking the preacher again . . . and now it was too late. His thoughts wandered, shying from the fate waiting for him outside. Think about Champol's book. Maybe it was a philosophical discourse? Something about gods, at any rate. He couldn't think why it was important. He tried to focus on the bookshelves, but his hands shook—withdrawal and fear. He needed more dust, more belief. Somewhere in the cemetery there was a source of dust. Yet there were no itinerant gods in the cemetery—he would have known if there had. Gods did not usually keep quiet about their presence.

Shouts from outside. They wouldn't come in, not after he'd killed those three Zambur, but they knew he had no way out. A book near the heart can save your life . . . too bad it had been too late, he thought, to save the caretaker's.

He needed to find a way out. Books offered a way out. Or so he'd been told. They provided escape. Escapism. He needed an escape. It didn't make much sense and yet it did—he could sense it in a part of him, perhaps the part that was starved of dust, that was sensitive to it—there was something down there, waiting, and the entrance was nearby.

He began searching the shelves, pulling out books. His search grew more frantic. He could hear a calling from down below, cold and ancient, guiding him . . . he thought he heard the caretaker's voice and shivered, but he kept on going. The shelves were growing bare, like trees in the fall. And yet—nothing.

Not the books then. Something else. Something in the room . . . he examined the floor but could see no hidden trapdoor, no opening into the underground. There must be something! His hands shook harder and then he remembered—yes . . . he had meant to follow it up, and hadn't had the chance. Preacher again. He kept coming up. Something about the man that wasn't right . . . when he found the corpse of Kelini Pashtill he had gone through her pockets. There had been a small, rolled packet in there. He fished in his pockets and drew it out. Dust. He had known it was dust the moment he took it, didn't know what had made him palm it, not showing it to the caretaker, keeping it secreted away. Had Pashtill bought from it the preacher? What did it mean? If he got out he would corner the man and beat an answer out of him, regardless of what had gone before. Right now all he could think of was the dust. He opened the packet. The white powder lay inside. He took a pinch between thumb and forefinger, brought it to his nose, sniffed it.

An explosion. For a moment he thought it was inside his head, but no— it was outside. They had broken down the wall. His head swam. They were coming after him. The dust rushed through his bloodstream, his heart pumping hard and dust going to his brain. He took another sniff, and another. His hands steadied. The packet was empty.

There was high-toned screeching outside and then the wall of the library disintegrated. But Gorel was no longer there.

Death waited underground for him. He could taste the flavor of it in the back of his throat, dust and bones and rust, a coldness and a shiver and the stench of a blood that had been spilled long ago.

There were nine stone sarcophagi in the cavern. He didn't wish to look inside them, but could sense a strange appraisal emanating from inside. They were watching him.

He had sought escape in books and found it in a drug. Yet was dust a drug? A god's black kiss, an enslaving, a desire, a need: yes, all those things, a distilled faith he had not wanted and could not now refuse. It had opened the door for him—he was sure of that. For there was a door, though to call it a door would be not to understand it. A hole, an absence, but hidden—a fall. It was as if, for just one moment, he had died, and in death was freed to fall. It only lasted for a moment, and when it was over he had landed there, in the cold dark cavern underground. The dead were there, but he could not see them, only sense them—for now. But they were watching him, aware, troubled somehow—he could sense that, a great agitation in them, a restlessness, as if their sleep has been disturbed.

He pushed them away from his mind. He needed to find a way out. A way back to the surface, back to the public face of the Garden of Statues, and there . . .

But what? He was wanted now, wanted for two murders he did not commit, and they would be looking for him, hunting him. He could, he thought, walk away. Steal out of the cemetery and continue on his way. For what, after all, did he owe this dismal place? He had been sidetracked here, lured with the promise of knowledge, a clue to help him on his way, back to his kingdom, his birthright, his home: back to Goliris, the greatest kingdom the World had ever seen, from which he had been banished, to which he will return, with the cold vengeance nurtured, forever nurtured inside himself. He could leave—but he knew he wouldn't, not now, for his anger was up, and someone would pay for trying to play with him, a prince of Goliris. There would be more dead in the Garden before Gorel would be finished.

He spoke his vow out loud then, and it seemed to him that the watchers in the darkness nodded, as if in agreement. A weight seemed to come off from his shoulders and the tomb felt warmer. Preacher, he thought. He would find the preacher and squeeze the information from him, squeeze very hard. His instincts told him there was an intelligence behind the two murders, an intelligent agency, and aware—alive. The dead seldom schemed, unless amongst themselves.

It would be underground, he thought then. Here it would hide, in the subterranean world of the cemetery. He thought then of the World, which was immense and ancient, a world above ground of sun and rain and stars. Yet how much of the World was hidden, was beneath the surface, how many lives and deaths were hidden in the flesh of the World?

"I'll find you," he said, speaking out loud, and had the sense that the silent sarcophagi approved.

He looked at his surroundings. A cavern, yes, and those nine stone coffins that seemed to exude an unnatural chill—he felt his hands grow numb with sudden cold—but there, beyond them—a door.

Who would set a door into the wall of a tomb?

He went over to it, ran his hands along its sides. The door was stone, and cold to the touch. There was no handle. He tried pushing it. To his surprise, it moved.

Turning his back on the coffins made him wary. He could sense them watching him, evaluating, measuring. He wondered who or what they had been. Former caretakers? He decided he didn't really want to know and pushed harder.

The door gave.

He stepped through it into warmth. It was dark and dank down there, the smell of rotting things, of fungus. As he began to shut the door behind him, pushing to close it, it seemed to him something emanated from the coffins and was reaching out for him, tendrils of intent, grasping to take hold of him like a ghostly hand. He shut the door with a curse and stood with its back to it, and heard something heavy bang against the door and fall to the ground.

Where was he?

It must have been an old service tunnel, he realized. The Garden must be riddled with them, miners' tunnels that ran between the tombs. There might be an entire other city underground, with avenues that ran between the houses of the dead.

He followed the tunnel. Somewhere down there, there might be an answer, he thought. He followed the tunnel and soon reached a place where the tunnel forked. He chose the left one and followed it. The tunnel slowly expanded around him as he walked. At intervals he passed doors. They were marked with etched symbols, dead alphabets he could not read. He searched for the script of Goliris but did not see it

There were places for lamps set in the walls but there were no lamps in them. Moss grew on the walls and glowed faintly in the dark. It was warm and humid. From time to time he thought he heard the tiny scuttling sound of minute creatures. Apart from them his footsteps were the only sound in the dark.

The tunnel forked again, and again he went left. On and on he walked, past untold graves, but all was silent. It occurred to him the Zambur, at least, must know of the tunnels, might come down there, looking for him. But how could they find him if he himself did not know where he was, or where he was going?

Slowly, he became aware of a thread in the dark. Something, some external influence was pulling him in a specific direction. It was like dust, like the black kiss: a binding tied in with the power he was enslaved to.

The corridors slowly changed, earth giving way to wood, wood to stone. He passed turnings that seemed to open when he followed them a short while, became grand caverns, dark palaces, but he knew his road led elsewhere. For a while the space around him expanded, then shrank again. He felt he was walking around in great circles, following a maze with no openings, no ways leading out. He came to a stream, a thin line of brackish water running in a crack in the ground. He bent down and touched it. It was very cold, and he drank it. When he rose it seemed to him he could see better than before.

He followed the water and it grew, a trickle becoming an underground river whose water was black and featureless.

The water he drank coursed through him. He felt at first restless, then lethargic. He began to see things that weren't there. Now the water of the river was very dark, and the river wide, so wide he could no longer see the other bank. He was going, he thought, into death.

They came to him underground. They came to him in the darkness of the subterranean city of tombs, the ghosts of those who had lived and were now in the shadow realm: the dead. They were not real. They were assemblages of memory and dream, fragments and snatches of recollections of encounters, of jumbled details. He was in a realm he knew well, that thin membrane that separates the worlds, but it was worse, worse than it had ever been, for the dead had noticed Gorel of Goliris, had turned the inward gaze of their attention to him, like metal shavings attracted, without control, to a powerful lodestone.

He tried to ignore them; he tried to keep his focus on the whisper of water, a thing that was real down there in the dark, or might have been. He wanted to know where the dark river flowed into. He tried to keep his eyes on a distant horizon, looking for a faint light, looking for a way out. Yet there were none, and he was afraid.

She came to him then, the goddess Shar, she who gave him the black kiss, she who enslaved him in the dark forbidding jungles of the south, in the realm of the tree-ghosts, the Urino-Dagg. She came, glistening naked black skin, yet he could see the burn marks where his cindergun had done its work. Her teeth were small and sharp, and she spat at him. He felt her close to him, unreal hands reaching to fondle and caress, and he knew she would hurt him if only she could, would drag him down into the levels below the world where the dead reside. He ignored her, and she cursed at him, though her voice did not carry. Still he kept on, and after a time she ebbed away, her essence pulled apart by the world of physicality.

Then came a succession of ghosts, which are no more or less than those who had passed and that we carry within us; those who are bound by shame and fear, love and excitement; those who, in their passing, had impacted us and left a sliver of themselves embedded in our consciousness. The old sorcerer of Goliris he had killed in the town called Prosperity, on the sands of Meskatel; though this time Gorel got a cold satisfaction from seeing the dead man's face, staring accusingly up at him from the darkness, for he was one of the men behind his exile, and well deserving of his fate. The merchant he had tortured—but did not kill!—on the banks of the river Tharat, frog-man with his stomach slit open and his bulging eyes haunted and sad. And others, many others, so many he had killed or caused to die, so many that at first he did not see her, and when he did he stopped, faltered, and was mute.

Not even death, she said to him, in a voice that was not a voice but a composite from his memories, his knowing of her. *Not even death can release a prince or princess of Goliris . . .*

In seeing, he remembered her. In remembering, he saw. His mother, who was proud and yet loving: a queen of Goliris—that greatest of empires—who held him in her lap and sang him to sleep, who commanded lands beyond lands and seas beyond seas. He said, "I am the last but I will return. I will avenge you."

Fool! his mother said. *We who are dead have no need for vengeance. We are not here, have gone beyond. Only the living have need of revenge.*

"Help me," he said. His voice was small there in the darkness, a little boy's, and lost. "Tell me how I could return!"

You must find your own way, she said. *Do not seek advice from the dead.*

He wanted to hold her, but she was not there. He wanted to tell her . . . but she was gone, offering nothing, giving nothing—yet perhaps she had . . .

There had been that old story. There had once been an exile from Goliris. His mother had mentioned both prince and princess. A princess of Goliris? The old story again . . . he never learned it fully. An ancient war, a split bloodline, and an exile . . .

His thoughts wandered. He didn't know how long he had been traveling there, underground, below the Kur-a-len, through the realms of the dead. The air was musty, and things rustled in corners; dark creatures that live in no-light scuttled away from him, frightened. There was no draft. Perhaps there had never been. It was airless down there, it was choking him. It was a tomb, and it would be his tomb. A princess of Goliris. What a nonsensical thing. Not even death.

Could it be?

Determination returned. He was a prince of Goliris—perhaps the last. He would not die here, like a rodent in a tunnel. The dead, his mother said, had no need of vengeance.

But he was not dead—and he did.

Part Four: Tomb of the Unknown God

He came to another opening, and the river flowed through it. He stepped in, and found himself in a wide cavern with a black lake at its center.

He stared at the lake. Around him the whispers of the dead dispersed like dry leaves. The black waves of the lake lapped gently at the shore.

He had come here for a reason. He had followed the pull of the goddess' curse, the black kiss of Shar, and it had led him here. He felt he was close to an answer, at least a part of one. What had he asked the preacher? The words came back to him—*What gods are there to track with in a cemetery?*

Ah, the preacher had said, and his smile grew obscene. There is your question and your answer right there, in one neat package . . .

One neat package . . . the preacher procured dust, somewhere in the cemetery. Where had it come from? What gods were there, in a . . .

Dead gods, he thought. He could taste the drug in the air all around him, enchantment raw and powerful. He could run it around his mouth with his tongue, could drink it, eat it, smoke it, fuck it. He could no more pull away from it than a night creature could pull away from the lure of bright light. He came closer to the shore and stared ahead into the darkness.

A glint of light. Something rose out of the middle of the lake. At first he thought it was an island, but it wasn't. It was . . .

Light glinted on metal and he thought he heard a scream, turning halfway into a quiet moan, of such intense misery that, for a moment, he froze. He bent down and ran his fingers through the dark water of the lake. They felt warm at the top, colder below, as if two separate currents were running simultaneously.

There was dust in the water. He did not need anything but his senses to tell him that his entire mind was enveloped in the feel of the drug, and it was overwhelming him. He bent down and cupped water in his hands, and drank and drank and drank.

How long he lay on that subterranean shore he did not know. It could have been hours, or days. He had no need for nourishment, for talk, for love. His only need was for the black kiss and it had been sated, at last, here, beside this tomb of an unknown god.

His senses were both dulled and made keen. He could not see the world around him, but could see the world beyond the world, could see through the membrane that separates the worlds of gods and men. He saw the lake as a whirlpool made not of water but of the remnants of the dead, flotsam and jetsam of lives, composed of memories, of dreams, of recollections and reflections and nightmares, all ebbing and eddying in the water, turning and turning around—

A great metal structure, greater than the space that held it—for it opened into that other, wider world—a rising moving spiral with great engines at the base that took in the death water and churned it and *processed* it and sent it up in jets through massive tubes, an enormous, terrible factory. Gorel, sitting up at last, stared at the geysers of death water, rising and disappearing beyond the steam, beyond the membrane of the world. Grave-robbing, he thought, and giggled.

The colors captivated him for a while. He exhaled, and watched and thought he saw mirages rising over the waters, anguished faces reaching out insubstantial hands in a plea for help. He stood at last and staggered, bewildered by the enormity of the place, by his eyes which could no longer see the world of physicality, that were focused now entirely into the world beyond. He stumbled into the water and waded, as if in a dream, toward the great metal edifice.

The water rose above his feet, over his ankles. Soon he was chest-deep with the water was rising still as he plodded forward, not thinking, his entire being dominated by this factory of gods' dust. The water came to his chin, his nose, his eyes. He giggled and bubbles rose to the surface, and then he breathed and there was no air; the death water came flooding into his mouth and nose and lungs and the world became a solid dark silence like a black stone.

He came to on cold hard ground. He was in darkness, the only sound that of the waves meeting the shore. He was himself again, though the dust was still in him, the drug still coursing through his body. It had reached some equilibrium inside of him, but he knew he could slip either way of it, into oblivion or reality, at any moment. Come to think of it, he wondered why he wasn't dead.

"You should be dead," a voice said, close by. The voice was raspy and weak, full of pain like fine threads of black through a worn cloth. It seemed familiar, as if someone he'd briefly known had spoken that way.

Gorel peered into the darkness. "Not the first one to say it," he mumbled. His tongue felt thick with disuse. Words were unfamiliar concepts. He heard a groan and came closer and said, suddenly shocked, "It's you."

The preacher was planted into the metal ground. A hollow tube rose up from the ground and traveled to his head, pinning him at the back. Another, horizontal tube held his arms spread out and away from him. This tube, too, was transparent. Gorel examined the apparatus. He had seen similar things, long ago, in the underground workshops of Goliris . . .

Blood ran through the tubes, the preacher's blood, but mixed. A grayish-green substance, a viscous liquid, ran through the tubes, and there were things inside the stream that seemed alive, strange globular clusters like mollusks or crabs. The liquid glowed as it moved sluggishly through the tubes. "What does it do?" Gorel said.

"It keeps me alive," the preacher said.

Gorel stared at him. The preacher's face was a map of pain. His single eye stared up at Gorel. Gorel said, "So this is where you get the dust from?"

"Help me out of this thing!" the preacher said.

Gorel said, "Don't shout. My head hurts." The preacher stared at him. Gorel came close, stroked the man's face. The preacher flinched. "Hush," Gorel said.

He remembered the workshops and labs below the palace of Goliris. There had been a room where a cluster of pipes trapped inside it two human shapes. The pipes led directly into their bodies. They seemed suspended in mid-air, but it was the tubes that held them there. Although they screamed there was no sound. The bodies only seemed human part of the time. Sometimes they would flicker and change, become snakes, dragons, water creatures, birds. But the device held them whatever shape they assumed. "What does it do?" he had asked his father, just as he had asked the preacher now. "It keeps them alive," his father had said. "But that is the least significant of its functions."

There had been experiments done constantly in Goliris. Had there not been treachery, had he not been sent across the World into his exile, he would have inherited the throne and learned the secrets. There were gods down there, he had once heard one of his tutors say. Captive gods, all but forgotten. "They are assisting the palace in its investigations," his tutor had said.

"What investigations?" the young Gorel had asked.

The tutor smirked. "Your father wants to know what makes a god," he said.

The preacher was breathing hard. "Please," he said.

Gorel looked at him, knowing he was a part of the treachery, and yet . . . he came closer, closed his lips on the preacher's mouth, kissed him. He did not taste of dust any more: he tasted of blood.

Gorel pulled away.

"Who built this?" he said.

"Release me and I'll tell you."

"If I release you, you'll die," Gorel said.

"Then kill me."

"I might still do that." He stared at the preacher. "Did you kill them?"

"I . . . " the preacher's mouth opened and closed, but no sound came.

"The first one," Gorel said. "Kelini Pashtill."

"Was that her name?"

"Did you take her face?"

"What would I want with a woman's face?"

"That," Gorel said patiently, "is what I would quite like to know."

"Kill me. Before he comes back."

"Your god?"

There was no answer. Something moved through the liquid in the tubes and the preacher screamed. Gorel looked up.

A factory of dust, he thought. A dead god—wanting to come back to life? No. There was more to it than that. "Who's the god?" he said.

The preacher tried to laugh, dribbled blood instead. "I don't know," he said. "Nobody does, not even him."

"What does he want, then?" Gorel said.

"Kill me?"

"Tell me," Gorel said.

The preacher shook his head—wildly, from side to side. Gorel had had enough. He took out his gun and put it to the preacher's head. "Kill me," the preacher said. "Do it now."

"Tell me," Gorel said, his finger on the trigger like a promise. "What does he want?"

"He wants her!" the preacher said, and before Gorel could pull the trigger the liquid in the tubes began to seethe and boil and the preacher screamed. Gorel took a step back and holstered his gun. He watched as the liquid seemed to pour into the preacher's body, the tubes emptying, the little scuttling creatures disappearing through holes into the preacher's body—the whole while the man's single eye was open and his mouth open in a scream.

Gorel took another step back. Realization hit him, and with it fear. He whispered, "What are you?"

"I . . . " the preacher tried to form words, couldn't. "I . . . "

Then he was gone. Gorel waited. The single eye grew empty, dead. It closed . . .

When it opened again it was no longer the preacher staring out. The tubes slid without sound back into the ground, and the body of the preacher stood up. "He was my avatar," the thing inside the preacher's body said. "But now it's time to deal with matters . . . personally."

Gorel stared at the god. The beat-up body of the preacher quivered, as if being held together with some effort. There was no longer anything handsome, anything attractive about the preacher's body. It was no longer a body, but a corpse.

He took another step back. The corpse moved toward him, the dead hand of the preacher reaching out for him, for his throat, caught him. He was being strangled, the air caught in his lungs, the dead hand forcing down to the ground. "I won't kill you," the unnamed god whispered, his face close to Gorel's. "Not yet. Not while I still need—"

Gorel kneed him between the legs. The hand slackened and he pushed and rolled away, both guns materializing in his hands. The god laughed. "You think you can kill *me*?"

The first two bullets caught the god's body in the head. The next two hit his torso. There was no blood. The god roared again, staggered back, regained his balance. "Guns," the god said, and spat. Where his spit hit the ground the metal hissed and dissolved. Gorel took a step back, and another, and found himself at the edge of the dark lake. "I need eyes," the god said. "She wants yours, but yours disgust me, man of Goliris. No." The god shook his head. "I would like a woman's eyes to stare at, a woman's eyes, fresh like morning dew."

For a moment, strangely, he seemed lost. "Do they still have morning dew?" he said. "Does the sun still rise every day?"

"Not in the Garden," Gorel said.

"Bring me eyes. I need eyes. It is a simple enough request," the god said.

"And in exchange?"

"Besides keeping you alive?"

Gorel nodded.

The god said, "Dust. As much dust as you would ever crave, human."

Dust. "Any particular color?"

The god seemed to think about the question. "Blue," he said at last. "Blue like a sea at noon. Blue like . . . " but he could not, it seem, put it into words. "Blue. Do they still have blue?"

"They still have blue," Gorel said, holstering his guns. "What sort of god *were* you?"

"I was a great god!" the god said. "Countless people prayed to me! Countless temples worshipped in my name! Countless sacrifices were made—"

He fell silent. "You don't remember," Gorel said.

The god turned away his head. Gorel could see where the bullets had hit, opening bloodless passageways through the skull.

"No," the god said.

Part Five: Blud & Deth

In his whole life, both as a prince of Goliris and later as an exile, mercenary, hired killer, thief, and what he liked to think of as odd jobs man, Gorel of Goliris had been asked to perform many strange deeds. Never, though, had he been given the task of obtaining a pair of living blue eyes for a nameless, dead, and quite possibly deranged god. He had to admit it made a change.

He wants *her*, the preacher had said before he—died? Ceased to exist? Had he existed at all to begin with? Gorel didn't know—but who was she? He had thought the events that had taken place due to the arrival in the Garden of Seraph Gadashtill. But, what if that were not the case? What if what had happened—what was happening now—were the result of something begun long ago?

He felt like hitting something. Someone. In fact, he had in mind two such someones. There was a conspiracy of sorts in the Garden of Statues, perhaps more than one. The living and the dead both seemed tangled in plans that made no sense. Perhaps it was a function of death, he thought. It confused the mind.

He made his way cautiously through silent tombstones. He wasn't sure where he was going, where they would be, but he knew that, sooner or later, he would find them.

But why bother? She was there then, gliding beside him, and the moon shone through her, and her face was that of a dead woman, and her heart belonged to someone else, and she was blind. He knew that now. He had thought her a specter, a thing of no substance conjured from his dreams. He knew better now. He stopped. "Not even death," he said, and it seemed to him she nodded, there beside him. *Yes,* she agreed. *Not even death . . .*

"Princess," he said, and it seemed to him she laughed, though the sound was like that of rattling bones. *Perhaps,* she said. *I no longer remember . . .*

This angered him, and he said, "So now you are a whore? The dead whore of a dead god?"

Careful, Gorel of Goliris, the voice that was only in his mind said. Her image shivered in the moonlight. *You have the eyes of Goliris,* she said. *Yes, though your manners are those of a barnyard animal, such as you were raised amongst in your exile, no doubt. Yes . . . your eyes might fit.* There was a kind of laughter in the voice. *Shall I take them from you?*

"Princess," he said, and bowed his head, though his hand was on the butt of his gun. A princess of Goliris, he thought. So the old story was true.

She laughed again. *Blud and Deth are by the Lake of the Drowned God,* she said.

"I've lost all desire to go near lakes," Gorel said, but she was already gone, and he was alone and speaking to himself. "Or any large body of water," he added as an afterthought. He trudged his way through the cemetery, encountering no one and nothing, heading for the watery graveyard of the Merlangai folk.

The clouds had gathered over the Garden and the closer he came to the Lake of the Drowned God the thicker the air became with fog and there was a hint of rain. Somewhere nearby lightning cracked. Gorel made his way blindly, groping through the soup of elements, fearing a fall into the water. Perhaps it would have been easier, he thought, to merely find a pair of eyes, blue or not, and get out of the Garden as quickly as was possible.

Perhaps.

Instinct made him follow the flash of lightning. Thunder broke periodically, shaking the ground. The sound came closer and closer, in great rapidity, and he knew he was getting close. Earlier, he had furtively slipped to where, when he had first taken the job, he had buried some of his arsenal. It was, naturally, an unused grave. Now, equipped with some of the material he thought he might need, he felt better, more himself.

At last, he heard voices through the fog, and stopped.

"They said I was unstable! A necrophile! And for what? For standing up for the rights of the dead? I will show them, I will—"

"Oh, shut up," another voice said.

Gorel recognized them: Blud and Deth, as promised by a dead princess. What were they really up to?

"You do go on, Blud. Let's just finish setting up the equipment."

"I really find this sort of work rather distasteful," said the voice of Dr. Blud. "I mean, what does he need with the Merlangai?"

"You just said—" Professor Deth, then sighed. "You keep changing your bloody mind."

"I'm just saying," Dr. Blud said.

"Shut up and let's get on with it."

"Let's."

Gorel crept closer. They were by the water. As he came closer the air seemed to clear a little, and through patches of fog he watched the two men.

They stood on the shore of the lake. A machine of sorts mounted on a metal tripod, stood with its legs in the water. Its bulbous upper body, made of a greenish metal, began to rotate, slowly at first, then growing faster, and the water of the lake began to churn.

"The parameters of control—" said Dr. Blud.

"Are within acceptable limits," said Professor Deth.

"There can be no full reincarnation in a semi-solid state—"

"That's not our concern."

"Still. Water zombies? Distasteful."

"Incidentally, do you think there is something buried in the lake?"

"Yes, corpses."

They both laughed.

"Nevertheless. She—"

"Yes, she—"

"She wants us to—"

"But what about—"

"Him? Yes, it is a concern—"

"A worry—"

"Are we in over our heads?"

"Always, my dear friend."

"Indeed."

And they laughed again.

Gorel stepped through the fog. His guns were pointed at the two men and their contraption. "Step away from the machine, gentlemen."

"Sheriff!"

"Man of Goliris?" Professor Deth looked confused. "Why are you hindering our progress? We are doing this on the behest of—"

"Yes, indeed—"

"Step away!"

The two men paid him no attention. "It's too late," Dr. Blud said cheerfully. "The machine is running—"

"Emitting the death-sounds of Greater Pond—"

"A rare and, until recently, thought of as lost—"

"Yet wasn't—"

"Was given to us—"

"To study and analyze—"

"To record—"

"To make use of—"

"The ancient ritual—"

"Automated—"

"Embedded within a machine construct—"

"Wonderful, isn't she?"

"Look."

Gorel looked.

The lightning fell over the water now, sparks flying where the surface boiled. Steam began to rise from the water, and with it . . .

First a skull, rising slowly out of the waves that began to slap against the shore. In its empty eye sockets an intelligence could still, perhaps, be discerned. The skull moved, this way and that, scanning the above-surface world. The rest of its skeletal body emerged slowly from the waters, and it began to advance toward the shore,

More followed. Some were little more than skeletons. Others were fresher. Some still had patches of flesh hanging from their bones, and some were well preserved—perhaps in the depths of that miniature sea—but had swelled up, intestinal gasses inflating them into obscene balloons. The dead sea-folk, the corpses of the Merlangai, were rising from their graves.

Gorel could not let that happen.

The top half of the machine was spinning faster and faster. Mud and boiling water churned between its three metal legs. "Shut it down!"

"It's too late—" Professor Deth said. "It would require re-calibration for the pacification protocols to take effect—" said Dr. Blud.

"Fuck it," Gorel said, and shot Deth in the chest.

The professor took a step back. His legs buckled. He put a hand to his thorax, placed his finger into the hole there, looked up at Gorel with what could have been amazement, and said, "You *shot* me."

"Turn it off!"

"You fucking *idiot*!"

"Gentlemen," Dr. Blud said. "Please. I abhor this sort of language."

"He *shot* me!"

The doctor made a sound something like, "Pffah."

Professor Deth shuddered. "I hate when this happens," he said.

"Unavoidable, in our line of work," Dr. Blud said.

"Nevertheless."

Gorel stared at them. The professor continued to shudder. Lights began to glow over his wrists, his neck, his knees. "Bastard," he said.

The hole in his chest grew smaller and disappeared. The professor stood up, cleared his throat for a long moment, and spat. A metal object flew from his mouth and bounced on the ground. It was Gorel's bullet. Gorel said, "Shit."

On the lake, more and more of the submerged dead appeared. They all waded toward the shore in unison. Where they mounted dry land they continued, passing Gorel and his two companions, completely ignoring them.

"What did you make them *do*?" Gorel said.

"*She* made us do it!" Dr. Blud said.

Gorel stopped. "They're going to the god's tomb," he said slowly.

"Well . . . " Professor Deth said.

"She doesn't like him, you see," Dr. Blud said.

"Though he does love her so."

"But she does not love him back."

"She loves another."

"Death is not a barrier to love."

"Quite. And rather poetic, my friend."

"Thank you. I shall write it down."

"Shut *up*!" beside them, the machine hummed one last time and was silenced.

"A war amongst the dead?" Gorel said.

"Unfortunate," Dr. Blud said.

"Fascinating," Professor Deth said.

"We shall present a paper on the subject at the next conference," said Dr. Blud.

"Perhaps a book—"

"Not a war, in any case—"

"A skirmish—"

"Internal conflict—"

Gorel tuned them out. Around them the clouds were dispersing, the lightning easing though not entirely disappearing. He watched the dance of blue on blue. A bolt hit one of the last corpses to come ashore, one of the bloated ones from the bottom, and the resulting explosion threw chunks of flesh and bones and a cloud of noxious gas around the immediate area.

"Dead or alive," Gorel said, after he had finished wiping off the more obvious bits of rotten flesh from his clothes, "you're coming with me."

"Gladly," said Dr. Blud.

"Wouldn't miss it for the world," said Professor Deth.

"*Who* gave you the—" what was it? "—the death sounds of Greater Pond?"

He knew of Greater Pond. It was once one of the great Merlangai cities—one of the forbidden, abandoned places, now. "Was it the god?"

"The god?"

"Why would—"

"You still haven't figured it out, have you—"

"Really, sheriff, you're pretty dense for someone with your responsibilities—"

"It was the lover."

"The necromancer."

"And so."

"And so."

And Gorel, realizing at last what was happening in the Garden, cursed and then said, "Not on my fucking watch."

Part Six: Death Wore a Veil

The tomb of the unknown god rose out of the cemetery ground, a pyramid of metal shining a sickly green. The makeshift army of dead Merlangai walked toward the tomb. Somewhere, Gorel knew, would be the instigator of their undead rebellion: Seraph Gadashtill, Ninth Caliph of Mindano Caliphate, last in the line of the necromancer-kings.

Last, Gorel thought, but not just that. He had been misled more than once, and it was because he had tried to think like a lawman, which he was not. Nothing was ever solved with clever deduction, with clues and witnesses and due process. But a lot of things could be solved with a gun.

He could have disposed of Blud and Deth. He had chosen not to. They thought he did not understand the ways of the dead, and perhaps he didn't. But he *did* know how to kill them, in a final sort of way. Instead, he and the two scientists followed the army of undead toward the god's tomb.

Death, dead, undead, whatever, Gorel thought. They were just words, and they all meant the same. There was no real life after death, whatever the necromancers and the spirit-talkers, the shamans and priests and wizards may say. The dead were words. They were a residue of what had been before. The dead could no more love than make love. They were fragments, torn pieces of what had been, what had gone before and was gone forever. None of this, he thought, was any of his business. Yet he did not like to be made a fool of—and besides . . .

He could smell the dust from here.

Dust. The great curse he had been afflicted with. The power of the gods, the drug with which they could enslave the living. The army of the dead Merlangai marched, and the fog cleared, and a moon shone down, yellow like a rotting tooth.

Before the great pyramid of the unnamed god, the plain of the cemetery was filled with the dead.

There were Avians there, with skeletal wings that kept them afloat against all probability; there were spider-like creatures the likes of which Gorel had never before seen; there were countless humans and those of the frog-tribes, the falangs; and coming forth from the direction of Gardentown, there was a group of Zambur, silent and pale, coming forward in a great wave of white foam.

Coming toward him.

"Perhaps—" Dr. Blud said.

"A war is an appropriate term—" said Professor Deth.

"A battle—" said Dr. Blud.

"Interesting how the dead Avians can still hover despite the lack of functioning wings," said Professor Deth.

"My dear fellow! We must take notes—"

"Make sketches—"

"Survey—"

"Annotate—"

Gorel said, "Who killed the women?"

"The women?" Blud and Deth, exchanging glances.

"Who can tell?" Dr. Blud said at last.

"Perhaps the god," Professor Deth said.

"The necromancer—" Dr. Blud said.

"Perhaps you," Professor Deth said.

The two men turned their gaze on Gorel.

"I don't think so," Gorel said, speaking slowly. He felt more irritation than outright anger.

"Sheriff?"

"Will you put down that knife?"

For the first time, the two men looked worried.

"It could have been you," Gorel pointed out. The point of the blade was aimed at the men. They took a step back, in unison.

"Not us."

"Why would we—"

"Put down the knife!"

Could he prove it? Did it matter, in the last count, just *who* had killed the caretaker, who stole the face of Kelini Pashtill? Perhaps he just found the two men irritating, perhaps . . .

The two didn't quite die. He hadn't expected them to.

Professor Deth, spitting blood, said, "What did you—?"

"But why?" Dr. Blud said.

There was a lot of blood.

Gorel worked with the knife. He preferred guns, but sometimes the situation called for knife work, and the knife seemed to sing its bloodied song in his hand. The knife felt right—it felt good. Gorel sliced away flesh, cut through bone. The two men never screamed or cried, even when Gorel had sliced the professor's nose clean off and both of the doctor's ears. They tried to reform, they tried to charge him. Gorel hit, using Professor Deth as a punching bag, his fists taking the podgy man in the face, in the stomach. The knife again, not killing but cutting, slicing, removing flesh. The pieces of the two men's flesh trembled and shook on the ground and, like crabs, tried to crawl back toward their masters.

"Where is she?" Gorel said.

"Fuck you!" Dr. Blud said. His head was hanging at an unnatural angle from his neck. Gorel kicked it. What remained of Professor Deth jumped on him, teeth sinking into Gorel's neck, blood pouring out. He punched and pummeled but the professor held on, teeth sinking deeper. He began to drink from the wound, sucking in Gorel's blood with great gulping sounds. Gorel cursed, reached, grabbed the man by an ear and pulled. He threw the professor to the ground and pointed his gun at him. "Where," he said, "is she?"

"In the tomb!" Professor Deth said.

The bands of light were glowing at full brightness along the remains of the body, the torn fragments slowly gathering back toward their master. Beside him, Dr. Blud was trying to straighten his head over his broken neck, similar light engulfing him. But their movements were slow and sluggish. "Where in the tomb?"

"Above ground," Dr. Blud said.

"Damn you."

"At the very top," Professor Deth said.

"The apex," Dr. Blud said.

"Peak—"

"Summit—"

In the end, they defeated him. Gorel gave up.

He left them to it. He did not think they would be going anywhere in a hurry but he had the feeling that, even if all else in the Garden, in Kur-a-len, was truly laid to rest at last, those two would somehow still be there, walking away, their flesh reassembling. In their way they were worse than the dead.

He left them strewn on the ground, angry eyes still staring up at him, and walked away.

"Where are you?" he said, but there was no answer, and he hadn't expected one. He walked toward the great pyramid, the tomb of the unknown god.

The dead swarmed between the graves.

Many of them human—some little more than bones strung together, like a shaman's talisman, some with flesh still hanging from their frames. The ghost of Nocturnes glided through shadows. There were falangs there, the frog-tribes of Tharat, Ebong with their great helmet heads. There were species he had never seen before—all who were once no doubt great—all reduced now to this makeshift shambling army of corpses, all enthralled in the command of the necromancer-king, Seraph Gadashtill, in quest of his one love. And yet there had been no response from the god's tomb, no army raised in reply, and Gorel, stalking toward the grave, suddenly stopped . . .

Something wasn't right. A piece still missing, a sudden suspicion rising—

He was nearly at the tomb. A sturdy door with many locks, and he shot them all, the sound lost in the groaning of the shambling creatures. Kicked it and it crashed back and he went in.

Silence.

The tomb was dark and empty, corridors leading into a silence of disuse. A staircase. She would be at the top . . . yet he hesitated. A thrumming under his feet, as if the entire structure was vibrating. Where was the god?

He thought of that entire edifice underground, the great churning factory. Yet there was nothing up here, an empty shell like all graves . . .

A piece of masonry fell, narrowly missing his head.

He thought: the god wasn't there.

Where would he be?

He began to run down the stairs.

Behind him the tomb was shaking. He thought of the energies trapped underground. They were being channeled—but for what purpose?

Out the door, and running still, pushing away the animated corpses. The wave of Zambur close now, in disarray. He had been charged with maintaining order in this hellish place, and he had failed.

He ran, his breath ragged. Away from the tomb. "Get away!" he shouted. The Zambur emitted high-pitch screams. "It's a trap!" He ran past them. Toward the town. He felt the ground shake beneath his feet.

When the explosion came it lifted him off his feet and threw him in the air. Bright light like jade illuminating the night. Tumbling, he saw the massive grave of the unknown god disintegrating, the jade light shooting out of it, the dead around it, caught in the light, turning to dust without a sound.

He fell—it felt to him very slowly—until he hit the ground.

It is too late for you now, she said. She was there again, and so was he, in the dark of forced sleep, and they were standing, he realized, outside the great palace of Goliris, and she was very beautiful.

"Tell me," he said, demanded. She shook her head. *It is far beyond even you, Gorel of Goliris,* she said. *We are both exiles. Forget Goliris, it is no more, not for you.*

"I will return," Gorel said. "Even death will not stop me."

A laudable sentiment, she said, wryly. *But being the lord of death is something you discover to be, essentially, empty of meaning. And you are mortal, and far from your home—and you are empty, too, are you not, Gorel of Goliris?*

"I don't—" he said, and fell silent. She nodded, and they walked together through the gardens, and saw no one and nothing living. *You have nothing but revenge,* she said, *and what is that but a crutch? Seek love, instead, my cousin.*

"And you," he said with a sneer, "who do you love, princess of Goliris?"

She sighed, and above their heads the sky darkened, and the palace seemed to grow distant again, and they were standing on the great shore of Goliris, and the waves were wild and dark like things alive. *I loved them both,* she said. *And now I am tired . . . how will it end?*

"Are you whole, now?"

She shrugged. *Have I ever been,* she said, half question, half statement.

"You have the face, and the heart . . . " he thought it through. The foam of the dark sea of Goliris fell on him, and he felt a chill. "What else do you need, to live again?"

She laughed. *Only you, my cousin,* she said. *Yet I see you are, despite a loving guiding hand, not dead.*

The tomb. The explosion. And he—

"No," he said. She was growing weaker, and Goliris was fading around them, a dream world of no substance.

I need your eyes, to see again, to live again. Only your eyes. Is that too much to ask, from family? She sighed then, the voice like wind stirring dead leaves. *I shall wait, then,* she said. *I have waited long enough, a little more time will make no change . . . And anyway you cannot help but come to me. Can you, Gorel of Goliris?*

And she was gone, and the world was dark, then jade.

When he opened his eyes he was lying on the ground and around him was a wasteland.

The graves had gone, the god's tomb, and with them the dead. The world was a flat expanse of land, with no markers. A memory of a dream came back to him—he was standing on a vast expanse of land, and the dead were calling to him, a multitude of voices—but there were no more voices here, only a profound silence. They were gone.

At that moment he craved dust, knew its absence with a black despair. His body shook uncontrollably. He took deep breaths, but the sensation would not go away: deprivation, of the worst kind, an absence that bore into the very core of him. He craved the drug, felt helpless in its abeyance.

Only revenge motivated him still. He took deep breaths and focused on that harder, impenetrable core inside himself: the heir of Goliris, exiled from his home, doomed to wander the World in search of those who doomed him so. Revenge was strong, still. The blood pulsed in his head. He craved the black kiss and cursed it. His guns seemed to whisper to him. *Use us. Avenge the dead. Kill something.*

But how do you kill something that is already dead?

Well, he thought—he'd done it before.

He rose slowly, the whispering of armaments loud in his ears. He had been so wrong . . .

Somewhere nearby—sound. He turned. The ground moved. He aimed the gun, then lowered it again. A small, pathetic figure climbed out of the ground. "Jais!" it said.

Gorel watched the creature come close. Its face was creased—in misery or happiness, he couldn't tell. Masonry shifted all around, and he watched them in the moonlight, hundreds of Jais.

"Jais!"

"I remember," Gorel said.

The creature came closer and, startling Gorel, reached out its hand, touching Gorel's. "Gorel!" it said.

It whistled, or so it seemed. Another of the Jais came close. He thought it could have been a female, but wasn't sure. The little creature squatted on the ground, rocking on its heels. Gorel said, "No, really—"

There was a burst of gas, a gasp of pain. A stone the size of a fist lay on the ground, a stone that wasn't diamond or ruby or emerald but, strangely, even more beautiful, wrapped in rainbows as it shone in the moonlight.

"Gorel!" the first Jais said, and it went over to the stone and picked it up. His small leathery face seemed to smile. He went up to Gorel again and put the stone at his feet, then stepped back. The other one scampered away.

Gorel picked up the stone.

"Thank you," he said.

"Gorel!" the Jais said. Then it darted off and returned, a moment later, holding two metallic objects in his hand.

"What is that?" Gorel said. The Jais, looking suddenly nervous, took a step back from him, then threw the two objects on the ground and ran away.

Gorel put away the stone, picked away the metal objects—they were bullets.

He examined them. A strange script ran along their sides. He had seen such ammunition before, long ago . . . there were such objects in the ruins of the Lower Kidron, the product of the races that had lived and died there before humans came, and the children of the Lower Kidron would hunt for them amidst the ruins, and sell them to the gunsmiths of that dark place. He had been one of those children, once . . .

"Where did you find these?" he said but, of course, there was no answer. Kur-a-len, he thought: it was the dumping ground to rival all others, the refuse and dead things of a thousand places all mingled together. He loaded the bullets into his gun and turned his back on the silent graveyard.

In the distance he could see a single light shining, in the direction of the town. Yes. They would be waiting, he thought. Well, let them wait. It won't be long, now. He smiled, and there was nothing pleasant in that smile. Then he began to march, stiffly, toward the town and that single source of light, his hands on the butts of his guns.

He came to the town and walked down the street and the light beckoned him on. He paused and changed the bullets in his guns. Only two, and they would have to suffice . . .

He came to the Last Homily and entered.

Nothing had changed. The same dim light, the same fat candles, the same bartender behind the bar, the grave-wraith leering as he polished a glass with his dirty rag.

No one sitting at the tables but for one figure, cloaked in shadows, in a far corner. Gorel went up to the bar.

"What can I get you, sheriff?"

Gorel's gun materialized in his hand, pointing at the grave-wraith. "You can die," he said, in a low voice.

The grave-wraith laughed. "An unpleasant experience," he said.

"And one you are thoroughly familiar with?"

For the first time, a flash of anger from that ruined face. "What can you possibly know of death, man of Goliris?" he said. "I should have killed you when I had the chance, and pulled out your eyes. I was wrong, too merciful."

"Is it my eyes you want?" Gorel said, and the grave-wraith grimaced. "One can have eyes and still not see," Gorel said. "Who were you, before?"

"Shut up!"

"What are you but a shadow?" Gorel said. "Perhaps the thing that you once were, was also once great. But you are shadow, not even a memory remaining . . ."

The grave-wraith shook his head. His eyes turned to the figure in the shadows and his eyes, for one moment, looked lost. "It is no matter, now," he said softly. His eyes turned to the door, watching, waiting.

Gorel followed his gaze. "You set a trap, not for me, but for him," he said, realizing. "Her lover. The necromancer—"

"Enough," the grave-wraith said. "He is gone."

"How can you be sure?"

The bartender's eyes flickered. There was a sound like a sigh from the seated shadow. "I will trade you my eyes," he said, speaking to *her*, knowing she was listening. "Tell me the way to return."

There is no way back, she said. *And I will take your eyes regardless, cousin.*

Anger consumed Gorel then, but he controlled it. "The necromancer," he said. "The ninth caliph. I was fooled, was I not?"

You are *a fool,* she said.

"There was a story I read in a book," Gorel said. "About a boy from Mindano who met a strange princess traveling through the mountains, a woman he loved and killed to become the first caliph . . . but there have never been any others, have there? The ninth caliph and the first, they were both the same."

He came for me, she said, and there was something in her voice, a catching, of wonder or fear, he didn't know. *After all those years, he came for me . . .*

"Enough!" the grave-wraith said. "He will not have you."

Gorel said, "Are you sure?"

"She is mine," the grave-wraith said. More quietly, he said, "I love her."

"Love." Gorel's finger was steady on the trigger, but he didn't know who to shoot.

And what do you know of love, Gorel of Goliris, she said softly from her shadows.

At last he turned to face her. "I know love is a poor second," he said, and she sighed, the voice of dead leaves blowing in a graveyard. *Let us be,* she said. *This is not your business.* There was some animation in her voice. *Go back to your quest, go back to Goliris, that heinous, ruinous place that shapes children like weapons, that made us . . .* she sighed again.

"Where is it?" he said, anger rising suddenly, hot and painful. "For the last time, where is Goliris?"

She laughed, and the sound was bitter. *So you are truly lost in the World . . . how sad. You will never find it, Gorel of Goliris, last in the line to the throne. Not with my help.*

"Then you are no good to me," Gorel said, the anger dissipating, replaced by an immense cold.

He shot her.

She fell back. From behind the counter, a howl of anger, and then the grave-wraith was on him, arms trying to strangle him. Gorel punched back, fell and rolled, throwing off his opponent—who stood back up and, facing him, began slowly, to change.

The costume of the grave-wraith was at last discarded: and the god who no longer had his name began to form in its place, a hideous, shapeless mass, a white star growing in the middle of the Last Homily, howling in languages long thought dead and buried, its true form that of no form.

What did you do? she said, and the god stopped suddenly. Both of them turned to her. She crawled away from the shadows, and he could see her now for the first time. Gorel involuntarily took a step back.

She had no eyes, she was blind, but inside the yellowing bone of her ribcage a heart beat, cloaked in shadows: the caretaker's heart which he had lost. She was unclothed with skin. A hole hissed through her chest, bones melting. The bullet had missed the heart.

A veil, made of the sheerest silk, covered her face. *What is this weapon?* she said, sounding confused.

The god rushed toward her, his white heat singeing the tables as he passed. "I will kill your cousin and give you his eyes," he said. "It is as we planned. We have waited so long!"

I can wait a while longer, she said, but still she sounded bewildered. He had only one bullet left, the Jais' gift to him. Bullets to kill the dead . . . but which one?

"I will kill you," the nameless god said, "slowly, and will enjoy it."

"Fuck you," Gorel said.

The god stopped and hovered, very still, above the floor of the tavern. "Or perhaps not . . . " he mused. "Perhaps there is something you want, Gorel of Goliris . . . "

"There is nothing I want from you?"

"No?" and suddenly the god had changed, its countenance that of his avatar, the one-eyed preacher, and his lips were full and dark like cherries. In the air there was a stench of enchantment that clenched Gorel's stomach, but would not allow him to draw away.

"You have been kissed before," the preacher said, his voice filled with relish. "You know the taste of the black kiss well. I can give you what you want."

"No . . . " Gorel whispered.

The god said, "Yes." He came closer to Gorel. His single eye shone in his head like a white star. "You crave it so . . . " he said.

"No," Gorel said again, but the hand holding the gun fell to his side, and he found it hard to breathe, or think, or act. The preacher's lips were coming closer all the while, coming for the kiss Gorel remembered so well, a god's kiss, a doom sweeter than life, more powerful than death. "Please," he said.

"Since you ask so nicely," the god said, and the preacher's face leered, his lips almost touching Gorel's, who closed his eyes—no longer fighting, thinking only of the touch of the god's lips on his, of the god's tongue penetrating into his mouth—and his body felt as light as air as he sank forward to welcome the kiss—

The door of the Last Homily exploded inwards, showering them with slivers of wood. Gorel fell to his knees and the preacher screamed with rage. "You!" he said. Woozily, Gorel turned his head. Sense returned, and with it purpose, and he rose to his feet, the gun raised again, the other gun leaping into his other hand, both of them aimed.

"Me," Seraph Gadashtill said.

Death had not changed the last—and first—caliph of Mindano. He was an urbane-looking man, the pallor of death permanent on his skin, and in his arms he held two weapons Gorel could not identify, but thought to be of Zul manufacture. The preacher had leaped behind the counter when the necromancer arrived and now faced both Gorel and the necromancer with what appeared to be a gigantic blunderbuss but which Gorel knew to be an ancient Merlangai weapon, a thing of sorcery, not artifice, and from the Drowned God's domain.

They aimed guns at each other: Gorel, the caliph, the nameless god, moving their gaze from one to the other, tense, waiting—and Gorel laughed suddenly.

It was a three-man standoff, and two of them were already dead.

They faced each other this way, and the necromancer said, "I have no business with you, man of Goliris, but will shoot you if I must."

"I'll kill you both," the preacher said.

Gorel alone did not speak. He knew then what he must do, but something inside him hurt at the thought. In his mind, he fashioned words: *Will you not tell me the way?*

She did not reply, which was a reply in itself. Somewhere that was not inside him and yet indelibly linked to his own being, he felt her relax.

The three opponents kept covering each other. Gorel knew they would kill him first. Their fight was their own and he was superfluous to it. There was only one way. He took it: he turned away from them and fired, and watched the caretaker's heart explode inside the stolen body of what had once been a princess of Goliris. Gorel watched the stolen face of Kelini Pashtill relax, and knew that, at last, some ghosts at least have been laid to rest.

He heard the god and the necromancer cry in unison, but he was already ducking, making for the window, and as he sailed out into the night he heard behind him two weapons discharge at once, and yet felt no pain. He hit the ground outside and rolled hard, and lay there, staring at the stars, and it was silent: there was a silence like death, and he knew that he was alone, and alone still alive in that terrible place called Kur-a-len: the Garden of Statues.

They were all dead: which was as it should be. In the Last Homily the necromancer and the nameless god had fallen almost side-by-side. In real death, at last, they seemed almost like brothers.

They were all dead, but no—perhaps not all. He thought of those strange, small figures he had met, who made their habitat in the rubble of the dead's once-proud mansions, who stole through shadows . . . Perhaps the Jais, at least, have found a peaceful place to call home. No one would disturb them there again. Only rubble remained of the Garden, and as for the town—

Gorel torched the place. He watched the Last Homily as it burned and then made his way slowly down the road, setting fire to the rest of the town. His graal was waiting for him and he rode him away then, the flames reflected in the graal's dark carapace. They rode together for most of the night until, at last, the fire disappeared behind them.

⋙═⟨♦⟩═⋘

Lavie Tidhar is the author of *A Man Lies Dreaming, The Violent Century,* and the World Fantasy Award winning *Osama*. His other works include the Bookman Histories trilogy, several novellas, two collections and a forthcoming comics mini-series, *Adler*. He currently lives in London.

⋙═⟨♦⟩═⋘

ACKNOWLEDGEMENTS

"The Screams of Dragons" © 2014 Kelley Armstrong. First publication: *Subterranean Press Magazine*, Spring 2014.

"The End of the End of Everything" © 2014 Dale Bailey. First publication: *Tor.com*, 23 April 2014.

"(Little Miss) Queen of Darkness" © 2014 Laird Barron. First publication: *Dark Discoveries #29*.

"Madam Damnable's Sewing Circle" © 2014 Elizabeth Bear. First Publication: *Dead Man's Hand*, ed. John Joseph Adams (Titan Books).

"Sleep Walking Now and Then" © 2014 Richard Bowes. First publication: *Tor.com*, 9 July 2014.

"Only Unity Saves the Damned" © 2014 Nadia Bulkin. First publication: *Letters to Lovecraft: Eighteen Whispers to the Darkness*, ed. Jesse Bullington (Stone Skin Press).

"A Wish From a Bone" © 2014 Gemma Files. First publication: *Fearful Symmetries*, ed. Ellen Datlow (ChiZine Publications).

"Mr. Hill's Death" © 2014 S. L. Gilbow. First publication: *The Dark*, Issue 4.

"The Female Factory" © 2014 Lisa L. Hannett & Angela Slatter. First publication: *The Female Factory* (Twelfth Planet Press).

"Who Is Your Executioner?" © 2014 Maria Dahvana Headley. First publication: *Nightmare*, November 2014.

"The Elvis Room" © 2014 Stephen Graham Jones. First publication: *The Elvis Room* (This Is Horror).

ABOUT THE EDITOR

Paula Guran is senior editor for Prime Books. She edited the Juno fantasy imprint from its small press inception through its incarnation as an imprint of Pocket Books. Guran edits the annual Year's Best Dark Fantasy and Horror series as well as a growing number of other anthologies—thirty-seven published by the end of 2015—as well as more than fifty novels and single-author collections.

In an earlier life she produced weekly email newsletter *DarkEcho* (winning two Stokers, an IHG award, and a World Fantasy Award nomination), edited *Horror Garage* (earning another IHG and a second World Fantasy nomination), and has contributed reviews, interviews, and articles to numerous professional publications. Mother of four, mother-in-law of two, grandmother to one (with another on the way), she lives in Akron, Ohio.